THE YEAR'S BEST

SCIENCE FICTION

ALSO BY GARDNER DOZOIS

THE YEAR'S BEST

SCIENCE FICTION

sixteenth annual collection

edited by Gardner Dozois

st. martin's press new york

For the Gibsons:
Shari, Jimmy, Jared,
Steven, and Melissa.

ISBN 0-312-20963-0 (hc)

acknowledgment is made for permission to print the following material:

contents

acknowledgments

The editor would like to thank the following people for their help and support: first and foremost, Susan Casper, for doing much of the thankless scut work involved in producing this anthology; Michael Swanwick, Ellen Datlow, Virginia Kidd, Jim Allen, Vaughne Lee Hansen, Sheila Williams, David Pringle, Charles C. Ryan, David G. Hartwell, Jack Dann, Janeen Webb, Warren Lapine, Jan Berriends, Ed McFadden, Tom Piccirilli, Nicola Griffith, Lawrence Person, Dwight Brown, Darrell Schweitzer, Corin See, and special thanks to my own editor, Gordon Van Gelder.

Thanks are also due to Charles N. Brown, whose magazine *Locus* (Locus Publications, P.O. Box 13305, Oakland, CA 94661, $43 for a one-year subscription [twelve issues] via second class; credit card orders [510] 339-9198) was used as a reference source throughout the Summation, and to Andrew Porter, whose magazine *Science Fiction Chronicle* (Science Fiction Chronicle, P.O. Box 022730, Brooklyn, NY 11202-0056, $35 for a one-year subscription [twelve issues]; $42 first class) was also used as a reference source throughout.

On the surface, 1998 was a relatively quiet year, although just below that surface, major changes swum like monstrous fish, changes that could affect the entire publishing world and make it a radically different place in 2008 than it is today.

It was in general a prosperous year, with the major chain bookstores reporting record earnings, and the relatively new area of online bookselling proving itself to be a serious money-maker, with online services such as Amazon.com and barnesandnoble.com bringing in serious bucks, and a great potential for growth still ahead in those areas. A good solid percentage of the money earned this year was earned by science fiction books, which I think pretty much serves to dismiss fears, discussed here last year, that the Death of Science Fiction as a publishing category is imminent. At this point, momentum and inertia alone would carry SF publishing into the next century, even if not another SF book ever sold a copy again—and, indeed, schedules into the first and second year of the new century have already been announced.

But all indications are that SF (even solid core SF, leaving the much dreaded media novels out of the equation altogether) is selling *better* than ever here at the brink of the new millennium. The big, dramatic, catastrophic recession/bust/slump that genre insiders have been predicting for more than a decade now did *not* happen in 1998; in fact, the overall totals for books published seemed to be on the rise again, after a couple of years of mild decline (although the *ways* in which SF books get published continue to change and evolve, with mass-market titles declining and the number of books that are published instead as hardcovers or trade paperbacks on the rise). There were some fairly hefty cutbacks in 1997, and some failing or faltering lines, but they were more than made up for this year in numbers of books released by the founding of major and ambitious new science fiction lines by Avon Eos and Simon & Schuster UK.

The field seems to be in good shape artistically and creatively, too; yes, the majority of the stuff available on the bookstore shelves at any given time is crap, but this has *always* been true, whatever decade you're talking about, whether it's the '50s, the '60s, the '70s, the '80s, or the '90s. Look beyond the crap, and you'll find an enormous and enormously varied number of top authors (from several different generations, stretching all the way from Golden Age giants of the '30s and '40s to the kid who made his first sale yesterday) producing an amazingly varied spectrum of first-rate work, from High Fantasy to the hardest of Hard Science Fiction—including a lot of material that could not have been published *at all* twenty years ago. There are still people around, some of them quite vocal, who will complain at length about how nobody's writing anything good anymore in the field, not like they did in the *old* days, but look closely and you'll find that most of those same people *don't read any new science fiction*, and haven't for years. Those of us who *do* read lots of new science fiction know better. When people are looking back nostalgically to the Golden Age twenty years from now, *this*, the present, this period we're in right *now*, is what they'll be looking at.

Like last year, there was little activity in the traditional game of Editorial Musical Chairs in 1998, with the only really significant change being that Shelley Shapiro was named Editorial Director of Del Rey Books, moving up from her former position as Executive Editor. Most of the other changes this year took place a lot farther up the food-chain, in the rarified corporate realms where the very top suits dwell. The giant German publishing conglomerate Bertelsmann, owner of Bantam Doubleday Dell, bought Random House, which includes under *its* corporate umbrella houses such as Del Rey, Ballantine, Knopf, and dozens of other imprints. Later in the year, Bertelsmann bought a 50 percent stake in barnesandnoble.com, the online arm of Barnes & Noble and direct head-to-head competitor with Amazon.com for the increasingly profitable online bookselling market. Viacom sold off all but the consumer division of Simon & Schuster to Pearson, the owner of Penguin and Putnam. In England, the Orion Publishing Group bought Cassell, which resulted in the merger of SF lines Gollancz and Millennium, with future SF books being published as Gollancz hardcovers and Millennium paperbacks; Jo Fletcher of Gollancz and Simon Spanton of Millennium will be the acquiring editors (with Caroline Oakley, in charge of Orion paperbacks, continuing to edit some authors) — they will report directly to Malcolm Edwards, himself a former SF editor (as is Anthony Cheetham, the head of Orion). And, late in the year, Barnes & Noble, the largest of the chain bookstores, bought Ingram, the largest book distributor. Since Ingram had been the major distributor for Amazon.com as well as for the remaining independent bookstores, news of the purchase sent shockwaves through the entire publishing industry, with the executive director of the Author's Guild, Paul Aiken, saying (as quoted in *Locus*), "The Godzilla of publishing is wedding the King Kong of distribution . . . If I were an independent bookseller, I would be scared to death by this." Other experts downplayed this implication, suggesting that business would carry on more or less as always despite the sale.

It may take a while for the effects of these changes to surface, but some of them — especially those things concerned with the online bookselling market — may be affecting the industry well into the next century.

And there are other potential changes just down the road, things that could radically alter the nature of the publishing world as we know it. The field of electronic books, e-books, is just now taking its first faltering baby steps, with Tor announcing this year that they plan to offer about 100 books as e-text for the Rocket eBook via direct downloading from barnesandnoble.com; Tor has already licensed electronic versions of new and reprint titles to digital publisher Peanut Press for the 3Com PalmPilot, which are downloadable from the net (Peanut Press has a Web store at www.peanut-press.com that offers versions of books from a number of publishers that can be downloaded into the 3Com PalmPilot). Other "electronic book" systems are in development, including Millennium Reader, EveryBook, and SoftBook. I have a feeling that this market may turn out to be very significant indeed before we're too many years into the new century—taken to an extreme, it could change the face of publishing itself.

Another development that could change the face of publishing forever is print-on-demand technology. Working models of such a system were demonstrated at this year's ABA. If it works as well as it's said to work, you may soon be able to walk into a bookstore that has such a system installed, and ask for, say, a copy of *The Sun Also Rises*, or any other book the system has on file, and it will print one out for you on the spot, indistinguishable from a regular trade product. The implications of such a system are staggering—only one such implication is that it would solve at a stroke the problem of the vanishing backlist that has plagued SF publishing throughout the last several decades, since the old mail-order backlist system more or less disappeared at the end of the '70s: if you decide that you like Poul Anderson, and you want to read some of his old stuff, like *The High Crusade* or *The Enemy Stars*, instead of waiting years for a reissue or haunting used book-stores trying to find those titles, you just go to the print-on-demand machine and have it whomp up some copies of them for you on the spot. (Other implications, already beginning to occur to some writers and agents, affect current understanding of out-of-print and rights reversions issues; if your book is always available on a print-on-demand system, how can it ever be said to have gone out of print? And how can you ever get the rights to that book reverted to you in order to be sold again? A supposed one-time sale of a book could become a de facto *to the end of time* sale, unless contractual limitations are applied to the situation somehow.) Print-on-demand, if it works as well as its promoters claim it will, would also change the face of publishing by eliminating the need for huge warehouses to store large numbers of physical copies of books, eliminate the need for fleets of trucks to ship the physical copies around, and, perhaps most significant, eliminate at another stroke a great deal of the waste and inefficiency built into today's system (including the returns system that has been a crushing Old-Man-of-the-Sea on the back of the publishing industry for most of the second half of the twentieth century), saving immense amounts in paper and production costs; you would print exactly as many copies of a book as customers wanted to buy, with no need to produce five copies to sell one. Postulate a print-on-demand system able to print books downloaded directly from the Internet, and the need for many of the world's bookstores disappears as well (I think there will always be some bookstores, places for people to browse and schmooze, although there probably wouldn't need to be as *many* of them in any given location).

This all sounds like utopian, pie-in-the-sky daydreaming, but it may not be as far off as you think. Similar technologies are already in place in many CD stores, where you can create your own CDs, mixing and matching songs as you like. Along the same lines, someday you may be able to go into a bookstore with a print-on-demand system and create your own anthology, drawing on a database of the year's stories (perhaps many of them published electronically online), selecting whatever stories you'd like for it, making anthologists like me obsolete.

I suppose it's inevitable to be thinking about the future, here at the end of the twentieth century, with a new century and a new millennium looming just ahead of us. (Yes, I know that the new millennium doesn't *really* start in 2000, starting instead in 2001, so don't bother to write letters to me indignantly pointing this out. That's a lost cause anyway, I'm afraid—for all except a handful of stubborn purists, the new millennium will start in 2000, which is when the vast majority of the population will celebrate the change . . . and I must admit that even though I know better, I'll probably feel a certain emotional *frisson* the first time I write "2000" as the year date on a check, after having spent a lifetime writing 19__-something instead!)

For most of my life, the year 2000 was THE FUTURE, the time when the majority of science fiction stories were set, unimaginably distant. Now THE FUTURE is suddenly just a few months away, sweeping relentlessly down on us. It's tempting to try to peek into the future, to predict what's to come, as I was just doing above, but I know better than that. Just as SF writers peering at 2000 from the 1950s could have no real understanding of what 2000 would *really* be like, just as people peering into the oncoming new century from the end of the nineteenth century couldn't possibly have imagined the horrors and wonders and vast social changes that awaited humanity in the twentieth century, so we ourselves, almost by definition, lack the imagination and the foresight to see the as-yet unimaginable changes that lie ahead of us in the twenty-first century and beyond, things that would seem just as bizarre and impossible to *us* as the atomic bomb or a laptop computer, or a microchip, or penicillin, or the death camp at Dachau, or organ-transplant surgery, or a female Senator, or racially mixed schools, or *Hustler* magazine, or the Space Shuttle, or the Internet, or the ability to see into our own bodies with fiber-optic cameras, or the ability to speak to someone on the other side of the world would have seemed to somebody back in 1898.

The future is always fundamentally unpredictable and unknowable. And in that lies perhaps our greatest hope.

It was another rocky year in the magazine market, although, for the first time in several years, there were a few upbeat notes, with *Amazing Stories* reborn and the circulation of a few of the magazines even beginning to creep up a bit for a change.

Asimov's Science Fiction and *Analog Science Fiction & Fact* both changed their "trim size" in mid-1998, going to a new format that added a little over an inch in height and about a quarter-inch in width to each issue (leaving *The Magazine of Fantasy & Science Fiction* as the only true digest-size magazine in the genre), and, as hoped, it seems to have helped with newsstand sales. *Asimov's* lost about 2,000 in subscriptions but more than doubled their newsstand sales, from 5,040 to 11,982, for an 11% gain in overall circulation. *Analog* gained about 383 in subscriptions and another 5,902 in newsstand sales, for an 11.8% gain in overall circulation; both magazines also improved their "sell-through" rate, from 29% to 52% for *Asimov's*, and from 32% to 51% for *Analog*. *The Magazine of Fantasy & Science Fiction* lost about 4,393 in subscriptions and another 495 in newsstand sales, for a 12.3% loss in overall circulation. *Science Fiction Age* lost about 4,740 in subscriptions and about another 4,462 in newsstand sales, for a 21.3% loss in overall circulation. *Realms of Fantasy* gained about 517 in subscriptions and about another 209 in newsstand sales, for a 1.6% gain in overall circulation.

The magazine business is a strange one, and some of these figures probably look worse than they actually are. The fact is that many of these magazines, even the ones with declining circulations, may have actually *increased* their profitability in the last couple of years by various strategies, including adjusting their "draw" (sending fewer issues to newsstands that habitually sell less, so that fewer issues overall need to be printed and distributed in order to sell one issue, increasing the magazine's efficiency, and thereby lowering costs—and so increasing profitability), instituting cost-saving procedures in printing and physical production, and working out better targeting of "direct-mail" outlets (bookstores—where SF magazines usually sell well) as opposed to scattershot mass markets (magazine racks in supermarkets—where SF magazines usually *don't* sell well). Also, a lot of the subscriptions that have been lost by various magazines in recent years are Publishers Clearing House–style cut-rate stamp-sheet subscriptions, lost when many of the stamp-sheet places dropped most genre magazines awhile back; stamp-sheet subscriptions can swell your circulation rate, and make it *look* as though you're doing great, but since they cost more to fulfill than they actually bring in in revenue, they can be dangerous—they're part of the reason the print *Omni* went under, despite an annual circulation of 700,000—and an argument can be made that the genre magazines are better off without them. Although the magazine field did suffer a postage increase in early 1999, it also got a break in that paper costs, projected to rise, not only held steady but actually declined somewhat in 1998. And, of course, one of the traditional advantages that has always helped the digest magazines to survive is that they're so *cheap* to produce in the first place that you don't have to sell very many of them to make a profit (this is still true of the now slightly larger *Asimov's* and *Analog*, where, owing to changes in production methods and the economies that result from the parent company, Penny Press, having lots of other magazines—mostly crossword magazines—that print at the same size, the larger trim size is not significantly more expensive to produce than the old digest-size editions were).

So, my cautious prediction—knock wood—is that it looks like most of the genre magazines will survive into the next century.

At the same time, it would be prudent not to underestimate the problems facing the magazine market. The dramatic contraction of the domestic distribution network that has been taking place in the last few years, with bigger distributors abruptly swallowing up the small independent distributors (one of the major reasons for precipitous circulation drops in almost all magazines, not just genre ones) continues—in 1996, there were 300 wholesale distributors; in 1999 that total is down to *five*, and the odds are good that it will be down to four before the year is over. There are so few distributors left that it's a buyer's market, and the surviving distributors often charge much higher fees for carrying titles or ask for greatly increased "discounts" and "cash incentives" for carrying them—because they *can*, basically. All of this makes it hard for low-circulation magazines without a company with deep pockets behind them (most SF magazines, basically) to get out on the newsstands effectively, and eats ever more deeply into their profit margin even when they can. Some distributors also set "subscription caps," refusing even to handle magazines with a circulation below a certain set figure, usually a higher circulation figure than that of most genre magazines. With so few distributors, fewer and fewer "sales-points" (individual newsstands) get serviced, because distributors now have such large areas to cover that they don't find it worthwhile to send trucks a long way to service a sales-point that may sell only a few magazines per month, so newsstands may not be able to get copies of genre magazines even if they *want* them; the loss of those one or two magazine sales per month may be negligible to big-circulation magazines like *Cosmo* or *Playboy*, but they can add up vitally for a science fiction magazine. Many newsstand managers have also become much more selective about which magazines they'll display, reducing the numbers of titles they'll put on their shelves, in some cases by as much as half; newsstands now will sometimes refuse to display magazines that fall below a certain circulation figure—again, a figure usually higher than that of most genre magazines.

The net result of all this is that it's a lot harder for genre magazines to get out on as many newsstands as they used to, and—with distributors demanding ever more—a lot harder to make a profit than it used to be, even if you *do* get out there. As I said above, the magazine field has evolved strategies for coping with this situation, and profitability actually seems to be up at many of the magazines, even those with declining circulations, but it's not difficult to envision a hardening economic situation that would drive genre magazines off the newsstands altogether, or at least make it so expensive for them to be there that it's not worth it.

This scenario is why I think it's important for the genre magazines to try to find ways to get around the potential newsstand bottleneck, to find ways to attract new subscribers even *without* a strong presence on the newsstand. Most SF magazines have always been subscription-driven, anyway. Being frozen out of the newsstands would hurt magazines the most by cutting them off from attracting new readers, casual newsstand browsers who might, with luck, eventually become new subscribers; without a constant flow of new suscribers, a magazine's circulation will continually dwindle as natural attrition eliminates a certain percentage of the *old* subscribers.

Which brings us to one of the other hopeful notes struck in the magazine market in 1998: the use of the Internet as a method to do an end-run around traditional distribution channels, potentially enabling the magazines to avoid the newsstand bottleneck and attract the attention of potential new subscribers to their product even *without* much traditional newsstand display. Early in 1998, Internet Web sites went up for both *Asimov's* and *Analog* (*Asimov's* site is at http://www.asimovs.com, and *Analog's* is at http://www.analogsf.com, both sites sponsored by *SF Site*) and, after a full year of operation, the results are encouraging — not only is a small but steady flow of new subscriptions coming through these Web sites every month, but, even more significant, many of them are from heretofore untapped new audiences, particularly from other parts of the world, where interested readers have formerly found it difficult to subscribe because of the difficulty of obtaining American currency and because of other logistical problems (*Asimov's*, for instance, has already picked up new subscribers from Australia, Great Britain, Russia, France, Ireland, Italy, and even the United Arab Emirites, and *Analog* has attracted subscribers from a similar range of countries); the availability of subscribing electronically online, with just the click of a few buttons required rather than a trip to the post office or at least a mailbox, is also proving attractive to domestic customers as well. *The Magazine of Fantasy & Science Fiction* now has a working Internet Web site as well (http://www.sfsite.com/fsf/), as do magazines such as *Absolute Magnitude* and *Weird Tales* (see below for more information), and it is to be hoped that this is an area that will continue to grow, helping the beleaguered genre magazines to survive into the next century.

One of the year's other big stories in the professional magazine market was the rebirth of *Amazing Stories*, reported to have died back in 1994. As it has done several times in its seventy-year-plus existence, *Amazing Stories* rose from the grave one more time in 1998, after memorial services had been read for it and the mourners were already home from the wake. This time, *Amazing Stories* was resurrected in a full-size, full-color format by Wizards of the Coast Inc., who recently bought TSR Inc., *Amazing's* former owner; the editor is Kim Mohan, who was the editor of *Amazing Stories* in its *last* incarnation. The new version features media fiction as well as more traditional science fiction; the first issue, debuted at the 1998 Worldcon, had a painting of the Starship *Enterprise* on the cover, and in its first three issues to date, the magazine has featured several *Star Trek* stories, a *Babylon 5* story, a *Star*Drive*™* story, and other media-and-gaming related stuff, including nonfiction media and gaming columns. On the other hand, the magazine has *also* featured some good to excellent *non*-media-oriented core science fiction by Ursula K. Le Guin, Kristine Kathryn Rusch, Eliot Fintushel, Uncle River, Orson Scott Card, and others, and has featured science columns by people such as Ben Bova and Gregory Benford, as well as book reviews. All of this gives the new *Amazing Stories* a curiously schizophrenic nature, split down the middle between two different kinds of beasts, fish on this side of the line, fowl on the other, and I wonder how the audience is going to react to this — how *either* of the potential audiences are going to react to this. Are the media fans who pick up the magazine looking for a good *Star Trek* story going to like the mainline science fiction stories that make up much of the magazine's contents? Is the media stuff going to appeal to the regular SF fans, or turn them off and drive them away from the magazine? Clearly the idea is that *Amazing Stories* will draw support from *both* audiences, but I can't help wondering if the magazine can long survive being half one thing and half another, if one kind of thing must not eventually drive the *other* kind of thing out of the magazine. Which audience might drive out the other will ultimately be determined by which sort of fans are actually buying the magazine. (And since Wizards of the Coast clearly thinks that it's the media fans who are going to end up paying the bills, would it be unreasonable to wonder if the media fans won't end up demanding that they get rid of all the *other* crap and replace it with *more media fiction* instead?) This is an experiment well worth keeping an eye on; if it works the way the Powers That Be behind the magazine obviously hope it will, then the new *Amazing Stories* may help print science fiction tap into whole new and largely untouched audiences. At the very worst, ignoring the whole media-fiction controversy, *Amazing Stories* will be very welcome as a new high-end market in a genre that needs all the markets it can get, and signs are that it may well prove to be a respectable player in the short-fiction market in the years to come.

Most of the news about *Asimov's* and *Analog* was covered above. *The Magazine of Fantasy & Science Fiction* completed its second full year under new editor Gordon Van Gelder, and although the game of "guess which stories were bought by Gordon and which were inventory left behind by former editor Kristine Kathryn Rusch" still goes on, the Rusch inventory must surely be growing rather thin by now, and chances are from here on in that something that appears in the magazine was bought by Gordon. Although the magazine's circulation declined to a record low, *F&SF* is a magazine blessed with a very low operating overhead (basically, it's run out of the living rooms of people such as Ed Ferman and Gordon, with no office rents to pay and only minimum staff costs), and it's a pretty good bet that *F&SF* is still quite profitable even at its present circulation. New science columnists Pat Murphy and Paul Doherty have come in to supplement Gregory Benford, and the book reviews seem to rotate on an irregular basis between Robert K.J. Killheffer, Michelle West, Elizabeth Hand, and Douglas E. Winter, with a review column by Charles De Lint also in most issues, and occasionally a review column by Gordon himself. Paul Di Fillipo's occasional "Plumage From Pegasus" column is a hoot, often at least as inventive and imaginative as the stories themselves (my favorite this year was the slyly amusing "Next Big Thing" column). As mentioned above, *F&SF* has a new Internet Web site (http: www.sfsite.com/fsf/), one of a cluster of genre-magazine sites on the *SF Site*'s new page, Fictionhome (see below).

The British magazine *Interzone* completed its eighth full year as a monthly publication. Circulation remained more or less steady this year, as it has for several years now, with a subscriber base of about 2,000 and newsstand/bookstore sales of another 2,000. Every year, year in and year out, *Interzone* publishes some of the best fiction to be found in the entire magazine market, and really deserves to be read much more widely than it is. The magazine has been almost impossible to find on newsstands in the United States, even in SF specialty bookstores, but it has recently been redesigned to a slightly smaller format that brings it more in line with other U.S. magazines such as *Science Fiction Age* and *Realms of Fantasy*, and has engaged a new U.S. distributor. Maybe those changes, with luck, will mean that this excellent magazine will be easier to find on this side of the Atlantic in 1999. *Interzone* does have a Web site (http://www.riviera.demon.co.uk/inter-zon.htm), although there's not a lot of content there—you *can* subscribe to the magazine there, though, which is what counts.

Science Fiction Age successfully completed its sixth full year of publication. Although the overall circulation of *Science Fiction Age* dropped again in 1998, following drops in 1997 and 1996, the magazine has several things going for it to offset these losses—for one thing, they attract a *lot* of paid advertisements, far more than any other magazine in the field (with the possible exception of their sister magazine, *Realms of Fantasy*); for another, as part of a parent company, Sovereign Media, that also runs four other magazines, with a fifth on the way, they can take advantage of "economy of scale" savings in printing and publishing costs, and the large number of magazines gives them all a bigger "footprint" on the newsstand (i.e., the amount of rack space devoted to all of the Sovereign Media magazines helps to insure that there's a place there for *Science Fiction Age*). Despite record low circulation figures, *Science Fiction Age*'s publisher states that 1998 was the magazine's most profitable year yet. Artistically, *Science Fiction Age* had another strong year; for the last couple of years, in fact, *Science Fiction Age* has been one of the most reliable sources for good fiction, particularly for good solid core science fiction, in the entire magazine market. Oddly, *Science Fiction Age* does *not* have a Web site, although you'd think that their connections with the media world, particularly the Sci-Fi Channel (which has an extensive Web site of its own) would make that a natural.

Realms of Fantasy is a companion magazine to *Science Fiction Age*, very similar to it in format (a slick, large-size, full-color magazine with lots of ads), except devoted to fantasy rather than science fiction. They completed their fourth full year of publication in 1998. In the last few years, under the editorship of veteran magazine editor Shawna McCarthy, *Realms of Fantasy* has established itself as by far the best of the all-fantasy magazines, with the best of the stories from it only rivaled for sophistication and eclecticism by the best of the fantasy stories published by *The Magazine of Fantasy & Science Fiction* and *Asimov's Science Fiction*. (The other two fantasy magazines, the much longer established *Marion Zimmer Bradley's Fantasy Magazine* — in its tenth year of publication in 1998 — and *Weird Tales* are much more erratic and undependable in literary quality and consistency.) *Realms of Fantasy* also does not have a Web site.

As usual, short SF and fantasy also appeared in many magazines outside genre boundaries, from *The New Yorker* to *Ellery Queen's Mystery Magazine* to *Playboy*.

(Subscription addresses follow for those magazines hardest to find on the newsstands: *The Magazine of Fantasy & Science Fiction*, Mercury Press, Inc., 143 Cream Hill Road, West Cornwall, CT, 06796, annual subscription — $33.97 in U.S.; *Asimov's Science Fiction*, Dell Magazines, P.O. Box 54033, Boulder, CO 80322-4033 — $33.97 for annual subscription in U.S.; *Analog*, Dell Magazines, P.O. Box 54625, Boulder, CO 80323 — $33.97 for annual subscription in U.S.; *Interzone*, 217 Preston Drove, Brighton BN1 6FL, United Kingdom, $60.00 for an airmail one year — twelve issues — subscription. Note that many of these magazines can also be subscribed to electronically online, at their various Web sites.)

With all of the problems — especially rising production costs — threatening the magazine market (and perhaps ultimately all of publishing in general), many cyber-geeks have been insisting for the last few years that the future of fiction publishing, especially short-fiction publishing, lies in the online world, where "online electronic magazines" can be "published" without having to worry about escalating paper and production costs, and can be "delivered" right into the homes of the consumers without having to use outdated physical distribution systems as middlemen.

What nobody has yet figured out is how you can reliably *make money* doing this, and therein lies the rub.

To date, although the promise of "online electronic publication" remains large, it also largely remains a promise that is as yet unfulfilled. So far, in fact, the track record for such "electronic magazines" or "e-zines" is not very good. In the last few years, magazines such as *Omni* and *Tomorrow* have fled the troubled print magazine world for the supposed refuge of electronic publishing, but, in those cases, the refuge proved to be illusionary. *Omni* abandoned their print edition and instead established the *Omni Online* Internet Web site, but that died early in 1998 after a couple of years of operation (although it's hard to say whether it died because it wasn't bringing in enough money or, as some of the people involved with running the site insist, because the top brass at General Media lost interest in supporting it after the death of publisher Kathy Keeton, who had been the real driving force behind *Omni*'s migration into the online world). *Tomorrow* magazine also abandoned its print edition and reinvented itself as an Internet e-zine called *Tomorrow SF*. Last year, I reported that *Tomorrow SF* was in the process of carrying out an interesting experiment, where, after "publishing" the first three online issues of *Tomorrow SF* for free, they had begun charging a "subscription fee" for access to the Web site, hoping that the audience would have been hooked enough by the free samples that they would continue to want the stuff enough to actually *pay* for it. Unfortunately, this experiment seems to have been a failure, which may raise doubts about the viability of the whole "e-zine" concept, since *Tomorrow SF* abruptly gave up its e-zine format in mid-1998. The *Tomorrow SF* site still exists (http://www.tomorrowsf.com), but it has switched over to being an archive site for reprint stories by editor Algis Budrys, rather than an ongoing "magazine" that publishes new stories by other hands.

The blunt fact is that there are not really that many good, professional-level science fiction stories being published online at the moment (at least original stories, stories that are making their initial "appearance" online; there *are* a fairly large number of good reprint stories archived here and there around the Internet, on one site or another). Cyber-optimists insist that this will soon change dramatically—and they may even be right.

At the moment, though, most publishers seem to be using their Web sites for pushing a physical product, selling subscriptions to print magazines and advertising forthcoming books, rather than using them as places to print original fiction online in electronic format. There are exceptions, though.

When the plug was pulled on *Omni Online*, the indomitable Ellen Datlow, fiction editor of *Omni Online* and, before that, longtime fiction editor of the print *Omni*, got together with Robert K. J. Killheffer, former editor of *Century* magazine, and a few other people, and launched a *new* Internet Web site and e-zine, *Event Horizon* (http://www.eventhorizon.com/eventhorizon), which started operation in mid-1998, and which has already become, as was *Omni Online* before it, perhaps your best bet for finding good professional-quality original science fiction, fantasy, and horror stories published in electronic format on the Internet. Since going up, *Event Horizon* has published good work by Howard Waldrop (a story which is reprinted in this anthology for the first time ever in print format, having "appeared" before that only as phosphor dots on a screen), Terry Dowling, Kelly Link, K. W. Jeter, Michaela Roessner, and others, reprints by Robert Silverberg, Carter Scholz, and Pat Cadigan, and "round-robin" stories (written by four authors in collaboration, each writing a section in term) by authors such as Gwyneth Jones, Susan

Casper, Scott Baker, Garry Kilworth, and others. *Event Horizon* also features reviews and other nonfiction pieces, regular columns by Barry N. Malzberg and Lucius Shepard, and hosts regularly scheduled live interactive interviews or "chats" with various prominent authors every Thursday night.

Another interesting experiment, with the jury still out on this one, is taking place at *Mind's Eye Fiction* (http://tale.com/genres.htm), where you can read the first half of a story for free, but if you want to read the *second* half of the story, you have to *pay* for the privilege, which you can do by setting up an electronic account online and then clicking a few buttons; the fees are small, less than fifty cents per story in most cases. I think that this concept actually has a chance of working, although it would probably work better if they had some Bigger Name authors involved with the project, the kind of authors with lots of intensely loyal fans who might be willing and eager to pay a few cents to get an advance look at a story by their favorite author. This is another experiment that's worth keeping a close eye on, and one whose success or failure could have large implications for the future of SF-oriented e-zines on the Internet.

A promising new SF-oriented e-zine is *Dark Planet* (http://www.sfsite.com/darkplanet/), which, in addition to reviews and other features, has published some professional-level work by Kelly Link, Gary A. Braunbeck, Ardath Mayhar, and others. Longer-established sites that are worth watching, although the quality of the fiction can be uneven and they are often not SF-oriented, include *InterText* (http://www.intertext.com/), and *E-Scape* (http://www.interink.com/escape.html). If none of these sites has satisfied your lust for e-zines, you can find *lots* of other genre "electronic magazines" by accessing http://dir.yahoo.com/Arts/Humanities/literature/genres/Science_Fiction_and_Fantasy/Magazines/, but be warned—much of the stuff you'll find on these sites is awful, no better than slush-pile quality (there's an unbelievable amount of it out there, too; you could wade through these sites for a solid year and still have oceans of it left to go by the time you gave up). Links to e-magazines and related sites of interest can also be found at sites such as *Locus Online*, *SF Site*, *Science Fiction Weekly*, and *SFF.NET* (see below).

After this point, original science fiction stories of professional quality become harder to find, rather scarce on the ground, in fact. Many of the remaining SF-oriented sites are associated with existent print magazines—*Eidolon: SF Online* (http://www.eidolon.net/); *Aurealis* (http://www.aurealis.hl.net/) *Asimov's Science Fiction* (http://www.asimovs.com/); *Analog Science Fiction and Fact* (http://www.analogsf.com/); *The Magazine of Fantasy & Science Fiction* (http: www.sfsite.com/fsf/); *Interzone* (http://www.riviera.demon.co.uk/interzon.htm); *Transversions* (http://www.salmar.com/transversions/); *Terra Incognita* (http://www.voicenet.com/~incognit/); *On Spec* (http://www.icomm.ca/onspec/); *Talebones* (http://www.nventure.com/talebones/)—and although many of them have extensive archives of material, both fiction and nonfiction, previously published by the print versions of the magazines, few of them publish original online–only fiction with any regularity; most don't publish it at all, in fact. Magazines like *Asimov's*, *Analog*, *The Magazine of Fantasy & Science Fiction*, and others, regularly run teaser excerpts from stories coming up in forthcoming issues, and occasionally a chunk from an upcoming novel will appear somewhere, but complete original stories are rarer (I've run one online original, by Michael Swanwick and Sean Swanwick, on the *Asimov's* site, and would like to do more of this, but finding the money to finance it is not easy). *Eidolon Online* published a good original story last year, which appeared in our Fifteenth Annual Collection, but don't seem to have done much along those lines since. *Talebones* seems to have published some original stories online (it's sometimes hard to tell, as attribution is often nonexistent) by Terry McGarry, Mary Soon Lee, Uncle River, Darell Schweitzer, and others. A good general site where you can be pretty sure of finding something of quality to read is the British *Infinity Plus* (http://www.users.zetnet.co.uk/iplus/), which features a very extensive selection of reprint stories, most by British authors, as well as extensive biographical and bibliographical information, book reviews, critical essays, and so forth — as far as I can tell, though, there are few if any original online–only stories published here, although they do publish novel extracts from upcoming novels.

Fiction is not the only SF-oriented stuff of interest to check out on the Internet, however. Some of the most prominent SF-related sites on the Internet, and some of the sites that I visit the most frequently, are the general-interest sites that, while they *don't* publish fiction, do publish lots of reviews, critical articles, and genre-oriented news of various kinds. One of the most substantial of these sites is *SF Site* (www.sfsite.com/), which over the last year has turned itself into one of the most important genre-related sites on the whole Web. Their home page features an extensive selection of reviews of books, games, and magazines, interviews, critical retrospective articles, letters, and so forth, plus a huge archive of past reviews; in addition, starting with *Asimov's* and *Analog* early in 1998, they've become the host site for the Web pages of a significant percentage of all the SF/fantasy print magazines in existence, including *The Magazine of Fantasy & Science Fiction*, and the recently assembled DNA Publishing group (see below) of *Absolute Magnitude*, *Pirate Writings*, *Weird Tales*, *Aboriginal SF*, and *Dreams of Decadence* (which can be accessed directly at http://www.sfsite.com/dnaweb/home.htm). In early 1999, they also instituted a section called *Fictionhome* (http://www.sfsite.com/ fiction/fichome.htm), where reviews of and links to all of the above magazines can be found, and which also plays host to the electronic version of *Tangent* called *Tangent Online*, one of the few places online where you can read regularly scheduled reviews of short fiction, and to the online version of *Science Fiction Chronicle*. Another general-interest site that's one of my most frequent destinations while net-surfing is *Locus Online* (http://www.locusmag.com), the online version of the newsmagazine *Locus*; *Locus Online* is a great source for fast-breaking genre-related news, where it sometimes shows up weeks before it even makes it into the print *Locus*, but I must admit that to a large extent I read the site for the online version of Mark Kelly's short fiction-review column, the *other* place on the net where you can find regularly appearing reviews of SF and fantasy short fiction; there are also book reviews, critical lists, database archives, links to other sites of interest, and the like here. Another valuable general-interest site, one that's been around long enough to be almost venerable by the mayfly standards of the Internet, is *Science*

Fiction Weekly (http://www.scifiweekly.com), which is somewhat more media-and-gaming oriented than *SF Site* or *Locus Online*, but which does feature book reviews every issue, of both new releases and classic reprints, and also features an erudite, opinionated, and occasionally fiercely controversial column by John Clute, perhaps SF's premiere critic. A new entry in this category is *SFRevu* (http://www.sfrevv.com//members.aol.com/sfrevu/), another site full of book and media reviews, and other genre-related information. *SFF NET* (http//www.sff.net) is a huge site that functions as a home away from home for many writers, featuring dozens of home pages for SF writers, genre-oriented "live chats," and, among other lists of data, the Locus Magazine Index 1984–1996, which is an extremely valuable research tool; you can also link to the Science Fiction Writers of America page from here, where valuable research data and reading lists are to be found as well, or you can link directly to the SFFWA Web Page at http://www.sfwa.org/. Live online interviews with prominent genre writers are now offered on a regular basis on many sites, including interviews sponsored by *Asimov's* and *Analog* and conducted by Gardner Dozois on the Sci-Fi Channel (http://www.scifi.com/chat/—there's also an enormous amount of SF-media-related stuff available here) every other Tuesday night at 9:00 P.M. EST, interviews conducted by Ellen Datlow every Thursday night at 9:00 P.M. EST on the *Event Horizon* site (http://www.even-thorizon.com/eventhorizon/), regular scheduled interviews on the *Cybling* site (http://www.cybling.com/), and occasional interviews on the *Talk City* site (http://www.talkcity.com/). Many Bulletin Board Services, such as *GEnie*, *Delphi* (which also now has a Web site, http://www0.delphi.com/sflit/), *Compuserve*, and *AOL*, have large online communities of SF writers and fans (with *GEnie* having perhaps the largest and most active such community). Most of these services also feature regularly scheduled live interactive real-time "chats" or conferences, in which anyone interested in SF is welcome to participate, as does *SFF NET*—the SF-oriented chat on *Delphi*, the one with which I'm most familiar, and one which gives you the opportunity to schmooze with well-known professional SF writers in a relaxed and informal atmosphere, starts every Wednesday at about 10:00 P.M. EST.

Many of the criticalzines also have Web sites, including *The New York Review of Science Fiction* (http://www.sfsite.com/isfdb/nyrsf.html), *Nova Express* (http://www.delphi.com/sflit/novaexpress/index.html), *Speculations* (http://www.speculations.com/), and *SF Eye* (http://www.empathy.com/eyeball/sfeye.html), although most of these sites are not particularly active ones. And for a funny and often iconoclastic slant on genre-oriented news, from multiple Hugo-winner David Langford, check out the online version of his fanzine *Ansible* (http://www.dcs.gla.ac.uk/Ansible/).

There may not be a lot of original SF being published on the Net as yet, but the whole SF community on the Web is growing so fast, and is not only becoming larger but, perhaps more importantly, becoming more intensely *interconnected*, with links being forged from site to site, that it's an area well worth keeping an eye on. I suspect that it's an area that will become more and more important as we penetrate ever deeper into the new century ahead.

• • •

It was a year of big changes in the semiprozine market, some of them potentially quite positive, others, alas, not so positive.

The big story in the semiprozine market for 1998 was the consolidation of several struggling fiction semiprozines under the same roof. Warren Lapine's DNA Publications (previously the publisher of *Absolute Magnitude*) bought up several competing magazines this year, ending up with six of them: *Absolute Magnitude, The Magazine of Science Fiction Adventures; Pirate Writings, Tales of Fantasy, Mystery & Science Fiction; Aboriginal Science Fiction; Weird Tales* (back to its old title again after several issues in exile as *Worlds of Fantasy and Horror*); the all-vampire-fiction magazine *Dreams of Decadence*; and the new Australian magazine *Altair* (see below) — Warren became owner of all of these but *Aboriginal Science Fiction*, which he is managing; the current editors of all the magazines continue to provide the editorial content for a fee or a percentage, and DNA Publications handles the production, circulation, and the business end. The hope is that this move will enable DNA Publications to take advantage of the economies of scale and an increased "footprint" on the newsstand — the same strategy employed by Sovereign Media — as well as generating savings by streamlining the whole operation and making it more efficient. This could well work, as long as Warren hasn't bitten off more than he can chew and becomes overextended and swamped — if he can handle the workload, this could be a big boost to all of the above magazines, some of which have been struggling in the marketplace and could frankly use a boost. So this could turn out to be one of the most positive developments in the semiprozine market in some years. (Warren's other challenge will be to stabilize publication schedules, if he can — most of the above magazines only produced two issues apiece this year instead of following their announced publication schedules, a chronic problem throughout all of the semiprozine market — and to try to produce a more reliable level of quality in the fiction published by those magazines; at the moment, quality is all over the place, from very good to at-best mediocre.) As mentioned above, the Web site for all of the DNA Publications magazines is http://www.sfsite.com/dnaweb/home.htm.

Much of the rest of the news in this market is not so positive — some of it is downright bad, in fact.

The eccentric and eclectic fiction semiprozine *Crank!* officially died this year, after publishing one last issue, as editor Bryan Cholfin announced that he was giving up the magazine so that he could concentrate on his publishing career; Cholfin is now working for Gordon Van Gelder at St. Martin's Press. With the death of *Century* — and, with no new issue in more than three years, I do consider it to be dead, in spite of occasional protests to the contrary, especially as editor Robert K. J. Killheffer has moved on to other projects — both of the most ambitious and literarily sophisticated American fiction semiprozines of the '90s are gone, a dispiriting track record for such magazines. With *Crank!* and *Century* dead, the most ambitious of the remaining American fiction semiprozines, and the one which is probably producing the highest percentage of high-end professional-level work, is newcomer *Terra Incognita*, which this year published an excellent story by Liz Williams, as well as good work by Kandis Elliot, John C. Waugh, Judy Klass, and others — the only problem is, they only managed to publish one out of their scheduled four issues this year, just like last year; they'll have to work hard on their reliability if they want to be the Contender that they potentially could be in this market; otherwise, they chance following *Century* into oblivion down the same old drain. The longer-established *Tales of the Unanticipated*, although not quite up to the same level of accomplishment, did publish some intriguing stuff this year by Eleanor Arnason, Lyda Morehouse, Sue Isle, Martha A. Hood, and others. *Talebones, Fiction on the Dark Edge*, although officially a horror semiprozine, seems to be adding a lot more science fiction and fantasy to its editorial mix these days (making it more attractive to *me*, anyway), and remains a lively and promising little magazine, definitely one to watch. *Space & Time* has been more uneven, but seems to be getting national distribution on some newsstands these days, and so may become more of a player in this market. If there were any issues of *Non-Stop, Xizquil, Argonaut Science Fiction, Next Phase, Plot Magazine*, or *The Thirteenth Moon Magazine* out this year, I didn't see them; I suspect at least some of these magazines are dead.

A new SF fiction semiprozine called *Age of Wonder* published its first issue in early 1998 and died before the middle of the year, perhaps a new record even in the semiprozine market, where magazines often come and go with the speed of mayflies. The lead story from that first (and only) issue, by Gregory Benford, appeared later in the year under a different title in *Science Fiction Age*.

Turning to our neighbor to the north, there are two Canadian fiction semiprozines, the long-established *On Spec*, one of the longest-running of all the fiction semiprozines, and a promising newcomer called *TransVersions*. *On Spec* has seemed a bit sunk in the doldrums for the last few years, with most of the fiction in it gray, oversolemn, and not particularly entertaining, publishing little good core science fiction, except for near-future dystopias (the magazine in general seems to take itself too seriously, as witness its annoying new slogan "more than just science fiction"—to which I must admit my immediate grumpy reaction was "*some* science fiction every once in a while would be nice, though"). Still, *On Spec* is one of the most reliably published of all the fiction semiprozines, and has published a lot of worthwhile stuff over the years, so we shouldn't give up on it; the magazine is set to go to a single editor instead of the "collective" that has been editing it (I don't believe that a committee is any better at selecting fiction than it is at any other task), which may perhaps perk up the fiction. *TransVersions* is also uneven, with some stuff at a decent professional level, and some not, but it seems to have more of a sense of fun about it than *On Spec* has had recently, and is livelier and less pretentious.

Turning our eyes overseas, two of the three longest-established fiction semiprozines (the other one is *On Spec*) are published in Australia: *Aurealis* and *Eidolon*. Although both magazines had their usual difficulty sticking to their quarterly publication schedule, they also published a fair amount of good professional-level fiction, by writers such as Terry Dowling, Simon Brown, Russell Blackford, and others in *Aurealis* (the Double Issue of *Aurealis*, *Aurealis 20/21*, also functions as an Alternate History anthology, about possible alternate futures of Australia), and writers such as William Dowding, Leanne Frahm, Sean Williams, and Simon Brown, and others in *Eidolon*; *Eidolon* is also home to perhaps the most technically difficult and formidable science column in the industry, likely over the head of even most *Analog* readers, by Greg Egan (the sort of column where the text says, "Therefore, we can see that" and then goes on to a solid page or two of equations) as well as a less-demanding new column by Howard Waldrop. Perhaps because of the "boom" that seems to be taking place in the Australian science fiction world, the Australian stuff seems to be more vigorous and substantial than a lot of the other material available elsewhere in the semiprozine market. Another new magazine joined the roster of Australian semiprozines this year, the promising newcomer *Altair*, which published two digest-size issues (the same format as *Aurealis* and *Eidolon*) this year out of a scheduled four, and which is soon going to be available in a full-size semiannual "American edition" from DNA Publications. The fiction in *Altair* is also uneven, as it is in most semiprozines, but they did feature some good professional-level work by Stephen Dedman, Ian Watson, Ben Jeapes, and others; they also publish a fair amount of nonfiction, but I think they could lose most of it without losing anything of real value (especially the beginner-level How to Write articles) and have more room for fiction. (*Altair* has a Web site at http://www.sfsite.com/altair/, and I suspect they'll soon be accessible at the DNA Publications site as well.)

Another promising newcomer, a full-size, full-color British magazine called *Odyssey*, published five issues this year, and seemed to be struggling to establish an identity for itself; torn between being a science fiction magazine, a horror/fantasy magazine, and a media/gaming-oriented magazine, it managed to be sort of all and none of the above at the same time. The fiction was wildly uneven, ranging from ameuter-level stuff to good professional-level work by Ian Watson, Peter T. Garratt, Charles Stross, Ben Jeapes, Constance Ash, Mary Gentle, and others. My advice would be to concentrate more on the fiction, especially good solid core science fiction, and let some of the other stuff go. The covers here were often quite attractive, among the most striking in the industry, but the interior layout is often of the "hip" sort that makes it difficult to read the text, and something has to be done about that—this problem actually seemed to be getting worse rather than better in later issues, culminating in issue 6, where printing stories like Charles Stross's "Extracts from the Club Diary" in light type over gray pages already printed with an illustration made large parts of the story almost impossible to read. A little less coolness and a little more legibility, please! Despite such problems, this is a promising magazine, and could be very good indeed if it manages to shape itself up. Most of the other British fiction semiprozines lean heavily toward "slipstream" and literary surrealism of various sorts; the most prominent of these at the moment seem to be *The Third Alternative* and the long-established *Back Brain Recluse*. I think there might have been an issue of Irish semiprozine *Albedo 1* this year, but, if so, I missed it.

I don't follow the horror semiprozine market much any more, but there the most prominent magazines seem to be the highly respected *Cemetery Dance*, and perhaps *Talebones*.

Turning to the critical magazines, as always, Charles N. Brown's *Locus* and Andy Porter's *SF Chronicle*, remain your best bets among that subclass of semiprozines known as "newszines," and are your best resources if you're looking for publishing news or an overview of what's happening in the genre. *The New York Review of Science Fiction*, edited by David G. Hartwell, completed its tenth full year of publication, once again not only publishing its scheduled twelve issues but publishing them all on time—in the entire semiprozine market, fiction and non-fiction, this is a trick that only *Locus* and *The New York Review of Science Fiction* seem to know how to do; most other magazines count themselves lucky if they can manage to bring out half their scheduled issues. As always, the magazine was full of tasty and informative stuff, articles and reviews that ran the gamut from fascinating to infuriating (sometimes both at once), and eclectic little gems such as "Read This" lists by various well-known authors. Other intriguing critical stuff can be found in Steve Brown's *Science Fiction Eye* and in Lawrence Person's *Nova Express*—when you can find them; actually, this was a red-letter year for *Nova Express*, which managed two issues in the same year, something of a record. There were big changes in the offing this year for David A. Truesdale's *Tangent*, which for several years now has performed an invaluable service by providing a place where interested readers can find reviews of most of the year's short fiction, something that can be found almost nowhere else in the field, except for Mark Kelly's short fiction review column in *Locus*. In late 1997 and early 1998, however, there were signs that *Tangent* was becoming bogged down, and they began delaying and missing issues (my own feeling was that Truesdale was making the magazine too complicated, taking on too many new columns and features, more every issue, it seemed; the basic task they had to do—covering the year's short fiction—was huge and complex enough by itself without having to deal with all of that other stuff as well). Only one issue of *Tangent* came out in 1998, a "Special Double Collector's Issue" released in time for the Baltimore Worldcon, and it was immediately evident that most of the reviews in the issue were of stuff from the previous year; clearly, *Tangent* was falling behind, and rumors began to circulate that the magazine would soon disappear and be heard from no more. Instead, I'm very pleased to say, it metamorphosed rather than died, and can now be found in a new form as *Tangent Online* (http://www.sfsite.com/tangent/index.htm), part of *SF Site*'s short-fiction-oriented new site, *Fictionhome*, and where, liberated from the constraints of printing, production, and distribution, it has already "published" four issues in electronic online format, with a return to something like its old vigor (although there are still too many columns and features, in my opinion, even in the online version; the other stuff we can get elsewhere—*Tangent* should stick to reviewing stories). Since the loss of *Tangent* would be a major blow to the field, we should all breathe a sigh of relief. An as-yet unanswered question is, What will be the fate of the print version of *Tangent*? Supposedly it will continue, as a semiannual supplement to the online version—but it wouldn't entirely surprise me to see the print version fade and *Tangent Online* become the "real" version instead. *Speculations*, which features writing-advice articles as well as extensive sections of market reports and market news, remains a useful resource for young or would-be authors.

(*Locus, The Newspaper of the Science Fiction Field*, Locus Publications, Inc.,

P.O. Box 13305, Oakland, California 94661, $53.00 for a one-year first-class sub-scription, 12 issues; *Science Fiction Chronicle*, P.O. Box 022730, Brooklyn, N.Y. 11202-0056, $25.00 for one-year first-class subscription, 12 issues; *The New York Review of Science Fiction*, Dragon Press, P.O. Box 78, Pleasantville, NY, 10570, $32.00 per year, 12 issues; *Science Fiction Eye*, P.O. Box 18539, Asheville, NC 28814, $12.50 for one year; *Nova Express*, P.O. Box 27231, Austin, Texas 78755-2231, $12 for a one-year (four-issue) subscription; *Tangent*, 5779 Norfleet, Ray-town, MO 64133, $20 for one year, four issues; *Speculations*, 111 West El Camino Real, Suite #109-400, Sunnyvale, CA 94087-1057, a first-class subscription, six issues, $25; *Aboriginal Science Fiction*, P.O. Box 2449, Woburn, MA 01888-0849, $19.00 for four issues; *Marion Zimmer Bradley's Fantasy Magazine*, P.O. Box 249, Berkeley, CA 94701, $16 for four issues in U.S.; *Odyssey*, Partizan Press 816-818 London Road, Leigh-on-Sea, Essex SS9 3NH, United Kingdom, $35 for a five-issue subscription, $75 for a twelve-issue subscription; *On Spec, More Than Just Science Fiction*, P.O. Box 4727, Edmonton, AB, Canada T6E 5G6, $18 for a one-year subscription; *Aurealis, the Australian Magazine of Fantasy and Science Fiction*, Chimaera Publications, P.O. Box 2164, Mt. Waverley, Victoria 3149, Australia, $43 for a four-issue overseas airmail subscription, "all cheques and money orders must be made out to Chimarea Publications in Australian dollars"; *Eidolon, the Journal of Australian Science Fiction and Fantasy*, Eidolon Publications, P.O. Box 225, North Perth, Western Australia 6906, $45 (Australian) for a four-issue overseas airmail subscription, payable to Eidolon Publications; *Altair, Alternate Airings of Speculative Fiction*, PO Box 475, Blackwood, South Australia, 5051, Australia, $36 for a four-issue subscription; *Back Brain Recluse*, P.O. Box 625, Sheffield S1 3GY, United Kingdom, $18 for four issues; *REM*, REM Publications, 19 Sandringham Road, Willesden, London NW2 5EP, United Kingdom, £7.50 for four issues; *Pirate Writings, Tales of Fantasy, Mystery & Science Fiction*, DNA Publications, PW Subscriptions, P.O. Box 2988, Radford, VA 24142, $15 for one year (four issues) *Absolute Magnitude, The Magazine of Science Fiction Adventures*, P.O Box 13, Greenfield, MA 01302, four issues for $14, all checks payable to "D.N.A. Publications"; *TransVersions*, Paper Orchid Press, 216 Woodfield Road, Toronto, Ontario, Canada M4L 2W7, four-issue subscription, $20 Can. or U.S.; *Terra Incognita*, Terra Incognita, 52 Windermere Avenue #3, Lansdowne, PA 19050-1812, $15 for four issues; *Talebones, Fiction on the Dark Edge*, Fairwood Press, 10531 SE 250th Pl. #104, Kent, WA 98031, $16 for four issues; *Cemetery Dance*, CD Publications, Box 18433, Baltimore, MD 21237.)

It was a fairly weak year for original anthologies, with a few moderately bright spots.

Starlight 2 (Tor), edited by Patrick Nielsen Hayden, was probably the best orig-inal science fiction anthology published this year in the United States, but the competition it had to overcome to claim the title this year was even weaker than the competition the original *Starlight 1* had to overcome back in 1996. *Starlight 2* is still a superior anthology, containing two of the year's best stories, by Robert Charles Wilson and Ted Chiang, and good, quirky, ambitious work by several other authors, but it is by no means as strong overall as *Starlight 1* was, and doesn't seem to be generating the same kind of critical buzz, either.

As mentioned, my favorites in *Starlight 2* were Ted Chiang's complex and subtle novella "Story of Your Life" and Robert Charles Wilson's clever metaphysical reductio ad absurdum "Divided by Infinity." A step below those was Ellen Kushner's "The Death of the Duke," an elegant fantasy story strongly reminiscent in mood of later-period Le Guin (a high compliment as far as *I'm* concerned), Geoffrey A. Landis's bitter "Snow," David Langford's somewhat less bitter but more complicated take on similar territory, "A Game of Consequences," and Esther M. Friesner's unflinchingly brutal "Brown Dust," definitely *not* an example of Friesner in her more characteristic Funny Stuff or Sentimental modes (considered in light of Roger Zelazny's well-known dictum that a short story should be the last chapter of a novel you don't actually write, it struck me as interesting that Friesner's "Brown Dust" reads more like the *first* chapter of a novel she didn't actually write; it wouldn't be hard for her to go on from here and actually *write* such a novel either, in spite of what happens to her protagonist in the course of the story).

A step below these were several stories I didn't have a strong reaction to one way or the other, competent but not (to me, anyway) exciting, including Susanna Clarke's kidnapped-by-faeries fantasy, "Mrs Mabb," Martha Soukup's better-watch-out-what-you-wish-for story on the borderline of science fiction, "The House of Expectations," and M. Shayne Bell's entertaining but somewhat unlikely time-travel story (I can't really believe that the minor change he posits would have the wide-sweeping effect he claims it would have), "Lock Down." Everything else in the book struck me as flawed to one degree or another. Raphael Carter's "Congenital Agenesis of Gender Ideation" has some very intriguing ideas, but, as fiction presented in the form of an academic paper, it is also as dry as the form it is mimicking. Carter Scholz's surrealistic "The Amount to Carry" is vividly and lyrically written, but probably a good deal too long; toward the end, it began to seem dull rather than nightmarish, and I doubt I would have finished it if I hadn't been paid to do so; it also breaks no new ground for Scholz, being the sort of territory he's covered several times in the past. Angélica Gorodischer's "The End of a Dynasty," elegantly translated by Ursula K. Le Guin, has some amusing touches, but again seems ultimately uninvolving and overly stylized to me. I responded least well to Jonathan Lethem's "Access Fantasy," which in spite of its pose of hip modernism comes across (to me, anyway) as recycled *Galaxy*-era satire, starting out in a traffic jam on the highway that's been locked in place so long that whole families have been living in their cars for decades, raising their children there, and going on to become a killer satire of the advertising industry.

Overall, a fair number of the stories here seem dry and abstract to me; not only is there not much color, action, or (with a few significant exceptions) sense-of-wonder stuff here, but there's really not a lot of genuine *emotion* of any sort generated by most of the stories. Highly intelligent, but cool and somewhat remote. I suppose that "dry" is as good an overall characterizing adjective as any for this volume.

The Chiang novella and the Robert Charles Wilson story, though, *are* among the best stories of the year, and, along with the Friesner, the Landis, the Kushner, and a few others, definitely make this anthology worth the price of admission, even as an expensive hardcover, even if it's not as memorable overall as the original *Starlight 1* had been. With these two volumes, *Starlight* has firmly established itself as one of the most important anthology series of recent years, and it is to be hoped that it will continue for many years to come.

A worthwhile follow-up candidate for the title of best original SF anthology of the year, behind *Starlight 2*, is harder to find, although I guess I would have to vote for *Lord of the Fantastic* (Avon Eos), edited by Martin H. Greenberg, the Roger Zelazny tribute anthology, even though it contains almost as much fantasy as it does science fiction, and some of the best stories in it are reprints, having appeared previously in *Science Fiction Age* and *Asimov's Science Fiction*.

The contents of the anthology break down roughly into two parts: those stories that really have nothing in particular to do with Roger Zelazny or his work, and that could have appeared with equal justification in any other market (several of these authors claim "inspiration" by Zelazny as a rationale for their inclusion here, but that inspiration often doesn't show up on the *page* to any noticeable degree), and those that either use Zelazny characters and settings or attempt to do a pastiche or homage to his characteristic and highly individual writing style, even when, as in Walter Jon Williams's "Lethe," they don't use any actual thematic material from Zelazny's published work (as a subset of this category, there are also several stories that use the author *himself* as a character, embroiling him with time-travelers or aliens, a type of story familiar from the earlier Jack Williamson and Ray Bradbury tribute anthologies, and from the Isaac Asimov memorial anthology; the most ingenious story of this type is Robert Silverberg's "Call Me Titan," which also does a moderately good job of pastiching Zelazny's exuberant style); both categories can then be broken down further into successful and less successful stories, with good and bad stuff in both.

It's an uneven anthology, with a lot of weak material in it—although only one story, Jennifer Roberson's "Mad Jack," was bad enough to make me throw the book across the room in disgust—but also with good to excellent work by William Browning Spencer, William Sanders, John Varley, and Neil Gaiman, solid entertaining work by Nina Kiriki Hoffman, Jack Williamson, Pati Nagle, Steven Brust, John J. Miller, Jane Lindskold, Jack C. Haldeman II, and others, plus the above-mentioned reprints by Robert Silverberg, Walter Jon Williams, and Gregory Benford, all of high quality, and all of which will still count toward the strength of the volume as far as the average reader is concerned.

It was interesting to me that so many of the authors who *did* use characters or settings from Zelazny's work chose fantasy rather than science fiction, and that much of their inspiration was drawn from Zelazny's later work rather than from his earlier, more famous stuff—there is nothing here that draws on *Lord of Light* or the *Amber* novels, for instance, but there are several stories that seem to have been inspired by Zelazny's late fantasy *A Night in the Lonesome October*, and at least one that draws its inspiration from Zelazny's Flying Dutchman fantasy, *And Only I Am Escaped to Tell Thee*, although that produces one of the book's strongest stories, the Varley (which is, however, a story that doesn't really seem to owe that much stylistically or conceptually to Zelazny, once given the basic theme, and could have appeared anywhere without the Zelazny connection being particularly noticeable). Steven Brust does draw on the background of an alien-dominated Earth from *This Immortal*, a background rich enough to support a dozen more stories, and I can see that this one might even have been a story Zelazny himself might have chosen to tell (although if he did, certainly he would have found a way to tell it that didn't bog the story down in technical poker terms to such a degree that the narrator has to call a halt to the narration to explain them every couple of paragraphs!), and Nina Kiriki Hoffman draws on *Isle of the Dead*, but I would like to have seen more such use made of Zelazny's colorful worlds and characters, especially the science fictional ones; with such material to draw on, it seems a shame to settle for standard bland contemporary-fantasy backgrounds, as several authors do. Some authors reflect Zelazny's fondness for playing mix-and-match with elements from different mythological systems, although only Silverberg and William Sanders really do this well, and only Sanders succeeds at catching a bit of the flavor of caustic humor and deliberate playful anachronism that usually characterized Zelazny's own ventures into this area. Of all the book's authors, only William Browning Spencer and Neil Gaiman come close to catching the flavor of high-spirited, rapid-fire, pyrotechnic *outrageousness* that characterized early Zelazny at his best, and only Neil Gaiman really plays with the language in anything like the exuberant, freewheeling, risk-taking way that Zelazny played with it in his prime.

At a rather modest (by today's standards) cover price of $14.00, *Lord of the Fantastic* is a fairly good reading bargain, and will certainly be worth the money to most readers.

Another of 1998's few worthwhile anthologies was *Bending the Landscape: Science Fiction, Original Gay and Lesbian Writing* (Overlook), edited by Nicola Griffith and Stephen Pagel, although this was not as strong an anthology overall as 1997's *Bending the Landscape: Fantasy*. The anthology contains a lot of minor material, and even most of the good stories here provide either a strong SF element or a strong gay element, but rarely integrate both elements in a balanced way in a single story. In some of the stories, such as Keith Hartman's "Sex, Guns, and Baptists," *both* elements are superficial and arbitrary, since there's no intrinsic reason why the story (a familiar one about a private investigator spying on an illicit couple in a hotel-room tryst, and the consequences that arise when his emotionally unstable client finds out what's going on inside) needed to be told about a gay couple in the first place, and the very minimal SF elements present, like the PI's "fiber-optic snake," are window-dressing, so that there was no compelling reason for this story to be *either* about gay people *or* a science fiction story. To show that SF and gay themes *can* be combined in such a way that each is dependent on the other, and the synthesis gives the author a way to say something about society that otherwise could not easily be said, one only needs to point to Greg Egan's "Cocoon" (only the first such example to come to mind), but there is little here that successfully integrates the anthology's two elements in an organic way. There *are* excellent stories here by Ellen Klages (the most successful of the book's authors in providing a story where both the SF element and the gay element are integral to the plot) and Jim Grimsley (whose story is the most emotionally powerful in the book—but also has so little to do with homosexuality that the gay element is almost subliminal), as well as good work by Rebecca Ore, Nancy Kress, Mark W. Tiedemann, L. Timmel Duchamp, Charles Sheffield, and others—but at $26.95, it's rather steeply priced for what you get, and some readers may be disappointed. (The Overlook Press, Peter Mayer Publishers, Inc., Lewis Hollow Road, Woodstock, New York 12498—$26.95 for *Bending the Landscape: Science Fiction*.)

Also interesting, if not quite in the same weight class as the anthologies above, is the mixed original-and-reprint anthology *More Amazing Stories* (Tor), edited by Kim Mohan. As I read this book, I found myself wondering how best to describe the flavor of the "typical *Amazing* story"; there *is* such a flavor, I think, but articulating it precisely is difficult. The typical *Amazing* story is less rigorous than an *Analog* story, less literarily intense than an *Asimov's* story . . . which ought to make it roughly the same as an *F&SF* story, but that's not quite it either; there are noticeable differences in flavor between the usual *Amazing* story and the usual *F&SF* story as well, although the stuff in *Amazing* is perhaps somewhat closer to *F&SF* material in feel than it is to either *Analog* or *Asimov's*.

About the closest I can come to it is that many of the stories in *Amazing* mix science fiction and fantasy in the same story, producing stories that can either be looked at as hybrids of SF and fantasy (if you're feeling charitable) or nonrigorous SF that doesn't concern itself much with scientific plausibility or social consistency (if you're not). The best story by a good margin in the anthology, for instance, Ursula K. Le Guin's reprint story "Unchosen Love," is a ghost story that takes place in a science fiction milieu. The best of the original stories here, Eleanor Arnason's "The Gauze Banner," is a "translation" into English of a consciously crafted bit of mythology, featuring gods with vast supernatural powers, created by an alien living in another science fiction milieu (and who probably doesn't believe in the actual existence of the gods he's describing either). SF, or fantasy? Or a bit of both? The life-transforming "miracles" for sale in Nancy Springer's "The Time of Her Life" are couched superficially in terms of technology, and yet that technology is never really explained or rationalized and makes little real sense either in itself or as part of a society, and the shopkeepers who proffer it are called "angels." Along the same lines, not even a token scientific double-talk explanation of the machine that keeps a mother's baby in some sort of suspension, waking it for an hour every few years, is ever offered in Marti McKenna's "Perchance to Dream," and little time is wasted wondering about what the overall effect on society such technology would be; it's merely an enabling device to allow the mother to grow old while her baby stays forever young, and a magic spell would have done the job just as effectively, if not more so. And so it goes with story after story here, many of which are presented as science fiction, and couched in SF's terminology, but where the fantastic element is so unexamined and unexplained, and exists in such isolation from the rest of the society, that the story might just as well be fantasy.

It strikes me that the closest relative to "the typical *Amazing* story," with its SF furniture and fantasy aesthetic, is probably not to be found in print literature at all, but rather in television—it's very close to the mix used in television's *The Twilight Zone*, where the premises could shock or amuse, but very rarely stood up under any sort of closer examination. Like *The Twilight Zone*, sometimes the results are very entertaining; sometimes they're just annoying.

The original stories here are, for the most part, solid and entertaining but not particularly memorable or first-rate; the best of the lot is the Arnason, with good work also being done by S. N. Dyer, L. A. Taylor, Don Webb, and others, but the anthology as a whole is strengthened by the presence of some good reprint work, including the above-mentioned Le Guin story and reprint stories by Howard Waldrop, Gregory Benford, James Alan Gardner, and Philip K. Dick, and is further bolstered by an interesting article about the work of Philip K. Dick by Robert Silverberg, so the package as a whole does deliver value for your money, although at a somewhat steep cover price of $24.95, it's probably a marginal buy; it would be a better deal if it was being offered as a cheaper trade paperback or mass-market.

An unusual item is *Dreaming Down-Under*, edited by Jack Dann and Janeen Webb, a huge mixed anthology of Australian science fiction, fantasy, horror, and "magic realism" (by which the editors seem to mean literary surrealism of various sorts), which may well be the best overall anthology of the year, pound for pound, although few American readers will have seen it, and it's so inclusive across so many genre lines that it's hard to know where to categorize it. In the United States, the different genres represented in *Dreaming Down-Under* are to a large extent kept discrete; you may see a couple of them represented in the same magazine or anthology, but rarely *all* of them. This mixing of different genres in one literary package seems to be characteristic of Australia, though — the new Australian Best of the Year anthology series edited by Jonathan Strahan and Jeremy G. Byrne is set up that way, and you'll find a similar mix of genres in most issues of Australian semiprozines such as *Eidelon* and *Aurealis*. (For what it's worth, the cover copy here refers to this mix as "wild-side fiction," listing its elements as "fantasy, horror, magic realism, cyberpunk and science fiction"; interesting that those last two seem to be considered to be separate subgenres!) For someone accustomed to American practice, it may seem as though there are really several *different* books here in one package, and, in fact, it would be easy enough to carve *Dreaming Down-Under* up into separate volumes of science fiction, fantasy, and horror (which would still leave a few literary "unclassifiables" left over!) . . . and I wonder if indeed this won't be its fate when the American publishing industry finally comes to grips with the problem of an American edition (or editions). Still, having so many different genres represented in one volume does give you a one-stop overview across the entire spectrum of the booming Australian publishing scene, and the anthology is worthwhile for that alone, as well as serving as an introduction to a great many writers of whom most of the American audience will not have heard before.

For me, the most effective stories here were usually the ones that had the most local color, the ones that, if science fiction, dealt the most centrally with the special problems and characteristics of Australian society and culture, or, if fantasy, the ones that centered around aboriginal mythology or the (sometimes hybrid) folkways developed by the Europeans after settlement; the further away from Australian settings, themes, and concerns the stories got, the weaker they became generally. There *is* a fair amount of weak material here: there's too much second-generation cyberpunk, which is beginning to feel a bit tired fifteen years after *Neuromancer*, the horror is mild by contemporary American standards, and some of the stories are minor enough that it seems likely that they were used only because of a (perhaps misplaced) desire to be as inclusive as possible across the wide spectrum of currently active Australian writers (although, in this context, the absence of Greg Egan, probably Australia's hottest genre writer of the '90s, may be remarked upon by some) — but the book is *so* huge that a strong still-larger-than-normal-size anthology could still be put together out of what's left. *Dreaming Down-Under* contains excellent science fiction by Chris Lawson, Cherry Wilder, Damien Broderick, Terry Dowling, David J. Lake, Sean Williams, Dirk Strasser, and others, good fantasy by Stephen Dedman, Lucy Sussex, Simon Brown, Jane Routley, Rosaleen Love, Sean McMullen, Kelly Greenwood, and others, and good horror by Wynne Whiteford, Sara Douglas, Ian Nichols, Paul Brandon, and others. The most frustrating item here is *part* of a science fiction novella by the late George Turner, left unfinished when he died; what there is of it here is first-rate work (if the rest of the story lived up to the promise of what's on the page here, it probably would have been the best story in the book, and one of the best of the year). It's a tragedy that Turner was unable to complete it, but I wonder if it was really a good idea to include an unfinished novella in the anthology, although no doubt Turner completists will be glad to have it; the casual reader, though, is likely to find it just frustrating.

On the whole, then, this is an anthology that's well worth the money, both in itself and as a window on a whole fascinating world of science fiction and fantasy that's developed in parallel to but distinct from American genre work and even British genre work, a world produced by convergent evolution, in some ways familiar, and yet also various and strange.

Alternate Generals (Baen), edited by Harry Turtledove, is both more substantial and less flamboyant than most of the long string of Alternate History anthologies edited in recent years by Mike Resnick, for both better *and* worse; there are no really first-rate stories here, as occasionally *did* crop up as the high points of the Resnick Alternate anthologies (Maureen McHugh's "The Lincoln Train," for instance, or Pat Cadigan's "Dispatches from the Revolution"), but if the highs are not as high, the lows are not as low, either. You get far fewer of the kind of stories that postulate the wildly improbable if not impossible (and often downright silly) scenarios ("Suppose Mother Teresa formed an outlaw gang during the Depression with Einstein and Albert Schweitzer!", "Suppose Buddy Holly became president of the United States!") that often filled the Resnick anthologies, stories that, in the more extreme cases, strike me as being just fantasy stories with all-star celebrity casts rather than valid science fiction at all (the same way I feel about Kim Newman and Eugene Byrne's "Alternate History" stories that have been running for years in *Interzone*). Not surprisingly, considering that Harry Turtledove is the editor, the stories here are less frothy and "playful" and more stick-to-your-ribs substantial, with less emphasis on the self-consciously "outrageous" juxtaposition of wild and crazy images and much more emphasis on historical scenarios that, although often unlikely, actually *could* happen — which, in my opinion, is where the interest of most good Alternate History stories lies: seeing how radical a change in subsequent history you can produce by altering only one or two historical parameters, things that might actually *have* happened but which (in this universe) did not. The trick is to do that without spinning away into anything-can-happen-What-if-Napoleon-had-a-B-52-at-Waterloo? fantasies, which for serious Alternate History writers is the equivalent of the hard science writers's famous complaint about "playing with the net down."

The authors here do a pretty good job of pulling off that trick, on the whole, walking the line between "imaginative" and "impossible." The overall mood of the anthology is serious, if not somber (in a few cases, almost a bit stodgy), and many of the alternate history scenarios are ingenious, and elegantly minimalist, producing substantial ultimate changes from small changes in initial conditions. "Substantial," in fact, is a good overall word to describe this particular book. It helps to be a history buff if you're really going to appreciate *Alternate Generals* — and, in fact, it helps to be a *military* history buff; if you're not, you may have difficulty here and there figuring out how and why things have changed from the actual history of our world; you may not even know what the actual events were in the *first* place, which diminishes the impact of seeing them cleverly changed, always a fundamental problem for Alternate History; without hitting the reference books, for instance, I find that I have no idea what the "real history" events are that are being altered in a story such as Elizabeth Moon's otherwise-rousing chase-and-battle-at-sea story "Tradition," and I doubt that many other readers will, either. There are a few other stories that suffer from this syndrome as well. The best stories here are William Sanders's vivid "Billy Mitchell's Overt Act" and Lois Tilton's ingenious "The Craft of War," but the book also features, yes, *substantial* work by Esther M. Friesner, David Weber, R. M. Meluch, Lillian Stewart Carl, S. M. Stirling, Turtledove himself, and others. At a cover price of $5.99, it's a solid reading value.

Interestingly, perhaps out of a fear that there *aren't* that many military history buffs out there after all, the publisher has done its best with its packaging and its cover copy to make this look like one of the Resnick-style wild-and-crazy juxtapositions kind of anthologies, instead of what it actually is. The cover painting, for instance, features a Roman soldier riding in a World War II–style tank, and the back-cover copy burbles "At Gaugemela the Macedonians had Alexander and the Persians had — Darius . . . . But what if the Persians had — Erwin Rommel. Or what if George S. Patton had commanded Southern forces at Bull Run, and Lincoln had become a Confederate prisoner?" — all scenarios which, as far as I can tell, do *not* occur in any of the stories in the book. I'm not sure of the wisdom of trying to fool the reading public into thinking they're buying one kind of thing when actually they're getting quite a different kind of thing altogether (if Baen wanted a Resnick-style alternate history anthology, why didn't they hire *Resnick* to do one for them in the first place?), as though consumers who thought they were buying chocolate ice cream won't notice they're been given strawberry instead, but that's pretty much what the packaging here attempts to do. Strange.

There was also an Alternate-History-of-Canada anthology this year, *Arrow-Dreams: An Anthology of Alternate Canadas* (Nuage Editions), edited by Mark Shainblum and John Dupuis, most of the contents of which were earnest but rather dull, although there is interesting work here by Eric Choi, Derryl Murphy, Glenn Grant, and others. (Nuage Editions, P.O. Box 206, RPO Corydon, Winnipeg, Manitoba, Canada R3M 3S7—CDN $19.95 for *ArrowDreams: An Anthology of Alternate Canadas*.) (We somehow missed another original anthology of Canadian fiction, *Tesseracts*⁶ [Tesseract], edited by Robert J. Sawyer and Carolyn Clink, which we'll have to save for next year.) The double issue of the Australian semiprozine *Aurealis*, *Aurealis* 20/21, also functions as an Alternate History anthology about the possible futures ahead for Australia, and is somewhat livelier and more entertaining than its Canadian counterpart, with good work by Simon Brown, Terry Dowling, Sue Isle, Russell Blackford, and others, although most of the scenarios here are not terribly likely either.

An even more specialized Alternate History item is *Alternate Skiffy* (Wildside Press), edited by Mike Resnick and Patrick Nielsen Hayden, which I missed when it appeared late last year. As the title indicates, this anthology makes no bones about being frivolous, even unabashedly silly; in effect, it's a sequence of in-jokes about science fiction fandom and prodom, with almost no chance of being appreciated by anyone who *isn't* seriously involved in those worlds: fan fiction, in other words, although sometimes superior examples of same. The best stories here are David Langford's droll and satirical "The Spear of the Sun" (which originally appeared in *Interzone*, and was reprinted in *Asimov's* a few years back, while this anthology presumably languished on the shelf) and Frederik Pohl's sly and ingenious "The Golden Years of *Astounding*," which makes a surprisingly plausible case for what science fiction would have been like if John W. Campbell had been fired early on and Donald Wollheim put in charge of *Astounding* instead (although I doubt if even the formidable Wollheim would really have been capable of talking J. R. R. Tolkien into writing his magnum opus as a space opera, *The Lord of Saturn's Rings*, rather than as a fantasy—it's a good joke, though, the best in the book). There's other good work here from Barry N. Malzberg, Gregory Feeley, Anthony R. Lewis, Greg Cox, and others. If you're a science fiction fan (particularly a convention-attending fan) or professional, or at least are moderately familiar with the history of the genre, you may well get a few chuckles, and even a belly laugh or two, out of this material. If you're not, I suspect that most of the stories might as well be written in Sanskrit, for all you're going to be able to get out of them. (The Wildside Press, 522 Park Avenue, Berkeley Heights, NJ 07922—$9 for *Alternate Skiffy*.)

There was also a reprint anthology of Alternate History stories, *Roads Not Taken* (Del Rey), edited by Gardner Dozois and Stanley Schmidt.

Although it has the odd distinction of having the second silliest idea for a theme anthology of the year (*Dangerous Vegetables* edges it out by a hair), *Alien Pets* (DAW), edited by Denise Little, turns out to be a decent although unexciting and unexceptional anthology, perhaps even worth the money at a cover price of $5.99, one made up for the most part of pleasant but minor stories. After "pleasant but minor," there really isn't a whole lot left to say about the book, except to observe that the template of the Alien Pet story seems to have been set by Robert Heinlein all the way back in *The Star Beast*, where the protagonist's alien pet actually turns out to be a sentient being of one degree or another of importance in the galactic scheme of things; several stories here ring minor changes on this basic idea. There's nothing even close to exceptional here, but the best work in the anthology is by Jack Williamson, Michelle West, Nina Kiriki Hoffman, Jane M. Lindskold, and Bruce Holland Rogers.

Oddball items included *Clones and Clones* (Norton), edited by Martha C. Nussbaum and Cass R. Sunstein, a mixed fiction and (mostly) nonfiction anthology about, what else, clones (the nonfiction stuff is rather elementary for a genre audience, with the exception of one nice piece by Stephen Jay Gould, and the fiction is largely uninspired, with the exception of one decent story by Lisa Tuttle), and, even odder, an anthology called *Lamps on the Brow* (James Cahill Publishing), edited by James Cahill, which was published in a print run of only 200 copies by a small press; even after reading the introduction and such front matter as there is, I have no idea what the ostensible theme of this anthology is, what the criterion for inclusion was, or why it's called *Lamps on the Brow*. The book contains an interesting "Introduction" about immortality by Ben Bova (various sorts of "immortality" — or at least of persistence after death — would be my guess as to a unifying theme here, if there is one, although it's a stretch), reprint stories by A. E. van Vogt and Gregory Benford, and mostly minor original stories by Bruce Bethke, David Brin, Andre Norton, Mike Resnick and Josepha Sherman, Harry C. Stubbs (not, note, "Hal Clement"), Gene Wolfe, and Laura Resnick, the most substantial of which is probably the Stubbs, a standard *Analog*-type struggle-to-survive-on-a-hostile-world planet with some good detail, interesting because the protagonist does *not* survive. Another offbeat, hard-to-classify item is *Leviathan 2, The Legacy of Boccaccio* (Ministry of Whimsy Press), edited by Jeff VanderMeer and Rose Secrest, an anthology of "slipstream" stories that may be too far out on the edge for most genre readers, although it does contain interesting work by L. Timmel Duchamp, Stepan Chapman, and others. (Ministry of Whimsy Press, Post Office Box 4248, Tallahassee, Florida 32315 — $10.99 for *Leviathan 2, The Legacy of Boccaccio*.) Also unusual is *Frontiers: On the Edge of the Empire, 3rd Encounters of Science Fiction & Fantasy* (Simetria), edited by Maria Augusta and Antonio de Macedo, a book from the Portuguese Science Fiction Association, with stories by a mixed group of Portuguese and English authors, the stories presented in Portuguese on one side of the book, the same stories presented in English on the flip side.

L. Ron Hubbard Presents Writers of the Future Volume XIV (Bridge), edited by Dave Wolverton, presents, as usual, novice work by beginning writers, some of whom may later turn out to be important talents. Much the same sort of thing could be said about *Spec-Lit, Speculative Fiction No 2*, edited by Phyllis Eisenstein, the second in a series of anthologies that collects student work from Eisenstein's writing class at Columbia College in Chicago — most of the work here is at a competent professional level, and this time there is work by more experienced hands such as Valerie J. Freireich and Phyllis Eisenstein herself, as well as good reprints by George R. R. Martin and Alfred Bester. (For *Spec-Lit, No 2*, send $11.95 to Phyllis Eisenstein, Editor-in-Chief, *Spec-Lit*, Fiction Writing Department, Columbia College Chicago, 600 South Michigan Avenue, Chicago, IL 60605-1996; make checks payable to Columbia College Chicago.)

Other original SF anthologies this year included the above-mentioned *Dangerous Vegetables* (Baen), "created by Keith Laumer," edited by Martin H. Greenberg; *Armageddon* (Baen), edited by David Drake and Billie Sue Mosiman; *The UFO Files* (DAW), edited by Ed Gorman and Martin H. Greenberg; and *The Conspiracy Files* (DAW), edited by Martin H. Greenberg and Scott H. Urban.

Shared-world anthologies this year included: *More Than Honor* (Baen), by David Weber, David Drake, and S. M. Stirling; *Worlds of Honor* (Baen), edited by David Weber; *The Man-Kzin Wars VIII: Choosing Names* (Baen), edited by Larry Niven; and *Dragonlance: The Dragons of Chaos* (TSR), edited by Margaret Weis and Tracy Hickman.

One of the big stories for next year will probably be the appearance of the science fiction version of *Legends*, new stories in a popular and long-running series by major authors called *Far Horizons*, edited by Robert Silverberg. There's also an as-yet untitled major new original anthology series that will be "like *Full Spectrum*," edited by many of the same people who worked on *Full Spectrum*, in the works from Avon Eos; the first volume of that may appear next year, and is keenly anticipated. Another volume of *Starlight* is also in the works. There was still no sign of an edition of George Zebrowski's long-delayed anthology series *Synergy* this year, or of a new edition of *New Worlds*, and, considering all the downsizing that has been going on at White Wolf, I think it's fair to wonder if either of those anthology series is still viable; we'll just have to wait and see.

In fantasy, the best original anthology of the year by far was *Legends* (Tor), edited by Robert Silverberg, an anthology of new stories set in various famous fantasy worlds. I was inclined to dislike *Legends*, turned off by the hype and hoopla about the record size of its advance (by far the largest ever paid for an anthology) and by the cynical "market savvy" of assembling a book composed *only* of bestselling authors—but I must admit that the finished book turns out to be a very substantial anthology, standing head and shoulders above the minor fantasy theme anthologies that make up the rest of this category, undoubtedly the best fantasy anthology of the year. The best story here is Ursula K. Le Guin's exquisitely crafted novella "Dragonfly," but the book also contains strong work by George R. R. Martin, Stephen King, Terry Prachett, Orson Scott Card, Robert Silverberg, Robert Jordan, Terry Goodkind, Anne McCaffrey, and others, all of which—since we're talking about novellas here and this is a *huge* anthology—makes *Legends* one of the best reading bargains, value received for money paid, of the year.

(I'm bemused, though, by the fact that Anne McCaffery's "Dragonrider" series and Robert Silverberg's "Majipoor" series, both of which started out as science fiction series, have seemingly now become fantasy series instead by some discretely unspoken understanding. Some of the series represented here, such as Stephen King's "Gunslinger" series—and, to a lesser extent, Orson Scott Card's "Alvin Maker" series—had strong cross-genre elements in them from the start, but the "Dragonrider" stories started out in *Analog*, for God's sake, as SF, competing for the Hugo with all the other SF stories, and the author herself denied indignantly for years the idea that they were fantasy rather than science fiction. To find these series suddenly an unquestioned part of the fantasy genre instead, as if they'd always been there, is a bit unnerving, smacking of historical revisionism.)

Sirens and other Daemon Lovers (HarperPrism), edited by Ellen Datlow and Terri Windling is also a fairly substantial anthology, although still considerably less so than *Legends*; a book of "erotic tales of magical, obsessional, and irresistible love," it could be considered to be either a fantasy anthology or a horror anthology depending on how you wink at it (it struck me, arbitrarily, as being a shade more fantasy than horror, which is why I'm listing it here, although there is also a good deal of moderately grotesque horror in it as well). The erotic element in the stories here is strong and unambiguous, making it one of the most "adult" (i.e., dirtiest) books of the year, although the stories themselves sometimes give you the impression that they've been created as a vehicle for carrying the erotic scenes rather than because of any intrinsic story that the author really wanted to tell. There is good work here, though, by Tanith Lee, Pat Murphy, Michael Swanwick, Delia Sherman, Brian Stableford, Jane Yolen, Kelly Eskridge, and others.

"Pleasant but minor," a phrase used to describe *Alien Pets*, above, could also be used to describe most of the rest of the year's original fantasy anthologies (which, in some cases, were more minor than pleasant). *Warrior Princesses* (DAW), edited by Elizabeth Ann Scarborough and Martin H. Greenberg, features interesting work by Jane Yolen, Bruce Holland Rogers, Megan Lindholm, Janet Berliner, Esther Friesner, and others. *Olympus* (DAW), edited by Martin H. Greenberg and Bruce D. Arthurs, features interesting work by Esther Friesner, Jane Yolen, Lawrence Watt-Evans, and others. *Black Cats and Broken Mirrors* (DAW), edited by Martin H. Greenberg and John Helfers, features interesting work by Bruce Holland Rogers, Elizabeth Ann Scarborough, Charles de Lint, Michelle West, Nancy Springer, and others. *Battle Magic* (DAW), edited by Martin H. Greenberg and Larry Segriff, features interesting work by Lois Tilton, Ed Gorman, John De Chancie, Nina Kiriki Hoffman, Michelle West, Charles de Lint, and others. And *Camelot Fantastic* (DAW), edited by Lawrence Schimel and Martin H. Greenberg, features interesting work by Ian McDowell, Brian Stableford, Nancy Springer, Mike Ashley, Rosemary Edghill, and others. Occasionally a story here thrusts itself up to a higher level than its fellows ("Thirteen Ways to Water," by Bruce Holland Rogers in *Black Cats and Broken Mirrors*; "Strays," by Megan Lindholm and "Becoming a Warrior" by Jane Yolen in *Warrior Princesses*; "The Miracle of Salamis," by Lois Tilton in *Battle Magic*; and "The Feasting of the Hungry Man," by Ian McDowell and "The Architect of Worlds," by Brian Stableford in *Camelot Fantastic*), but for the most part the stories are pleasant but minor at best, just minor at worst.

The best of these overall, especially if you like Arthurian fantasy, is probably *Camelot Fantastic*, followed by *Warrior Princesses*.

Other original fantasy anthologies this year included *Did You Say Chicks?* (Baen), edited by Esther M. Friesner, *On Crusade: More Tales of the Knights Templar* (Warner Aspect), edited by Katherine Kurtz, and *Mob Magic* (DAW), edited by Brian Thomsen and Martin H. Greenberg.

I'm not following the horror field closely these days, but the most prominent original horror anthology of the year would seem to be *Dark Terrors 4* (Gollancz), edited by Stephen Jones, followed by *Sirens and other Daemon Lovers*, if you list it as a horror anthology instead of a fantasy anthology. (*Dreaming Down-Under*, which contains a lot of horror material, should probably be considered in here somewhere as well.) Other original horror anthologies this year included *In the Shadow of the Gargoyle* (Ace), edited by Nancy Kilpatrick and Thomas S. Roche; *Robert Bloch's Psychos* (Pocket), edited by Robert Bloch; *Horrors! 365 Scary Stories* (Barnes & Noble), edited by Stefan R. Dziemianowicz, Robert Weinberg, and Martin H. Greenberg; *Going Postal* (Space & Time), edited by Gerard D. Houraner; and *Hot Blood X* (Pocket), edited by Jeff Gelb and Michael Garrett.

As you can see, there were a lot of anthologies published this year, but only a few, such as *Starlight 2* and *Legends*, of any real quality. As for the rest, although you may well find some of these books entertaining enough to be worth the money you spend on them, especially with the cheaper ones that are only $5.99 a shot, the money you'd need to buy *all* of them still adds up to a substantial amount. You could take that same amount of money and use it to buy subscriptions to several SF/fantasy magazines instead (if you don't like *Asimov's*, try *Interzone* and *F&SF*, or *Science Fiction Age* and *Realms of Fantasy*), with a far greater assurance of actually getting your money's worth of good stories during the course of the year—but, of course, since I'm a magazine editor myself, this suggestion can be dismissed as self-serving.

Despite several years of gloomy recessionary talk (and recent panicky chatter about the imminent Death of Science Fiction), the novel market appeared to be on the rebound in 1998 after two years of decline, with last year's cutbacks at houses like HarperCollins being more than compensated for by the founding of major new SF lines at places such as Avon and Simon & Schuster UK. Although the *ways* in which science fiction typically gets published continue to alter—mass-market paperback originals, for instance, which once made up the bulk of the field, continued to dwindle, hitting a thirteen-year low in 1998, part of a trend away from mass-market that has persisted for the past several years, while the percentage of titles that are now being done in hardcover or trade paperback instead continued to grow, with original hardcover titles up 21% and original trade paperback titles up 23%—the overall totals of novels published not only held their own rather than slumping disastrously, as had been predicted, but showed some significant growth.

According to the newsmagazine *Locus*, there were 1,959 books "of interest to the SF field," both original and reprint, published in 1998, up 8% from the total of 1,816 such books in 1997, an increase after two years of decline which comes close to reaching the record total of 1,990 in 1991. Original books were up to 1,122 titles, a strong 12% gain over last year's total of 999. The number of new SF novels was up, with 242 novels published as opposed to 229 in 1997 (although still a bit down from the total of 253 in 1996), fantasy was up, with 233 novels published as opposed to 220 in 1997 (the highest total since 234 in 1994), and horror managed to halt and even turn around slightly the precipitous drops it's been suffering since 1995, publishing 110 novels in 1998 as opposed to 106 in 1997 (still down considerably from its high of 193 titles in 1995, though). So,

1998 was not a record year, perhaps, but neither does it show anything like the kind of recessionary, total bust, through-the-floor disastrous crash in overall numbers that some of our gloomier pundits were forecasting. In fact, overall totals are trending *up*, not down, as we near the new century ahead.

As usual, I haven't had time to read many novels this year, and so can contribute no really definitive overview, but of those I have seen, *Mission Child*, Maureen F. McHugh (Avon Eos), *The Alien Years*, Robert Silverberg (HarperPrism), *Distraction*, Bruce Sterling (Bantam Spectra), *The Golden Globe*, John Varley (Ace), *Tea from an Empty Cup*, Pat Cadigan (Tor), *Kirinyaga* (if considered as a novel rather than a collection, as Resnick insists it should be considered), Mike Resnick (Del Rey), *Ports of Call*, Jack Vance (Tor), and *To Say Nothing of the Dog*, Connie Willis (Bantam Spectra), alone should be sufficient to indicate that 1998 was a fairly good year for novels.

Other novels that have received a lot of attention and acclaim in 1998 include: *Starfarers*, Poul Anderson (Tor); *A Clash of Kings*, George R. R. Martin (Bantam Spectra); *Cosm*, Gregory Benford (Avon Eos); *Parable of the Talents*, Octavia E. Butler (Seven Stories); *Dinosaur Summer*, Greg Bear (Warner Aspect); *Maximum Light*, Nancy Kress (Tor); *Moonseed*, Stephen Baxter (HarperPrism); *Flanders*, Patricia Anthony (Ace); *Kirinya*, Ian McDonald (Gollancz); *Darwinia*, Robert Charles Wilson (Tor); *Children of God*, Mary Doria Russell (Villard); *Child of the River*, Paul J. McAuley (Avon Eos); *Deepdrive*, Alexander Jablokov (Avon Eos); *Proxies*, Laura J. Mixon (Tor); *Mockingbird*, Sean Stewart (Ace); *Earth Made of Glass*, John Barnes (Tor) ; *Vast*, Linda Nagata (Bantam Spectra); *Bloom*, Wil McCarthy (Del Rey); *The Children Star*, Joan Slonczewski (Tor); *Irrational Fears*, William Browning Spencer (White Wolf); *Inherit the Earth*, Brian Stableford (Tor); *Girl in Landscape*, Jonathan Lethem (Doubleday Anchor); *Prince of Dogs*, Kate Elliot (DAW); *The Cassini Division*, Ken MacLeod (Orbit); *O Pioneer!*, Frederik Pohl (Tor); *Mother of Plenty*, Colin Greenland (Avon); *Dragon's Winter*, Elizabeth A. Lynn (Ace); *Dreaming in Smoke*, Tricia Sullivan (Bantam Spectra); *Inversions*, Iain M. Banks (Orbit); *Playing God*, Sarah Zettel (Warner); *The Centurion's Empire*, Sean McMullen (Tor); *Newton's Cannon*, J. Gregory Keyes (Del Rey); *Six Moon Dance*, Sheri S. Tepper (Avon Eos); *Climb the Wind*, Pamela Sargent (HarperPrism); *The One-Armed Queen*, Jane Yolen (Tor); *Bag of Bones*, Stephen King (Scribner); and *Faces Under Water*, Tanith Lee (Overlook). (The Overlook Press, Peter Mayer Publishers, Inc., Lewis Hollow Road, Woodstock, New York 12498 — $23.95 for *Faces Under Water*, Tanith Lee.)

Jack Vance's *Ports of Call* is not as good as 1996's *The Night Lamp* (Vance is never at his best when he succumbs to the picaresque plot, and here he's so picaresque that there's hardly any plot at all), but deserves a special mention anyway for the richness of imagination, imagery, and invention that he displays here, and for Vance's deadpan humor and dour irony, something often overlooked and underrated by critics, although *Ports of Call* makes it clear that P. G. Wodehouse is one of Vance's most important literary ancestors. I'd also like to single out for praise Greg Bear's *Dinosaur Summer* for managing to do successfully what a number of other authors have tried and failed to do in recent years, writing a

Young Adult SF novel that manages to be good science fiction *and* entertaining enough to hold the interest of younger readers, all at the same time. The field desperately needs more such books, the '90s equivalent of the so-called juvenile novels by Robert A. Heinlein and Andre Norton that addicted whole generations of readers to science fiction in the '50s and '60s; if we had them, perhaps fewer young readers would be inclined to turn to *Star Trek* and *Star Wars* novels instead for the kind of fast, "fun" read they're looking for. A few conscious attempts have been made in the last couple of years to duplicate the Heinlein-style "juvenile," but they've mostly been faintly dull and weighted down with heavy indigestible lumps of stodgy libertarian polemic. Bear has avoided this trap and instead written a rousing, vivid story about a boy's adventures with living dinosaurs that I certainly would have appreciated when I was fourteen. More power to him. (It would make a great movie, too, if anybody bothered to make good kid's movies anymore.) Special mention should also be made of an odd item, *Psychoshop* (Vintage), an uncompleted novel by the late Alfred Bester that was finished by Roger Zelazny just before his *own* tragic death—alas, this is more of interest for nostalgic value than as a successful novel on its own terms, although flashes of the vivid prose styles of both authors do shine through here and there. Mention should also be made of an omnibus reissue of three classic novels of space travel, A. E. van Vogt's *Voyage of the Space Beagle*, Barry N. Malzberg's *Galaxies*, and Poul Anderson's *The Enemy Stars*, all packaged together in one book as *Three in Space* (White Wolf), edited by Jack Dann, Pamela Sargent, and George Zebrowski; get them while—fleetingly—they're available again.

The first novels that seemed to attract the most attention and arouse the most heat this year were *Halfway Human* (Avon Eos), by Carolyn Ives Gilman, and *Brown Girl in the Ring* (Warner Aspect), by Nalo Hopkinson. Also getting a fair amount of comment were *Dawn Song*, Michael Marano (Tor); *The Iron Bridge*, David Morse (Harcourt Brace); *Silk*, Caitlín R. Kiernan (Roc); *Green Rider*, Kristen Britain (DAW); *The Last Dragonlord*, Joanne Bertin (Tor); and *A Scientific Romance*, Ronald Wright (Picador USA). Tor, Roc, Harcourt Brace, and Avon Eos all published several first novels this year, and are to be commended for it, as all publishers should be who are willing to publish first novels, taking a chance on unknown writers with no track record, a very risky proposition—it's a chance that must be taken by *someone*, though, if the genre is going to continue to grow . . . or even to survive.

It seemed like a pretty good year for novels to me, even if I only actually got to read a handful of them. Avon Eos produced an impressive lineup in its first year of existence under the new imprint, and Tor, Bantam Spectra, and HarperPrism had strong years as well. As has been true more often than not in the last five or six years, there's plenty of hardcore, sure-enough, pure-quill *science fiction* here, with perhaps the majority of titles fitting into that category—giving the lie to the tired old line about how nobody publishes "real" science fiction anymore; read the Sterling, the Varley, the Baxter, the McHugh, the Jablokov, the Anderson, the McDonald, the Stableford, the Cadigan, the Silverberg, or a dozen of the others, and then come back and tell me that—but there's also plenty of fine fantasy of many different types, from George R. R. Martin's *A Clash of Kings* to Sean Stewart's *Mockingbird*, with plenty of room left over for harder-to-classify stuff that mixes several different genres, such as William Browning Spencer's *Irrational Fears*, Jonathan Lethem's *Girl in Landscape*, or Patricia Anthony's *Flanders*. In fact, it's amazing just how wide the spectrum of first-rate work being produced today really is—chances are, no matter what your tastes are, from hard SF to high fantasy, you'll find something you like out there somewhere.

As usual, predicting what's going to take the major awards this year is a daunting task. Connie Willis's *To Say Nothing of the Dog* might have a shot at the Nebula Award, unless last year's Hugo winner, Joe Haldeman's *Forever Peace* (still eligible for this year's Nebulas under SFWA's bizarre "rolling eligibility" rule) takes it away from her. It's much too early to call the Hugo contest, I'm afraid, although the fact that the Worldcon is taking place in Australia this year may end up skewing the voting results to some degree.

A borderline novel by an SF writer (mainstream with a few touches that could be construed as mild fantastic elements) that may be of interest to some is 253 (St. Martin's Griffin), by Geoff Ryman, the "print remix" of an "interactive hypertext novel" that Ryman ran on his Web site, one of the most successful examples to date of electronically published fiction that utilizes "hypertext" features. The novel examines in fascinating detail 253 passengers who are taking a fateful seven-and-a-half-minute ride on a London Underground tube train. It has very little plot, instead devoting a page to a description of each of the characters (including internal thoughts, fears, and aspirations), each description exactly 253 words long—this sounds boring and awful, I know, but in practice it has a great fascination, simply because of Ryman's huge abilities as an author and prose stylist. It's probably better to read a section at a time rather than trying to read the "novel" in one sitting (this format supposedly worked better online, where you could jump from one character description to the other, and also read the hypertext footnotes, in any order you chose—but here, the very fact that it's in print, pages bound in a book, imposes a certain structure on the text, like it or not). The character descriptions are fascinating, rich and detailed and vivid, and the book is often quite funny (particularly in the "hypertext" bits—mock advertisements, "reader satisfaction surveys," and so forth—with which Ryman surrounds the character-description capsules), although there's a pervasive underlying tang of bitterness and sorrowing compassion for the everyday tragedies of life. (Buried and rather lost in the midst of all this is the idea of Anne Frank as the modern-day incarnation of the Wandering Jew—something that immediately resonated with me and gave me the frisson of witnessing a new myth being created before my very eyes . . . or what might become a new myth if enough people read this book—probably, alas, a rather unlikely scenario.) All of this gave me a slight feeling of immense skills and talents being utilized to create something that is not quite worth the time and effort that went into it, like watching Michaelangelo make a Jello sculpture—nevertheless, although I wouldn't want to see Ryman spend the rest of his career turning out this sort of thing, 253 is definitely worth the cover price, and I think I can safely say that you're unlikely to come across anything else even remotely like it anywhere else this year. Another eccentric and highly eclectic performance, dancing on the borderline between horror, fantasy, and what almost might be called "imaginary scholarship" is the posthumously published *The Boss in the Wall, A Treatise on the House Devil* (Tachyon Publications), by Avram Davidson and Grania Davis, a short novel completed by Grania Davis from rough drafts Avram Davidson left behind after his death; the plot here is rather sketchy, but the material dealt with in the book is rich and strange enough (and creepy enough), all served up with Davidson's wonderfully flavorful and idiosyncratic prose, that few readers will feel that they haven't gotten more than their money's worth. (*The Boss in the Wall, A Treatise on the House Devil*—$12 from Tachyon Publications, 1459 18th St. #139, San Francisco, CA 94107.) *Blue Light* (Little, Brown), by Walter Mosley, represents the first foray into science fiction by this best-selling mystery writer, and although it was largely slammed by genre critics, may still be of interest to Mosley fans.

Associational novels by genre authors this year included a Gothic suspense novel by Kate Wilhelm, *The Good Children* (St. Martin's), Philip José Farmer's *noir* novel *Nothing Burns in Hell* (Forge), and mystery novels by Ron Goulart, *Groucho Marx, Master Detective* (St. Martin's) and by James Sallis, *Bluebottle* (Walker).

It was a good year for collections, especially in the area of retrospective collections that return long-unavailable work by dead (and in danger of being unjustly forgotten) authors to print. The best of these retrospective collections, as well as being the best collection of the year and one of the best collections of the decade, was *The Avram Davidson Treasury: A Tribute Collection* (Tor), by Avram Davidson, edited by Robert Silverberg and Grania Davis, a well-named trove of long-out-of-print material by a man who was one of SF and fantasy's best (and most underrated) writers. *First Contacts: The Essential Murray Leinster* (NESFA Press), by Murray Leinster, edited by Joe Rico, *An Ornament to His Profession* (NESFA Press), by Charles L. Harness, *The Perfect Host: The Complete Short Stories of Theodore Sturgeon, Vol. 5* (North Atlantic), by Theodore Sturgeon, *Farwell to Lankhmar* (White Wolf), by Fritz Leiber, and *Collected Fictions* (Viking), by Jorge Luis Borges also belong in the library of any serious student of the genre.

First-rate collections by more contemporary writers this year included *Beaker's Dozen*, Nancy Kress (Tor); *Luminous*, Greg Egan (Millennium); *The Invisible Country*, Paul J. McAuley (Avon Eos); *Frankensteins and Foreign Devils*, Walter Jon Williams (NESFA Press); *The Moon Maid and Other Fantastic Adventures*, R. Garcia y Robertson (Golden Gryphon); *Kirinyaga* (if considered as a collection—where most commentators placed it—instead of a novel), Mike Resnick (Del Rey); *A Second Chance at Eden*, Peter F. Hamilton (Warner); *Black Glass*, Karen Joy Fowler (Holt); and *Traces*, by Stephen Baxter (Voyager). Other strong collections included: *Last Summer at Mars Hill*, Elizabeth Hand (HarperPrism); *Lost Pages*, Paul Di Filippo (Four Walls Eight Windows); *The Night We Buried Road Dog*, Jack Cady (DreamHaven); *Smoke and Mirrors*, Neil Gaiman (Avon); *One Day Closer to Death*, Bradley Denton (St. Martin's Press); *Extremities*, Kathe Koja (Four Walls Eight Windows); *Weird Women, Wired Women*, Kit Reed (Wesleyan); *This Is the Year Zero*, Andrew Weiner (Pottersfield Press); *Moonlight and Vines*, Charles de Lint (Tor); *Reave the Just and Other Tales*, Stephen R. Donaldson (Bantam Spectra) ; *Black Butterflies: A Flock on the Dark Side*, John Shirley (Zeising); *Burning Sky*, Rachel Pollack (Cambrian); and *The Cleft and Other Odd Tales*, Gahan Wilson (Tor).

It's worth noting that just one story in the Hamilton collection, the title story, "A Second Chance at Eden," is all by itself longer than many of the novels I remember from my childhood—well over 50,000 words long—and that it would have been in *this* collection if I could have found room for it, but that it was too long even for me to be able to handle, even with all the space I have to fill! The Hamilton collection is unusually hefty for a comtemporary collection, and thus a good reading bargain.

An unusual item is *The Alchemy of Love* (Triple Tree Publishing), by Elizabeth Engstrom and Alan M. Clark, an art book/collection, eight stories by Engstrom and eight pieces of art by Clark, with four stories by Engstrom based on Clark's artwork, and four artworks by Clark based on Engstrom's stories. (A similar gimmick is used in the anthology *Imagination Fully Dilated*—see below—in which stories by various authors are based on Clark's artwork.)

Small presses like NESFA Press, DreamHaven, and Golden Gryphon Press remain important (with NESFA particularly vital for the retrospective collections full of older, long-out-of-print stuff), but it's encouraging to see both middle-level trade publishers such as Four Walls Eight Windows and big commercial houses such as Tor, St. Martin's, HarperPrism, Warner, Avon, Bantam Spectra, Del Rey, Holt, and Avon Eos taking a chance with short-story collections again, especially after so many years in the '80s and early '90s when they mostly did *not*.

(Very few small-press titles will be findable in the average bookstore, or even in the average chain store, which means that mail order is your best bet, and so I'm going to list the addresses of the small-press publishers mentioned above: NESFA Press, P.O. Box 809, Framingham, MA 01701-0203—$25 for *First Contacts: The Essential Murray Leinster*, by Murray Leinster, $25 for *An Ornament to His Profession*, by Charles L. Harness, and $23 for *Frankensteins and Foreign Devils*, by Walter Jon Williams; Golden Gryphon Press, 364 West Country Lane, Collinsville, IL 62234—$22.95 for *The Moon Maid and Other Fantastic Adventures*, by R. Garcia y Robertson; North Atlantic Books, P.O. Box 12327, Berkeley, CA, 94701—$25 for *The Perfect Host: Volume V: The Complete Stories of Theodore Sturgeon*, by Theodore Sturgeon; Pottersfield Press, Lawrencetown Beach, 83 Leslie Road, East Lawrencetown, Nova Scotia, Canada B2Z 1P8—$16.95 for *This Is the Year Zero*, by Andrew Weiner; University Press of New England/Wesleyan, 23 South Main St., Hanover, NH 03755—$16.95 plus $2.50 postage for *Weird Women, Wired Women*, by Kit Reed; Cambrian Publications, P.O. Box 112170, Campbell, CA 95011-2170—$34 for *Burning Sky*, by Rachel Pollack; TripleTree Publishing, P.O. Box 5684, Eugene, OR 97405—$49.95 plus $5.00 postage for *The Alchemy of Love*, by Alan M. Clark and Elizabeth Engstrom; DreamHaven Books, 912 West Lake St., Minneapolis, NM 55408—$27 for *The Night We Buried Road Dog*, by Jack Cady; Mark V. Ziesing, P.O. Box 76, Shingletown, CA 96088—$16.95 for *Black Butterflies: A Flock on the Dark Side*, by John Shirley.)

• • •

There was some good solid stuff in the reprint anthology field this year, although perhaps no single especially impressive blockbuster volume, of the sort that has turned up occasionally in other years.

As usual, the best bets for your money in this category were the various "Best of the Year" anthologies, and the annual Nebula Award anthology, *Nebula Awards 32* (Harcourt Brace), edited by Jack Dann. Science fiction is now being covered by *two* "Best of the Year" anthology series, the one you are holding in your hand, and the *Year's Best SF* series (HarperPrism), edited by David G. Hartwell, now up to its fourth annual volume. It would be inappropriate for me to review Hartwell's *Year's Best SF*, since it's a direct competitor to *this* volume, and anything critical I might have to say about it could be seen as suspect and self-serving — but, in general, I think that the relatively small amount of overlap between my selections and Hartwell's demonstrates that the field is wide enough for there to be more than one Best anthology every year, and that it's probably a healthy thing for the genre for there to be more than one. Since no anthology can be big enough or comprehensive enough to include *all* the worthwhile SF of different varieties that comes out in the course of a year, having two volumes gives more authors a chance to be showcased every year, and the parallax provided by comparing Hartwell's slant on what was the year's best fiction to my own slant may be informative. A somewhat more specialized kind of Best of the Year anthology, running a year behind mine and Hartwell's, and including fantasy, horror, and some harder-to-classify literary surrealism as well as science fiction, is a new series called *The Year's Best Australian Science Fiction and Fantasy* (HarperCollins Australia Voyager), edited by Jonathan Strahan and Jeremy G. Byrne, now up to Volume Two. There were two Best of the Year anthologies covering horror in 1998: the latest edition in the British series *The Mammoth Book of Best New Horror* (Robinson), edited by Stephen Jones, now up to Volume 9, and the Ellen Datlow half of a huge volume covering both horror *and* fantasy, *The Year's Best Fantasy and Horror* (St. Martin's Press), edited by Ellen Datlow and Terri Windling, this year up to its Eleventh Annual Collection. Fantasy, as opposed to horror, is still only covered by the Windling half of the Datlow/Windling anthology, a surprising lapse considering how popular fantasy is these days.

Turning to retrospective SF anthologies, books that provide a historical/critical overview of the evolution of the field, there was nothing as strong as last year's *A Science Fiction Century* or the similarly titled *A Century of Science Fiction 1950–1959*, but solid value and some interesting insights on SF from outside the familiar American perspective are provided by *The Road to Science Fiction Volume 5: The British Way* (White Wolf) and *The Road to Science Fiction Volume 6: Around the World* (White Wolf), both edited by James Gunn. Noted without comment is *The Good Old Stuff* (St. Martin's Griffin), edited by Gardner Dozois, a retrospective overview of the evolution of "Adventure SF" from the '40s to the '70s.

There were also some good singleton reprint SF anthologies this year. In spite of its silly title, the best of these might be *Flying Cups and Saucers: Gender Explorations in Science Fiction and Fantasy* (Edgewood Press), edited by Debbie Notkin and "the Secret Feminist Cabal," being referred to informally by most commentators as "the Tiptree Award anthology" — appropriately enough, since it assembles thirteen stories from among the winners and the stories "shortlisted" for the Tiptree Award (the award for the most effective "exploration of genre roles" in SF and fantasy) since its inception in 1991. It makes for an impressive list, including first-rate stories such as Ursula K. Le Guin's "Forgiveness Day" and "The Matter of Seggri," Eleanor Arnason's "The Lovers," R. Garcia y Robertson's "The Other Magpie," Lisa Tuttle's "Food Man," Delia Sherman's "Young Woman in a Garden," Ian R. MacLeod's "Grownups," and a half-dozen others, almost all of which will make you think, often about things that don't get thought about much. (Edgewood Press, P.O. Box 380264, Cambridge, MA 02238 — $17 for a trade paperback, $38.50 for a hardcover edition for *Flying Cups and Saucers: Gender Explorations in Science Fiction and Fantasy.*) *The Playboy Book of Science Fiction* (HarperPrism), edited by Alice K. Turner, turns out to be surprisingly substantial as well, though, and gives *Flying Cups and Saucers* a decent run for its money; in addition to the lighter satirical/comic stuff you might expect, the anthology also reprints some powerful and sobering tales such as Damon Knight's "Masks," Arthur C. Clarke's "Transit of Earth," Ursula K. Le Guin's "Nine Lives," Joe Haldeman's "More Than the Sum of His Parts," Howard Waldrop's "Heirs of the Perisphere," Lucius Shepard's "Fire Zone Emerald," and many others (including, of course, the above-mentioned satirical/comic stuff, by an array of practiced hands from Vonnegut to Effinger to Bisson, which will increase the entertainment value of the book for most readers). Another solid grouping of stories is to be found in *Future on Ice* (Tor), edited by Orson Scott Card, the long-delayed sequel to 1991's *Future on Fire*. (Ironically, considering the title, the book has been sitting around "on ice" for almost a decade, and it shows its age sometimes. Whether the storynotes are new or years old is hard to tell for sure from internal evidence; if they're old, then they should have been replaced; if they're *new*, however, then in them Card inadvertently paints a rather sad portrait of himself as a man clearly still deeply embroiled in fighting the Cyberpunk Wars of the mid-'80s, taking potshots at his enemies and obviously at times himself feeling the throbbing of old wounds — a display of passion and choler that looks rather quaint and dusty, like arguing over which end of the egg to break, here at the end of the '90s, at a time when most young readers are probably not even aware that there *were* any Cyberpunk Wars, let alone who the participants were or what issues they were fighting over. It may be possible to argue with Card's highly charged and deliberately provocative polemics in the front matter and storynotes here — and, indeed, I've heard many people, including some of the book's authors, doing just that — but it's hard to argue with the quality of most of the *stories* reprinted inside, including John Kessel's "The Pure Product," John Crowley's "Snow," Nancy Kress's "Out of All Them Bright Stars," Greg Bear's "Blood Music," Lisa Goldstein's "Tourists," Walter Jon Williams's "Dinosaurs," Card's own "The Fringe," and almost a dozen others, all also of high quality. *The Best of Crank!* (Tor), edited by Bryan Cholfin, comes along, ironically, just as the idiosyncratic semiprozine from which its stories are drawn, *Crank!*, has been officially pronounced dead (see magazine section, above); this anthology gives a good representative cross section of the kind of thing for which the magazine was known, quirky, offbeat stories that often tried consciously (sometimes too hard) to avoid easy genre classification, always ambitious, sometimes pretentious, often full of in-your-face Attitude—the best story here by far, and the best thing *Crank!* ever published, is Ursula K. Le Guin's "The Matter of Seggri," but the book also features good (and idiosyncratic) work by Eliot Fintushel, Jonathan Lethem, Lisa Tuttle, Michael Bishop, Gwyneth Jones, R. A. Lafferty, and others. *Tales in Space* (White Wolf), edited by Peter Crowther, provides a solid grouping of, well, tales in space, including first-rate work by Paul J. McAuley, Ursula K. Le Guin, John Varley, Brian W. Aldiss, and others. *The Reel Stuff* (DAW) edited by Brian Thomson and Martin H. Greenberg, provides an unusual twist, reprinting the original short stories from which SF movies and TV shows have later been made—not surprisingly, most of them were better in the original print versions than in their later film incarnations, including William Gibson's "Johnny Mnemonic," George R. R. Martin's "Sandkings" and "Nightflyers," John Varley's "Air Raid," and Philip K. Dick's "Second Variety" and "We Can Remember It for You Wholesale," all making for a worthwhile reading experience.

Noted without comment are *Clones* (Ace), edited by Jack Dann and Gardner Dozois, *Immortals* (Ace), edited by Jack Dann and Gardner Dozois, *Nanotech* (Ace), edited by Jack Dann and Gardner Dozois, the Alternate History anthology *Roads Not Taken* (Del Rey), edited by Gardner Dozois and Stanley Schmidt, and *Isaac Asimov's Detectives* (Ace), edited by Gardner Dozois and Sheila Williams.

There were also some good values in the reprint fantasy anthology market this year, a sort of anthology that has been thinly represented in recent times. Although it received scathing criticism from some critics for concentrating too much on American genre fantasy and not including enough European and academically oriented fantasy, I doubt that too many readers are going to be bothered by this to any significant degree when they dip into *The Fantasy Hall of Fame* (HarperPrism), edited by Robert Silverberg, and find it chock-full of stories by writers such as L. Sprague de Camp, Jack Vance, Fritz Leiber, Tanith Lee, Ursula K. Le Guin, Terry Bisson, Roger Zelazny, Avram Davidson, Ray Bradbury, and twenty-one other first-rate authors. I suppose that it *is* skewed heavily toward American genre fantasy, probably not a big surprise when you realize that it was largely selected by vote of the membership of the Science Fiction and Fantasy Writers of America, and I agree that a volume titled "The Fantasy Hall of Fame" probably should have made an effort to include different sorts of fantasy and cast its net further afield—the ordinary reader, though, who's merely looking to find the most good reading for his money that he can, will probably not be all that concerned about such matters . . . and considered in that light, value received for money paid, this enormous anthology of mostly good-to-excellent stories for a cover price of $14 is one of the best reading bargains of the year. (This has been a good year for Silverberg the Fantasy Anthology editor, a hat he doesn't often wear—he's edited the best original fantasy anthology of the year *and* the best reprint fantasy anthology of the year; not too shabby!)

Other good fantasy reprint anthologies this year included *two* solid volumes of comic fantasy, a specialized subgenre even rarer than reprint fantasy anthologies in general—a big, well-named mostly reprint (with a few originals) volume called *The Mammoth Book of Comic Fantasy* (Carroll & Graf), edited by Mike Ashley, featuring good work by Esther Friesner, Terry Prachett, Avram Davidson, Neil Gaiman, Terry Bisson, Jane Yolen, and many others, and *The Flying Sorcerers* (Ace), edited by Peter Haining, with good (and mostly older) reprint stories by P. G. Wodehouse, John Collier, L. Sprague de Camp and Fletcher Pratt, Angela Carter, Kurt Vonnegut Jr., Roald Dahl, Robert Bloch, Nelson Bond, and many others. Noted without comment is *Isaac Asimov's Camelot* (Ace), edited by Gardner Dozois and Sheila Williams.

Reprint anthologies seem even rarer in horror, where most of the anthologies are originals. The best reprint horror anthology I saw this year—although, in fairness, I should say that I didn't search assiduously for them—was *Eternal Lovecraft: The Persistence of HPL in Popular Culture* (Golden Gryphon), edited by Jim Turner, a smart and solid anthology of Lovecraft-inspired work that gives some fresh, inventive, and eclectic twists to this familiar material, by writers such as Ian R. MacLeod, Fritz Leiber, Gene Wolfe, Stephen King, Steve Utley and Howard Waldrop, Harlan Ellison, Robert Charles Wilson, and others. Other reprint horror anthologies this year included: *Mistresses of the Dark: 25 Macabre Tales by Master Storytellers* (Barnes & Noble), edited by Stefan R. Dziemianowicz, Denise Little, and Robert Weinberg; *100 Twisted Little Tales of Torment* (Barnes & Noble), edited by Stefan Dziemianowicz, Robert Weinberg, and Martin H. Greenberg; *The Best of Cemetery Dance* (Cemetery Dance Publications), edited by Richard Chizmar; *Fields of Blood: Vampire Stories of the Heartland* (Cumberland House), edited by Lawrence Schimel and Martin H. Greenberg; and *Streets of Blood: Vampire Stories from New York City* (Cumberland House), edited by Lawrence Schimel and Martin H. Greenberg. I'm not watching horror closely anymore, so no doubt there are some I've missed.

An offbeat small press item is *Stranger Kaddish* (Aardwolf Publishing), edited by Jim Reeber and Clifford Lawrence Meth, a follow-up to last year's *Strange Kaddish*, another anthology of Jewish science fiction featuring work by Harlan Ellison, Neil Gaiman, and others. (Aardwolf Publishing, 45 Park Place South, suite 270, Morristown, NJ 07960—$12.95 for *Stranger Kaddish*.)

It was a relatively quiet year in the SF-and-fantasy-oriented nonfiction and reference book field, with nothing published anywhere near as substantial as last year's mammoth *The Encyclopedia of Fantasy*. The closest we came to this level of quality this year is *The Ultimate Encyclopedia of Fantasy: The Definitive Illustrated Guide* (Carlton), edited by David Pringle, which has plenty of useful and entertaining information, but lacks the scope, comprehensiveness, and heft of Clute and Grant's *Encyclopedia of Fantasy*. The critical book that aroused the most comment—and controversy—was undoubtedly Thomas M. Disch's sharp-edged and deliberately provocative study of science fiction and popular culture, *The Dreams Our Stuff Is Made Of: How Science Fiction Conquered the World* (Free Press); I disagree with many if not most of Disch's theoretical conclusions about the nature of and the future of SF, and he gets a fair number of his facts wrong, but Disch is so entertainingly bitchy, witty, and acid-tongued in many places here that it's hard to deny the overall appeal of the book as mean-spirited fun, especially when he's attacking bloated media darlings such as Whitley Streiber, upon whom he performs a spectacular hatchet job. Drier, more academically oriented reference books included that invaluable research tool, *Hugo, Nebula and World Fantasy Awards* (Advent), by Howard DeVore, *Science-Fiction: The Gernsback Years* (Kent State), by Everett F. Bleiler, and the *St. James Guide to Horror, Ghost & Gothic Writers* (St. James), edited by David Pringle. Books *about* writers included *The Tall Adventurer: The Works of E. C. Tubb* (Beacon), by Sean Wallace and Philip Harbottle, *Lovecraft Remembered* (Arkham House), edited by Peter Cannon, *The Works of Jack Williamson: An Annotated Bibliography and Guide* (NESFA Press), by Richard A. Hauptmann, and *British Fantasy and Science Fiction Writers Before World War I* (Gale), edited by Darren Harris-Fain. *Northern Dreamers: Interviews with Famous Science Fiction, Fantasy, and Horror Writers* (Quarry Press), by Edo van Belkom, is a book of interviews with various Canadian writers, and *Windows of the Imagination* (Borgo), by Darrell Schweitzer, is a book of essays by a well-known genre critic.

There were also two books of reminiscences *by* writers this year: *Lemady: Episodes of a Writer's Life* (Borgo), by Keith Roberts, and *Writer at Large* (Gryphon), by Richard A. Lupoff. The Roberts is particularly recommended as a vivid, if sometimes depressing, look at life in the publishing world by one of the most significant talents of the '60s. (Borgo Press, PO Box 2845, San Bernardino, CA 92406-2845 — $21 plus $3 shipping for *Lemady: Episodes of a Writer's Life*, by Keith Roberts; Gryphon Publications, P.O. Box 209, Brooklyn NY 11228-0209 — $15 for *Writer at Large*, by Richard A. Lupoff.) An interesting book of correspondence by two very dissimilar writers is *Arthur C. Clarke and Lord Dunsany: A Correspondence* (Anamensis Press).

The art book field also seemed weaker this year, or at least it didn't come anywhere near producing anything as comprehensive and valuable as last year's retrospective survey of science fiction art, *Infinite Worlds: The Fantastic Visions of Science Fiction Art*. The closest approach in quality, and the art book to buy if you're only going to buy one SF art book this year, is *Pulp Culture: The Art of Fiction Magazines* (Collectors Press), by Frank M. Robinson and Lawrence Davidson, which not only features lots of beautiful reproductions of old pulp magazine covers, but an overview of the evolution of pulp magazines as well.

The latest edition of a sort of "Best of the Year" series that compiles the year's fantastic art, *Spectrum 5: The Best in Contemporary Fantastic Art* (Underwood), edited by Arnie Fenner and Cathy Fenner, provides a valuable overview of what's happening in the *current* SF and fantasy art scene. An overview of the career of an individual artist, one of the most famous in modern fantastic art, is to be found in *Icon: A Retrospective by the Grand Master of Fantastic Art, Frank Frazetta* (Underwood), also edited by Arnie and Cathy Fenner. Similar retrospective overviews are offered by *The Fantastic Art of Beksinski* (Morpheus International) and *H. R. Giger's Retrospective 1964–1984* (Morpheus International), while Wayne Barlowe takes us on a harrowing journey through Hell in *Barlowe's Inferno* (Morpheus International). Everyone who loved Brian Froud's famous art book *Faeries* (as I did), will want his new cut through the same mythic material, *Good Faeries/Bad Faeries* (Simon & Schuster), edited by Terri Windling, where half of the book is printed upside-down to distinguish the good faeries from the bad faeries; Froud's rendering here is as luminous and beautifully evocative as ever, but the book at times becomes much too twee: "the credit card faery lurks in cash dispensers . . ." Give me a break! The cuteness level here ought to have been turned down several notches, and will be too much for some readers, but the art *is* often stunning, which I suppose is the real selling point. Comics fans will probably want *Dustcovers: The Collected Sandman Covers* (DC/Vertigo), by Dave McKean.

An offbeat item is *Imagination Fully Dilated* (Cemetery Dance Publications), edited by Alan M. Clark and Elizabeth Engstrom (see also the original anthology section, above), an anthology of stories by writers such as Poppy Z. Brite, Lucy Taylor, Steve Rasnic Tem and Melanie Tem, and twenty-five others, all inspired by the horror art of Alan M. Clark, which is included as tipped-in color plates, so that the book functions either as a horror anthology *or* as an art book, depending on which factor you choose to emphasize.

There weren't a lot of general genre-related nonfiction books of interest this year. The strongest, and my personal favorite, was *The Life of Birds* (Princeton University Press), by David Attenborough, a fascinating and richly detailed examination of the lifeways and evolutionary strategies of birds, including behaviors much more alien than those exhibited by most SF writers' aliens; SF writers, in fact, could do worse than to dip into this endlessly surprising book for inspiration. Another intriguing book, offering us the science fictional kick of suddenly reevaluating known facts from an entirely new perspective, is *The Victorian Internet: The Remarkable Story of the Telegraph and the Nineteenth Century's On-Line Pioneers* (Walker), by Tom Standage, which argues cogently that almost all of the culture- and mind-set-altering effects and social changes driven by the Internet today were *anticipated* in the Victorian Age by the introduction of the telegraph: "A world-wide communications network whose cables spanned continents and oceans, it revolutionized business practice, gave rise to new forms of crime, and inundated its users with a deluge of information." As Standage points out, it even changed courtship patterns, with lovers meeting and marrying "online," and spurred the development of cryptology, as businessmen tried to come up with codes to protect the privacy of information sent by telegraph, and other businessmen tried to crack those codes to gain a business advantage. (Standage also points out that the effect of this technology on the Victorians was perhaps even *greater* than the effect of the Internet on society today, since they went in one jump from a world where messages took months to cross the oceans to a world of instant communications where such messages could be received in minutes: "If any generation has the right to claim that it bore the full bewildering, world-shrinking brunt of such a revolution, it is not us—it is our nineteenth-century forebears." The parallels for our own times are interesting, and instructive, as is the lesson in how a shift in perspective can change the emotional weight and shading we give to facts without actually changing any of the facts themselves. Also probably of interest to some genre fans, dealing as it does with perspectives of "deep time," giving us a series of pictures of what portions of our world were like millions of years ago, and how they got to be the way they are today, is *Annals of the Former World* (Farrar, Straus, and Giroux), by John McPhee, an omnibus collection of McPhee's four earlier books on geology, rounded out by a new book about the geology of the Great Plains. Most genre fans remain interested in space travel, of course, and so might be interested in a trade paperback reprint of *A Man on the Moon* (Penguin), by Andrew Chaikin, giving a behind-the-scenes look at the Apollo missions, or in *Dragonfly, NASA and the Crisis aboard MIR* (Harper Collins), by Bryan Burrough. Another object of interest to many genre fans is the dinosaur, which gets an interesting cultural examination in *The Last Dinosaur Book* by W. J. T. Mitchell (Univ. of Chicago Press). I can find no even *remotely* plausible genre-connection to justify mentioning one of my favorite nonfiction books this year, *A Walk in the Woods* (Broadway Books), by Bill Bryson, unless it's that this hilarious account of two middle-aged, pudgy, out-of-shape, unathletic men with no previous camping experience or outdoorsmanlike expertise trying to cope with the rigors of walking the Appalachian Trail may remind many of us of ourselves — except that Bryson is probably funnier telling about it all than *we* would be.

There were a lot of genre movies out in 1998, including some box office blockbusters, some much-hyped immensely expensive films that "performed below expectations" (i.e., bombed out), some unmitigated stinkers, some movies that were actually pretty good, some that could have been better, and some movies where the thought that they were making a genre film probably never crossed the producers' minds in the first place.

This could also be thought of as the Year of the Dueling Twin Movies, so that we had *two* Giant-Asteroids-Will-Slam-into-Earth-Unless-a-Desperate-Space-Mission-Can-Deflect-Them movies, two animated movies about cute talking bugs, two movies about "reality" actually being a show-business illusion, two big, glossy, gorgeously photographed After-Death Fantasy/angel movies, and so on. All of this, of course, is sheer coincidence, nothing more. (Cough.)

The best genre movie I saw this year, and, agreeably, one of the box office champs as well, was *The Truman Show*. There are no surprises here for the experienced genre reader, of course — it's pretty much Philip K. Dick's *Time Out of Joint* crossed with D. G. Compton's *The Unsleeping Eye*, as far as content is concerned — but it's rare to see relatively sophisticated genre concepts translated to the screen with this degree of style, intelligence, and grace, with little or no talking down or prechewing of the material, a movie in which the director (a foreigner, of course) actually *trusts* his audience to be intelligent enough to understand it. This is certainly the most successful translation of Philip K. Dick–like material to the screen since a couple of inspired bits from 1974's *Dark Star*, and I think Dick would have liked it, even if he isn't credited anywhere here. Even Jim Carrey is surprisingly effective, with his patented mugging-and-leering routine slipping out only once or twice when the director's attention faltered. Visually, there are a couple of moments that are simply stunning: when the full moon suddenly turns into a searchlight, for instance, and begins sweeping over the town looking for the fugitive Carrey, or when Carrey's sailboat, supposedly taking him out over the open ocean, *runs into* the sky at the horizon, getting its mast stuck in it, or even the quieter moment when one of the stars falls from the sky, and proves to be a spotlight labeled "Polaris" (or whatever it was) — pure cognitive dissonance, of the sort that science fiction delivers best. Yes, I think Phil Dick would have liked this movie. (And to answer a question posed by *TV Guide* last year, "Would we actually watch The Truman Show?"—you bet your ass we would. That's the scariest thing about it.)

Similar ground in some ways, although more openly satirical and Twilight Zone–ish, is covered in *Pleasantville*, an intelligent little comic nightmare about two '90s teens getting stuck in the black-and-white, white-bread, keep-smiling-no-matter-what world of a 1950s TV sitcom, a good little movie unfairly overshadowed by the (mostly justified) attention given to *The Truman Show*.

Next we turn to the two Giant-Rocks-Bash-the-Earth movies. One of these, the second one out of the gate, *Armageddon*, was immensely successful at the box office, perhaps the highest-grossing movie of the year; the other one, the more self-consciously "serious" *Deep Impact*, didn't do nearly as well. Although I wasn't—ha ha—blown away by either of these movies, both of which contain immensely embarrassing scientific howlers and huge holes in the plot-logic, I must say that my own reaction supports that of the boxoffice. *Deep Impact* was weepy and New Agey, more of a soap opera than a disaster movie, with most of its special effects reserved for the very impressive—and frighteningly convincing—giant tsunami scenes at the end (one thing that annoyed me about this movie was that with days if not weeks of prior warning as to where the asteroid is going to hit, the government makes no effort to evacuate most of the population to higher ground, something that would have saved millions of lives, even if they *had* been forced to rough it in makeshift refugee camps in West Virginia; nor does the public react realistically, so you have scenes of crowds going about their business as usual in midtown Manhattan, strolling around as if nothing was happening, while the giant wave sweeps in on them). The special effects were worse in *Armageddon*, with the on-the-surface-of-the-"comet" scenes surprisingly poor, but the movie as a whole was considerably more vigorous and less self-important, loud, vulgar, fast-paced, full of MTV-style jump cuts and blaring rock music, with Bruce Willis doing an almost self-parodying turn as a crude, vulgar, cigar-chomping (but superhumanly competent) oil driller, supported by a cast of eccentric, crude, vulgar, two-fisted, hard-drinking, "colorful" roughnecks who might as well have stepped out of a *Blackhawks* or *Sgt. Fury* comic book. If *Armageddon* is junk—and it is—it's at least robust and entertaining junk, a relief after the slow, syrupy, self-congratulatory pretentiousness of *Deep Impact*. My least favorite scene in *Deep Impact* is where the estranged daughter gives up any last chance of survival so that she can share a sensitive, reconciling, New Age hug with her father on the beach as the giant tsunami sweeps down on them. The hard-bitten, tough and competent, ass-kicking Survivor Types of *Armageddon* would sneer at this—and rightly so. (You actually could have made a better movie out of *Deep Impact* by dropping the Earth-based story line altogether and instead concentrating exclusively on the space-mission story line, the best part of the film, mostly because of Robert Duvall's quiet, assured underplaying; less soap opera content that way, too.)

Reaction was mixed to the other big-budget, special effects–heavy spectaculars of the year, the kind of movies that have to earn big in order to earn back at all. *Star Trek: Insurrection* seemed to do okay, although not spectacularly, at the box office, and audience reaction to it seemed similarly lukewarm, with nobody liking it as much as 1996's *Star Trek: First Contact*, and nobody loathing it as much as some of the franchise's low spots, such as the William Shatner–directed *Star Trek V: The Final Frontier*; most people seemed to agree that it was like an average episode of the TV show writ large, no better and no worse. Perhaps not the reaction that was hoped for, but it certainly keeps the option of another *Star Trek* movie alive; I'd be surprised if there *wasn't* one, at this point. Much the same thing—an episode of the TV show writ large—could be said of *The X-Files* movie, *Fear the Future*, which fared okay commercially. The immensely expensive *Godzilla*, on the other hand, one of the costliest movies ever made, was a major box-office disaster, a bomb of epic proportions—even the spin-off merchandising didn't sell; my local supermarket still has a half-dozen containers of *Godzilla* ice cream in the freezer. This failure was richly deserved; the movie was just awful, with few if any redeeming virtues. The redesigned monster, trumpeted in advance as a triumph of the CGI art, was surprisingly fake-looking (and faintly silly-looking, too), and not particularly scary; the monster from the original *Godzilla* film actually had more gravitas and presence, even though I knew even as a little kid that it was just a guy in a rubber suit. *Lost in Space* also seems to have "performed below expectations," although I don't think it was as major a bomb as *Godzilla*. *Lost in Space* actually had the best special effects and the most handsome and lavish set-dressing of any movie this year, and a good cast that it largely wasted—too bad they hadn't thought to put in a decent story and some good writing as well, while they were at it. The decision to do *Lost in Space* straight rather than camp (although Gary Oldman doing a shameless Jonathan Harris imitation throughout for his interpretation of Doctor Smith is an eyebrow-raiser) was probably the initial mistake here; for a slambang action-adventure space spectacular, the movie has surprisingly little sense of fun, and is downright brooding at times, although with little of substance to actually brood *about*, for the most part. (I find it interesting, culturally, that the producers felt it necessary to load a lot of sodden stuff about '90s-style dysfunctional families, and a lot of New Age psychobabble, into even this brainless bit of fluff—it would have been a lot better off without it.) The movie ends with an obvious setup for a sequel, which, with luck, we'll never actually get. (I'm struck, in passing, with wonder and bemusement at the immense amounts of money Hollywood spent bringing a long-dead and not-terribly-important-in-the-first-place science fiction TV show back to fitful life, probably more money than has been spent on *all* of print science fiction in the last ten years. If you add in the immense budget for *Godzilla*, more than the Gross National Product of some small countries, the money spent on these two cinematic turkeys would comfortably support print science fiction publishing through a good hefty percentage of the coming century. Am I alone in thinking that this money could be better spent than it's being spent at present, for more worthwhile ends? Yes, I know that I am, pretty much, so don't bother to answer.)

The Avengers sucked, completely lacking the mischievous flair and elan that made the original series such tongue-in-cheek wink-wink fun, and also bombed big at the box office; it was also perhaps the most critically savaged movie of the year, with almost nobody having anything good to say about it, a negative reaction so ubiquitous that one could imagine fans of the old TV show who hadn't agreed on anything *else* or even spoken in twenty years shaking hands and commiserating with each other about how awful it was. (The humiliating failure of movies such as *Lost in Space* and *The Avengers* won't keep the movie industry from visiting *more* big-budget resurrections of long-dead TV series on us, though, of course; several more are already on the way, in fact, including *The Wild, Wild West*, *The Mod Squad*, and even, heaven help us, *Hogan's Heroes*.) *Dark City* was a stylish and strikingly set-dressed exercise in future noir, although perhaps too obviously and heavily influenced by *Bladerunner*.

Sphere wasted an even better cast than *Lost in Space*, including Dustin Hoffman and Samuel L. Jackson, in a movie that tried to be intellectually challenging, but somehow ended up rather muddled and emotionally flat instead. They'd have been better off, in my opinion, sticking with investigating the real-world consequences of the intriguing initial setup, a crashed spaceship found on the bottom of the ocean, rather than flying off into two-a-penny mysticism, where the special effects equivalent of a Magic Wishing Ball makes anything they dream about come true, thus enabling the director to devote the rest of the movie to investigating their fears in gooshy horror movie–style sequences where they're assailed by various monsters from the id of their own conjuring (how come only subconscious *fears* are made real by the Magic Wishing Ball?, I kept asking myself. How come none of them dreams that Sharon Stone has jumped into the sack with them, or that they found the puppy they lost when they were six, or that their brother isn't dead after all?). In the end, in spite of good intentions and some good efforts, *Sphere* is vaguely disappointing. (I haven't read the Michael Crichton novel from which this is taken, so I don't know how many of these tropes are drawn from the book, but the movie certainly tempts you to picture some executives sitting around somewhere and saying "Hey! Let's cross *The Abyss* with *Event Horizon*! That ought to sell!")

A Bug's Life is the more successful and the more imaginative of the two talking bug movies (the best capsule description I've heard of it is Greg Feeley's remark that it was "*Seven Samurai* with ants"), and was a huge hit at the box office. The other one, *Antz*, is more obviously satirical (as might be expected from a movie in which Woody Allen voices the lead ant) and less adventurous and colorful, and didn't seem to have as much of an impact on the kids as *A Bug's Life* did (although both movies are full of satiric humor that probably flies way over the heads of most of the target audience, *A Bug's Life* depends less on this element than *Antz* does). *What Dreams May Come* is a gorgeously photographed but not terribly involving after-death fantasy, also bungful of New Age philosophy and jargon, as is *City of Angels*, a stylish but rather bleak romance between a mortal woman and an angel who must decide whether to give up his immortality to be with her. A retake on the Cinderella story, *Ever After* is more sentimental and less obviously satirical than *The Princess Bride*, say, but also has its revisionist moments; this seemed to be something of a sleeper hit. I'm sure that the producers of *Sliding Doors* didn't think of themselves as making a genre film, but it's hard to think of this film in any other terms: it follows the experiences of a young woman in two parallel worlds, one in which she *did* catch a subway train and one in which she *didn't*, cutting back and forth between the two realities, and even coyly hinting at the end that the experiences from one reality can leak into and color the other. It's interesting that these concepts, once unquestionably science-fictional, are now so taken for granted and absorbed into the mainstream culture that people look at you in surprise when you suggest that *Sliding Doors* is a genre movie — although it is, by any fair standard, and a rather intelligent, quietly effective, and well-acted one, at that. (I'll bet nobody thinks to nominate it for this year's Hugo, though.) I could go on to make an argument that *Shakespeare in Love* appeals to the same audience that enjoys reading Alternate History stories, but trying to include it as a genre movie stretches the definition of an SF film beyond any useful limits, in my opinion, so I won't bother.

I never managed to catch a small, independent film called *Pi*, which apparently deals with the Kabbalah and mathematical mysticism, but many of those who did were enthusiastic about it.

Still on the horizon: everyone's waiting impatiently for the release of the new *Star Wars* movie, which will probably be the big story next year. Considering the wildly enthusiastic reaction even to the *trailer* for the movie, with audiences paying to get into theaters just to see the trailer, and then leaving before the actual film that was showing came on, it's probably not too risky a prediction to forecast immense commercial success for it. Whether it's artistically successful or not remains to be seen (although that trailer *was* pretty damn good, and made even cynics like myself look forward to seeing the film; some real expertise going on there, on the part of the trailer-makers).

Frankly, I didn't pay a whole lot of attention to SF and fantasy on television this year. Several of the long-dominant genre shows have ended or are just about to end (or at least metamorphose), though, so obviously there will be some big changes next year. *Babylon 5* concluded its initial five-year series this year, much to the dismay of the show's unbelievably dedicated fans, although there's a spin-off series in the works for next season. *Star Trek: Deep Space Nine* is supposedly set to end this year too, which, if true, leaves the Star Trek empire with only the relatively unpopular (even with stone Star Trek fans) *Star Trek: Voyager* in place, the most attenuated that the Star Trek franchise has been in many years; it wouldn't surprise me if a new show were in the works there, too, although no official announcement of such has been made that I know of. Cult favorite *The X-Files* is also making noises about be nearing the end of its run, although speculation is rife as to whether the show will actually end or will just continue with a different cast; it seems a pretty good bet that Mulder and Scully will be leaving, though, whether the show continues or not. *Highlander* finally died, and was replaced by a spin-off show, *Highlander: The Raven*, featuring Amanda, one of the female Immortals from the old series, although in practice the show actually turns out to be more like *La Femme Nikita* than, as speculated, like *Xena: Warrior Princess*; it still fits well into the category of what I once called "Beautiful Women Kick Male Butt" shows, though.

Leaving to one side those shows like *Babylon 5* or *Star Trek: Deep Space Nine* or *The X-Files* that have ended or are supposedly ending, the most popular genre shows on television probably include *Xena: Warrior Princess, Buffy, the Vampire Slayer, La Femme Nikita, Hercules: The Legendary Journeys,* and *Third Rock From the Sun*—not all of these could fairly be fitted into the subgenre of "Beautiful Women Kick Male Butt" shows (I suppose we could refer to "Hercules" as a "Guys with Blow-Dried Hair Kick Butt" show, but it doesn't have the same ring to it somehow), but, with the exception of *Third Rock from the Sun,* most of them seem to involve serious butt-kicking of one sort or another. Butt-kicking, then, is obviously the wave of the future for TV, especially when you consider nongenre shows such as *Martial Law* and *Walker: Texas Ranger* (to say nothing of the World Wrestling Federation, the Ultimate Fighting Challenge shows, and MTV'S *Celebrity Deathmatch*) that feature quite a bit of it. Maybe the Star Trek franchise should consider a "Star Trek Characters Kick Butt" show for its next series. Perhaps we could have WWF/Ultimate Fighting Challenge–style steel-cage deathmatch competitions between characters from *Star Trek: Deep Space Nine* and *Babylon 5....*

Minor new genre shows came and—in some cases—went throughout the year, but none of them so far seems to have made much of an impression on the viewing public. *Mystery Science Theater 3000* just ended its long run, which is fine by me since I didn't find it very interesting for its last year anyway. Some of the critical buzz about last year's hot cult show, *South Park,* seems to have died away, perhaps because of overexposure—certainly you couldn't go into a gift shop last year without falling over a stack of *South Park* T-shirts, Kenny dolls, and Cartman key chains; they even put out boxes of Cheesy Poofs. The show is still intermittently funny, and still uses a lot of genre tropes, but it's beginning to grow repetitive, and I have a feeling its prime period of influence is already past.

I still think that, for the most part, you'd be better off turning the set off and reading a book instead.

The 56th World Science Fiction Convention, Bucconeer, was held in Baltimore, Maryland, from August 5 to 9, 1998, a month earlier than the traditional Labor Day date, and drew an estimated attendance of 5,474. The 1998 Hugo Awards, presented at Bucconeer, were: Best Novel, *Forever Peace,* by Joe Haldeman; Best Novella, "... Where Angels Fear To Tread," by Allen Steele; Best Novelette, "We Will Drink a Fish Together...," by Bill Johnson; Best Short Story, "The 43 Antarean Dynasties," by Mike Resnick; Best Related Book, *The Encyclopedia of Fantasy,* edited by John Clute and John Grant; Best Professional Editor, Gardner Dozois; Best Professional Artist, Bob Eggleton; Best Dramatic Presentation, *Contact*; Best Semiprozine, *Locus,* edited by Charles N. Brown; Best Fanzine, *Mimosa,* edited by Nicki and Richard Lynch; Best Fan Writer, David Langford; Best Fan Artist, Joe Mayhew; plus the John W. Campbell Award for Best New Writer to Mary Doria Russell.

The 1997 Nebula Awards, presented at a banquet at the Hotel Santa Fe in Santa Fe, New Mexico, on May 2, 1998, were: Best Novel, *The Moon and the Sun,* by Vonda N. McIntyre; Best Novella, "Abandon in Place," by Jerry Oltion; Best Novelette, "The Flowers of Aulit Prison," by Nancy Kress; Best Short Story,

"Sister Emily's Lightship"; plus an Author Emeritus award to Nelson S. Bond and the Grand Master award to Poul Anderson.

The World Fantasy Awards, presented at the Twenty-Fourth Annual World Fantasy Convention in Monterey, California, on November 1, 1998, were: Best Novel, *The Physiognomy*, by Jeffrey Ford; Best Novella, "Streetcar Dreams," by Richard Bowes; Best Short Fiction, "Dust Motes," by P. D. Cacek; Best Collection, *The Throne of Bones*, by Brian McNaughton; Best Anthology, *Bending the Landscape: Fantasy*, edited by Nicola Griffith and Stephen Pagel; Best Artist, Alan Lee; Special Award (Professional), to John Clute and John Grant, for *The Encyclopedia of Fantasy*; Special Award (Nonprofessional), to Fedogan & Bremer, for book publishing; plus a Life Achievement Award to Edward L. Ferman and Andre Norton (tie).

The 1998 Bram Stoker Awards, presented by the Horror Writers of America during a banquet at the New York Marriott East Side in New York City on June 6, 1998, were: Best Novel, *Children of the Dusk*, by Janet Berliner and George Guthridge; Best First Novel, *Lives of the Monster Dogs*, by Kirsten Bakis; Best Collection, *Exorcisms and Ecstasies*, by Karl Edward Wagner; Best Long Fiction, "The Big Blow," by Joe R. Lansdale; Best Short Story, "Rat Food," by Edo van Belkom and David Nickle; Nonfiction, *Dark Thoughts: On Writing*, by Stanley Wiater; a Specialty Press Award to Richard Chizmar of Cemetery Dance Publications; and the Hammer Award to Sheldon Jaffery, plus a Life Achievement Award to Jack Williamson and William Peter Blatty.

The 1997 John W. Campbell Memorial Award was won by *Forever Peace*, by Joe Haldeman.

The 1997 Theodore Sturgeon Award for Best Short Story was won by "House of Dreams," by Michael F. Flynn.

The 1997 Philip K. Dick Memorial Award went to *The Troika*, by Stepan Chapman, with a Special Citation to *Acts of Conscience*, by William Barton.

The 1997 Arthur C. Clarke award was won by *The Sparrow*, by Mary Doria Russell.

The 1997 James Tiptree, Jr., Memorial Award was won by *Black Wine*, by Candas Jane Dorsey and "Travels with the Snow Queen," by Kelly Link (tie).

Dead in 1998 or early 1999 were: **Jerome Bixby**, 75, prolific short-story writer and screenwriter, author of the collection *Space by the Tale*, whose best-known story "It's a *Good* Life" was made into one of the most famous *Twilight Zone* episodes ever; **Robert A. W. ("Doc") Lowndes** 81, veteran SF editor, writer, and member of the Futurians (the famous New York City fan group whose other members included Isaac Asimov, Frederik Pohl, Donald Wollheim, and other notables), one-time editor of magazines such as *Future Fiction*, *Original Science Fiction Stories*, and *Startling Mystery Stories*; **Paul Lehr,** 68, acclaimed SF artist, at one time among the most celebrated and widely used cover artists in the SF publishing world; **Naomi Mitchison,** 101, writer, socialist, "freethinker," and prominent feminist, probably best known to the genre for her historical fantasy *The Corn King and the Spring Queen*, also the author of books such as *Solution Three, Not by Bread Alone*, and *Memoirs of a Spacewoman*; **Rachel Cosgrove Payes,** 75, veteran writer, author of *Bridge to Yesterday*; **John W. Pritchard,** 85, who wrote SF as "Ian Wallace," author of novels such as *Croyd, The Rape of the Sun,* and *Pan Sagittarius*; **T. A. Waters,** 60, writer, actor, and stage magician, author of the SF novel *The Probability Pad*; **Jo Clayton,** 58, SF/fantasy writer, author of thirty-five books, including *Diadem from the Stars* and *Moongather*; **Bob Kane,** 83, comic-book artist, famous as the creator of *Batman*; **Jean-Claude Forest,** 68, French writer and artist, best known as the creator of the comic strip *Barbarella,* which was later adapted into a well-known SF movie; **Eric Ambler,** 89, best known for his spy novels such as *The Mask of Dimitrios,* author of the associational SF thriller *The Dark Frontier*; **Allen Drury,** 80, political novelist best known for *Advise and Consent,* also author of the near-future SF novel *The Throne of Saturn*; **Lawrence Sanders,** 78, thriller writer, best known for *The First Deadly Sin* and *The Anderson Tapes,* whose books included borderline SF novels *The Sixth Commandment* and *The Tomorrow File*; **Brian Moore,** 77, noted literary novelist best known to the genre audience for the screenplay for the near-future TV movie *Catholics*; **Alain Doremieux,** 64, leading French writer, editor, and translator; **Shin'ichi Hoshi,** 71, Japanese SF writer; Henrik Altov, 52, leading Russian SF writer; **Sean A. Moore,** 33, fantasy novelist and game designer; **Robert Marasco,** 62, playwright and novelist, author of the horror novel *Burnt Offerings*; **Ernst Junger,** 102, German writer; **Peter Nilson,** 60, Swedish astronomer and author; **Jose Paulo Paes,** 72, Brazilian critic, editor, and translator; **Wayland Drew,** 66, author of film novelizations and the SF trilogy "The Erthring Cycle"; **Miichael D. Weaver,** 36, SF/fantasy writer, author of *Mercedes Nights* and other novels; **Ted Hughes,** 68, Britain's Poet Laureate, author of occasional SF poetry, as well as two Young Adult SF novels *The Iron Man* and *The Iron Woman*; **Ian Gunn,** 40, Australian fan artist and writer, winner of nine Ditmar Awards; **Frank D. McSherry, Jr.,** 69, coeditor (with Martin H. Greenberg and Charles G. Waugh) of more than thirty SF and fantasy anthologies; **Alan D. Williams,** 72, noted New York book editor, the editor on many of Stephen King's most famous novels; **Archie Goodwin,** 60, leading comic-book editor; **Lee Elias,** 77, comics artist who drew the Jack Williamson–scripted comic strip *Beyond Mars*; **John L. Millard,** 80, longtime Canadian fan, chairman of the 1973 World Science Fiction Convention, Torcon; **Aubery Vincent Clarke,** 76, longtime British fan; **John V. Baltadonis,** longtime Philadelphia-area fan, one of the founding members of the Philadelphia Science Fiction Society; **T. Bruce Yerke,** 75, longtime fan; **Richard Wright,** 55, longtime fan; **Ardis Waters,** 56, fan and writer, sister of writer Melisa Michaels; and **Margaret Brady Martin,** 80, mother of SF writer George R. R. Martin.

oceanic

GREG EGAN

*As the new century approaches, it's become obvious that Australian writer Greg Egan is one of the Big Names to emerge in SF in the nineties, probably the best new "hard-science" writer to enter the field since Greg Bear, and already one of the most widely known of all Australian genre writers. In the last few years, he has become a frequent contributor to In-*terzone *and* Asimov's Science Fiction, *and has made sales as well to* Pulphouse, Analog, Aurealis, Eidolon, *and elsewhere; many of his stories have also appeared in various Best of the Year series, and he was on the Hugo final ballot in 1995 for his story "Cocoon," which won the Ditmar Award and the* Asimov's Readers *Award. His first novel,* Quarantine, *appeared in 1992 to wide critical acclaim, and was followed by a second novel in 1994,* Permutation City, *which won the John W. Campbell Memorial Award. His most recent books are two new novels,* Distress *and* Diaspora, *and three collections of his short fiction,* Axiomatic, Luminous, *and* Our Lady of Chernobyl. *Upcoming is a new novel,* Teranesia. *He has had stories in our Seventh, Eighth, Ninth, Tenth, Eleventh, Twelfth, Thirteenth, and Fifteenth Annual Collections. He has a Web site at http:// www.netspace.net.au/˜gregegan/.*

Here he takes us into the far future and across the galaxy for a powerful, evocative, and compelling study of a young boy's coming-of-age, as that boy struggles to understand the world and his place in it and grapples with controversial and perhaps potentially deadly issues of faith and acceptance and God's Plan For The World, as well as diving deep into a literal ocean of mystery in search of answers to the kinds of questions it has always been dangerous to ask, in any age and on any world. . . .

ONE

The swell was gently lifting and lowering the boat. My breathing grew slower, falling into step with the creaking of the hull, until I could no longer tell the difference between the faint rhythmic motion of the cabin and the sensation of filling and emptying my lungs. It was like floating in darkness: every inhalation buoyed me up, slightly; every exhalation made me sink back down again.

In the bunk above me, my brother Daniel said distinctly, "Do you believe in God?"

My head was cleared of sleep in an instant, but I didn't reply straight away. I'd never closed my eyes, but the darkness of the unlit cabin seemed to shift in front of me, grains of phantom light moving like a cloud of disturbed insects.

"Martin?"

"I'm awake."

"Do you believe in God?"

"Of course." Everyone I knew believed in God. Everyone talked about Her, everyone prayed to Her. Daniel most of all. Since he'd joined the Deep Church the previous summer, he prayed every morning for a kilotau before dawn. I'd often wake to find myself aware of him kneeling by the far wall of the cabin, muttering and pounding his chest, before I drifted gratefully back to sleep.

Our family had always been Transitional, but Daniel was fifteen, old enough to choose for himself. My mother accepted this with diplomatic silence, but my father seemed positively proud of Daniel's independence and strength of conviction. My own feelings were mixed. I'd grown used to swimming in my older brother's wake, but I'd never resented it, because he'd always let me in on the view ahead: reading me passages from the books he read himself, teaching me words and phrases from the languages he studied, sketching some of the mathematics I was yet to encounter first-hand. We used to lie awake half the night, talking about the cores of stars or the hierarchy of transfinite numbers. But Daniel had told me nothing about the reasons for his conversion, and his ever-increasing piety. I didn't know whether to feel hurt by this exclusion, or simply grateful; I could see that being Transitional was like a pale imitation of being Deep Church, but I wasn't sure that this was such a bad thing if the wages of mediocrity included sleeping until sunrise.

Daniel said, "Why?"

I stared up at the underside of his bunk, unsure whether I was really seeing it or just imagining its solidity against the cabin's ordinary darkness. "Someone must have guided the Angels here from Earth. If Earth's too far away to see from Covenant . . . how could anyone find Covenant from Earth, without God's help?"

I heard Daniel shift slightly. "Maybe the Angels had better telescopes than us. Or maybe they spread out from Earth in all directions, launching thousands of expeditions without even knowing what they'd find."

I laughed. "But they had to come *here*, to be made flesh again!" Even a less-than-devout ten-year-old knew that much. God prepared Covenant as the place for the Angels to repent their theft of immortality. The Transitionals believed that in a million years we could earn the right to be Angels again; the Deep Church believed that we'd remain flesh until the stars fell from the sky.

Daniel said, "What makes you so sure that there were ever really Angels? Or that God really sent them Her daughter, Beatrice, to lead them back into the flesh?"

I pondered this for a while. The only answers I could think of came straight out of the Scriptures, and Daniel had taught me years ago that appeals to authority counted for nothing. Finally, I had to confess: "I don't know." I felt foolish, but I was grateful that he was willing to discuss these difficult questions with me. I wanted to believe in God for the right reasons, not just because everyone around me did.

He said, "Archaeologists have shown that we must have arrived about twenty thousand years ago. Before that, there's no evidence of humans, or any co-ecological plants and animals. That makes the Crossing older than the Scriptures say, but there are some dates that are open to interpretation, and with a bit of poetic license everything can be made to add up. And most biologists think the native microfauna could have formed by itself over millions of years, starting from simple chemicals, but that doesn't mean God didn't guide the whole process. Everything's compatible, really. Science and the Scriptures can both be true."

I thought I knew where he was headed, now. "So you've worked out a way to use science to prove that God exists?" I felt a surge of pride; my brother was a genius!

"No." Daniel was silent for a moment. "The thing is, it works both ways. What-ever's written in the Scriptures, people can always come up with different expla-nations for the facts. The ships might have left Earth for some other reason. The Angels might have made bodies for themselves for some other reason. There's no way to convince a non-believer that the Scriptures are the word of God. It's all a matter of faith."

"Oh."

"Faith's the most important thing," Daniel insisted. "If you don't have faith, you can be tempted into believing anything at all."

I made a noise of assent, trying not to sound too disappointed. I'd expected more from Daniel than the kind of bland assertions that sent me dozing off during sermons at the Transitional church.

"Do you know what you have to do to get faith?"

"No."

"Ask for it. That's all. Ask Beatrice to come into your heart and grant you the gift of faith."

I protested, "We do that every time we go to church!" I couldn't believe he'd forgotten the Transitional service already. After the priest placed a drop of seawater on our tongues, to symbolize the blood of Beatrice, we asked for the gifts of faith, hope, and love.

"But have you received it?"

I'd never thought about that. "I'm not sure." I believed in God, didn't I? "I might have."

Daniel was amused. "If you had the gift of faith, you'd *know*."

I gazed up into the darkness, troubled. "Do you have to go to the Deep Church, to ask for it properly?"

"No. Even in the Deep Church, not everyone has invited Beatrice into their hearts. You have to do it the way it says in the Scriptures: 'like an unborn child again, naked and helpless.' "

"I was Immersed, wasn't I?"

"In a metal bowl, when you were thirty days old. Infant Immersion is a gesture by the parents, an affirmation of their own good intentions. But it's not enough to save the child."

I was feeling very disoriented now. My father, at least, approved of Daniel's conversion . . . but now Daniel was trying to tell me that our family's transactions with God had all been grossly deficient, if not actually counterfeit.

Daniel said, "Remember what Beatrice told Her followers, the last time She appeared? 'Unless you are willing to drown in My blood, you will never look upon the face of My Mother.' So they bound each other hand and foot, and weighted themselves down with rocks."

My chest tightened. "And you've done that?"

"Yes."

"When?"

"Almost a year ago."

I was more confused than ever. "Did Ma and Fa go?"

Daniel laughed. "No! It's not a public ceremony. Some friends of mine from the Prayer Group helped; someone has to be on deck to haul you up, because it would be arrogant to expect Beatrice to break your bonds and raise you to the surface, like She did with Her followers. But in the water, you're alone with God."

He climbed down from his bunk and crouched by the side of my bed. "Are you ready to give your life to Beatrice, Martin?" His voice sent gray sparks flowing through the darkness.

I hesitated. "What if I just dive in? And stay under for a while?" I'd been swimming off the boat at night plenty of times, there was nothing to fear from that.

"No. You have to be weighted down." His tone made it clear that there could be no compromise on this. "How long can you hold your breath?"

"Two hundred tau." That was an exaggeration; two hundred was what I was aiming for.

"That's long enough."

I didn't reply. Daniel said, "I'll pray with you."

I climbed out of bed, and we knelt together. Daniel murmured, "Please, Holy Beatrice, grant my brother Martin the courage to accept the precious gift of Your blood." Then he started praying in what I took to be a foreign language, uttering a rapid stream of harsh syllables unlike anything I'd heard before. I listened apprehensively; I wasn't sure that I wanted Beatrice to change my mind, and I was afraid that this display of fervor might actually persuade Her.

I said, "What if I don't do it?"

"Then you'll never see the face of God."

I knew what that meant: I'd wander alone in the belly of Death, in darkness, for eternity. And even if the Scriptures weren't meant to be taken literally on this, the reality behind the metaphor could only be worse. Indescribably worse.

"But . . . what about Ma and Fa?" I was more worried about them, because I knew they'd never climb weighted off the side of the boat at Daniel's behest.

"That will take time," he said softly.

My mind reeled. He was absolutely serious.

I heard him stand and walk over to the ladder. He climbed a few rungs and opened the hatch. Enough starlight came in to give shape to his arms and shoulders, but as he turned to me I still couldn't make out his face. "Come on, Martin!" he whispered. "The longer you put it off, the harder it gets." The hushed urgency of his voice was familiar: generous and conspiratorial, nothing like an adult's impatience. He might almost have been daring me to join him in a midnight raid on the pantry—not because he really needed a collaborator, but because he honestly didn't want me to miss out on the excitement, or the spoils.

I suppose I was more afraid of damnation than drowning, and I'd always trusted Daniel to warn me of the dangers ahead. But this time I wasn't entirely convinced that he was right, so I must have been driven by something more than fear, and blind trust.

Maybe it came down to the fact that he was offering to make me his equal in this. I was ten years old, and I ached to become something more than I was; to reach, not my parents' burdensome adulthood, but the halfway point, full of freedom and secrets, that Daniel had reached. I wanted to be as strong, as fast, as quick-witted and widely read as he was. Becoming as certain of God would not have been my first choice, but there wasn't much point hoping for divine intervention to grant me anything else.

I followed him up onto the deck.

He took cord, and a knife, and four spare weights of the kind we used on our nets from the toolbox. He threaded the weights onto the cord, then I took off my shorts and sat naked on the deck while he knotted a figure-eight around my ankles. I raised my feet experimentally; the weights didn't seem all that heavy. But in the water, I knew, they'd be more than enough to counteract my body's slight buoyancy.

"Martin? Hold out your hands."

Suddenly I was crying. With my arms free, at least I could swim against the tug of the weights. But if my hands were tied, I'd be helpless.

Daniel crouched down and met my eyes. "Ssh. It's all right."

I hated myself. I could feel my face contorted into the mask of a blubbering infant.

"Are you afraid?"

I nodded.

Daniel smiled reassuringly. "You know why? You know who's doing that? Death doesn't want Beatrice to have you. He wants you for himself. So he's here on this boat, putting fear into your heart, because he *knows* he's almost lost you."

I saw something move in the shadows behind the toolbox, something slithering into the darkness. If we went back down to the cabin now, would Death follow us? To wait for Daniel to fall asleep? If I'd turned my back on Beatrice, who could I ask to send Death away?

I stared at the deck, tears of shame dripping from my cheeks. I held out my arms, wrists together.

When my hands were tied—not palm-to-palm as I'd expected, but in separate loops joined by a short bridge—Daniel unwound a long stretch of rope from the winch at the rear of the boat, and coiled it on the deck. I didn't want to think about how long it was, but I knew I'd never dived to that depth. He took the blunt hook at the end of the rope, slipped it over my arms, then screwed it closed to form an unbroken ring. Then he checked again that the cord around my wrists was neither so tight as to burn me, nor so loose as to let me slip. As he did this, I saw something creep over his face: some kind of doubt or fear of his own. He said, "Hang on to the hook. Just in case. Don't let go, no matter what. Okay?" He whispered something to Beatrice, then looked up at me, confident again.

He helped me to stand and shuffle over to the guard rail, just to one side of the winch. Then he picked me up under the arms and lifted me over, resting my feet on the outer hull. The deck was inert, a mineralized endoshell, but behind the guard rails the hull was palpably alive: slick with protective secretions, glowing softly. My toes curled uselessly against the lubricated skin; I had no purchase at all. The hull was supporting some of my weight, but Daniel's arms would tire eventually. If I wanted to back out, I'd have to do it quickly.

A warm breeze was blowing. I looked around, at the flat horizon, at the blaze of stars, at the faint silver light off the water. Daniel recited: "Holy Beatrice, I am ready to die to this world. Let me drown in Your blood, that I might be redeemed, and look upon the face of Your Mother."

I repeated the words, trying hard to mean them.

"Holy Beatrice, I offer You my life. All I do now, I do for You. Come into my heart, and grant me the gift of faith. Come into my heart, and grant me the gift of hope. Come into my heart, and grant me the gift of love."

"And grant me the gift of love."

Daniel released me. At first, my feet seemed to adhere magically to the hull, and I pivoted backward without actually falling. I clung tightly to the hook, pressing the cold metal against my belly, and willed the rope of the winch to snap taut, leaving me dangling in midair. I even braced myself for the shock. Some part of me really did believe that I could change my mind, even now.

Then my feet slipped and I plunged into the ocean and sank straight down.

It was not like a dive—not even a dive from an untried height, when it took so long for the water to bring you to a halt that it began to grow frightening. I was falling through the water ever faster, as if it was air. The vision I'd had of the rope keeping me above the water now swung to the opposite extreme: my acceleration seemed to prove that the coil on the deck was attached to nothing, that its frayed end was already beneath the surface. *That's what the followers had done, wasn't it? They'd let themselves be thrown in without a lifeline.* So Daniel had cut the rope, and I was on my way to the bottom of the ocean.

Then the hook jerked my hands up over my head, jarring my wrists and shoulders, and I was motionless.

I turned my face toward the surface, but neither starlight nor the hull's faint phosphorescence reached this deep. I let a stream of bubbles escape from my mouth; I felt them slide over my upper lip, but no trace of them registered in the darkness.

I shifted my hands warily over the hook. I could still feel the cord fast around my wrists, but Daniel had warned me not to trust it. I brought my knees up to my chest, gauging the effect of the weights. If the cord broke, at least my hands would be free, but even so I wasn't sure I'd be able to ascend. The thought of trying to unpick the knots around my ankles as I tumbled deeper filled me with horror.

My shoulders ached, but I wasn't injured. It didn't take much effort to pull myself up until my chin was level with the bottom of the hook. Going further was awkward—with my hands so close together I couldn't brace myself properly—but on the third attempt I managed to get my arms locked, pointing straight down.

I'd done this without any real plan, but then it struck me that even with my hands and feet tied, I could try shinning up the rope. It was just a matter of getting started. I'd have to turn upside-down, grab the rope between my knees, then curl up—dragging the hook—and get a grip with my hands at a higher point.

And if I couldn't reach up far enough to right myself?

I'd ascend feet-first.

I couldn't even manage the first step. I thought it would be as simple as keeping my arms rigid and letting myself topple backward, but in the water even two-thirds of my body wasn't sufficient to counterbalance the weights.

I tried a different approach: I dropped down to hang at arm's length, raised my legs as high as I could, then proceeded to pull myself up again. But my grip wasn't tight enough to resist the turning force of the weights; I just pivoted around my center of gravity—which was somewhere near my knees—and ended up, still bent double, but almost horizontal.

I eased myself down again, and tried threading my feet through the circle of my arms. I didn't succeed on the first attempt, and then on reflection it seemed like a bad move anyway. Even if I managed to grip the rope between my bound feet—rather than just tumbling over backward, out of control, and dislocating my shoulders—climbing the rope *upside-down with my hands behind my back* would either be impossible, or so awkward and strenuous that I'd run out of oxygen before I got a tenth of the way.

I let some more air escape from my lungs. I could feel the muscles in my diaphragm reproaching me for keeping them from doing what they wanted to do; not urgently yet, but the knowledge that I had no control over when I'd be able to draw breath again made it harder to stay calm. I knew I could rely on Daniel to bring me to the surface on the count of two hundred. But I'd only ever stayed down for a hundred and sixty. Forty more tau would be an eternity.

I'd almost forgotten what the whole ordeal was meant to be about, but now I started praying. *Please Holy Beatrice, don't let me die. I know You drowned like this to save me, but if I die it won't help anyone. Daniel would end up in the deepest shit . . . but that's not a threat, it's just an observation.* I felt a stab of anxiety; on top of everything else, had I just offended the Daughter of God? I struggled on, my confidence waning. *I don't want to die. But You already know that. So I don't know what You want me to say.*

I released some more stale air, wishing I'd counted the time I'd been under: you weren't supposed to empty your lungs too quickly—when they were deflated it was even harder not to take a breath—but holding all the carbon dioxide in too long wasn't good either.

Praying only seemed to make me more desperate, so I tried to think other kinds of holy thoughts. I couldn't remember anything from the Scriptures word for word, but the gist of the most important part started running through my mind.

After living in Her body for thirty years, and persuading all the Angels to become mortal again, Beatrice had gone back up to their deserted spaceship and flown it straight into the ocean. When Death saw Her coming, he took the form of a giant serpent, coiled in the water, waiting. And even though She was the Daughter of God, with the power to do anything, She let Death swallow Her.

That's how much She loved us.

Death thought he'd won everything. Beatrice was trapped inside him, in the darkness, alone. The Angels were flesh again, so he wouldn't even have to wait for the stars to fall before he claimed them.

But Beatrice was part of God. Death had swallowed part of God. This was a mistake. After three days, his jaws burst open and Beatrice came flying out, wreathed in fire. Death was broken, shriveled, diminished.

My limbs were numb but my chest was burning. Death was still strong enough to hold down the damned. I started thrashing about blindly, wasting whatever oxygen was left in my blood, but desperate to distract myself from the urge to inhale.

Please Holy Beatrice—

Please Daniel—

Luminous bruises blossomed behind my eyes and drifted out into the water. I watched them curling into a kind of vortex, as if something was drawing them in.

It was the mouth of the serpent, swallowing my soul. I opened my own mouth and made a wretched noise, and Death swam forward to kiss me, to breathe cold water into my lungs.

Suddenly, everything was seared with light. The serpent turned and fled, like a pale timid worm. A wave of contentment washed over me, as if I was an infant again and my mother had wrapped her arms around me tightly. It was like basking in sunlight, listening to laughter, dreaming of music too beautiful to be real. Every muscle in my body was still trying to prize my lungs open to the water, but now I found myself fighting this almost absentmindedly while I marveled at my strange euphoria.

Cold air swept over my hands and down my arms. I raised myself up to take a mouthful, then slumped down again, giddy and spluttering, grateful for every breath but still elated by something else entirely. The light that had filled my eyes was gone, but it left a violet afterimage everywhere I looked. Daniel kept winding until my head was level with the guard rail, then he clamped the winch, bent down, and threw me over his shoulder.

I'd been warm enough in the water, but now my teeth were chattering. Daniel wrapped a towel around me, then set to work cutting the cord. I beamed at him. "I'm so happy!" He gestured to me to be quieter, but then he whispered joyfully, "That's the love of Beatrice. She'll always be with you now, Martin."

I blinked with surprise, then laughed softly at my own stupidity. Until that moment, I hadn't connected what had happened with Beatrice at all. But of course it was Her. I'd asked Her to come into my heart, and She had.

And I could see it in Daniel's face: a year after his own Drowning, he still felt Her presence.

He said, "Everything you do now is for Beatrice. When you look through your telescope, you'll do it to honor Her creation. When you eat, or drink, or swim, you'll do it to give thanks for Her gifts." I nodded enthusiastically.

Daniel tidied everything away, even soaking up the puddles of water I'd left on the deck. Back in the cabin, he recited from the Scriptures, passages that I'd never really understood before, but which now all seemed to be about the Drowning, and the way I was feeling. It was as if I'd opened the book and found myself mentioned by name on every page.

When Daniel fell asleep before me, for the first time in my life I didn't feel the slightest pang of loneliness. The Daughter of God was with me: I could feel Her presence, like a flame inside my skull, radiating warmth through the darkness behind my eyes.

Giving me comfort, giving me strength.

Giving me faith.

TWO

The monastery was almost four milliradians northeast of our home grounds. Daniel and I took the launch to a rendezvous point, and met up with three other small vessels before continuing. It had been the same routine every tenth night for almost a year—and Daniel had been going to the Prayer Group himself for a year before that—so the launch didn't need much supervision. Feeding on nutrients in the ocean, propelling itself by pumping water through fine channels in its skin, guided by both sunlight and Covenant's magnetic field, it was a perfect example of the kind of legacy of the Angels that technology would never be able to match.

Bartholomew, Rachel, and Agnes were in one launch, and they traveled beside us while the others skimmed ahead. Bartholomew and Rachel were married, though they were only seventeen, scarcely older than Daniel. Agnes, Rachel's sister, was sixteen. Because I was the youngest member of the Prayer Group, Agnes had fussed over me from the day I'd joined. She said, "It's your big night tonight, Martin, isn't it?" I nodded, but declined to pursue the conversation, leaving her free to talk to Daniel.

It was dusk by the time the monastery came into sight, a conical tower built from at least ten thousand hulls, rising up from the water in the stylized form of Beatrice's spaceship. Aimed at the sky, not down into the depths. Though some commentators on the Scriptures insisted that the spaceship itself had sunk forever, and Beatrice had risen from the water unaided, it was still the definitive symbol of Her victory over Death. For the three days of Her separation from God, all such buildings stood in darkness, but that was half a year away, and now the monastery shone from every porthole.

There was a narrow tunnel leading into the base of the tower; the launches detected its scent in the water and filed in one by one. I knew they didn't have souls, but I wondered what it would have been like for them if they'd been aware of their actions. Normally they rested in the dock of a single hull, a pouch of boatskin that secured them but still left them largely exposed. Maybe being drawn instinctively into this vast structure would have felt even safer, even more comforting, than docking with their home boat. When I said something to this effect, Rachel, in the launch behind me, sniggered. Agnes said, "Don't be horrible."

The walls of the tunnel phosphoresced pale green, but the opening ahead was filled with white lamplight, dazzlingly richer and brighter. We emerged into a canal circling a vast atrium, and continued around it until the launches found empty docks.

As we disembarked, every footstep, every splash, echoed back at us. I looked up at the ceiling, a dome spliced together from hundreds of curved triangular hull sections, tattooed with scenes from the Scriptures. The original illustrations were more than a thousand years old, but the living boatskin degraded the pigments on a time scale of decades, so the monks had to constantly renew them.

"Beatrice Joining the Angels" was my favorite. Because the Angels weren't flesh, they didn't grow inside their mothers; they just appeared from nowhere in the streets of the Immaterial Cities. In the picture on the ceiling, Beatrice's immaterial body was half-formed, with cherubs still working to clothe the immaterial bones of Her legs and arms in immaterial muscles, veins, and skin. A few Angels in luminous robes were glancing sideways at Her, but you could tell they weren't particularly impressed. They'd had no way of knowing, then, who She was.

A corridor with its own smaller illustrations led from the atrium to the meeting room. There were about fifty people in the Prayer Group—including several priests and monks, though they acted just like everyone else. In church, you followed the liturgy; the priest slotted in his or her sermon, but there was no room for the worshippers to do much more than pray or sing in unison and offer rote responses. Here it was much less formal. There were two or three different speakers every night—sometimes guests who were visiting the monastery, sometimes members of the group—and after that anyone could ask the group to pray with them, about whatever they liked.

I'd fallen behind the others, but they'd saved me an aisle seat. Agnes was to my left, then Daniel, Bartholomew and Rachel. Agnes said, "Are you nervous?"

"No."

Daniel laughed, as if this claim was ridiculous.

I said, "I'm not." I'd meant to sound loftily unperturbed, but the words came out sullen and childish.

The first two speakers were both lay theologians, Firmlanders who were visiting the monastery. One gave a talk about people who belonged to false religions, and how they were all—in effect—worshipping Beatrice, but just didn't know it. He said they wouldn't be damned, because they'd had no choice about the cultures they were born into. Beatrice would know they'd meant well, and forgive them.

I wanted this to be true, but it made no sense to me. Either Beatrice *was* the Daughter of God, and everyone who thought otherwise had turned away from Her into the darkness, or . . . there was no "or." I only had to close my eyes and feel Her presence to know that. Still, everyone applauded when the man finished, and all the questions people asked seemed sympathetic to his views, so perhaps his arguments had simply been too subtle for me to follow.

The second speaker referred to Beatrice as "the Holy Jester," and rebuked us severely for not paying enough attention to Her sense of humor. She cited events in the Scriptures which she said were practical jokes, and then went on at some length about "the healing power of laughter." It was all about as gripping as a lecture on nutrition and hygiene; I struggled to keep my eyes open. At the end, no one could think of any questions.

Then Carol, who was running the meeting, said, "Now Martin is going to give witness to the power of Beatrice in his life."

Everyone applauded encouragingly. As I rose to my feet and stepped into the aisle, Daniel leaned toward Agnes and whispered sarcastically, "This should be good."

I stood at the lectern and gave the talk I'd been rehearsing for days. Beatrice, I said, was beside me now whatever I did: whether I studied or worked, ate or swam, or just sat and watched the stars. When I woke in the morning and looked into my heart, She was there without fail, offering me strength and guidance. When I lay in bed at night, I feared nothing, because I knew She was watching over me. Before my Drowning, I'd been unsure of my faith, but now I'd never again be able to doubt that the Daughter of God had become flesh, and died, and conquered Death, because of Her great love for us.

It was all true, but even as I said these things I couldn't get Daniel's sarcastic words out of my mind. I glanced over at the row where I'd been sitting, at the people I'd traveled with. What did I have in common with them, really? Rachel and Bartholomew were married. Bartholomew and Daniel had studied together, and still played on the same dive-ball team. Daniel and Agnes were probably in love. And Daniel was my brother . . . but the only difference that seemed to make was the fact that he could belittle me far more efficiently than any stranger.

In the open prayer that followed, I paid no attention to the problems and blessings people were sharing with the group. I tried silently calling on Beatrice to dissolve the knot of anger in my heart. But I couldn't do it; I'd turned too far away from Her.

When the meeting was over, and people started moving into the adjoining room to talk for a while, I hung back. When the others were out of sight, I ducked into the corridor, and headed straight for the launch.

Daniel could get a ride home with his friends; it wasn't far out of their way. I'd wait a short distance from the boat until he caught up; if my parents saw me arrive on my own I'd be in trouble. Daniel would be angry, of course, but he wouldn't betray me.

Once I'd freed the launch from its dock, it knew exactly where to go: around the canal, back to the tunnel, out into the open sea. As I sped across the calm, dark water, I felt the presence of Beatrice returning, which seemed like a sign that She understood that I'd had to get away.

I leaned over and dipped my hand in the water, feeling the current the launch was generating by shuffling ions in and out of the cells of its skin. The outer hull glowed a phosphorescent blue, more to warn other vessels than to light the way. In the time of Beatrice, one of her followers had sat in the Immaterial City and designed this creature from scratch. It gave me a kind of vertigo, just imagining the things the Angels had known. I wasn't sure why so much of it had been lost, but I wanted to rediscover it all. Even the Deep Church taught that there was nothing wrong with that, so long as we didn't use it to try to become immortal again.

The monastery shrank to a blur of light on the horizon, and there was no other beacon visible on the water, but I could read the stars, and sense the field lines, so I knew the launch was heading in the right direction.

When I noticed a blue speck in the distance, it was clear that it wasn't Daniel and the others chasing after me; it was coming from the wrong direction. As I watched the launch drawing nearer I grew anxious; if this was someone I knew, and I couldn't come up with a good reason to be traveling alone, word would get back to my parents.

Before I could make out anyone on board, a voice shouted, "Can you help me? I'm lost!"

I thought for a while before replying. The voice sounded almost matter-of-fact, making light of this blunt admission of helplessness, but it was no joke. If you were sick, your diurnal sense and your field sense could both become scrambled, making the stars much harder to read. It had happened to me a couple of times, and it had been a horrible experience — even standing safely on the deck of our boat. This late at night, a launch with only its field sense to guide it could lose track of its position, especially if you were trying to take it somewhere it hadn't been before.

I shouted back our coordinates, and the time. I was fairly confident that I had them down to the nearest hundred microradians, and few hundred tau.

"That can't be right! Can I approach? Let our launches talk?"

I hesitated. It had been drummed into me for as long as I could remember that if I ever found myself alone on the water, I should give other vessels a wide berth unless I knew the people on board. But Beatrice was with me, and if someone needed help it was wrong to refuse them.

"All right!" I stopped dead, and waited for the stranger to close the gap. As the launch drew up beside me, I was surprised to see that the passenger was a young man. He looked about Bartholomew's age, but he'd sounded much older.

We didn't need to tell the launches what to do; proximity was enough to trigger a chemical exchange of information. The man said, "Out on your own?"

"I'm traveling with my brother and his friends. I just went ahead a bit."

That made him smile. "Sent you on your way, did they? What do you think they're getting up to, back there?" I didn't reply; that was no way to talk about people you didn't even know. The man scanned the horizon, then spread his arms in a gesture of sympathy. "You must be feeling left out."

I shook my head. There was a pair of binoculars on the floor behind him; even before he'd called out for help, he could have seen that I was alone.

He jumped deftly between the launches, landing on the stern bench. I said, "There's nothing to steal." My skin was crawling, more with disbelief than fear. He was standing on the bench in the starlight, pulling a knife from his belt. The details — the pattern carved into the handle, the serrated edge of the blade — only made it seem more like a dream.

He coughed, suddenly nervous. "Just do what I tell you, and you won't get hurt."

I filled my lungs and shouted for help with all the strength I had; I knew there was no one in earshot, but I thought it might still frighten him off. He looked around, more startled than angry, as if he couldn't quite believe I'd waste so much effort. I jumped backward, into the water. A moment later I heard him follow me.

I found the blue glow of the launches above me, then swam hard, down and away from them, without wasting time searching for his shadow. Blood was pounding in my ears, but I knew I was moving almost silently; however fast he was, in the darkness he could swim right past me without knowing it. If he didn't catch me soon he'd probably return to the launch and wait to spot me when I came up for air. I had to surface far enough away to be invisible — even with the binoculars.

I was terrified that I'd feel a hand close around my ankle at any moment, but Beatrice was with me. As I swam, I thought back to my Drowning, and Her presence grew stronger than ever. When my lungs were almost bursting, She helped me to keep going, my limbs moving mechanically, blotches of light floating in front of my eyes. When I finally knew I had to surface, I turned face-up and ascended slowly, then lay on my back with only my mouth and nose above the water, refusing the temptation to stick my head up and look around.

I filled and emptied my lungs a few times, then dived again.

The fifth time I surfaced, I dared to look back. I couldn't see either launch. I raised myself higher, then turned a full circle in case I'd grown disoriented, but nothing came into sight.

I checked the stars, and my field sense. The launches should *not* have been over the horizon. I trod water, riding the swell, and tried not to think about how tired I was. It was at least two milliradians to the nearest boat. Good swimmers — some younger than I was — competed in marathons over distances like that, but I'd never even aspired to such feats of endurance. Unprepared, in the middle of the night, I knew I wouldn't make it.

If the man had given up on me, would he have taken our launch? When they cost so little, and the markings were so hard to change? That would be nothing but an admission of guilt. *So why couldn't I see it?* Either he'd sent it on its way, or it had decided to return home itself.

I knew the path it would have taken; I would have seen it go by, if I'd been looking for it when I'd surfaced before. But I had no hope of catching it now.

I began to pray. I knew I'd been wrong to leave the others, but I asked for forgiveness, and felt it being granted. I watched the horizon almost calmly — smiling at the blue flashes of meteors burning up high above the ocean — certain that Beatrice would not abandon me.

I was still praying — treading water, shivering from the cool of the air — when a blue light appeared in the distance. It disappeared as the swell took me down again, but there was no mistaking it for a shooting star. *Was this Daniel and the others — or the stranger?* I didn't have long to decide; if I wanted to get within earshot as they passed, I'd have to swim hard.

I closed my eyes and prayed for guidance. *Please Holy Beatrice, let me know.* Joy flooded through my mind, instantly: it was them, I was certain of it. I set off as fast as I could.

I started yelling before I could see how many passengers there were, but I knew Beatrice would never allow me to be mistaken. A flare shot up from the launch, revealing four figures standing side by side, scanning the water. I shouted with jubilation, and waved my arms. Someone finally spotted me, and they brought the launch around toward me. By the time I was on board I was so charged up on adrenaline and relief that I almost believed I could have dived back into the water and raced them home.

I thought Daniel would be angry, but when I described what had happened all he said was, "We'd better get moving."

Agnes embraced me. Bartholomew gave me an almost respectful look, but Rachel muttered sourly, "You're an idiot, Martin. You don't know how lucky you are."

I said, "I know."

Our parents were standing on deck. The empty launch had arrived some time ago; they'd been about to set out to look for us. When the others had departed I began recounting everything again, this time trying to play down any element of danger.

Before I'd finished, my mother grabbed Daniel by the front of his shirt and started slapping him. "I trusted you with him! *You maniac!* I trusted you!" Daniel half raised his arm to block her, but then let it drop and just turned his face to the deck.

I burst into tears. "It was my fault!" Our parents never struck us; I couldn't believe what I was seeing.

My father said soothingly, "Look . . . he's home now. He's safe. No one touched him." He put an arm around my shoulders and asked warily, "That's right, Martin, isn't it?"

I nodded tearfully. This was worse than anything that had happened on the launch, or in the water; I felt a thousand times more helpless, a thousand times more like a child.

I said, "Beatrice was watching over me."

My mother rolled her eyes and laughed wildly, letting go of Daniel's shirt. "Beatrice? *Beatrice?* Don't you know what could have happened to you? You're too young to have given him what he wanted. He would have had to use the knife."

The chill of my wet clothes seemed to penetrate deeper. I swayed unsteadily, but fought to stay upright. Then I whispered stubbornly, "Beatrice was there."

My father said, "Go and get changed, or you're going to freeze to death."

I lay in bed listening to them shout at Daniel. When he finally came down the ladder I was so sick with shame that I wished I'd drowned.

He said, "Are you all right?"

There was nothing I could say. I couldn't ask him to forgive me.

"Martin?" Daniel turned on the lamp. His face was streaked with tears; he laughed softly, wiping them away. "Fuck, you had me worried. Don't ever do anything like that again."

"I won't."

"Okay." That was it; no shouting, no recriminations. "Do you want to pray with me?"

We knelt side by side, praying for our parents to be at peace, praying for the man who'd tried to hurt me. I started trembling; everything was catching up with me. Suddenly, words began gushing from my mouth — words I neither recognized nor understood, though I knew I was praying for everything to be all right with Daniel, praying that our parents would stop blaming him for my stupidity.

The strange words kept flowing out of me, an incomprehensible torrent somehow imbued with everything I was feeling. I knew what was happening: *Beatrice had given me the Angels' tongue.* We'd had to surrender all knowledge of it when we became flesh, but sometimes She granted people the ability to pray this way, because the language of the Angels could express things we could no longer put into words. Daniel had been able to do it ever since his Drowning, but it wasn't something you could teach, or even something you could ask for.

When I finally stopped, my mind was racing. "Maybe Beatrice planned everything that happened tonight? Maybe She arranged it all, to lead up to this moment!"

Daniel shook his head, wincing slightly. "Don't get carried away. You have the gift; just accept it." He nudged me with his shoulder. "Now get into bed, before we're both in more trouble."

I lay awake almost until dawn, overwhelmed with happiness. Daniel had forgiven me. Beatrice had protected and blessed me. I felt no more shame, just humility and amazement. I knew I'd done nothing to deserve it, but my life was wrapped in the love of God.

THREE

According to the Scriptures, the oceans of Earth were storm-tossed, and filled with dangerous creatures. But on Covenant, the oceans were calm, and the Angels created nothing in the ecopoiesis that would harm their own mortal incarnations. The four continents and the four oceans were rendered equally hospitable, and just as women and men were made indistinguishable in the sight of God, so were Freelanders and Firmlanders. (Some commentators insisted that this was literally true: God chose to blind Herself to where we lived, and whether or not we'd been born with a penis. I thought that was a beautiful idea, even if I couldn't quite grasp the logistics of it.)

I'd heard that certain obscure sects taught that half the Angels had actually become embodied as a separate people who could live in the water and breathe beneath the surface, but then God destroyed them because they were a mockery of Beatrice's death. No legitimate church took this notion seriously, though, and archaeologists had found no trace of these mythical doomed cousins. Humans were humans, there was only one kind. Freelanders and Firmlanders could even intermarry—if they could agree where to live.

When I was fifteen, Daniel became engaged to Agnes from the Prayer Group. That made sense: they'd be spared the explanations and arguments about the Drowning that they might have faced with partners who weren't so blessed. Agnes was a Freelander, of course, but a large branch of her family, and a smaller branch of ours, were Firmlanders, so after long negotiations it was decided that the wedding would be held in Ferez, a coastal town.

I went with my father to pick a hull to be fitted out as Daniel and Agnes's boat. The breeder, Diana, had a string of six mature hulls in tow, and my father insisted on walking out onto their backs and personally examining each one for imperfections.

By the time we reached the fourth I was losing patience. I muttered, "It's the skin underneath that matters." In fact, you could tell a lot about a hull's general condition from up here, but there wasn't much point worrying about a few tiny flaws high above the waterline.

My father nodded thoughtfully. "That's true. You'd better get in the water and check their undersides."

"I'm not doing that." We couldn't simply trust this woman to sell us a healthy hull for a decent price; that wouldn't have been sufficiently embarrassing.

"Martin! This is for the safety of your brother and sister-in-law."

I glanced at Diana to show her where my sympathies lay, then slipped off my shirt and dived in. I swam down to the last hull in the row, then ducked beneath it. I began the job with perverse thoroughness, running my fingers over every square nanoradian of skin. I was determined to annoy my father by taking even longer than he wanted—and determined to impress Diana by examining all six hulls without coming up for air.

An unfitted hull rode higher in the water than a boat full of furniture and junk, but I was surprised to discover that even in the creature's shadow there was enough light for me to see the skin clearly. After a while I realized that, paradoxically, this was because the water was slightly cloudier than usual, and whatever the fine particles were, they were scattering sunlight into the shadows.

Moving through the warm, bright water, feeling the love of Beatrice more strongly than I had for a long time, it was impossible to remain angry with my father. He wanted the best hull for Daniel and Agnes, and so did I. As for impressing Diana . . . who was I kidding? She was a grown woman, at least as old as Agnes, and highly unlikely to view me as anything more than a child. By the time I'd finished with the third hull I was feeling short of breath, so I surfaced and reported cheerfully, "No blemishes so far!"

Diana smiled down at me. "You've got strong lungs."

All six hulls were in perfect condition. We ended up taking the one at the end of the row, because it was easiest to detach.

Ferez was built on the mouth of a river, but the docks were some distance upstream. That helped to prepare us; the gradual deadening of the waves was less of a shock than an instant transition from sea to land would have been. When I jumped from the deck to the pier, though, it was like colliding with something massive and unyielding, the rock of the planet itself. I'd been on land twice before, for less than a day on both occasions. The wedding celebrations would last ten days, but at least we'd still be able to sleep on the boat.

As the four of us walked along the crowded streets, heading for the ceremonial hall where everything but the wedding sacrament itself would take place, I stared uncouthly at everyone in sight. Almost no one was barefoot like us, and after a few hundred tau on the paving stones—much rougher than any deck—I could understand why. Our clothes were different, our skin was darker, our accent was unmistakably foreign . . . but no one stared back. Freelanders were hardly a novelty here. That made me even more self-conscious; the curiosity I felt wasn't mutual.

In the hall, I joined in with the preparations, mainly just lugging furniture around under the directions of one of Agnes's tyrannical uncles. It was a new kind of shock to see so many Freelanders together in this alien environment, and stranger still when I realized that I couldn't necessarily spot the Firmlanders among us; there was no sharp dividing line in physical appearance, or even clothing. I began to feel slightly guilty; if God couldn't tell the difference, what was I doing hunting for the signs?

At noon, we all ate outside, in a garden behind the hall. The grass was soft, but it made my feet itch. Daniel had gone off to be fitted for wedding clothes, and my parents were performing some vital task of their own; I only recognized a handful of the people around me. I sat in the shade of a tree, pretending to be oblivious to the plant's enormous size and bizarre anatomy. I wondered if we'd take a siesta; I couldn't imagine falling asleep on the grass.

Someone sat down beside me, and I turned.

"I'm Lena. Agnes's second cousin."

"I'm Daniel's brother, Martin." I hesitated, then offered her my hand; she took it, smiling slightly. I'd awkwardly kissed a dozen strangers that morning, all distant prospective relatives, but this time I didn't dare.

"Brother of the groom, doing grunt work with the rest of us." She shook her head in mocking admiration.

I desperately wanted to say something witty in reply, but an attempt that failed would be even worse than merely being dull. "Do you live in Ferez?"

"No, Mitar. Inland from here. We're staying with my uncle." She pulled a face. "Along with ten other people. No privacy. It's awful."

I said, "It was easy for us. We just brought our home with us." *You idiot. As if she didn't know that.*

Lena smiled. "I haven't been on a boat in years. You'll have to give me a tour sometime."

"Of course. I'd be happy to." I knew she was only making small talk; she'd never take me up on the offer.

She said, "Is it just you and Daniel?"

"Yes."

"You must be close."

I shrugged. "What about you?"

"Two brothers. Both younger. Eight and nine. They're all right, I suppose." She rested her chin on one hand and gazed at me coolly.

I looked away, disconcerted by more than my wishful thinking about what lay behind that gaze. Unless her parents had been awfully young when she was born, it didn't seem likely that more children were planned. So did an odd number in the family mean that one had died, or that the custom of equal numbers carried by each parent wasn't followed where she lived? I'd studied the region less than a year ago, but I had a terrible memory for things like that.

Lena said, "You looked so lonely, off here on your own."

I turned back to her, surprised. "I'm never lonely."

"No?"

She seemed genuinely curious. I opened my mouth to tell her about Beatrice, but then changed my mind. The few times I'd said anything to friends—ordinary friends, not Drowned ones—I'd regretted it. Not everyone had laughed, but they'd all been acutely embarrassed by the revelation.

I said, "Mitar has a million people, doesn't it?"

"Yes."

"An area of ocean the same size would have a population of ten."

Lena frowned. "That's a bit too deep for me, I'm afraid." She rose to her feet. "But maybe you'll think of a way of putting it that even a Firmlander can understand." She raised a hand goodbye and started walking away.

I said, "Maybe I will."

The wedding took place in Ferez's Deep Church, a spaceship built of stone, glass, and wood. It looked almost like a parody of the churches I was used to, though it probably bore a closer resemblance to the Angels' real ship than anything made of living hulls.

Daniel and Agnes stood before the priest, beneath the apex of the building. Their closest relatives stood behind them in two angled lines on either side. My father—Daniel's mother—was first in our line, followed by my own mother, then me. That put me level with Rachel, who kept shooting disdainful glances my way. After my misadventure, Daniel and I had eventually been allowed to travel to the Prayer Group meetings again, but less than a year later I'd lost interest, and soon after I'd also stopped going to church. Beatrice was with me, constantly, and no gatherings or ceremonies could bring me any closer to Her. I knew Daniel disapproved of this attitude, but he didn't lecture me about it, and my parents had accepted my decision without any fuss. If Rachel thought I was some kind of apostate, that was her problem.

The priest said, "Which of you brings a bridge to this marriage?"

Daniel said, "I do." In the Transitional ceremony, they no longer asked this; it was really no one else's business—and in a way the question was almost sacrilegious. Still, Deep Church theologians had explained away greater doctrinal inconsistencies than this, so who was I to argue?

"Do you, Daniel and Agnes, solemnly declare that this bridge will be the bond of your union until death, to be shared with no other person?"

They replied together, "We solemnly declare."

"Do you solemnly declare that as you share this bridge, so shall you share every joy and every burden of marriage—equally?"

"We solemnly declare."

My mind wandered; I thought of Lena's parents. Maybe one of the family's children was adopted. Lena and I had managed to sneak away to the boat three times so far, early in the evenings while my parents were still out. We'd done things I'd never done with anyone else, but I still hadn't had the courage to ask her anything so personal.

Suddenly the priest was saying, "In the eyes of God, you are one now." My father started weeping softly. As Daniel and Agnes kissed, I felt a surge of contradictory emotions. I'd miss Daniel, but I was glad that I'd finally have a chance to live apart from him. And I wanted him to be happy—I was jealous of his happiness already—but at the same time, the thought of marrying someone like Agnes filled me with claustrophobia. She was kind, devout, and generous. She and Daniel would treat each other, and their children, well. But neither of them would present the slightest challenge to the other's most cherished beliefs.

This recipe for harmony terrified me. Not least because I was afraid that Beatrice approved, and wanted me to follow it myself.

Lena put her hand over mine and pushed my fingers deeper into her, gasping. We were sitting on my bunk, face to face, my legs stretched out flat, hers arching over them.

She slid the palm of her other hand over my penis. I bent forward and kissed her, moving my thumb over the place she'd shown me, and her shudder ran through both of us.

"Martin?"

"What?"

She stroked me with one fingertip; somehow it was far better than having her whole hand wrapped around me.

"Do you want to come inside me?"

I shook my head.

"Why not?"

She kept moving her finger, tracing the same line; I could barely think. *Why not?* "You might get pregnant."

She laughed. "Don't be stupid. I can control that. You'll learn, too. It's just a matter of experience."

I said, "I'll use my tongue. You liked that."

"I did. But I want something more now. And you do, too. I can tell." She smiled imploringly. "It'll be nice for both of us, I promise. Nicer than anything you've done in your life."

"Don't bet on it."

Lena made a sound of disbelief, and ran her thumb around the base of my penis. "I can tell you haven't put this inside anyone before. But that's nothing to be ashamed of."

"Who said I was ashamed?"

She nodded gravely. "All right. Frightened."

I pulled my hand free, and banged my head on the bunk above us. Daniel's old bunk.

Lena reached up and put her hand on my cheek.

I said, "I can't. We're not married."

She frowned. "I heard you'd given up on all that."

"All what?"

"Religion."

"Then you were misinformed."

Lena said, "This is what the Angels made our bodies to do. How can there be anything sinful in that?" She ran her hand down my neck, over my chest.

"But the bridge is meant to . . ." *What?* All the Scriptures said was that it was meant to unite men and women, equally. And the Scriptures said God couldn't tell women and men apart, but in the Deep Church, in the sight of God, the priest had just made Daniel claim priority. So why should I care what any priest thought?

I said, "All right."

"Are you sure?"

"Yes." I took her face in my hands and started kissing her. After a while, she reached down and guided me in. The shock of pleasure almost made me come, but I stopped myself somehow. When the risk of that had lessened, we wrapped our arms around each other and rocked slowly back and forth.

It wasn't better than my Drowning, but it was so much like it that it had to be blessed by Beatrice. And as we moved in each other's arms, I grew determined to ask Lena to marry me. She was intelligent and strong. She questioned everything. It didn't matter that she was a Firmlander; we could meet halfway, we could live in Ferez.

I felt myself ejaculate. "I'm sorry."

Lena whispered, "That's all right, that's all right. Just keep moving."

I was still hard; that had never happened before. I could feel her muscles clenching and releasing rhythmically, in time with our motion, and her slow exhalations. Then she cried out, and dug her fingers into my back. I tried to slide partly out of her again, but it was impossible, she was holding me too tightly. This was it. There was no going back.

Now I was afraid. "I've never—" Tears were welling up in my eyes; I tried to shake them away.

"I know. And I know it's frightening." She embraced me more tightly. "Just feel it, though. Isn't it wonderful?"

I was hardly aware of my motionless penis anymore, but there was liquid fire flowing through my groin, waves of pleasure spreading deeper. I said, "Yes. Is it like that for you?"

"It's different. But it's just as good. You'll find out for yourself, soon enough."

"I hadn't been thinking that far ahead," I confessed.

Lena giggled. "You've got a whole new life in front of you, Martin. You don't know what you've been missing."

She kissed me, then started pulling away. I cried out in pain, and she stopped. "I'm sorry. I'll take it slowly." I reached down to touch the place where we were joined; there was a trickle of blood escaping from the base of my penis.

Lena said, "You're not going to faint on me, are you?"

"Don't be stupid." I did feel queasy, though. "What if I'm not ready? What if I can't do it?"

"Then I'll lose my hold in a few hundred tau. The Angels weren't completely stupid."

I ignored this blasphemy, though it wasn't just any Angel who'd designed our bodies—it was Beatrice Herself. I said, "Just promise you won't use a knife."

"That's not funny. That really happens to people."

"I know." I kissed her shoulder. "I think—"

Lena straightened her legs slightly, and I felt the core break free inside me. Blood flowed warmly from my groin, but the pain had changed from a threat of damage to mere tenderness; my nervous system no longer spanned the lesion. I asked Lena, "Do you feel it? Is it part of you?"

"Not yet. It takes a while for the connections to form." She ran her fingers over my lips. "Can I stay inside you, until they have?"

I nodded happily. I hardly cared about the sensations anymore; it was just contemplating the miracle of being able to give a part of my body to Lena that was wonderful. I'd studied the physiological details long ago, everything from the exchange of nutrients to the organ's independent immune system—and I knew that Beatrice had used many of the same techniques for the bridge as She'd used with gestating embryos—but to witness Her ingenuity so dramatically at work in my own flesh was both shocking and intensely moving. Only giving birth could bring me closer to Her than this.

When we finally separated, though, I wasn't entirely prepared for the sight of what emerged. "Oh, that is disgusting!"

Lena shook her head, laughing. "New ones always look a bit . . . encrusted. Most of that stuff will wash away, and the rest will fall off in a few kilotau."

I bunched up the sheet to find a clean spot, then dabbed at my—her—penis. My newly formed vagina had stopped bleeding, but it was finally dawning on me just how much mess we'd made. "I'm going to have to wash this before my parents get back. I can put it out to dry in the morning, after they're gone, but if I don't wash it now they'll smell it."

We cleaned ourselves enough to put on shorts, then Lena helped me carry the sheet up onto the deck and drape it in the water from the laundry hooks. The fibers in the sheet would use nutrients in the water to power the self-cleaning process.

The docks appeared deserted; most of the boats nearby belonged to people who'd come for the wedding. I'd told my parents I was too tired to stay on at the celebrations; tonight they'd continue until dawn, though Daniel and Agnes would probably leave by midnight. To do what Lena and I had just done.

"Martin? Are you shivering?"

There was nothing to be gained by putting it off. Before whatever courage I had could desert me, I said, "Will you marry me?"

"Very funny. Oh—" Lena took my hand. "I'm sorry, I never know when you're joking."

I said, "We've exchanged the bridge. It doesn't matter that we weren't married first, but it would make things easier if we went along with convention."

"Martin—"

"Or we could just live together, if that's what you want. I don't care. We're already married in the eyes of Beatrice."

Lena bit her lip. "I don't want to live with you."

"I could move to Mitar. I could get a job."

Lena shook her head, still holding my hand. She said firmly, "No. You knew, before we did anything, what it would and wouldn't mean. You don't want to marry me, and I don't want to marry you. So snap out of it."

I pulled my hand free, and sat down on the deck. *What had I done?* I'd thought I'd had Beatrice's blessing, I'd thought this was all in Her plan . . . but I'd just been fooling myself.

Lena sat beside me. "What are you worried about? Your parents finding out?"

"Yes." That was the least of it, but it seemed pointless trying to explain the truth. I turned to her. "When could we —?"

"Not for about ten days. And sometimes it's longer after the first time."

I'd known as much, but I'd hoped her experience might contradict my theoretical knowledge. *Ten days.* We'd both be gone by then.

Lena said, "What do you think, you can never get married now? How many marriages do you imagine involve the bridge one of the partners was born with?"

"Nine out of ten. Unless they're both women."

Lena gave me a look that hovered between tenderness and incredulity. "My estimate is about one in five."

I shook my head. "I don't care. We've exchanged the bridge, we have to be together." Lena's expression hardened, then so did my resolve. "Or I have to get it back."

"Martin, that's ridiculous. You'll find another lover soon enough, and then you won't even know what you were worried about. Or maybe you'll fall in love with a nice Deep Church boy, and then you'll both be glad you've been spared the trouble of getting rid of the extra bridge."

"Yeah? Or maybe he'll just be disgusted that I couldn't wait until I really *was* doing it for him!"

Lena groaned, and stared up at the sky. "Did I say something before about the Angels getting things right? Ten thousand years without bodies, and they thought they were qualified —"

I cut her off angrily. "Don't be so fucking blasphemous! Beatrice knew exactly what She was doing. If we mess it up, that's our fault!"

Lena said, matter-of-factly, "In ten years' time, there'll be a pill you'll be able to take to keep the bridge from being passed, and another pill to make it pass when it otherwise wouldn't. We'll win control of our bodies back from the Angels, and start doing exactly what we like with them."

"That's sick. That really is sick."

I stared at the deck, suffocating in misery. *This was what I'd wanted, wasn't it? A lover who was the very opposite of Daniel's sweet, pious Agnes?* Except that in my fantasies, we'd always had a lifetime to debate our philosophical differences. Not one night to be torn apart by them.

I had nothing to lose, now. I told Lena about my Drowning. She didn't laugh; she listened in silence.

I said, "Do you believe me?"

"Of course." She hesitated. "But have you ever wondered if there might be another explanation for the way you felt, in the water that night? You were starved of oxygen —"

"People are starved of oxygen all the time. Freelander kids spend half their lives trying to stay underwater longer than the last time."

Lena nodded. "Sure. But that's not quite the same, is it? You were pushed beyond the time you could have stayed under by sheer willpower. And . . . you were cued, you were told what to expect."

"That's not true. Daniel never told me what it would be like. I was *surprised* when it happened." I gazed back at her calmly, ready to counter any ingenious hypothesis she came up with. I felt chastened, but almost at peace now. This was what Beatrice had expected of me, before we'd exchanged the bridge: not a dead ceremony in a dead building, but the honesty to tell Lena exactly who she'd be making love with.

We argued almost until sunrise; neither of us convinced the other of anything. Lena helped me drag the clean sheet out of the water and hide it below deck. Before she left, she wrote down the address of a friend's house in Mitar, and a place and time we could meet.

Keeping that appointment was the hardest thing I'd ever done in my life. I spent three solid days ingratiating myself with my Mitar-based cousins, to the point where they would have had to be openly hostile to get out of inviting me to stay with them after the wedding. Once I was there, I had to scheme and lie relentlessly to ensure that I was free of them on the predetermined day.

In a stranger's house, in the middle of the afternoon, Lena and I joylessly reversed everything that had happened between us. I'd been afraid that the act itself might rekindle all my stupid illusions, but when we parted on the street outside, I felt as if I hardly knew her.

I ached even more than I had on the boat, and my groin was palpably swollen, but in a couple of days, I knew, nothing less than a lover's touch or a medical examination would reveal what I'd done.

In the train back to the coast, I replayed the entire sequence of events in my mind, again and again. *How could I have been so wrong?* People always talked about the power of sex to confuse and deceive you, but I'd always believed that was just cheap cynicism. Besides, I hadn't blindly surrendered to sex; I'd thought I'd been guided by Beatrice.

If I could be wrong about that—

I'd have to be more careful. Beatrice always spoke clearly, but I'd have to listen to Her with much more patience and humility.

That was it. That was what She'd wanted me to learn. I finally relaxed and looked out the window, at the blur of forest passing by, another triumph of the ecopoiesis. If I needed proof that there was always another chance, it was all around me now. The Angels had traveled as far from God as anyone could travel, and yet God had turned around and given them Covenant.

FOUR

I was nineteen when I returned to Mitar, to study at the city's university. Originally, I'd planned to specialize in the ecopoiesis—and to study much closer to home— but in the end I'd had to accept the nearest thing on offer, geographically and intellectually: working with Barat, a Firmlander biologist whose real interest was native microfauna. "Angelic technology is a fascinating subject in its own right," he told me. "But we can't hope to work backward and decipher terrestrial evolution from anything the Angels created. The best we can do is try to understand what Covenant's own biosphere was like, before we arrived and disrupted it."

I managed to persuade him to accept a compromise: my thesis would involve the impact of the ecopoiesis on the native microfauna. That would give me an excuse to study the Angels' inventions, alongside the drab unicellular creatures that had inhabited Covenant for the last billion years.

"The impact of the ecopoiesis" was far too broad a subject, of course; with Barat's help, I narrowed it down to one particular unresolved question. There had long been geological evidence that the surface waters of the ocean had become both more alkaline, and less oxygenated, as new species shifted the balance of dissolved gases. Some native species must have retreated from the wave of change, and perhaps some had been wiped out completely, but there was a thriving population of zooytes in the upper layers at present. So had they been there all along, adapting *in situ*? Or had they migrated from somewhere else?

Mitar's distance from the coast was no real handicap in studying the ocean; the university mounted regular expeditions, and I had plenty of library and lab work to do before embarking on anything so obvious as gathering living samples in their natural habitat. What's more, river water, and even rainwater, was teeming with closely related species, and since it was possible that these were the reservoirs from which the "ravaged" ocean had been recolonized, I had plenty of subjects worth studying close at hand.

Barat set high standards, but he was no tyrant, and his other students made me feel welcome. I was homesick, but not morbidly so, and I took a kind of giddy pleasure from the vivid dreams and underlying sense of disorientation that living on land induced in me. I wasn't exactly fulfilling my childhood ambition to uncover the secrets of the Angels—and I had fewer opportunities than I'd hoped to get side-tracked on the ecopoiesis itself—but once I started delving into the minutiae of Covenant's original, wholly undesigned biochemistry, it turned out to be complex and elegant enough to hold my attention.

I was only miserable when I let myself think about sex. I didn't want to end up like Daniel, so seeking out another Drowned person to marry was the last thing on my mind. But I couldn't face the prospect of repeating my mistake with Lena; I had no intention of becoming physically intimate with anyone unless we were already close enough for me to tell them about the most important thing in my life. But that wasn't the order in which things happened here. After a few humiliating attempts to swim against the current, I gave up on the whole idea, and threw myself into my work instead.

Of course, it *was* possible to socialize at Mitar University without actually exchanging bridges with anyone. I joined an informal discussion group on Angelic culture, which met in a small room in the students' building every tenth night— just like the old Prayer Group, though I was under no illusion that this one would be stacked with believers. It hardly needed to be. The Angels' legacy could be analyzed perfectly well without reference to Beatrice's divinity. The Scriptures were written long after the Crossing by people of a simpler age; there was no reason to treat them as infallible. If non-believers could shed some light on any aspect of the past, I had no grounds for rejecting their insights.

"It's obvious that only one faction came to Covenant!" That was Céline, an anthropologist, a woman so much like Lena that I had to make a conscious effort to remind myself, every time I set eyes on her, that nothing could ever happen between us. "*We're* not so homogeneous that we'd all choose to travel to another planet and assume a new physical form, whatever cultural forces might drive one small group to do that. So why should the Angels have been unanimous? The other factions must still be living in the Immaterial Cities, on Earth, and on other planets."

"Then why haven't they contacted us? In twenty thousand years, you'd think they'd drop in and say hello once or twice." David was a mathematician, a Free-lander from the southern ocean.

Céline replied, "The attitude of the Angels who came here wouldn't have encouraged visitors. If all we have is a story of the Crossing in which Beatrice persuades every last Angel in existence to give up immortality—a version that simply erases everyone else from history—that doesn't suggest much of a desire to remain in touch."

A woman I didn't know interjected, "It might not have been so clear-cut from the start, though. There's evidence of settler-level technology being deployed for more than three thousand years after the Crossing, long after it was needed for the ecopoiesis. New species continued to be created, engineering projects continued to use advanced materials and energy sources. But then in less than a century, it all stopped. The Scriptures merge three separate decisions into one: renouncing immortality, migrating to Covenant, and abandoning the technology that might have provided an escape route if anyone changed their mind. But we *know* it didn't happen like that. Three thousand years after the Crossing, something changed. The whole experiment suddenly became irreversible."

These speculations would have outraged the average pious Freelander, let alone the average Drowned one, but I listened calmly, even entertaining the possibility that some of them could be true. The love of Beatrice was the only fixed point in my cosmology; everything else was open to debate.

Still, sometimes the debate was hard to take. One night, David joined us straight from a seminar of physicists. What he'd heard from the speaker was unsettling enough, but he'd already moved beyond it to an even less palatable conclusion.

"Why did the Angels choose mortality? After ten thousand years without death, why did they throw away all the glorious possibilities ahead of them, to come and die like animals on this ball of mud?" I had to bite my tongue to keep from replying to his rhetorical question: because God is the only source of eternal life, and Beatrice showed them that all they really had was a cheap parody of that divine gift.

David paused, then offered his own answer—which was itself a kind of awful parody of Beatrice's truth. "Because they discovered that they weren't immortal, after all. They discovered that *no one can be.* We've always known, as they must have, that the universe is finite in space and time. It's destined to collapse eventually: 'the stars will fall from the sky.' But it's easy to *imagine* ways around that." He laughed. "We don't know enough physics yet, ourselves, to rule out anything. I've just heard an extraordinary woman from Tia talk about coding our minds into waves that would orbit the shrinking universe so rapidly that we could think *an infinite number of thoughts* before everything was crushed!" David grinned joyfully at the sheer audacity of this notion. I thought primly: what blasphemous nonsense.

Then he spread his arms and said, "Don't you see, though? If the Angels *had* pinned their hopes on something like that—some ingenious trick that would keep them from sharing the fate of the universe—*but then they finally gained enough knowledge to rule out every last escape route*, it would have had a profound effect on them. Some small faction could then have decided that since they were mortal after all, they might as well embrace the inevitable, and come to terms with it in the way their ancestors had. In the flesh."

Céline said thoughtfully, "And the Beatrice myth puts a religious gloss on the whole thing, but that might be nothing but a *post hoc* reinterpretation of a purely secular revelation."

This was too much; I couldn't remain silent. I said, "If Covenant really was founded by a pack of terminally depressed atheists, what could have changed their minds? Where did the desire to impose a '*post hoc* reinterpretation' *come from?* If the revelation that brought the Angels here was 'secular,' why isn't the whole planet still secular today?"

Someone said snidely, "Civilization collapsed. What do you expect?"

I opened my mouth to respond angrily, but Céline got in first. "No, Martin has a point. If David's right, the rise of religion needs to be explained more urgently than ever. And I don't think anyone's in a position to do that yet."

Afterward, I lay awake thinking about all the other things I should have said, all the other objections I should have raised. (And thinking about Céline.) Theology aside, the whole dynamics of the group was starting to get under my skin; maybe I'd be better off spending my time in the lab, impressing Barat with my dedication to his pointless fucking microbes.

Or maybe I'd be better off at home. I could help out on the boat; my parents weren't young anymore, and Daniel had his own family to look after.

I climbed out of bed and started packing, but halfway through I changed my mind. I didn't really want to abandon my studies. And I'd known all along what the antidote was for all the confusion and resentment I was feeling.

I put my rucksack away, switched off the lamp, lay down, closed my eyes, and asked Beatrice to grant me peace.

I was awakened by someone banging on the door of my room. It was a fellow boarder, a young man I barely knew. He looked extremely tired and irritable, but something was overriding his irritation.

"There's a message for you."

My mother was sick, with an unidentified virus. The hospital was even further away than our home grounds; the trip would take almost three days.

I spent most of the journey praying, but the longer I prayed, the harder it became. I *knew* that it was possible to save my mother's life with one word in the Angels' tongue to Beatrice, but the number of ways in which I could fail, corrupting the purity of the request with my own doubts, my own selfishness, my own complacency, just kept multiplying.

The Angels created nothing in the ecopoiesis that would harm their own mortal incarnations. The native life showed no interest in parasitizing us. But over the millennia, our own DNA had shed viruses. And since Beatrice Herself chose every last base pair, that must have been what She intended. Aging was not enough. Mortal injury was not enough. Death had to come without warning, silent and invisible.

That's what the Scriptures said.

The hospital was a maze of linked hulls. When I finally found the right passageway, the first person I recognized in the distance was Daniel. He was holding his daughter Sophie high in his outstretched arms, smiling up at her. The image dispelled all my fears in an instant; I almost fell to my knees to give thanks.

Then I saw my father. He was seated outside the room, his head in his hands. I couldn't see his face, but I didn't need to. He wasn't anxious, or exhausted. He was crushed.

I approached in a haze of last-minute prayers, though I knew I was asking for the past to be rewritten. Daniel started to greet me as if nothing was wrong, asking about the trip — probably trying to soften the blow — then he registered my expression and put a hand on my shoulder.

He said, "She's with God now."

I brushed past him and walked into the room. My mother's body was lying on the bed, already neatly arranged: arms straightened, eyes closed. Tears ran down my cheeks, angering me. Where had my love been when it might have prevented this? When Beatrice might have heeded it?

Daniel followed me into the room, alone. I glanced back through the doorway and saw Agnes holding Sophie.

"She's with God, Martin." He was beaming at me as if something wonderful had happened.

I said numbly, "She wasn't Drowned." I was almost certain that she hadn't been a believer at all. She'd remained in the Transitional church all her life — but that had long been the way to stay in touch with your friends when you worked on a boat nine days out of ten.

"I prayed with her, before she lost consciousness. She accepted Beatrice into her heart."

I stared at him. Nine years ago he'd been certain: you were Drowned, or you were damned. It was as simple as that. My own conviction had softened long ago; I couldn't believe that Beatrice really was so arbitrary and cruel. But I knew my mother would not only have refused the full-blown ritual; the whole philosophy would have been as nonsensical to her as the mechanics.

"Did she say that? Did she tell you that?"

Daniel shook his head. "But it was clear." Filled with the love of Beatrice, he couldn't stop smiling.

A wave of revulsion passed through me; I wanted to grind his face into the deck. *He didn't care what my mother had believed.* Whatever eased his *own* pain, whatever put his own doubts to rest, had to be the case. To accept that she was damned — or even just dead, gone, erased — was unbearable; everything else flowed from that. *There was no truth in anything he said, anything he believed. It was all just an expression of his own needs.*

I walked back into the corridor and crouched beside my father. Without looking at me, he put an arm around me and pressed me against his side. I could feel the blackness washing over him, the helplessness, the loss. When I tried to embrace him he just clutched me more tightly, forcing me to be still. I shuddered a few times, then stopped weeping. I closed my eyes and let him hold me.

I was determined to stay there beside him, facing everything he was facing. But after a while, unbidden, the old flame began to glow in the back of my skull: the old warmth, the old peace, the old certainty. Daniel was right, my mother was with God. *How could I have doubted that?* There was no point asking how it had come about; Beatrice's ways were beyond my comprehension. But the one thing I knew firsthand was the strength of Her love.

I didn't move, I didn't free myself from my father's desolate embrace. But I was an impostor now, merely praying for his comfort, interceding from my state of grace. Beatrice had raised me out of the darkness, and I could no longer share his pain.

FIVE

After my mother's death, my faith kept ceding ground, without ever really wavering. Most of the doctrinal content fell away, leaving behind a core of belief that was a great deal easier to defend. It didn't matter if the Scriptures were superstitious nonsense or the Church was full of fools and hypocrites; Beatrice was still Beatrice, the way the sky was still blue. Whenever I heard debates between atheists and believers, I found myself increasingly on the atheists' side — not because I accepted their conclusion for a moment, but because they were so much more honest than their opponents. Maybe the priests and theologians arguing against them had the same kind of direct, personal experience of God as I did — or maybe not, maybe they just desperately needed to believe. But they never disclosed the true source of their conviction; instead, they just made laughable attempts to "prove" God's existence from the historical record, or from biology, astronomy, or mathematics. Daniel had been right at the age of fifteen — you couldn't prove any such thing — and listening to these people twist logic as they tried made me squirm.

I felt guilty about leaving my father working with a hired hand, and even guiltier when he moved onto Daniel's boat a year later, but I knew how angry it would have made him if he thought I'd abandoned my career for his sake. At times, that was the only thing that kept me in Mitar: even when I honestly wanted nothing more than to throw it all in and go back to hauling nets, I was afraid that my decision would be misinterpreted.

It took me three years to complete my thesis on the migration of aquatic zooytes in the wake of the ecopoiesis. My original hypothesis, that freshwater species had replenished the upper ocean, turned out to be false. Zooytes had no genes as such, just families of enzymes that resynthesized each other after cell division, but comparisons of these heritable molecules showed that, rather than rain bringing new life from above, an ocean-dwelling species from a much greater depth had moved steadily closer to the surface, as the Angels' creations drained oxygen from the water. That wouldn't have been much of a surprise, if the same techniques hadn't also shown that several species found in river water were even closer relatives of the surface dwellers. But those freshwater species weren't anyone's ancestors; they were the newest migrants. Zooytes that had spent a billion years confined to the depths had suddenly been able to survive (and reproduce, and mutate) closer to the surface than ever before, and when they'd stumbled on a mutation that let them thrive in the presence of oxygen, they'd finally been in a position to make use of it. The ecopoiesis might have driven other native organisms into extinction, but the invasion from Earth had enabled this ancient benthic species to mount a long overdue invasion of its own. Unwittingly or not, the Angels had set in motion the sequence of events that had released it from the ocean to colonize the planet.

So I proved myself wrong, earned my degree, and became famous amongst a circle of peers so small that we were all famous to each other anyway. Vast new territories did not open up before me. Anything to do with native biology was rapidly becoming an academic cul-de-sac; I'd always suspected that was how it would be, but I hadn't fought hard enough to end up anywhere else.

For the next three years, I clung to the path of least resistance: assisting Barat with his own research, taking the teaching jobs no one else wanted. Most of Barat's other students moved on to better things, and I found myself increasingly alone in Mitar. But that didn't matter; I had Beatrice.

At the age of twenty-five, I could see my future clearly. While other people deciphered — and built upon — the Angels' legacy, I'd watch from a distance, still messing about with samples of seawater from which all Angelic contaminants had been scrupulously removed.

Finally, when it was almost too late, I made up my mind to jump ship. Barat had been good to me, but he'd never expected loyalty verging on martyrdom. At the end of the year, a bi-ecological (native and Angelic) microbiology conference was being held in Tia, possibly the last event of its kind. I had no new results to present, but it wouldn't be hard to find a plausible excuse to attend, and it would be the ideal place to lobby for a new position. My great zooyte discovery hadn't been entirely lost on the wider community of biologists; I could try to rekindle the memory of it. I doubted there'd be much point offering to sleep with anyone; ethical qualms aside, my bridge had probably rusted into place.

Then again, maybe I'd get lucky. Maybe I'd stumble on a fellow Drowned Freelander who'd ended up in a position of power, and all I'd have to do was promise that my work would be for the greater glory of Beatrice.

Tia was a city of ten million people on the east coast. New towers stood side-by-side with empty structures from the time of the Angels, giant gutted machines that might have played a role in the ecopoiesis. I was too old and proud to gawk like a child, but for all my provincial sophistication I wanted to. These domes and cylinders were twenty times older than the illustrations tattooed into the ceiling of the monastery back home. They bore no images of Beatrice; nothing of the Angels did. But why would they? They predated Her death.

The university, on the outskirts of Tia, was a third the size of Mitar itself. An underground train ringed the campus; the students I rode with eyed my unstylish clothes with disbelief. I left my luggage in the dormitory and headed straight for the conference center. Barat had chosen to stay behind; maybe he hadn't wanted to witness the public burial of his field. That made things easier for me; I'd be free to hunt for a new career without rubbing his face in it.

Late additions to the conference program were listed on a screen by the main entrance. I almost walked straight past the display; I'd already decided which talks I'd be attending. But three steps away, a title I'd glimpsed in passing assembled itself in my mind's eye, and I had to backtrack to be sure I hadn't imagined it.

Carla Reggia: "Euphoric Effects of Z/12/80 Excretions"

I stood there laughing with disbelief. I recognized the speaker and her co-workers by name, though I'd never had a chance to meet them. If this wasn't a hoax . . . what had they done? Dried it, smoked it, and tried writing that up as research? Z/12/80 was one of "my" zooytes, one of the escapees from the ocean; the air and water of Tia were swarming with it. If its excretions were euphoric, the whole city would be in a state of bliss.

I knew, then and there, what they'd discovered. I knew it, long before I admitted it to myself. I went to the talk with my head full of jokes about neglected culture flasks full of psychotropic breakdown products, but for two whole days, I'd been steeling myself for the truth, finding ways in which it didn't have to matter.

Z/12/80, Carla explained, excreted among its waste products an amine that was able to bind to receptors in our Angel-crafted brains. Since it had been shown by other workers (no one recognized me; no one gave me so much as a glance) that Z/12/80 hadn't existed at the time of the ecopoiesis, this interaction was almost certainly undesigned, and unanticipated. "It's up to the archaeologists and neurochemists to determine what role, if any, the arrival of this substance in the environment might have played in the collapse of early settlement culture. But for the past fifteen to eighteen thousand years, we've been swimming in it. Since we still exhibit such a wide spectrum of moods, we're probably able to compensate for its presence by down-regulating the secretion of the endogenous molecule that was designed to bind to the same receptor. That's just an educated guess, though. Exactly what the effects might be from individual to individual, across the range of doses that might be experienced under a variety of conditions, is clearly going to be a matter of great interest to investigators with appropriate expertise."

I told myself that I felt no disquiet. Beatrice acted on the world through the laws of nature; I'd stopped believing in supernatural miracles long ago. The fact that someone had now identified the way in which She'd acted on *me*, that night in the water, changed nothing.

I pressed ahead with my attempts to get recruited. Everyone at the conference was talking about Carla's discovery, and when people finally made the connection with my own work, their eyes stopped glazing over halfway through my spiel. In the next three days, I received seven offers—all involving research into *zooyte biochemistry*. There was no question, now, of side-stepping the issue, of escaping into the wider world of Angelic biology. One man even came right out and said to me: "You're a Freelander, and you know that the ancestors of Z/12/80 live in much greater numbers in the ocean. Don't you think *oceanic* exposure is going to be the key to understanding this?" He laughed. "I mean, you swam in the stuff as a child, didn't you? And you seem to have come through unscathed."

"Apparently."

On my last night in Tia, I couldn't sleep. I stared into the blackness of the room, watching the gray sparks dance in front of me. (Contaminants in the aqueous humor? Electrical noise in the retina? I'd heard the explanation once, but I could no longer remember it.)

I prayed to Beatrice in the Angels' tongue; I could still feel Her presence, as strongly as ever. The effect clearly wasn't just a matter of dosage, or trans-cutaneous absorption; merely swimming in the ocean at the right depth wasn't enough to make anyone feel Drowned. But in combination with the stress of oxygen starvation, and all the psychological build-up Daniel had provided, the jolt of zooyte piss must have driven certain neuroendocrine subsystems into new territory—or old territory, by a new path. *Peace, joy, contentment, the feeling of being loved* weren't exactly unknown emotions. But by short-circuiting the brain's usual practice of summoning those feelings only on occasions when there was a *reason* for them, I'd been "blessed with the love of Beatrice." I'd found happiness on demand.

And I still possessed it. That was the eeriest part. Even as I lay there in the dark, on the verge of reasoning everything I'd been living for out of existence, my ability to work the machinery was so ingrained that I felt as loved, as blessed as ever.

Maybe Beatrice was offering me another chance, making it clear that She'd still forgive this blasphemy and welcome me back. But why did I believe that there was anyone there to "forgive me"? You couldn't reason your way to God; there was only faith. And I knew, now, that the source of my faith was a meaningless accident, an unanticipated side-effect of the ecopoiesis.

I still had a choice. I could, still, decide that the love of Beatrice was immune to all logic, a force beyond understanding, untouched by evidence of any kind.

No, I couldn't. I'd been making exceptions for Her for too long. Everyone lived with double standards—but I'd already pushed mine as far as they'd go.

I started laughing and weeping at the same time. It was almost unimaginable: all the millions of people who'd been misled the same way. All because of the zooytes, and . . . what? One Freelander, diving for pleasure, who'd stumbled on a strange new experience? Then tens of thousands more repeating it, generation after generation—until one vulnerable man or woman had been driven to invest the novelty with meaning. Someone who'd needed so badly to feel loved and protected that the illusion of a real presence behind the raw emotion had been impossible to resist. Or who'd desperately wanted to believe that—in spite of the Angels' discovery that they, too, were mortal—death could still be defeated.

I was lucky: I'd been born in an era of moderation. I hadn't killed in the name of Beatrice. I hadn't suffered for my faith. I had no doubt that I'd been far happier for the last fifteen years than I would have been if I'd told Daniel to throw his rope and weights overboard without me.

But that didn't change the fact that the heart of it all had been a lie.

I woke at dawn, my head pounding, after just a few kilotau's sleep. I closed my eyes and searched for Her presence, as I had a thousand times before. *When I woke in the morning and looked into my heart, She was there without fail, offering me strength and guidance. When I lay in bed at night, I feared nothing, because I knew She was watching over me.*

There was nothing. She was gone.

I stumbled out of bed, feeling like a murderer, wondering how I'd ever live with what I'd done.

SIX

I turned down every offer I'd received at the conference, and stayed on in Mitar. It took Barat and me two years to establish our own research group to examine the effects of the zooamine, and nine more for us to elucidate the full extent of its activity in the brain. Our new recruits all had solid backgrounds in neuro-chemistry, and they did better work than I did, but when Barat retired I found myself the spokesperson for the group.

The initial discovery had been largely ignored outside the scientific community; for most people, it hardly mattered whether our brain chemistry matched the Angels' original design, or had been altered fifteen thousand years ago by some unexpected contaminant. But when the Mitar zooamine group began publishing detailed accounts of the biochemistry of religious experience, the public at large rediscovered the subject with a vengeance.

The university stepped up security, and despite death threats and a number of unpleasant incidents with stone-throwing protesters, no one was hurt. We were flooded with requests from broadcasters—though most were predicated on the notion that the group was morally obliged to "face its critics," rather than the broadcasters being morally obliged to offer us a chance to explain our work, calmly and clearly, without being shouted down by enraged zealots.

I learned to avoid the zealots, but the obscurantists were harder to dodge. I'd expected opposition from the Churches—defending the faith was their job, after all—but some of the most intellectually bankrupt responses came from academics in other disciplines. In one televised debate, I was confronted by a Deep Church priest, a Transitional theologian, a devotee of the ocean god Marni, and an an-thropologist from Tia.

"This discovery has no real bearing on any belief system," the anthropologist explained serenely. "All truth is local. Inside every Deep Church in Ferez, Beatrice *is* the daughter of God, and we're the mortal incarnations of the Angels, who traveled here from Earth. In a coastal village a few milliradians south, Marni is the supreme creator, and it was She who gave birth to us, right here. Going one step further and moving from the spiritual domain to the scientific might appear to 'negate' certain spiritual truths . . . but equally, moving from the scientific do-main to the spiritual demonstrates the same limitations. We are nothing but the stories we tell ourselves, and no one story is greater than another." He smiled beneficently, the expression of a parent only too happy to give all his squabbling children an equal share in some disputed toy.

I said, "How many cultures do you imagine share your definition of 'truth'? How many people do you think would be content to worship a God who consisted of literally nothing but the fact of their belief?" I turned to the Deep Church priest. "Is that enough for you?"

"Absolutely not!" She glowered at the anthropologist. "While I have the greatest respect for my brother here," she gestured at the devotee of Marni, "you can't draw a line around those people who've been lucky enough to be raised in the true faith, and then suggest that *Beatrice's* infinite power and love is confined to that group of people . . . like some collection of folk songs!"

The devotee respectfully agreed. Marni had created the most distant stars, along with the oceans of Covenant. Perhaps some people called Her by another name, but if everyone on this planet was to die tomorrow, She would still be Marni: unchanged, undiminished.

The anthropologist responded soothingly, "Of course. But in context, and with a wider perspective—"

"I'm perfectly happy with a God who resides within us," offered the Transitional theologian. "It seems . . . *immodest* to expect more. And instead of fretting uselessly over these ultimate questions, we should confine ourselves to matters of a suitably human scale."

I turned to him. "So you're actually indifferent as to whether an infinitely powerful and loving being created everything around you, and plans to welcome you into Her arms after death . . . or if the universe is a piece of quantum noise that will eventually vanish and erase us all?"

He sighed heavily, as if I was asking him to perform some arduous physical feat just by responding. "I can summon no enthusiasm for these issues."

Later, the Deep Church priest took me aside and whispered, "Frankly, we're all very grateful that you've debunked that awful cult of the Drowned. They're a bunch of fundamentalist hicks, and the Church will be better off without them. But you mustn't make the mistake of thinking that your work has anything to do with ordinary, civilized believers!"

I stood at the back of the crowd that had gathered on the beach near the rock pool, to listen to the two old men who were standing ankle-deep in the milky water. It had taken me four days to get here from Mitar, but when I'd heard reports of a zooyte bloom washing up on the remote north coast, I'd had to come and see the results for myself. The zooamine group had actually recruited an anthropologist for such occasions—one who could cope with such taxing notions as the existence of objective reality, and a biochemical substrate for human thought—but Céline was only with us for part of the year, and right now she was away doing other research.

"This is an ancient, sacred place!" one man intoned, spreading his arms to take in the pool. "You need only observe the shape of it to understand that. It concentrates the energy of the stars, and the sun, and the ocean."

"The focus of power is there, by the inlet," the other added, gesturing at a point where the water might have come up to his calves. "Once, I wandered too close. I was almost lost in the great dream of the ocean, when my friend here came and rescued me!"

These men weren't devotees of Marni, or members of any other formal religion. As far as I'd been able to tell from old news reports, the blooms occurred every eight or ten years, and the two had set themselves up as "custodians" of the pool more than fifty years ago. Some local villagers treated the whole thing as a joke, but others revered the old men. And for a small fee, tourists and locals alike could be chanted over, then splashed with the potent brew. Evaporation would have concentrated the trapped waters of the bloom; for a few days, before the zooytes ran out of nutrients and died *en masse* in a cloud of hydrogen sulphide, the amine would be present in levels as high as in any of our laboratory cultures back in Mitar.

As I watched people lining up for the ritual, I found myself trying to downplay the possibility that anyone could be seriously affected by it. It was broad daylight, no one feared for their life, and the old men's pantheistic gobbledy-gook carried all the gravitas of the patter of streetside scam merchants. Their marginal sincerity, and the money changing hands, would be enough to undermine the whole thing. This was a tourist trap, not a life-altering experience.

When the chanting was done, the first customer knelt at the edge of the pool. One of the custodians filled a small metal cup with water and threw it in her face. After a moment, she began weeping with joy. I moved closer, my stomach tightening. *It was what she'd known was expected of her, nothing more. She was playing along, not wanting to spoil the fun—like the good sports who pretended to have their thoughts read by a carnival psychic.*

Next, the custodians chanted over a young man. He began swaying giddily even before they touched him with the water; when they did, he broke into sobs of relief that racked his whole body.

I looked back along the queue. There was a young girl standing third in line now, looking around apprehensively; she could not have been more than nine or ten. Her father (I presumed) was standing behind her, with his hand against her back, as if gently propelling her forward.

I lost all interest in playing anthropologist. I forced my way through the crowd until I reached the edge of the pool, then turned to address the people in the queue. "These men are frauds! There's nothing mysterious going on here. I can tell you exactly what's in the water: it's just a drug, a natural substance given out by creatures that are trapped here when the waves retreat."

I squatted down and prepared to dip my hand in the pool. One of the custodians rushed forward and grabbed my wrist. He was an old man, I could have done what I liked, but some people were already jeering, and I didn't want to scuffle with him and start a riot. I backed away from him, then spoke again.

"I've studied this drug for more than ten years, at Mitar University. It's present in water all over the planet. We drink it, we bathe in it, we swim in it every day. But it's concentrated here, and if you don't understand what you're doing when you use it, that misunderstanding can harm you!"

The custodian who'd grabbed my wrist started laughing. "The dream of the ocean is powerful, yes, but we don't need your advice on that! For fifty years, my friend and I have studied its lore, until we were strong enough to *stand* in the sacred water!" He gestured at his leathery feet; I didn't doubt that his circulation had grown poor enough to limit the dose to a tolerable level.

He stretched out his sinewy arm at me. "So fuck off back to Mitar, Inlander! Fuck off back to your books and your dead machinery! What would you know about the sacred mysteries? *What would you know about the ocean?*"

I said, "I think you're out of your depth."

I stepped into the pool. He started wailing about my unpurified body polluting the water, but I brushed past him. The other custodian came after me, but though my feet were soft after years of wearing shoes, I ignored the sharp edges of the rocks and kept walking toward the inlet. The zooamine helped. I could feel the old joy, the old peace, the old "love"; it made a powerful anesthetic.

I looked back over my shoulder. The second man had stopped pursuing me; it seemed he honestly feared going any further. I pulled off my shirt, bunched it up, and threw it onto a rock at the side of the pool. Then I waded forward, heading straight for the "focus of power."

The water came up to my knees. I could feel my heart pounding, harder than it had since childhood. People were shouting at me from the edge of the pool—some outraged by my sacrilege, some apparently concerned for my safety in the presence of forces beyond my control. Without turning, I called out at the top of my voice, "There is no 'power' here! There's nothing 'sacred'! There's nothing here but a drug—"

Old habits die hard; I almost prayed first. *Please, Holy Beatrice, don't let me regain my faith.*

I lay down in the water and let it cover my face. My vision turned white; I felt like I was leaving my body. The love of Beatrice flooded into me, and nothing had changed: Her presence was as palpable as ever, as undeniable as ever. I *knew* that I was loved, accepted, forgiven.

I waited, staring into the light, almost expecting a voice, a vision, detailed hallucinations. That had happened to some of the Drowned. How did anyone ever claw their way back to sanity, after that?

But for me, there was only the emotion itself, overpowering but unembellished. It didn't grow monotonous; I could have basked in it for days. But I understood, now, that it said no more about my place in the world than the warmth of sunlight on skin. I'd never mistake it for the touch of a real hand again.

I climbed to my feet and opened my eyes. Violet afterimages danced in front of me. It took a few tau for me to catch my breath, and feel steady on my feet again. Then I turned and started wading back toward the shore.

The crowd had fallen silent, though whether it was in disgust or begrudging respect I had no idea.

I said, "It's not just here. It's not just in the water. It's part of us now; it's in our blood." I was still half-blind; I couldn't see whether anyone was listening. "But as long as you know that, you're already free. As long as you're ready to face the possibility that everything that makes your spirits soar, everything that lifts you up and fills your heart with joy, *everything that makes your life worth living* . . . is a lie, is corruption, is meaningless—then you can never be enslaved!"

They let me walk away unharmed. I turned back to watch as the line formed again; the girl wasn't in the queue.

I woke with a start, from the same old dream.

I was lowering my mother into the water from the back of the boat. Her hands were tied, her feet weighted. She was afraid, but she'd put her trust in me. "You'll bring me up safely, won't you, Martin?"

I nodded reassuringly. But once she'd vanished beneath the waves, I thought: What am I doing? I don't believe in this shit any more.

So I took out a knife and started cutting through the rope—

I brought my knees up to my chest, and crouched on the unfamiliar bed in the darkness. I was in a small town on the railway line, halfway back to Mitar. Halfway between midnight and dawn.

I dressed, and made my way out of the hostel. The center of town was deserted, and the sky was thick with stars. Just like home. In Mitar, everything vanished in a fog of light.

All three of the stars cited by various authorities as the Earth's sun were above the horizon. If they weren't all mistakes, perhaps I'd live to see a telescope's image of the planet itself. But the prospect of seeking contact with the Angels—if there really was a faction still out there, somewhere—left me cold. I shouted silently up at the stars: *Your degenerate offspring don't need your help! Why should we rejoin you? We're going to surpass you!*

I sat down on the steps at the edge of the square and covered my face. Bravado didn't help. Nothing helped. Maybe if I'd grown up facing the truth, I would have been stronger. But when I woke in the night, knowing that my mother was simply dead, that everyone I'd ever loved would follow her, that I'd vanish into the same emptiness myself, it was like being buried alive. It was like being back in the water, bound and weighted, with the certain knowledge that there was no one to haul me up.

Someone put a hand on my shoulder. I looked up, startled. It was a man about my own age. His manner wasn't threatening; if anything, he looked slightly wary of me.

He said, "Do you need a roof? I can let you into the Church if you want." There was a trolley packed with cleaning equipment a short distance behind him.

I shook my head. "It's not that cold." I was too embarrassed to explain that I had a perfectly good room nearby. "Thanks."

As he was walking away, I called after him, "Do you believe in God?"

He stopped and stared at me for a while, as if he was trying to decide if this was a trick question—as if I might have been hired by the local parishioners to vet him for theological soundness. Or maybe he just wanted to be diplomatic with anyone desperate enough to be sitting in the town square in the middle of the night, begging a stranger for reassurance.

He shook his head. "As a child I did. Not anymore. It was a nice idea . . . but it made no sense." He eyed me skeptically, still unsure of my motives.

I said, "Then isn't life unbearable?"

He laughed. "Not all the time!"

He went back to his trolley, and started wheeling it toward the Church.

I stayed on the steps, waiting for dawn.

Approaching perimelasma

GEOFFREY A. LANDIS

A physicist who works for NASA and who has recently been working on the Martian Lander program, Geoffrey A. Landis is a frequent contributor to Analog *and to* Asimov's Science Fiction, *and has also sold stories to markets such as* Interzone, Amazing, *and* Pulphouse. *Landis is not a prolific writer by the high-production standards of the genre, but he is popular. His story "A Walk in the Sun" won him a Nebula and a Hugo Award in 1992, his story "Ripples in the Dirac Sea" won him a Nebula Award in 1990, and his story "Elemental" was on the final Hugo ballot a few years back. His first book was the collection,* Myths, Legends, and True History, *and he has just sold his first novel,* Mars Crossing. *His stories have appeared in our Ninth and Fifteenth Annual Collections. He has a Web site at http://www.sff.net/people/Geoffrey.Landis. He lives in Brook Park, Ohio.*

Here he takes us along on a suspenseful and hair-raising cosmic ride in company with an intrepid future adventurer bound for someplace nobody has ever gone before: a headlong plunge into a black hole, and out of it again—if he can figure a way to get out of it, that is, with all the forces of the universe against him. . . .

There is a sudden frisson of adrenaline, a surge of something approaching terror (if I could still feel terror), and I realize that this is it, this time I am the one who is doing it.

I'm the one who is going to drop into a black hole.

Oh, my god. This time I'm not you.

This is real.

Of course, I have experienced this exact feeling before. We both know exactly what it feels like.

My body seems weird, too big and at once too small. The feel of my muscles, my vision, my kinesthetic sense, everything is wrong. Everything is strange. My vision is fuzzy, and colors are oddly distorted. When I move, my body moves unexpectedly fast. But there seems to be nothing wrong with it. Already I am getting used to it. "It will do," I say.

There is too much to know, too much to be all at once. I slowly coalesce the fragments of your personality. None of them are you. All of them are you.

A pilot, of course, you must have, you must be, a pilot. I integrate your pilot persona, and he is me. I will fly to the heart of a darkness far darker than any mere unexplored continent. A scientist, somebody to understand your experience, yes. I synthesize a persona. You are him, too, and I understand.

And someone to simply *experience* it, to tell the tale (if any of me will survive to tell the tale) of how you dropped into a black hole, and how you survived. If you survive. *Me.* I will call myself Wolf, naming myself after a nearby star, for no reason whatsoever, except maybe to claim, if only to myself, that I am not you.

All of we are me are you. But, in a real sense, you're not here at all. None of me are you. You are far away. Safe.

Some black holes, my scientist persona whispers, are decorated with an accretion disk, shining like a gaudy signal in the sky. Dust and gas from the interstellar medium fall toward the hungry singularity, accelerating to nearly the speed of light in their descent, swirling madly as they fall. It collides; compresses; ionizes. Friction heats the plasma millions of degrees, to emit a brilliant glow of hard X-rays. Such black holes are anything but black; the incandescence of the infalling gas may be the most brilliantly glowing thing in a galaxy. Nobody and nothing would be able to get near it; nothing would be able to survive the radiation.

The Virgo hole is not one of these. It is ancient, dating from the very first burst of star-formation when the universe was new, and has long ago swallowed or ejected all the interstellar gas in its region, carving an emptiness far into the interstellar medium around it.

The black hole is fifty-seven light years from Earth. Ten billion years ago, it had been a supermassive star, and exploded in a supernova that for a brief moment had shone brighter than the galaxy, in the process tossing away half its mass. Now there is nothing left of the star. The burned-out remnant, some thirty times the mass of the sun, has pulled space itself around it, leaving nothing behind but gravity.

Before the download, the psychologist investigated my—your—mental soundness. We must have passed the test, obviously, since I'm here. What type of man would allow himself to fall into a black hole? That is my question. Maybe if I can answer that, I would understand ourself.

But this did not seem to interest the psychologist. She did not, in fact, even look directly at me. Her face had the focusless abstract gaze characteristic of somebody hotlinked by the optic nerve to a computer system. Her talk was perfunctory. To be fair, the object of her study was not the flesh me, but my computed reflection, the digital maps of my soul. I remember the last thing she said.

"We are fascinated with black holes because of their depth of metaphor," she said, looking nowhere. "A black hole is, literally, the place of no return. We see it as a metaphor for how we, ourselves, are hurled blindly into a place from which no information ever reaches us, the place from which no one ever returns. We live our lives falling into the future, and we will all inevitably meet the singularity." She paused, expecting, no doubt, some comment. But I remained silent.

"Just remember this," she said, and for the first time her eyes returned to the outside world and focused on me. "This is a real black hole, not a metaphor. Don't treat it like a metaphor. Expect reality." She paused, and finally added, "Trust the math. It's all we really know, and all that we have to trust."

Little help.

Wolf versus the black hole! One might think that such a contest is an unequal one, that the black hole has an overwhelming advantage.

Not quite so unequal.

On my side, I have technology. To start with, the wormhole, the technological sleight-of-space which got you fifty-seven light years from Earth in the first place.

The wormhole is a monster of relativity no less than the black hole, a trick of curved space allowed by the theory of general relativity. After the Virgo black hole was discovered, a wormhole mouth was laboriously dragged to it, slower than light, a project that took over a century. Once the wormhole was here, though, the trip became only a short one, barely a meter of travel. Anybody could come here and drop into it.

A wormhole—a far too cute name, but one we seem to be stuck with—is a shortcut from one place to another. Physically, it is nothing more than a loop of exotic matter. If you move through the hoop on this side of the wormhole, you emerge out the hoop on that side. Topologically, the two sides of the wormhole are pasted together, a piece cut out of space glued together elsewhere.

Exhibiting an excessive sense of caution, the proctors of Earthspace refused to allow the other end of the Virgo wormhole to exit at the usual transportation nexus, the wormhole swarm at Neptune-Trojan 4. The far end of the wormhole opens instead to an orbit around Wolf-562, an undistinguished red dwarf sun circled by two airless planets that are little more than frozen rocks, twenty-one light-years from Earthspace. To get here we had to take a double wormhole hop: Wolf, Virgo.

The black hole is a hundred kilometers across. The wormhole is only a few meters across. I would think that they were overly cautious.

The first lesson of relativity is that time and space are one. For a long time after the theoretical prediction that such a thing as a traversable wormhole ought to be possible, it was believed that a wormhole could also be made to traverse time as well. It was only much later, when wormhole travel was tested, that it was found that the Cauchy instability makes it impossible to form a wormhole that leads backward in time. The theory was correct—space and time are indeed just aspects of the same reality, spacetime—but any attempt to move a wormhole in such a way that it becomes a timehole produces a vacuum polarization to cancel out the time effect.

After we—the spaceship I am to pilot, and myself/yourself—come through the wormhole, the wormhole engineers go to work. I have never seen this process close up, so I stay nearby to watch. This is going to be interesting.

A wormhole looks like nothing more than a circular loop of string. It is, in fact, a loop of exotic material, negative-mass cosmic string. The engineers, working telerobotically via vacuum manipulator pods, spray charge onto the string. They charge it until it literally glows with Paschen discharge, like a neon light in the dirty vacuum, and then use the electric charge to manipulate the shape. With the application of invisible electromagnetic fields, the string starts to twist. This is a slow process. Only a few meters across, the wormhole loop has a mass roughly equal to that of Jupiter. Negative to that of Jupiter, to be precise, my scientist persona reminds me, but either way, it is a slow thing to move.

Ponderously, then, it twists further and further, until at last it becomes a lemniscate, a figure of eight. The instant the string touches itself, it shimmers for a moment, and then suddenly there are two glowing circles before us, twisting and oscillating in shape like jellyfish.

The engineers spray more charge onto the two wormholes, and the two wormholes, arcing lightning into space, slowly repel each other. The vibrations of the cosmic string are spraying out gravitational radiation like a dog shaking off water—even where I am, floating ten kilometers distant, I can feel it, like the swaying of invisible tides—and as they radiate energy, the loops enlarge. The radiation represents a serious danger. If the engineers lose control of the string for even a brief instant, it might enter the instability known as "squiggle mode," and catastrophically enlarge. The engineers damp out the radiation before it gets critical, though—they are, after all, well practiced at this—and the loops stabilize into two perfect circles. On the other side, at Wolf, precisely the same scene has played out, and two loops of exotic string now circle Wolf-562 as well. The wormhole has been cloned.

All wormholes are daughters of the original wormhole, found floating in the depths of interstellar space eleven hundred years ago, a natural loop of negative cosmic string as ancient as the Big Bang, invisible to the eyes save for the distortion of spacetime. That first one led from nowhere interesting to nowhere exciting, but from that one we bred hundreds, and now we casually move wormhole mouths from star to star, breeding new wormholes as it suits us, to form an ever-expanding network of connections.

I should not have been so close. Angry red lights have been flashing in my peripheral vision, warning blinkers that I have been ignoring. The energy radiated in the form of gravitational waves had been prodigious, and would have, to a lesser person, been dangerous. But in my new body, I am nearly invulnerable, and if I can't stand a mere wormhole cloning, there is no way I will be able to stand a black hole. So I ignore the warnings, wave briefly to the engineers—though I doubt that they can even see me, floating kilometers away—and use my reaction jets to scoot over to my ship.

The ship I will pilot is docked to the research station, where the scientists have their instruments and the biological humans have their living quarters. The wormhole station is huge compared to my ship, which is a tiny ovoid occupying a berth almost invisible against the hull. There is no hurry for me to get to it.

I'm surprised that any of the technicians can even see me, tiny as I am in the void, but a few of them apparently do, because in my radio I hear casual greetings called out: how's it, *ohayo gozaimasu*, hey glad you made it, how's the bod? It's hard to tell from the radio voices which ones are people I know, and which are only casual acquaintances. I answer back: how's it, *ohayo*, yo, surpassing spec. None of them seem inclined to chat, but then, they're busy with their own work.

They are dropping things into the black hole.

Throwing things in, more to say. The wormhole station orbits a tenth of an astronomical unit from the Virgo black hole, closer to the black hole than Mercury is to the sun. This is an orbit with a period of a little over two days, but, even so close to the black hole, there is nothing to see. A rock, released to fall straight downward, takes almost a day to reach the horizon.

One of the scientists supervising, a biological human named Sue, takes the time to talk with me a bit, explaining what they are measuring. What interests me most is that they are measuring whether the fall deviates from a straight line. This will let them know whether the black hole is rotating. Even a slight rotation would mess up the intricate dance of the trajectory required for my ship. However, the best current theories predict that an old black hole will have shed its angular momentum long ago, and, as far as the technicians can determine, their results show that the conjecture holds.

The black hole, or the absence in space where it is located, is utterly invisible from here. I follow the pointing finger of the scientist, but there is nothing to see. Even if I had a telescope, it is unlikely that I would be able to pick out the tiny region of utter blackness against the irregular darkness of an unfamiliar sky.

My ship is not so different from the drop probes. The main difference is that I will be on it.

Before boarding the station, I jet over in close to inspect my ship, a miniature egg of perfectly reflective material. The hull is made of a single crystal of a synthetic material so strong that no earthly force could even dent it.

A black hole, though, is no earthly force.

Wolf versus the black hole! The second technological trick I have in my duel against the black hole is my body.

I am no longer a fragile, fluid-filled biological human. The tidal forces at the horizon of a black hole would rip a true human apart in mere instants; the accelerations required to hover would squash one into liquid. To make this journey, I have downloaded your fragile biological mind into a body of more robust material. As important as the strength of my new body is the fact that it is tiny. The force produced by the curvature of gravity is proportional to the size of the object. My new body, a millimeter tall, is millions of times more resistant to being stretched to spaghetti.

The new body has another advantage as well. With my mind operating as software on a computer the size of a pinpoint, my thinking and my reflexes are thousands of times faster than biological. In fact, I have already chosen to slow my thinking down, so that I can still interact with the biologicals. At full speed, my microsecondreactions are lightning compared to the molasses of neuron speeds in biological humans. I see far in the ultraviolet now, a necessary compensation for the fact that my vision would consist of nothing but a blur if I tried to see by visible light.

You could have made my body any shape, of course, a tiny cube or even a featureless sphere. But you followed the dictates of social convention. A right human should be recognizably a human, even if I am to be smaller than an ant, and so my body mimics a human body, although no part of it is organic, and my brain faithfully executes your own human brain software. From what I see and feel, externally and internally, I am completely, perfectly human.

As is right and proper. What is the value of experience to a machine?

Later, after I return — *if* I return — I can upload back. I can become you.

But return is, as they say, still somewhat problematical.

You, my original, what do you feel? Why did I think I would do it? I imagine you laughing hysterically about the trick you've played, sending me to drop into the black hole while you sit back in perfect comfort, in no danger. Imagining your laughter comforts me, for all that I know that it is false. I've been in the other place before, and never laughed.

I remember the first time I fell into a star.

We were hotlinked together, that time, united in online-realtime, our separate brains reacting as one brain. I remember what I thought, the incredible electric feel: ohmigod, am I really going to do this? Is it too late to back out?

The idea had been nothing more than a whim, a crazy idea, at first. We had been dropping probes into a star, Groombridge 1830B, studying the dynamics of a flare star. We were done, just about, and the last-day-of-project party was just getting in swing. We were all fuzzed with neurotransmitter randomizers, creativity spinning wild and critical thinking nearly zeroed. Somebody, I think it was Jenna, said, we could ride one *down*, you know. Wait for a flare, and then plunge through the middle of it. Helluva ride!

Helluva *splash* at the end, too, somebody said, and laughed.

Sure, somebody said. It might have been me. What do you figure? Download yourself to temp storage and then uplink frames from yourself as you drop?

That works, Jenna said. Better: we copy our bodies first, then link the two brains. One body drops; the other copy hotlinks to it.

Somehow, I don't remember when, the word "we" had grown to include me.

"Sure," I said. "And the copy on top is in null-input suspension; experiences the whole thing realtime!"

In the morning, when we were focused again, I might have dismissed the idea as a whim of the fuzz, but for Jenna the decision was already immovable as a droplet of neutronium. *Sure* we're dropping, let's start now.

We made a few changes. It takes a long time to fall into a star, even a small one like Bee, so the copy was reengineered to a slower thought-rate, and the original body in null-input was frame-synched to the drop copy with impulse-echoers. Since the two brains were molecule by molecule identical, the uplink bandwidth required was minimal.

The probes were reworked to take a biological, which meant mostly that a cooling system had to be added to hold the interior temperature within the liquidus range of water. We did that by the simplest method possible: we surrounded the probes with a huge block of cometary ice. As it sublimated, the ionized gas would carry away heat. A secondary advantage of the ice was that our friends, watching from orbit, would have a blazing cometary trail to cheer on. When the ice was used up, of course, the body would slowly vaporize. None of us would actually survive to hit the star.

But that was no particular concern. If the experience turned out to be too undesirable, we could always edit the pain part of it out of the memory later.

It would have made more sense, perhaps, to have simply recorded the brain-uplink from the copy onto a local high-temp buffer, squirted it back, and linked to it as a memory upload. But Jenna would have none of that. She wanted to experience it in realtime, or at least in as close to realtime as speed-of-light delays allow.

Three of us—Jenna, Martha, and me—dropped. Something seems to be missing from my memory here; I can't remember the reason I decided to do it. It must have been something about a biological body, some a-rational consideration that seemed normal to my then-body, that I could never back down from a crazy whim of Jenna's.

And I had the same experience, the same feeling then, as I, you, did, always do, the feeling that my god *I* am the copy and I am going to die. But that time, of course, thinking every thought in synchrony, there was no way at all to tell the copy from the original, to split the me from you.

It is, in its way, a glorious feeling.

I dropped.

You felt it, you remember it. Boring at first, the long drop with nothing but freefall and the chatter of friends over the radio-link. Then the ice shell slowly flaking away, ionizing and beginning to glow, a diaphanous cocoon of pale violet, and below the red star getting larger and larger, the surface mottled and wrinkled, and then suddenly we fell into and through the flare, a huge luminous vault above us, dwarfing our bodies in the immensity of creation.

An unguessable distance beneath me, the curvature of the star vanished, and, still falling at three hundred kilometers per second, I was hanging motionless over an infinite plane stretching from horizon to horizon.

And then the last of the ice vaporized, and I was suddenly suspended in nothing, hanging nailed to the burning sky over endless crimson horizons of infinity, and pain came like the inevitability of mountains—I didn't edit it—pain like infinite oceans, like continents, like a vast, airless world.

Jenna, now I remember. The odd thing is, I never did really connect in any significant way with Jenna. She was already in a quadrad of her own, a quadrad she was fiercely loyal to, one that was solid and accepting to her chameleon character, neither needing nor wanting a fifth for completion.

Long after, maybe a century or two later, I found out that Jenna had disassembled herself. After her quadrad split apart, she'd downloaded her character to a mainframe, and then painstakingly cataloged everything that made her Jenna: all her various skills and insights, everything she had experienced, no matter how minor, each facet of her character, every memory and dream and longing: the myriad subroutines of personality. She indexed her soul, and she put the ten thousand pieces of it into the public domain for download. A thousand people, maybe a million people, maybe even more, have pieces of Jenna, her cleverness, her insight, her skill at playing antique instruments.

But nobody has her sense of self. After she copied her subroutines, she deleted herself.

And who am I?

Two of the technicians who fit me into my spaceship and who assist in the ten thousand elements of the preflight check are the same friends from that drop, long ago; one of them even still in the same biological body as he had then, although eight hundred years older, his vigor undiminished by biological reconstruction. My survival, if I am to survive, will be dependent on microsecond timing, and I'm embarrassed not to be able to remember his name.

He was, I recall, rather stodgy and conservative even back then.

We joke and trade small talk as the checkout proceeds. I'm still distracted by my self-questioning, the implications of my growing realization that I have no understanding of why I'm doing this.

Exploring a black hole would be no adventure if only we had faster-than-light travel, but of the thousand technological miracles of the third and fourth millennia, this one miracle was never realized. If I had the mythical FTL motor, I could simply drive out of the black hole. At the event horizon, space falls into the black hole at the speed of light; the mythical motor would make that no barrier.

But such a motor we do not have. One of the reasons I'm taking the plunge — not the only one, not the main one, but one — is in the hope that scientific measurements of the warped space inside the black hole will elucidate the nature of space and time, and so I myself will make one of the innumerable small steps to bring us closer to an FTL drive.

The spaceship I am to pilot has a drive nearly — but not quite — as good. It contains a microscopic twist of spacetime inside an impervious housing, a twist that will parity-reverse ordinary matter into mirror-matter. This total conversion engine gives my ship truly ferocious levels of thrust. The gentlest nudge of my steering rockets will give me thousands of gravities of acceleration. Unthinkable acceleration for a biological body, no matter how well cushioned. The engine will allow the rocket to dare the unthinkable, to hover at the very edge of the event horizon, to maneuver where space itself is accelerating at nearly light-speed. This vehicle, no larger than a peanut, contains the engines of an interstellar probe.

Even with such an engine, most of the ship is reaction mass.

The preflight checks are all green. I am ready to go. I power up my instruments, check everything out for myself, verify what has already been checked three times, and then check once again. My pilot persona is very thorough. Green.

"You still haven't named your ship," comes a voice to me. It is the technician, the one whose name I have forgotten. "What is your call sign?"

One way journey, I think. Maybe something from Dante? No, Sartre said it better: no exit. *"Huis Clos,"* I say, and drop free.

Let them look it up.

Alone.

The laws of orbital mechanics have not been suspended, and I do not drop into the black hole. Not yet. With the slightest touch of my steering engines — I do not dare use the main engine this close to the station — I drop into an elliptical orbit, one with a perimelasma closer to, but still well outside, the dangerous zone of the black hole. The black hole is still invisible, but inside my tiny kingdom I have enhanced senses of exquisite sensitivity, spreading across the entire spectrum from radio to gamma radiation. I look with my new eyes to see if I can detect an X-ray glow of interstellar hydrogen being ripped apart, but if there is any such, it is too faint to be visible with even my sensitive instruments. The interstellar medium is so thin here as to be essentially nonexistent. The black hole is invisible.

I smile. This makes it better, somehow. The black hole is pure, unsullied by any outside matter. It consists of gravity and nothing else, as close to a pure mathematical abstraction as anything in the universe can ever be.

It is not too late to back away. If I were to choose to accelerate at a million gravities, I would reach relativistic velocities in about thirty seconds. No wormholes would be needed for me to run away; I would barely even need to slow down my brain to cruise at nearly the speed of light to anywhere in the colonized galaxy.

But I know I won't. The psychologist knew it, too, damn her, or she would never have approved me for the mission. Why? What is it about me?

As I worry about this with part of my attention, while the pilot persona flies the ship, I flash onto a realization, and at this realization another memory hits. It is the psychologist, and in the memory I'm attracted to her sexually, so much so that you are distracted from what she is saying.

I feel no sexual attraction now, of course. I can barely remember what it is. That part of the memory is odd, alien.

"We can't copy the whole brain to the simulation, but we can copy enough that, to yourself, you will still feel like yourself," she said. She is talking to the air, not to you. "You won't notice any gaps."

I'm brain-damaged. This is the explanation.

You frowned. "How could I not notice that some of my memories are missing?"

"The brain makes adjustments. Remember, at any given time, you never even use 1 percent of 1 percent of your memories. What we'll be leaving out will be stuff that you will never have any reason to think about. The memory of the taste of strawberries, for example; the floor-plan of the house you lived in as a teenager. Your first kiss."

This bothered you somewhat — you want to remain yourself. I concentrate, hard. What do strawberries taste like? I can't remember. I'm not even certain what color they are. Round fruits, like apples, I think, only smaller. And the same color as apples, or something similar, I'm sure, except I don't remember what color that is.

You decided that you can live with the editing, as long as it doesn't change the essential you. You smiled. "Leave in the first kiss."

So I can never possibly solve the riddle: what kind of a man is it that would deliberately allow himself to drop into a black hole. I cannot, because I don't have the memories of you. In a real sense, I am *not* you at all.

But I do remember the kiss. The walk in the darkness, the grass wet with dew, the moon a silver sliver on the horizon, turning to her, and her face already turned up to meet my lips. The taste indescribable, more feeling than taste (not like strawberries at all), the small hardness of her teeth behind the lips—all there. Except the one critical detail: I don't have any idea at all who she *was*.

What else am I missing? Do I even know what I don't know?

I was a child, maybe nine, and there was no tree in the neighborhood that you could not climb. I was a careful, meticulous, methodical climber. On the tallest of the trees, when you reached toward the top, you were above the forest canopy (did I live in a forest?) and, out of the dimness of the forest floor, emerged into brilliant sunshine. Nobody else could climb like you; nobody ever suspected how high I climbed. It was your private hiding place, so high that the world was nothing but a sea of green waves in the valley between the mountains.

It was my own stupidity, really. At the very limit of the altitude needed to emerge into sunlight, the branches were skinny, narrow as your little finger. They bent alarmingly with your weight, but I knew exactly how much they would take. The bending was a thrill, but I was cautious, and knew exactly what I was doing.

It was further down, where the branches were thick and safe, that I got careless. Three points of support, that was the rule of safety, but I was reaching for one branch, not paying attention, when one in my other hand broke, and I was off balance. I slipped. For a prolonged instant I was suspended in space, branches all about me, I reached out and grasped only leaves, and I fell and fell and fell, and all I could think as leaves and branches fell upward past me was, oh my, I made a miscalculation; I was really stupid.

The flash memory ends with no conclusion. I must have hit the ground but I cannot remember it. Somebody must have found me, or else I wandered or crawled back, perhaps in a daze, and found somebody, but I cannot remember it.

Half a million kilometers from the hole. If my elliptical orbit were around the sun instead of a black hole, I would already have penetrated the surface. I now hold the record for the closest human approach. There is still nothing to see with unmagnified senses. It seems surreal that I'm in the grip of something so powerful that is utterly invisible. With my augmented eyes used as a telescope, I can detect the black hole by what isn't there, a tiny place of blackness nearly indistinguishable from any other patch of darkness except for an odd motion of the stars near it.

My ship is sending a continuous stream of telemetry back to the station. I have an urge to add a verbal commentary—there is plenty of bandwidth—but I have nothing to say. There is only one person I have any interest in talking to, and you are cocooned at absolute zero, waiting for me to upload myself and become you.

My ellipse takes me inward, moving faster and faster. I am still in Newton's grip, far from the sphere where Einstein takes hold.

A tenth of a solar radius. The blackness I orbit is now large enough to see without a telescope, as large as the sun seen from Earth, and swells as I watch with time-distorted senses. Due to its gravity, the blackness in front of the star pattern is a bit larger than the disk of the black hole itself. Square root of twenty-seven over two—about two and a half times larger, the physicist persona notes. I watch in fascination.

What I see is a bubble of purest blackness. The bubble pushes the distant stars away from it as it swells. My orbital motion makes the background stars appear to sweep across the sky, and I watch them approach the black hole and then, smoothly pushed by the gravity, move off to the side, a river of stars flowing past an invisible obstacle. It is a gravitational lensing effect, I know, but the view of flowing stars is so spectacular that I cannot help but watch it. The gravity pushes each star to one side or the other. If a star were to pass directly behind the hole, it would appear to split and for an instant become a perfect circle of light, an Einstein ring. But this precise alignment is too rare to see by accident.

Closer, I notice an even odder effect. The sweeping stars detour smoothly around the bubble of blackness, but very close to the bubble, there are other stars, stars that actually move in the opposite direction, a counterflowing river of stars. It takes me a long time (microseconds perhaps) before my physicist persona tells me that I am seeing the image of the stars in the Einstein mirror. The entire external universe is mirrored in a narrow ring outside the black hole, and the mirror image flows along with a mirror of my own motion.

In the center of the ring there is nothing at all.

Five thousand kilometers, and I am moving fast. The gravitational acceleration here is over ten million gees, and I am still fifty times the Schwarzschild radius from the black hole. Einstein's correction is still tiny, though, and if I were to do nothing, my orbit would whip around the black hole and still escape into the outside world.

One thousand kilometers. Perimelasma, the closest point of my elliptical orbit. Ten times the Schwarzschild radius, close enough that Einstein's correction to Newton now makes a small difference to the geometry of space. I fire my engines. My speed is so tremendous that it takes over a second of my engine firing at a million gravities to circularize my orbit.

My time sense has long since speeded up back to normal, and then faster than normal. I orbit the black hole about ten times per second.

My god, this is why I exist, this is why I'm here!

All my doubts are gone in the rush of naked power. No biological could have survived this far; no biological could have even survived the million-gee circularization burn, and I am only at the very beginning! I grin like a maniac, throb with a most unscientific excitement that must be the electronic equivalent of an adrenaline high.

Oh, this ship is good. This ship is sweet. A million-gee burn, smooth as magnetic levitation, and I barely cracked the throttle. I should have taken it for a spin before dropping in, should have hot-rodded *Huis Clos* around the stellar neighborhood. But it had been absolutely out of the question to fire the main engine close to the wormhole station. Even with the incredible efficiency of the engine, that million-gee perimelasma burn must have lit up the research station like an unexpected sun.

I can't wait to take *Huis Clos* in and see what it will *really* do.

My orbital velocity is a quarter of the speed of light.

The orbit at nine hundred kilometers is only a parking orbit, a chance for me to configure my equipment, make final measurements, and, in principle, a last chance for me to change my mind. There is nothing to reconnoiter that the probes have not already measured, though, and there is no chance that I will change my mind, however sensible that may seem.

The river of stars swirls in a dance of counterflow around the blackness below me. The horizon awaits.

The horizon below is invisible, but real. There is no barrier at the horizon, nothing to see, nothing to feel. I will even be unable to detect it, except for my calculations.

An event horizon is a one-way membrane, a place you can pass into but neither you nor your radio signals can pass out of. According to the mathematics, as I pass through the event horizon, the directions of space and time change identity. Space rotates into time; time rotates into space. What this means is that the direction to the center of the black hole, after I pass the event horizon, will be the future. The direction out of the black hole will be the past. This is the reason that no one and nothing can ever leave a black hole; the way inward is the one direction we always must go, whether we will it or not: into the future.

Or so the mathematics says.

The future, inside a black hole, is a very short one.

So far the mathematics has been right on. Nevertheless, I go on. With infinitesimal blasts from my engine, I inch my orbit lower.

The bubble of blackness gets larger, and the counterflow of stars around it becomes more complex. As I approach three times the Schwarzschild radius, 180 kilometers, I check all my systems. This is the point of no rescue: inside three Schwarzschild radii, no orbits are stable, and my automatic systems will be constantly thrusting to adjust my orbital parameters to keep me from falling into the black hole or being flung away to infinity. My systems are all functional, in perfect form for the dangerous drop. My orbital velocity is already half the speed of light. Below this point, centrifugal force will decrease toward zero as I lower my orbit, and I must use my thrusters to increase my velocity as I descend, or else plunge into the hole.

When I grew up, in the last years of the second millennium, nobody thought that they would live forever. Nobody would have believed me if I told them that by my thousandth birthday, I would have no concept of truly dying.

Even if all our clever tricks fail, even if I plunge through the event horizon and am stretched into spaghetti and crushed by the singularity, I will not die. You, my original, will live on, and if *you* were to die, we have made dozens of back-ups and spin-off copies of myselves in the past, some versions of which must surely still be living on. My individual life has little importance. I can, if I chose, uplink my brain-state to the orbiting station right at this instant, and reawake, whole, continuing this exact thought, unaware (except on an abstract intellectual level) that I and you are not the same.

But we are not the same, you and I. I am an edited-down version of you, and the memories that have been edited out, even if I never happen to think them, make me different, a new individual. Not *you*.

On a metaphorical level, a black hole stands for death, the blackness that is sucking us all in. But what meaning does death have in a world of matrix back-ups and modular personality? Is my plunge a death wish? Is it thumbing my nose at death? Because I intend to survive. Not you. *Me*.

I orbit the black hole over a hundred times a second now, but I have revved my brain processing speed accordingly, so that my orbit seems to me leisurely enough. The view here is odd. The black hole has swollen to the size of a small world below me, a world of perfect velvet darkness, surrounded by a belt of madly rotating stars.

No engine, no matter how energetic, can put a ship into an orbit at 1.5 times the Schwarzschild radius; at this distance, the orbital velocity is the speed of light, and not even my total-conversion engine can accelerate me to that speed. Below that, there are no orbits at all. I stop my descent at an orbit just sixty kilometers from the event horizon, when my orbital velocity reaches 85 percent of the speed of light. Here I can coast, ignoring the constant small adjustments of the thrusters that keep my orbit from sliding off the knife-edge. The velvet blackness of the black hole is almost half of the universe now, and if I were to trust the outside view, I am diving at a slant downward into the black hole. I ignore my pilot's urge to override the automated navigation and manually even out the trajectory. The downward slant is only relativistic aberration, nothing more, an illusion of my velocity.

And 85 percent of the speed of light is as fast as I dare orbit; I must conserve my fuel for the difficult part of the plunge to come.

In my unsteady orbit sixty kilometers above the black hole, I let my ship's computer chat with the computer of the wormhole station, updating and downloading my sensors' observations.

At this point, according to the mission plan, I am supposed to uplink my brain state, so that should anything go wrong further down the well, you, my original, will be able to download my state and experiences to this point. To hell with that, I think, a tiny bit of rebellion. I am not you. If you awaken with my memories, I will be no less dead.

Nobody at the wormhole station questions my decision not to upload.

I remember one other thing now. "You're a type N personality," the psychologist had said, twitching her thumb to leaf through invisible pages of test results. The gesture marked her era; only a person who had grown up before computer hotlinks would move a physical muscle in commanding a virtual. She was twenty-first century, possibly even twentieth. "But I suppose you already know that."

"Type N?" you asked.

"Novelty-seeking," she said. "Most particularly, one not prone to panic at new situations."

"Oh," you said. You did already know that. "Speaking of novelty seeking, how do you feel about going to bed with a type N personality?"

"That would be unprofessional." She frowned. "I think."

"Not even one who is about to jump down a black hole?"

She terminated the computer link with a flick of her wrist, and turned to look at you. "Well—"

From this point onward, microsecond timing is necessary for the dance we have planned to succeed. My computer and the station computer meticulously compare clocks, measuring Doppler shifts to exquisite precision. My clocks are running slow, as expected, but half of the slowness is relativistic time dilation due to my velocity. The gravitational redshift is still modest. After some milliseconds—a long wait for me, in my hyped-up state—they declare that they agree. The station has already done their part, and I begin the next phase of my descent.

The first thing I do is fire my engine to stop my orbit. I crack the throttle to fifty million gees of acceleration, and the burn takes nearly a second, a veritable eternity, to slow my flight.

For a moment I hover, and start to drop. I dare not drop too fast, and I ramp my throttle up, to a hundred megagee, five hundred, a billion gravities. At forty billion gravities of acceleration, my engine thrust equals the gravity of the black hole, and I hover.

The blackness has now swallowed half of the universe. Everything beneath me is black. Between the black below and the starry sky above, a spectacularly bright line exactly bisects the sky. I have reached the altitude at which orbital velocity is just equal to the speed of light, and the light from my rocket exhaust is in orbit around the black hole. The line I see around the sky is my view of my own rocket, seen by light that has traveled all the way around the black hole. All I can see is the exhaust, far brighter than anything else in the sky.

The second brightest thing is the laser beacon from the wormhole station above me, shifted from the original red laser color to a greenish blue. The laser marks the exact line between the station and the black hole, and I maneuver carefully until I am directly beneath the orbiting station.

At forty billion gravities, even my ultrastrong body is at its limits. I cannot move, and even my smallest finger is pressed against the form-fitting acceleration couch. But the controls, hardware-interfaced to my brain, do not require me to lift a finger to command the spacecraft. The command I give *Huis Clos* is: down.

My engine throttles down slightly, and I drop inward from the photon sphere, the bright line of my exhaust vanishes. Every stray photon from my drive is now sucked downward.

Now my view of the universe has changed. The black hole has become the universe around me, and the universe itself, all the galaxies and stars and the wormhole station, is a shrinking sphere of sparkling dust above me.

Sixty billion gravities. Seventy. Eighty.

Eighty billion gravities is full throttle. I am burning fuel at an incredible rate, and only barely hold steady. I am still twenty kilometers above the horizon.

There is an unbreakable law of physics: incredible accelerations require incredible fuel consumption. Even though my spaceship is, by mass, comprised mostly of fuel, I can maintain less than a millisecond worth of thrust at this acceleration. I cut my engine and drop.

It will not be long now. This is my last chance to uplink a copy of my mind back to the wormhole station to wake in your body, with my last memory the decision to upload my mind.

I do not.

The stars are blueshifted by a factor of two, which does not make them notice-ably bluer. Now that I have stopped accelerating, the starlight is falling into the hole along with me, and the stars do not blueshift any further. My instruments probe the vacuum around me. The theorists say that the vacuum close to the horizon of a black hole is an exotic vacuum, abristle with secret energy. Only a ship plunging through the event horizon would be able to measure this. I do, recording the results carefully on my ship's on-board recorders, since it is now far too late to send anything back by radio.

There is no sign to mark the event horizon, and there is no indication at all when I cross it. If it were not for my computer, there would be no way for me to tell that I have passed the point of no return.

Nothing is different. I look around the tiny cabin, and can see no change. The blackness below me continues to grow, but is otherwise not changed. The outside universe continues to shrink above me; the brightness beginning to concentrate into a belt around the edge of the glowing sphere of stars, but this is only an effect of my motion. The only difference is that I have only a few hundred microseconds left.

From the viewpoint of the outside world, the light from my spacecraft has slowed down and stopped at the horizon. But I have far outstripped my lagging image, and am falling toward the center at incredible speed. At the exact center is the singularity, far smaller than an atom, a mathematical point of infinite gravity and infinite mystery.

Whoever I am, whether or not I survive, I am now the first person to penetrate the event horizon of a black hole. That's worth a cheer, even with nobody to hear. Now I have to count on the hope that the microsecond timing of the technicians above me had been perfect for the second part of my intricate dance, the part that might, if all goes well, allow me to survive.

Above me, according to theory, the stars have already burned out, and even the most miserly red dwarf has sputtered the last of its hydrogen fuel and grown cold. The universe has already ended, and the stars have gone out. I still see a steady glow of starlight from the universe above me, but this is fossil light, light that has been falling down into the black hole with me for eons, trapped in the infinitely stretched time of the black hole.

For me, time has rotated into space, and space into time. Nothing feels different to me, but I cannot avoid the singularity at the center of the black hole any more than I can avoid the future. Unless, that is, I have a trick.

Of course, I have a trick.

At the center of the spherical universe above me is a dot of bright blue-violet; the fossil light of the laser beacon from the orbiting station. My reaction jets have kept on adjusting my trajectory to keep me centered in the guidance beam, so I am directly below the station. Anything dropped from the station will, if everything works right, drop directly on the path I follow.

I am approaching close to the center now, and the tidal forces stretching my body are creeping swiftly toward a billion gees per millimeter. Much higher, and even my tremendously strong body will be ripped to spaghetti. There are only microseconds left for me. It is time.

I hammer my engine, full throttle. Far away, and long ago, my friends at the wormhole station above dropped a wormhole into the event horizon. If their timing was perfect—

From a universe that has already died, the wormhole cometh.

Even with my enhanced time sense, things happen fast. The laser beacon blinks out, and the wormhole sweeps down around me like the vengeance of God, far faster than I can react. The sparkle-filled sphere of the universe blinks out like a light, and the black hole—and the tidal forces stretching my body—abruptly disappears. For a single instant I see a black disk below me, and then the wormhole rotates, twists, stretches, and then silently vanishes.

Ripped apart by the black hole.

My ship is vibrating like a bell from the abrupt release of tidal stretching. "I did it," I shout. "It worked! God damn it, it really worked!"

This was what was predicted by the theorists, that I would be able to pass through the wormhole before it was shredded by the singularity at the center. The other possibility, that the singularity itself, infinitesimally small and infinitely powerful, might follow me through the wormhole, was laughed at by everyone who had any claim to understand wormhole physics. This time, the theorists were right.

But where am I?

There should be congratulations pouring into my radio by now, teams of friends and technicians swarming over to greet me, cheering and shouting.

"Huis Clos," I say, over the radio. "I made it! Huis Clos here. Is anybody there?"

In theory, I should have reemerged at Wolf-562. But I do not see it. In fact, what I see is not recognizably the universe at all.

There are no stars.

Instead of stars, the sky is filled with lines, parallel lines of white light by the uncountable thousands. Dominating the sky, where the star Wolf-562 should have been, is a glowing red cylinder, perfectly straight, stretching to infinity in both directions.

Have I been transported into some other universe? Could the black hole's gravity sever the wormhole, cutting it loose from our universe entirely, and connect it into this strange new one?

If so, it has doomed me. The wormhole behind me, my only exit from this strange universe, is already destroyed. Not that escaping through it could have done me any good—it would only have brought me back to the place I escaped, to be crushed by the singularity of the black hole.

I could just turn my brain off, and I will have lost nothing, in a sense. They will bring you out of your suspended state, tell you that the edition of you that dropped into the black hole failed to upload, and they lost contact after it passed the event horizon. The experiment failed, but you had never been in danger.

But, however much you think we are the same, *I am not you.* I am a unique individual. When they revive you, without your expected new memories, I will still be gone.

I want to survive, I want to return.

A universe of tubes of light! Brilliant bars of an infinite cage. The bright lines in the sky have slight variations in color, from pale red to plasma-arc blue. They must be similar to the red cylinder near me, I figure, but light-years away. How could a universe have lines of light instead of stars?

I am amazingly well equipped to investigate that question, with senses that range from radio through X-ray, and I have nothing else to do for the next thousand years or so. So I take a spectrum of the light from the glowing red cylinder.

I have no expectation that the spectrum will reveal anything I can interpret, but oddly, it looks normal. Impossibly, it looks like the spectrum of a star.

The computer can even identify, from its data of millions of spectra, precisely which star. The light from the cylinder has the spectral signature of Wolf-562.

Coincidence? It cannot possibly be coincidence, out of billions of possible spectra, that this glowing sword in the sky has exactly the spectrum of the star that should have been there. There can be no other conclusion but that the cylinder *is* Wolf-562.

I take a few more spectra, this time picking at random three of the lines of light in the sky, and the computer analyzes them for me. A bright one: the spectrum of 61 Virginis. A dimmer one: a match to Wolf-1061. A blue-white streak: Vega.

The lines in the sky are stars.

What does this mean?

I'm not in another universe. I am in *our* universe, but the universe has been transformed. Could the collision of a wormhole with a black hole destroy our entire universe, stretching suns like taffy into infinite straight lines? Impossible. Even if it had, I would still see far-away stars as dots, since the light from them has been traveling for hundreds of years.

The universe cannot have changed. Therefore, by logic, it must be *me* who has been transformed.

Having figured out this much, the only possible answer is obvious.

When the mathematicians describe the passage across the event horizon of a black hole, they say that the space and time directions switch identity. I had always thought this only a mathematical oddity, but if it were true, if I had rotated when I passed the event horizon, and was now perceiving time as a direction in space, and one of the space axes as time—this would explain everything. Stars extend from billions of years into the past to long into the future; perceiving time as space, I see lines of light. If I were to come closer and find one of the rocky planets of Wolf-562, it would look like a braid around the star, a helix of solid rock. Could I land on it? How would I interact with a world where what I perceive as time is a direction in space?

My physicist persona doesn't like this explanation, but is at a loss to find a better one. In this strange sideways existence, I must be violating the conservation laws of physics like mad, but the persona could find no other hypothesis and must reluctantly agree: time is rotated into space.

To anybody outside, I must look like a string, a knobby long rope with one end at the wormhole and the other at my death, wherever that might be. But nobody could see me fast enough, since with no extension in time I must only be a transient event that bursts everywhere into existence and vanishes at the same instant. There is no way I can signal, no way I can communicate —

Or? Time, to me, is now a direction I can travel in as simply as using my rocket. I could find a planet, travel parallel to the direction of the surface —

But, no, all I could do would be to appear to the inhabitants briefly as a disk, a cross-section of myself, infinitely thin. There is no way I could communicate.

But I can travel in time, if I want. Is there any way I can use this?

Wait. If I have rotated from space into time, then there is one direction in space that I cannot travel. Which direction is that? The direction that used to be away from the black hole.

Interesting thoughts, but not ones which help me much. To return, I need to once again flip space and time. I could dive into a black hole. This would again rotate space and time, but it wouldn't do me any good: once I left the black hole — if I could leave the black hole — nothing would change.

Unless there were a wormhole inside the black hole, falling inward to destruction just at the same instant I was there? But the only wormhole that has fallen into a black hole was already destroyed. Unless, could I travel forward in time? Surely some day the research team would drop a new wormhole into the black hole —

Idiot. Of course there's a solution. Time is a spacelike dimension to me, so I can travel either direction in time now, forward or back. I need only to move back to an instant just after the wormhole passed through the event horizon, and, applying full thrust, shoot through. The very moment that my original self shoots through the wormhole to escape the singularity, I can pass through the opposite direction, and rotate myself back into the real universe.

The station at Virgo black hole is forty light years away, and I don't dare use the original wormhole to reach it. My spacetime-rotated body must be an elongated snake in this version of space-time, and I do not wish to find out what a wormhole passage will do to it until I have no other choice. Still, that is no problem for me. Even with barely enough fuel to thrust for a few microseconds, I can reach an appreciable fraction of light-speed, and I can slow down my brain to make the trip appear only an instant.

To an outside observer, it takes literally no time at all.

"No," says the psych tech, when I ask her. "There's no law that compels you to uplink back into your original. You're a free human being. Your original can't force you."

"Great," I say. Soon I'm going to have to arrange to get a biological body built for myself. This one is superb, but it's a disadvantage in social intercourse being only a millimeter tall.

The transition back to real space worked perfectly. Once I figured out how to navigate in time-rotated space, it had been easy enough to find the wormhole and the exact instant it had penetrated the event horizon.

"Are you going to link your experiences to public domain?" the tech asks. "I think he would like to see what you experienced. Musta been pretty incredible."

"Maybe," I said.

"For that matter," the psych tech added, "I'd like to link it, too."

"I'll think about it."

So I am a real human being now, independent of you, my original.

There had been cheers and celebrations when I had emerged from the wormhole, but nobody had an inkling quite how strange my trip had been until I told them. Even then, I doubt that I was quite believed until the sensor readings and computer logs of *Huis Clos* confirmed my story with hard data.

The physicists had been ecstatic. A new tool to probe time and space. The ability to rotate space into time will open up incredible capabilities. They were already planning new expeditions, not the least of which was a trip to probe right to the singularity itself.

They had been duly impressed with my solution to the problem, although, after an hour of thinking it over, they all agreed it had been quite obvious. "It was lucky," one of them remarked, "that you decided to go through the wormhole from the opposite side, that second time."

"Why?" I asked.

"If you'd gone through the same direction, you'd have rotated an additional ninety degrees, instead of going back."

"So?"

"Reversed the time vector. Turns you into antimatter. First touch of the interstellar medium — Poof."

"Oh," I said. I hadn't thought of that. It made me feel a little less clever.

Now that the mission is over, I have no purpose, no direction for my existence. The future is empty, the black hole that we all must travel into. I will get a biological body, yes, and embark on the process of finding out who I am. Maybe, I think, this is a task that everybody has to do.

And then I will meet you. With luck, perhaps I'll even like you.

And maybe, if I should like you enough, and I feel confident, I'll decide to upload you into myself, and once more, we will again be one.

craphound

CORY DOCTOROW

Here's a wry, quirky, nostalgic, and oddly lyrical reexamination of an old question—what do the vintners buy one-half so precious as the stuff they sell?

New writer Cory Doctorow has sold fiction to Science Fiction Age, Asimov's Science Fiction, Amazing, Northern Suns, On Spec, Air Fish, *and* Tesseracts[7], *and nonfiction pieces to* Wired *and* Sci-Fi Entertainment. *He also contributes a regular column about interesting stuff to find on the Internet to* Science Fiction Age. *He has a Web site at http:// www.craphound.com. He lives in Toronto, Canada.*

Craphound had wicked yard-sale karma, for a rotten, filthy, alien bastard. He was too good at panning out the single grain of gold in a raging river of uselessness for me not to like him—respect him, anyway. But then he found the cowboy trunk. It was two months' rent to me and nothing but some squirrely alien kitsch-fetish to Craphound.

So I did the unthinkable. I violated the Code. I got into a bidding war with a buddy. Never let them tell you that women poison friendships: In my experience, wounds from women-fights heal quickly; fights with men over garbage leave nothing behind but scorched earth.

Craphound spotted the sign—his karma, plus the goggles in his exoskeleton, gave him the advantage when we were doing 80 kmh on some stretch of back-highway in cottage country. He was riding shotgun while I drove, and we had the radio tuned to the summer-Saturday programming: eight weekends with eight hours of old radio dramas: *The Shadow, Quiet Please, Tom Mix, The Crypt-Keeper* with Bela Lugosi. It was hour three, and Bogey was phoning in his performance on a radio adaptation of *The African Queen*. I had the windows of the old truck rolled down so that I could smoke without fouling Craphound's breather. My arm was hanging out the window, the radio was booming, and Craphound said "Turn around! Turn around, now, Jerry, now, turn around!"

When Craphound gets that excited, it's a sign that he's spotted a rich vein. I checked the side-mirror quickly, pounded the brakes, and spun around. The transmission creaked, the wheels squealed, and then we were creeping along the way we'd come.

"There," Craphound said, gesturing with his long, skinny arm. I saw it. A wooden A-frame real-estate sign, a piece of hand-lettered cardboard stuck overtop of the realtor's name:

EAST MUSKOKA VOLUNTEER FIRE DEPT
LADIES AUXILIARY RUMMAGE SALE
SAT 25 JUNE

"Hoo-eee!" I hollered, and spun the truck onto the dirt road. I gunned the engine as we cruised along the tree-lined road, trusting Craphound to spot any deer, signs, or hikers in time to avert disaster. The sky was a perfect blue and the smells of summer were all around. I snapped off the radio and listened to the wind rushing through the truck. Ontario is beautiful in the summer.

"There!" Craphound shouted. I hit the turn-off and down-shifted and then we were back on a paved road. Soon, we were rolling into a country fire station, an ugly brick barn. The hall was lined with long folding tables, stacked high. The mother lode!

Craphound beat me out the door, as usual. His exoskeleton is programmable, so he can record little scripts for it like: move left arm to door handle, pop it, swing legs out to running-board, jump to ground, close door, move forward. Meanwhile, I'm still making sure I've switched off the headlights and that I've got my wallet.

Two blue-haired grannies had a card table set up in front of the hall, with a big tin pitcher of lemonade and three boxes of Tim Horton assorted donuts. That stopped us both, since we share the superstition that you always buy food from old ladies and little kids, as a sacrifice to the crap-gods. One of the old ladies poured out the lemonade while the other smiled and greeted us.

"Welcome, welcome! My, you've come a long way for us!"

"Just up from Toronto, ma'am," I said. It's an old joke, but it's also part of the ritual, and it's got to be done.

"I meant your friend, sir. This gentleman."

Craphound smiled without baring his gums and sipped his lemonade. "Of course I came, dear lady. I wouldn't miss it for the worlds!" His accent is pretty good, but when it comes to stock phrases like this, he's got so much polish you'd think he was reading the news.

The biddie *blushed* and *giggled*, and I felt faintly sick. I walked off to the tables, trying not to hurry. I chose my first spot, about halfway down, where things wouldn't be quite so picked over. I grabbed an empty box from underneath and started putting stuff into it: four matched highball glasses with gold crossed bowling-pins and a line of black around the rim; an Expo '67 wall-hanging that wasn't even a little faded; a shoebox full of late '60s O-Pee-Chee hockey cards; a worn, wooden-handled steel cleaver that you could butcher a steer with.

I picked up my box and moved on: a deck of playing cards copyrighted '57, with the logo of the Royal Canadian Dairy, Bala Ontario printed on the backs; a fireman's cap with a brass badge so tarnished I couldn't read it; a three-story wedding-cake trophy for the 1974 Eastern Region Curling Championships. The cash-register in my mind was ringing, ringing, ringing. God bless the East Muskoka Volunteer Fire Department Ladies' Auxiliary.

I'd mined that table long enough. I moved to the other end of the hall. Time was, I'd start at the beginning and turn over each item, build one pile of maybes and another pile of definites, try to strategize. In time, I came to rely on instinct and on the fates, to whom I make my obeisances at every opportunity.

Let's hear it for the fates: a genuine collapsible tophat; a white-tipped evening cane; a hand-carved cherry-wood walking stick; a beautiful black lace parasol; a wrought-iron lightning rod with a rooster on top; all of it in an elephant-leg umbrella-stand. I filled the box, folded it over, and started on another.

I collided with Craphound. He grinned his natural grin, the one that showed row on row of wet, slimy gums, tipped with writhing, poisonous suckers. "Gold! Gold!" he said, and moved along. I turned my head after him, just as he bent over the cowboy trunk.

I sucked air between my teeth. It was magnificent: a leather-bound miniature steamer trunk, the leather worked with lariats, Stetson hats, war-bonnets, and six-guns. I moved toward him, and he popped the latch. I caught my breath.

On top, there was a kid's cowboy costume: miniature leather chaps; a tiny Stetson; a pair of scuffed white leather cowboy boots with long, worn spurs affixed to the heels. Craphound moved it reverently to the table and continued to pull more magic from the trunk's depths: a stack of cardboard-bound Hopalong Cassidy 78s; a pair of tin six-guns with gunbelt and holsters; a silver star that said Sheriff; a bundle of Roy Rogers comics tied with twine, in mint condition; and a leather satchel filled with plastic cowboys and Indians, enough to reenact the Alamo.

"Oh, my God," I breathed, as he spread the loot out on the table.

"What are these, Jerry?" Craphound asked, holding up the 78s.

"Old records, like LPs, but you need a special record player to listen to them." I took one out of its sleeve. It gleamed, scratch-free, in the overhead fluorescents.

"I got a 78 player here," said a member of the East Muskoka Volunteer Fire Department Ladies' Auxiliary. She was short enough to look Craphound in the eye, a hair under five feet, and had a skinny, rawboned look to her. "That's my Billy's things, 'Billy the Kid' we called him. He was dotty for cowboys when he was a boy. Couldn't get him to take off that fool outfit—nearly got him thrown out of school. He's a lawyer now, in Toronto, got a fancy office on Bay Street. I called him to ask if he minded my putting his cowboy things in the sale, and you know what? He didn't know what I was talking about! Doesn't that beat everything? He was dotty for cowboys when he was a boy."

It's another of my rituals to smile and nod and be as polite as possible to the erstwhile owners of crap that I'm trying to buy, so I smiled and nodded and examined the 78 player she had produced. In lariat script, on the top, it said, "Official Bob Wills Little Record Player," and had a crude watercolor of Bob Wills and His Texas Playboys grinning on the front. It was the kind of record player that folded up like a suitcase when you weren't using it. I'd had one as a kid, with Yogi Bear silkscreened on the front.

Billy's mom plugged the yellowed cord into a wall jack and took the 78 from me, touched the stylus to the record. A tinny ukelele played, accompanied by horse-clops, and then a narrator with a deep, whisky voice said, "Howdy, Pardners! I was just settin' down by the ole campfire. Why don't you stay an' have some beans, an' I'll tell y'all the story of how Hopalong Cassidy beat the Duke Gang when they come to rob the Santa Fe."

In my head, I was already breaking down the cowboy trunk and its contents, thinking about the minimum bid I'd place on each item at Sotheby's. Sold individually, I figured I could get over two grand for the contents. Then I thought about putting ads in some of the Japanese collectors' magazines, just for a lark, before I sent the lot to the auction house. You never can tell. A buddy I knew had sold a complete packaged set of *Welcome Back, Kotter* action figures for nearly eight grand that way. Maybe I could buy a new truck. . . .

"This is wonderful," Craphound said, interrupting my reverie. "How much would you like for the collection?"

I felt a knife in my guts. Craphound had found the cowboy trunk, so that meant it was his. But he usually let me take the stuff with street-value—he was interested in *everything*, so it hardly mattered if I picked up a few scraps with which to eke out a living.

Billy's mom looked over the stuff. "I was hoping to get twenty dollars for the lot, but if that's too much, I'm willing to come down."

"I'll give you thirty," my mouth said, without intervention from my brain.

They both turned and stared at me. Craphound was unreadable behind his goggles.

Billy's mom broke the silence. "Oh, my! Thirty dollars for this old mess?"

"I will pay fifty," Craphound said.

"Seventy-five," I said.

"Oh, my," Billy's mom said.

"Five hundred," Craphound said.

I opened my mouth, and shut it. Craphound had built his stake on Earth by selling a complicated biochemical process for nonchlorophyll photosynthesis to a Saudi banker. I wouldn't ever beat him in a bidding war: "A thousand dollars," my mouth said.

"Ten thousand," Craphound said, and extruded a roll of hundreds from somewhere in his exoskeleton.

"My Lord!" Billy's mom said. "Ten thousand dollars!"

The other pickers, the firemen, the blue-haired ladies, all looked up at that and stared at us, their mouths open.

"It is for a good cause," Craphound said.

"Ten thousand dollars!" Billy's mom said again.

Craphound's digits ruffled through the roll as fast as a croupier's counter, separated off a large chunk of the brown bills, and handed them to Billy's mom.

One of the firemen, a middle-aged paunchy man with a comb-over, appeared at Billy's mom's shoulder.

"What's going on, Eva?" he said.

"This . . . gentleman is going to pay ten thousand dollars for Billy's old cowboy things, Tom."

The fireman took the money from Billy's mom and stared at it. He held up the top note under the light and turned it this way and that, watching the holographic stamp change from green to gold, then green again. He looked at the serial number, then the serial number of the next bill. He licked his forefinger and started counting off the bills in piles of ten. Once he had ten piles, he counted them again. "That's ten thousand dollars, all right. Thank you very much, mister. Can I give you a hand getting this to your car?"

Craphound, meanwhile, had repacked the trunk and balanced the 78 player on top of it. He looked at me, then at the fireman.

"I wonder if I could impose on you to take me to the nearest bus station. I think I'm going to be making my own way home."

The fireman and Billy's mom both stared at me. My cheeks flushed. "Aw, c'mon," I said. "I'll drive you home."

"I think I prefer the bus," Craphound said.

"It's no trouble at all to give you a lift, friend," the fireman said.

I called it quits for the day, and drove home alone with the truck only half-filled. I pulled into the coach-house and threw a tarp over the load and went inside and cracked a beer and sat on the sofa, watching a nature show on a desert reclamation project in Arizona, where the state legislature had traded a derelict mega-mall and a custom-built habitat to an alien for a local-area weather-control machine.

The following Thursday, I went to the little crapauction house on King Street. I'd put my finds from the weekend in the sale: lower minimum bid, and they took a smaller commission than Sotheby's. Fine for moving the small stuff.

Craphound was there, of course. I knew he'd be. It was where we met, when he bid on a case of Lincoln Logs I'd found at a fire-sale.

I'd known him for a kindred spirit when he bought them, and we'd talked afterward, at his place, a sprawling, two-story warehouse amid a cluster of auto-wrecking yards where the junkyard dogs barked, barked, barked.

Inside was paradise. His taste ran to shrines—a collection of '50s bar kitsch that was a shrine to liquor, a circular waterbed on a raised podium that was nearly buried under '70s bachelor pad-inalia; a kitchen that was nearly unusable, so packed it was with old barnboard furniture and rural memorabilia; a leather-appointed library straight out of a Victorian gentlemen's club; a solarium dressed in wicker and bamboo and tiki-idols. It was a hell of a place.

Craphound had known all about the Goodwills and the Sally Anns, and the auction houses, and the kitsch boutiques on Queen Street, but he still hadn't figured out where it all came from.

"Yard sales, rummage sales, garage sales," I said, reclining in a vibrating Naugahyde easy chair, drinking a glass of his pricey single-malt that he'd bought for the beautiful bottle it came in.

"But where are these? Who is allowed to have them?" Craphound hunched opposite me, his exoskeleton locked into a coiled, semiseated position.

"Who? Well, anyone. You just one day decide that you need to clean out the basement, you put an ad in the *Star*, tape up a few signs, and *voila*—yard sale. Sometimes, a school or a church will get donations of old junk and sell it all at one time, as a fundraiser."

"And how do you locate these?" he asked, bobbing up and down slightly with excitement.

"Well, there're amateurs who just read the ads in the weekend papers, or just pick a neighborhood and wander around, but that's no way to go about it. What I do is, I get in a truck, and I sniff the air, catch the scent of crap, and vroom! — I'm off like a bloodhound on a trail. You learn things over time: like stay away from Yuppie yard sales; they never have anything worth buying, just the same crap you can buy in any mall."

"Do you think I might accompany you some day?"

"Hell, sure. Next Saturday? We'll head over to Cabbagetown — those old coach houses, you'd be amazed what people get rid of. It's practically criminal."

"I would like to go with you next Saturday very much Mr. Jerry Abington." He used to talk like that, without commas or question marks. Later, he got better, but then, it was all one big sentence.

"Call me Jerry. It's a date, then. Tell you what, though: there's a Code you got to learn before we go out. The Craphound's Code."

"What is a craphound?"

"You're lookin' at one. You're one, too, unless I miss my guess. You'll get to know some of the local craphounds, you hang around with me long enough. They're the competition, but they're also your buddies, and there're certain rules we have."

And then I explained to him all about how you never bid against a craphound at a yard sale, how you get to know the other fellows' tastes, and when you see something they might like you haul it out for them, and they'll do the same for you, and how you never buy something that another craphound might be looking for, if all you're buying it for is to sell it back to him. Just good form and common sense, really, but you'd surprised how many amateurs just fail to make the jump to pro because they can't grasp it.

There was a bunch of other stuff at the auction, other craphounds' weekend treasures. This was high season, when the sun comes out and people start to clean out the cottage, the basement, the garage. There were some collectors in the crowd, and a whole whack of antique and junk dealers, and a few pickers, and me, and Craphound. I watched the bidding listlessly, waiting for my things to come up and sneaking out for smokes between lots. Craphound never once looked at me or acknowledged my presence, and I became perversely obsessed with catching his eye, so I coughed and shifted and walked past him several times, until the auctioneer glared at me, and one of the attendants asked if I needed a throat lozenge.

My lot came up. The bowling glasses went for five bucks to one of the Queen Street junk dealers; the elephant-foot fetched $350 after a spirited bidding war between an antique dealer and a collector — the collector won; the dealer took the tophat for $100. The rest of it came up and sold, or didn't, and at the end of the lot I'd made $800, which was rent for the month plus beer for the weekend plus gas for the truck.

Craphound bid on and bought more cowboy things — a box of Super 8 cowboy movies, the boxes moldy, the stock itself running to slime; a Navajo blanket; a plastic donkey that dispensed cigarettes out of its ass; a big neon armadillo sign.

One of the other nice things about that place over Sotheby's, there was none of this waiting thirty days to get a check. I waited in line with the other pickers after the bidding was through, collected a wad of bills, and headed for my truck.

I spotted Craphound loading his haul into a minivan with handicapped plates. It looked like some kind of fungus was growing over the hood and side-panels. On closer inspection, I saw that the body had been covered in closely glued Legos.

Craphound popped the hatchback and threw his gear in, then opened the driver's side door, and I saw that his van had been fitted out for a legless driver, with brake and accelerator levers. A paraplegic I knew drove one just like it. Craphound's exoskeleton levered him into the seat, and I watched the eerily precise way it executed the macro that started the car, pulled the shoulder-belt, put it into drive, and switched on the stereo. I heard tape-hiss, then, loud as a b-boy cruising Yonge Street, an old-timey cowboy voice: "Howdy pardners! Saddle up, we're ridin'!" Then the van backed up and sped out of the lot.

I got into the truck and drove home. Truth be told, I missed the little bastard.

Some people said that we should have run Craphound and his kin off the planet, out of the Solar System. They said that it wasn't fair for the aliens to keep us in the dark about their technologies. They say that we should have captured a ship and reverse-engineered it, built our own and kicked ass.

Some people!

First of all, nobody with human DNA could survive a trip in one of those ships. They're part of Craphound's people's bodies, as I understand it, and we just don't have the right parts. Second of all, they *were* sharing their tech with us — they just weren't giving it away. Fair trades every time.

It's not as if space was off-limits to us. We can, any one of us, visit their home-world, just as soon as we figure out how. Only they wouldn't hold our hands along the way.

I spent the week haunting the "Secret Boutique," AKA the Goodwill As-Is Center on Jarvis. It's all there is to do between yard sales, and sometimes it makes for good finds. Part of my theory of yard-sale karma holds that if I miss one day at the thrift shops that'll be the day they put out the big score. So I hit the stores diligently and came up with crapola. I had offended the fates, I knew, and wouldn't make another score until I placated them. It was lonely work, and I missed Craphound's good eye and obsessive delight.

I was at the cash register with a few items at the Goodwill when a guy in a suit tapped me on the shoulder.

"Sorry to bother you," he said. His suit looked expensive, as did his manicure and his haircut and his wire-rimmed glasses. "I was just wondering where you found that." He gestured at a rhinestone-studded ukelele, with a cowboy hat wood-burned into the body. I had picked it up with a guilty little thrill, thinking that Craphound might buy it at the next auction.

"Second floor, in the toy section."

"There wasn't anything else like it, was there?"

" 'Fraid not," I said, and the cashier picked it up and started wrapping it in newspaper.

"Ah," he said, and he looked like a little kid who'd just been told that he couldn't have a puppy. "I don't suppose you'd want to sell it, would you?"

I held up a hand and waited while the cashier bagged it with the rest of my stuff, a few old clothbound novels I thought I could sell at a used bookstore, and a *Grease* belt buckle with Olivia Newton John on it. I led him out the door by the elbow of his expensive suit.

"How much?" I had paid a dollar.

"Ten bucks?"

I nearly said, "Sold!" but I caught myself. "Twenty."

"Twenty dollars?"

"That's what they'd charge at a boutique on Queen Street."

He took out a slim leather wallet and produced a twenty. I handed him the uke. His face lit up like a lightbulb.

After the cowboy trunk episode, I didn't run into Craphound again until the annual Rotary Club charity rummage sale at the Upper Canada Brewing Company. He was wearing the cowboy hat, six-guns, and the silver star from the cowboy trunk. It should have looked ridiculous, but the net effect was naive and somehow charming, like he was a little boy whose hair you wanted to muss.

I found a box of nice old melamine dishes, in various shades of green — four square plates, bowls, salad plates, and a serving tray. I threw them in the duffel bag I'd brought and kept browsing, ignoring Craphound as he charmed a salty old Rotarian while fondling a box of leather-bound books.

I browsed a stack of old Ministry of Labour licenses — barber, chiropodist, bartender, watchmaker. They all had pretty seals and were framed in stark green institutional metal. They all had different names, but all from one family, and I made up a little story to entertain myself, about the proud mother saving her sons' accreditations and framing and hanging them in the spare room with their diplomas. "Oh, George Junior's just opened his own barbershop, and little Jimmy's still fixing watches. . . ."

I bought them.

In a box of crappy plastic Little Ponies and Barbies and Care Bears I found a leather Indian headdress, a wooden bow-and-arrow set, and a fringed buckskin vest. Craphound was still buttering up the leather books' owner. I bought them quick, for five bucks.

"Those are beautiful," a voice said at my elbow. I turned around and smiled at the snappy dresser who'd bought the uke at the Secret Boutique. He'd gone casual for the weekend, in an expensive, L.L. Bean button-down way.

"Aren't they, though."

"You sell them on Queen Street? Your finds, I mean?"

"Sometimes. Sometimes at auction. How's the uke?"

"Oh, I got it all tuned up," he said, and smiled the same smile he'd given me when he'd taken hold of it at Goodwill. "I can play 'Don't Fence Me In' on it." He looked at his feet. "Silly, huh?"

"Not at all. You're into cowboy things, huh?" As I said it, I was overcome with the knowledge that this was 'Billy the Kid,' the original owner of the cowboy trunk. I don't know why I felt that way, but I did, with utter certainty.

"Just trying to relive a piece of my childhood, I guess. I'm Scott," he said, extending his hand.

Scott? I thought wildly. *Maybe it's his middle name?* "I'm Jerry."

The Upper Canada Brewery sale has many things going for it, including a beer garden where you can sample their wares and get a BBQ burger. We gently gravitated to it, looking over the tables as we went.

"You're a pro, right?" he asked after we had plastic cups of beer.

"You could say that."

"I'm an amateur. A rank amateur. Any words of wisdom?"

I laughed and drank some beer, lit a cigarette. "There's no secret to it, I think. Just diligence: you've got to go out every chance you get, or you'll miss the big score."

He chuckled. "I hear that. Sometimes, I'll be sitting in my office, and I'll just know that they're putting out a piece of pure gold at the Goodwill and that someone else will get to it before my lunch. I get so wound up, I'm no good until I go down there and hunt for it. I guess I'm hooked, eh?"

"Cheaper than some other kinds of addictions."

"I guess so. About that Indian stuff—what do you figure you'd get for it at a Queen Street boutique?"

I looked him in the eye. He may have been something high-powered and cool and collected in his natural environment, but just then, he was as eager and nervous as a kitchen-table poker-player at a high-stakes game.

"Maybe fifty bucks," I said.

"Fifty, huh?" he asked.

"About that," I said.

"Once it sold," he said.

"There is that," I said.

"Might take a month, might take a year," he said.

"Might take a day," I said.

"It might, it might." He finished his beer. "I don't suppose you'd take forty?"

I'd paid five for it, not ten minutes before. It looked like it would fit Craphound who, after all, was wearing Scott/Billy's own boyhood treasures as we spoke. You don't make a living by feeling guilty over eight hundred percent markups. Still, I'd angered the fates, and needed to redeem myself.

"Make it five," I said.

He started to say something, then closed his mouth and gave me a look of thanks. He took a five out of his wallet and handed it to me. I pulled the vest and bow and headdress from my duffel.

He walked back to a shiny black Jeep with gold detail work, parked next to Craphound's van. Craphound was building onto the Lego body, and the hood had a miniature Lego town attached to it.

Craphound looked around as he passed, and leaned forward with undisguised interest at the booty. I grimaced and finished my beer.

• • •

It's not that my adulthood is particularly unhappy. Likewise, it's not that my childhood was particularly happy.

There are memories I have, though, that are like a cool drink of water. My grandfather's place near Milton, an old Victorian farmhouse, where the cat drank out of a milk-glass bowl; and where we sat around a rough pine table that, in my memory, is as big as my whole apartment; and where my playroom was the drafty old barn with hay-filled lofts bulging with old farm junk and Tarzan-ropes I could swing on.

There was Grampa's friend Fyodor, and we took a trip out to his wrecking yard every evening so that he and Grampa could talk and smoke on the porch while I scampered around in the twilight, scaling mountains of auto-junk. The glove-boxes yielded treasure troves: crumpled photos of college boys mugging in front of tourist signs, roadmaps of faraway places, other things. I found a guidebook from the 1964 New York World's Fair, once. And a lipstick like a chrome bullet, and a pair of white leather ladies' gloves.

Fyodor dealt in scrap, too, and once he had half of a carny carousel, a few horses and part of the canopy, paint flaking and sharp torn edges protruding; next to it, a Korean War tank minus its turret and caterpillar treads, and inside the tank were peeling old pinup girls and a rotation schedule and a crudely sketched Kilroy. The control room in the middle of the carousel had a stack of paperback sci-fi novels with lurid covers, Ace Doubles that had two books bound back-to-back, and when you finished the first, you turned it over and read the other. Fyodor let me keep them, and there was a pawn ticket in one from Macon, GA, for a transistor radio.

My parents left me alone in the house when I got old enough, fourteen or fifteen, and then I couldn't keep myself from sneaking into their room and snooping. Mom's jewelry box had books of matches from the Acapulco hotel where they'd honeymooned, printed with a bad palm-tree motif, and the matches had green heads and wooden bodies, though they were bound like paper matches. My Dad kept an old photo in his sock drawer, of himself on Muscle Beach, shirtless, flexing his biceps, and he had a silver turnip pocket-watch that had his grandfather's initials engraved on the front.

My grandmother saved every scrap of my mother's life in her basement, in dusty old Army trunks. I entertained myself endlessly by pulling then out and taking it in: her Mouse Ears from the big family train trip to Disneyland in '57, and her record albums, and the glittery pasteboard sign from her sweet sixteen. There were endless photo albums, and well-chewed stuffed animals, and school exercise books in which she'd practiced variations on her signature for page after page.

It all told a story. The penciled Kilroy in the tank made me see one of those Canadian soldiers in Korea, unshaven and crew cut like an extra on $M*A*S*H$, sitting bored hour after hour, staring at the pinup girls, fiddling with a crossword, finally laying it down and sketching his Kilroy quickly, before anyone saw.

The photo of my dad posing sent me whirling through time to Toronto's old Muscle Beach in the east end, near Kew Beach, and hearing the tinny AM radios playing weird old psychedelic rock while teenagers lounged on their Mustangs and the girls sunbathed in bikinis that made their tits into torpedoes.

It all made poems. The old pulp novels and the pawn ticket, when I spread them out in the living room in front of the TV, and arranged them just so, they made up a poem that could take my breath away.

They say that when my mom was a kid, little kids imagined their dream-houses in obsessive, hyperreal clarity. That they knew what kind of dog they'd have, and what kind of fridge, and what kind of sofa, and what kind of end tables and what kind of husband, and how many kids they'd have and what they'd name them and what they'd wear.

I must've inherited the gene. I'd walk into our kitchen and just stand in the center of the linoleum, and think about what was missing—the curtains, for example, should be more like Grandma's, with bright floral prints. And there was a stove in Fyodor's yard that he used as a workbench, an old cast-iron gas-fired piece from a Deco diner, that had elegant ivory knobs and a grill big enough to cook thirty burgers on at once. That would nicely replace the greenish electric stove we had.

And our glasses were all wrong: Grampa had milk glasses with Li'l Orphan Annie, and Grandma's place had anodized aluminum cups in bright metallic colors that were so cold when you filled them with chocolate milk.

A restaurant we'd eaten at once while on a camping trip had a mahogany-paneled lounge with solid, lion's-footed horsehair sofas. They'd look great in the living room, especially with cutglass and chrome tablelamps.

Our garage had nothing but tools and bikes and spare tires. It should have had tin signs advertising nickel bottles of Coca-Cola, and Burma Shave, and patented quack remedies with hand-painted smiling babies endorsing them.

The shed shouldn't have been a Sears prefab tin special—it should have been peeling old boards, with rickety wooden shelves inside and sawdust on the floor, and oiled iron tools on the walls.

I knew what was wrong with every square inch of my bedroom. I needed some old patchwork quilts to sleep under, instead of the synthetic-filled comforter, and my desk should have been a salvaged steel office desk with a worn green blotter and a solid oak chair on brass wheels. The basketball-hoop light fixture had to go, and in its place I wanted wall sconces made from brutally simple wrought iron rings with blown-glass shades.

The bathroom needed a bookcase. The books needed to be old and leather bound, swollen with the damp of a thousand showers, dog-eared and much-annotated.

I live in an apartment almost west enough to be in High Park. I've got two bedrooms at the top of the three-story house that was once a Victorian but was rebuilt after a fire in the mid-'70s. It's nice enough, in a generic, post-war kind of way.

It has a tremendous plus going for it: a coach-house out back that I pay another hundred bucks a month for. It's where I store my treasures, and there are three locks on the door.

The apartment came furnished in no-taste Late Canadian Thrift Store, and I never got around to redecorating it, strangely enough.

What I did do, though, was hang three long shelves at the foot of my bed. That's all the space I have to keep treasures on. It's a self-regulating mechanism, preventing me from sampling too much of the merchandise. If I find a piece that I have to keep, something from the shelf has to be moved out to the coach-house and taken away to an auction or a consignment store.

I have a milk-glass bowl on the shelves; a Made-in-Occupied-Japan tin tank that is pieced together from old tuna cans and hand-painted; a mint-condition Ace Double with bug-eyed monsters on both covers; a souvenir ashtray from the 1964 World's Fair; four anodized aluminum cups in brilliant metallic colors; a set of pink Mouse Ears with a girl's name stitched in cursive writing on the reverse; a silver turnip pocket watch; a small postcard with a 3-D Jesus who winks at you when you move your head; a lighter made from burnished shrapnel; other treasures that come and go.

Over the years, I've found the steel desk and the wall sconces and carousel animals and tin Coca-Cola signs galore. Finding them feels right, like I've checked off an item on a checklist. They go straight into my garage without gracing my apartment even once, and selling them is never painful — it's touching them again, just once, having them pass through my possession that makes it good.

When I can't bring myself to switch on the TV, I take an armload of things down from my shelves and sit on the living room floor and spread them out in front of me and see if I can't make a poem. Sometimes I laugh and sometimes I cry, but usually I just stare at them and let my mind caress each piece and match it up with a memory.

I met Scott/Billy three times more at the Secret Boutique that week. He was a lawyer, and specialized in alien-technology patents. He had a practice on Bay Street, with two partners, and despite his youth, he was the senior man.

I didn't let on that I knew about Billy the Kid and his mother in the East Muskoka Volunteer Fire Department Ladies' Auxiliary. But I felt a bond with him, as though we shared an unspoken secret. I pulled any cowboy finds for him, and he developed a pretty good eye for what I was after and returned the favor.

The fates were with me again, and no two ways about it. I took home a ratty old Oriental rug that on closer inspection was a 19th-century hand-knotted Persian; an upholstered Turkish footstool; a collection of hand-painted silk Hawaiiana pillows and a carved Meerschaum pipe. Scott/Billy found the last for me, and it cost me two dollars. I knew a collector who would pay thirty in an eye-blink, and from then on, as far as I was concerned, Scott/Billy was a fellow craphound.

"You going to the auction tomorrow night?" I asked him at the checkout line.

"Wouldn't miss it," he said. He'd barely been able to contain his excitement when I told him about the Thursday night auctions and the bargains to be had there. He sure had the bug.

"Want to get together for dinner beforehand? The Rotterdam's got a good patio."

He did, and we did, and I had a glass of framboise that packed a hell of a kick and tasted like fizzy raspberry lemonade; and doorstopper fries and a club sandwich.

I had my nose in my glass when he kicked my ankle under the table.

"Look at that!"

It was Craphound in his van, cruising for a parking spot. The Lego village had been joined by a whole postmodern spaceport on the roof, with a red-and-blue castle, a football-sized flying saucer, and a clown's head with blinking eyes.

I went back to my drink and tried to get my appetite back.

"Was that an extee driving?"

"Yeah. Used to be a friend of mine."

"He's a picker?"

"Uh-huh." I turned back to my fries and tried to kill the subject.

"Do you know how he made his stake?"

"The chlorophyll thing, in Saudi Arabia."

"Sweet!" he said. "Very sweet. I've got a client who's got some secondary patents from that one. What's he go after?"

"Oh, pretty much everything," I said, resigning myself to discussing the topic after all. "But lately, the same as you—cowboys and Injuns."

He laughed and smacked his knee. "Well, what do you know? What could he possibly want with the stuff?"

"What do they want with any of it? He got started one day when we were cruising the Muskokas," I said carefully, watching his face. "Found a trunk of old cowboy things at a rummage sale. East Muskoka Volunteer Fire Department Ladies' Auxiliary." I waited for him to shout or startle. He didn't.

"Yeah? A good find, I guess. Wish I'd made it."

I didn't know what to say to that, so I took a bite of my sandwich.

Scott continued. "I think about what they get out of it a lot. There's nothing we have here that they couldn't make for themselves. I mean if they picked up and left today, we'd still be making sense of everything they gave us in a hundred years. You know, I just closed a deal for a biochemical computer that's ten thousand times faster than anything we've built out of silicon. You know what the extee took in trade? Title to a defunct fairground outside of Calgary—they shut it down ten years ago because the midway was too unsafe to ride. Doesn't that beat all? This thing is worth a billion dollars right out of the gate, I mean, within twenty-four hours of the deal closing, the seller can turn it into the GDP of Bolivia. For a crummy real-estate dog that you couldn't get five grand for!"

It always shocked me when Billy/Scott talked about his job—it was easy to forget that he was a high-powered lawyer when we were jawing and fooling around like old craphounds. I wondered if maybe he wasn't Billy the Kid; I couldn't think of any reason for him to be playing it all so close to his chest.

"What the hell is some extee going to do with a fairground?"

Craphound got a free Coke from Lisa at the check-in when he made his appearance. He bid high, but shrewdly, and never pulled $10,000 stunts. The bidders were wandering the floor, previewing the week's stock, and making notes to themselves.

I rooted through a box-lot full of old tins, and found one with a buckaroo at the Calgary Stampede, riding a bucking bronc. I picked it up and stood to inspect it. Craphound was behind me.

"Nice piece, huh?" I said to him.

"I like it very much," Craphound said, and I felt my cheeks flush.

"You're going to have some competition tonight, I think," I said, and nodded at Scott/Billy. "I think he's Billy; the one whose mother sold us — you — the cowboy trunk."

"Really?" Craphound said, and it felt like we were partners again, scoping out the competition. Suddenly I felt a knife of shame, like I was betraying Scott/Billy somehow. I took a step back.

"Jerry, I am very sorry that we argued."

I sighed out a breath I hadn't known I was holding in. "Me, too."

"They're starting the bidding. May I sit with you?"

And so the three of us sat together, and Craphound shook Scott/Billy's hand and the auctioneer started into his harangue.

It was a night for unusual occurrences. I bid on a piece, something I told myself I'd never do. It was a set of four matched Li'l Orphan Annie Ovaltine glasses, like Grandma's had been, and seeing them in the auctioneer's hand took me right back to her kitchen, and endless afternoons passed with my coloring books and weird old-lady hard candies and Liberace albums playing in the living room.

"Ten," I said, opening the bidding.

"I got ten, ten, ten, I got ten, ten, ten, who'll say twenty, who'll say twenty, twenty for the four."

Craphound waved his bidding card, and I jumped as if I'd been stung.

"I got twenty from the space cowboy, I got twenty, sir, will you say thirty?"

I waved my card.

"That's thirty to you sir."

"Forty," Craphound said.

"Fifty," I said even before the auctioneer could point back to me. An old pro, he settled back and let us do the work.

"One hundred," Craphound said.

"One fifty," I said.

The room was perfectly silent. I thought about my overextended MasterCard, and wondered if Scott/Billy would give me a loan.

"Two hundred," Craphound said.

Fine, I thought. Pay two hundred for those. I can get a set on Queen Street for thirty bucks.

The auctioneer turned to me. "The bidding stands at two. Will you say two-ten, sir?"

I shook my head. The auctioneer paused a long moment, letting me sweat over the decision to bow out.

"I have two — do I have any other bids from the floor? Any other bids? Sold, two hundred dollars, to number fifty-seven." An attendant brought Craphound the tumblers. He took them and tucked them under his seat.

I was fuming when we left. Craphound was at my elbow. I wanted to punch him — I'd never punched anyone in my life, but I wanted to punch him.

We entered the cool night air and I sucked in several lungfuls before lighting a cigarette.

"Jerry," Craphound said.

I stopped, but didn't look at him. I watched the taxis pull in and out of the garage next door instead.

"Jerry, my friend," Craphound said.

"*What?*" I said, loud enough to startle myself. Scott, beside me, jerked as well.

"We're going. I wanted to say goodbye, and to give you some things that I won't be taking with me."

"What?" I said again, Scott just a beat behind me.

"My people — we're going. It has been decided. We've gotten what we came for."

Without another word, he set off toward his van. We followed along behind, shell-shocked.

Craphound's exoskeleton executed another macro and slid the panel door aside, revealing the cowboy trunk.

"I wanted to give you this. I will keep the glasses."

"I don't understand," I said.

"You're all leaving?" Scott asked, with a note of urgency.

"It has been decided. We'll go over the next twenty-four hours."

"But *why?*" Scott said, sounding almost petulant.

"It's not something that I can easily explain. As you must know, the things we gave you were trinkets to us — almost worthless. We traded them for something that was almost worthless to you — a fair trade, you'll agree — but it's time to move on."

Craphound handed me the cowboy trunk. Holding it, I smelled the lubricant from his exoskeleton and the smell of the attic it had been mummified in before making its way into his hands. I felt like I almost understood.

"This is for me," I said slowly, and Craphound nodded encouragingly. "This is for me, and you're keeping the glasses. And I'll look at this and feel . . ."

"You understand," Craphound said, looking somehow relieved.

And I *did*. I understood that an alien wearing a cowboy hat and six-guns and giving them away was a poem and a story, and a thirtyish bachelor trying to spend half-a-month's rent on four glasses so that he could remember his grandma's kitchen was a story and a poem, and that the disused fairground outside Calgary was a story and a poem, too.

"You're craphounds!" I said. "All of you!"

Craphound smiled so I could see his gums and I put down the cowboy trunk and clapped my hands.

Scott recovered from his shock by spending the night at his office, crunching numbers, talking on the phone, and generally getting while the getting was good. He had an edge — no one else knew that they were going.

He went pro later that week, opened a chi-chi boutique on Queen Street, and hired me on as chief picker and factum factotum.

Scott was not Billy the Kid. Just another Bay Street shyster with a cowboy jones. From the way they come down and spend, there must be a million of them.

Our draw in the window is a beautiful mannequin I found, straight out of the '50s, a little boy we call The Beaver. He dresses in chaps and a sheriff's badge and six-guns and a miniature Stetson and cowboy boots with worn spurs, and rests one foot on a beautiful miniature steamer trunk whose leather is worked with cowboy motifs.

He's not for sale at any price.

TANITH LEE

JEDELLA GHOST

*Here's a new kind of ghost story, unlike any you've ever read before, fea-
turing a new kind of "ghost," one who lives in the world and yet at the
same time is isolated from it in a very peculiar way . . . perhaps forever.*

*Tanith Lee is one of the best-known and most prolific of modern fanta-
sists, with more than sixty books to her credit, including (among many
others)* The Birthgrave, Drinking Sapphire Wine, Don't Bite the Sun,
Night's Master, The Storm Lord, Sung in Shadow, Volkhavaar, Anackire,
Night's Sorceries, Black Unicorn, Days of Grass, The Blood of Roses,
Vivia, Reigning Cats and Dogs, When the Lights Go Out, Elephantasm,
and The Gods Are Thirsty, *and the collections* Tamastara, The Gorgon,
Dreams of Dark and Light, Nightshades, *and* Forests of the Night. *Her
short story "The Gorgon" won her a World Fantasy Award in 1983, and
her short story "Elle Est Trois (La Mort)" won her another World Fantasy
Award in 1984. Her brilliant collection of retold folk tales,* Red As Blood,
*was also a finalist that year, in the Best Collection category. Her most
recent book is a new novel,* Faces Under Water. *Her stories have appeared
in our First, Second, and Fourth Annual Collections. She lives with her
husband in the south of England.*

That fall morning, Luke Baynes had been staying a night with his grandmother
up on the ridge, and he was tramping back to town through the woods. It was
about an hour after sun-up, and the soft level light was caught broadcast in all the
trees, molasses-red and honey-yellow. The birds sang, and squirrels played across
the tracks. As he stepped on to the road above the river, Luke looked down into
the valley. There was an ebbing mist, sun-touched like a bridal veil, and out of
this he saw her come walking, up from the river, like a ghost. He knew at once
she was a stranger, and she was young, pale and slight in an old-fashioned long
dark dress. Her hair was dark, too, hanging down her back like a child's. As he
got closer he saw she was about 18, a young woman. She had, he said, not a pretty
face, but serene, pleasing; he liked to look at her. And she, as she came up to

him, looked straight at him, not boldly or rudely, but with an open interest. Luke took off his hat, and said, "Good morning." And the girl nodded. She said, "Is there a house near here?" Luke said there was, several houses, the town was just along the way. She nodded again, and thanked him. It was, he said, a lovely voice, all musical and lilting upward, like a smile. But then she went and sat at the roadside, where a tree had been cut and left a stump. She looked away from him now, up into the branches. It was as if there was nothing more to say. He did ask if he could assist her. She answered at once, "No, thank you." And so, after a moment, he left her there, though he was not sure he should do. But she did not appear concerned or worried.

"She had the strangest shoes," he said.

"Her shoes?" I asked. Luke had never seemed a man for noting the footware of women, or of anyone.

"They were the colours of the woods," he said, "crimson and gold and green. And—they seemed to me like they were made of glass."

"Cinderella," I said, "run off from the ball."

"But she had on both," he said, and grinned.

After this we went for coffee and cake at Millie's.

I had no doubt he had seen this woman, but I thought perhaps he had made more of her than there was. Because I am a writer people sometimes try to work spells on me—Oh, John Cross, this will interest you. You can *write* about this. It does them credit, really, to make their imaginations work. But they should take up the pen, not I. Usually, I have enough ideas of my own.

About ten, I went back to my room to work, and did not come out again until three. And then I, too, saw Luke's lady of the mist. She was standing in the square, under the old cobweb trees, looking up at the white tower of the church, on which the clock was striking the hour.

People going about were glancing at her curiously, and even the old-timers on the bench outside the stables were eying her. She was a stranger, and graceful as a lily. And sure enough, she seemed to have on sparkling stained-glass shoes.

When the clock stopped, she turned and looked around her. Do any of us look about that way? Human things are cautious, circumspect—or conversely arrogant. And she was none of these. She looked the way a child does, openly, perhaps not quite at ease, but not on guard. And then she saw—evidently she saw—the old men on the bench, Will Marks and Homer Avory and Nut Warren. She became very still, gazing at them, until they in turn grew uneasy. They did not know what to do, I could see, and Nut, who was coming on for 90 years, he turned belligerent.

I stepped out and crossed the square, and came right up to her, standing between her and the old boys.

"Welcome to our town. My name's John Cross."

"I'm Jedella," she said at once.

"I'm glad to meet you. Can I help?"

"I'm lost," she said. I could not think at once what to say. Those that are lost do not speak in this way. I knew it even then. Jedella said presently, "You see, I've lived all my life in one place, and now—here I am."

"Do you have kin here?"

"Kin?" she said. "I have no kin."

"I'm sorry. But is there someone—?"

"No," she said. "Oh, I'm tired. I'd like a drink of water. To sit down."

I said, and I thought myself even then hard and cruel, "Your shoes."

"Oh. That was my fault. I should have chosen something else."

"Are they glass?"

"I don't know," she said.

I took her straight across to Millie's, and in the big room sat her at a table, and when the coffee came, she drank it down. She seemed comfortable with coffee, and I was surprised. I had already realized, maybe, that the things of civilized life were not quite familiar to her.

Hannah returned and refilled our cups—Jedella had refused my offer of food. But as Hannah went away Jedella looked after her. The look was deep and sombre. She had eyes, Jedella, like the rivers of the Greek Hell—melancholy, and so dark.

"What's wrong with her?"

"With—?"

"With that woman who brought the coffee."

Hannah was a robust creature, about 40. She was the wife of Abel Sorrensen, and had five children, all bright and sound—a happy woman, a nice woman. I had never seen her sick or languishing.

"Hannah Sorrensen is just fine."

"But—" said Jedella. She stared at me, then the stare became a gaze. "Oh, those men outside . . ."

"The old men on the bench," I said.

Jedella said, "I'm sorry, I don't mean to be impertinent."

I said, squaring my shoulders, "I think you should see Doc McIvor. He's bound to have some plan of how to go on."

I had formed the impression she was a little mad. And, I confess, I wondered how she would react to the notion of a doctor.

But Jedella smiled at me, and then I saw what Luke had only heard in her voice. Her smile made her beautiful. For a moment I saw her as my muse. I wondered if I would fall in love with her, and feed upon her mystery. The writer can be selfish. But, in my own defence, I knew that here was something rare, precious—rich and strange.

"Of course I'll see him," she said. "I have no one, and nowhere to go. How kind you are."

What happens when the doctor is sick? An old adage to be sure. But Doc McIvor had gone to visit his niece in the city, who was expecting her first baby. Everyone knew but me. But then, I had only lived in the town for five years.

I did not want, I admit, to give Jedella, with her Lethe eyes and Cinderella shoes and heavenly smile, over to the law, so I took her to my rooming-house, and there Abigail Anchor came sweeping forth in her purple dress.

"I can give her that little room on the west side," said Abigail. "This girl has run away. I know it."

"Do you think so?" I asked.

"Oh, to be sure. Her daddy is some harsh man. Perhaps forcing her to marry. I won't sit in judgement, Mr. Cross. Indeed, Mr. Cross, you may know more than you say. But I won't ask it—"

"I don't know anything, Mrs. Anchor."

"That's as you say, Mr. Cross."

I met Luke Baynes that night in the Tavern. We had a beer. He grinned at me again.

"They're talking. Your sweetheart's stashed away at Ma Anchor's."

"Yours and mine. You saw her first."

"Then it *is* the girl with glass shoes."

"A strange one," I said. "She keeps to herself. But when I came out tonight, she was at her window and the blind was raised. She was looking along the street."

Luke said, "Don't you know anything?"

"Not a thing. Abigail has sheltered her from the goodness of her heart. Her name's Jedella."

"I don't believe," said Luke, "she's real. She's a ghost."

"I took her arm," I said. "She's real as you or I."

"What is it then?" he said.

"I think she's crazy. A little crazy. Probably someone will come after her. She can't have come far."

"But," he said, "she's—*wonderful*."

"Yes," I said. "A fascinating woman. The woman you can't have is always fascinating."

"You're too clever," he said. "I fancy going courting."

"Don't," I said. I frowned into my drink. "Don't."

Two weeks passed, and Jedella lived in the room on the west side of the Anchor house. She gave no trouble, and I had had a word with Abigail about the rent. I believe Abigail helped with any female things that Jedella might have needed, and certainly, I was presented with a bill before too long. My trade had brought me moderate success, and I did not flinch.

Otherwise, I saw no reason to interfere. I gathered from Abigail that Jedella did not much wish to go out, yet seemed quite well. She ate her meals in private, and enjoyed the services of the house. Now and then I noted Jedella at her window, gazing along the street. Once I lifted my hand, but she did not respond. I let it go at that.

Of course, word had got around about the unknown young woman. I was sometimes pestered, but knowing next to nothing myself, could be of little assistance.

Did I want to draw Jedella out? Rather, I was inclined to avoid her. Real life that takes the form of a story, or appears to, is so often disappointing. Or, if one learns some gem, must one become a traitor who can no longer be trusted with anything? I prefer to invent, and that keeps me busy enough.

Luke did try to introduce himself to the woman on the west side. He took her flowers one afternoon, and a box of sweets in a green bow another. But, Jedella apparently seemed only amazed. She did not respond as a woman should, hopefully a flirtatious, willing woman. He was baffled, and retreated, to the relief of the two or three young ladies of the town who had such hopes of him, some day.

On the last Friday of that second week, just as I had finished a long story for the *Post*, I heard at Millie's that Homer Avory had died in his bed. He was nearly 80, which for the town is quite a youngster, and his daughter was in a rage, it seemed, for she had always loved him and had been planning a birthday dinner.

Everyone went to a funeral then, and presently I heard it was fixed for Tuesday. I looked out my black suit with a sensation of the droll and the sad. My father had once warned me, "You don't feel a death, John, not truly, till you start to feel your own." He was 50 when he said this, and he died two years after, so I may not argue. But I felt it was a shame about Homer, and about his daughter, who was 60 herself, and had lost her husband ten months before to a fever.

On Monday evening I was reading some books that had come in the mail, when a light knock sounded on my door.

It was not Abigail, evidently, who thundered, nor Luke, who burst in. I went to see, and there stood the apparition called Jedella, still in her dark dress, but with a new pair of simple shoes. Her hair was done up on her head.

"Good evening, Miss Jedella. Can I help you?"

"Mr. Cross," she said, "something is happening tomorrow."

"Tomorrow? Oh, do you mean poor old Homer's funeral?"

"That," she said, "is what Abigail Anchor called it."

"Abigail? Well, what else. A burial, a funeral."

She stared straight at me. She said, still and low, "But what is that?"

Abigail had her rules, but it was just light. I drew Jedella into the room and left the door an inch ajar.

I made her sit down in my comfortable chair, and moved the books.

"How do you mean, Miss Jedella?"

She seemed for a moment disturbed. Then she composed her pale face and said, "They say the—old man—has *died*."

"He has."

"Was he one of the three men I saw in the square that day?"

"Yes, just so."

"He has some terrible illness," she said. She looked about distractedly. "Am I right?"

This unnerved me. I could not put it together. I recalled, I had thought her slightly insane. I said, quietly, "Unfortunately, he was old, and so he died. But, please believe, he had no ailment. He passed away peacefully in his sleep, I gather."

"But what do you mean?" she said.

"He's dead," I answered. "I'm afraid it happens." I had intended irony, but she gazed at me with such pathos, I felt myself colour, as if I had insulted her. I did not know what to say next. She spoke first.

"This funeral, what is it?"

"Jedella," I said firmly, "do you say you don't know what a funeral is?"

"No," said Jedella, "I have no idea."

If I had been three years younger, I suspect I would have thought myself the victim or some game. But peculiar things happen. Oddities, differences.

I sat down in the other chair.

"When a man dies, we put him in the earth. If you are religious, you reckon he waits there for the last trumpet, which summons him up to God."

"In the earth," she said. "But how can he stand it—is it some punishment?"

"He's dead," I replied, like stone. "He won't know."

"How can he not know?"

In the window, the light of day was going out. And it came to me, as sometimes it did when a child, that perhaps this was the end, and the sun would never return.

In ten minutes or so, Abigail's boy would sound the bell for dinner. Jedella did not join the communal table.

"Jedella," I said, "I can't help you. It's too profound a question for me. Can I ask the minister to call on you?"

She said, "Why?"

"He may be able to assist you."

She said, looking at me, her countenance bewildered and yet serene even now, as if *she* had seen that I and all the world were mad—"This is a terrible place. I wish that I could help you, but I don't know how. How can you bear it, Mr. Cross, when you witness such suffering?"

I smiled. "I agree, it can be difficult. But then, it could have been worse. We all come to it."

She said, "To what?"

The bell rang. Perhaps it was early, or I had misjudged. I said, "Well, you're very young, Jedella." Some phantom of my father's words, perhaps.

But Jedella went on looking at me with her Lethe eyes. She said, flatly, "What does that mean?"

"Now this is silly. You keep asking me that. I mean that you're young. About sixteen, maybe."

I confess, I tried to flatter, making her a little less than she appeared to be. One should always be careful with a woman's age, one way or the other. In those days 16 was the dividing line; now it is more 20.

But Jedella, who Luke had thought a ghost, stared into my face. She was not flattered.

She said, "Sixteen years do you mean? Of course not."

"Sixteen, eighteen, whatever it may be."

Outside, my fellow boarders were going down the stairs; they would hear us talking and realize that John Cross had the woman in his room.

Jedella stood up. The last glimmer of light was behind her, and played about her slender shape, making her seem suddenly thin and despoiled. Abigail must have persuaded her to put up her hair. She was a shadow, and all at once, the shadow of someone else, as if I had seen through her—but to what?

"I am," she said, "sixty-five years of age."

I laughed. But it was a laugh of fright. For I could see her there like a little old lady, five years on from Homer's daughter.

"I'm going down to my meal, Jedella. Are you willing to come?"

"No," she said.

She turned, moved; the new lamplight from beyond the door caught her. She was 18. She went out on to the landing, and away up the house.

What we ate that night I have no notion. Someone—Clark, I think—regaled us with jokes, and everyone guffawed, but for Miss Pim, and Abigail, who did not approve. I chuckled, too—but God knows why. Did I even hear what was said?

In the end we remembered, Homer was to go into the ground tomorrow, and a silence fell. I recall how Abigail lighted a candle in the window, a touching gesture, old superstition, but kind and sweet, to guide a soul home.

I had mentioned nothing of what Jedella had said to me, and no one had ventured to ask what she and I had had to converse on.

In my room, I walked about. I lit the lamp and picked up my books, and put them down.

Over in the west end of the house, she was, that girl with dark hair, who had come up from the morning mist, like a ghost.

In God's name, what had she been talking of? What did she suggest? What did she want?

I have said, if I had been a few years younger, I would have thought it a game. And, 40 years older, as now I am, I might have deemed it quite proper, to go across the house and knock on the door. Times change, and customs with them. It was not possible then.

At length I went to bed, and lay in the dark, with all the gentle quiet of that place about me, my haven from the city. But I could not rest. She said she did not know what a funeral was, she inquired how he could bear it, Homer, going into the ground. She told me she was 65 years old.

She was mad. She had come from the river in stained glass shoes, and she was crazy.

I dreamed I was at my father's burial, which once I had been, but no one else was there, save for Jedella. And she looked down into the pit of black earth, and she said to me, "Will you leave him here?"

I woke with tears on my face. I had not wanted to leave him there. Not my father, that lovable and good man, who had given me so much. But surely it had not been my father any more, down there in the dark?

The first light was coming, and I got up and sat by the window. The town was calm and the birds sang. Far off beyond the woods and the forests of pines, I could see, it was so clear, the transparent aurora of the mountains.

I knocked on Jedella's door about 9.30 in the morning, and when she opened it, I said, "Will you walk with me?" I wanted no more clandestine meetings in the rooms.

The funeral was at two. Outside there was nothing out of the ordinary going on. The trees had on their scalding full colour. The stores were open, and a dog or two were nosing down the street. Jedella looked at all this, in a sad, silent way. She reminded me of a widow.

We went into the square, and sat on the vacant bench under the cobweb trees.

"I want you to tell me, Jedella, where you come from. If you will."

She said, "Beyond the woods. Up in the pines. A house there."

"How far away?" I said. I was baffled.

"I don't know. It took me a day to reach this town. A day, and the night before."

"Why did you come here?"

"I didn't know what else to do. I didn't mean to come. I was only walking."

"Why then did you leave the house—the house in the pines?"

"They had all gone," she said. For a moment she looked the way I have only seen human things look after some great disaster, the wreck of a train, the random horror of a war. I did not know it then. What she spoke of was a terror beyond her grasp. It had hurt her, but it had no logic, like the acts of God.

"Who had gone?"

"The people who were there with me. Often they did, of course, but not all at once. The house was empty. I looked."

"Tell me about the house."

Then she smiled. It was the lovely, lilting smile. This memory made her happy.

"It was where I was, always."

"Where you were born?" I asked.

As if from far off, she smiled on at me. "The first thing I remember," she said.

She sat on the bench, and I realized absently that in her old-fashioned dress, she was clad as an old lady, like Homer's daughter or Elsie Baynes, or some other elder woman of our town. The air was sweet and crisp and summer had died. I said, "I'd like to hear."

"It's a big white house," she said, "and there are lots of rooms. I was usually in the upper house, though sometimes I went down. All around was a high wall, but I could see the tops of the trees. There were trees inside the garden, too, and I walked there every day, except in winter. Then it was too cold, when the snow was down."

"Who was in the house with you?"

"Many people. Oh, lots of people, Mr. Cross. They looked after me."

Curiously I said, as if encouraging a child. "Who did you like the best?"

"I liked them all—but you see, they didn't stay for long. No one ever stayed."

She was sad once more, but in a deeper, softer way. She was indeed like a child, that was what I finally saw then, a child in an old lady's dress, which fitted. "When I was a girl," she said, oddly mimicking my thought, "I used to be upset by it, the going away. But in the end, I knew that it had to be."

"Why did it have to be?" I asked, blindly.

"That was their lives. But I remained. That was mine."

"Tell me more about the house," I said.

"Oh, it was only a house. It was where I lived. Some of the rooms were large, and some, my bedroom, for example, quite small."

"What did you do there?"

"I read the books, and I painted on paper. And I played the piano. There was always something to do."

"Your father and mother," I said.

Jedella glanced at me. "What do you mean?"

The sun was warm on my face and hands, and yet the air was cool. A blue shadow descended from the tower of the church. Something had hold of me now, it held me back. I said, "Well, tell me about something that you enjoyed especially."

She laughed. Her laugh was so pretty, so truthful and young. "There were a great many things. I used to imagine places, places I'd never been — cities of towers from the books I'd read, and rivers and seas. And animals, too. There are lions and tigers and bears, aren't there?"

"So I believe."

"Yes, I believe it, too. Have you ever seen them?"

"In cages," I said.

She looked startled a moment. But then she brushed that away from her like a fallen leaf. "I longed to see them, and they said, one day."

I said, "Did they tell you when?"

"No. I suppose it was meant to be now. After I left the house."

"Then they told you you must leave?"

"Oh no. But when they were gone, the doors were all open. And the big door in the wall, that, too."

I was trying now, quite hard, to follow along with her, not to delay or confuse by protestations. I thought how, when I had spoken of her being born, she had had that look of the polite guest at the party, when you say something he does not understand, but is too nice to debate on.

"The door had never been open before?"

"No, never."

"Did — they — say why not?"

"I never asked, because, you see, it was the way I lived. I didn't need anything else."

She was young — or was she young? — yet surely there had been some yearning, like her wish to see the animals from the books. The young feel they are prisoners even when they are not, or not decidedly. Something came to me. I said, "Did you see pictures in your books of lion cubs?"

"Oh yes," she said.

I said, "And once, you were a child."

"Of course."

Above us the clock struck — it must have done so before. Now it was noon.

Jedella looked about her. She said, "Something's very wrong here. Can't you tell me what it is?"

"It's the way we are, the way *we* live," I said.

She sighed. She said, and there was that in her voice that filled me with a sort of primeval fear, "Is it like this everywhere?"

I said, intuitively, "Yes, Jedella."

Then she said, "Abigail Anchor brought some books up to me. It was a kindness. I didn't understand them."

"In what way?"

"Things happen in those books — that don't happen."

I could have said this might be true of much poor fiction. But clearly she did not imply this.

"You had books in your house," I said. "What about those books?"

"Parts had been cut away," she said. I said nothing, but as if I had, she added, "I used to ask where those pieces were. But they said the books had been there a long time, that was all."

I said, blindly, as before, "For example, the lion cubs were there, and they grew up into lions. But you didn't know how they had arrived there." She was silent. I said, "And how long did the lions live, Jedella? Did the books say?"

Jedella the ghost, turned her dark eyes on me. She was no longer a temptation, not my muse. She said, "Always, of course. To live — is to live."

"For ever?"

She said and she did nothing. I felt my heart beat in a wild random crescendo, and all at once that peaceful square, that town where I had come to be quiet, was rushing all apart, like a jigsaw, broken. Then it settled. My heart settled.

"Will you come," I said, "to Homer's funeral?"

"If you think so," she said.

I got up and offered her my arm. "We'll take some lunch in Millie's. Then we'll go on."

Her hand was light on me, as a leaf of the fall.

She was quiet and nearly motionless all through the ceremony, and though she looked down at his old, creased, vacant face, before the coffin was closed, she made no fuss about it.

But when everything was done, and we stood alone on the path, she said, "I used to watch the squirrels playing, in the trees and along the tops of the wall. They were black squirrels. I used to throw them little bits of cake. One day, John Cross, I saw a squirrel lying there on the grass in the garden. It didn't move. It was so still I was able to stroke its side. Then someone came from the house. I think it was a man called Orlen. And he picked up the squirrel. He said to me, 'Poor thing, it's fallen and stunned itself. Sometimes they do. Don't fret, Jedella. I'll take it back to its tree, and it will get better.'"

Over the lawn, Homer's daughter walked, leaning on the arm of her son. She was rubbing at her face angrily muttering about the meat dishes and the sweet pie she had been going to make for the birthday. Her son held his hat across his middle, head bowed, troubled the way we often are at grief we cannot share.

"So the squirrel was stunned," I said.

"Yes. And later he pointed it out to me, running along the wall."

"That same squirrel."

"He told me that it was."

"And you think now that Homer is only stunned, and we've thrown him down into the ground, and now they'll cover him with earth, so he can't get out."

We stood, two respectful and well-behaved figures. Her life had been an acceptance, and she was coming to accept even now the unacceptable.

"Jedella, will you describe for me very carefully the way you came here, from your house in the pines?"

"If you want."

"It would be a great help," I said. "You see, I mean to go there."

"I can't go back," she said.

I thought she was like Eve, cast out of Eden because she had failed to eat the Forbidden fruit.

"No, I won't make you. But I think I must. There may be some clue to all of this."

She did not argue with me. She had begun to accept also her utter difference, and that she was outnumbered. She guessed something had been done to her; as I did. She had ceased to debate, and would never resist.

When I first took up my life here, I went frequently to walk or ride in the wooded country. Then I got down to my work and adventured less. To ride out on this cold bright morning was no penance, though I had grown a little stiff, and guessed I should feel it later, which I did. The horse was a pretty mare by the name of May.

We went with care along the route Jedella had outlined, even drawing—she had a fair hand with a pencil—landmarks I might look for. Beyond the road we climbed into the woods and so up the hill called Candy Crag, and over into the pines.

I was high up by nightfall, and I could feel the cold blowing down from the distant snow-lined mountains. I thought, as I made my camp, I might hear a wolf call up on the heights, but there was only stillness and the swarm of the stars. Such great calm is in those places and the sense of Infinity. Some men can only live there, but for me, I should be lost. I like the little things. This was enough, a night or two, a day or two, up so close to the sky. At dawn I went on.

A couple of times I saw my fellow humans. A trapper with his gun, a man far down on the river. Both glimpsed me, and hailed me, and I them. For the rest the wild things of the woods came and went, a porcupine, a deer, the birds, the insects. May stepped mildly through their landscape, her skin shining like a flame. I spoke to her now and then, and sang her a few songs.

I found the house with no trouble in the afternoon of that second day. Jedella had travelled more quickly than I, unless she had lost track of time.

You could see the mountains from there very well, a vast white battlement rising from the pelt of the pines. But near at hand, the forest was thick, so dense we had to pick our way. The house was in a clearing, as Jedella had told me, shut round with its tall white wall. It had a strange look, as if it had no proper architecture, no style of anywhere at all. Like boxes put together, and roofs put on, and windows set in. Something a child had made, but a child without fantasies.

The gate was open, and the sunlight slanted down through the trees and showed me a man standing there, on the path. He wore a white suit, and was smoking a cigarette. I had become used to the pipes and chewing-tobacco of my town. And somehow I had anticipated—God knows what. He was a very old man, too, but spare and upright, with a mane of thick, whitish hair, and eyebrows dark as bands of iron.

He lifted his hand, as he saw me. And this was not the lonely greeting of the trapper or the river man. I could see, he had expected me, or someone. Had he come there to wait for me?

I am not given to drama, except sometimes when I write, and can have it there on my own terms. But I eased myself off the horse and undid my saddlebag and took out the two brightly coloured shoes that looked as if they were made of glass, and holding these out, I walked up to him.

"Jedella's slippers," he said. "Did she get so far in them?"

"Quite far."

"They're not glass," he said, "something I fashioned, when I was younger. A sort of resin."

"I'd hoped," I said, "you would come and fetch her."

"No, I can't do that. I haven't time now. It had to end, and she has to go on as best she can. She wouldn't know me now, in any case. She saw me for five or six years, when she was a child, and I was in my twenties."

"That would make her old," I said.

"Sixty-five is her age."

"So she said."

"And of course," he said, "it can't be, for she is eighteen or nineteen, a girl."

Behind me, May shook her amber head, as if in warning, and a bird hammered a moment on the trunk of a tree.

"I came here," I said, "hoping to find out."

"Yes, I know it. And I shall tell you. I am Jedediah Goëste, and for now this house is mine. Will you step inside?"

I went with him up the path, leading May, who I settled in a sunny place. The trees were all around inside the wall, the trees where the black squirrels played. I had been struck by his name—Scandinavian, perhaps, and its affinity of sound to what Luke and I had come to call her: Miss Ghost. *Jedediah*, too, the father's name, and the daughter taking a feminized version, Jedella. Was it so simple? For yes, if he had been in his 20s, he would be near his 90s now, and she would be 65.

Inside the door was an open room, white-walled, quite pleasant, with ornaments and pictures, and with a large fireplace where some logs and cones were burning. Hot coffee stood on a table. Had he known the hour of my coming? No, that was too fanciful. It seemed to me I had better be as careful as I had been when riding through the denseness of the pines. Something strange there was, but not all of it could or need be.

A wide staircase ran up from the room and above was a sort of gallery. I noticed another man standing there, and Jedediah Goëste gestured to him quietly, and the man went away.

"My servant. He won't disturb us."

"Is that Orlen?" I said.

"Oh, no. Orlen is long gone. But Orlen was a favourite of Jedella's, I believe, when she was still a child. It was a pity they all had to leave her. She used to cry in the beginning. She cried when I left her. But later, they told me, she was philosophical. She had grown accustomed."

I had given him in turn my name, and he had taken the privilege of the old to call me at once *John*. We sat down in two large velvet armchairs, and I drank some of the coffee, hot and sweet and good.

"I have come back here," he said, "to die. It's comfortable for me here, and I have all I want. A few months, no more."

I said, "Then shouldn't you have kept her here?"

"She was given, implicitly, the choice. She might have remained, although I didn't think she would. If she had been here when I returned, I would, I think, have had to pretend to be someone else. And even then, the shock—"

"Your age. But it's your death that was the reason for letting her go."

"Yes. I can't anymore manage things, you see. The experiment is over."

"Experiment," I said.

"Come now," he said, "I believe you grasp it, John. I truly believe you do."

"I've read rather widely," I said. "Years ago, I came across the legend of the Buddha." Goëste folded his hands. He smiled his old strong teeth. "Buddha was originally a prince," I said, "and they resolved to keep all ugly things from him— poverty, disease, old age and death. He saw only beauty. Until one day something went wrong, and he found out the truth."

Jedediah Goëste said. "You see, John, I began to think of it even when I was quite young. From the start, everything comes our way. Even when they tell us lies, the facts are still before us. There is a moment when we must work it out. The old lady in the mauve dress with her hands crippled by rheumatics. The dead dog the cart ran over. The bird shot for the table. In Europe in the Middle Ages they fixed a skull over the church door. Under that skull was written, *Remember thou shall be as me.*" He leaned back. His eyes were black, like hers, but, paler with the watery encroachment of old age. "How does the infant learn?" he said. "He copies. The sounds from the mouths that become language. The gestures that become manners. The opinions that he will either adopt or rebel against. And he learns that the sun rises and sets, and as the days and the years go by, he grows, he changes. All around, the lesson is we grow to our fullness, but after that we decline. From the summit of that hill, the path leads downwards. Down to weakness and sickness, down to the first lines and wrinkles, the stiffening and the lessening. Down to the bowed spine and the loss of teeth and sight and hearing. Down into the grave that awaits us all. *Remember thou shall be as me.* We are taught from the commencement, and reminded over and over."

He pointed at the rug before the fire, where I had laid the glass shoes that were not.

"I made those, to show it could be done. I've done many things like that. I had money, John, and time, and a brain. And, I confess, here and there I have experimented with living things—not to hurt them, never that. But to see. Always, to see."

"Jedella," I said, "was never told about old age, or death. Illness was for some reason mentioned, but as something that no longer existed. Pages were cut from books. The people of the house were always young and fit, and when it became likely they would cease to be, they were sent away. And when a squirrel died under her window, Orlen told her it was stunned, and took it back to its tree, and later he showed her the squirrel running on the wall."

"A girl came to me in the city," said Jedediah Goëste, "it was shocking, I had given her a child. She didn't want it. So she was paid, and I took the child to myself. That was Jedella. She was a baby—younger than Buddha, who I believe was twelve—too young to have learned anything at all. It was so perfect, John, and I had the means. I brought her here, and for those first years I was her friend. And after, of necessity, I had gone, those who came after me carried on my work. They were well-recompensed, and clever. There were no mistakes. She grew up in a world where no one sickened or aged or died. Where *nothing* died, and no death was seen, not even the dead animals for her food. Not even the leaves of the trees."

It was true. She had seen only the pines, renewal but not obvious slough—and then she had come from the open door and down into the woods of fall, where ruby and yellow and wine, the death descends from every tree.

"*Now* she sees it," I said. "She saw it as sickness to begin with. Or something that made no sense. But she's turning towards the terrible fact, Mr Goëste, that all things perish."

"Recollect," he said, "that she is sixty-five years old. She's like a girl. So many lessons, all the same. Can they be unlearned?"

I stood up. I was not angry, I have no word for what I was. But I could no longer sit in the chair before the fire nor drink the fragrant coffee, nor look in that old man's face that was so strong and sure.

"You've acted God, Mr Goëste."

"Have I? How can we presume to know how God has acted, or would act?"

"You think you've made her eternally young. You think you've made her *immortal*."

"I may have done," he said.

I answered him, "In a world where all things come to an end—what will become of her?"

"You will take care of her now," he said, so easily, so gently. "Your quiet little town. Good people. Kind people."

"But her pain," I said, "her *pain*."

Jedediah Goëste looked at me with her look. He was innocent, in her way. There was no chance against such innocence. "Pain, I think, is after all in the unfathomable jurisdiction of God. I've never been able to believe that mankind, for all its faults, could devise so horrible and so complex a thing."

"She never questioned?" I asked.

"Questions spring from doubt. Now she questions, I imagine?"

A log cracked in the fire. There was a small ache in my back I would not have had a year ago.

"If you wish, I should be happy for you to be my guest tonight, John."

I thanked him and made some excuse. Even then, even there, the etiquette of my father stayed with me. Those first lessons.

As I reached the door, Jedediah Goëste said one final thing to me: "I'm glad that she found her way to you."

But she had not found her way to me, nor to anyone, how could she? She had not found her way.

. . .

The years have passed in the town, and it has been faithful to Jedella. She has been protected as best we might. She has her little house behind the church, and her piano that we sent for from the city, her paints, her books—all kinds of books now. She reads for days on end, with her clear dark eyes. Sometimes she will read something out for me when even my glasses fail to help with the small print.

More people have come to the town with time, and for them she is a mystery that, largely, they are indifferent to. The new creatures of the world are very self-involved and this has taken away some of the curiosity, the prying, that came to us so naturally. But then, the avalanches of war, and fear of war, the wonderful inventions that cause so much harm and confusion and noise, all these things change us, the children of this other world, much more so.

Luke died in a war. I have said elsewhere, and will not here, what I did there. Many were lost, or lost themselves. But others take those places. I was even famous for a year, and travelled in the cities and on other continents, and grew tired and came home. And there the town was in its misty morning silence that the new cacophony cannot quite break.

That was a morning like this one, a fall morning, with the colours on the trees, and the new restaurant, where Millie's used to be, was having its windows washed.

But today the restaurant is old and familiar, and instead I passed Jedella's house, and she came out and I knew I should go in, just for an hour, maybe, and drink coffee, and eat her chocolate cake which she vaunts, and rightly so.

I went with caution over that road, for now there are sometimes motor-bikes upon it, and as I did I saw her waiting, pale and slender, a girl, with her hair cut short and permed and a touch of lipstick on her mouth.

She touched my arm at her door.

"Look, John," she said.

My eyes are not so good as I would like, but there in the pure, sheer sunlight, I did my best to see. She pointed at her cheek, and then, she put one finger to her hair.

"Is it your powder, Jedella? Yes, your hair looks grand."

And then I did see, as she stood smiling up at me, her eyes full of the morning, of the new beginning of all things, I did see what she had found to show me with such pride. The little crease that had grown in her cheek. The single bright silver hair.

Taklamakan

BRUCE STERLING

One of the most powerful and innovative talents to enter SF in recent decades, a man with a rigorously worked out and aesthetically convincing vision of what the future may have in store for humanity, Bruce Sterling as yet may still be better known to the cognoscenti than to the SF-reading population at large, in spite of a recent Hugo win. If you look behind the scenes, though, you will find him everywhere, and he had almost as much to do—as writer, critic, propagandist, aesthetic theorist, and tireless polemicist—with the shaping and evolution of SF in the eighties and nineties as Michael Moorcock did with the shaping of SF in the sixties. It is not for nothing that many of the other writers of the eighties and nineties refer to him, half ruefully, half admiringly, as "Chairman Bruce."

Bruce Sterling sold his first story in 1976. By the end of the eighties, he had established himself—with a series of stories set in his exotic Shaper/Mechanist future, with novels such as the complex and Stapeldonian Schismatrix and the well-received Islands in the Net (as well as with his editing of the influential cyberpunk anthology Mirrorshades and the infamous critical magazine Cheap Truth)—as perhaps the prime driving force behind the revolutionary cyberpunk movement in science fiction (rivaled for that title only by his friend and collaborator, William Gibson), and also as one of the best new "hard-science" writers to enter the field in some time. His other books include a critically acclaimed nonfiction study of First Amendment issues in the world of computer networking, The Hacker Crackdown: Law and Disorder on the Electronic Frontier; the novels The Artificial Kid, Involution Ocean, Heavy Weather, Holy Fire; a novel in collaboration with William Gibson, The Difference Engine; and the landmark collections Crystal Express and Globalhead. His most recent books include the omnibus collection, (containing the novel Schismatrix as well as most of his Shaper/Mechanist stories) Schismatrix Plus, and a new novel, Distraction. Coming up is a new collection, A Good Old-Fashioned Future. His story "Bicycle Repairman" earned him a long-overdue Hugo in 1997. His stories have appeared in our First, Second, Third, Fourth, Fifth, Sixth, Seventh, Eighth, Eleventh, and Fourteenth Annual Collections. He lives with his family in Austin, Texas. His Web site is at http://www.well.com/conf/mirrorshades.

In the fast-paced and ingenious story that follows, he takes us along with *two ambitious freelance, high-tech spies who have the grit and chutzpah to penetrate a bizarre lost world no outsider has ever seen before, where strange dangers and even stranger wonders await them—some of which may well turn out to be fatal!*

A bone-dry frozen wind tore at the earth outside, its lethal howling cut to a muffled moan. Katrinko and Spider Pete were camped deep in a crevice in the rock, wrapped in furry darkness. Pete could hear Katrinko breathing, with a light rattle of chattering teeth. The neuter's yeasty armpits smelled like nutmeg.

Spider Pete strapped his shaven head into his spex.

Outside their puffy nest, the sticky eyes of a dozen gelcams splayed across the rock, a sky-eating web of perception. Pete touched a stud on his spex, pulled down a glowing menu, and adjusted his visual take on the outside world.

Flying powder tumbled through the yardangs like an evil fog. The crescent moon and a billion desert stars, glowing like pixelated bruises, wheeled above the eerie wind-sculpted landscape of the Taklamakan. With the exceptions of Antarctica, or maybe the deep Sahara—locales Pete had never been paid to visit—this central Asian desert was the loneliest, most desolate place on Earth.

Pete adjusted parameters, etching the landscape with a busy array of false colors. He recorded an artful series of panorama shots, and tagged a global positioning fix onto the captured stack. Then he signed the footage with a cryptographic time-stamp from a passing NAFTA spy-sat.

1/15/2052 05:24:01.

Pete saved the stack onto a gelbrain. This gelbrain was a walnut-sized lump of neural biotech, carefully grown to mimic the razor-sharp visual cortex of an American bald eagle. It was the best, most expensive piece of photographic hardware that Pete had ever owned. Pete kept the thing tucked in his crotch.

Pete took a deep and intimate pleasure in working with the latest federally subsidized spy gear. It was quite the privilege for Spider Pete, the kind of privilege that he might well die for. There was no tactical use in yet another spy-shot of the chill and empty Taklamakan. But the tagged picture would prove that Katrinko and Pete had been here at the appointed rendezvous. Right here, right now. Waiting for the man.

And the man was overdue.

During their brief professional acquaintance, Spider Pete had met the Lieutenant Colonel in a number of deeply unlikely locales. A parking garage in Pentagon City. An outdoor seafood restaurant in Cabo San Lucas. On the ferry to Staten Island. Pete had never known his patron to miss a rendezvous by so much as a microsecond.

The sky went dirty white. A sizzle, a sparkle, a zenith full of stink. A screaming-streaking-tumbling. A nasty thunderclap. The ground shook hard.

"Dang," Pete said.

They found the Lieutenant Colonel just before eight in the morning. Pieces of his landing pod were violently scattered across half a kilometer.

Katrinko and Pete skulked expertly through a dirty yellow jumble of wind-grooved boulders. Their camou gear switched coloration moment by moment, to match the landscape and the incidental light.

Pete pried the mask from his face, inhaled the thin, pitiless, metallic air, and spoke aloud. "That's our boy all right. Never missed a date."

The neuter removed her mask and fastidiously smeared her lips and gums with silicone anti-evaporant. Her voice fluted eerily over the insistent wind. "Space-defense must have tracked him on radar."

"Nope. If they'd hit him from orbit, he'd really be spread all over. . . . No something happened to him really close to the ground." Pete pointed at a violent scattering of cracked ochre rock. "See, check out how that stealth-pod hit and tumbled. It didn't catch fire till after the impact."

With the absent ease of a gecko, the neuter swarmed up a three-story-high boulder. She examined the surrounding forensic evidence at length, dabbing carefully at her spex controls. She then slithered deftly back to earth. "There was no anti-aircraft fire, right? No interceptors flyin' round last night."

"Nope. Heck, there's no people around here in a space bigger than Delaware."

The neuter looked up. "So what do you figure, Pete?"

"I figure an accident," said Pete.

"A what?"

"An accident. A lot can go wrong with a covert HALO insertion."

"Like what, for instance?"

"Well, G-loads and stuff. System malfunctions. Maybe he just blacked out."

"He was a federal military spook, and you're telling me he *passed out?*" Katrinko daintily adjusted her goggled spex with gloved and bulbous fingertips. "Why would that matter anyway? He wouldn't fly a spacecraft with his own hands, would he?"

Pete rubbed at the gummy line of his mask, easing the prickly indentation across one dark, tattooed cheek. "I kinda figure he would, actually. The man was a pilot. Big military prestige thing. Flyin' in by hand, deep in Sphere territory, covert insertion, way behind enemy lines. . . . That'd really be something to brag about, back on the Potomac."

The neuter considered this sour news without apparent resentment. As one of the world's top technical climbers, Katrinko was a great connoisseur of pointless displays of dangerous physical skill. "I can get behind that." She paused. "Serious bad break, though."

They resealed their masks. Water was their greatest lack, and vapor exhalation was a problem. They were recycling body-water inside their suits, topped off with a few extra cc's they'd obtained from occasional patches of frost. They'd consumed the last of the trail-goop and candy from their glider shipment three long days ago.

They hadn't eaten since. Still, Pete and Katrinko were getting along pretty well, living off big subcutaneous lumps of injected body fat.

More through habit than apparent need, Pete and Katrinko segued into evidence-removal mode. It wasn't hard to conceal a HALO stealth pod. The spycraft was radar-transparent and totally biodegradable. In the bitter wind and cold of the Taklamakan, the bigger chunks of wreckage had already gone all brown and crispy, like the shed husks of locusts. They couldn't scrape up every physical trace, but they'd surely get enough to fool aerial surveillance.

The Lieutenant Colonel was extremely dead. He'd come down from the heavens in his full NAFTA military power-armor, a leaping, brick-busting, lightning-spewing exoskeleton, all acronyms and input jacks. It was powerful, elaborate gear, of an entirely different order than the gooey and fibrous street tech of the two urban intrusion freaks.

But the high-impact crash had not been kind to the armored suit. It had been crueler still to the bone, blood, and tendon housed inside.

Pete bagged the larger pieces with a heavy heart. He knew that the Lieutenant Colonel was basically no good: deceitful, ruthlessly ambitious, probably crazy. Still, Pete sincerely regretted his employer's demise. After all, it was precisely those qualities that had led the Lieutenant Colonel to recruit Spider Pete in the first place.

Pete also felt sincere regret for the gung-ho, clear-eyed young military widow, and the two little redheaded kids in Augusta, Georgia. He'd never actually met the widow or the little kids, but the Lieutenant Colonel was always fussing about them and showing off their photos. The Lieutenant Colonel had been a full fifteen years younger than Spider Pete, a rosy-cheeked cracker kid really, never happier than when handing over wads of money, nutty orders, and expensive covert equipment to people whom no sane man would trust with a burnt-out match. And now here he was in the cold and empty heart of Asia, turned to jam within his shards of junk.

Katrinko did the last of the search-and-retrieval while Pete dug beneath a ledge with his diamond hand-pick, the razored edges slashing out clods of shale.

After she'd fetched the last blackened chunk of their employer, Katrinko perched birdlike on a nearby rock. She thoughtfully nibbled a piece of the pod's navigation console. "This gelbrain is good when it dries out, man. Like trail mix, or a fortune cookie."

Pete grunted. "You might be eating part of him, y'know."

"Lotta good carbs and protein there, too."

They stuffed a final shattered power-jackboot inside the Colonel's makeshift cairn. The piled rock was there for the ages. A few jets of webbing and thumbnail dabs of epoxy made it harder than a brick wall.

It was noon now, still well below freezing, but as warm as the Taklamakan was likely to get in January. Pete sighed, dusted sand from his knees and elbows, stretched. It was hard work, cleaning up; the hardest part of intrusion work, because it was the stuff you had to do after the thrill was gone. He offered Katrinko the end of a fiber-optic cable, so that they could speak together without using radio or removing their masks.

Pete waited until she had linked in, then spoke into his mike. "So we head on back to the glider now, right?"

The neuter looked up, surprised. "How come?"

"Look, Trink, this guy that we just buried was the actual spy in this assignment. You and me, we were just his gophers and backup support. The mission's an abort."

"But we're searching for a giant, secret, rocket base."

"Yeah, sure we are."

"We're supposed to find this monster high-tech complex, break in, and record all kinds of crazy top secrets that nobody but the mandarins have ever seen. That's a totally hot assignment, man."

Pete sighed. "I admit it's very high-concept, but I'm an old guy now, Trink. I need the kind of payoff that involves some actual money."

Katrinko laughed. "But Pete! It's a *starship!* A whole fleet of 'em, maybe! Secretly built in the desert, by Chinese spooks and Japanese engineers!"

Pete shook his head. "That was all paranoid bullshit that the flyboy made up, to get himself a grant and a field assignment. He was tired of sitting behind a desk in the basement, that's all."

Katrinko folded her lithe and wiry arms. "Look, Pete, you saw those briefings just like me. You saw all those satellite shots. The traffic analysis, too. The Sphere people are up to something way big out here."

Pete gazed around him. He found it painfully surreal to endure this discussion amid a vast and threatening tableau of dust-hazed sky and sand-etched mudstone gullies. "They built something big here once, I grant you that. But I never figured the Colonel's story for being very likely."

"What's so unlikely about it? The Russians had a secret rocket base in the desert a hundred years ago. American deserts are full of secret mil-spec stuff and space-launch bases. So now the Asian Sphere people are up to the same old game. It all makes sense."

"No, it makes no sense at all. Nobody's space-racing to build any starships. Starships aren't a space race. It takes four hundred years to fly to the stars. Nobody's gonna finance a major military project that'll take four hundred years to pay off. Least of all a bunch of smart and thrifty Asian economic-warfare people."

"Well, they're sure building *something.* Look, all we have to do is find the complex, break in, and document some stuff. We can do that! People like us, we never needed any federal bossman to help us break into buildings and take photos. That's what we always do, that's what we live for."

Pete was touched by the kid's game spirit. She really had the City Spider way of mind. Nevertheless, Pete was fifty-two years old, so he found it necessary to at least try to be reasonable. "We should haul our sorry spook asses back to that glider right now. Let's skip on back over the Himalayas. We can fly on back to Washington, tourist class out of Delhi. They'll debrief us at the puzzle-palace. We'll give 'em the bad news about the bossman. We got plenty of evidence to prove *that,* anyhow. . . . The spooks will give us some walkin' money for a busted job, and tell us to keep our noses clean. Then we can go out for some pork chops."

Katrinko's thin shoulders hunched mulishly within the bubblepak warts of her insulated camou. She was not taking this at all well. "Peter, I ain't looking for pork chops. I'm looking for some professional validation, okay? I'm sick of that lowlife kid stuff, knocking around raiding network sites and mayors' offices. . . . This is my chance at the big-time!"

Pete stroked the muzzle of his mask with two gloved fingers.

"Pete, I know that you ain't happy. I know that already, okay? But you've *already made it* in the big-time, Mr. City Spider, Mr. Legend, Mr. Champion. Now here's my big chance come along, and you want us to hang up our cleats."

Pete raised his other hand. "Wait a minute, I never said that."

"Well, you're tellin' me you're walking. You're turning your back. You don't even want to check it out first."

"No," Pete said weightily, "I reckon you know me too well for that, Trink. I'm still a Spider. I'm still game. I'll always at least check it out."

Katrinko set their pace after that. Pete was content to let her lead. It was a very stupid idea to continue the mission without the overlordship of the Lieutenant Colonel. But it was stupid in a different and more refreshing way than the stupid idea of returning home to Chattanooga.

People in Pete's line of work weren't allowed to go home. He'd tried that once, really tried it, eight years ago, just after that badly busted caper in Brussels. He'd gotten a straight job at Lyle Schweik's pedal-powered aircraft factory. The millionaire sports tycoon had owed him a favor. Schweik had been pretty good about it, considering.

But word had swiftly gotten around that Pete had once been a champion City Spider. Dumb-ass co-workers would make significant remarks. Sometimes they asked him for so-called favors, or tried to act street-wise. When you came down to it, straight people were a major pain in the ass.

Pete preferred the company of seriously twisted people. People who really cared about something, cared enough about it to really warp themselves for it. People who looked for more out of life than mommy-daddy, money, and the grave.

Below the edge of a ridgeline they paused for a recce. Pete whirled a tethered eye on the end of its reel and flung it. At the peak of its arc, six stories up, it recorded their surroundings in a panoramic view.

Pete and Katrinko studied the image together through their linked spex. Katrinko highlit an area downhill with a fingertip gesture. "Now there's a tipoff."

"That gully, you mean?"

"You need to get outdoors more, Pete. That's what we rockjocks technically call a road."

Pete and Katrinko approached the road with professional caution. It was a paved ribbon of macerated cinderblock, overrun with drifting sand. The road was made of the coked-out clinker left behind by big urban incinerators, a substance that Asians used for their road surfaces because all the value had been cooked out of it.

The cinder road had once seen a great deal of traffic. There were tire-shreds here and there, deep ruts in the shoulder, and post-holes that had once been traffic signs, or maybe surveillance boxes.

They followed the road from a respectful distance, cautious of monitors, trip-wires, landmines, and many other possible unpleasantries. They stopped for a rest in a savage arroyo where a road bridge had been carefully removed, leaving only neat sockets in the roadbed and a kind of conceptual arc in midair.

"What creeps me out is how clean this all is," Pete said over cable. "It's a road, right? Somebody's gotta throw out a beer can, a lost shoe, something."

Katrinko nodded. "I figure construction robots."

"Really."

Katrinko spread her swollen-fingered gloves. "It's a Sphere operation, so it's bound to have lots of robots, right? I figure robots built this road. Robots used this road. Robots carried in tons and tons of whatever they were carrying. Then when they were done with the big project, the robots carried off everything that was worth any money. Gathered up the guideposts, bridges everything. Very neat, no loose ends, very Sphere-type way to work." Katrinko set her masked chin on her bent knees, gone into reverie. "Some very weird and intense stuff can happen, when you got a lot of space in the desert, and robot labor that's too cheap to meter."

Katrinko hadn't been wasting her time in those intelligence briefings. Pete had seen a lot of City Spider wannabes, even trained quite a few of them. But Katrinko had what it took to be a genuine Spider champion: the desire, the physical talent, the ruthless dedication, and even the smarts. It was staying out of jails and morgues that was gonna be the tough part of Katrinko. "You're a big fan of the Sphere, aren't you, kid? You really like the way they operate."

"Sure, I always liked Asians. Their food's a lot better than Europe's."

Pete took this in stride. NAFTA, Sphere, and Europe: the trilateral super-powers jostled about with the uneasy regularity of sunspots, periodically brewing storms in the proxy regimes of the South. During his fifty-plus years, Pete had seen the Asian Cooperation Sphere change its public image repeatedly, in a weird political rhythm. Exotic vacation spot on Tuesdays and Thursdays. Baffling alien threat on Mondays and Wednesdays. Major trading partner each day and every day, includ-ing weekends and holidays.

At the current political moment, the Asian Cooperation Sphere was deep into its Inscrutable Menace mode, logging lots of grim media coverage as NAFTA's chief economic adversary. As far as Pete could figure it, this basically meant that a big crowd of goofy North American economists were trying to act really macho. Their major complaint was that the Sphere was selling NAFTA too many neat, cheap, well-made consumer goods. That was an extremely silly thing to get killed about. But people perished horribly for much stranger reasons than that.

At sunset, Pete and Katrinko discovered the giant warning signs. They were titanic vertical plinths, all epoxy and clinker, much harder than granite. They were four stories tall, carefully rooted in bedrock, and painstakingly chiseled with menacing horned symbols and elaborate textual warnings in at least fifty different languages. English was language number three.

"Radiation waste," Pete concluded, deftly reading the text through his spex, from two kilometers away. "This is a radiation waste dump. Plus, a nuclear test site.

Old Red Chinese hydrogen bombs, way out in the Taklamakan desert." He paused thoughtfully. "You gotta hand it to 'em. They sure picked the right spot for the job."

"No way!" Katrinko protested. "Giant stone warning signs, telling people not to trespass in this area? That's got to be a con-job."

"Well, it would sure account for them using robots, and then destroying all the roads."

"No, man. It's like—you wanna hide something big nowadays. You don't put a safe inside the wall any more, because hey, everybody's got magnetometers and sonic imaging and heat detection. So you hide your best stuff in the garbage."

Pete scanned their surroundings on spex telephoto. They were lurking on a hillside above a playa, where the occasional gullywasher had spewed out a big alluvial fan of desert varnished grit and cobbles. Stuff was actually growing down there—squat leathery grasses with fat waxy blades like dead men's fingers. The evil vegetation didn't look like any kind of grass that Pete had ever seen. It struck him as the kind of grass that would blithely gobble up stray plutonium. "Trink, I like my explanations simple. I figure that so-called giant starship base for a giant radwaste dump."

"Well, maybe," the neuter admitted. "But even if that's the truth, that's still news worth paying for. We might find some busted up barrels, or some badly managed fuel rods out there. That would be a big political embarrassment, right? Proof of that would be worth something."

"Huh," said Pete, surprised. But it was true. Long experience had taught Pete that there were always useful secrets in other people's trash. "Is it worth glowin' in the dark for?"

"So what's the problem?" Katrinko said. "I ain't having kids. I fixed that a long time ago. And you've got enough kids already."

"Maybe," Pete grumbled. Four kids by three different women. It had taken him a long sad time to learn that women who fell head-over-heels for footloose, sexy tough guys would fall repeatedly for pretty much any footloose, sexy tough guy.

Katrinko was warming to the task at hand. "We can do this, man. We got our suits and our breathing masks, and we're not eating or drinking anything out here, so we're practically radiation-tight. So we camp way outside the dump tonight. Then before dawn we slip in, we check it out real quick, we take our pictures, we leave. Clean, classic intrusion job. Nobody living around here to stop us, no problem there. And then, we got something to show the spooks when we get home. Maybe something we can sell."

Pete mulled this over. The prospect didn't sound all that bad. It was dirty work, but it would complete the mission. Also—this was the part he liked best—it would keep the Lieutenant Colonel's people from sending in some other poor guy. "Then, back to the glider?"

"Then back to the glider."

"Okay, good deal."

Before dawn the next morning, they stoked themselves with athletic performance enhancers, brewed in the guts of certain gene-spliced ticks that they had kept hibernating in their armpits. Then they concealed their travel gear, and swarmed like ghosts up and over the great wall.

They pierced a tiny hole through the roof of one of the dun-colored, half-buried containment hangars, and oozed a spy-eye through.

Bombproofed ranks of barrel-shaped sarcophagi, solid glossy as polished granite. The big fused radwaste containers were each the size of a tanker truck. They sat there neatly-ranked in hermetic darkness, mute as sphinxes. They looked to be good for the next twenty thousand years.

Pete liquefied and retrieved the gelcam, then re-sealed the tiny hole with rock putty. They skipped down the slope of the dusty roof. There were lots of lizard tracks in the sand drifts, piled at the rim of the dome. These healthy traces of lizard cheered Pete up considerably.

They swarmed silently up and over the wall. Back uphill to the grotto where they'd stashed their gear. Then they removed their masks to talk again.

Pete sat behind a boulder, enjoying the intrusion afterglow. "A cakewalk," he pronounced it. "A pleasure hike." His pulse was already normal again, and, to his joy, there were no suspicious aches under his caraco-acromial arch.

"You gotta give them credit, those robots sure work neat."

Pete nodded. "Killer application for robots, your basic lethal waste gig."

"I telephoto'ed that whole cantonment," said Katrinko, "and there's no water there. No towers, no plumbing, no wells. People can get along without a lot of stuff in the desert, but nobody lives without water. That place is stone dead. It was always dead." She paused. "It was all automated robot work from start to finish. You know what that means, Pete? It means no human being has ever seen that place before. Except for you and me."

"Hey, then it's a first! We scored a first intrusion! That's just dandy," said Pete, pleased at the professional coup. He gazed across the cobbled plain at the walled cantonment, and pressed a last set of spex shots into his gelbrain archive. Two dozen enormous domes, built block by block by giant robots, acting with the dumb persistence of termites. The sprawling domes looked as if they'd congealed on the spot, their rims settling like molten taffy into the desert's little convexities and concavities. From a satellite view, the domes probably passed for natural features. "Let's not tarry, okay? I can kinda feel those X-ray fingers kinking my DNA."

"Aw, you're not all worried about that, are you, Pete?"

Pete laughed and shrugged. "Who cares? Job's over, kid. Back to the glider."

"They do great stuff with gene damage nowadays, y'know. Kinda reweave you, down at the spook lab."

"What, those military doctors? I don't wanna give them the excuse."

The wind picked up. A series of abrupt and brutal gusts. Dry, and freezing, and peppered with stinging sand.

Suddenly, a faint moan emanated from the cantonment. Distant lungs blowing the neck of a wine bottle.

"What's that big weird noise?" demanded Katrinko, all alert interest.

"Aw no," said Pete. "Dang."

. . .

Steam was venting from a hole in the bottom of the thirteenth dome. They'd missed the hole earlier, because the rim of that dome was overgrown with big thriving thornbushes. The bushes would have been a tip-off in themselves, if the two of them had been feeling properly suspicious.

In the immediate area, Pete and Katrinko swiftly discovered three dead men. The three men had hacked and chiseled their way through the containment dome—from the inside. They had wriggled through the long, narrow crevice they had cut, leaving much blood and skin.

The first man had died just outside the dome, apparently from sheer exhaustion. After their Olympian effort, the two survivors had emerged to confront the sheer four-story walls.

The remaining men had tried to climb the mighty wall with their handaxes, crude woven ropes, and pig-iron pitons. It was a nothing wall for a pair of City Spiders with modern handwebs and pinpression cleats. Pete and Katrinko could have camped and eaten a watermelon on that wall. But it was a very serious wall for a pair of very weary men dressed in wool, leather, and homemade shoes.

One of them had fallen from the wall, and had broken his back and leg. The last one had decided to stay to comfort his dying comrade, and it seemed he had frozen to death.

The three men had been dead for many months, maybe over a year. Ants had been at work on them, and the fine salty dust of the Taklamakan, and the freeze-drying. Three desiccated Asian mummies, black hair and crooked teeth and wrinkled dusky skin, in their funny bloodstained clothes.

Katrinko offered the cable lead, chattering through her mask. "Man, look at these *shoes!* Look at this shirt this guy's got—would you call this thing a *shirt?*"

"What I would call this is three very brave climbers," Pete said. He tossed a tethered eye into the crevice that the men had cut.

The inside of the thirteenth dome was a giant forest of monitors. Microwave antennas, mostly. The top of the dome wasn't sturdy sintered concrete like the others, it was some kind of radar-transparent plastic. Dark inside, like the other domes, and hermetically sealed—at least before the dead men had chewed and chopped their hole through the wall. No sign of any rad-waste around here.

They discovered the little camp where the men had lived. Their bivouac. Three men, patiently chipping and chopping their way to freedom. Burning their last wicks and oil lamps, eating their last rations bite by bite, emptying their leather canteens and scraping for frost to drink. Surrounded all the time by a towering jungle of satellite relays and wavepipes. Pete found that scene very ugly. That was a very bad scene. That was the worst of it yet.

Pete and Katrinko retrieved their full set of intrusion gear. They then broke in through the top of the dome, where the cutting was easiest. Once through, they sealed the hole behind themselves, but only lightly, in case they should need a rapid retreat. They lowered their haul bags to the stone floor, then rappelled down on their smart ropes. Once on ground level, they closed the escape tunnel with web and rubble, to stop the howling wind, and to keep contaminants at bay.

With the hole sealed, it grew warmer in the dome. Warm, and moist. Dew was collecting on walls and floor. A very strange smell, too. A smell like smoke and old socks. Mice and spice. Soup and sewage. A cozy human reek from the depths of the earth.

"The Lieutenant Colonel sure woulda have loved this," whispered Katrinko over cable, spexing out the towering machinery with her infrareds. "You put a clip of explosive ammo through here, and it sure would put a major crimp in somebody's automated gizmos."

Pete figured their present situation for an excellent chance to get killed. Automated alarm systems were the deadliest aspect of his professional existence, somewhat tempered by the fact that smart and aggressive alarm systems frequently killed their owners. There was a basic engineering principle involved. Fancy, paranoid alarm systems went false-positive all the time: squirrels, dogs, wind, hail, earth tremors, horny boyfriends who forgot the password. . . . They were smart, and they had their own agenda, and it made them troublesome.

But if these machines were alarms, then they hadn't noticed a rather large hole painstakingly chopped in the side of their dome. The spars and transmitters looked bad, all patchy with long-accumulated rime and ice. A junkyard look, the definite smell of dead tech. So somebody had given up on these smart, expensive, paranoid alarms. Someone had gotten sick and tired of them, and shut them off.

At the foot of a microwave tower, they found a rat-sized manhole chipped out, covered with a laced-down lid of sheep's hide. Pete dropped a spy-eye down, scoping out a machine-drilled shaft. The tunnel was wide enough to swallow a car, and it dropped down as straight as a plumb bob for farther than his eye's wiring could reach.

Pete silently yanked a rusting pig-iron piton from the edge of the hole, and replaced it with a modern glue anchor. Then he whipped a smart-rope through and carefully tightened his harness.

Katrinko began shaking with eagerness. "Pete, I am way hot for this. Lemme lead point."

Pete clipped a crab into Katrinko's harness, and linked their spex through the fiber-optic embedded in the rope. Then he slapped the neuter's shoulder. "Get bold, kid."

Katrinko flared out the webbing on her gripgloves, and dropped in feet-first.

The would-be escapes had made a lot of use of cabling already present in the tunnel. There were ceramic staples embedded periodically, to hold the cabling snug against the stone. The climbers had scrabbled their way up from staple to staple, using ladder-runged bamboo poles and iron hooks.

Katrinko stopped her descent and tied off. Pete sent their haulbags down. Then he dropped and slithered after her. He stopped at the lead chock, tied off, and let Katrinko take lead again, following her progress with the spex.

An eerie glow shone at the bottom of the tunnel. Pay day. Pete felt a familiar transcendental tension overcome him. It surged through him with mad intensity. Fear, curiosity, and desire: the raw, hot, thieving thrill of a major-league intrusion.

A feeling like being insane, but so much better than craziness, because now he felt so *awake*. Pete was awash in primal spiderness, cravings too deep and slippery to speak about.

The light grew hotter in Pete's infrareds. Below them was a slotted expanse of metal, gleaming like a kitchen sink, louvers with hot slots of light. Katrinko planted a foamchock in the tunnel wall, tied off, leaned back, and dropped a spy eye through the slot.

Pete's hands were too busy to reach his spex. "What do you see?" he hissed over cable.

Katrinko craned her head back, gloved palms pressing the goggles against her face. "I can see *everything*, man! Gardens of Eden, and cities of gold!"

The cave had been ancient solid rock once, a continental bulk. The rock had been pierced by a Russian-made drilling rig. A dry well, in a very dry country. And then some very weary, and very sunburned, and very determined Chinese Communist weapons engineers had installed a one-hundred-megaton hydrogen bomb at the bottom of their dry hole. When their beast in its nest of layered casings achieved fusion, seismographs jumped like startled fawns in distant California.

The thermonuclear explosion had left a giant gasbubble at the heart of a crazy webwork of faults and cracks. The deep and empty bubble had lurked beneath the desert in utter and terrible silence, for ninety years.

Then Asia's new masters had sent in new and more sophisticated agencies.

Pete saw that the distant sloping walls of the cavern were daubed with starlight. White constellations, whole and entire. And amid the space—that giant and sweetly damp airspace—were three great glowing lozenges, three vertical cylinders the size of urban high rises. They seemed to be suspended in midair.

"Starships," Pete muttered.

"Starships," Katrinko agreed. Menus appeared in the shared visual space of their linked spex. Katrinko's fingertip sketched out a set of tiny moving sparks against the walls. "But check *that* out."

"What are those?"

"Heat signatures. Little engines." The envisioned world wheeled silently. "And check out over here too—and crawlin' around deep in there, dozens of the things. And Pete, see these? Those big ones? Kinda on patrol?"

"Robots."

"Yep."

"What the hell are they up to, down here?"

"Well, I figure it this way, man. If you're inside one of those fake starships, and you look out through those windows—those *portholes*, I guess we call 'em—you can't see anything but shiny stars. Deep space. But with spex, we can see right through all that business. And Pete, that whole stone sky down there is crawling with machinery."

"Man oh man."

"And nobody inside those starships can see *down*, man. There is a whole lot of very major weirdness going on down at the bottom of that cave. There's a lot of hot steamy water down there, deep in those rocks and those cracks."

"Water, or a big smelly soup maybe," Pete said. "A chemical soup."

"Biochemical soup."

"Autonomous self-assembly proteinaceous biotech. Strictly forbidden by the Nonproliferation Protocols of the Manila Accords of 2037," said Pete. Pete rattled off this phrase with practiced ease, having rehearsed it any number of times during various background briefings.

"A whole big lake of way-hot, way-illegal, self-assembling goo down there."

"Yep. The very stuff that *our* covert-tech boys have been messing with under the Rockies for the past ten years."

"Aw, Pete, everybody cheats a little bit on the accords. The way we do it in NAFTA, it's no worse than bathtub gin. But this is *huge!* And Lord only know what's inside those starships."

"Gotta be people, kid."

"Yep."

Pete drew a slow moist breath. "This is a big one, Trink. This is truly major-league. You and me, we got ourselves an intelligence coup here of historic proportions."

"If you're trying to say that we should go back to the glider now," Katrinko said, "don't even start with me."

"We need to go back to the glider," Pete insisted, "with the photographic proof that we got right now. That was our mission objective. It's what they pay us for."

"Whoop-tee-do."

"Besides, it's the patriotic thing. Right?"

"Maybe I'd play the patriot game, if I was in uniform," said Katrinko. "But the Army don't allow neuters. I'm a total freak and I'm a free agent, and I didn't come here to see Shangri-La and then turn around first thing."

"Yeah," Pete admitted. "I really know that feeling."

"I'm going down in there right now," Katrinko said. "You belay for me?"

"No way, kid. This time, I'm leading point."

Pete eased himself through a crudely broken louver and out onto the vast rocky ceiling. Pete had never much liked climbing rock. Nasty stuff, rock — all natural, no guaranteed engineering specifications. Still, Pete had spent a great deal of his life on ceilings. Ceilings he understood.

He worked his way out on a series of congealed lava knobs, till he hit a nice solid crack. He did a rapid set of fist-jams, then set a pair of foam-clamps, and tied himself off on anchor.

Pete panned slowly in place, upside down on the ceiling, muffled in his camou gear, scanning methodically for the sake of Katrinko back on the fiber-optic spex link. Large sections of the ceiling looked weirdly worm-eaten, as if drills or acids had etched the rock away. Pete could discern in the eerie glow of infrared that the three fake starships were actually supported on columns. Huge hollow tubes, lacelike and almost entirely invisible, made of something black and impossibly strong, maybe carbon-fiber. There were water pipes inside the columns, and electrical power.

Those columns were the quickest and easiest ways to climb down or up to the starships. Those columns were also very exposed. They looked like excellent places to get killed.

Pete knew that he was safely invisible to any naked human eye, but there wasn't much he could do about his heat signature. For all he knew, at this moment he was glowing like a Christmas tree on the sensors of a thousand heavily armed robots. But you couldn't leave a thousand machines armed to a hair-trigger for years on end. And who would program them to spend their time watching ceilings?

The muscular burn had faded from his back and shoulders. Pete shook a little extra blood through his wrists, unhooked, and took off on cleats and gripwebs. He veered around one of the fake stars, a great glowing glassine bulb the size of a laundry basket. The fake star was cemented into a big rocky wart, and it radiated a cold, enchanting, and gooey firefly light. Pete was so intrigued by this bold deception that his cleat missed a smear. His left foot swung loose. His left shoulder emitted a nasty-feeling, expensive-sounding pop. Pete grunted, planted both cleats, and slapped up a glue patch, with tendons smarting and the old forearm clock ticking fast. He whipped a crab through the patchloop and sagged within his harness, breathing hard.

On the surface of his spex, Katrinko's glowing fingertip whipped across the field of Pete's vision, and pointed. Something moving out there. Pete had company.

Pete eased a string of flashbangs from his sleeve. Then he hunkered down in place, trusting to his camouflage, and watching.

A robot was moving toward him among the dark pits of the fake stars. Wobbling and jittering.

Pete had never seen any device remotely akin to this robot. It had a porous, foamy hide, like cork and plastic. It had a blind compartmented knob for a head, and fourteen long fibrous legs like a frayed mess of used rope, terminating in absurdly complicated feet, like a boxful of grip pliers. Hanging upside down from bits of rocky irregularity too small to see, it would open its big warty head and flick out a forked sensor like a snake's tongue. Sometimes it would dip itself close to the ceiling, for a lingering chemical smooch on the surface of the rock.

Pete watched with murderous patience as the device backed away, drew nearer, spun around a bit, meandered a little closer, sucked some more ceiling rock, made up its mind about something, replanted its big grippy feet, hoofed along closer yet, lost its train of thought, retreated a bit, sniffed the air at length, sucked meditatively on the end of one of its ropy tentacles.

It finally reached him, walked deftly over his legs, and dipped up to lick enthusiastically at the chemical traces left by his gripweb. The robot seemed enchanted by the taste of the glove's elastomer against the rock. It hung there on its fourteen plier feet, loudly licking and rasping.

Pete lashed out with his pick. The razored point slid with a sullen crunch right through the thing's corky head.

It went limp instantly, pinned there against the ceiling. Then with a nasty rustling it deployed a whole unsuspected set of waxy and filmy appurtenances.

Complex bug-tongue things, mandible scrapers, delicate little spatulas, all reeling and trembling out of its slotted underside.

It was not going to die. It couldn't die, because it had never been alive. It was a piece of biotechnical machinery. Dying was simply not on its agenda anywhere. Pete photographed the device carefully as it struggled with obscene mechanical stupidity to come to workable terms with its new environmental parameters. Then Pete levered the pick loose from the ceiling, shook it loose, and dropped the pierced robot straight down to hell.

Pete climbed more quickly now, favoring the strained shoulder. He worked his way methodically out to the relative ease of the vertical wall, where he discovered a large mined-out vein in the constellation Sagittarius. The vein was a big snaky recess where some kind of ore had been nibbled and strained from the rock. By the look of it, the rock had been chewed away by a termite host of tiny robots with mouths like toenail clippers.

He signaled on the spex for Katrinko. The neuter followed along the clipped and anchored line, climbing like a fiend while lugging one of the haulbags. As Katrinko settled in to their new base camp, Pete returned to the louvers to fetch the second bag. When he'd finally heaved and grappled his way back, his shoulder was aching bitterly and his nerves were shot. They were done for the day.

Katrinko had put up the emission-free encystment web at the mouth of their crevice. With Pete returned to relative safety, she reeled in their smart-ropes and fed them a handful of sugar.

Pete cracked open two capsules of instant fluff, then sank back gratefully into the wool.

Katrinko took off her mask. She was vibrating with alert enthusiasm. Youth, thought Pete—youth, and the 8 percent metabolic advantage that came from lacking sex organs. "We're in so much trouble now," Katrinko whispered, with a feverish grin in the faint red glow of a single indicator light. She no longer resembled a boy or a young woman. Katrinko looked completely diabolical. This was a nonsexed creature. Pete liked to think of her as a "she," because this was somehow easier on his mind, but Katrinko was an "it." Now it was filled with glee, because finally it had placed itself in a proper and pleasing situation. Stark and feral confrontation with its own stark and feral little being.

"Yeah, this is trouble," Pete said. He placed a fat medicated tick onto the vein inside of his elbow. "And you're taking first watch."

Pete woke four hours later, with a heart-fluttering rise from the stunned depths of chemically assisted delta-sleep. He felt numb, and lightly dusted with a brain-clouding amnesia, as if he'd slept for four straight days. He had been profoundly helpless in the grip of the drug, but the risk had been worth it, because now he was thoroughly rested. Pete sat up, and tried the left shoulder experimentally. It was much improved.

Pete rubbed feeling back into his stubbled face and scalp, then strapped his spex on. He discovered Katrinko squatting on her haunches, in the radiant glow of her own body heat, pondering over an ugly mess of spines, flakes, and goo.

Pete touched spex knobs and leaned forward. "What you got there?"

"Dead robots. They ate our foamchocks, right out of the ceiling. They eat anything. I killed the ones that tried to break into camp." Katrinko stroked at a midair menu, then handed Pete a fiber lead for his spex. "Check this footage I took."

Katrinko had been keeping watch with the gelcams, picking out passing robots in the glow of their engine heat. She'd documented them on infrared, saving and editing the clearest live-action footage. "These little ones with the ball-shaped feet, I call them keets," she narrated, as the captured frames cascaded across Pete's spex-clad gaze. "They're small, but they're really fast, and all over the place—I had to kill three of them. This one with the sharp spiral nose is a drillet. Those are a pair of dubits. The dubits always travel in pairs. This big thing here, that looks like a spilled dessert with big eyes and a ball on a chain, I call that one a lurchen. Because of the way it moves, see? It's sure a lot faster than it looks."

Katrinko stopped the spex replay, switched back to live perception, and poked carefully at the broken litter before her booted feet. The biggest device in the heap resembled a dissected cat's head stuffed with cables and bristles. "I also killed this piteen. Piteens don't die easy, man."

"There's lots of these things?"

"I figure hundreds, maybe thousands. All different kinds. And every one of 'em as stupid as dirt. Or else we'd be dead and disassembled a hundred times already."

Pete stared at the dissected robots, a cooling mass of nerve-netting, batteries, veiny armor plates, and gelatin. "Why do they look so crazy?"

"Cause they grew all by themselves. Nobody ever designed them." Katrinko glanced up. "You remember those big virtual spaces for weapons design, that they run out in Alamagordo?"

"Yeah, sure, Alamagordo. Physics simulations on those super-size quantum gel-brains. Huge virtualities, with ultra-fast, ultra-fine detail. You bet I remember New Mexico! I love to raid a great computer lab. There's something so traditional about the hack."

"Yeah. See, for us NAFTA types, physics virtualities are a military app. We always give our tech to the military whenever it looks really dangerous. But let's say you don't share our NAFTA values. You don't wanna test new weapons systems inside giant virtualities. Let's say you want to make a can-opener, instead."

During her sleepless hours huddling on watch, Katrinko had clearly been giving this matter a lot of thought. "Well, you could study other people's can-openers and try to improve the design. Or else you could just set up a giant high-powered virtuality with a bunch of virtual cans inside it. Then you make some can-opener simulations, that are basically blobs of goo. They're simulated goo, but they're also programs, and those programs trade data and evolve. Whenever they pierce a can, you reward them by making more copies of them. You're running, like, a million generations of a million different possible can-openers, all day every day, in a simulated space."

The concept was not entirely alien to Spider Pete. "Yeah, I've heard the rumors. It was one of those stunts like Artificial Intelligence. It might look really good on paper, but you can't ever get it to work in real life."

"Yeah, and now it's illegal too. Kinda hard to police, though. But let's imagine you're into economic warfare and you figure out how to do this. Finally, you evolve this super weird, super can-opener that no human being could ever have invented. Something that no human being could even *imagine*. Because it grew like a mushroom in an entire alternate physics. But you have all the specs for its shape and proportions, right there in the supercomputer. So to make one inside the real world, you just print it out like a photograph. And it works! It runs! See? Instant cheap consumer goods."

Pete thought it over. "So you're saying the Sphere people got that idea to work, and these robots here were built that way?"

"Pete, I just can't figure any other way this could have happened. These machines are just too alien. They had to come from some totally nonhuman, autonomous process. Even the best Japanese engineers can't design a jelly robot made out of fuzz and rope that can move like a caterpillar. There's not enough money in the world to pay human brains to think that out."

Pete prodded at the gooey ruins with his pick. "Well, you got that right."

"Whoever built this place, they broke a lot of rules and treaties. But they did it all *really cheap*. They did it in a way that is so cheap that it is *beyond economics*." Katrinko thought this over. "It's *way* beyond economics, and that's exactly *why* it's against all those rules and the treaties in the first place."

"Fast, cheap, and out of control."

"Exactly, man. If this stuff ever got loose in the real world, it would mean the end of everything we know."

Pete liked this last statement not at all. He had always disliked apocalyptic hype. He liked it even less now because under these extreme circumstances it sounded very plausible. The Sphere had the youngest and the biggest population of the three major trading blocs, and the youngest and the biggest ideas. People in Asia knew how to get things done. "Y'know, Lyle Schweik once told me that the weirdest bicycles in the world come out of China these days."

"Well, he's right. They do. And what about those Chinese circuitry chips they've been dumping in the NAFTA markets lately? Those chips are dirt cheap and work fine, but they're full of all this crazy leftover wiring that doubles back and gets all snarled up. . . . I always thought that was just shoddy workmanship. Man, 'workmanship' had nothing to do with those chips."

Pete nodded soberly. "Okay. Chips and bicycles, that much I can understand. There's a lot of money in that. But who the heck would take the trouble to create a giant hole in the ground that's full of robots and fake stars? I mean, *why*?"

Katrinko shrugged. "I guess it's just the Sphere, man. They still do stuff just because it's wonderful."

The bottom of the world was boiling over. During the passing century, the nuclear test cavity had accumulated its own little desert aquifer, a pitch-black subterranean oasis. The bottom of the bubble was an unearthly drowned maze of shattered cracks and chemical deposition, all turned to simmering tidepools of mechanical self-assemblage. Oxygen-fizzing geysers of black fungus tea.

Steam rose steadily in the darkness amid the crags, rising to condense and run in chilly rivulets down the spherical star-spangled walls. Down at the bottom, all the water was eagerly collected by aberrant devices of animated sponge and string. Katrinko instantly tagged these as "smits" and "fuzzens."

The smits and fuzzens were nightmare dishrags and piston-powered spaghetti, leaping and slopping wetly from crag to crag. Katrinko took an unexpected ease and pleasure in naming and photographing the machines. Speculation boiled with sinister ease from the sexless youngster's vulpine head, a swift off-the-cuff adjustment to this alien toy world. It would seem that the kid lived rather closer to the future than Pete did.

They cranked their way from boulder to boulder, crack to liquid crack. They documented fresh robot larvae, chewing their way to the freedom of darkness through plugs of goo and muslin. It was a whole miniature creation, designed in the senseless gooey cores of a Chinese supercomputing gelbrain, and transmuted into reality in a hot broth of undead mechanized protein. This was by far the most amazing phenomenon that Pete had ever witnessed. Pete was accordingly plunged into gloom. Knowledge was power in his world. He knew with leaden certainty that he was taking on far too much voltage for his own good.

Pete was a professional. He could imagine stealing classified military secrets from a superpower, and surviving that experience. It would be very risky, but in the final analysis it was just the military. A rocket base, for instance — a secret Asian rocket base might have been a lot of fun.

But this was not military. This was an entire new means of industrial production. Pete knew with instinctive street-level certainty that tech of this level of revolutionary weirdness was not a spy thing, a sports thing, or a soldier thing. This was a big, big *money* thing. He might survive discovering it. He'd never get away with revealing it.

The thrilling wonder of it all really bugged him. Thrilling wonder was at best a passing thing. The sober implications for the longer term weighed on Pete's soul like a damp towel. He could imagine escaping this place in one piece, but he couldn't imagine any plausible aftermath for handing over nifty photographs of thrilling wonder to military spooks on the Potomac. He couldn't imagine what the powers-that-were would do with that knowledge. He rather dreaded what they would do to him for giving it to them.

Pete wiped a sauna cascade of sweat from his neck.

"So I figure it's either geothermal power, or a fusion generator down there," said Katrinko.

"I'd be betting thermonuclear, given the circumstances." The rocks below their busy cleats were a-skitter with bugs: gippers and ghents and kebbits, dismantlers and glue-spreaders and brain-eating carrion disassemblers. They were profoundly dumb little devices, specialized as centipedes. They didn't seem very aggressive, but it surely would be a lethal mistake to sit down among them.

A barnacle thing with an iris mouth and long whipping eyes took a careful taste of Katrinko's boot. She retreated to a crag with a yelp.

"Wear your mask," Pete chided. The damp heat was bliss after the skin-eating chill of the Taklamakan, but most of the vents and cracks were spewing thick smells of hot beef stew and burnt rubber, all varieties of eldritch mechano-metabolic byproduct. His lungs felt sore at the very thought of it.

Pete cast his foggy spex up the nearest of the carbon-fiber columns, and the golden, glowing, impossibly tempting lights of those starship portholes up above.

Katrinko led point. She was pitilessly exposed against the lacelike girders. They didn't want to risk exposure during two trips, so they each carried a haul bag.

The climb went well at first. Then a machine rose up from wet darkness like a six-winged dragonfly. Its stinging tail lashed through the thready column like the kick of a mule. It connected brutally. Katrinko shot backwards from the impact, tumbled ten meters, and dangled like a ragdoll from her last backup chock.

The flying creature circled in a figure eight, attempting to make up its nonexistent mind. Then a slower but much larger creature writhed and fluttered out of the starry sky, and attacked Katrinko's dangling haulbag. The bag burst like a Christmas piñata in a churning array of taloned wings. A fabulous cascade of expensive spy gear splashed down to the hot pools below.

Katrinko twitched feebly at the end of her rope. The dragonfly, cruelly alerted, went for her movement. Pete launched a string of flashbangs.

The world erupted in flash, heat, concussion, and flying chaff. Impossibly hot and loud, a thunderstorm in a closet. The best kind of disappearance magic: total overwhelming distraction, the only real magic in the world.

Pete soared up to Katrinko like a balloon on a bungee-cord. When he reached the bottom of the starship, twenty-seven heart-pounding seconds later, he had burned out both the smart-ropes.

The silvery rain of chaff was driving the bugs to mania. The bottom of the cavern was suddenly a-crawl with leaping mechanical heat-ghosts, an instant menagerie of skippers and humpers and floppers. At the rim of perception, there were new things rising from the depths of the pools, vast and scaly, like golden carp to a rain of fish chow.

Pete's own haulbag had been abandoned at the base of the column. That bag was clearly not long for this world.

Katrinko came to with a sudden winded gasp. They began free-climbing the outside of the starship. It surface was stony, rough and uneven, something like pumice, or wasp spit.

They found the underside of a monster porthole and pressed themselves flat against the surface.

There they waited, inert and unmoving, for an hour. Katrinko caught her breath. Her ribs stopped bleeding. The two of them waited for another hour, while crawling and flying heat-ghosts nosed furiously around their little world, following the tatters of their programming. They waited a third hour.

Finally they were joined in their haven by an oblivious gang of machines with suckery skirts and wheelbarrows for heads. The robots chose a declivity and began filling it with big mandible trowels of stony mortar, slopping it on and jaw-chiseling it into place, smoothing everything over, tireless and pitiless.

Pete seized this opportunity to attempt to salvage their lost equipment. There had been such fabulous federal bounty in there: smart audio bugs, heavy-duty gelcams, sensors and detectors, pulleys, crampons and latches, priceless vials of programmed neural goo. . . . Pete crept back to the bottom of the spacecraft.

Everything was long gone. Even the depleted smart-ropes had been eaten, by a long trail of foraging keets. The little machines were still squirreling about in the black lace of the column, sniffing and scraping at the last molecular traces, with every appearance of satisfaction.

Pete rejoined Katrinko, and woke her where she clung rigid and stupefied to her hiding spot. They inched their way around the curved rim of the starship hull, hunting for a possible weakness. They were in very deep trouble now, for their best equipment was gone. It didn't matter. Their course was very obvious now, and the loss of alternatives had clarified Pete's mind. He was consumed with a burning desire to break in.

Pete slithered into the faint shelter of a large, deeply pitted hump. There he discovered a mess of braided rope. The rope was woven of dead and mashed organic fibers, something like the hair at the bottom of a sink. The rope had gone all petrified under a stony lacquer of robot spit.

These were climber's ropes. Someone had broken out here—smashed through the hull of the ship, from the inside. The robots had come to repair the damage, carefully resealing the exit hole, and leaving this ugly hump of stony scar tissue.

Pete pulled his gelcam drill. He had lost the sugar reserves along with the haulbags. Without sugar to metabolize, the little enzyme-driven rotor would starve and be useless soon. That fact could not be helped. Pete pressed the device against the hull, waited as it punched its way through, and squirted in a gelcam to follow.

He saw a farm. Pete could scarcely have been more astonished. It was certainly farmland, though. Cute, toy farmland, all under a stony blue ceiling, crisscrossed with hot grids of radiant light, embraced in the stony arch of the enclosing hull. There were fishponds with reeds. Ditches, and a wooden irrigation wheel. A little bridge of bamboo. There were hairy melon vines in rich black soil and neat, entirely weedless fields of dwarfed red grain. Not a soul in sight.

Katrinko crept up and linked in on cable. "So where is everybody?" Pete said.

"They're all at the portholes," said Katrinko, coughing.

"What?" said Pete, surprised. "Why?"

"Because of those flashbangs," Katrinko wheezed. Her battered ribs were still paining her. "They're all at the portholes, looking out into the darkness. Waiting for something else to happen."

"But we did that stuff hours ago."

"It was very big news, man. Nothing ever happens in there."

Pete nodded, fired with resolve. "Well then. We're breakin' in."

Katrinko was way game. "Gonna use caps?"

"Too obvious."

"Acids and fibrillators?"

"Lost 'em in the haulbags."

"Well, that leaves cheesewires," Katrinko concluded. "I got two."

"I got six."

Katrinko nodded in delight. "Six cheesewires! You're loaded for bear, man!"

"I love cheesewires," Pete grunted. He had helped to invent them.

Eight minutes and twelve seconds later they were inside the starship. They reset the cored-out plug behind them, delicately gluing it in place and carefully obscuring the hair-thin cuts.

Katrinko sidestepped into a grove of bamboo. Her camou bloomed in green and tan and yellow, with such instant and treacherous ease that Pete lost her entirely. Then she waved, and the spex edge-detectors kicked in on her silhouette.

Pete lifted his spex for a human naked-eye take on the situation. There was simply nothing there at all. Katrinko was gone, less than a ghost, like pitchforking mercury with your eyelashes.

So they were safe now. They could glide through this bottled farm like a pair of bad dreams.

They scanned the spacecraft from top to bottom, looking for dangerous and interesting phenomena. Control rooms manned by Asian space technicians maybe, or big lethal robots, or video monitors—something that might cramp their style or kill them. In the thirty-seven floors of the spacecraft, they found no such thing.

The five thousand inhabitants spent their waking hours farming. The crew of the starship were preindustrial, tribal, Asian peasants. Men, women, old folks, little kids.

The local peasants rose every single morning, as their hot networks of wiring came alive in the ceiling. They would milk their goats. They would feed their sheep, and some very odd, knee-high, dwarf Bactrian camels. They cut bamboo and netted their fishponds. They cut down tamarisks and poplar trees for firewood. They tended melon vines and grew plums and hemp. They brewed alcohol, and ground grain, and boiled millet, and squeezed cooking oil out of rapeseed. They made clothes out of hemp and raw wool and leather, and baskets out of reeds and straw. They ate a lot of carp.

And they raised a whole mess of chickens. Somebody not from around here had been fooling with the chickens. Apparently these were super space-chickens of some kind, leftover lab products from some serious long-term attempt to screw around with chicken DNA. The hens produced five or six lumpy eggs every day. The roosters were enormous, and all different colors, and very smelly, and distinctly reptilian.

It was very quiet and peaceful inside the starship. The animals made their lowing and clucking noises, and the farm workers sang to themselves in the tiny round-edged fields, and the incessant foot-driven water pumps would clack rhythmically, but there were no city noises. No engines anywhere. No screens. No media.

There was no money. There were a bunch of tribal elders who sat under the blossoming plum trees outside the big stone granaries. They messed with beads on wires, and wrote notes on slips of wood. Then the soldiers, or the cops—they were a bunch of kids in crude leather armor, with spears—would tramp in groups, up and down the dozens of stairs, on the dozens of floors. Marching like crazy, and requisitioning stuff, and carrying stuff on their backs, and handing things out to people. Basically spreading the wealth around.

Most of the weird bearded old guys were palace accountants, but there were some others too. They sat cross-legged on mats in their homemade robes, and straw sandals, and their little spangly hats, discussing important matters at slow and extreme length. Sometimes they wrote stuff down on palm-leaves.

Pete and Katrinko spent a special effort to spy on these old men in the spangled hats, because, after close study, they had concluded that this was the local government. They pretty much had to be the government. These old men with the starry hats were the only part of the population who weren't being worked to a frazzle.

Pete and Katrinko found themselves a cozy spot on the roof of the granary, one of the few permanent structures inside the spacecraft. It never rained inside the starship, so there wasn't much call for roofs. Nobody ever trespassed up on the roof of the granary. It was clear that the very idea of doing this was beyond local imagination. So Pete and Katrinko stole some bamboo water jugs, and some lovely handmade carpets, and a lean-to tent, and set up camp there.

Katrinko studied an especially elaborate palm-leaf book that she had filched from the local temple. There were pages and pages of dense alien script. "Man, what do you suppose these yokels have to write about?"

"The way I figure it," said Pete, "they're writing down everything they can remember from the world outside."

"Yeah?"

"Yeah. Kinda building up an intelligence dossier for their little starship regime, see? Because that's all they'll ever know, because the people who put them inside here aren't giving 'em any news. And they're sure as hell never gonna let 'em out."

Katrinko leafed carefully through the stiff and brittle pages of the handmade book. The people here spoke only one language. It was no language Pete or Katrinko could even begin to recognize. "Then this is their history. Right?"

"It's their lives, kid. Their past lives, back when they were still real people, in the big real world outside. Transistor radios, and shoulder-launched rockets. Barbed-wire, pacification campaigns, ID cards. Camel caravans coming in over the border, with mortars and explosives. And very advanced Sphere mandarin bosses, who just don't have the time to put up with armed, Asian, tribal fanatics."

Katrinko looked up. "That kinda sounds like *your* version of the outside world, Pete."

Pete shrugged. "Hey, it's what happens."

"You suppose these guys really believe they're inside a real starship?"

"I guess that depends on how much they learned from the guys who broke out of here with the picks and the ropes."

Katrinko thought about it. "You know what's truly pathetic? The shabby illusion of all this. Some spook mandarin's crazy notion that ethnic separatists could be squeezed down tight, and spat out like watermelon seeds into interstellar space. . . . Man, what a *come-on*, what an enticement, what an empty promise!"

"I could sell that idea," Pete said thoughtfully. "You know how *far away* the stars really are, kid? About *four hundred years* away, that's how far. You seriously want to get human beings to travel to another star, you gotta put human beings inside of a sealed can for four hundred solid years. But what are people supposed to do in there, all that time? The only thing they can do is quietly run a farm. Because that's what a starship is. It's a desert oasis."

"So you want to try a dry-run starship experiment," said Katrinko. "And in the meantime, you happen to have some handy religious fanatics in the backwoods of Asia, who are shooting your ass off. Guys who refuse to change their age-old lives, even though you are very, very high-tech."

"Yep. That's about the size of it. Means, motive, and opportunity."

"I get it. But I can't believe that somebody went through with that scheme in real life. I mean, rounding up an ethnic minority, and sticking them down in some godforsaken hole, just so you'll never have to think about them again. That's just impossible!"

"Did I ever tell you that my grandfather was a Seminole?" Pete said.

Katrinko shook her head. "What's that mean?"

"They were American tribal guys who ended up stuck in a swamp. The Florida Seminoles, they called 'em. Y'know, maybe they just *called* my grandfather a Seminole. He dressed really funny. . . . Maybe it just *sounded good* to call him a Seminole. Otherwise, he just would have been some strange, illiterate geezer."

Katrinko's brow wrinkled. "Does it *matter* that your grandfather was a Seminole?"

"I used to think it did. That's where I got my skin color—as if that matters, nowadays. I reckon it mattered plenty to my grandfather, though. . . . He was always stompin' and carryin' on about a lot of weird stuff we couldn't understand. His English was pretty bad. He was never around much when we needed him."

"Pete . . ." Katrinko sighed. "I think it's time we got out of this place."

"How come?" Pete said, surprised. "We're safe up here. The locals are not gonna hurt us. They can't even see us. They can't touch us. Hell, they can't even *imagine* us. With our fantastic tactical advantages, we're just like gods to these people."

"I know all that, man. They're like the ultimate dumb straight people. I don't like them very much. They're not much of a challenge to us. In fact, they kind of creep me out."

"No way! They're fascinating. Those baggy clothes, the acoustic songs, all that menial labor . . . These people got something that we modern people just don't have any more."

"Huh?" Katrinko said. "Like *what*, exactly?"

"I dunno," Pete admitted.

"Well, whatever it is, it can't be very important." Katrinko sighed. "We got some serious challenges on the agenda, man. We gotta sidestep our way past all those angry robots outside, then head up that shaft, then hoof it back, four days through a freezing desert, with no haulbags. All the way back to the glider."

"But Trink, there are two other starships in here that we didn't break into yet. Don't you want to see those guys?"

"What I'd like to see right now is a hot bath in a four-star hotel," said Katrinko. "And some very big international headlines, maybe. All about *me*. That would be lovely." She grinned.

"But what about the *people*?"

"Look, I'm not 'people,' " Katrinko said calmly. "Maybe it's because I'm a neuter, Pete, but I can tell you're way off the subject. These people are none of our business. Our business now is to return to our glider in an operational condition, so that we can complete our assigned mission, and return to base with our data. Okay?"

"Well, let's break into just one more starship first."

"We gotta move, Pete. We've lost our best equipment, and we're running low on body fat. This isn't something that we can kid about and live."

"But we'll never come back here again. Somebody will, but it sure as heck won't be *us*. See, it's a Spider thing."

Katrinko was weakening. "One more starship? Not both of 'em?"

"Just one more."

"Okay, good deal."

The hole they had cut through the starship's hull had been rapidly cemented by robots. It cost them two more cheesewires to cut themselves a new exit. Then Katrinko led point, up across the stony ceiling, and down the carbon column to the second ship. To avoid annoying the lurking robot guards, they moved with hypnotic slowness and excessive stealth. This made it a grueling trip.

This second ship had seen hard use. The hull was extensively scarred with great wads of cement, entombing many lengths of dried and knotted rope. Pete and Katrinko found a weak spot and cut their way in.

This starship was crowded. It was loud inside, and it smelled. The floors were crammed with hot and sticky little bazaars, where people sold handicrafts and liquor and food. Criminals were being punished by being publicly chained to posts and pelted with offal by passers-by. Big crowds of ragged men and tattooed women gathered around brutal cockfights, featuring spurred mutant chickens half the size of dogs. All the men carried knives.

The architecture here was more elaborate, all kinds of warrens, and courtyards, and damp, sticky alleys. After exploring four floors, Katrinko suddenly declared that she recognized their surroundings. According to Katrinko, they were a physical replica of sets from a popular Japanese interactive samurai epic. Apparently the starship's designers had needed some preindustrial Asian village settings, and they hadn't wanted to take the expense and trouble to design them from scratch. So they had programmed their construction robots with pirated game designs.

This starship had once been lavishly equipped with at least three hundred armed video camera installations. Apparently, the mandarins had come to the stunning realization that the mere fact that they were recording crime didn't mean that they could control it. Their spy cameras were all dead now. Most had been vandalized. Some had gone down fighting. They were all inert and abandoned.

The rebellious locals had been very busy. After defeating the spy cameras, they had created a set of giant hullbreakers. These were siege engines, big crossbow torsion machines, made of hemp and wood and bamboo. The hullbreakers were starship community efforts, elaborately painted and ribboned, and presided over by tough, aggressive gang bosses with batons and big leather belts.

Pete and Katrinko watched a labor gang, hard at work on one of the hullbreakers. Women braided rope ladders from hair and vegetable fiber, while smiths forged pitons over choking, hazy charcoal fires. It was clear from the evidence that these restive locals had broken out of their starship jail at least twenty times. Every time they had been corralled back in by the relentless efforts of mindless machines. Now they were busily preparing yet another breakout.

"These guys sure have got initiative," said Pete admiringly. "Let's do 'em a little favor, okay?"

"Yeah?"

"Here they are, taking all this trouble to hammer their way out. But we still have a bunch of caps. We got no more use for 'em, after we leave this place. So the way I figure it, we blow their wall out big-time, and let a whole bunch of 'em loose at once. Then you and I can escape real easy in the confusion."

Katrinko loved this idea, but had to play devil's advocate. "You really think we ought to interfere like that? That kind of shows our hand, doesn't it?"

"Nobody's watching any more," said Pete. "Some technocrat figured this for a big lab experiment. But they wrote these people off, or maybe they lost their anthropology grant. These people are totally forgotten. Let's give the poor bastards a show."

Pete and Katrinko planted their explosives, took cover on the ceiling, and cheerfully watched the wall blow out.

A violent gust of air came through as pressures equalized, carrying a hemorrhage of dust and leaves into interstellar space. The locals were totally astounded by the explosion, but when the repair robots showed up, they soon recovered their morale. A terrific battle broke out, a general vengeful frenzy of crab-bashing and sponge-skewering. Women and children tussled with the keets and bibbets. Soldiers in leather cuirasses fought with the bigger machines, deploying pikes, crossbow quarrels, and big robot-mashing mauls.

The robots were profoundly stupid, but they were indifferent to their casualties, and entirely relentless.

The locals made the most of their window of opportunity. They loaded a massive harpoon into a torsion catapult, and fired it into space. Their target was the neighboring starship, the third and last of them.

The barbed spear bounded off the hull. So they reeled it back in on a monster bamboo hand-reel, cursing and shouting like maniacs.

The starship's entire population poured into the fight. The walls and bulkheads shook with the tramp of their angry feet. The outnumbered robots fell back. Pete and Katrinko seized this golden opportunity to slip out the hole. They climbed swiftly up the hull, and out of reach of the combat.

The locals fired their big harpoon again. This time the barbed tip struck true, and it stuck there quivering.

Then a little kid was heaved into place, half-naked, with a hammer and screws, and a rope threaded through his belt. He had a crown of dripping candles set upon his head.

Katrinko glanced back, and stopped dead.

Pete urged her on, then stopped as well.

The child began reeling himself industriously along the trembling harpoon line, trailing a bigger rope. An airborne machine came to menace him. It fell back twitching, pestered by a nasty scattering of crossbow bolts.

Pete found himself mesmerized. He hadn't felt the desperation of the circumstances, until he saw this brave little boy ready to fall to his death. Pete had seen many climbers who took risks because they were crazy. He'd seen professional climbers, such as himself, who played games with risk as masters of applied technique. He'd never witnessed climbing as an act of raw, desperate sacrifice.

The heroic child arrived on the grainy hull of the alien ship, and began banging his pitons in a hammer-swinging frenzy. His crown of candles shook and flickered with his efforts. The boy could barely see. He had slung himself out into stygian darkness to fall to his doom.

Pete climbed up to Katrinko and quickly linked in on cable. "We gotta leave now, kid. It's now or never."

"Not yet," Katrinko said. "I'm taping all this."

"It's our big chance."

"We'll go later." Katrinko watched a flying vacuum cleaner batting by, to swat cruelly at the kid's legs. She turned her masked head to Pete and her whole body stiffened with rage. "You got a cheesewire left?"

"I got three."

"Gimme. I gotta go help him."

Katrinko unplugged, slicked down the starship's wall in a daring controlled slide, and hit the stretched rope. To Pete's complete astonishment, Katrinko lit there in a crouch, caught herself atop the vibrating line, and simply ran for it. She ran along the humming tightrope in a thrumming blur, stunning the locals so thoroughly that they were barely able to fire their crossbows.

Flying quarrels whizzed past and around her, nearly skewering the terrified child at the far end of the rope. Then Katrinko leapt and bounded into space, her gloves and cleats outspread. She simply vanished.

It was a champion's gambit if Pete had ever seen one. It was a legendary move.

Pete could manage well enough on a tightrope. He had experience, excellent balance, and physical acumen. He was, after all, a professional. He could walk a rope if he was put to the job.

But not in full climbing gear, with cleats. And not on a slack, handbraided, homemade rope. Not when the rope was very poorly anchored by a homemade pig-iron harpoon. Not when he outweighed Katrinko by twenty kilos. Not in the middle of a flying circus of airborne robots. And not in a cloud of arrows.

Pete was simply not that crazy any more. Instead, he would have to follow Katrinko the sensible way. He would have to climb the starship, traverse the ceiling, and climb down to the third starship onto the far side. A hard three hours' work at the very best—four hours, with any modicum of safety.

Pete weighed the odds, made up his mind, and went after the job.

Pete turned in time to see Katrinko busily cheesewiring her way through the hull of Starship Three. A gout of white light poured out as the cored plug slid aside. For a deadly moment, Katrinko was a silhouetted goblin, her camou useless as the starship's radiance framed her. Her clothing fluttered in a violent gust of escaping air.

Below her, the climbing child had anchored himself to the wall and tied off his second rope. He looked up at the sudden gout of light, and he screamed so loudly that the whole universe rang.

The child's many relatives reacted by instinct, with a ragged volley of crossbow shots. The arrows veered and scattered in the gusting wind, but there were a lot of them. Katrinko ducked, and flinched, and rolled headlong into the starship. She vanished again.

Had she been hit? Pete set an anchor, tied off, and tried the radio. But without the relays in the haulbag, the weak signal could not get through.

Pete climbed on doggedly. It was the only option left.

After half an hour, Pete began coughing. The starry cosmic cavity had filled with a terrible smell. The stench was coming from the invaded starship, pouring slowly from the cored-out hole. A long-bottled, deadly stink of burning rot.

Climbing solo, Pete gave it his best. His shoulder was bad and, worse yet, his spex began to misbehave. He finally reached the cored-out entrance that Katrinko had cut. The locals were already there in force, stringing themselves a sturdy rope bridge, and attaching it to massive screws. The locals brandished torches, spears, and crossbows. They were fighting off the incessant attacks of the robots. It was clear from their wild expressions of savage glee that they had been longing for this moment for years.

Pete slipped past them unnoticed, into Starship Three. He breathed the soured air for a moment, and quickly retreated again. He inserted a new set of mask filters, and returned.

He found Katrinko's cooling body, wedged against the ceiling. An unlucky crossbow shot had slashed through her suit and punctured Katrinko's left arm. So, with her usual presence of mind, she had deftly leapt up a nearby wall, tied off on a chock, and hidden herself well out of harm's way. She'd quickly stopped the bleeding. Despite its awkward location, she'd even managed to get her wound bandaged.

Then the foul air had silently and stealthily overcome her.

With her battered ribs and a major wound, Katrinko hadn't been able to tell her dizziness from shock. Feeling sick, she had relaxed, and tried to catch her breath. A fatal gambit. She was still hanging there, unseen and invisible, dead.

Pete discovered that Katrinko was far from alone. The crew here had all died. Died months ago, maybe years ago. Some kind of huge fire inside the spacecraft. The electric lights were still on, the internal machinery worked, but there was no one left here but mummies.

These dead tribal people had the nicest clothes Pete had yet seen. Clearly they'd spent a lot of time knitting and embroidering, during the many weary years of their imprisonment. The corpses had all kinds of layered sleeves and tatted aprons, and braided belt-ties, and lacquered hairclips, and excessively nifty little sandals. They'd all smothered horribly during the sullen inferno, along with their cats and dogs and enormous chickens, in a sudden wave of smoke and combustion that had filled their spacecraft in minutes.

This was far too complicated to be anything as simple as mere genocide. Pete figured the mandarins for gentlemen technocrats, experts with the best of intentions. The lively possibility remained that it was mass suicide. But on mature consideration, Pete had to figure this for a very bad, and very embarrassing, social-engineering accident.

Though that certainly wasn't what they would say about this mess, in Washington. There was no political mess nastier than a nasty ethnic mess. Pete couldn't help but notice that these well-behaved locals hadn't bothered to do any harm to their spacecraft's lavish surveillance equipment. But their cameras were off and their starship was stone dead anyway.

The air began to clear inside the spacecraft. A pair of soldiers from Starship Number Two came stamping down the hall, industriously looting the local corpses. They couldn't have been happier about their opportunity. They were grinning with awestruck delight.

Pete returned to his comrade's stricken body. He stripped the camou suit—he needed the batteries. The neuter's lean and sexless corpse was puffy with subcutaneous storage pockets, big encystments of skin where Katrinko stored her last-ditch escape tools. The battered ribs were puffy and blue. Pete could not go on.

Pete returned to the break-in hole, where he found an eager crowd. The invaders had run along the rope-bridge and gathered there in force, wrinkling their noses and cheering in wild exaltation. They had beaten the robots; there simply weren't enough of the machines on duty to resist a whole enraged population. The robots just weren't clever enough to out-think armed, coordinated human resistance—not without killing people wholesale, and they hadn't been designed for that. They had suffered a flat-out defeat.

Pete frightened the cheering victors away with a string of flash-bangs.

Then he took careful aim at the lip of the drop, and hoisted Katrinko's body, and flung her far, far, tumbling down, into the boiling pools.

Pete retreated to the first spacecraft. It was a very dispiriting climb, and when he had completed it, his shoulder had the serious, familiar ache of chronic injury. He hid among the unknowing population while he contemplated his options.

He could hide here indefinitely. His camou suit was slowly losing its charge, but he felt confident that he could manage very well without the suit. The starship seemed to feature most any number of taboo areas. Blocked-off no-go spots, where there might have been a scandal once, or bloodshed, or a funny noise, or a strange, bad, panicky smell.

Unlike the violent, reckless crowd in Starship Two, these locals had fallen for the cover story. They truly believed that they were in the depths of space bound for some better, brighter pie in their starry stone sky. Their little stellar ghetto was full of superstitious kinks. Steeped in profound ignorance, the locals imagined that their every sin caused the universe to tremble.

Pete knew that he should try to take his data back to the glider. This was what Katrinko would have wanted. To die, but leave a legend—a very City Spider thing.

But it was hard to imagine battling his way past resurgent robots, climbing the walls with an injured shoulder, then making a four-day bitter trek through a freezing desert, all completely alone. Gliders didn't last forever, either. Spy gliders weren't built to last. If Pete found the glider with its batteries flat, or its cute little brain gone sour, Pete would be all over. Even if he'd enjoyed a full set of equipment, with perfect health, Pete had few illusions about a solo spring outing, alone and on foot, over the Himalayas.

Why risk all that? After all, it wasn't like this subterranean scene was breaking news. It was already many years old. Someone had conceived, planned and executed this business a long time ago. Important people with brains and big resources had known all about this for years. *Somebody* knew. Maybe not the Lieutenant Colonel, on the lunatic fringe of NAFTA military intelligence. But.

When Pete really thought about the basic implications . . . This was a great deal of effort, and for not that big a payoff. Because there just weren't that many people cooped up down here. Maybe fifteen thousand of them, tops. The Asian Sphere must have had tens of thousands of unassimilated tribal people, maybe hundreds of thousands. Possibly millions. And why stop at that point? This wasn't just an Asian problem. It was a very general problem. Ethnic, breakaway people, who just plain couldn't, or wouldn't, play the twenty-first century's games.

How many Red Chinese atom-bomb tests had taken place deep in the Taklamakan? They'd never bothered to brief him on ancient history. But Pete had to wonder if, by now, maybe they hadn't gotten this stellar concept down to a fine art. Maybe the Sphere had franchised their plan to Europe and NAFTA. How many forgotten holes were there, relic pockets punched below the hide of the twenty-first century, in the South Pacific, and Australia, and Nevada? The deadly trash of a long-derailed Armageddon. The sullen trash heaps where no one would ever want to look.

Sure, he could bend every nerve and muscle to force the world to face all this. But why? Wouldn't it make better sense to try to think it through first?

Pete never got around to admitting to himself that he had lost the will to leave.

As despair slowly loosened its grip on him, Pete grew genuinely interested in the locals. He was intrigued by the stark limits of their lives and their universe, and in what he could do with their narrow little heads. They'd never had a supernatural being in their midst before; they just imagined them all the time. Pete started with a few poltergeist stunts, just to amuse himself. Stealing the spangled hats of the local greybeards. Shuffling the palm leaf volumes in their sacred libraries. Hijacking an abacus or two.

But that was childish.

The locals had a little temple, their special holy of holies. Naturally Pete made it his business to invade the place.

The locals kept a girl locked up in there. She was very pretty, and slightly insane, so this made her the perfect candidate to become their Sacred Temple Girl. She was the Official Temple Priestess of Starship Number One. Apparently, their modest community could only afford one, single, awe-inspiring Virgin High Priestess. But they were practical folks, so they did the best with what they had available.

The High Priestess was a pretty young woman with a stiflingly pretty life. She had her own maidservants, a wardrobe of ritual clothing, and a very time-consuming hairdo. The High Priestess spent her entire life carrying out highly complex, totally useless, ritual actions. Incense burnings, idol dustings, washings and purifications, forehead knocking, endless chanting, daubing special marks on her hands and feet. She was sacred and clearly demented, so they watched her with enormous interest, all the time. She meant everything to them. She was doing all these crazy, painful things so the rest of them wouldn't have to. Everything about her was completely and utterly foreclosed.

Pete quite admired the Sacred Temple Girl. She was very much his type, and he felt a genuine kinship with her. She was the only local that Pete could bear to spend any personal time with.

So after prolonged study of the girl and her actions, one day, Pete manifested himself to her. First, she panicked. Then she tried to kill him. Naturally that effort failed. When she grasped the fact that he was hugely powerful, totally magical, and utterly beyond her ken, she slithered around the polished temple floor, rending her garments and keening aloud, clearly in the combined hope/fear of being horribly and indescribably defiled.

Pete understood the appeal of her concept. A younger Pete would have gone for the demonic subjugation option. But Pete was all grown up now. He hardly saw how that could help matters any, or, in fact, make any tangible difference in their circumstances.

They never learned each other's languages. They never connected in any physical, mental, or emotional way. But they finally achieved a kind of status quo, where they could sit together in the same room, and quietly study one another, and fruitlessly speculate on the alien contents of one another's heads. Sometimes, they would even get together and eat something tasty.

That was every bit as good as his connection with these impossibly distant people was ever going to get.

It had never occurred to Pete that the stars might go out.

He'd cut himself a sacred, demonic bolt-hole, in a taboo area of the starship. Every once in a while, he would saw his way through the robots' repair efforts and nick out for a good long look at the artificial cosmos. This reassured him, somehow. And he had other motives as well. He had a very well founded concern that the inhabitants of Starship Two might somehow forge their way over, for an violent racist orgy of looting, slaughter, and rapine.

But Starship Two had their hands full with the robots. Any defeat of the bubbling gelbrain and its hallucinatory tools could only be temporary. Like an onrushing mudslide, the gizmos would route around obstructions, infiltrate every evolutionary possibility, and always, always keep the pressure on.

After the crushing defeat, the bubbling production vats went into biomechanical overdrive. The old regime had been overthrown. All equilibrium was gone. The machines had gone back to their cybernetic dreamtime. Anything was possible now.

The starry walls grew thick as fleas with a seething mass of new-model jailers. Starship Two was beaten back once again, in another bitter, uncounted, historical humiliation. Their persecuted homeland became a mass of grotesque cement. Even the portholes were gone now, cruelly sealed in technological spit and ooze. A living grave.

Pete had assumed that this would pretty much finish the job. After all, this clearly fit the parameters of the system's original designers.

But the system could no longer bother with the limits of human intent.

When Pete gazed through a porthole and saw that the stars were fading, he knew that all bets were off. The stars were being robbed. Something was embezzling their energy.

He left the starship. Outside, all heaven had broken loose. An unspeakable host of creatures were migrating up the rocky walls, bounding, creeping, lurching, rappelling on a web of gooey ropes. Heading for the stellar zenith.

Bound for transcendence. Bound for escape.

Pete checked his aging cleats and gloves, and joined the exodus at once.

None of the creatures bothered him. He had become one of them now. His equipment had fallen among them, been absorbed, and kicked open new doors of evolution. Anything that could breed a can opener could breed a rock chock and a piton, a crampon, and a pulley, and a carabiner. His haul bags, Katrinko's bags, had been stuffed with generations of focused human genius, and it was all about one concept: UP. Going up. Up and *out*.

The unearthly landscape of the Taklamakan was hosting a robot war. A spreading mechanical prairie of inching, crawling, biting, wrenching, hopping mutations. And pillars of fire: Sphere satellite warfare. Beams pouring down from the authentic heavens, invisible torrents of energy that threw up geysers of searing dust. A bio-engineer's final nightmare. Smart, autonomous hell. They couldn't kill a thing this big and keep it secret. They couldn't burn it up fast enough. No, not without breaking the containment domes, and spilling their own ancient trash across the face of the earth.

A beam crossed the horizon like the finger of God, smiting everything in its path. The sky and earth were thick with flying creatures, buzzing, tumbling, sculling. The beam caught a big machine, and it fell spinning like a multiton maple seed. It bounded from the side of a containment dome, caromed like a dying gymnast, and landed below Spider Pete. He crouched there in his camou, recording it all.

It looked back at him. This was no mere robot. It was a mechanical civilian journalist. A brightly painted, ultramodern, European network drone, with as many cameras on board as a top-flight media mogul had martinis. The machine had smashed violently against the secret wall, but it was not dead. Death was not on its agenda. It was way game. It had spotted him with no trouble at all. He was a human interest story. It was looking at him.

Glancing into the cold spring sky, Pete could see that the journalist had brought a lot of its friends.

The robot rallied its fried circuits, and centered him within a spiraling focus. Then it lifted a multipronged limb, and ceremonially spat out every marvel it had witnessed, up into the sky and out into the seething depths of the global web.

Pete adjusted his mask and his camou suit. He wouldn't look right, otherwise.

"Dang," he said.

The island of the immortals

URSULA K. LE GUIN

Ursula K. Le Guin is one of the best-known and most universally respected SF writers in the world today. Her famous novel The Left Hand of Darkness *may have been the most influential SF novel of its decade, and shows every sign of becoming one of the enduring classics of the genre — even ignoring the rest of Le Guin's work, the impact of this one novel alone on future SF and future SF writers would be incalculably strong. (Her 1968 fantasy novel,* A Wizard of Earthsea, *would be almost as influential on future generations of high fantasy writers.) The* Left Hand of Darkness *won both the Hugo and Nebula Awards, as did Le Guin's monumental novel* The Dispossessed *a few years later. Her novel* Tehanu *won her another Nebula in 1990, and she has also won three other Hugo Awards and two Nebula Awards for her short fiction, as well as the National Book Award for children's literature for her novel* The Farthest Shore, *part of her acclaimed Earthsea trilogy. Her other novels include* Planet of Exile, The Lathe of Heaven, City of Illusions, Rocannon's World, The Beginning Place, The Eye of the Heron, The Tombs of Atuan, Searoad, *and the controversial multimedia novel* Always Coming Home. *She has had seven collections:* The Wind's Twelve Quarters, Orsinian Tales, The Compass Rose, Buffalo Gals and Other Animal Presences, A Fisherman of the Inland Sea, Four Ways to Forgiveness, *and most recently,* Unlocking the Air. *Last year she published* Steering the Craft, *a slim book on the craft of writing fiction. Her stories have appeared in our Second, Fifth, Eighth, Twelfth, and Thirteenth Annual Collections. She lives with her husband in Portland, Oregon.*

In the quiet little story that follows, as sharply, exquisitely, and perfectly drawn as a miniature on tortoiseshell, she shows us that everything has a price . . . and that the more valuable the object of desire is, the higher that price is likely to be. . . .

Somebody asked me if I'd heard that there were immortal people on the Yendian Plane, and somebody else told me that there were, so when I go there, I asked about them. The travel agent rather reluctantly showed me a place called the Island of the Immortals on her map. "You don't want to go there," she said.

"I don't?"

"Well, it's dangerous," she said, looking at me as if she thought I was not the danger-loving type, in which she was entirely correct. She was a rather unpolished local agent, not an employee of the Interplanary Service. Yendi is not a popular destination. In many ways it's so like our own plane that it seems hardly worth the trouble of visiting. There are differences, but they're subtle.

"Why is it called the Island of the Immortals?"

"Because some of the people there are immortal."

"They don't die?" I asked, never quite sure of the accuracy of my translatomat.

"They don't die," she said indifferently. "Now, the Prinjo Archipelago is a lovely place for a restful fortnight." Her pencil moved southward across the map of the Great Sea of Yendi. My gaze remained on the large, lonely Island of the Immortals. I pointed to it.

"Is there a hotel—there?"

"There are no tourist facilities. Just cabins for the diamond hunters."

"There are diamond mines?"

"Probably," she said. She had become dismissive.

"What makes it dangerous?"

"The flies."

"Biting flies? Do they carry disease?"

"No." She was downright sullen by now.

"I'd like to try it for a few days," I said, as winningly as I could. "Just to find out if I'm brave. If I get scared, I'll come right back. Give me an open flight back."

"No airport."

"Ah," said I, more winningly than ever. "So how would I get there?"

"Ship," she said, unwon. "Once a week."

Nothing rouses an attitude like an attitude. "Fine!" I said.

At least, I thought as I left the travel agency, it won't be anything like Laputa. I had read *Gulliver's Travels* as a child, in a slightly abridged and probably greatly expurgated version. My memory of it was like all my childhood memories, immediate, broken, vivid—bits of bright particularity in a vast drift of oblivion. I remembered that Laputa floated in the air, so you had to use an airship to get to it. And really I remembered little else, except that the Laputans were immortal, and that I had liked it the least of Gulliver's four Travels, deciding it was *for grown-ups*, a damning quality at the time. Did the Laputans have spots, moles, something like that, which distinguished them? And were they scholars? But they grew senile, and lived on and on in incontinent idiocy—or did I imagine that? There was something nasty about them, something like that, something for grown-ups.

But I was on Yendi, where Swift's works are not in the library. I could not look it up. Instead, since I had a whole day before the ship sailed, I went to the library and looked up the Island of the Immortals.

The Central Library of Undund is a noble old building full of modern conveniences, including book-translatomats. I asked a librarian for assistance and he brought me Postwand's *Explorations*, written about a hundred and sixty years earlier, from which I copied what follows. At the time Postwand wrote, the port city where I was staying, An Ria, had not been founded; the great wave of settlers from the east had not begun; the peoples of the coast were scattered tribes of shepherds and farmers. Postwand took a rather patronizing but intelligent interest in their stories.

"Among the legends of the peoples of the West Coast," he writes, "one concerned a large island two or three days west from Undund Bay, where live *the people who never die*. All whom I asked about it were familiar with the reputation of the Island of the Immortals, and some even told me that members of their tribe had visited the place. Impressed with the unanimity of this tale, I determined to test its veracity. When at length Vong had finished making repairs to my boat, I sailed out of the Bay and due west over the Great Sea. A following wind favored my expedition.

"About noon on the fifth day, I raised the island. Low-lying, it appeared to be at least fifty miles long from north to south.

"In the region in which I first brought the boat close to the land, the shores were entirely salt marsh. It being low tide, and the weather unbearably sultry, the putrid smell of the mud kept us well away, until at length sighting sand beaches I sailed into a shallow bay and soon saw the roofs of a small town at the mouth of a creek. We tied up at a crude and decrepit jetty and with indescribable emotion, on my part at least, set foot on this isle reputed to hold the secret of ETER-NAL LIFE."

I think I shall abbreviate Postwand; he's long-winded, and besides, he's always sneering at Vong, who seems to do most of the work and have none of the indescribable emotions. So he and Vong trudged around the town, finding it all very shabby and nothing out of the way, except that there were dreadful swarms of flies. Everyone went about in gauze clothing from head to toe, and all the doors and windows had screens. Postwand assumed the flies would bite savagely, but found they didn't; they were annoying, he says, but one scarcely felt their bites, which didn't swell up or itch. He wondered if they carried some disease. He asked the islanders, who disclaimed all knowledge of disease, saying nobody ever got sick except mainlanders.

At this, Postwand got excited, naturally, and asked them if they ever died. "Of course," they said.

He does not say what else they said, but one gathers they treated him as yet another idiot from the mainland asking stupid questions. He becomes quite testy, and makes comments on their backwardness, bad manners, and execrable cookery. After a disagreeable night in a hut of some kind, he explored inland for several miles, on foot since there was no other way to get about. In a tiny village near a marsh he saw a sight that was, in his words, "proof positive that the islanders' claim of being free from disease was mere boastfulness, or something yet more sinister: for a more dreadful example of the ravages of udreba I have never seen, even in the wilds of Rotogo. The sex of the poor victim was indistinguishable; of the legs, nothing remained but stumps; the whole body was as if it had been melted in fire; only the hair, which was quite white, grew luxuriantly, long, tangled, and filthy—a crowning horror to this sad spectacle."

I looked up udreba. It's a disease the Yendians dread as we dread leprosy, which it resembles, though it is far more immediately dangerous; a single contact with saliva or any exudation can cause infection. There is no vaccine and no cure. Postwand was horrified to see children playing close by the udreb. He apparently lectured a woman of the village on hygiene, at which she took offense and lectured him back, telling him not to stare at people. She picked up the poor udreb "as if it were a child of five," he says, and took it into her hut. She came out with a bowl full of something, muttering loudly. At this point Vong, with whom I sympathize, suggested that it was time to leave. "I acceded to my companion's groundless apprehensions," Postwand says. In fact, they sailed away that evening.

I can't say that this account raised my enthusiasm for visiting the island. I sought some more modern information. My librarian had drifted off, the way Yendians always seemed to do. I didn't know how to use the subject catalogues, or it was even more incomprehensibly organized than our electronic subject catalogues, or there was singularly little information concerning the Island of the Immortals in the library. All I found was a treatise on the *Diamonds of Aya* — a name sometimes given the island. The article was too technical for the translatomat. I couldn't understand much except that apparently there were no mines; the diamonds did not occur deep in the earth but were to be found lying on the surface of it, as I think is the case in a southern African desert. As the island of Aya was forested and swampy, its diamonds were exposed by heavy rains or mudslides in the wet season. People went and wandered around looking for them. A big one turned up just often enough to keep people coming. The islanders apparently never joined in the search. In fact, some baffled diamond hunters claimed that the natives buried diamonds when they found them. If I understood the treatise, some that had been found were immense by our standards: they were described as shapeless lumps, usually black or dark, occasionally clear, and weighing up to five pounds. Nothing was said about cutting these huge stones, what they were used for, or their market price. Evidently the Yendi didn't prize diamonds as we do. There was a lifeless, almost furtive tone to the treatise, as if it concerned something vaguely shameful.

Surely if the islanders actually knew anything about "the secret of ETERNAL LIFE," there'd be a bit more about them, and it, in the library?

It was mere stubbornness, or reluctance to go back to the sullen travel agent and admit my mistake, that impelled me to the docks the next morning.

I cheered up no end when I saw my ship, a charming miniliner with about thirty pleasant staterooms. Its fortnightly round took it to several islands farther west than Aya. Its sister ship, stopping by on the homeward leg, would bring me back to the mainland at the end of my week. Or perhaps I would simply stay aboard and have a two-week cruise? That was fine with the ship's staff. They were informal, even lackadaisical, about arrangements. I had the impression that low energy and a short attention span were quite common among Yendians. But my companions on the ship were undemanding, and the cold fish salads were excellent. I spent two days on the top deck watching sea-birds swoop, great red fish leap, and translucent vane-wings hover over the sea. We sighted Aya very early in the morning of the third day. At the mouth of the bay the smell of the marshes was truly discouraging; but a conversation with the ship's captain had decided me to visit Aya after all, and I disembarked.

The captain, a man of sixty or so, had assured me that there were indeed immortals on the island. They were not born immortal, but contracted immortality from the bite of the island flies. It was, he thought, a virus. "You'll want to take precautions," he said. "It's rare. I don't think there's been a new case in the last hundred years—longer, maybe. But you don't want to take chances."

After pondering awhile I inquired, as delicately as possible, though delicacy is hard to achieve on the translatomat, whether there weren't people who *wanted* to escape death—people who came to the island *hoping* to be bitten by one of these lively flies. Was there a drawback I did not know about, some price too high to pay even for immortality?

The captain considered my question for a while. He was slow-spoken, unexcitable, verging on the lugubrious. "I think so," he said. He looked at me. "You can judge," he said. "After you've been there."

He would say no more. A ship's captain is a person who has that privilege.

The ship did not put into the bay, but was met out beyond the bar by a boat that took passengers ashore. The other passengers were still in their cabins. Nobody but the captain and a couple of sailors watched me (all rigged out head to foot in a suit of strong but gauzy mesh which I had rented from the ship) clamber down into the boat and wave goodbye. The captain nodded. One of the sailors waved. I was extremely frightened. It was no help at all that I didn't know what I was frightened of.

Putting the captain and Postwand together, it sounded as if the price of immortality was the horrible disease, udreba. But I really had very little evidence, and my curiosity was intense. If a virus that made you immortal turned up in my country, vast sums of money would be poured into studying it, and if it had bad effects they'd alter it genetically to get rid of the bad effects, and the talk shows would yatter on about it, and news anchors would pontificate about it, and the Pope would do some pontificating too, and so would all the other holy men, and meanwhile the very rich would be cornering not only the market, but the supplies. And then the very rich would be even more different from you and me.

What I was really curious about was the fact that none of this had happened. The Yendians were apparently so uninterested in their chance to be immortal that there was scarcely anything about it in the library.

But I could see, as the boat drew close to the town, that the travel agent had been a bit disingenuous. There had been hotels here—big ones, six or eight stories. They were all visibly derelict, signs askew, windows boarded or blank.

The boatman, a shy young man, rather nice-looking as well as I could tell through my gauzy envelope, said, "Hunters' lodge, ma'am?" into my translatomat. I nodded and he sailed us neatly to a small jetty at the north end of the docks. The waterfront too had seen better days. It was now sagging and forlorn, no ships, only a couple of trawlers or crabbers. I stepped up onto the dock, looking about nervously for flies; but there were none at the moment. I tipped the boatman a couple of radlo, and he was so grateful he took me up the street, a sad little street, to the diamond hunters' lodge. It consisted of eight or nine decrepit cabins managed by a dispirited woman who, speaking slowly but without any commas or periods, said to take Number Four because the screens were the best ones breakfast at eight dinner at seven eighteen radlo and did I want a lunch packed a radlo fifty extra.

All the other cabins were unoccupied. The toilet had a little, internal, eternal leak, *tink . . . tink*, which I could not find the source of. Dinner and breakfast arrived on trays, and were edible. The flies arrived with the heat of the day, plenty of them, but not the thick fearsome swarms I had expected. The screens kept them out, and the gauze suit kept them from biting. They were small, weak-looking, brownish flies.

That day and the next morning, walking about the town, the name of which I could not find written anywhere, I felt that the Yendian tendency to depression had bottomed out here, attained nadir. The islanders were a sad people. They were listless. They were lifeless. My mind turned up that word and stared at it.

I realized I'd waste my whole week just getting depressed if I didn't rouse up my courage and ask some questions. I saw my young boatman fishing off the jetty and went to talk to him.

"Will you tell me about the immortals?" I asked him, after some halting amenities.

"Well, most people just walk around and look for them. In the woods," he said.

"No, not the diamonds," I said, checking the translatomat. "I'm not really very interested in diamonds."

"Nobody much is any more," he said. "There used to be a lot of tourists and diamond hunters. I guess they do something else now."

"But I read in a book that there are people here who live very, very long lives — who actually don't die."

"Yes," he said, placidly.

"Are there any immortal people in town? Do you know any of them?"

He checked his fishing line. "Well, no," he said. "There was a new one, way back in my grandpa's time, but it went to the mainland. It was a woman. I guess there's an old one in the village." He nodded toward the island. "Mother saw it once."

"If you could, would you like to live a long time?"

"Sure!" he said, with as much enthusiasm as a Yendian is capable of. "You know."

"But you don't want to be immortal. You wear the fly-gauze."

He nodded. He saw nothing to discuss in all this. He was fishing with gauze gloves, seeing the world through a mesh veil. That was life.

The storekeeper told me that you could walk to the village in a day and showed me the path. My dispirited landlady packed me a lunch. I set out next morning, attended at first by thin, persistent swarms of flies. It was a dull walk across a low, damp landscape, but the sun was mild and pleasant, and the flies finally gave up. To my surprise, I got to the village before I was even hungry for lunch. The islanders must walk slowly and seldom. It had to be the right village, though, because they spoke of only one, "the village," again no name.

It was small and poor and sad: six or seven wooden huts, rather like Russian izbas, stilted up a bit to keep them from the mud. Poultry, something like guinea fowl but mud-brown, scuttled about everywhere, making soft, raucous noises. A couple of children ran away and hid as I approached.

And there, propped up next to the village well, was the figure Postwand had described, just as he had described it—legless, sexless, the face almost featureless, blind, with skin like badly burned bread, and thick, matted, filthy white hair.

I stopped, appalled.

A woman came out of the hut to which the children had run. She came down the rickety steps and walked up to me. She gestured at my translatomat, and I automatically held it out to her so she could speak into it.

"You came to see the Immortal," she said.

I nodded.

"Two radlo fifty," she said.

I got out the money and handed it to her.

"Come this way," she said. She was poorly dressed and not clean, but was a fine-looking woman, thirty-five or so, with unusual decisiveness and vigor in her voice and movements.

She led me straight to the well and stopped in front of the being propped up in a legless canvas fisherman's chair next to it. I could not look at the face, nor the horribly maimed hand. The other arm ended in a black crust above the elbow. I looked away from that.

"You are looking at the Immortal of our village," the woman said in the practiced singsong of the tour guide. "It has been with us for many many centuries. For over one thousand years it has belonged to the Roya family. In this family it is our duty and pride to look after the Immortal. Feeding hours are six in the morning and six in the evening. It lives on milk and barley broth. It has a good appetite and enjoys good health with no sicknesses. It does not have udreba. Its legs were lost when there was an earthquake one thousand years ago. It was also damaged by fire and other accidents before it came into the care of the Roya family. The legend of my family says that the Immortal was once a handsome young man who made his living for many lifetimes of normal people by hunting in the marshes. This was two or three thousand years ago, it is believed. The Immortal cannot hear what you say or see you, but is glad to accept your prayers for its wellbeing and any offerings for its support, as it is entirely dependent on the Roya family for food and shelter. Thank you very much. I will answer questions."

After a while I said, "It can't die."

She shook her head. Her face was impassive; not unfeeling, but closed.

"You aren't wearing gauze," I said, suddenly realizing this. "The children weren't. Aren't you—"

She shook her head again. "Too much trouble," she said, in a quiet, unofficial voice. "The children always tear the gauze. Anyhow, we don't have many flies. And there's only one."

It was true that the flies seemed to have stayed behind, in the town and the heavily manicured fields near it.

"You mean there's only one immortal at a time?"

"Oh, no," she said. "There are others all around. In the ground. Sometimes people find them. Souvenirs. The really old ones. Ours is young, you know." She looked at the Immortal with a weary but proprietary eye, the way a mother looks at an unpromising infant.

"The diamonds?" I said. "The diamonds are immortals?"

She nodded. "After a really long time," she said. She looked away, across the marshy plain that surrounded the village, and then back at me. "A man came from the mainland, last year, a scientist. He said we ought to bury our Immortal. So it could turn to diamond, you know. But then he said it takes thousands of years to turn. All that time it would be starving and thirsty in the ground and nobody would look after it. It is wrong to bury a person alive. It is our family duty to look after it. And no tourists would come."

It was my turn to nod. The ethics of this situation were beyond me. I accepted her choice.

"Would you like to feed it?" she asked, apparently liking something about me, for she smiled at me.

"No," I said, and I have to admit that I burst into tears.

She came closer and patted my shoulder.

"It is very, very sad," she said. She smiled again. "But the children like to feed it," she said. "And the money helps."

"Thank you for being so kind," I said, wiping my eyes, and I gave her another five radlo, which she took gratefully. I turned around and walked back across the marshy plains to the town, where I waited four more days until the sister ship came by from the west, and the nice young man took me out in the boat, and I left the Island of the Immortals, and soon after that I left the Yendian Plane.

We are a carbon-based life form, as the scientists say, but how a human body could turn to diamond I do not know, unless through some spiritual factor, perhaps the result of genuinely endless suffering.

Perhaps "diamond" is only a name the Yendians give these lumps of ruin, a kind of euphemism.

I am still not certain what the woman in the village meant when she said, "There's only one." She was not referring to the immortals. She was explaining why she didn't protect herself or her children from the flies, why she found the risk not worth the bother. It is possible that she meant that among the swarms of flies in the island marshes there is only one fly, one immortal fly, whose bite infects its victim with eternal life.

sea change, with monsters

PAUL J. McAULEY

Here's a vivid and suspenseful scientific thriller that takes us to the outer reaches of the solar system, to a brooding Gothic monastery on the frozen surface of the Jovian moon Europa, where an intrepid investigator must match wits with a sinister group of fanatical monks in order to unravel a high-tech mystery with chilling implications for all of human civilization. . . .

Born in Stroud, England, in 1955, Paul J. McAuley now makes his home in London. He is considered to be one of the best of the new breed of British writers (although a few Australian writers could be fit in under this heading as well) who are producing that sort of revamped, updated, wide-screen Space Opera sometimes referred to as "radical hard science fiction." He is a frequent contributor to Interzone, *as well as to markets such as* Amazing, The Magazine of Fantasy & Science Fiction, Asimov's Science Fiction, When the Music's Over, *and elsewhere. His first novel,* Four Hundred Billion Stars, *won the Philip K. Dick Award, and his most recent collection,* The Invisible Country, *was also a finalist for the award. His other books include the novels* Of the Fall, Eternal Light, *and* Pasquale's Angel, *a collection of his short work,* The King of the Hill and Other Stories, *and an original anthology co-edited with Kim Newman,* In Dreams. *His acclaimed novel,* Fairyland, *won both the Arthur C. Clarke Award and the John W. Campbell Award in 1996. His most recent books are* Child of the River *and* Ancient of Days, *the first two volumes of a major trilogy of ambitious scope and scale,* Confluence, *set ten million years in the future. Currently he is working on a new novel,* Life on Mars. *His Web site is at http:/www.omegacom.demon.co.uk.*

S he made it clear that she was taking the job as a favor.

Vlad Simonov pretended to be slighted by her reluctance. He said, "But Indira, what's the problem? It's a fantastic job, and it's not as if you are working."

"I have been working," Indira said. "Now I'm resting."

She had spent two weeks supervising the clearance of an infestation of urchins at the perimeter of a farm collective. It had been difficult, dangerous, tiring work, and she had nearly been killed in almost exactly the same way she had nearly been killed on her first job, when she hadn't really known what she had been doing. She had come full circle. She was beginning to believe that she had killed enough monsters.

Vlad snapped his fingers and leaned close to the camera of his phone. "After that picayune little job, you need to *rest*? That kind of thing, I do as an exercise. I do it for relaxation! I do it in my sleep, after a proper day's work. Listen, Indira, I would take this job myself, it is so good, except already I am committed to three others. So I give it to you. With my usual commission of course, but the terms are so generous you will not notice the little I have kept to take home to feed my children."

Vlad's restless, good-humored energy was apparent even over the phone. Indira laughed.

He said chidingly, "Indira, Indira. You are getting old. You are getting bored. Urchins, spinners, makos, they're all the same to you. Routine, routine, routine. It hurts me to see you like this. So, I put some pep in your life. To make you think again. To make you love life. Say yes. You will have fun, I promise."

"Vlad . . . we are all getting old."

"Not the *monsters*. While you sit around in your nice, warm, comfortable apt, the monsters are swimming in the cold and the dark, pumping sulfides, getting strong. Indira, this is a very exciting job, and the people who commission it are some kind of funny monks who know nothing about the value of money. You will be rich, even after my tiny percentage is removed. They claim it is a dragon, Indira. You have never hunted a dragon, but I know you can do it. That is why I ask only you."

"And that's why I'm taking it as a favor to *you*, Vlad. Because I know no one else will do it."

Indira had started out as an apprentice to Vlad Simonov; now she freelanced for him. He was one of the first generation of hunters, one of the few to have survived the early days of tracking the biowar macroforms, the monsters, which had been set loose during the Quiet War. Vlad liked to project a buccaneering image. He had two wives and five children. He drank brandy and smoked huge cigars. He had a wild mane of black hair with little lights spidering inside its curls. But there was no safer or more cautious hunter in all of Europa's ocean.

She said, "A dragon."

"*Perhaps* a dragon. Are you scared?"

"I'm always scared."

A pod of urchins had ambushed her toward the end of the last job. She had been finning down a long flaw in pure water ice, leading her diving buddy, a nervous farm worker. The flaw had been polished smooth by methane seep. It had reflected her lights in a blue-white glare that had prevented her seeing very much of what was ahead. The urchins had fallen down on her from a crevice. She had doubled up, knocking two urchins off her face mask—their spines left deep scratches in the glass—and had started firing her flechette pistol even as she kicked backward. Her diving buddy had been frozen in fear, blocking her escape; the urchins had bobbed toward her through a dancing dazzle of reflected light. She had coldly and methodically killed every one of them in a Zen-like calm that had thawed to violent trembling as soon as the slaughter was over.

She told Vlad, "I can't go solo against a dragon. If it *is* a dragon."

He said, "You won't need to go solo. The monks have a big weed farm and their workers will help you. Anyway, it's probably no more than a mako. No one has seen a dragon for years—they're probably extinct. The monks see something lurking just beyond their perimeter and make it bigger than it is. Let me tell you what I know."

Indira's daughter, Alice, came in two hours later. She found her mother in the workshop, with the luggage pod open on the floor. She said, "You only just came home."

"I know, sweet."

Alice stood in the doorway, bouncing up and down as gently as a tethered balloon. Seven years old, smart and determined. She wore baggy shorts and a nylon vest with many pockets and an iridescent flared collar that rose above her head like a lizard's ruff. Fluorescent tattoos braided her thin brown arms. She had changed them since she had gone off to school that morning. They had been interlocking lizards and birds then; now they were long fluttering banners, red and violet and maroon. Her hair was done up in tight cornrows and decorated with little tags that flashed in random patterns of yellow and green.

Alice said, "Have you told Carr yet?"

Indira didn't look up. She was concentrating on fitting her dry suit into the pod, taking great care not to crease it. She said, "He'll be home soon. How was school?"

"I'm doing a project."

"You must tell me all about it."

"It's a secret."

A pause. Indira knew that her daughter had been down to the service levels of the city again, at the bottom of the ice. She had beeped Alice's location after she had finalized the contract with Vlad. And Alice knew that she knew. She watched solemnly as her mother checked the weapon cases. They were flat metal shells with foam plastic bedding inside. The smallest contained three kinds of specific neurotoxin in glass snap-top vials. Indira made very sure that these were packed properly.

At last, Alice said, "Did you know that the city once had another name?"

"Of course."

"It was called Minos. Why was that?"

"Because Minos was one of the sons of Europa. Of Europa and Zeus."

When Alice stamped her foot, she bounced a meter into the air. "I know that! It means creature of the moon. He was the king who built a maze under his palace. But why did it *change*?"

"Politics."

"Oh. You mean the war."

Alice had been born ten years after the Quiet War. Like all of her generation, she couldn't understand why the adults around her spent so much time talking about it when it clearly made them so unhappy.

"Yes, the war. Where did you find this out?"

"I saw a sign."

"A sign? In school?"

Alice shook her head. "Of course not in school. The Goonies—" which was the latest nickname for the soldiers of the Three Powers Occupying Force—"have changed all the signs they know about. But they don't know everything."

"Then where was it?"

Alice said, "Carr will be cross because you're going away again so soon."

"That's because he loves me almost as much as he loves you. Where was this sign, Alice?"

"It's to do with my project. So it's a secret until my project's finished."

Indira closed the luggage pod. It made a little whirring noise as it sealed itself up. She didn't want an argument just before she went away, but she didn't want Alice to think that she could disobey her. She said, "I think we had better have a little talk, you and I."

Later, Carr said, "There's nothing to harm her down there."

"Don't take sides," Indira said.

"I'm not. I'm trying to be realistic. Kids go down there all the time. They like staring out into the dark."

"She dresses like a Ring smuggler. Those lights in her hair . . ."

"All the kids her age dress like that. They get it from the sagas. It's harmless."

"Why are you so fucking reasonable?"

"It's a talent I have."

Indira snuggled closer to him. They had just made love, and were both sweating on the big bed, beneath a simulated starscape. Carr liked to keep their room warm and humid. Bamboos and ferns and banana plants surrounded them. The walls were set to show misty distances above a moonlit rainforest. Carr had been born on Earth. His family had migrated from Greater Brazil to Europa a few years before the Quiet War. He was one of the ecological maintenance team of the city; once upon a time, he would have been called a gardener. He was a strong, solid, dependable man. He and Indira had been a couple for nine years now; several months ago, they had started to buy tickets in the child lottery for the second time.

Carr said, "I think it's nice that she wants to make gardens under the ice. A little bit of me, a little bit of you. Did she show you her drawings?"

"Of course she did. Once we had made up after the argument about her going down to the service levels. All those friendly crabs and fish."

Carr stretched luxuriously and asked the bed's treacher for a glass of water. "Citrus, fizzy, ice." He told Indira, "She wants to think that one day there might be a world without monsters." He took a sip of water. He said, "She wants to be a gengineer."

"She wanted to be a tractor driver last week."

"That was two months ago. She has been asking all sorts of questions about gengineering. She asked me why there weren't any fish out there in the ocean. You know, I think sometimes she tells me things because she knows I'll tell you."

"She's smart."

Carr sipped his water. After a while he said, "Why do you have to go away so soon?"

"Because of a monster. One of the angry fish Alice wants to replace with happy, smiling fish."

"There are other hunters."

"You knew what I did when we met, Carr. That hasn't changed. And we need the money to pay for the lottery tickets."

Carr put his water down and folded his arms around her. The hand which had held the glass was cool on her flank. He said, "I didn't even know there was a nunnery on Europa."

"It's a monastery. For monks. Male nuns. Vlad was a bit vague about them and I can't find anything about them on the net. They're some kind of Christians, but not of any of the mainstream sects."

"Whatever. Tell me again why they can't kill this monster for themselves."

"I think they tried." A silence. She took a deep breath and said, "I haven't told you everything, and it's only fair that you know. Vlad thinks it might be a dragon."

Carr said, "They're extinct, aren't they?"

"The last time one was killed was over ten years ago. No one has seen one since. But absence of evidence—"

"—is not evidence of absence. So Vlad the Impaler wants to send you out against a dragon all by yourself."

"We're not certain it is a dragon. And I won't exactly be alone. There will be the monks."

Indira had met Vlad Simonov almost twenty years before, just after the end of the Quiet War. She had been a construction diver then, helping build the city's first weed farm. Biowar macroforms were getting past the sonar and electrical barriers that were supposed to keep them away from the city's underside, and Vlad had been hired to clear out a nest of urchins. The things had learned to passively drift through the barriers on currents and reactivate in the lights of the construction site. They were etching away support pylons, and in those days there were still a few of the kind of urchin that manufactured explosives in their cores. Two construction divers had been killed.

Indira volunteered to assist Vlad, and they quickly located the place where the urchins were breeding. It was five kilometers east of the weed farm, downstream of the currents driven by the upwelling plume. It was an area of rotten ice eroded by the relatively warm water of the upwelling, riddled with caves and crevices and half-collapsed tunnels, rich in precipitated sulfides. Indira didn't panic when urchins started dropping out of crevices in the ice. They seemed like harmless toys, spiny, fist-sized black balls that wobbled this way and that on pulsed jets of water. She forgot that some could be carrying explosive charges and coolly and methodically killed them with neurotoxin-tipped flechettes, not wasting a shot. Afterward,

Vlad said that he liked her style, and that evening they got drunk together to celebrate their victory. She thought no more about it, but a few weeks later he called her up to ask if she would like to help out again.

The gengineered biowar macroforms had been delivered to Europa's ocean by penetrator probes during the Quiet War. Viruses had destroyed the food yeasts (and incidentally had caused the extinction of the indigenous microbes that had lived around the hydrothermal vents at the bottom of the ocean); the macroforms had wrecked the yeast reactors, the mines and the cargo submarines, the heat exchangers and the tidal generators.

Earth had not expected to win the Quiet War quickly. The Three Powers Occupying Force had no plans to decommission the monsters they had set loose, and no one knew how many there were now. They reproduced by parthenogenesis, like certain insects, and they had contained dormant embryos when they had been released. Hunters like Vlad Simonov were the only reliable line of defense against their depredations.

The second job was against a mako that had been systematically destroying mine intakes at Taliesin. Vlad and Indira spent a dozen hours hanging by the probe of one intake, following it as, like a giant articulated proboscis, it moved this way and that in the black water, tracking mineral-rich currents. The mako came in hard and fast out of the darkness, straight at Indira. She held steady and Vlad hit it with his second shot. Afterward, he offered her a permanent job, and she accepted.

She discovered a talent for killing. She got no pleasure from it, except to do it as cleanly and professionally as possible, and it did not diminish the guilt she felt because she had survived the Quiet War and her parents had not. Only time did that. But she was good at killing monsters. She cleaned out hundreds of urchin nests, destroyed infestations of fireworms that had wrapped themselves around electrical cables and caused crippling over-voltages, went up against and killed makos and mantas and spinners. But she had never before had to face a dragon, the smartest and most dangerous of all the monsters.

Indira took the railway west from Phoenix, along Phineus Linea to Cadmus. The scarp stood to the north, an endless fault wall half a kilometer high. It was one of the highest features of Europa's flat surface. Mottled terrain stretched away to the south, textured by small hills and cut by numerous dikes and fracture lines. Lobes of brown and grey ice flows were fretted by sublimation and lightly spattered with small craters. This was one of the oldest landscapes of Europa. The ice here was almost five kilometers thick.

It was early morning, four hours after sunrise. Europa's day was exactly the length of its orbit around Jupiter, and so, from any point on Europa's subjovian hemisphere, Jupiter hung in the same spot in the sky, waxing and waning through the eighty-five hour day. At present, Jupiter was completely dark, a glowering circular black hole in the sky that was nearly thirty times as big as Earth's moon. Indira was in the train's observation car, sipping iced peach tea and watching the beginning of the day's eclipse. It would last three hours, and was the nearest thing to true night on the sub-jovian hemisphere, for when the Sun set, Jupiter was full, and there was almost always one or more of the other three Galilean moons in the sky.

There was a sudden flash of light that briefly defined Jupiter's lower edge as the diamond point of the Sun disappeared behind it. Darkness swept across the ice plain; stars suddenly bestrode the sky in their rigid patterns. As her eyes adapted, Indira could make out the flicker of a lightning storm near the upper edge of Jupiter's black disc—a storm bigger than Europa.

Indira talked with Carr. She talked with Alice and told her what she could see, and tried to patch up the row they'd had.

"Carr misses you already," Alice said. She was on one of the slideways of the city's commercial center. "He says he's going to change your room. It's a surprise." She didn't want to talk about her project. When Indira tried to press her about it, she said, "I have to go. This is where I should be."

The train was full of miners. They were all flying on some drug or other. This was their last chance to get high before they returned to work. They were native Europans, originally from South Africa. They wore leather jackets and fancy high-topped boots over pressure suit liners. One of them played a slow blues on a steel-bodied guitar; another, egged on by his comrades, tried to chat up Indira. He was a young man, tall and very handsome, with very black skin and chiseled cheekbones. He spent more time looking at his reflection in the diamond window of the observation car, ghosting over the speeding, star-lit landscape, than he did looking at Indira. His name was Champion Khumalo. Indira thought that it was a nickname, but no, all his friends had names like that, or names out of the Bible. Trinity Adepoju. Gospel Motloheloa. Ruth and Isaac Mahlungu.

Once Champion gave up his half-hearted attempt to sweet-talk Indira, they all became friends. Indira learnt that two of Champion's brothers went to the same school as Alice. They passed around a bottle of pear brandy and tubes of something called haze. It smelt sharply of ketones and delivered an immediate floating feeling of bonhomie.

The miners were fascinated by her profession. "To clean all the ocean of monsters," Gospel Motloheloa said, "is a noble calling!"

"Well, I don't see why we need to go into the world below," Isaac Mahlungu said. "I have been a miner for thirty years and I have never needed to go there. This is our land, the world all around us."

"But the ocean is part of our world," Gospel said. She was the oldest of the miners. Her iron-grey hair was done up in medusa ropes wound with plastic wire. There were keloid scars on her forehead; because they spent their working lives on the surface, most miners suffered from radiation-induced cancers. She said, "The ocean makes the land what it is, and so it is important to get rid of the monsters that infest it."

"The monsters are from Earth," Trinity Adepoju said. "That's why we have to get rid of them." He was the guitar player, a tall man even for a Europan, with a ready smile and fingers so long they seemed to have several extra joints as he moved them idly up and down the neck of his guitar.

Indira remembered a conversation she had once had with Alice. She had been trying to explain to her daughter why Earth had won the Quiet War.

"They have more wealth, more processing power, more people. They have used up their world and now they want to use up all the others."

"Then we'll have to do things they can't," Alice had said, so solemnly that Indira had laughed.

Champion said, "Even with the monsters gone, we will still live on Earth's sufferance."

His friends nodded, and began to tell Indira their war stories. Many of the miners had been on Europa throughout the Quiet War. Although the population of the capital, then called Minos (the miners called it that still), had at last been evacuated to Ganymede, the miners had been left in their camps. Most had managed to synthesize enough oxygen from water ice, but there had not been enough food.

"We were so hungry," Gospel told Indira, "that we were thinking of eating our boots at the end of it."

Ruth Mahlungu said, "What are you talking about, woman! You are so vain that you would starve to death and be buried in your boots rather than eat them!"

The others laughed. It was true: Gospel's boots were extraordinary, even for a miner, green suede decorated with intricate patterns made from little bits of mirror and red and gold thread.

There were stories of cannibalism. Several camps had been vaporized by the nuclear device that had broken through the crust to allow the penetrators containing the biowar organisms to reach the ocean. This was at Tyre Macula, on Europa's anti-jovian hemisphere. Although the area had been lightly populated, the blast had killed more than a hundred miners and had left a flat plain of radioactive ice and radial grooves hundreds of kilometers long: a bright sunburst scar on Europa's mottled brown face.

Indira had heard all these stories before; it seemed that Europans would never tire of telling and retelling stories about the war. She had stories of her own, but they were all too sad to bear telling. The death of her family, the two years she had spent as an orphaned refugee on Ganymede. At last, she managed to steer the conversation to the monastery.

Champion grinned. "You're going *there?* That's a good joke!"

The miners exchanged words in a language full of glottal clicks. They all laughed, but the young miner would not tell Indira what they found funny.

"They're very rich there, those people," Champion said, "They have a very big weed farm. They supply fixed carbon to half the mines."

"Their leader is a gengineer," Gospel said.

Trinity said, "He calls himself Rothar. I don't think it's his real name. They say he ran from Earth because they caught him doing something illegal. He's probably doing something illegal out there, too."

"Maybe making more monsters," Champion said. "Maybe he makes one monster too many and wants you to kill it."

"They are strange people," Gospel said. "Not Christian at all, although they claim to be. They call themselves Adamists."

This was more than Indira had managed to glean about the monastery from the net. The miners didn't know many hard facts, but they had plenty of gossip. Their talk grew lively and wild. Three hours after the beginning of the eclipse, the double star of Earth and Venus rose above Jupiter's dark bulk, and then the Sun followed and flooded the ice plain with its light. Trinity took up his guitar again and had half the observation car singing along by the time the train reached Cadmus.

Cadmus was an industrial settlement, several clusters of stilt buildings, storage tanks, a big spaceport that was essentially an ice field pitted with black exhaust blasts, the long track of a mass driver. Indira caught a few hours rest in a rented cubicle. Before she fell asleep, she talked with Carr about the small change of his day. Alice was sleeping. She missed her mother, Carr said.

"I miss her, too."

"Be careful," Carr said.

Soldiers of the Three Powers Occupying Force were much in evidence. Two officers were talking loudly in the canteen where Indira ate breakfast, oblivious to the resentful stares of the miners around them, and she had to endure a fifteen-minute interrogation before she could board the rolligon bus that would carry her to the monastery of Scyld Shield.

The journey took ten hours. As the bus traveled west, the diamond point of the Sun descended ahead of it, while Jupiter hung low in the east — Indira had traveled a long way, a quarter of the way around the icy little moon. Jupiter was almost full, banded vertically with the intricately ruffled yellow and whites of his perpetual storms. Their slow churning was visible if Indira watched long enough. Io's yellow disc fell below the horizon and an hour later rose, renewed.

The road was a single track raised on an embankment above a wide plain of crustal plates. Some were more than ten kilometers across; most were much smaller.

Changes in currents in Europa's ocean had broken the plates apart again and again, rafting them into new positions. It was like crossing the shaken pieces of a jigsaw puzzle of simple Euclidean shapes. You could see here that the surface of Europa was a thin skin of ice over the ocean, as fragile as the craquelure on an ancient painting. Triplet ridge and groove features cut across the plates. They were caused by the upwelling of water through stress fractures. The ridges were breccia dikes, ice mixed with mineralized silicates, complexly faulted and folded; the grooves between them were almost pure water-ice. They were like a vast freeway system half-built and abruptly abandoned, cut across where the ice plates had fractured or had been buried by blue-white icy flows that had spewed from newer fissures.

The road the bus was following crossed a groove so wide that the ridge on one side disappeared over the horizon before the ridge on the far side appeared. Beyond it, geysers powered by convective upwellings had built clusters of low hills that shone amidst patches of darker material.

Like Io, Europa's core was kept molten by heat generated by tidal distortions that pulled it this way and that as the moon orbited Jupiter, heat leaking through underwater vents and volcanoes kept the ocean from freezing beneath its icy crust and drove big cellular currents from bottom to top. Cadmus was at the edge of the Nemo Chaos, where a huge upwelling current kept the ice crust less than a kilometer thick. The same upwelling currents that eroded and shaped the icy crust brought up minerals from the bottom of the ocean. It was why the miners were there. Indira saw a solitary cabin crawling away toward the horizon, its red beacon flashing. Every twenty or thirty kilometers, the bus passed the drill-head of a mine, with one or two or three cabins raised high on stilts like so many copies of Baba Yaga's hut. The mines pumped mineral-rich water into huge settling basins. Vacuum organisms grew on the ice and extracted metals, and the miners harvested them.

Alice called Indira. She was enthusiastic about her project. Indira pretended to be enthusiastic, too, but she resolved that she would talk with Alice's monitors when this was over. Her daughter's education was taking a direction she didn't like.

"Spend some time with Carr," Indira told Alice. "Help him out."

"I don't like the flowers. Some of them make me sneeze. And the light is too bright in the greenhouses."

"It helps them grow."

"The weeds don't need light."

"That's because they don't photosynthesize."

"I know that. They're—" Alice scrunched up her face and said slowly and carefully—"chemolithotrophs. They absorb the chemicals in the water and make biomass, which we eat."

They talked about the metabolism of the weeds for a while. Alice promised that she would ask Carr about photosynthesis. She said that she was doing some gene splicing in the garden labs, using the cell gun. Indira was encouraging. The more time Alice spent in the labs and the gardens, the less she spent skulking around the lower levels of the city.

The bus had low priority and had to keep pulling into laybys to allow trucks to pass. Indira was its only passenger, and its first for several weeks. It seemed that very few people went to Scyld Shield. The bus grumbled that the monks weren't friendly.

"They tell me to be quiet, and it is a long drive out. I like to talk. It's part of my personality design." The bus paused. It added, "I hope you don't mind talking with me."

"What do you know about the monastery?"

"It was a mine, before the war. The monks have built around the old shaft. But of course, I have never been inside. They don't have a garage. If I broke down, someone would have to come all the way out from Cadmus. It's irresponsible, but that's the way things are these days in the free market economy. No one wants to pay for the upkeep of publicly owned infrastructure."

Someone had probably dumped a bunch of anti-libertarian propaganda in the bus's memory. Indira was sympathetic, but hastily told it that she wasn't interested in discussing politics. There was a silence. At last the bus said:

"Many of the trucks come from the monastery. They supply huge amounts of cheap fixed carbon. Glycogens, proteins, cellulose, starches. They supply the bio-reactors of most of the mines in this region."

"There must be a lot of monks in the monastery."

"I wouldn't know," the bus said. "Only two of them regularly travel to and from Cadmus. The rest keep themselves to themselves."

Which was what the dispatcher at the bus garage had told Indira. She could have called Vlad Simonov, of course, but she had her pride.

The Sun set. Jupiter's hard yellow light spread across the ice plains. Io had disappeared behind him; a few of the brightest stars had come out. Ahead, something briefly glittered on the horizon, vanishing before Indira could see what it was. The bus crawled on, and an hour later, Indira saw the fugitive glitter again, much closer now. A plume of gas, shining in Jupiter's sullen light.

"There she blows," the bus said.

"What is it?"

"Scyld Shield's methane vent," the bus said. "Most of the mines around here have them."

"Of course."

Methane bubbled up from the hydrothermal vents and collected under the ice crust, occasionally breaking the rafts apart as it escaped through fault lines. Mines vented excess methane to keep themselves stabilized. The methane dispersed, of course, for at $-150°C$ Europa's surface was just above its triple point, but the vent had deposited drifts of dirty white water snow across a huge polygonal plate. The monastery was on a ridge of brecciated ice beyond.

It was not as large as Indira expected, no more than a single silvered dome. The bus took a spur off the main road. It climbed a winding switchback up the face of the ridge and dived into a wide apron hacked out of an ice bench, where half a dozen tanker trucks were parked in front of a mass of insulated pipes, presumably taking on loads of raw biomass. The bus reversed onto a airlock coupling and said goodbye to Indira.

"I'll be back in three days," it said. "I come here every three days even when there isn't anyone who wants to ride. That is, if I don't break down. Perhaps you can tell me about the monastery when I take you back to Cadmus."

The luggage pod followed Indira through the freezing cold flexible coupling into a big, echoing, brightly lit room. Two monks were waiting there. Both wore black robes and a kind of cowl around their heads, topped with square headdresses. Both had untrimmed patriarchal beards, with big pectoral crosses hung over them. The older monk was impassive, but the younger was the first man Indira had ever seen do a double-take in real life.

They had been expecting a man. Sending Indira had been Vlad Simonov's idea of a joke.

The two monks left Indira with her luggage pod in the middle of the big, empty space. There were marks on the concrete floor that suggested that it had once been partitioned into many small rooms. A gutted air compressor sat in one corner. She sat down on the pod and tried to call Carr, but her phone wasn't getting any signal. It was so cold that the smoke of each breath crystallized into a floating frost with a tiny tinkling sound, too cold to sit still and wait.

She began to prowl around. The empty room took up half the dome; a corridor looped around the other half, with little rooms opening off on either side. None showed any sign of recent habitation. There were two service tunnels. One led downward, curving out of sight; she had just opened the door of the other, its ribbed wall rimed with ice and stopped with a locked hatch, when the older of the two monks found her. It seemed that Brother Rothar, the abbot of the monastery, would talk with her.

The old monk's name was Halga. Indira asked him about the other tunnel as they walked down, and he said that it led to the old mine structure, which had sunk into the ice after it had been abandoned during the war.

"We cut a tunnel to it to see what we could salvage. Now we use it for storage."

"I didn't mean to pry. I was just looking around and wondering where I should stow my gear."

"I think you should talk with Brother Rothar," the old monk said.

"Is there a problem?"

"Brother Rothar will explain."

The tunnel wound down a long way. Indira realized that the monastery was like a pin piercing the ice—a pin a kilometer long, with the dome at its head and a winding series of chambers and passages built around its shaft. Brother Halga explained that the whole structure had been synthesized from glass and silicates extracted from the brecciated ice and bound together by diamond wire. Indira wondered how often they had to adjust the shaft because of stress in the icy crust, and Brother Halga told her that the monastery was built on a breccia intrusion that went almost all the way down to the ocean.

"The surface is covered with ice, but a hundred meters below the surface it is quite stable."

The old monk had a mild, diffident manner. He did not look at her when he spoke.

She said, "I don't mean to make you uncomfortable by asking all these questions."

"We are not used to people like you. To women, I mean." His brown face, framed by the black cowl, darkened. He was blushing.

They walked on in silence, and at last took a side corridor whose walls, floor, and ceiling were covered in thick red fur. The air was at blood heat. Double doors at the end were covered in some kind of hide, dyed the same red as the fur. Brother Halga opened them, ushered her in, and announced her to the man who stood at the far end of the dimly lit room.

"Brother Rothar," the old monk whispered, and stepped backward and pulled the double doors shut behind him.

On one side of the room, shelves holding printed books stepped up into darkness. On the other, a stone wall was muffled by an ancient tapestry: an enlarged reproduction of a section of the ceiling of the Vatican's Sistine Chapel, God reaching out from the clouds to a casually reclining Adam. At the far end of the room, a man was standing in front of a huge fireplace, watching a bank of holos that floated in the darkness to one side. The fireplace was as big as an emergency shelter and held an actual, real fire. The flames crackled and danced above a bed of white-hot pressed carbon chunks and sent little licks of aromatic smoke curling over the monumental lintel, and firelight beat over the Persian carpets that layered the floor.

Indira had been told that the monastery was wealthy, but she had not realized *how* wealthy.

"Welcome," the man said. His voice was subtly amplified. It boomed and rolled, mellow as good whisky, around the corners of the sumptuous room.

He was an old man, thin and straight-backed, with a shrewd, hawkish face. His dusty white skin was marked with dark blotches. He wore the same black robes as the monks, but instead of a cowl, his bald pate was covered with a black skullcap on which molecular shapes were embroidered in gold wire. Heavy gold rings extended the lobes of his large, papery ears.

"I have arranged for some food," he said.

He crossed to the side of the fireplace, tracked by a spotlight that came on somewhere high above, and pulled a Florentine chair from a little burred walnut table. A plastic tray of food was set on the table: a sloppy puree of some kind of green leaf; a slab of gelatin seamed with chunks of uncooked vegetable; dry salty biscuits. A plastic beaker held pure water.

Rothar watched Indira push the puree around and said, "The same food is served in our refectory. We are an ascetic order."

He gestured, and one of the holos floating to the side of the fireplace inflated. It showed a view looking down on a refectory in which about a hundred black-robed monks sat in rows, ten by ten, along white plastic tables.

She said, "I ate at Cadmus, and then on the bus. This isn't quite —"

"What you expected? No. It is not what I expected, either. And there is the problem."

The holo shrank back into the array. Others showed views of a weed farm that seemed to stretch forever. Indira realized that Rothar was showing off. This room; his army of monks; the vast farm.

Rothar said, "I have been trying to talk with Vlad Simonov about this . . . problem. But he is nowhere on the net."

He was rubbing his hands over each other. She noticed that when he thought she wasn't looking at him, he made little grabby glances at her body. She wished that she had worn something over the skintight suit liner.

She said, "Vlad is working at a mine on the anti-jovian hemisphere. He's probably under the ice. What is this problem? When do I start to work? Perhaps I can see the echo traces, and any video you have."

When Rothar looked at her for a moment, she added, "Of the monster. The monster I've come to kill."

"Ah. Now. I'm afraid that there has been a misunderstanding."

"A misunderstanding? You have reported a Dragon Class biowar macroform in your area. You made a contract with Vlad Simonov, and Vlad sent me."

"There is the misunderstanding. You see, we did not expect him to send us a woman."

"One of Vlad's little jokes."

"A very embarrassing joke for both of us, Ms. Dzurisin."

"That's between you and him. Meanwhile, I have a job to do."

"I'm afraid not, Ms. Dzurisin. I am revoking your contract."

Indira sat back in the chair and stared at Rothar, who still would not meet her gaze. It came out slowly. Rothar did not want her to hunt the dragon. The monastery was forbidden to women. The bus would return in three days; she would leave then.

"Meanwhile, we cannot work our farm," Rothar said. "It will cost us a great deal of money. We are very angry with Mr. Simonov."

He did not seem angry; he had not raised or varied his voice at any time during the interview. He added, "I have arranged for accommodation. Breakfast will be brought to you tomorrow. Expect it at six o'clock."

"You really do want me out of here."

"We are a contemplative order. We rise early. By the time you receive your breakfast, we will have already celebrated our first service. We will serve you at the same time that we eat."

She said, "I need to tell my family about the change of plan, but my phone isn't working."

"Something to do with the structure, I understand."

"Then perhaps I could plug into your net. Or are you cut off here?"

"I suppose that you could go outside," Rothar said. A pause. He added, "You will be quite safe here. We have been freed of the normal Satanic lust that blinds men. Not by chemical or physical castration. Both are unreliable and have unsatisfactory side-effects. And, of course, chemical castration would involve use of those very hormones that taint you and your kind. No. We have all submitted to nanosurgery that has isolated the neurons that control the lordotic response. We are incapable of being tempted because we are incapable of arousal."

Indira stared at him. "I see," she said, although she did not understand why he had told her this. Unless it was another form of boasting. At last she said, "I still want my fee."

"Of course. We would not dream of reneging on the contract. Goodbye, Ms. Dzurisin."

Rothar made no signal, but at the far end of the room, Brother Halga opened the big double doors.

The old monk took Indira back up the helical tunnel and left her in one of the dome's empty cells. It was as spartan as the room in which Indira had lived with her foster parents in the refugee center on Ganymede, three meters long and two wide, a bare concrete floor and fiberboard walls sprayed with thick resin, the only furniture a fold-down shelf bunk and a combination shower and shit-stool. Brother Halga assured her that it was like all the other cells in the monastery. If that was true, then no wonder Rothar could afford a real fire, all those old books, the ostentatious decor. Like any other pseudo-religious sect, the devotees did the work and the leader got the geld.

Her phone still wasn't working. And she could not lock the door of the cell. She left the luggage pod outside and told it to keep watch, but found that she could not sleep. It was too cold and she could not switch off the light, only dim it. And something somewhere in the dome made a roaring noise at unpredictable intervals, shutting off with an explosive bang and a dying series of rattles that emphasized the unnatural silence that followed.

Memories of hiding in the city's service tunnels crept around the edges of her consciousness. She resisted them.

The whole thing was ridiculous. An order of misogynist monks, a megalomaniac leader who was quite possibly a mad scientist, a secret passage. And a monster, of course, haunting the vast dark ocean at the basement of the monastery . . . It was like one of those old gothic sagas.

The monks had some kind of religious phobia about women. Fine. Europa was big enough for all kinds of eccentrics. The original charter, drawn up by the first settlers and suspended but not revoked after the Quiet War, had expressly allowed freedom of belief and speech. Let them get on with their devotions; maybe they could keep off the monster by prayer alone.

It was nothing to do with her. And yet, of course, it was. Rothar's cold indifferent dismissal had cut her deeper than she liked to admit.

She tried the phone again. Still no luck. It was two in the morning, and she knew that she would not sleep now. She decided to go outside and try her luck with the phone there, and opened the door and told the luggage pod that she needed her pressure suit.

Indira supposed that the airlock was monitored, but found that she didn't care. She crossed the brightly lit apron, where the trucks squatted over their shadows all in a row, like supplicants, and left the road and climbed to the top of the ridge. Jupiter sat at the eastern horizon, exactly where he had been sitting when the bus had arrived. A crescent of darkness was eating into the bottom of his disc. His yellow light tangled long shadows across the rough, dark ice.

The phone still wasn't working. Indira went a long way, in long easy lopes that barely touched the ground, until, about two kilometers out, the phone suddenly woke and started scanning channels. She had to go another kilometer before she could get a steady signal.

It was half past three in the morning. It was half past three in the morning all over Europa. No one had been able to divide the moon's 85.2-hour day in a sensible way, so Europans kept universal time. Indira left a message with Carr's avatar, saying that she was fine but the job hadn't panned out, and she would be coming back in a couple of days. She put a priority call to Vlad, and his avatar made various excuses until she cut it off and said, "This is an emergency. *I'm flying the black flag.*"

Which was the ridiculous piratical code phrase that gave access to the less public of the avatar's functions.

The avatar, which looked exactly like Vlad, down to the tiny lights crawling in its bushy black hair, suddenly froze in the little window in the upper right-hand corner of her helmet's visor, then reformatted. It said, in a voice that was clipped and neutral, now not Vlad's at all, "Of course, *druzhok*. What do you wish me to do?"

The avatar could not contact Vlad—he really was working—but it was able to give her some more information about the Adamists. As the miners had told her, Rothar was some kind of gengineer. His birth name was Gregory Janes. He had been born in Canberra. Presently he was claiming asylum as a political refugee in the occupied territory of the Outer System. He had been working for the government of Earth's Pacific Community, but precisely on what was obscured by contradictory rumors, most of which were almost certainly black propaganda. There was speculation that he had worked on the biowar macroforms before the Quiet War, and that the monastery was able to supply so much biomass because he had improved on the productivity and growth of standard weeds.

Rothar had not founded the Adamists, but had taken them over after the death of the charismatic mystic whose acolyte he had become—another crime lurking there, perhaps. The Adamists were an extremist separatist group, the kind that only the pressure cooker of Earth could have evolved. Their creed was simple. They believed that God had created Adam and Lilith as the first of a race who would worship God on Earth as angels did in Heaven. But Lilith had been murdered by Satan, who had then created Eve by ripping a rib from Adam while he had been sleeping. All men since Adam had been tainted by Satan's mark, fallen but redeemable; all women were the handmaidens of Satan. The avatar told Indira that much of the Adamists' creed was mixed up with considerable misuse of genetics, involving the Y chromosome and homeoboxes, and asked her if she wanted a précis. She told the avatar to skip it. She had heard enough to know that she was glad Rothar didn't want her to work for him.

"And tell Vlad that I'll see him when I get back," she said. "We'll have a lot to talk about."

She had kept walking as she talked with the avatar, along a folded ridge above the silver dome that capped the monastery's shaft (and the shape of the monastery, she thought, was as graphically symbolic as the tapestry in Rothar's palatial office). The regolith here was gravelly, marked with tracks and the cleated prints of boots, scored and ridged with fretted humps of bare ice. She had begun to follow a road, she realized, a wide road that had once taken a lot of traffic.

Europa's surface was one of the youngest in the Solar System. Every part had been flooded and reflooded by eruptions of water and slush ice from the ocean that covered the moon from pole to pole beneath its icy crust; Europa had very few craters because most had been buried or eroded by the constant resurfacing. The landscapes of Mars were billions of years old and the planet was covered in gardened regolith—debris from meteorite strikes—to a depth of more than a kilometer. Ganymede's much younger regolith was merely meters deep; Europa's was no more than a few centimeters. But like any moon with almost no atmosphere, the ordinary processes of erosion were so slow that they might as well be non-existent. A footprint could last a million years before it was erased by micrometeorite bombardment.

And so it was here. Indira had stumbled upon the road that had served the original mine. All around, the surface was marked by dozens of years of activity. Parts of the road had been worn through to ice; the ice had been eroded into knobs and long slides, shot through with cracks and columns of bubbles frozen into place. They glittered like diamonds in the helmet light of Indira's pressure suit, diamonds glittering up at her wherever she looked.

She still had a couple of hours before she was due to be woken. She did not relish spending it in the spartan cell of the creepily uninhabited dome. Instead, she decided to explore.

The suit's radar soon gave her the location of the old mining station; it was below her, buried in the ice. It had probably been built on some kind of insulated raft with superconducting thread dispersing waste heat to radiators in the ocean far below, and its systems must have been left running when it had been abandoned. Presumably, its owners had expected to return in a few weeks. But something—perhaps a quake caused by the Tyre Macula nuclear device—had deflated its insulating raft, and perhaps some biowar macroform had destroyed its heat sink. The dome had sunk slowly through ice melted by its own waste heat.

Indira was tracing the perimeter of the dome when her proximity alarm beeped. A moment later she saw a figure duck behind a fold of ice. Someone was following her.

She circled around, keeping as low as the pressure suit would allow. No sign of the figure, either visually or on radar. She crossed the old road again, crept in toward the place where she had last seen the figure.

A square hole had been cut into the ice, and steps led down into darkness.

The monks had excavated the old entrance and later reburied it, but a stress fracture had collapsed and partly reopened the long, steep shaft. Indira climbed over a flow of glassy ice and found the airlock.

It was still operational.

The mysterious figure could be behind the door. What the hell. She cycled through.

The airlock walls had been deformed by the pressure of the ice into which it had slowly sunk, but someone had sealed up the cracked seams with swathes of black resin. There was air beyond it, the usual seven hundred millibar nitrox mix of Europan habitats, but Indira kept her suit sealed. It was very cold, $-50°C$, although not as cold as the surface. If the monks had wanted to store things, they could have just left them outside the dome. Unless they were things that would be damaged by vacuum ablation. Unless they were things that the monks didn't want others to see.

Speculating about just what those things might be, senses alert for any sign of the person she had followed, Indira wandered through the old mining base.

It had been abandoned in a hurry. Perhaps its crew had spotted the incoming missile whose nuclear warhead had blown a hole in the crust to the northwest.

Metal equipment lockers lined the corridor that led away from the airlock. Their locks had been cut out and their doors hung open. There was a big rec room in what must be the center of the dome. Food boxes were stacked along one wall; broken furniture along another. Ice crystals had gathered here and there in little drifts, crunching under her pressure suit's boots like dry beach sand. Overhead, the curved ceiling groaned and creaked: the structure was compressed all around by the ice into which it had sunken.

The dormitory corridor was littered with paper and infoneedles. The rooms were as small as the cell Indira had been assigned. She looked into one. It was half-filled with a shocking intrusion of ice, its surface glistening blue-white and smoothly sculptured like a muscle flayed of skin, its depths dirty with suspended silicates. In the next room, bedclothes were frozen with the impress of the man who had last slept there twenty years ago. His clothes were still scattered on the floor, stiff and sparkling with frost. Posters of lithe young women scaled the wall. One pin-up stirred against a feeble backglow. She cupped her breasts and began to say something, then froze and rastered back to the beginning of her cycle and stirred again.

As she turned away, Indira heard something above the poster's scratchy entreaties and the creaking of the stressed dome. Footsteps were coming along the curving corridor—then a beam of light slashed through the air, turning suspended ice crystals into fugitive diamonds! Somehow, the person she had been following had managed to get behind her.

Fearing a trap, Indira dodged clumsily back into the room. In her bulky pressure suit, she was like a monster intruding on a child's bedroom. The poster lit up again, and she tore it down and wadded it in her stiff gloves until its scratchy voice died. She killed her helmet's light and hunkered inside her suit, listening intently, her heart beating quickly and lightly.

She had hidden from the soldiers of the Three Powers Occupation Force when they had begun to evacuate Minos. She had been eleven, as stubborn then as Alice was now. The city had been a prime target for the biowar macroforms. Its heat exchangers and its turbines had been destroyed, its yeast reactors had been poisoned. With no food, no power except feeble battery power, and its environmental cycling running out of control, Minos had surrendered while the rest of Europa was still notionally at war. Indira had hidden during the evacuation because she had been possessed with the romantic notion that she would join rebels who in reality were little more than an invention of the Occupation Force's black propaganda unit.

She had been found, of course, but she had missed boarding the heavy lifter that had evacuated the rest of her family. And which, in the long slow orbit between Europa and Ganymede, had been crippled by an explosion in its antimatter pod and lost all power. Its crew and passengers had either suffocated or died of cold. Indira hadn't known about that until she had arrived at Ganymede. She had spent the two years as a refugee convinced that she had killed her parents.

Now her suit's microphone picked up the sound of footsteps, boots rattling loudly on plastic tiles whose adhesive had given way in the intense cold. Going past, dying away.

Indira stayed in the dark for two minutes, then cracked the door. Dark and silence beyond. She used infrared to track the footprints of whoever had been following her. One set, leading away down the curving corridor.

The airlock must have been alarmed. Someone had come to check. To look for her.

A new section of corridor had been roughly welded to an opening cut in the dome's skin. Metal stairs led down. As Indira descended, her suit reported that it was growing warmer, a strange inversion given that warm air should rise. But then she reached the high-ceilinged corridor at the foot of the stairwell and discovered the heat engines that crouched on either side, humming laboriously, their coils shining with frost. Heat was being pumped out of the dome and transferred . . . where?

To somewhere behind a dog-latched door with the universal trefoil symbol for biological hazard in black on fluorescent orange.

Indira hesitated only for a moment. She was still fully suited. If she was exposed to any biological agent she could sterilize her suit by returning to the near-vacuum and −150°C of Europa's surface.

The heavy metal door was latched but not locked. Its seals gave only momentary resistance. It swung open on its massive hinges and she stepped over the sill.

It was an airlock. She waited while it cycled. When the door on the far side opened, her suit's temperature sensor registered a sudden rise of fifty degrees as air gusted unfelt around her, and lamps came on in the big room beyond. They hung from chains under the high ceiling. They registered only in the infrared. Indira swept the beam of her helmet's light from side to side. Beneath the lamps were rows of big square tanks linked by grey plastic pipework, crusted with yellowish salts and holding various levels of still, black water. Seawater, she realized, the salty, sulfurous water of Europa's ocean. The temperature was just above zero. The air was 90 percent nitrogen and 10 percent carbon dioxide, with traces of hydrogen sulfide, sulfur dioxide, and hydrogen.

All of the tanks were empty. The recirculating pumps were switched off; the incubators ranked along one wall held only racks of flaccid salt-crusted plastic sleeves. The tiled workbench that ran along one wall was marked with chemical stains and the places where machines had once rested. A brown glass vial had fallen behind a strut; Indira turned it over in her clumsy gloves, smudged frost from its label. It had held the mixture of restriction nucleases and DNA ligases that was commonly used to insert genes into bacterial plasmids for cloning, either for identification of gene product or use in gengineering.

Indira secured a sample of water from one of the tanks and went out through the lock on the other side of the room. It cycled her into a long, rising corridor. At its far end, she stepped through an open hatch and found herself in the curved corridor of the dome which capped the monastery. Down the curve of the corridor, a red light flashed insistently. It was the emergency beacon of her luggage pod.

Without prompting, the luggage pod said, "Several people came after you left. They tried to open me. I responded with a class two defense as specified in subsection two paragraph three of the—"

Indira set the helmet of her pressure suit on the floor and said, "What did you do, exactly?"

"I activated my alarm and gave two warnings. After these were ignored, I passed a high amperage, low voltage current through my outer frame. One of the men who was trying to force me open was rendered unconscious."

"Did they manage to open you?"

"Of course not. After I defended myself, they went away." The pod added, "Two of them had to carry the man who had been incapacitated."

"By incapacitated, do you mean dead?"

"The shock was sufficient to cause unconsciousness but not death in a healthy adult human, as specified in subsection—"

"You've probably landed me in a whole world of shit."

The pod said that it did not understand this remark.

"Trouble."

"I am sorry," the pod said. "I had believed that I had contained the problem."

"Open up. I need to stow my pressure suit."

By the time Brother Halga appeared, to announce that Rothar would speak with her again, Indira had desuited and run the sample of water through her chemical sniffer. Brother Halga did not mention the attempt to open the luggage pod; neither did Indira.

As before, Rothar was standing in front of the roaring fire. If the room was a symbol of his power, then the fire was its focus. Her breakfast waited for her on the little table. Gruel, watery coffee, and a sticky, pale yellow liquid that was, Rothar said, mango juice.

Her pressure suit could supply better food, but she drank the coffee to be polite. It was weaker than any of the excuses she had made up, as she had walked down the helical corridor with Brother Halga, to try and explain why she had trespassed in the old mining station.

"You will work for me after all," Rothar said. "There have been . . . developments."

"I'm not sure that I want to. And surely a man would be better than a mere woman."

"Ah. You have been researching us."

"A little. But I only need to know a little to realize how much I dislike the entire idea of you and your crew."

Rothar smiled. He had small, widely spaced teeth, like those of a young boy prematurely grown up. He said, "We do not despise women. We pity them, as we pity all of humanity. We are a contemplative order that prays for redemption from the mark of Satan that is imprinted in each of our cells."

"That's very nice of you."

His smile went away. "You will work for us, Ms. Dzurisin. Or forfeit the penalty clauses of the contract you have already signed."

"From which you released me."

"Only verbally. Do you have a recording? I thought not. Then you have no proof that it ever took place."

"For a holy man, you don't set much store by the truth."

"None of us are holy, child. And besides, a small lie will sometimes serve a higher truth."

Which could justify anything, Indira thought. No wonder religions had caused so much trouble on Earth.

Rothar said, "It should not take long. You are an experienced hunter, and I will provide experienced divers to help you. We have men here from all trades. We aim to be self-sufficient. By the way, I hope our laboratory impressed you."

Indira looked at Rothar but said nothing. If he wanted to accuse her, she could accuse him of trying to tamper with her equipment. She had a pretty good idea of what the monks had been after. And there was the matter of what she had found in the water sample from the laboratory.

"We no longer use that facility," Rothar said, "but it has provided the basis of our farm's profitability. Which is why—" his smile came back—"we will have to search you thoroughly after you have finished. Whether you catch the monster or not."

"Oh, I'll catch it."

Meaning, I'll show you what a woman can do, and shame you for your presumption that I'm less than you are merely because of my sex.

She didn't put the two things together. Her discovery, Rothar's about-face. After all, the story about the weed was entirely plausible; he couldn't know that she had evidence that he must be lying. She thought that it was a matter of pride. His. Hers.

The two men who had been assigned to accompany her, Brother Fergus and Brother Finn, were competent and professional, but did not bother to hide their disgust at having to work with a woman. Fergus was dark and wiry and nervous; Finn was blond and burly and quiet, and one of the tallest men Indira had seen, overtopping her by half a meter. His head, covered with the hood of his dry suit so that only his face showed, was as big and bumpy as a boulder. His beard was white, and as fine as cornsilk; like Fergus's, it was done up in a kind of net. Both monks made it quite clear that they thought that this duty was an insult to their dignity. Neither offered any information about the dragon. No sonar signals, no video grabs, no chemical traces.

"We know it is there," Finn said.

"Still, I would like to see what evidence you have," Indira said. "It would confirm that it is a dragon. The neurotoxins I use are class specific."

"It is a terrible monster," Fergus said. "That's all you need to know. We can no longer work the farm because of it."

He folded his arms defiantly. They were suited up and sitting in the pressure chamber. Finn and Fergus wore black dry suits and black stabilization jackets; Indira's suit was white, her stab jacket yellow. Their scooters made the chamber crowded; they had to rest their feet on them. They were ready to go, but Indira insisted on talking first. She wanted to establish a plan of action and emphasize that they must stick to it. She did not trust them. She had filled her air-tanks herself, and done all her suit checks alone.

Finn said, "We know where its lair is."

"Lair?"

None of the big macroforms lived in the ice. They were creatures of the open water, spending long periods drifting in upwelling plumes, fixing carbon and storing energy for their attacks. And occasionally reproducing. They had been designed to operate for years—overdesigned, as it turned out. The Quiet War had been a rout.

"It lives in the ice," Finn said.

"Near the farm," Fergus said.

They were a double act. The idea appeared to be to give away as little information as possible. It didn't matter. Indira had worked with less—although of course she had never worked against a dragon.

"We can do most of the work," Fergus said.

"In fact," Finn said, "if you give us the neurotoxins we can do it all."

Neurotoxins were the major expense of hunting monsters. They had been tailored to specific classes of biowar macroforms by the wizards who had gengineered them. They were bought on license from the Three Powers Occupying Force, and only hunters were licensed to use them. Grey chemists had tried to isolate the specifics, but they were mixed with several thousand closely related chemicals. Indira had guessed that the vials of neurotoxin were what the monks had been trying to take from her luggage pod when it had zapped one of them. Having failed to get the neurotoxins, they were stuck with her.

"I have already caught and killed one like it," Finn said, deadpan.

"She doesn't need to hear that," Fergus said, with sudden violence. "You were told—"

Finn punched him on the side of the head and the little monk banged against the steel wall of the airlock and shut up, although he glared at Finn with genuine hatred. But Finn was smiling at Indira. He had about a hundred teeth, as gleaming white as an ice cliff. His blue eyes glittered with psychotic intensity.

He said, "I really did. Do you want to know how?"

Indira laughed.

"You're making a fool of yourself," Fergus said, and flinched when Finn stuck his massive fist in front of his face.

Finn said, "I didn't have any fancy gear. No nets or shock bombs or toxins. I fought it one on one. We fought for days. The water boiled with the fury of our struggle. It took me down to the bottom of the ocean, thinking it would crush me and drown me. But I was too strong. It tried to escape then, but I held onto it. I broke open a vent and seared off its fins and its teeth with the lava that spewed out."

As he spoke, in a low voice as monotonous as Rothar's, he brought his face closer and closer to Indira's. His pupils were huge, so that his eyes were all black and white. Sweat stood out like oily droplets on his smooth, pale skin. His breath smelled bad: acetone, butanol, sweet rot.

Indira was sure that he was flying on something. Perhaps drugs were part of the devotions of these strange, sinister monks. She said, as calmly as she could, "That's a good story."

"It's the truth," Finn said. "You don't believe it but that doesn't mean it isn't true."

"We don't know how many are out there," Fergus said. "No one knows how often they reproduce. There could be hundreds out there. Thousands."

"We don't need to bring anyone in," Finn said, still staring at Indira. "I can handle it."

Indira thought of the tanks in the laboratory under the old mining camp. The analysis had showed traces of metabolites and degradation products consistent with the presence of animal metabolism, although her sniffer had not been able to identify the type of animal. Perhaps Finn had caught a monster. Perhaps they had kept it in one of the tanks they had used to develop their strains of weed, although she doubted that it had been a dragon. A spinner, perhaps a juvenile mako. But not a dragon; even a newborn dragon would have torn up the lab. But why hadn't they simply killed it? What had they used it for?

Fergus leaned over and dared touch Indira's knee. His black eyes were liquid with what Indira thought was genuine concern. "He gets wired up," he said. "Don't worry. We'll look after you."

Finn said, "No more talk. We go."

Indira told him to wait. She had already checked her equipment, but now she wanted to check it again in front of the two monks, to show them what she had, to show them that she meant business, to puncture their contempt. The spear gun with its hollow tipped spears. The taser. The percussion bomblets, the sticky bomblets, the flares. The diamond mesh drift nets. The sonar. The motion detector. The sniffer.

Both monks watched her closely, but said nothing. They carried nothing but ordinary spear guns and knives; a pouch of the kind of explosive charges used by construction workers hung from Finn's harness.

"All right," she said at last. "Let's do it."

Fergus allowed a little water in. Although it was filtered to remove its chemical load, it still had the rotten egg stench of hydrogen sulfide. Indira could feel its cold through the layers of her suit.

They busied themselves in the small space, rinsing their face masks in the water and then spitting in them and rubbing the spittle over the inside of the glass of the visors so they would not fog up, checking the seals of their hoods and the straps that fastened the fins to their feet, their weight-belts and the harnesses that held their tanks, putting on their face masks and adjusting regulator mouthpieces.

Fergus carried a little video rack and he switched on its lamp for a moment; harsh light flooded the chamber, bleaching out all colors. Then he opened the valve all the way and water gushed from the floor vent, filling the chamber in a few moments.

The water of Europa's ocean was at an average temperature of minus ten degrees centigrade. Although its freezing point was reduced because of its heavy concentration of salts, much of the water beneath the icy crust was half frozen into slush: grease ice and firn ice; brash ice and bergy bits. In places, though, currents driven by plumes from hydrothermal vents at the bottom of the sea, fifty kilometers below the surface, carried relatively warm, mineral-rich water to the bottom of the ice crust. Sometimes, currents driven by especially active vents melted the ice crust, and water and slush spilled across the surface of Europa like lava.

Mines and farms were built over vent plumes. Mines sucked up the mineral-rich water; farms grew gengineered weed in the Europa equivalent of tropical seawater enriched with fertilizer.

Even so, the water that flooded the chamber was at a freezing two degrees centigrade. As it rose around Indira, an intense ring of cold gripped her body, rising with the water and inducing a terrific headache right between her eyes. It was as if she had gulped down a liter of ice cream. The cold of the water was already sucking heat through her thin gloves. It stung the little bits of exposed skin where the seal of her face mask did not quite meet the seal of her hood; then the skin went numb. She bit down hard on the soft plastic regulator that filled her mouth and concentrated on her breathing until the first agony of immersion passed. The air that hissed through the regulator at each breath was dry and metallic.

Fergus was staring at a little hand-held videoscreen. It switched every two seconds to show different views of black water under ice. His voice said in her earpiece, "Looks clear."

Finn said impatiently, "They said it was clear. They switched on the lights to make sure that it was clear."

"But the thing can travel fast."

Their voices were thin and muffled and flat, sub-vocalizations picked up by throat mikes and processed for clarity.

Indira said, "I hope it does come to us. Then we won't have to go far."

"We'll find it," Finn said, and hit a big red button with his fist.

The chamber rotated with a grinding noise. They spilled out into the black water, dragging their scooters with them.

They were in a wide shaft. The bottom of the shaft loomed above, a massive blister of steel studded with grab rails and red and green lights. Someone moved behind one of the thick bullseye ports. The two men angled away and Indira followed. The white vee of her scooter hummed, its vents pushing out water in muscular streams on either side of her, pulling her toward the open water below.

The two men were heading straight out at a fast clip past the finned radiators that bled waste heat into the ocean. They had not waited for her. It was a challenge, a typical male gesture. Indira paused to gauge the current, chose a long flat curve that would carry her ahead of them, and throttled up her scooter's reaction motor.

She had expected the farm to be big, but it was more than twice the size of her wildest estimate. The maintenance lights were on, and she could see that racks of weed stretched away on all sides of the bottom of the shaft, hundreds upon hundreds of them. Each rack was thirty meters long and five meters wide, bolted to its neighbors in a hexagonal array with orange flotation buoys at each corner, each array was linked at its six points to neighboring arrays and to pylons fixed in the ice roof of the ocean. Weed dangled down from ropes attached to the wire stretchers of the racks, filmy ribbons that in the weak lights glistened violet or purplish red or the reddish brown of dried blood. Mature weeds were a hundred meters long. The whole—weed, racks, rack arrays—flexed sinuously in the current, like the hide of a gently breathing beast. A haze of molecular sulfur, the waste product of the weeds' carbon fixation, smoked off it.

Unlike the green plants that decorated Phoenix's public and private spaces, weeds did not need light to grow; the lights were for the workers who maintained the rafts and cropped mature blades. Green plants harvested light energy and used it to transfer hydrogen ions and electrons from water to carbon dioxide, forming the simple sugar glucose, with oxygen as a byproduct. But no light penetrated Europa's kilometers-thick ice crust and there was no free oxygen in all its deep ocean: a fish would drown as quickly as a human. Like the indigenous microbes of Europa and chemolithotrophic bacteria of Earth, the weed used reduced inorganic compounds containing nitrogen or sulfur or iron instead of water and light to turn carbon dioxide into sugars.

Most available carbon on Europa was in the form of carbon dioxide dissolved in the ocean beneath its thick icy crust. There had been proposals to crash a carbonaceous chondrite asteroid onto Europa to supply carbon that could be processed by vacuum organisms, but no one had been able to work out how to do this without splitting the crust and resurfacing half the moon. Shortly before the Quiet War, there had been a half-hearted attempt to reach agreement between the five inhabited moons to establish a carbon-mining facility at one of Jupiter's Lagrangian points, but the plan had foundered in acrimonious arguments about sharing the start-up costs of purchasing mining rights to a suitable asteroid and moving it into orbit.

Before the war, Europans had augmented their expensive greenhouses by drawing up water and using it to grow gengineered yeasts in big tanks, utilizing metabolic pathways copied from the indigenous microbes that grew in the crushing blackness at the bottom of the ocean, around the hydrothermal vents that opened along ridge faults. The Europan vent microbes had been the only known extant life-forms in the Solar System other than those of Earth. Their genetic code had been based on triplet base sequences strung on a DNA double helix, reinforcing the modified Hoyle-Wickramasinghe panspermia hypothesis that all life in the Solar System, including the long-extinct Martian microflora, had a common ancestor. On Earth, certain bacteria had combined and evolved into multicellular eukaryotes, into plants and fungi and animals. Perhaps this step required an oxygen atmosphere and the more efficient energy-generating metabolic pathways it could support; in Europa's anaerobic ocean, nothing had evolved beyond the level of colonial microbes, which had formed crusts and sheets, lacework baskets and vases, and vast beds of long filaments, around the hot, black, mineral-rich water that issued from the vents. Life had not spread from these refugia; the rest of the ocean had been a sterile desert.

Tailored biowarfare viruses released in the Quiet War had destroyed the industrial yeasts and the native microflora. Afterward, a Pacific Community cartel had introduced licensed strains of chemolithotrophic weed. Even with the premium license tax, the weeds were a cheaper source of fixed carbon than algal ponds or hydroponic greenhouses. Those supplied luxury food items; the weed provided the base input of fixed carbon to Europa's expanding population, just as vacuum organisms growing on the methane and carbon monoxide ices and tars of carbonaceous chondrites supplied fixed carbon to the new Kuiper Belt settlements.

In the midst of the monastery's huge weed farm, Indira overtook Finn and Fergus and turned her scooter to face them as they vectored toward her. Her arms ached slightly and she worked one and then the other. Her headache had crept downward, a mantle of numbing cold that penetrated the dry suit and its three underlayers—a fleece liner, a quilted undersuit with a little skull cap, the liner from her vacuum suit. Her fingertips were numb inside the thin gloves; the little bits of exposed skin between hood and face mask were slivers of stinging pain. This would not go away. This would get worse. Yet she felt a thrill of elation vibrating in her core. She was here. She was doing her job. The close possibility of death made her more alive than at any other time. It was not something she could talk about, even with Carr. Only other hunters could understand it.

Above was a rippling ceiling of hexagonal arrays of racks, with blades of weed trailing down like hair; below, fifty kilometers of black water. No sign of any movement down there on her sonar. The chemical sniffer that sampled water every few seconds showed no trace of metabolites specific to biowar macroforms. Her regulator valve rattled; dry air hissed. She checked the elapsed time on her mask's head-up display—she had six hours of air in the two tanks she carried on her back, another hour in the emergency bottle clipped to the scooter.

"I think she's made a point," Fergus's thin, processed voice said in her earpiece, as the two monks swung in beside her.

Boys' games.

She said, "I want to look at the damage this monster did."

Finn: "That's where we're going."

Fergus: "It's at the southern edge of the farm."

Finn: "You follow us. Enough hot-dogging."

Yes, boys' games.

She let the men lead.

They traveled a long way through the cold and the dark. Two kilometers, three. An endless skimming fall below waving ranks of weed. It occurred to Indira that she had seen no one working the farm's racks. Surely there should be at least a hundred people out here, harvesting mature plants and stringing new ropes thick with sporelings. When she asked, Fergus said, "That's because of the monster. Which is why *we're* out here."

"You must have a lot of pressure chambers to handle the traffic."

"We manage."

Was that Finn or Fergus? Now she began to wonder how the monastery managed such a huge farm. Where were the facilities for servicing the huge numbers of divers that must be needed? Rothar had shown her the refectory filled with monks as a demonstration of his power—but there had been no more than a hundred men. Did all of them work the farm?

The creepy feeling, which she had shed as soon as she had powered out into the cold dark water of the ocean, began to return.

At last, an hour after they had set out, they finally reached the damaged section.

It was near the edge of the farm. It was extensive: at least a hectare. Lights were blown or dimmed to a greenish glow. Whole sections of racks had been twisted free of the supporting pylons, and dangled disjointedly. Other sections were completely missing; presumably they had fallen away to crushing darkness at the bottom of the deep ocean.

Weed grew over broken racks and twisted wire stringers, made complex knotted barricades that waved to and fro in a strong southerly current. Indira had to keep blipping her scooter's throttle to stay in place. There were patches in the weed that looked as if they had been harvested very recently. It had been done by someone who knew not to cut at the gnarly node where the weed gripped the rope, knew to leave a length of blade to allow swift regeneration. The cuts were fresh, no more than two or three days old. Had the monks tried to salvage their crop after the monster had wrecked this section? If so, then why hadn't they salvaged all of it?

She said at last, "I've only seen pictures of what a dragon can do, but the damage to the racks is consistent."

"I told you," Finn said. "I told you that I caught one."

Indira ignored this. She repeated what she had told them when they had first met. "This is a snoop dive. We'll look around and then we'll go back and make plans. It should take no more than another hour."

"She feels the cold," Finn said.

"*I* feel the cold," Fergus said, and switched on his lights and took shots of Indira against the wreckage, moving around her with dainty frog-kicks. "Just for the record," he said, when she protested that they were wasting time.

"We do waste time," Finn said. "We go to its lair. Time to finish this. One way or the other."

"Not here," Fergus said. The thin synthesized voice somehow conveyed alarm. "I know not here. Come."

And then the big man was powering off into the dark beyond the wrecked edge of the farm. Indira followed hard on his heels, riding the smooth water in his scooter's wake to conserve her own scooter's power. She did not believe the story about a lair, but she knew that she would have to look. And then she could begin to make her own plans. She would kill the monster today or tomorrow, and then she could go home.

Another long fall through black cold water. Once, she looked over her shoulder to check that Fergus was following, and saw that already the lights of the farm had dwindled far behind: a linear constellation of little sparks set in the vast cold night of the ocean. They were skimming along just beneath the icy roof. It was not flat, but undulated in long smooth swales, eroded by the relatively warm upwelling current. It glistened blue and green in the wide beam of the lamp of Indira's scooter. Fringes of ferny platelet ice hung down everywhere, delicate growths that softened the swelling contours of the ice.

Now the roof angled down—a smooth intrusion in the undulating ice, an upside-down hill. Indira followed Finn down the long slope. Her depth gauge pinged at every twenty-meter contour. She had nanoformed scavengers in her blood that prevented both nitrogen narcosis caused by high pressure and bubble formation caused by too-swift ascents, but the scavengers only worked within certain limits.

They went down almost two hundred meters; then the slope steepened into a vertical wall, and they dragged below its inverted crest. Beyond was a chaos of slab ice where part of the crust had broken away and reformed. Habitat-sized chunks of ice stuck out at all angles, transparent blue ice shot through with white stress marks, like a jumble of giant, rough-cut gems. Finn slowed and Indira slowed, too. They drifted beneath the jagged chaos and came to a stop near a black rift that led back into the ice — a long gently curving slot like a grinning mouth.

"This is where they went."

Indira did not know if Finn or Fergus had spoken — the distortion of their treated subvocalizations and a sudden surge of adrenaline in her blood obliterated the subtle distinction.

"We will get them back."

Was that the same voice? Fergus had drifted a little way beneath Finn, who was shining a strong lamp into the rift. Fluted ice reflected its red light in a thousand splinters.

"We finish the matter now."

That was definitely Finn.

Indira's chemical sniffer was flashing urgently. She called up the display. Strong metabolic traces, but no positive identification. Were there several types of macroform here? She started the sniffer's analytical program and said, "There's something in there. In a few minutes I'll know what it is."

She turned up all her lights and cautiously edged into the mouth of the rift. A faint but steady current issued from it. The sniffer's HPLC kicked in and started to flash spiky lines as it separated the unknown metabolites. She called up the chemical signature of a dragon as an overlay. And there it was buried amongst traces of other complex chemicals which the sniffer was unable to match against its library.

"Got you," she said, and something flew past her, a quick flash leaving a wake of bubbles that rose around her like a silvery rope.

Her backbrain recognized what it was and she turned away in reflex before she realized that someone — Finn or Fergus — had fired some kind of self-propelled explosive charge into the rift.

Then it exploded.

The pressure wave clamped around Indira, lifted her, shoved her against the roof of the rift, took her again and dragged her down amongst the glistening smooth hummocks of its floor. Big chunks of ice fell with her, through a haze of chips and fragments that washed to and fro in the cross-hatched froth of aftershock currents.

Someone was shouting, a thin voice like tearing metal. "Not this way! Not yet!"

Somehow, Indira had kept hold of her scooter. She killed her lights and crouched amongst ice rubble. Strong, freezing cold currents washed back and forth over her. There were lights hung beyond the slot of the rift's mouth, two clusters of lights, shining their high beams here and there. She realized that she had been set up. They would kill her here and blame the monster. Because of what she had seen, even if she did not understand what she had seen. Because she was a woman who had dared to trespass on men's territory.

And then something big shot past her. Someone screamed and one of the clusters of lights went out.

It was the dragon.

It doubled back, quick as thought. Indira tried to untangle her spear gun. She had an impression of something black and sleek, with two big fins or flippers that curled around a man-sized bundle.

Then it was past, swimming strongly into the depths of the rift. Gone.

It had taken Finn. Fergus's small figure hung some distance from the entrance. "Keep away," he said, as she angled toward him. "Keep away. I'm armed."

She kept going. A spear shot wide, disappearing into the black water to her right. She gunned her scooter and slammed into Fergus before he could recock his gun, spun him around, uncoupled the air hose from his face mask.

His masked face was obscured by a sudden flood of silvery bubbles. He waved his arms in blind panic. She counted to ten and stuck the hose in his hand. "All right," he said, when he had it back in place. "All right."

"You wanted me dead."

"Rothar said it was necessary. He said you would be bait for the monster."

"You were going to video it. You thought I would be almost certainly killed by the dragon. After all, I'm only a woman. And if I *had* killed it, you would have killed me, and made up a story."

Fergus didn't deny it. He said, "Finn wouldn't wait."

"He was a coward. Well, he's dead now. That's what dragons do."

"It has our workers," Fergus said, pointing toward the rift. It was just visible as a shadow crescent cut into the ice blocks of the tumbled roof, at the edge of the overlapping circles of their lights.

Indira said, "If it took them in there, then they're as dead as Finn."

How many had the dragon killed? There were about a hundred monks now, but many more than that would have been needed to maintain the farm. . . . Indira was very cold, and found it hard to follow any thought to its conclusion. Every few seconds, a tremor passed over her entire skin. That sleek black shape. Bigger and faster than anything she had ever seen before . . .

Fergus made a choking, squealing noise. It was laughter, translated by his throat mike. "Oh no," he said. "At least, they were alive a couple of days ago. They came out to feed. The dragon was with them. They ripped up the perimeter of the farm and disappeared before we could get them. *You*, you're one of the dead, though. Rothar has seen to it."

Then he kicked out with surprising strength and broke free. She let him go. If Rothar was determined to kill her, one little monk wouldn't be much of a bargaining chip.

Fergus was a solitary star dwindling through the ocean's black volume toward the distant constellation of the farm. His voice came faintly to her.

He said, "Finn really did kill one. It was small, but he killed it."

And then: "Don't try to follow me. You don't have enough air. . . ."

Indira had almost used up one of her two air-tanks. Apprehensive alarm suddenly fluttered in her chest. She switched to the second. Gas hissed through the regulator but there was no oxygen, and suddenly she couldn't get her breath. Nitrogen. The fuckers had somehow filled her second tank with nitrogen! She switched back as red and black began to blot out her vision. She had about half an hour's worth of air left, and the trip back would take at least an hour and a half. She had insisted on filling her air-tanks herself, but Finn or Fergus must have done some kind of switch, changing the compressor's inlet from the standard nitrox mix to pure nitrogen. She checked the emergency bottle in her scooter, but she already knew. It had been filled with nitrogen, too.

She did not have enough air to get back, but there was one place within reach where she could get air. The two men had not planned on the monster killing one of them. Finn's scooter with its emergency bottle was gone, still falling toward the true surface of Europa, a fifty-kilometer fall that might take three days. But perhaps his main tanks were still intact.

She had no other choice. And there was the mystery of the workers. Still alive, Fergus had said. Something had harvested patches of weed. Something was producing the chemical traces that overlay the dragon's metabolic signature.

She realized then what the workers must be. What the laboratory had been used for.

She turned and powered back into the rift.

Finn's explosive charge had brought down a big ice fall, but the dragon had punched a hole in the middle of it. Indira shot straight through the ragged gap. She didn't have time to waste.

The passage went a long way, rising in a gentle left-handed curve. It was as smooth as a gullet. The gleaming ice walls confused Indira's sonar, and she switched it off. The sniffer told her all she needed to know: increasing concentrations of the complex mixture of metabolic exudations, including the dragon's fingerprint of methylmalonic acid semialdehyde, α-ketoisovaleric acid, and a triple peak of phosphatidic acids.

When the passage suddenly opened out on all sides, Indira slewed to a stop and fired off a fan of flares. They ignited as they floated away, a string of harsh white stars that starkly illuminated the lower half of a vast chamber. Indira's heart was beating quickly and lightly, driven by anticipation and dread. If this was *not* the monster's lair, then she was fucked. She didn't have enough air to get back out into open water.

The flares floated higher. The chamber was easily twice the size of the Buddhist Temple in Phoenix. Chambers like this were common in the lower part of Europa's icy crust, opened by stress flow and carved wider by intrusive currents until they grew too big, even in Europa's low gravity, and collapsed. It was floored with chunks of ice that had fallen from the ceiling high above and fans of ice rubble slumped from the fluted walls. The chunks had been worn as smooth as pebbles by currents of relatively warm water.

Movement at the edge of the shifting shadows cast by the string of floating flares sharpened the quick beat of her heart. Belatedly, she remembered to switch on her sonar. A cluster of small signals, things the size of a human child. Had the monster reproduced, then? Yes, but not more than once. That was why it had killed Finn. As for these . . .

She guessed what they must be a moment before she worked out that the regular signal beyond the cluster of child-sized creatures was that of a set of racks bolted to the ceiling of the chamber. Of course. They had started their own weed farm; the currents that flowed through the chamber were as rich in sulfides and ammonium as those in the open water.

Then a big signal was suddenly coming straight at her, angling down like a guided missile, brushing through the picket line of flares and sending them spinning. She barely had time to get out her spear gun and aim it. There was a very fine tremor in her arms, but now that it was happening she was quite calm.

The thing came on and she did not fire. It was so very fast! She did not fire, and at the last moment revved the scooter and shot under the monster as it swept over her.

She rolled in its wake and brought up her spear gun again as she came around. The dragon had already turned. It hung there in the glare of her lights and the drifting stars of the flares.

She had seen pictures and brief video sequences of dragons, but she had never seen one in real life. No one had seen one in real life for more than ten years. Until now, she had not realized how beautiful they were.

The dragon's body was streamlined and compact, a long wedge of muscle twice her length, gloved in a flexible carapace of long black bony scales. Its fused rear flippers fanned out horizontally like a whale's fluke, far wider than the span of her arms. Its pectoral fins were stretched out like bat's wings. Three of the long fingers grew through the thick membrane they supported; they were tipped with long, sharp, black claws. Its mouth was wide and had a shark's humorless grin, with several rows of backward-tilted ripsaw teeth. Not for feeding—it had no digestive system, fueling itself by pumping sulfide-rich water through internal lamellae dense with symbiotic carbon-fixing bacteria—but for attack. It was gaping wide now. Its forehead was humped and swollen, with a band of warty protrusions, electrical sensory organs on which it relied more than sight, although it kept one rolling blue eye on Indira. That eye was unnervingly human; she had the uncanny impression that someone was buried inside the monster's carapace, peering out at her.

No, not at her, she realized. At the spear gun and the spear racked ready for firing, at the spear's explosive hypodermic tip, its charge of tailored neurotoxin. Even if it discharged into the water, the neurotoxin would be enough to paralyze the dragon, perhaps for long enough to kill it. If it could not pump sulfide-rich water over its symbionts, it could not generate energy, and after all this activity, it must have depleted the stored energy in its battery muscles. It would quickly die.

Indira raised the spear gun and watched the dragon shift with precise flicks of its winglike pectoral fins, keeping its rolling blue eye on the tip of the cocked spear. For the first time in her life, she saw her quarry not as a monster, but as another thinking creature.

Carefully, slowly, she inverted in the water and laid the spear gun amongst water-smoothed ice rubble on the floor. Came back right-side-up.

The dragon hung there, watching her. Smaller shapes gathered high above and behind it, shadows moving to and fro against the guttering light of the flares, which had floated up amongst the hanging blocks of the ceiling. She could hear a faint chirruping of cross-talk.

Still moving with dreamlike slowness, she took the emergency bottle from her scooter and vented it. The dragon sculled backward from the column of bubbles. Oxygen was poisonous to its symbiotic bacteria. But this was only nitrogen, and the dragon eased back to its original position.

Still moving slowly, Indira took off her harness. She was careful not to tangle the hose that led from the one functional air-tank to the regulator in her face mask. She vented nitrogen from the second tank. This time the dragon did not shy back.

It knew.

The regulator valve rattled more deeply each time she drew a breath. The air-tank was almost exhausted. She hung there in front of the monster, staring at its blue eye, small under the ridge of its swollen bony forehead. It must know that she was not like its enemies. Her dry suit was white and her stab jacket was yellow: compared to the monks' utilitarian black, she was a tropical bloom. And all biowar macroforms had a good sense of taste. It must be able to tell that she was releasing a different set of chemical signals into the cold water, that she was not a man.

The regulator rattled, and suddenly she could not breathe. It rattled again and her rib cage fully inflated, but she could not draw any air. She tried not to panic. She knew that she could hold her breath for more than three minutes. She tapped the regulator, tapped the air-tank.

The monster watched, immobile, unfathomable.

Indira stripped off her face mask, spat out her regulator and clamped her lips against the pressure of the freezing water. She wanted so much to breathe.

A rapid fire of clicks and chirps.

The cold salty water stung her eyes when she opened them. Something shot down, swooped between her and the dragon, dropped something, and shot away.

Finn's harness and his air-tanks.

Indira dove for it. The mouthpiece of the regulator was half-bitten through, and the air-tank it drew on was empty. She prayed that Finn had not switched over to his second tank before the dragon had killed him, jammed the regulator in her mouth, tasting Finn's blood and sputum, twisted the valve to the second tank, and drew a deep shuddering breath.

A bullet of freezing cold sulfurous water hit the back of her throat. She choked on it, bubbles leaking from her mouth, and then realized that she was breathing again.

More clicks tapped through the water. Small figures swooped down out of the darkness beyond and above the dragon. They hung in the black water on either side of its smooth bulk, gazing down as she hooked the hose of Finn's air-tank to her face mask and turned it on full to purge the mask of water as she fastened it over her face. They were half her size—Alice's size. Thick smooth coats of lustrous grey fur, sad brown human eyes, long vibrissae on either side of snouts swollen to the size of melons—they must rely on echo location as much as sight. They had the long, half-fused rear flippers of seals, but short, stout human arms where their pectoral flippers should be. Their hands were long-fingered, spread wide to show the webs between.

The farm workers. The creatures Rothar had gengineered and used as slaves to increase the wealth of the monastery. The creatures that the dragon had freed.

They clicked to each other using the flat, grinding teeth in their narrow jaws. They did not have the symbionts that fed the biowar macroforms. They needed to eat weed. They had to stay near the farm. But the dragon had shown them how they could live free. They could steal racks of weed and use them to start their own farm.

The dragon moved forward. The long terminal finger of one of its pectoral fins scratched something on a table of ice. And then it flicked its body like a whip and shot away into the darkness. The workers trailed after it, kicking strongly through the water. One hovered for a moment, watching Indira, and then a sharp chorus of clicks sounded and it turned and followed its companions.

Indira was alone. Cold and dark pressed all around the little bubble of light cast by her scooter's lamp. She finned over to the flat table of ice, traced the crude but legible letters the monster had gouged with its clawed finger.

No more war.

Indira got back to the lock with less than an hour of air left. They had to let her in. She showed Finn's explosive charges to the cameras and mimed slapping them against the hatch to make it clear that she would blow her way in if she had to.

Rothar came to her as soon as she had cycled through. A burly monk stood just behind him. Indira was cold and exhausted, and her dry suit stank of hydrogen sulfide, but she straightened her back and looked right at Rothar. She did not bother to look at the bodyguard.

She said, "Finn is dead."

"I know."

"The dragon killed him. Your workers were with it. They gave me Finn's airtank. That's how I survived your attempt to kill me."

She glared at Rothar defiantly. He was looking at a point somewhere behind her left shoulder. The dark blotches on his white face were vivid in the red light of the chamber. Only a slight tremor in his jaw betrayed the effort with which he was suppressing his emotions.

Indira said in an angry rush, "You tried to steal my neurotoxins, but when you failed, you knew you would have to let me go after the dragon. And you wanted me out of the way after I saw the laboratory, but you couldn't just get rid of me— too many people knew I was here. So you sent me out without enough air. The plan was that either the dragon would kill me and Finn would take my spear gun and kill the dragon, or I would kill the dragon and run out of air, and Finn would mutilate my body to make it look like I'd been fatally wounded by the dragon."

Rothar told his bodyguard to stand outside the door, and said mildly, "If you had given us the neurotoxins or let us take them, none of this would have happened."

"You had to kill me after I found the laboratory."

"Not at all. We tried to open your luggage pod as soon as you went outside to use your phone. But it was too well-defended and I had to implement a second plan. The only way to get your neurotoxins was to take them from you in the ocean, and the only way to take them from you was to kill you. I let you find the laboratory so that my community would condone your death because you had discovered our secrets."

Indira was too tired to feel either hatred or fear. She said, "You were certain the dragon would kill me. You expected it. After all, I'm only a woman. Fergus was supposed to video my death. And if I did kill the dragon, then I couldn't be allowed to live because it would make a mockery of your creed. Either way, I had to die."

Rothar did not deny it.

"Instead, the dragon took Finn because he had killed one of its scions. I don't know what happened to his body."

"We will hold a service in memory of his soul."

"Your workers have escaped you. They will start their own farm."

Rothar said, "They will have to come back. They need certain vitamins and amino acids that the weed cannot provide. They know this."

Perhaps they had eaten Finn's body. Or perhaps they had taken it with them. It would take a long time to even begin to decay in the cold anaerobic ocean. She said, "I don't think they'll be back."

"Then I will raise some more."

"And meanwhile, your farm will fail. And perhaps your new workers will escape, too. How intelligent did you make them?"

Rothar smiled. "Intelligent enough." He paused. He said, "Not as intelligent as the dragons."

She understood. She said, "You were a gengineer, on Earth."

Rothar looked at her for a moment, looked away. He said, "I was part of a team, Ms. Dzurisin. Unfortunately, I was not working on the dragons, or I would not have needed your neurotoxin."

"But you used that knowledge to gengineer your workers when you came here. Those blotches on your face—they're from some kind of accident, aren't they? You couldn't get it treated, because then people would know that you had been working illegally. Finn killed a dragon, a juvenile. At first, I thought you caught it because you wanted to learn the secret of how the macroforms can live off the ocean, but now I think he killed it because he could."

"Finn was a useful man, but his propensity for violence could not always be contained. I did not need to learn any secret, Ms. Dzurisin. I already know how the dragons and the other biowar macroforms live. My workers are a type of macroform that was not used in the Quiet War. I altered their genotype to make them dependent on the weed they grow, but otherwise they are just as they were designed."

"The dragon that sired the one Finn killed came here looking for its scion. And found the workers." Indira stared right at Rothar. She said, "I didn't kill it. But you'll want to pay me anyway."

Rothar said, with a note of amusement, "I don't think so."

"I think so. I found the dragon but I didn't kill it, and that's why you'll need me to negotiate with it."

Rothar folded his arms. He said, "We will talk, in my study. Get changed, Ms. Dzurisin. Get warm. Think about what story you will tell your colleagues once you leave here."

She knew then that she had won.

The bus pulled away from the monastery and began to descend the road that switchbacked down toward the plain. By human clocks, it was the middle of the night; on the surface of Europa, at 2°S 84 °W, it was just after dawn. The small, shrunken Sun stood just above the flat eastern horizon. Above it, Jupiter showed a wide, narrow crescent, a bow of yellow light bent toward Europa. Out there, on the plain of ice plates cross-hatched by triple-banded ridges, everything had two shadows.

The bus said, "Did you find the monster? Did you kill it?"

"I found something else," Indira said.

She thought of her daughter and her dreams of sea gardens full of benign animals. She thought of all the children of Phoenix, staring with avid fascination into the darkness of the ocean. She thought of the workers, and the monster that had adopted them. It was smarter than its makers knew. Perhaps it had learned wisdom in the black depths of the sea. Who knew what thoughts, what philosophies, the dragons spun as they hung in the cold and the dark and pumped life-giving water through symbiont-rich lamellae? Perhaps one day, Alice and her generation would find out.

Indira would have to talk with the other hunters. There must be no more hunting for dragons. *No more war.* Perhaps they could help the workers, set up feeding stations where the creatures could get their dietary supplements of vitamins and essential amino acids. Perhaps they could learn the workers' chattering *patois.* Make contact. Cooperate. And begin to make the ocean a place in which to live.

Indira said, "I think I might have found something that Earth can't do."

The bus didn't understand. Indira wasn't sure that she did, either, but it didn't matter. Alice and all the other children would.

Divided by Infinity

ROBERT CHARLES WILSON

Here's a tricky, brilliant, inventive story that brings you the glad news that you will never die. Well, then, in that case, you've got nothing to worry about, do you? Do you?

Robert Charles Wilson made his first sale in 1974, to Analog, *but little more was heard from him until the late eighties, when he began to publish a string of ingenious and well-crafted novels and stories that have since established him among the top ranks of the writers who came to prominence in the last two decades of the twentieth century. His first novel,* A Hidden Place, *appeared in 1986. He won the Philip K. Dick Award for his 1995 novel* Mysterium, *and the Aurora Award for his story "The Perseids." His other books include the novels* Memory Wire, Gypsies, The Divide, The Harvest, *and* A Bridge of Years. *His most recent book is a new novel,* Darwinia, *and he is currently working on another novel. He lives in Toronto, Canada.*

ONE

In the year after Lorraine's death I contemplated suicide six times. Contemplated it seriously, I mean: six times sat with the fat bottle of Clonazepam within reaching distance, six times failed to reach for it, betrayed by some instinct for life or disgusted by my own weakness.

I can't say I wish I had succeeded, because in all likelihood I *did* succeed, on each and every occasion. Six deaths. No, not just six. An infinite number.

Times six.

There are greater and lesser infinities.

But I didn't know that then.

I was only sixty years old.

I had lived all my life in the city of Toronto. I worked thirty-five years as a senior accountant for a Great Lakes cargo brokerage called Steamships Forwarding,

Ltd., and took an early retirement in 1997, not long before Lorraine was diagnosed with the pancreatic cancer that killed her the following year. Back then she worked part-time in a Harbord Street used-book shop called Finders, a short walk from the university district, in a part of the city we both loved.

I still loved it, even without Lorraine, though the gloss had dimmed considerably. I lived there still, in a utility apartment over an antique store, and I often walked the neighborhood—down Spadina into the candy-bright intricacies of Chinatown, or west to Kensington, foreign as a Bengali marketplace, where the smell of spices and ground coffee mingled with the stink of sun-ripened fish.

Usually I avoided Harbord Street. My grief was raw enough without the provocation of the bookstore and its awkward memories. Today, however, the sky was a radiant blue, and the smell of spring blossoms and cut grass made the city seem threatless. I walked east from Kensington with a mesh bag filled with onions and Havarti cheese, and soon enough found myself on Harbord Street, which had moved another notch upscale since the old days, more restaurants now, fewer macrobiotic shops, the palm readers and bead shops banished for good and all.

But Finders was still there. It was a tar-shingled Victorian house converted for retail, its hanging sign faded to illegibility. A three-legged cat slumbered on the cracked concrete stoop.

I went in impulsively, but also because the owner, an old man by the name of Oscar Ziegler, had put in an appearance at Lorraine's funeral the previous year, and I felt I owed him some acknowledgement. According to Lorraine, he lived upstairs and seldom left the building.

The bookstore hadn't changed on the inside, either, since the last time I had seen it. I didn't know it well (the store was Lorraine's turf and as a rule I had left her to it), but there was no obvious evidence that more than a year had passed since my last visit. It was the kind of shop with so much musty stock and so few customers that it could have survived only under the most generous circumstances—no doubt Ziegler owned the building and had found a way to finesse his property taxes. The store was not a labor of love, I suspected, so much as an excuse for Ziegler to indulge his pack-rat tendencies.

It was a full nest of books. The walls were pineboard shelves, floor to ceiling. Free-standing shelves divided the small interior into box canyons and dimly-lit hedgerows. The stock was old and, not that I'm any judge, largely trivial, forgotten jazz-age novels and *belles-lettres*, literary flotsam.

I stepped past cardboard boxes from which more books overflowed, to the rear of the store, where a cash desk had been wedged against the wall. This was where, for much of the last five years of her life, Lorraine had spent her weekday afternoons. I wondered whether book dust was carcinogenic. Maybe she had been poisoned by the turgid air, by the floating fragments of ivoried Frank Yerby novels, vagrant molecules of *Peyton Place* and *The Man in the Gray Flannel Suit*.

Someone else sat behind the desk now, a different woman, younger than Lorraine, though not what anyone would call young. A baby-boomer in denim overalls and a pair of eyeglasses that might have better suited the Hubble Space Telescope. Shoulder-length hair, gone gray, and an ingratiating smile, though there was something faintly haunted about the woman.

"Hi," she said amiably. "Anything I can help you find?"

"Is Oscar Ziegler around?"

Her eyes widened. "Uh, Mr. Ziegler? He's upstairs, but he doesn't usually like to be disturbed. Is he expecting you?"

She seemed astonished at the possibility that Ziegler would be expecting anyone, or that anyone would want to see Ziegler. Maybe it was a bad idea. "No," I said, "I just dropped by on the chance . . . you know, my wife used to work here."

"I see."

"Please don't bother him. I'll just browse for a while."

"Are you a book collector, or—?"

"Hardly. These days I read the newspaper. The only books I've kept are old paperbacks. Not the sort of thing Mr. Ziegler would stock."

"You'd be surprised. Mysteries? Chandler, Hammett, John Dickson Carr? Because we have some firsts over by the stairs. . . ."

"I used to read some mysteries. Mostly, though, it was science fiction I liked."

"Really? You look more like a mystery reader."

"There's a look?"

She laughed. "Tell you what. Science fiction? We got a box of paperbacks in last week. Right over there, under the ladder. Check it out, and I'll tell Mr. Ziegler you're here. Uh—"

"My name is Keller. Bill Keller. My wife was Lorraine."

She held out her hand. "I'm Deirdre. Just have a look; I'll be back in a jiff."

I wanted to stop her but didn't know how. She went through a bead curtain and up a dim flight of stairs while I pulled a leathery cardboard box onto a chair seat and prepared for some dutiful time-killing. Certainly I didn't expect to find anything I wanted, though I would probably have to buy something as the price of a courtesy call, especially if Ziegler was coaxed out of his lair to greet me. But what I had told Deirdre was true; though I had been an eager reader in my youth, I hadn't bought more than an occasional softcover since 1970. Fiction is a young man's pastime. I had ceased to be curious about other people's lives, much less other worlds.

Still, the box was full of forty-year-old softcover books, Ace and Ballantine paperbacks mainly, and it was nice to see the covers again, the Richard Powers abstracts, translucent bubbles on infinite plains, or Jack Gaughan sketches, angular and insectile. Titles rich with key words: *Time, Space, Worlds, Infinity*. Once I had loved this sort of thing.

And then, amongst these faded jewels, I found something I did *not* expect—

And another. And another.

The bead curtain parted and Ziegler entered the room.

He was a bulky man, but he moved with the exaggerated caution of the frail. A plastic tube emerged from his nose, was taped to his cheek with a dirty Band-Aid and connected to an oxygen canister slung from his shoulder. He hadn't shaved for a couple of days. He wore what looked like a velveteen frock coat draped over a T-shirt and a pair of pinstriped pajama-bottoms. His hair, what remained of it, was feathery and white. His skin was the color of thrift-shop Tupperware.

Despite his appearance, he gave me a wide grin.

"Mr. Ziegler," I said. "I'm Bill Keller. I don't know if you remember—"

He thrust his pudgy hand forward. "Of course! No need to explain. Terrible about Lorraine. I think of her often." He turned to Deirdre, who emerged from the curtain behind him. "Mr. Keller's wife . . ." He drew a labored breath. "Died last year."

"I'm sorry," Deirdre said.

"She was . . . a wonderful woman. Friendly by nature. A joy. Of course, death isn't final . . . we all *go on*, I believe, each in his own way. . . ."

There was more of this—enough that I regretted stopping by—but I couldn't doubt Ziegler's sincerity. Despite his intimidating appearance there was something almost willfully childlike about him, a kind of embalmed innocence, if that makes any sense.

He asked how I had been and what I had been doing. I answered as cheerfully as I could and refrained from asking after his own health. His cheeks reddened as he stood, and I wondered if he shouldn't be sitting down. But he seemed to be enjoying himself. He eyed the five slender books I'd brought to the cash desk.

"Science fiction!" he said. "I wouldn't have taken you for a science fiction reader, Mr. Keller."

(Deirdre glanced at me: *Told you so!*)

"I haven't been a steady reader for a long time," I said. "But I found some interesting items."

"The good old stuff," Ziegler gushed. "The pure quill. Does it strike you, Mr. Keller, that we live every day in the science fiction of our youth?"

"I hadn't noticed."

"There was a time when science seemed so *sterile*. It didn't yield up the wonders we had been led to expect. Only a bleak, lifeless solar system . . . a half-dozen desert worlds, baked or frozen, take your pick, and the gas giants . . . great roaring seas of methane and ammonia . . ."

I nodded politely.

"But now!" Ziegler exclaimed. "Life on Mars! Oceans under Europa! Comets plunging into Jupiter—!"

"I see what you mean."

"And here on Earth—the human genome, cloned animals, mind-altering drugs! Computer networks! Computer *viruses*!" He slapped his thigh. "I have a *Teflon hip*, if you can imagine such a thing!"

"Pretty amazing," I agreed, though I hadn't thought much about any of this.

"Back when we read these books, Mr. Keller, when we read Heinlein or Simak or Edmond Hamilton, we longed to immerse ourselves in the strange . . . the *outré*. And now—well—here we are!" He smiled breathlessly and summed up his thesis. "*Immersed in the strange*. All it takes is time. Just . . . time. Shall I put these in a bag for you?"

He bagged the books without looking at them. When I fumbled out my wallet, he raised his hand.

"No charge. This is for Lorraine. And to thank you for stopping by."

I couldn't argue . . . and I admit I didn't want to draw his attention to the paperbacks, in the petty fear that he might notice how unusual they were and refuse to part with them. I took the paper bag from his parchment hand, feeling faintly guilty.

"Perhaps you'll come back," he said.

"I'd like to."

"Anytime," Ziegler said, inching toward his bead curtain and the musty stairway behind it, back into the cloying dark. "Anything you're looking for, I can help you find it."

Crossing College Street, freighted with groceries, I stepped into the path of a car, a yellow Hyundai racing a red light. The driver swerved around me, but it was a near thing. The wheel wells brushed my trouser legs. My heart stuttered a beat.

. . . and I died, perhaps, a small infinity of times.

Probabilities collapse. I become increasingly *unlikely*.

"Immersed in the strange," Ziegler had said.

But had I ever wanted that? *Really* wanted that?

"Be careful," Lorraine told me one evening in the long month before she died. Amazingly, she had seemed to think of it as my tragedy, not hers. "Don't despise life."

Difficult advice.

Did I "despise life"? I think I did not; that is, there were times when the world seemed a pleasant enough place, times when a cup of coffee and a morning in the sun seemed a good enough reason to continue to draw breath. I remained capable of smiling at babies. I was even able to look at an attractive young woman and feel a response more immediate than nostalgia.

But I missed Lorraine terribly, and we had never had children, neither of us had any close living relations or much in the way of friends; I was unemployed and unemployable, confined forevermore within the contracting walls of my pension and our modest savings . . . all the joy and much of the simple structure of my life had been leeched away, and the future looked like more of the same, a protracted fumble toward the grave.

If anything postponed the act of suicide it wasn't courage or principle but the daily trivia. I would kill myself (I decided more than once), but not until after the news . . . not until I paid the electric bill . . . not until I had taken my walk.

Not until I solved the mystery I'd brought home from Finders.

I won't describe the books in detail. They looked more or less like others of their kind. What was strange about them was that I didn't recognize them, although this was a genre (paperback science fiction of the 1950s and '60s) I had once known in intimate detail.

The shock was not just unfamiliarity, since I might have missed any number of minor works by minor writers; but these were major novels by well-known names, not re-titled works or variant editions. A single example: I sat down that night with a book called *The Stone Pillow*, by a writer whose identity any science fiction follower would instantly recognize. It was a Signet paperback circa 1957, with a cover by the artist Paul Lehr in the period style. According to the credit slug, the story had been serialized in *Astounding* in 1946. The pages were browned at the margins; the glued spine was brittle as bone china. I handled the book carefully, but I couldn't resist reading it, and insofar as I was able to judge it was a plausible example of the late author's well-known style and habits of thought. I enjoyed it a great deal and went to bed convinced of its authenticity. Either I had missed it, somehow—in the days when *not* missing such things meant a great deal to me—or it had slipped out of memory. No other explanation presented itself.

One such item wouldn't have worried me. But I had brought home four more volumes equally inexplicable.

Chalk it up to age, I thought. Or worse. Senility. Alzheimer's. Either way, a bad omen.

Sleep was elusive.

The next logical step might have been to see a doctor. Instead, the next morning I thumbed through the yellow pages for a used-book dealer who specialized in period science fiction. After a couple of calls I reached a young man named Niemand who offered to evaluate the books if I brought them to him that afternoon.

I told him I'd be there by one.

If nothing else, it was an excuse to prolong my life one more interminable day.

Niemand—his store was an overheated second-story loft over a noisy downtown street—gave the books a long, thoughtful examination.

"Fake," he said finally. "They're fake."

"Fake? You mean . . . counterfeit?"

"If you like, but that's stretching a point. Nobody counterfeits books, even valuable books. The idea is ludicrous. I mean, what do you do, set up a press and go through all the work of producing a bound volume, duplicate the type, flaws and all, and then flog it on the collector's market? You'd never recoup your expenses, not even if you came up with a convincing Gutenberg Bible. In the case of books like this the idea's doubly absurd. Maybe if they were one-off from an abandoned print run or something, but hell, people would *know* about that. Nope. Sorry, but these are just . . . fake."

"But—well, obviously, somebody *did* go to the trouble of faking them."

He nodded. "Obviously. It's flawless work, and it can't have been cheap. And the books are genuinely old. *Contemporary* fakes, maybe . . . maybe some obsessive fan with a big disposable income, rigging up books he *wanted* to exist. . . ."

"Are they valuable?"

"They're certainly odd. Valuable? Not to me. Tell you the truth, I kind of wish you hadn't brought them in."

"Why?"

"They're creepy. They're *too* good. Kind of *X-Files.*" He gave me a sour grin. "Make up your own science fiction story."

"Or live in it," I said. *We live in the science fiction of our youth.*

He pushed the books across his cluttered desk. "Take 'em away, Mr. Keller. And if you find out where they came from—"

"Yes?"

"I really don't want to know."

• • •

Items I noticed in the newspaper that evening:

GENE THERAPY RENDERS HEART BYPASS OBSOLETE

BANK OF ZURICH FIRST WITH QUANTUM ENCRYPTION

SETI RESEARCHERS SPOT "POSSIBLE" ET RADIO SOURCE

I didn't want to go back to Ziegler, not immediately. It felt like admitting defeat—like looking up the answer to a magazine puzzle I couldn't solve.

But there was no obvious next step to take, so I put the whole thing out of my mind, or tried to; watched television, did laundry, shined my shoes.

None of this pathetic sleight-of-hand provided the slightest distraction.

I was not (just as I had told Deirdre) a mystery lover, and I didn't love this mystery, but it was a turbulence in the flow of the passing days, therefore interesting. When I had savored the strangeness of it to a satisfying degree I took myself in hand and carried the books back to Finders, meaning to demand an explanation.

Oscar Ziegler was expecting me.

The late-May weather was already too humid, a bright sun bearing down from the ozone-depleted sky. Walking wasn't such a pleasure under the circumstances. I arrived at Finders plucking my shirt away from my body. Graceless. The woman Deirdre looked up from her niche at the rear of the store. "Mr. Keller, right?" She didn't seem especially pleased to see me.

I meant to ask if Ziegler was available, but she waved me off: "He said if you showed up you were to go on upstairs. That's, uh, really unusual."

"Shouldn't you let him know I'm here?"

"Really, he's expecting you." She waved at the bead curtain, almost a challenge: *Go on, if you must.*

The curtain made a sound like chattering teeth behind me. The stairway was dim. Dustballs quivered on the risers and clung to the threadbare coco-mat tread. At the top was a door silted under so many layers of ancient paint that the moulding had softened into gentle dunes.

Ziegler opened the door and waved me in.

His room was lined with books. He stepped back, settled himself into an immense overstuffed easy chair, and invited me to look at his collection. But the titles at eye level were disappointing. They were old cloth volumes of Gurdjieff and Ouspenski, Velikovsky and Crowley—the usual pseudo-gnostic spiritualist bullshit, pardon my language. Like the room itself, the books radiated dust and boredom. I felt obscurely disappointed. So this was Oscar Ziegler, one more pathetic old man with a penchant for magic and cabbalism.

Between the books, medical supplies: inhalers, oxygen tanks, pill bottles.

Ziegler might be old, but his eyesight was still keen. "Judging by the expression on your face, you find my den distasteful."

"Not at all."

"Oh, fess up, Mr. Keller. You're too old to be polite and I'm too old to pretend I don't notice."

I gestured at the books. "I was never much for the occult."

"That's understandable. It's claptrap, really. I keep those volumes for nostalgic reasons. To be honest, there was a time when I looked there for answers. That time is long past."

"I see."

"Now tell me why you came."

I showed him the softcover books, told him how I'd taken them to Niemand for a professional assessment. Confessed my own bafflement.

Ziegler took the books into his lap. He looked at them briefly and took a long drag from his oxygen mask. He didn't seem especially impressed. "I'm hardly responsible for every volume that comes into the store."

"Of course not. And I'm not complaining. I just wondered—"

"If I knew where they came from? If I could offer you a meaningful explanation?"

"Basically, yes."

"Well," Ziegler said. "Well. Yes and no. Yes and no."

"I'm sorry?"

"That is . . . no, I can't tell you precisely where they came from. Deirdre probably bought them from someone off the street. Cash or credit, and I don't keep detailed records. But it doesn't really matter."

"Doesn't it?"

He took another deep drag from the oxygen bottle. "Oh, it could have been anyone. Even if you tracked down the original vendor—which I guarantee you won't be able to do—you wouldn't learn anything useful."

"You don't seem especially surprised by this."

"Implying that I know more than I'm saying." He smiled ruefully. "I've never been in this position before, though you're right, it doesn't surprise me. Did you know, Mr. Keller, that I am immortal?"

Here we go, I thought. The pitch. Ziegler didn't care about the books. I had come for an explanation; he wanted to sell me a religion.

"And you, Mr. Keller. You're immortal, too."

What was I doing here, in this shabby place with this shabby old man? There was nothing to say.

"But I can't explain it," Ziegler went on; "that is, not in the depth it deserves. There's a volume here—I'll lend it to you—" He stood, precariously, and huffed across the room.

I looked at his books again while he rummaged for the volume in question. Below the precambrian deposits of the occult was a small sediment of literature. First editions, presumably valuable.

And not all familiar.

Had Ernest Hemingway written a book called *Pamplona*? (But here it was, its Scribners dust jacket protected in brittle Mylar.) *Cromwell and Company*, by Charles Dickens? *Under the Absolute*, by Aldous Huxley?

"Ah, books." Ziegler, smiling, came up behind me. "They bob like corks on an ocean. Float between worlds, messages in bottles. This will tell you what you need to know."

The book he gave me was cheaply made, with a utilitarian olive-drab jacket. *You Will Never Die*, by one Carl G. Soziere.

"Come back when you've read it."

"I will," I lied.

"I had a feeling," Deirdre said, "you'd come downstairs with one of those."

The Soziere book. "You've heard of it?"

"Not until I took this job. Mr. Ziegler gave me a copy. But I speak from experience. Every once in a long while, somebody comes in with a question or a complaint. They go upstairs. And they come back down with *that*."

At which point I realized I had left the paperbacks in Ziegler's room. I suppose I could have gone back for them, but it seemed somehow churlish. But it was a loss. Not that I loved the books, particularly, but they were the only concrete evidence I had of the mystery—they *were* the mystery. Now Ziegler had them back in his possession. And I had *You Will Never Die*.

"It looks like a crank book."

"Oh, it is," Deirdre said. "Kind of a parallel-worlds argument, you know, J. W. Dunne and so on, with some quantum physics thrown in; actually, I'm surprised a major publisher didn't pick it up."

"You've read it?"

"I'm a sucker for that kind of thing, if you want the truth."

"Don't tell me. It changed your life." I was smiling.

She smiled back. "It didn't even change my mind."

But there was an odd note of worry in her voice.

Of course I read it.

Deirdre was right about *You Will Never Die*. It had been published by some private or vanity press, but the writing wasn't crude. It was slick, even witty in places.

And the argument was seductive. Shorn of the babble about Planck radii and Prigogine complexity and the Dancing Wu-Li Masters, it came down to this:

Consciousness, like matter, like energy, is preserved.

You are born, not an individual, but an *infinity* of individuals, in an infinity of identical worlds. "Consciousness," your individual awareness, is shared by this infinity of beings.

At birth (or at conception; Soziere wasn't explicit), this span of selves begins to divide, as alternate possibilities are indulged or rejected. The infant turns his head not to the left or to the right, but both. One infinity of worlds becomes two; then four; then eight, and so on, exponentially.

But the underlying *essence of consciousness* continues to connect all these disparate possibilities.

The upshot? Soziere says it all in his title.

You cannot die.

Consider. Suppose, tomorrow afternoon, you walk in front of a speeding eighteen-wheeler. The grillwork snaps your neck and what remains of you is sausaged under the chassis. Do you die? Well, yes; an infinity of you *does* die; but infinity is divisible by itself. Another infinity of you steps out of the path of the truck, or didn't leave the house that day, or recovers in hospital. The *you-ness* of you doesn't die; it simply continues to reside in those remnant selves.

An infinite set has been subtracted from infinity; but what remains, remains infinite.

The *subjective* experience is that the accident simply doesn't happen.

Consider that bottle of Clonazepam I keep beside the bed. Six times I reached for it, meaning to kill myself. Six times stopped myself.

In the great wilderness of worlds, I must have succeeded more often than I failed. My cold and vomit-stained corpse was carted off to whatever grave or urn awaits it, and a few acquaintances briefly mourned.

But that's not *me*. By definition, you can't experience your own death. Death is the end of consciousness. And consciousness persists. In the language of physics, consciousness is *conserved*.

I am the one who wakes up in the morning.

Always.

Every morning.

I don't die.

I just become increasingly *unlikely*.

I spent the next few days watching television, folding laundry, trimming my nails— spinning my wheels.

I tossed Soziere's little tome into a corner and left it there.

And when I was done kidding myself, I went to see Deirdre.

I didn't even know her last name. All I knew was that she had read Soziere's book and remained skeptical of it, and I was eager to have my own skepticism refreshed.

You think odd things, sometimes, when you're too often alone.

I caught Deirdre on her lunch break. Ziegler didn't come downstairs to man the desk; the store simply closed between noon and one every weekday. The May heat wave had broken; the sky was a soft, deep blue, the air balmy. We sat at a sidewalk table outside a lunch-and-coffee restaurant.

Her full name was Deirdre Frank. She was fifty and unmarried and had run her own retail business until some legal difficulty closed her down. She was working at Finders while she reorganized her life. And she understood why I had come to her.

"There's a couple of tests I apply," she said, "whenever I read this kind of book. First, is it likely to improve anyone's life? Which is a trickier question than it sounds. Any number of people will tell you they found happiness with the Scientologists or the Moonies or whatever, but what that usually means is they narrowed their focus—they can't see past the bars of their cage. Okay, *You Will Never Die* isn't a cult book, but I doubt it will make anybody a better person.

"Second, is there any way to test the author's claims? Soziere aced that one beautifully, I have to admit. His argument is that there's no *subjective* experience of death—your family might die, your friends, your grade-school teachers, the Princess of Wales, but never *you*. And in some other world, *you* die and other people go on living. How do you prove such a thing? Obviously, you can't. What Soziere tries to do is *infer* it, from quantum physics and lots of less respectable sources. It's a bubble theory—it floats over the landscape, touching nothing."

I was probably blushing by this time.

Deirdre said, "You took it seriously, didn't you? Or half seriously . . ."

"Half at most. I'm not stupid. But it's an appealing idea."

Her eyes widened. "*Appealing?*"

"Well—there are people who've died. People I miss. I like to think of them going on somewhere, even if it isn't a place I can reach."

She was aghast. "God, no! Soziere's book isn't a fairy tale, Mr. Keller—it's a horror story!"

"Pardon me?"

"Think about it! At first it sounds like an invitation to suicide. You don't like where you are, put a pistol in your mouth and go somewhere else—somewhere better, maybe, even if it is inherently less *likely*. But take you for example. You're what, sixty years old? Or so? Well, great, you inhabit a universe where a healthy human being can obtain the age of sixty, fine, but what next? Maybe you wake up tomorrow morning and find out they cured cancer, say, or heart disease—excluding you from all the worlds where William Keller dies of a colon tumor or an aneurism. And then? You're a hundred years old, a hundred and twenty—do you turn into some kind of freak? So *unlikely*, in Soziere's sense, that you end up in a circus or a research ward? Do they clone you a fresh body? Do you end up as some kind of half-human robot, a brain in a bottle? And in the meantime the world changes around you, everything familiar is left behind, you see others die, maybe millions of others, maybe the human race dies out or evolves into something else, and you go on, and on, while the universe groans under the weight of your unlikeliness, and there's no escape, every death is just another rung up the ladder of weirdness and disorientation. . . ."

I hadn't thought of it that way.

Yes, the *reductio ad absurdum* of Soziere's theory was a kind of relativistic paradox: as the observer's life grows more unlikely, he perceives the world around him becoming proportionately more strange; and down those unexplored, narrow rivers of mortality might well lie a cannibal village.

Or the Temple of Gold.

What if Deirdre was too pessimistic? What if, among all the unlikely worlds, there was one in which Lorraine had survived her cancer?

Wouldn't that be worth waiting for?

Worth *looking* for, no matter how strange the consequences might be?

News items that night:

NEURAL IMPLANTS RESTORE VISION
IN FIFTEEN PATIENTS

"TELOMERASE COCKTAIL" CREATES
IMMORTAL LAB MICE

TWINNED NEUTRON STARS POSE
POTENTIAL THREAT, NASA SAYS

My sin was longing.

Not grief. Grief isn't a sin, and is anyway unavoidable. Yes, I grieved for Lorraine, grieved long and hard, but I don't remember having a choice. I miss her still. Which is as it should be.

But I had given in too often to the vulgar yearnings. Mourned youth, mourned better days. Made an old man's map of roads not taken, from the stale perspective of a dead end.

Reached for the Clonazepam and turned my hand away, freighted every inch with deaths beyond counting.

I wonder if my captors understand this?

I went back to Ziegler — nodding at Deirdre, who was disappointed to see me, as I vanished behind the bead curtain.

"This doesn't explain it." I gave him back *You Will Never Die.*

"Explain," Ziegler said guilelessly, "what?"

"The paperbacks I bought from you."

"I don't recall."

"Or these —"

I turned to his bookshelf.

Copies of *In Our Time, Our Mutual Friend, Beyond the Mexique Bay.*

"I didn't realize they needed explaining."

I was the victim of a conjuror's trick, gulled and embarrassed. I closed my mouth.

"Anomalous experience," Ziegler said knowingly. "You're right, Soziere doesn't explain it. Personally I think there must be a kind of critical limit — a degree of accumulated unlikeliness so great that the illusion of normalcy can no longer be wholly sustained." He smiled, not pleasantly. "Things *leak.* I think especially books, books being little islands of mind. They trail their authors across phenomenological borders, like lost puppies. That's why I love them. But you're awfully young to experience such phenomena. You must have made yourself very unlikely indeed — more and more unlikely, day after day! What have you been *doing* to yourself, Mr. Keller?"

I left him sucking oxygen from a fogged plastic mask.

Reaching for the bottle of Clonazepam.

Drawing back my hand.

But how far must the charade proceed? Does the universe gauge intent? What if I touch the bottle? What if I open it and peer inside?

(These questions, of course, are answered now. I have only myself to blame.)

· · ·

I had tumbled a handful of the small white tablets into my hand and was regarding them with the cool curiosity of an entomologist when the telephone rang.

Pills or telephone?

Both, presumably, in Soziere's multiverse.

I answered the phone.

It was Deirdre. "He's dead," she told me. "Ziegler. I thought you should know."

I said, "I'm sorry."

"I'm taking care of the arrangements. He was so alone . . . no family, no friends, just nothing."

"Will there be a service?"

"He wanted to be cremated. You're welcome to come. It might be nice if somebody besides me showed up."

"I will. What about the store?"

"That's the crazy part. According to the bank, he left it to me." Her voice was choked with emotion. "Can you imagine that? I never even called him by his first name! To be honest—oh, God, I didn't even *like* him! Now he leaves me this tumbledown business of his!"

I told her I'd see her at the mortuary.

I paid no attention to the news that night, save to register the lead stories, which were ominous and strange.

We live, Ziegler had said, in the science fiction of our youth.

The "ET signals" NASA scientists had discovered were, it turned out, a simple star map, at the center of which was—not the putative aliens' home world—but a previously undiscovered binary neutron star in the constellation Orion.

The message, one astronomer speculated, might be a warning. Binary neutron stars are unstable. When they eventually collide, drawn together by their enormous gravity, the collision produces a black hole—and in the process a burst of gamma rays and cosmic radiation, strong enough to scour the Earth of life if the event occurs within some two or three thousand light-years of us.

The freshly discovered neutron stars were well within that range. As for the collision, it might happen in ten years, a thousand, ten thousand—none of the quoted authorities would commit to a date, though estimates had been shrinking daily.

Nice of our neighbors to warn us, I thought.

But how long had that warning bell been ringing, and for how many centuries had we ignored it?

Deirdre's description of the Soziere book as a "bubble theory" haunted me.

No proof, no evidence could exist: that was ruled out by the theory itself—or at least, as Ziegler had implied, there would be no evidence one could share.

But there *had* been evidence, at least in my case: the paperback books, "anomalous" books imported, presumably, from some other timeline, a history I had since lost to cardiac arrest, a car accident, Clonazepam.

But the books were gone.

I had traded them, in effect, for *You Will Never Die*.

Which I had returned to Oscar Ziegler.

Cup your hands as you might. The water runs through your fingers.

There was only the most rudimentary service at the crematorium where Ziegler's body was burned. A few words from an Episcopal minister Deirdre had hired for the occasion, an earnest young man in clerical gear and neatly pressed Levis who pronounced his consolations and hurried away as if late for another function. Deirdre said, afterward, "I don't know if I've been given a gift or an obligation. For a man who never left his room, Mr. Ziegler had a way of weaving people into his life." She shook her head sadly. "If any of it really matters. I mean, if we're not devoured by aliens or god knows what. You can't turn on the news these days. . . . Well, I guess he bailed out just in time."

Or moved on. Moved someplace where his emphysema was curable, his failing heart reparable, his aging cells regenerable. Shunting the train Oscar Ziegler along a more promising if less plausible track . . .

"The evidence," I said suddenly.

"What?"

"The books I told you about."

"Oh. Right. Well, I'm sorry, but I didn't get a good look at them." She frowned. "Is *that* what you're thinking? Oh, shit, that fucking Soziere book of his! It's *bait*, Mr. Keller, don't you get it? Not to speak ill of the dead, but he loved to suck people into whatever cloistered little mental universe he inhabited, misery loves company, and that book was always the bait—"

"No," I said, excited despite my best intentions, as if Ziegler's cremation had been a message, his personal message to me, that the universe discarded bodies like used Kleenex but that consciousness was continuous, seamless, immortal. . . . "I mean about the evidence. You didn't see it—but *someone* did."

"Leave it alone. You don't understand about Ziegler. Oscar Ziegler was a sour, poisonous old man. Maybe older than he looked. That's what I thought of when I read Soziere's book: Oscar Ziegler, someone so ridiculously old that he wakes up every morning surprised he's still a human being." She stared fiercely at me. "What exactly are you contemplating here—*serial suicide?*"

"Nothing so drastic."

I thanked her and left.

The paradox of proof.

I went to Niemand's store as soon as I left Deirdre.

I had shown the books to Niemand, the book dealer. He was the impossible witness, the corroborative testimony. If Niemand had seen the books, then I was sane; if Niemand had seen the books they might well turn up among Ziegler's possessions, and I could establish their true provenance and put all this dangerous Soziere mythology behind me.

But Niemand's little second-story loft store had closed. The sign was gone. The door was locked and the space was for lease.

Neither the jeweller downstairs nor the coffee-shop girl next door remembered the store, its clientele, or Niemand himself.

There was no Niemand in the phone book. Nor could I find his commercial listing. Not even in my yellow pages at home, where I had first looked it up.

Or remembered looking it up.

Anomalous experience.

Which constituted proof, of a kind, though Ziegler was right; it was not transferable. I could convince no one, ultimately, save myself.

The television news was full of apocalypse that night. A rumor had swept the Internet that the great gamma-ray burst was imminent, only days away. No, it was not, scientists insisted, but they allowed themselves to be drawn by their CNN inquisitors into hypothetical questions. Would there be any safe place? A half-mile underground, say, or two, or three? (*Probably not*, they admitted; or, *We don't have the full story yet.*)

To a man, or woman, they looked unsettled and skittish.

I went to bed knowing she was out there, Lorraine, I mean, out among the plenitude of worlds and stars. Alone, perhaps, since I must have died to her—infinities apart, certainly, but enclosed within the same inconceivably vast multiuniverse, as alike, in our way, as two snowflakes in an avalanche.

I slept with the pill bottle cradled in my hand.

The trick, I decided, was to abandon the charade, to *mean* the act.

In other words, to swallow twenty or thirty tablets—a more difficult act than you might imagine—and wash them down with a neat last shot of Glenlivet.

But Deirdre called.

Almost too late.

Not late enough.

I picked up the phone, confused, my hands butting the receiver like antagonistic parade balloons. I said, or meant to say, "Lorraine?"

But it was Deirdre, only Deirdre, and before long Deirdre was shouting in an annoying way. I let the phone drop.

I suppose she called 911.

TWO

I woke in a hospital bed.

I lay there passively for more than an hour, by the digital clock on the bedstand, cresting waves of sleep and wondering at the silence, until I was visited by Candice. Her name was written on her lapel tag. Candice was a nurse, with a throaty Jamaican accent and wide, sad eyes.

"You're awake," she said, barely glancing at me.

My head hurt. My mouth tasted of ashes and quicklime. I needed to pee, but there was a catheter in the way.

"I think I want to see a doctor," I managed.

"Prob'ly you do," Candice agreed. "And prob'ly you should. But our last resident went home yesterday. I can take the catheter out, if that's what you want."

"There are no *doctors?*"

"Home with their families like everybody else." She fluffed my pillow. "Only us pathetic lonelyhearts left, Mr. Keller. You been unconscious ten days."

Later she wheeled me down the corridor—though I insisted I could have walked—to a lounge with a tall plate glass window, where the ward's remaining patients had gathered to talk and weep and watch the fires that burned fitfully through the downtown core.

Soziere's curse. We become—or we make ourselves—less "likely." But it's not our own unlikeliness we perceive; instead, we see the world growing strange around us.

The lights are out all over the city. The hospital, fortunately, has its own generator. I tried to call Deirdre from a hospital phone, but there was no dial tone, just a crackling hiss, like the last groove in an LP record.

The previous week's newspapers, stacked by the door of the hospital lounge, were dwindling broadsheets containing nothing but stark outlines of the impending gamma-ray disaster.

The extraterrestrial warning had been timely. Timely, though we read it far too late. Apparently it not only identified the threatening binary neutron stars—which were spiralling at last into gaudy destruction, about to emit a burst of radiation brighter than a billion galaxies—but provided a calculable time scale.

A countdown, in other words, which had already closed in on its ultimate zero. Too close to home, a black hole was about to be born.

None of us would survive that last flash of annihilating fire.

Or, at least, if we did, we would all become *extremely* unlikely.

I remember a spot of blue luminescence roughly the size of a dinner plate at arm's length, suspended above the burning city: Cherenkov radiation. Gamma rays fractured molecules in the upper atmosphere, loading the air with nitric oxides the color of dried blood. The sky was frying like a bad picture tube.

The hard, ionizing radiation would arrive within hours. Cosmic rays striking the wounded atmosphere would trigger particle cascades, washing the crust of the Earth with what the papers called "high energy muons."

I was tired of the ward lounge, the incessant weeping and periodic shouting.

Candice took me aside. "I'll tell you," she said, "what I told the others. I been into the medicine cupboard. If you don't want to wait, there are pills you can take."

The air smelled suddenly of burning plastic. Static electricity drew bright blue sparks from metal shelves and gurney carts. Surely this would be the end: the irrevocable death, the utter annihilation, if there can ever be an end.

I told Candice a nightcap might be a good idea, and she smiled wanly and brought me the pills.

III

They want me to keep on with my memoirs.

They take the pages away from me, exchange them for greater rations of food.

The food is pale, chalky, with the claylike texture of goat cheese. They excrete it from a sort of spinerette, white obscene lumps of it, like turds.

I prefer to think of them as advanced machines rather than biological entities—vending machines, say, not the eight-foot-long centipedes they appear to be.

They've mastered the English language. (I don't know how.) They say "please" and "thank you." Their voices are thin and reedy, a sound like tree branches creaking on a windy winter night.

They tell me I've been dead for ten thousand years.

Today they let me out of my bubble, let me walk outside, with a sort of mirrored umbrella to protect me from the undiluted sunlight.

The sunlight is intense, the air cold and thin. They have explained, in patient but barely intelligible whispers, that the gamma ray burst and subsequent bath of cosmic radiation stripped the earth of its ozone layer as well as much of the upper atmosphere. The oxygen that remains, they say, is "fossil" oxygen, no longer replenished. The soil is alive with radioactive nuclei: samarium 146, iodine 129, isotopes of lead, of plutonium.

There is no macroscopic life on Earth. Present company excepted.

Everything died. People, plants, plankton, everything but the bacteria inhabiting the rocks of the deep mantle or the scalding water around undersea volcanic vents. The surface of the planet—here, at least—has been scoured by wind and radiation into a rocky desert.

All this happened ten thousand years ago. The sun shines placidly on the lifeless soil, the distant blue-black mountains.

Everything I loved is dead.

I can't imagine the technology they used to resurrect me, to *re-create* me, as they insist, from desiccated fragments of biological tissue tweezed from rocks. It's not just my DNA they have recovered but (apparently, somehow) my memories, my self, my consciousness.

I suppose Carl Soziere wouldn't be surprised.

I ask about others, other survivors reclaimed from the waterless desert. My captors (or saviours) only spindle their sickeningly mobile bodies: a gesture of negation, I've come to understand, the equivalent of a shake of the head. There are no other survivors.

And yet I can't help wondering whether Lorraine waits to be salvaged from her grave—some holographic scrap of her, at least; information scattered by time, like the dust of an ancient book.

There is nothing in my transparent cell but bowls of water and food, a floor soft enough to serve as a mattress, and the blunted writing instruments and clothlike paper. (Are they afraid I might commit suicide?)

The memoirs run out. I want the extra food, and I enjoy the diversion of writing, but what remains to be said? And to whom?

I've learned to distinguish between my captors.

The "leader" (that is, the individual most likely to address me directly and see that others attend to my needs) is a duller shade of silver-white, his cartilaginous shell dusted with fine powder. He (or she) possesses many orifices, all visible when he sways back to speak. I have identified his speaking-orifice and his food-excreting orifice, but there are three others I haven't seen in use, including a tooth-lined maw that must be a kind of mouth.

"We are the ones who warned you," he tells me. "For half of a million years we warned you. If you had known, you might have protected yourself." His grammar is impeccable, to my ears anyway, although consonants in close proximity make him stumble and hiss. "You might have deconstructed your moon, created a shield, as we did. Numerous strategies might have succeeded in preserving your world."

The tocsin had sounded, in other words, for centuries. We had simply been too dull to interpret it, until the very end, when nothing could be done to counter the threat.

I try not interpret this as a rebuke.

"Now we have learned to transsect distance," the insectile creature explains. "Then, we could only signal."

I ask whether he could re-create the Earth, revive the dead.

"No," he says. Perhaps the angle of his body signifies regret. "One of you is puzzle enough."

They live apart from me, in an immense silver half-sphere embedded in the alkaline soil. Their spaceship?

For a day they haven't come. I sit alone in my own much smaller shelter, its bubble walls polarized to filter the light but transparent enough to show the horizon with vicious clarity. I feel abandoned, a fly on a vast pane of dusty glass. And hungry. And thirsty.

They return — apologetically — with water, with paper and writing implements, and with a generous supply of food, thoughtfully pre-excreted.

They are compiling, they tell me, a sort of interstellar database, combining the functions of library, archeological museum, and telephone exchange. They are most grateful for my writings, which have been enthusiastically received. "Your cosmology," by which they must mean Soziere's cosmology, "is quite distinctive."

I thank them but explain that there is nothing more to write — and no audience I can even begin to imagine.

The news perplexes them. The leader asks, "Do you need a human audience?"

Yes. Yes, that's what I need. A human audience. Lorraine, warning me away from despair, or even Deirdre, trying vainly to shield me from black magic.

They confer for another day.

I walk outside my bubble at sunset, alone, with my silver umbrella tilted toward the western horizon. When the stars appear, they are astonishingly bright and crisp. I can see the frosted breath of the Milky Way.

"We cannot create a human audience for you," the leader says, swaying in a chill noon breeze like a stately elm. "But there is perhaps a way."

I wait. I am infinitely patient.

"We have experimented with time," the creature announces. Or I think the word is "experimented." It might as easily have been the clacking buzz of a cricket or a cicada.

"Send me back," I demand at once.

"No, not you, not physical objects. It cannot be done. Thoughts, perhaps. Dreams. Speaking to minds long dead. Of course, it changes nothing."

I rather like the idea—when they explain it—of my memoirs circulating through the Terrestrial past, appearing fragmented and unintelligible among the night terrors of Neanderthals, Cro-Magnons, Roman slaves, Chinese peasants, science fiction writers, drunken poets. And Deirdre Frank, and Oscar Ziegler. And Lorraine.

Even the faintest touch—belated, impossible—is better than none at all.

But still, I find it difficult to write.

"In that case," the leader says, "we would like to salvage you."

"Salvage me?"

They consult in their own woody, windy language, punctuated by long silences or sounds I cannot hear.

"Preserve you," they conclude. "Yourself. Your soul."

And how would they do that?

"I would take you into my body," the leader says.

Eat me, in other words. They have explained this more than once. Devour my body, *hoc est corpus*, and spit out my soul like a cherry pit into the great galactic telephone exchange.

"But this is how we must do it," the leader says apologetically.

I don't fear them.

I take a long last walk, at night, bundled against the cold in layers of flexible foil. The stars have not changed visibly in the ten thousand years of my absence, but there is nothing else familiar, no recognizable landmarks, I gather, anywhere on the surface of the planet. This might be an empty lakebed, this desert of mine, saline and ancient and, save for the distant mountains, flat as a chessboard.

I don't fear them. They might be lying, I know, although I doubt it; surely not even the most alien of creatures would travel hundreds of light-years to a dead planet in search of a single exotic snack.

I do fear their teeth, however, sharp as shark's teeth, even if (as they claim) their bodies secrete an anaesthetic and euphoriant venom.

And death?

I don't fear death.

I dread the absence of it.

• • •

Maybe Soziere was wrong. Maybe there's a teleological escape clause, maybe all the frayed threads of time will be woven back together at the end of the world, assembled in the ultimate library, where all the books and all the dreams are preserved and ordered in their multiple infinities.

Or not.

I think, at last, of Lorraine: really think of her, I mean; imagine her next to me, whispering that I ought to have taken her advice, not lodged this grief so close to my heart; whispering that death is not a door through which I can follow her, no matter how hard or how often I try. . . .

"Will you accept me?" the leader asks, rearing up to show his needled mouth, his venom sacs oozing a pleasant narcotic.

"I've accepted worse," I tell him.

US

HOWARD WALDROP

Here's an ironic, wise, funny, and (as is usual for this author) meticulously researched look at three different lives that might have arisen from one particular fork in the Road of Time, if things had worked out just a bit differently . . . and the impact that each of those lives might have had on the world around it.

Howard Waldrop is widely considered to be one of the best short-story writers in the business, and his famous story "The Ugly Chickens" won both the Nebula and the World Fantasy Awards in 1981. His work has been gathered in the collections Howard Who?, All About Strange Monsters of the Recent Past, *and* Night of the Cooters, *with more collections in the works. Waldrop is also the author of the novel* The Texas-Israeli War: 1999 *in collaboration with Jake Saunders, and of two solo novels,* Them Bones *and* A Dozen Tough Jobs. *He is at work on a new novel, tentatively entitled* The Moon World. *His most recent book is a new collection,* Going Home Again. *His stories have appeared in our First, Third, Fourth, Fifth, Sixth, Twelfth, and Fifteenth Annual Collections. While he has neither telephone nor computer, he has a Web site at http://www.sff.net/people/waldrop. A longtime Texan, Waldrop now lives in the tiny town of Arlington, Washington, outside Seattle, as close to a trout stream as he can possibly get without actually living in it.*

PROLOGUE

The ladder, though ingeniously made, was flimsy and the rungs were too far apart. He had pushed the dowels into the holes in each of the three sections. It had been made to fit inside the car, parked a mile away off the road to Hopewell. The night was cold and it had not been easy to put the sections of the ladder together with the leather gloves he wore.

Construction stuff lay all around. The house wasn't landscaped yet, borders and walks were laid out but not yet rocked in. The house was big, two stories and a gable-windowed third narrow one set in the steeply pitched roof. The outside was stucco.

He put the ladder against the upstairs window, the one with the shutter that, though new, was already warped and wouldn't close completely.

He picked up the gunnysack, checked in his pocket for the envelope, and started up. There were two lights on downstairs, the sitting room and the kitchen.

The ladder swayed and groaned. He had to lift one leg at a time, more crawl up than climb, then pull the other one after it up to the same rung. When both feet were on one, he could feel the vibration of the strain.

He reached the next from the top, pulled the shutter the rest of the way open without a sound. He raised the window, the sack flopping over his face as he used one hand to steady himself and the other to lift.

His eyes adjusted to the dim light inside. There was a stack of trunks and suitcases under the window, the sill of which was concrete rather than wood. A crib across the way. Beside the window a fireplace and mantel, some bird toys along the top. A scooter on the floor. Just past the fireplace a big parabolic electric heater and a chair. The room was almost hot.

He smelled Mentholatum or Vicks salve. He eased himself over the sill, swung the sack and his feet to the floor. He went to the crib, where the medicine smell was strongest.

The kid was safety-pinned under the blankets, its breathing a little rough and croupy. He undid one of the pins, eased the toddler out of the crib. It began to move.

"Sh-sh-sh," he said, holding it close and swinging it slightly back and forth. He noticed the kid was in some kind of cut-down larger garment rather than Dr. Denton's or a nightshirt. The child subsided.

He pulled a blanket out of the sack, wrapped the kid in it, put both back in the bag, lifted it gently by the center top. He went to the windowsill, laid the bag down, eased himself over. He had to search around for the first rung, turned, put one leg down, then the other. He reached back inside, lifted the child by the sack onto the concrete sill. He felt inside his pocket, took out the envelope, put it on the inside of the sill.

Then with both hands, he lifted the sack.

ONE: "THE LITTLE EAGLET"

He had been born just after Clyde Tombaugh discovered the planet Pluto. He was the most famous child in the world for a year or two, until Shirley Temple came along. He was the son of a famous man and a celebrated mother. Somebody'd tried to kidnap him when he was twenty months old, but they'd caught the guy on the way to his car, and Charles Jr. was back in his crib by 10:00 P.M. and didn't remember a thing about it.

But it convinced his father (a very private man) and his mother (from a distinguished family) that they would be hounded all their lives by newspapermen, gossip columnists, and radio reporters if they stayed where they were.

They moved out of the house in New Jersey and moved out to Roswell, New Mexico, so his father could be near his friend Dr. Robert H. Goddard, who fooled around with rockets.

"The Little Eaglet," as the press had dubbed him, grew up watching six-foot-long pieces of metal rise, wobble, and explode themselves all over the remote scrub country of the Eden Valley that "Uncle" Robert used as a range.

It was a great place to be a kid. His mother and father were often away on flights, surveying airline routes, or his father was off consulting with Boeing or Curtiss, or there'd be pictures of him in a zeppelin somewhere. His mother, when she was around, wrote books and was always off in her study, or having another of his brothers and sisters.

He had the run of the place. The first time he'd walked over on his own to the worksheds, Uncle Robert had stooped down to his level and said, "Do anything you want here, kid, but don't *ever* play with matches."

They let him have pieces of metal, old tubing, burnt-out frozen-up fuel pumps, and that neat stuff that looks like tortoiseshell. They had to run him out of the place when they closed up at night.

He went unwillingly to school in 1936, each day an agony of letters and numbers. Of course he had to poke a few three-foot jerks in the snoot because they made fun of his curly golden hair.

He learned a phrase early and used it often: "So's your old man."

His own old man, after some vacillation, jumped on the Preparedness bandwagon and was out with Hap Arnold, beefing up the army air corps.

You wouldn't have known there'd just been a Depression.

Uncle Robert finally got something right. When he was eight, Charles Jr. watched a rocket go up and actually get out of sight before it exploded. He, Uncle Robert, and everybody else ran back inside the small blockhouse while it rained metal for a couple of minutes.

Of course his father taught him how to fly, but since he'd been driving the converted mail van and rocket trailer from the shed three miles out to the range since he was six (he'd put blocks on the brakes and accelerator and stood on a box to see out the windshield), he thought flying was a lot like driving a car, only the road was bigger.

One time he and his father talked about it. "I like flying too, I guess," said Charles Jr. "But the air's so *thick*. That's for sissies."

"You'll think sissy when you pull three Gs on an inside turn sometime," said the Lone Eagle.

He spent most of his time with his aunt and uncle, and by the time he was ten he was working for Uncle Robert after school and full time in the summers, at whatever needed to be done.

Uncle Robert was getting older—he'd always looked old with his bald head and mustache, but now his head was wrinkled and the mustache was gray and white like a dollop of cream cheese across his lip.

The war had already started in Europe. One day a shady character in a cheap suit brought in some plans and left.

The whole crew gathered around. Uncle Robert tapped the blueprints. *"That's* what the Germans are working on," he said. "They're not very serious yet, but they will be. They're on the right track, but they're spending most of their time trying to get a good centrifugal pump, and haven't thought about regenerative cooling yet. On the other hand, look at this. Graphite vanes in the exhaust, and I assume if it's ballistic they'll be set beforehand; if it's guidable, they'll have to make room for steering mechanisms and radio controls."

He looked at all of them. "The army and air corps have their thumbs up their wazoos right now, so we'll have to do it ourselves on the Smithsonian and Guggenheim money. I figure the Nazis are six months behind us in some things, a couple of years ahead in others."

They went to work and they worked hard, especially after the U.S. got in the war when the Japanese bombed the Phillipines.

It wasn't easy, but they did it by the middle of 1942. They fired it off. It went 143 miles and punched a thirty-foot hole in the desert even without a warhead.

They showed it to the air corps.

World War II was over late in 1944, just after Charles Jr. turned 14.

It was a bright and sunny day in the winter of 1945. He and Uncle Robert were looking at one of the German A-4s that had been lying around everywhere in Europe when the war ended and then shipped to America, along with their scientists. The army had given Goddard five or six to play with.

Uncle Robert had been sick the year before, recurrence of the TB of his youth, but had gotten better. Now he seemed to have some of the old spark back. He looked at the pumps, the servo-mechanisms. He looked in the empty warhead section, then he looked at Charles Jr.

"How'd you like to take a little ride?" he asked.

"Yippee yahoo!"

"As many times as you've seen things I built turn into firecrackers?"

"You didn't build this one. The Germans did."

"At White Sands, they're maybe kinda going to send up mice and monkeys."

"Phooey!" said Charles Jr.

"Double phooey," said Uncle Robert.

On March 13, 1946, Charles Jr. went for a little ride. They hadn't told his mother or father, and no one else either, until after the fact.

The front section separated and fired some JATO units as retro rockets, and the surplus cargo parachute opened, and the thing came down sixty-eight miles away, within two miles of where Goddard and the crew were waiting.

The trucks drove up. Charles Jr. was sitting in the shade of the parachute canopy.

Uncle Robert jumped out of the truck and ran up to him.

There was a small cut above his eye.

"She rides a little rough," he said, and smiled.

On July 4th, 1963, *The Great Speckled Bird* came down on the surface of the Moon, backwards, rockets firing, and settled to the lunar dust.

The commander was Col. Chuck Yeager. The pilot was Lt. Col. David Simons, M.D., the navigator was Maj. Joe Kittinger, and the civilian mission specialist was Charles Lindbergh, Jr.

After a few hours of yammer and instrument readings that were hunky-dory, Charles Jr. suited up in one of the big bulky space suits the navy had built for them.

Yeager checked him over, then said, "You're on, kid."

It was being carried live by all the radios in the world; they'd have to wait till they got back to see it, as both Early Bird and Echo III satellites weren't cooperating.

The big ladder came out from the ship and Charles Jr. backed down it, unable to see well behind him because of the size of the oxygen equipment on the suit.

He paused just as he got to the bottom, looked up at Kittinger who was filming him with an Eymo camera (besides the official one on the side of the airlock), and stretched his foot out, inches above the dust.

He swung one foot out in a small circle, almost touching, then the other.

He said, "Here's one for Mom, and one for Pop, and one for Uncle Robert and"—he jumped onto the ground with both feet—"one for the good old USA."

TWO: "CALL ME CHUCKY"

He could say he'd been around since Pluto was a pup. Disney made the first cartoon with Mickey's mutt a few months after he was born.

When he was twenty months old he was kidnapped. It was the most sensational story of the decade. After much police activity and several copycat ransom notes, his father, the most famous man in the world, and, after Babe Ruth, in America, paid the right people and went in a coast guard plane to find his son in the boat—as the kidnapper's message said, "boad"—*Nelly* between Horseneck Beach and Gay Head near Elizabeth Island.

Charles Jr. was sleeping like a log in a built-in bureau drawer belowdecks on the stolen and deserted boat. The kidnappers were never found and the ransom money, much of it in marked gold certificates, which became illegal tender a couple of years later, never showed up.

Colonel H. N. Schwarzkopf of the New Jersey State Police had put a twenty-four-hour guard around the Lindbergh house in Hopewell and up at the Morrow house just after the kidnapping. His father hired his own bodyguards and dismissed the state troopers once Charles Jr. was recovered. But they moved from New Jersey soon anyway.

Famous father, famous mother, most famous child in America.

Of course he ended up in Hollywood.

Later in interviews, Charles Jr.—"Call me Chucky"—said, "Yeah, yeah, child of the Depression. We had to cut down to *two* cooks. And don't ask *me* how somebody with such a publicity-shy father and mother ended up doing one, count 'em, one *Our Gang* short. I think they felt sorry for me—guys with big guns walking around wherever we were; people watching me like a hawk day and night.

"Warhol used to run that damn clip at the Factory all the time. There I am, three years old, sitting in a beer-barrel airplane, replica of the *Spirit*, with an aviator's cap. There I am, me and the new kid Spanky—whatever happened to him, huh?—racing all these other kids down that damn long hill in L.A.; soap-box racers, fire engines, tanks, and me and Spanky McFarland win 'cause all the other kids have a wooden demo-derby.

"They tell me Roach creamed his shorts; wanted to sign me, team with Spanky; already had a name picked out, Sankandank, you know, Spank and Sankandank, anyway, lifetime contract; Louis B. Mayer would honor it once I got too old for the *Gang* stuff.

"Yeah, I coulda had it all. Been as big as Buckwheat or Alfalfa. Coulda stayed on, beat up on Butch and Woim.

"What happened. Dad said no way, José."

His father had visited Italy and Germany several times, and they had lived in England for a while, only to find British newspapermen just like the ones in America, so they moved back. His father was convinced that since it wasn't ready and couldn't afford it, the U.S. should stay neutral in any coming conflict in Europe or Asia. He'd become a major spokesman for America First.

One day at school, Chucky came out to find one of his best friends beating the snot out of another. He pulled them apart while they were swinging in blind rage at each other, noses bloodied, eyes shut.

"Geez, guys!" he said.

One pointed to the other. "He said your father was a Jew-hater. That made *me* mad. I said no, he wasn't, he was just dumb as a post. That made *him* mad."

Chucky, age eleven, went home. His father was packing for a trip to Des Moines where he was going to make a terrifically ill-timed speech about staying out of the European war which had been going on for a year and a half already.

"Dad," said Chucky to his father, who looked just like him only bigger, and was putting shirts in a leather bag. "Dad, *somebody* has to kick some Hitler butt."

He was sent to his room without his supper.

"Yeah, yeah," said Chucky in another interview in 1989, "that was the first time any kid of his expressed an opinion that wasn't his. It started me on that downward spiral that led me to where I am today. For which, thanks . . ."

After the war was over and things got back to normal, Chucky went off to college in 1948.

And fell in with evil companions. Some guys who endlessly drove back and forth across the country because they couldn't stand wherever they were. Poets, artists, weirdos, and Old Lefties, white folksingers who spent all their money on bus trips to Alabama to learn exactly what it was Cornbread Joe hollered on that record across the fields when he wanted someone to bring the water jug or oats for the mule. There were a zillion guys loose in New York City on the GI bill, finding out what life was all about. Chucky: "Say what you will. The guys who shot heroin are all still alive; the boozers have been dead these thirty years."

Then he started to make things. Birdhouses made out of old airplane parts.

Small ones at first, made from old propeller hubs and radio aerials, exhaust stacks, parts of instrument panels. Then they got larger and more complicated. He had a few small gallery shows, then a couple at museums. He dropped out of college his sophomore year, rented a studio and went to work.

One day Calder came by, took a look around, and whistled. Rauschenberg and all those guys dropped in; Mailer, smarting from *Barbary Shore*, came in and smoked some tea and talked about Chucky's pop, whom he'd met in the Pacific, and said he was going to start a Village newspaper sometime.

His first real show was called "Birdhouses for the Stratosphere" and it all went fine from then on. He went on to use parts from jets. His *Birdhouse for the Rukh* used most of a Super Constellation he'd gotten cheap from the NATSB. They had to build an extra plaza in front of the rededicated O'Hare before he could install it.

Even with that going on, he continued to make the smaller houses all through the fifties and sixties and have shows in little galleries; people actually bought them and used them for birdhouses. His wren series—made from an old Curtiss Wren—was the best and most popular.

At one of these small-show openings in the early sixties, Chucky was a little high from reefer and a little tight from wine and a little up from some innocuous-looking red tablets someone had given him. He was 32 and good at what he did, and knew he'd be doing it the rest of his life.

An old man was looking at some of the things ("Houses for the Bluebird of Sadness," the show was) and waited until the people who'd been around Chucky went over for the free cheese and beer.

The old man caught his eye. "You did these?"

"Yep."

"I have something to tell you," said the old man. "But I can't tell you until you promise it goes no further."

"Oh, this is serious? Wait a sec." Chucky quit smiling and set his face in a calm mask with a wipe of his hand.

"There," he said. "Try me."

"Between you and me?"

"My word as a Video Ranger," said Chucky.

The old man eyed him, then sagged his shoulders.

"I kidnapped you once."

"Sonofabitch!" said Chucky. "Not you. The situation. Why'd you ever do that?"

"I went *messhuganeh*," said the old man. "It was the Depression. I was desperate. I borrowed a stranger's boat. I kipped you from the crib, sent the notes."

"Well, they never caught you."

"It was very fucked over, from beginning to end. I couldn't believe it, that I was getting away with it, I was so excited. And I lost it, all $50,000 of it, between the time I put you in the boat and the time they came to get you. I took it from the satchel your father brought it to the graveyard in and put it in a big tin box. I had it with me when I put you on the boat. I was so excited, I dropped it. I watched my life getting smaller and smaller and further away. If only I'd put it in a *wooden* box . . ."

"Could I give you a few bucks?" asked Chucky.

"I didn't come here, Mr. Lindbergh, Jr., to ask for money. I came here to ask forgiveness."

Chucky laughed and reached out and grabbed him by the shoulders, causing him to wince.

"Forgive? Mister, that was probably the best thing that ever happened to me. Thank you!"

"You mean that? All these years, nobody knew but me, and I was so sorry that I'd done it. I've lived a clean life since. . . ."

"Gaffer," said Chucky. "Go with my blessing. I mean that. Thanks for telling me."

"Good-bye, then."

"Good-bye." He watched the old man leave.

"Whowazzat?" asked a friend. "It looked intense."

"A stranger," said Chucky, smiling. "He wanted to put the touch on my old man."

When his father died in the 1970s, Chucky called up a bunch of old engineers and mechanics and tool-and-die men. He had them make an exact replica of the Ryan *Spirit of St. Louis*.

Then he took it apart, piece by piece, and built the *Birdhouse for Pop*.

It's outside the Air and Space Museum.

THREE: "CRAZY CHARLIE"

After seventeen years in the Plutonian depths of being a famous man's son, he took off.

In 1953, just at the end of the Korean War, a guy showed up in Concrete, Washington. He walked with a slight gimp. He drove a secondhand two-door purple Kaiser. He rented a place on the edge of town for $8.40 a month. Once a week or so he'd drive out of town; one of the locals saw him over at the Veterans' Hospital in Mt. Vernon. Otherwise he walked everywhere in the town of Concrete, shopped at the local grocery store. Slowly it got out that his name was Charles.

Mostly what he did was fish the Skagit River, 365 days a year if he could, less if it was muddied up, though the flow was now controlled through Diablo and Gorge Dams. Sometimes the Sauk and Cascade were muddied up and put the lower river out for fishing for four or five days at a time.

He used a Gladding Ike Walton model 8 fiberglass fly rod and a Pfleuger 1498 reel, and he caught more fly-fishing than all the other people around there caught with bait or casting reels or the new spinning reels. People over on the Skykomish and Stillaguamish fly-fished, but not many yet on the Skagit.

One day right downtown, in a pouring rain, fifteen or twenty people stood on the bridge to watch him. There was already both ends of about an eight-pounder sticking out of the back pouch of his homemade fishing jacket, and they watched for twenty-two minutes by the watch, as he played and landed what was by the best estimate a steelhead that would go twenty-five pounds.

He reached down with a pair of pliers and jerked the Brad's Brat out of the fish's lip and watched it swim back out to the deeper water against the far bank.

"What the hell?" yelled someone from the bridge.

"They won't be around forever, you know?" said Charles

"Then why the hell did you catch it if you were going to let it go?"

"Because I can't help myself," said Charles, and began casting again.

From then on he was Crazy Charlie.

In 1957, over in Sedro-Wooley, he met a girl at the Dairy Delight. She moved in with him in a slightly larger shack on the edge of Concrete that cost $12.00 a month.

They ate trout and salmon; she canned salmonberries and blackberries; they smoked steelhead and came out of the woods with mushrooms and roots and nuts and skunk cabbage; they drove in the purple Kaiser.

In 1958 they had twin boys, whom people learned to call Key and Matt. They assumed they were family names for something like Keyes or Keynard and Matthew or even Mattias. If you go to the Skagit County Courthouse and look up their birth certificates, you'll find their names are Quemoy and Matsu. It was 1958 after all.

The one peculiarity other fishermen and the people in town noticed was that wherever he was, whatever he was doing, even playing a fish, if a plane flew over he would watch it until it disappeared. They assumed it had something to do with the Korean War.

One day one of the town blowhards came into the cafe shaking his head. Everybody was ready for a story.

"Goddamnedest thing. Give me that Seattle paper," he said. He looked through it quickly. "Here, damn, Ed, you look."

"What'm I lookin' for?"

"Well look with your eyes and just lissen. I was up in Marblemount at the Rocky Ford Cafe. Over in the corner was Crazy Charlie and that girl of his—the two boys being most likely in school this time of day. And you know who was in the booth with them, talkin' to them? Huh?"

"Dwight David Eisenhower," said someone. They all laughed.

"Charles Lindbergh. The Lone Eagle."

"Shit," said someone. "What would he be doin' talkin to Crazy Charlie?"

"You got me. He's older now, Lindbergh, but I knew it was him from when he used to come to the plant during the war. As big as life. Sure as shootin'." They all knew the blowhard had retired from Boeing with a disability a few years before.

"He used to be a practical joker, give old man Boeing a hotfoot soon as look at him," he continued. "Always cutting up."

"Well, what was they doin'?"

"Eating hamburgers, shakes, and fries."

"I didn't think Charlie and his girl ate that kind of stuff. The kids neither."

"I said the kids wasn't there. And they was sure as hell eatin' that way today."

"Did they see you?"

"Hell, no. I was so astounded it was Lindbergh I just sat down in that far booth, the one halfway in the kitchen. Couldn't hear 'em neither, place was crowded. Had a roast beef sandwich."

"We don't care what you had for lunch. What'd Lindbergh do?"

"Talked. Ate. Went outside. By the time I was through they was gone."

"Nothing about Lindbergh in the papers," said Ed.

"Can you beat that? Guy like that in town, nobody thinks it's a big deal."

"Well, it was more than thirty years ago," said the blowhard. "Still, you'd think somebody would mention it."

"Maybe it was personal," said someone.

"Yeah, right. The Lone Eagle and Crazy Charlie and his girl."

They all laughed.

Charlie died in 1985. His common-law wife Estelle died in 1989. Quemoy and Matsu own motion picture production in Seattle like the Krays owned London in the sixties. Neither fishes.

EPILOGUE:

He reached in his pocket, took out the envelope, put it on the inside of the sill.

Then, with both hands he lifted the sack.

The rung broke with a sharp snap and his foot hit the next one.

There was a sudden instant of chill blind panic. The sack had thudded onto the concrete sill. He eased his other foot down the outside of the ladder to the rung he'd fallen to. He made it the rest of the way down, filled with adrenaline, cradled the bundle in his arms, and made off for the woods and his car.

Halfway through the trees, he realized the kid hadn't moved.

When he got within sight of the car, he put the sack down, lifted the blanket and child out. The kid was limp as a bunch of leather. One side of the head was misshapen. He felt around for a heartbeat.

He went further back into the woods from the road, laid the kid down, kicked some leaves over him, and took the blanket and sack to his car and sped away toward Manhattan.

The biggest manhunt in history was on. There were shady intermediaries, ransom was paid. There was no Boad Nelly, no child.

Two truck drivers, one black, one white, on their way into Hopewell two months later, stopped their truck and went into the woods to take a pee.

They saw what was left of the kid on the ground. He had been gnawed by animals.

They ran for the cops.

Three years later, Bruno Richard Hauptmann, on trial for his life for essentially passing hot gold certificates, was shown the ladder used in the kidnapping. "I did not make *that*," he said. "I am a *carpenter*."

The Days of Solomon Gursky

IAN McDONALD

Here's a fast-paced, gorgeously colored, richly detailed, and wildly inventive story that sweeps us along on a journey of almost unimaginable scope and grandeur, tracing one man's journey through life and into death and then out the other side. McDonald takes us from a troubled near-future to the distant stars and on to the very end of the universe and the end of time itself—and beyond!

British author Ian McDonald is an ambitious and daring writer with a wide range and an impressive amount of talent. His first story was published in 1982, and since then he has appeared with some frequency in Interzone, Asimov's Science Fiction, New Worlds, Zenith, Other Edens, Amazing, and elsewhere. He was nominated for the John W. Campbell Award in 1985, and in 1989 he won the Locus Best First Novel Award for Desolation Road. He won the Philip K. Dick Award in 1992 for his novel King of Morning, Queen of Day. His other books include the novels Out on Blue Six; Hearts, Hands and Voices; Terminal Café; Sacrifice of Fools; and the acclaimed Evolution's Shore, and two collections of his short fiction, Empire Dreams and Speaking in Tongues. His most recent book is a new novel, Kirinya. His stories have appeared in our Eighth, Ninth, Tenth, Fourteenth, and Fifteenth Annual Collections. Born in Manchester, England, in 1960, McDonald has spent most of his life in Northern Ireland, and now lives and works in Belfast.

MONDAY

Sol stripped the gear on the trail over Blood of Christ Mountain. Clickshifted down to sixth for the steep push up to the ridge, and there was no sixth. No fifth, no fourth; nothing, down to zero.

Elena was already up on the divide, laughing at him pushing and sweating up through the pines, muscles twisted and knotted like the trunks of the primeval bristlecones, tubes and tendons straining like bridge cable. Then she saw the gear train sheared through and spinning free.

They'd given the bikes a good hard kicking down in the desert mountains south of Nogales. Two thousand apiece, but the salesperson had sworn on the virginity of all his unmarried sisters that these MTBs would go anywhere, do anything you wanted. Climb straight up El Capitan, if that was what you needed of them. Now they were five days on the trail—three from the nearest Dirt Lobo dealership, so Elena's palmtop told her—and a gear train had broken clean in half. Ten more days, four hundred more miles, fifty more mountains for Solomon Gursky, in high gear.

"Should have been prepared for this, engineer," Elena said.

"Two thousand a bike, you shouldn't need to," Solomon Gursky replied. It was early afternoon up on Blood of Christ Mountain, high and hot and resinous with the scent of the old, old pines. There was haze down in the valley they had come from, and in the one they were riding to. "And you know I'm not that kind of engineer. My gears are a lot smaller. And they don't break."

Elena knew what kind of engineer he was, as he knew what kind of doctor she was. But the thing was new between them and at the stage where research colleagues who surprise themselves by becoming lovers like to pretend that they are mysteries to each other.

Elena's palmtop map showed a settlement five miles down the valley. It was called Redención. It might be the kind of place they could get welding done quick and good for *norte* dollars.

"Be happy, it's downhill," Elena said as she swung her electric-blue padded ass onto the saddle and plunged down off the ridge. One second later, Sol Gursky in his shirt and shorts and shoes and shades and helmet came tearing after her through the scrub sage. The thing between them was still at the stage where desire can flare at a flash of electric-blue Lycra-covered ass.

Redención it was, of the kind you get in the border mountains; of gas and food and trailers to hire by the night, or the week, or, if you have absolutely nowhere else to go, the lifetime; of truck stops and recreational Jacuzzis at night under the border country stars. No welding. Something better. The many-branched saguaro of a solar tree was the first thing of Redención the travelers saw lift out of the heat haze as they came in along the old, cracked, empty highway.

The factory was in an ugly block annex behind the gas and food. A truck driver followed Sol and Elena round the back, entranced by these fantastic macaw-bright creatures who kept their eyes hidden behind wrap-around shades. He was chewing a sandwich. He had nothing better to do in Redención on a hot Monday afternoon. Jorge, the proprietor, looked too young and ambitious to be pushing gas, food, trailers, and molecules in Redención on any afternoon. He was thirty-wise, dark, serious. There was something tight-wound about him. Elena said in English that he had the look of a man of sorrows. But he took the broken gear train seriously, and helped Sol remove it from the back wheel. He looked at the smooth, clean shear plane with admiration.

"This I can do," he declared. "Take an hour, hour and a half. Meantime, maybe you'd like to take a Jacuzzi?" This, wrinkling his nose, downwind of two MTBers come over Blood of Christ Mountain in the heat of the day. The truck driver grinned. Elena scowled. "Very private," insisted Jorge the nanofacturer.

"Something to drink?" Elena suggested.

"Sure. Coke, Sprite, beer, *agua minerale*. In the shop."

Elena went the long way around the trucker to investigate the cooler. Sol followed Jorge into the factory and watched him set the gears in the scanner.

"Actually, this is my job," Sol said to make conversation as the lasers mapped the geometry of the ziggurat of cogs in three dimensions. He spoke Spanish. Everyone did. It was the universal language up in the *norte* now, as well as down *el sur*.

"You have a factory?"

"I'm an engineer. I build these things. Not the scanners, I mean; the tectors. I design them. A nano-engineer."

The monitor told Jorge the mapping was complete.

"For the Tesler *corporada*," Sol added as Jorge called up the processor system. "How do you want it?"

"I'd like to know it's not going to do this to me again. Can you build it in diamond?"

"All just atoms, friend."

Sol studied the processor chamber. It pleased him that they looked like whisky stills; round-bellied, high-necked, rising through the roof into the spreading fingers of the solar tree. Strong spirits in that still, spirits of the vacuum between galaxies, the cold of absolute zero, and the spirits of the tectors moving through cold and emptiness, shuffling atoms. He regretted that the physics did not allow viewing windows in the nanofacturers. Look down through a pane of pure and perfect diamond at the act of creation. Maybe creation was best left unseen, a mystery. All just atoms, friend. Yes, but it was what you *did* with those atoms, where you made them go. The weird troilisms and menages you forced them into.

He envisioned the minuscule machines, smaller than viruses, clever knots of atoms, scavenging carbon through the nanofacturer's roots deep in the earth of Redención, passing it up the buckytube conduits to the processor chamber, weaving it into diamond of his own shaping.

Alchemy.

Diamond gears.

Sol Gursky shivered in his light biking clothes, touched by the intellectual chill of the nanoprocessor.

"This is one of mine," he called to Jorge. "I designed the tectors."

"I wouldn't know." Jorge fetched beers from a crate on the factory floor, opened them in the door. "I bought the whole place from a guy two years back. Went up north, to the *Tres Valles*. You from there?"

The beer was cold. In the deeper, darker cold of the reactor chamber, the nanomachines swarmed. Sol Gursky held his arms out: Jesus of the MTB wear.

"Isn't everyone?"

"Not yet. So, who was it you said you work for? Nanosis? Ewart-OzWest?"

"Tesler Corp. I head up a research group into biological analogs."

"Never heard of them."

You will, was what Solomon Gursky would have said, but for the scream. Elena's scream.

Not, he thought as he ran, that he had heard Elena's scream—the thing was not supposed to be at that stage—but he knew it could not belong to anyone else.

She was standing in the open back door of the gas and food, pale and shaky in the high bright light.

"I'm sorry," she said. "I just wanted to get some water. There wasn't any in the cooler, and I didn't want Coke. I just wanted to get some water from the faucet."

He was aware that Jorge was behind him as he went into the kitchen. Man mess: twenty coffee mugs, doughnut boxes, beer cans, and milk cartons. Spoons, knives, forks. He did that too, and Elena told him off for having to take a clean one every time.

Then he saw the figures through the open door.

Somewhere, Jorge was saying, "Please, this is my home."

There were three of them; a good-looking, hard-worked woman, and two little girls, one newly school-age, the other not long on her feet. They sat in chairs, hands on thighs. They looked straight ahead.

It was only because they did not blink, that their bodies did not rock gently to the tick of pulse and breath, that Sol could understand.

The color was perfect. He touched the woman's cheek, the coil of dark hair that fell across it. Warm soft. Like a woman's should feel. Texture like skin. His fingertips left a line in dust.

They sat unblinking, unmoving, the woman and her children, enshrined in their own memorabilia. Photographs, toys, little pieces of jewelry, loved books and ornaments, combs, mirrors. Pictures and clothes. Things that make up a life. Sol walked among the figures and their things, knowing that he trespassed in sacred space, but irresistibly drawn by the simulacra.

"They were yours?" Elena was saying somewhere. And Jorge was nodding, and his mouth was working but no words were manufactured. "I'm sorry, I'm so sorry."

"They said it was a blow-out." Jorge finally said. "You know, those tires they say repair themselves, so they never blow out? They blew out. They went right over the barrier, upside down. That's what the truck driver said. Right over, and he could see them all, upside down. Like they were frozen in time, you understand?" He paused.

"I went kind of dark for a long time after that; a lot crazy, you know? When I could see things again, I bought this with the insurance and the compensation. Like I say, it's all just atoms, friend. Putting them in the right order. Making them go where you want, do what you want."

"I'm sorry we intruded," Elena said, but Solomon Gursky was standing there among the reconstructed dead and the look on his face was that of a man seeing something far beyond what is in front of him, all the way to God.

"Folk out here are accommodating." But Jorge's smile was a tear of sutures. "You can't live in a place like this if you weren't a little crazy or lost."

"She was very beautiful," Elena said.

"She is."

Dust sparkled in the float of afternoon light through the window.

"Sol?"

"Yeah. Coming."

The diamond gears were out of the tank in twenty-five minutes. Jorge helped Sol fit them to the two thousand *norte* dollar bike. Then Sol rode around the factory and the gas-food-trailer house where the icons of the dead sat unblinking under the slow fall of dust. He clicked the gears up and clicked them down. One two three four five six. Six five four three two one. Then he paid Jorge fifty *norte*, which was all he asked for his diamond. Elena waved to him as they rode down the highway out of Redención.

They made love by firelight on the top of Blessed Virgin Mountain, on the pine needles, under the stars. That was the stage they were at: ravenous, unselfconscious, discovering. The old deaths, down the valley behind them, gave them urgency. Afterward, he was quiet and withdrawn, and when she asked what he was thinking about, he said, "The resurrection of the dead."

"But they weren't resurrected," she said, knowing instantly what he meant, for it haunted her too, up on their starry mountain. "They were just *representations*, like a painting or a photograph. Sculpted memories. Simulations."

"But they were real for *him*." Sol rolled onto his back to gaze at the warm stars of the border. "He told me he talked to them. If his nanofactory could have made them move and breathe and talk back, he'd have done it, and who *could* have said that they weren't real?"

He felt Elena shiver against his flesh.

"What is it?"

"Just thinking about those faces, and imagining them in the reactor chamber, in the cold and the emptiness, with the tectors crawling over them."

"Yeah."

Neither spoke for a time long enough to see the stars move. Then Solomon Gursky felt the heat stir in him again and he turned to Elena and felt the warmth of her meat, hungry for his second little death.

TUESDAY

Jesus was getting fractious in the plastic cat carrier; heaving from side to side, shaking the grille.

Sol Gursky set the carrier on the landing mesh and searched the ochre smog haze for the incoming liftercraft. Photochromic molecules bonded to his irises polarized: another hot, bright, poisonous day in the TVMA.

Jesus was shrieking now.

"Shut the hell up," Sol Gursky hissed. He kicked the cat carrier. Jesus gibbered and thrust her arms through the grille, grasping at freedom.

"Hey, it's only a monkey," Elena said.

But that was the thing. Monkeys, by being monkeys, annoyed him. Frequently enraged him. Little homunculus things masquerading as human. Clever little fingers, wise little eyes, expressive little faces. Nothing but dumb animal behind that face, running those so-human fingers.

He knew his anger at monkeys was irrational. But he'd still enjoyed killing Jesus, taped wide open on the pure white slab. Swab, shave, slip the needle.

Of course, she had not been Jesus then. Just Rhesus; nameless, a tool made out of meat. Experiment 625G.

It was probably the smog that was making her scream. Should have got her one of those goggle things for walking poodles. But she would have just torn it off with her clever little human fingers. Clever enough to be dumb, monkey-thing.

Elena was kneeling down, playing baby-fingers with the clutching fists thrust through the bars.

"It'll bite you."

His hand still throbbed. Dripping, shivering, and spastic from the tank, Jesus had still possessed enough motor control to turn her head and lay his thumb open to the bone. Vampire monkey: the undead appetite for blood. Bastard thing. He would have enjoyed killing it again, if it were still killable.

All three on the landing grid looked up at the sound of lifter engines detaching themselves from the aural bedrock of two million cars. The ship was coming in from the south, across the valley from the big site down on Hoover where the new *corporada* headquarters was growing itself out of the fault line. It came low and fast, nose down, ass up, like a big bug that thrives on the taste of hydrocarbons in its spiracles. The backwash from its jets flustered the palm trees as it configured into vertical mode and came down on the research facility pad. Sol Gursky and Elena Asado shielded their sunscreened eyes from flying grit and leaf-storm.

Jesus ran from end to end of her plastic cage, gibbering with fear.

"Doctor Gursky." Sol did not think he had seen this *corporadisto* before, but it was hard to be certain; Adam Tesler liked his personal assistants to look as if he had nanofactured them. "I can't begin to tell you how excited Mr. Tesler is about this."

"You should be there with me," Sol said to Elena. "It was your idea." Then, to the suit, "Dr. Asado should be with me."

Elena swiped at her jet-blown hair.

"I shouldn't, Sol. It was your baby. Your gestation, your birth. Anyway, you know how I hate dealing with suits." This for the smiling PA, but he was already guiding Sol to the open hatch.

Sol strapped in and the ship lurched as the engines screamed up into lift. He saw Elena wave and duck back toward the facility. He clutched the cat carrier hard as his gut kicked when the lifter slid into horizontal flight. Within, the dead monkey burbled to herself in exquisite terror.

"What happened to your thumb?" the *corporadisto* asked.

When he'd cracked the tank and lifted Jesus the Rhesus out of the waters of rebirth, the monkey had seemed more pissed off at being sopping wet than at having been dead. There had been a pure, perfect moment of silence, then the simultaneous oath and gout of blood, and the Lazarus team had exploded into whooping exultation. The monkey had skittered across the floor, alarmed by the hooting and cheering, hunting for height and hiding. Elena had caught it spastically trying—and failing—to hurl itself up the side of a desk. She'd swaddled Jesus up in thermal sheeting and put the spasming thing in the observation incubator.

Within the hour, Jesus had regained full motor control and was chewing at the corners of her plastic pen, scratching imaginary fleas and masturbating ferociously. While delivery companies dropped off pizza stacks and cases of cheap Mexican champagne, someone remembered to call Adam Tesler.

The dead monkey was not a good flier. She set up a wailing keen that had even the pilot complaining.

"Stop that," Sol Gursky snapped. It would not do anything for him, though, and rocked on its bare ass and wailed all the louder.

"What way is that to talk to a piece of history?" the PA said. He grinned in through the grille, waggled fingers, clicked tongue. "Hey there, little fellow. Whatcha call him?"

"Little bitch, actually. We call her Jesus; also known as Bride of Frankenstein."

Bite him, Solomon Gursky thought as ten thousand mirrored swimming pools slipped beneath the belly of the Tesler *Corporada* lifter.

Frankenstein's creations were dead. That was the thing. That was the revelation.

It was the Age of Everything, but the power to make anything into anything else was not enough, because there was one thing the tectors of Nanosis and Aristide-Tlaxcalpo and the other founders of the nanotech revolution could not manipulate into anything else, and that was death. A comment by a pioneer nanotechnologist captured the optimism and frustration of the Age of Everything: Watson's Postulate. *Never mind turning trash into oil or asteroids into heaps of Volkswagens, or hanging exact copies of Van Goghs in your living room; the first thing we get with nanotechnology is immortality.*

Five billion Rim dollars in research disproved it. What tectors touched, they transformed; what they transformed, they killed. The Gursky-Asado team had beaten its rivals to the viral replicators, that infiltrated living cells and converted them into a different, tector-based matrix, and from their DNA spored a million copies. It had shaped an algorithm from the deadly accuracy of carcinomas. It had run tests under glass and in tanks. It had christened that other nameless Rhesus Frankenstein and injected the tectors. And Sol and Elena had watched the tiny machines slowly transform the monkey's body into something not even gangrene could imagine.

Elena wanted to put it out of its misery, but they could not open the tank for fear of contamination. After a week, it ended.

The monster fell apart. That was the thing. And then Asado and Gursky remembered a hot afternoon when Sol got a set of diamond gears built in a place called Redención.

If death was a complex thing, an accumulation of microdeath upon minideath upon little death upon middling death, life might obey the same power law. Escalating anti-entropy. Pyramid-plan life.

Gursky's Corollary to Watson's Postulate: *The first thing we get with nanotechnology is the resurrection of the dead.*

The Dark Tower rose out of the amber haze. Sol and Elena's private joke had escaped and replicated itself; everyone in R&D now called the thing Adam Tesler was building down in the valley Barad Dur, in Mordor, where the smogs lie. And Adam Tesler, its unresting, all-seeing Eye.

There were over fifty levels of it now, but it showed no signs of stopping. As each section solidified and became dormant, another division of Adam Tesler's corporate edifice was slotted in. The architects were unable to say where it would stop. A kilometer, a kilometer and a half; maybe then the architectors would stabilize and die. Sol loathed its glossy black excrescences and crenellations, a miscegeny of the geological and the cancerous. Gaudi sculpting in shit.

The lifter came in high over the construction, locked into the navigation grid and banked. Sol looked down into its open black maw.

All just atoms, the guy who owned the factory had said. Sol could not remember his name now. The living and the dead have the same atoms.

They'd started small: paramecia, amoebae. Things hardly alive. Invertebrates. Reanimated cockroaches, hurtling on their thin legs around the observation tank. Biological machine, nanotech machine, still a machine. Survival machine. Except now you couldn't stomp the bastards. They came back.

What good is resurrection, if you are just going to die again?

The cockroaches came back, and they kept coming back.

He had been the cautious one this time, working carefully up the evolutionary chain. Elena was the one who wanted to go right for it. Do the monkey. Do the monkey and you do the man.

He had watched the tectors swarm over it, strip skin from flesh, flesh from bone, dissolve bones. He had watched the nanomachines put it all back together into a monkey. It lay in the liquid intact, but, its signs said, dead. Then the line kicked, and kicked again, and another twitched in harmony, and a third came in, and then they were all playing together on the vital signs monitor, and that which was dead was risen.

The lifter was into descent, lowering itself toward the exact center of the white cross on the landing grid fastened to the side of the growing tower. Touchdown. The craft rocked on its bug legs. Seat-belt sign off, steps down.

"You behave yourself," Solomon Gursky told Jesus.

The All-Seeing Eye was waiting for him by the upshaft. His Dark Minions were with him.

"Sol."

The handshake was warm and strong, but Sol Gursky had never trusted Adam Tesler in all the years he had known him; as nanoengineering student or as head of the most dynamic nanotech *corporada* in the Pacific Rim Co-Prosperity Sphere.

"So this is it?" Adam Tesler squatted down and choo-choo-chooked the monkey.

"She bites."

"I see." Jesus grabbed his thumb in her tiny pink homunculus hand. "So, you are the man who has beaten the final enemy."

"Not beaten it. Found something on the far side of it. It's resurrection, not immortality."

Adam Tesler opened the cage. Jesus hopped up his arm to perch on the shoulder of his Scarpacchi suit. Tesler tickled the fur of her belly.

"And humans?"

"Point one percent divergence between her DNA and yours."

"Ah." Adam Tesler closed his eyes. "This makes it all the harder."

Fear pulsed through Solomon Gursky like a sickness.

"Leave us, please," Adam Tesler said to his assistants. "I'll join you in a moment."

Unspeaking, they filed to the lifter.

"Adam?"

"Sol. Why did you do it?"

"What are you talking about, Adam?"

"You know, Sol."

For an instant, Sol Gursky died on the landing grid fused to the fifty-third level of the Tesler *corporada* tower. Then he returned to life, and knew with cool and beautiful clarity that he could say it all, that he *must* say it all, because he was dead now and nothing could touch him.

"It's too much for one person. Adam. This isn't building cars or growing houses or nanofacturing custom pharmaceuticals. This is the resurrection of the dead. This is every human being from now to the end of the universe. You can't be allowed to own that. Not even God should have a monopoly on eternal life."

Adam Tesler sighed. His irises were photochromed dark, their expression unreadable.

"So. How long is it?"

"Thirteen years."

"I thought I knew you, Sol."

"I thought I knew you." The air was clear and fresh and pure, here on this high perch. "How did you find out?"

Adam Tesler stroked the monkey's head. It tried to push his fingers away, baring sharp teeth.

"You can come here now, Marisa."

The tall, muscular woman who walked from the upshaft across the landing grid was no stranger to Sol. He knew her from the Yucatán resort mastaba and the Alaskan ski-lodge and the gambling complex grown out of the nanoengineered reef in the South China Sea. From clandestine conversations through secure channels and discreet meetings, he knew that her voice would be soft and low and tinted Australian.

"You dressed better when you worked for Aristide Tlaxcalpo," Sol said. The woman was dressed in street leathers. She smiled. She had smiled better then as well.

"Why them?" Adam Tesler said. "Of all the ones to betray me to, *those* clowns!"

"That's why," said Solomon Gursky. "Elena had nothing to do with this, you know."

"I know that. She's safe. For the moment."

Sol Gursky knew then what must happen, and he shivered with the sudden, urgent need to destroy before he was destroyed. He pushed down the shake of rage by force of will as he held his hand out and clicked his fingers to the monkey. Jesus frowned and frisked off Tesler's shoulder to Sol's hand. In an instant, he had stretched, twisted, and snapped its neck. He flung the twitching thing away from him. It fell to the red mesh.

"I can understand that," Adam Tesler said. "But it will come back again, and again, and again." He turned on the bottom step of the lifter. "Have you any idea how disappointed I am, Sol?"

"I really don't give a shit!" Solomon Gursky shouted but his words were swallowed by the roar of engine power-up. The lifter hovered and swooped down over the great grid of the city toward the northern hills.

Sol Gursky and Marisa were alone on the platform.

"Do it!" he shouted.

Those muscles he had so admired, he realized, were augments; her fingers took a fistful of his neck and lifted him off the ground. Strangling, he kicked at air, snatched at breath. One-armed, she carried him to the edge.

"Do it," he tried to say, but her fingers choked all words in his throat. She held him out over the drop, smiling. He shat himself, and realized as it poured out of him that it was ecstasy, that it always had been, and the reason that adults forbade it was precisely because it was such a primal joy.

Through blood haze, he saw the tiny knotted body of Jesus inching toward him on pink man-fingers, its neck twisted over its back, eyes staring unshielded into the sun. Then the woman fingers at last released their grip, and he whispered "thank you" as he dropped toward the hard white death-light of Hoover Boulevard.

WEDNESDAY

The *seguridados* were on the boulevards tonight, hunting the trespassing dead. The meat were monsters, overmoneyed, understimulated, *cerristo* males and females who deeply enjoyed playing angels of Big Death in a world where any other kind of death was temporary. The meat were horrors, but their machines were beautiful. *Mechadors*: robot mantises with beaks of vanadium steel and two rapid fire MIST 27s throwing fifty self-targeting drones per second, each separating into a hail of sun-munitions half a second before impact. Fifteen wide-spectrum senses analyzed the world; the machines maneuvered on tightly focused impeller fields. And absolutely no thought or mercy. Big beautiful death.

The window in the house in the hills was big and wide and the man stood in the middle of it. He was watching the *mechadors* hunt. There were four of them, two pairs working each side of the avenue. He saw the one with *Necroslayer* painted on its tectoplastic skin bound over the shrubbery from the Sifuentes place in a single pulse of focused electrogravitic force. It moved over the lawn, beaked head sensing. It paused, scanned the window. The man met its five cluster eyes for an instant. It moved on. Its impeller drive left eddy patterns on the shaved turf. The man watched until the *mechadors* passed out of sight, and the *seguridados* in their over-emphatic battle-armor came up the avenue, covering imagined threats with their hideously powerful weapons.

"It's every night now," he said. "They're getting scared."

In an instant, the woman was in the big, wood-floored room where the man stood. She was dressed in a virtuality bodyglove; snapped tendrils retracting into the suit's node points indicated the abruptness with which she had pulled out of the web. She was dark and very angry. Scared angry.

"Jesus Joseph Mary, how many times do I have to tell you? Keep away from that window! They catch you, you're dead. Again. *Permanently.*"

Solomon Gursky shrugged. In the few weeks that he had lived in her house, the woman had come to hate that shrug. It was a shrug that only the dead can make. She hated it because it brought the chill of the abyss into her big, warm, beautiful house in the hills.

"It changes things," the dead man said.

Elena Asado pulled smart-leather pants and a mesh top over the body-glove. Since turning traitor, she'd lived in the thing. Twelve hours a day hooked into the web by eye and ear and nose and soul, fighting the man who had killed her lover. As well fight God, Solomon Gursky thought in the long, empty hours in the airy, light-filled rooms. He is lord of life and death. Elena only removed the bodyglove to wash and excrete and, in those early, blue-lit mornings that only this city could do, when she made chilly love on the big white bed. Time and anger had made her thin and tough. She'd cut her hair like a boy's. Elena Asado was a tight wire of a woman, femininity jerked away by her need to revenge herself on Adam Tesler by destroying the world order his gift of resurrection had created.

Not gift. Never gift. He was not Jesus, who offered eternal life to whoever believed. No profit in belief. Adam Tesler took everything and left you your soul. If you could sustain the heavy *inmortalidad* payments, insurance would take you into post-life debt-free. The other 90 percent of Earth's dead worked out their salvation through indenture contracts to the Death House, the Tesler Thanos *corporada's* agent of resurrection. The *contratos* were centuries long. Time was the province of the dead. They were cheap.

"The Ewart/OzWest affair has them rattled," Elena Asado said.

"A handful of *contradados* renege on their contracts out on some asteroid, and they're afraid the sky is going to fall on their heads?"

"They're calling themselves the Freedead. You give a thing a name, you give it power. They know it's the beginning. Ewart/OzWest, all the other orbital and deep-space manufacturing *corporadas*; they always knew they could never enforce their contracts off Earth. They've lost already. Space belongs to the dead," the meat woman said.

Sol crossed the big room to the other window, the safe window that looked down from the high hills over the night city. His palm print deconfigured the glass. Night, city night perfumed with juniper and sex and smoke and the dusky heat of the heat of the day, curled around him. He went to the balcony rail. The boulevards shimmered like a map of a mind, but there was a great dark amnesia at its heart, an amorphous zone where lights were not, where the geometry of the grid was abolished. St. John. Necroville. Dead town. The city of the dead, a city within a city, walled and moated and guarded with the same weapons that swept the boulevards. City of curfew. Each dusk, the artificial aurora twenty kilometers above the Tres Valles Metropolitan Area would pulse red: the skysign, commanding all the three million dead to return from the streets of the living to their necrovilles. They passed through five gates, each in the shape of a massive V bisected by a horizontal line. The entropic flesh life descending, the eternal resurrected life ascending, through the dividing line of death. That was the law, that plane of separation. Dead was dead, living was living. As incompatible as night and day.

That same sign was fused into the palm of every resurrectee that stepped from the Death House Jesus tanks.

Not true, he thought. Not all are reborn with stigmata. Not all obey curfew. He held his hand before his face, studied the lines and creases, as if seeking a destiny written there.

He had seen the deathsign in the palm of Elena's housegirl, and how it flashed in time to the aurora.

"Still can't believe it's real?"

He had not heard Elena come onto the balcony behind him. He felt the touch of her hand on his hair, his shoulder, his bare arm. Skin on skin.

"The Nez Perce tribe believe the world ended on the third day, and what we are living in are the dreams of the last night. I fell. I hit that white light and it was hard. Hard as diamond. Maybe I dream I live, and my dreams are the last shattered moments of my life."

"Would you dream it like this?"

"No," he said after a time. "I can't recognize anything any more. I can't see how it connects to what I last remember. So much is missing."

"I couldn't make a move until I was sure he didn't suspect. He'd done a thorough job."

"He would."

"I never believed that story about the lifter crash. The universe may be ironic, but it's never neat."

"I think a lot about the poor bastard pilot he took out as well, just to make it neat." The air carried the far sound of drums from down in the dead town. Tomorrow was the great feast, the Night of All the Dead. "Five years," he said. He heard the catch in her breathing and knew what she would say next, and what would follow.

"What is it like, being dead?" Elena Asado asked.

In his weeks imprisoned in the hill house, an unlawful dead, signless and contractless, he had learned that she did not mean, what was it like to be resurrected. She wanted to know about the darkness before.

"Nothing," he answered, as he always did, but though it was true, it was not the truth, for nothing is a product of human consciousness and the darkness beyond the shattering hard light at terminal vee on Hoover Boulevard was the end of all consciousness. No dreams, no time, no loss, no light, no dark. No thing.

Now her fingers were stroking his skin, feeling for some of the chill of the nothing. He turned from the city and picked her up and carried her to the big empty bed. A month of new life was enough to learn the rules of the game. He took her in the big, wide white bed by the glow from the city beneath, and it was as chill and formulaic as every other time. He knew that for her it was more than sex with her lover come back from a far exile. He could feel in the twitch and splay of her muscles that what made it special for her was that he was *dead*. It delighted and repelled her. He suspected that she was incapable of orgasm with fellow meat. It did not trouble him, being her fetish. The body once known as Solomon Gursky knew another thing, that only the dead could know. It was that not everything that died was resurrected. The shape, the self, the sentience came back, but love did not pass through death.

Afterward, she liked him to talk about his resurrection, when no-thing became thing and he saw her face looking down through the swirl of tectors. This night he did not talk. He asked. He asked, "What was I like?"

"Your body?" she said. He let her think that. "You want to see the morgue photographs again?"

He knew the charred grin of a husk well enough. Hands flat at his sides. That was how she had known right away. Burn victims died with their fists up, fighting incineration.

"Even after I'd had you exhumed, I couldn't bring you back. I know you told me that he said I was safe, for the moment, but that moment was too soon. The technology wasn't sophisticated enough, and he would have known right away. I'm sorry I had to keep you on ice."

"I hardly noticed," he joked.

"I always meant to. It was planned; get out of Tesler Thanos, then contract an illegal Jesus tank down in St. John. The Death House doesn't know one tenth of what's going on in there."

"Thank you," Sol Gursky said, and then he felt it. He felt it and he saw it as if it were his own body. She felt him tighten.

"Another flashback?"

"No," he said. "The opposite. Get up."

"What?" she said. He was already pulling on leather and silk.

"That moment Adam gave you."

"Yes?"

"It's over."

The car was morphed into low and fast configuration. At the bend where the avenue slung itself down the hillside, they both felt the pressure wave of something large and flying pass over them, very low, utterly silent.

"Leave the car," he ordered. The doors were already gull-winged open. Three steps and the house went up behind them in a rave of white light. It seemed to suck at them, drawing them back into its annihilating gravity, then the shock swept them and the car and every homeless thing on the avenue before it. Through the screaming house alarms and the screaming householders and the rush and roar of the conflagration, Sol heard the aircraft turn above the vaporized hacienda. He seized Elena's hand and ran. The lifter passed over them and the car vanished in a burst of white energy.

"Jesus, nanotok warheads!"

Elena gasped as they tumbled down through tiered and terraced gardens. The lifter turned high on the air, eclipsing the hazy stars, hunting with extra-human senses. Below, formations of *seguridados* were spreading out through the gardens.

"How did you know?" Elena gasped.

"I saw it," said Solomon Gursky as they crashed a pool party and sent bacchanalian *cerristos* scampering for cover. Down, down. Augmented cyber-hounds growled and quested with long-red eyes; domestic defense grids stirred, captured images, alerted the police.

"Saw?" asked Elena Asado.

APVs and city pods cut smoking hexagrams in the highway blacktop as Sol and Elena came crashing out of the service alley onto the boulevard. Horns. Lights. Fervid curses. Grind of wheels. Shriek of brakes. Crack of smashing tectoplastic, doubled, redoubled. Grid-pile on the westway. A mopedcab was pulled in at a *tortilleria* on the right shoulder. The *cochero* was happy to pass up his enchiladas for Elena's hard, black currency. Folding, clinking stuff.

"Where to?"

The destruction his passengers had wreaked impressed him. Taxi drivers universally hate cars.

"Drive," Solomon Gursky said.

The machine kicked out onto the strip.

"It's still up there," Elena said, squinting out from under the canopy at the night sky.

"They won't do anything in this traffic."

"They did it up there on the avenue." Then: "You said you saw. What do you mean, *saw?*"

"You know death, when you're dead," Solomon Gursky said. "You know its face, its mask, its smell. It has a perfume, you can smell it from a long way off, like the pheromones of moths. It blows upwind in time."

"Hey," the *cochero* said, who was poor, but live meat. "You know anything about that big boom up on the hill? What was that, lifter crash or something?"

"Or something," Elena said. "Keep driving."

"Need to know where to keep driving to, lady."

"Necroville," Solomon Gursky said. St. John. City of the Dead. The place beyond law, morality, fear, love, all the things that so tightly bound the living. The outlaw city. To Elena he said, "If you're going to bring down Adam Tesler, you can only do it from the outside, as an outsider." He said this in English. The words were heavy and tasted strange on his lips. "You must do it as one of the dispossessed. One of the dead."

To have tried to run the fluorescent vee-slash of the Necroville gate would have been as certain a Big Death as to have been reduced to hot ion dust in the nanotok flash. The mopedcab prowled past the samurai silhouettes of the gate *seguridados*. Sol had the driver leave them beneath the dusty palms on a deserted boulevard pressed up hard against the razor wire of St. John. Abandoned by the living, the grass verges had run verdant, scum and lilies scabbed the swimming pools, the generous Spanish-style houses softly disintegrating, digested by their own gardens.

It gave the *cochero* spooky vibes, but Sol liked it. He knew these avenues. The little machine putt-putted off for the lands of the fully living.

"There are culverted streams all round here," Sol said. "Some go right under the defenses, into Necroville."

"Is this your dead sight again?" Elena asked as he started down an overhung service alley.

"In a sense. I grew up around here."

"I didn't know that."

"Then I can trust it."

She hesitated a step.

"What are you accusing me of?"

"How much did you rebuild, Elena?"

"Your memories are your own, Sol. We loved each other, once."

"Once," he said, and then he felt it, a static purr on his skin, like Elena's fingers over his whole body at once. This was not the psychic bloom of death foreseen. This was physics, the caress of focused gravity fields.

They hit the turn of the alley as the *mechadors* came dropping soft and slow over the roofs of the old moldering *residencias*. Across a weed-infested tennis court was a drainage ditch defended by a rusted chicken-wire fence. Sol heaved away an entire section. Adam Tesler had built his dead strong, and fast. The refugees followed the seeping, rancid water down to a rusted grille in a culvert.

"Now we see if the Jesus tank grew me true," Sol said as he kicked in the grille. "If what I remember is mine, then we come up in St. John. If not, we end up in the bay three days from now with our eyes eaten out by chlorine."

They ducked into the culvert as a *mechador* passed over. MIST 27s sent the mud and water up in a blast of spray and battle tectors. The dead man and the living woman splashed on into darkness.

"He loved you, you know," Sol said. "That's why he's doing this. He is a jealous God. I always knew he wanted you, more than that bitch he calls a wife. While I was dead, he could pretend that it might still be. He could overlook what you were trying to do to him; you can't hurt him, Elena, not on your own. But when you brought me back, he couldn't pretend any longer. He couldn't turn a blind eye. He couldn't forgive you."

"A pretty God," Elena said, water eddying around her leather-clad calves. Ahead, a light from a circle in the roof of the culvert marked a drain from the street. They stood under it a moment, feeling the touch of the light of Necroville on their faces. Elena reached up to push open the grate. Solomon Gursky stayed her, turned her palm upward to the light.

"One thing." he said. He picked a sharp shard of concrete from the tunnel wall. With three strong savage strokes he cut the vee and slash of the death sign in her flesh.

THURSDAY

He was three kilometers down the mass driver when the fleet hit Marlene Dietrich. St. Judy's Comet was five AU from perihelion and out of ecliptic, the Clade thirty-six degrees out, but for an instant two suns burned in the sky.

The folds of transparent tectoplastic skin over Solomon Gursky's face opaqued. His *sur*-arms gripped the spiderwork of the interstellar engine, rocked by the impact on his electromagnetic senses of fifty minitok warheads converting into bevawatts of hard energy. The death scream of a nation. Three hundred Freedead had cluttered the freefall warren of tunnels that honeycombed the asteroid. Marlene Dietrich had been the seed of the rebellion. The *corporadas* cherished their grudges.

Solomon Gursky's face-shield cleared. The light of Marlene Dietrich's dying was short-lived but its embers faded in his infravision toward the stellar background.

Elena spoke in his skull.

You know?

Though she was enfolded in the command womb half a kilometer deep within the comet, she was naked to the universe through identity links to the sensor web in the crust and a nimbus of bacterium-sized spyships weaving through the tenuous gas halo.

I saw it, Solomon Gursky subvocalized.

They'll come for us now, Elena said.

You think. Using his *bas*-arms Sol clambered along the slender spine of the mass driver toward the micro meteorite impact.

I know. When long-range cleared after the blast, we caught the signatures of blip-fusion burns.

Hand over hand over hand over hand. One of the first things you learn, when the Freedead change you, is that in space it is all a question of attitude. A third of the way down a nine-kilometer mass driver with several billion tons of Oort comet spiked on it, you don't think up, you don't think down. *Up*, and it is vertigo. *Down*, and a two kilometer sphere of grubby ice is poised above your head by a thread of superconducting tectoplastic. *Out*, that was the only way to think of it and stay sane. Away, and back again.

How many drives? Sol asked. The impact pin-pointed itself; the smart plastic fluoresced orange when wounded.

Eight.

A sub-voiced blasphemy. *They didn't even make them break sweat. How long have we got?*

Elena flashed the projections through the em-link onto his visual cortex. Curves of light through darkness and time, warped across the gravitation marches of Jupiter. Under current acceleration, the Earth fleet would be within strike in eighty-two hours.

The war in heaven was in its twelfth year. Both sides had determined that this was to be the last. The NightFreight War would be fought to an outcome. They called themselves the Clades, the outlaw descendants of the original Ewart/OzWest asteroid rebellion: a handful of redoubts scattered across the appalling distances of the solar system. Marlene Dietrich, the first to declare freedom; Neruro, a half-completed twenty kilometer wheel of tectoplastic attended by O'Neill can utilities, agriculture tanks, and habitation bubbles, the aspirant capital of the space Dead. Ares Orbital, dreaming of tectoformed Mars in the pumice pore spaces of Phobos and Deimos; the Pale Gallileans, surfing over the icescapes of Europa on an improbable raft of cables and spars; the Shepherd Moons, dwellers on the edge of the abyss, sailing the solar wind through Saturn's rings. Toe-holds, shallow scratchings, space-hovels; but the stolen nanotechnology burgeoned in the energy-rich environment of space. An infinite ecological niche. The Freedead knew they were the inheritors of the universe. The meat *corporadas* had withdrawn to the orbit of their planet. For a time. When they struck, they struck decisively. The Tsiolkovski Clade on the dark side of the moon was the first to fall as the battle groups of the *corporadas* thrust outward. The delicate film of vacuum-compatible tectoformed forest that carpeted the crater was seared away in the alpha strike. By the time the last strike went in, a new five-kilometer-deep crater of glowing tufa replaced the tunnels and excavations of the old lunar mining base. Earth's tides had trembled as the moon staggered in its orbit.

Big Big Death.

The battle groups moved toward their primary targets. The *corporadas* had learned much embargoed under their atmosphere. The new ships were lean, mean, fast: multiple missile racks clipped to high-gee blip-fusion motors, pilots suspended in acceleration gel like flies in amber, hooked by every orifice into the big battle virtualizers.

Thirteen-year-old boys had the best combination of reaction time and viciousness.

Now the blazing teenagers had wantonly destroyed the Marlene Dietrich Clade. Ares Orbital was wide open; Neruro, where most of the Freedead slamship fleet was based, would fight hard. Two *corporada* ships had been dispatched Jupiterward. Orbital mechanics gave the defenseless Pale Gallileans fifteen months to contemplate their own annihilation.

But the seed has flown, Solomon Gursky thought silently, out on the mass driver of St. Judy's Comet. Where we are going, neither your most powerful ships nor your most vicious boys can reach us.

The micrometeorite impact had scrambled the tectoplastic's limited intelligence: fibers and filaments of smart polymer twined and coiled, seeking completion and purpose. Sol touched his *sur*-hands to the surfaces. He imagined he could feel the order pass out of him, like a prickle of tectors osmosing through vacuum-tight skin.

Days of miracles and wonder, Adam, he thought. And because you are jealous that we are doing things with your magic you never dreamed, you would blast us all to photons.

The breach was repaired. The mass driver trembled and kicked a pellet into space, and another, and another. And Sol Gursky, working his way hand over hand over hand over hand down the device that was taking him to the stars, saw the trick of St. Judy's Comet. A ball of fuzzy ice drawing a long tail behind it. Not a seed, but a sperm, swimming through the big dark. Thus we impregnate the universe.

St. Judy's Comet. Petite as Oort cloud family members go: two point eight by one point seven by two point two kilometers. (Think of the misshaped potato you push to the side of your plate because anything that looks that weird is sure to give you cramps.) Undernourished, at sixty-two billion tons. Waif and stray of the solar system, wandering slow and lonely back out into the dark after her hour in the sun (but not too close, burn you real bad, too much sun) when these dead people snatch her, grope her all over, shove things up her ass, mess with her insides, make her do strange and unnatural acts, like shitting tons of herself away every second at a good percentage of the speed of light. Don't you know you ain't no comet no more? You're a *starship*. See up there, in the Swan, just to the left of that big bright star? There's a little dim star you can't see. That's where you're going, little St. Judy. Take some company. Going to be a long trip. And what will I find when I get there? A big bastard MACHO of gas supergiant orbiting 61 Cygni at the distance of Saturn from the sun, that's what you'll find. Just swarming with moons; one of them should be right for terrestrial life. And if not, no matter; sure, what's the difference between tectoforming an asteroid, or a comet, or the moon of an extra-solar gas super-giant? Just scale. You see, we've got everything we need to tame a new solar system right here *with* us. It's all just carbon, hydrogen, nitrogen, and oxygen, and you have that in abundance. And maybe we like you so much that we find we don't even need a world at all. Balls of muck and gravity, hell; we're the Freedead. Space and time belong to us.

It was Solomon Gursky, born in another century, who gave the ship its name. In that other century, he had owned a large and eclectic record collection. On vinyl.

The twenty living dead crew of St. Judy's Comet gathered in the command womb embedded in sixty-two billion tons of ice to plan battle. The other five hundred and forty were stored as superconducting tector matrices in a helium ice core; the dead dead, to be resurrected out of comet stuff at their new home. The crew hovered in nanogee in a score of different orientations around the free-floating instrument clusters. They were strange and beautiful, as gods and angels are. Like angels, they flew. Like gods in some pantheons, they were four-armed. Fine, manipulating *sur*-arms; strong grasping *bas*-arms growing from a lower spine reconfigured by Jesus tanks into powerful anterior shoulder-blades. Their vacuum-and-radiation-tight skins were photosynthetic, and as beautifully marked and colored as a hunting animal's. Stripes, swirls of green on orange, blue on black, fractal patterns, flags of legendary nations, tattoos. Illustrated humans.

Elena Asado, caressed by tendrils from the sensor web gave them the stark news. Fluorescent patches on shoulders, hips, and groin glowed when she spoke.

"The bastards have jumped vee. They must have burned every last molecule of hydrogen in their thruster tanks to do it. Estimated to strike range is now sixty-four hours."

The *capitan* of St. Judy's Comet, a veteran of the Marlene Dietrich rebellion, shifted orientation to face Jorge, the ship's reconfiguration engineer.

"Long range defenses?" *Capitan* Savita's skin was an exquisite mottle of pale green bamboo leaves in sun yellow, an incongruous contrast to the tangible anxiety in the command womb.

"First wave missiles will be fully grown and launch-ready in twenty-six hours. The fighters, no. The best I can push the assemblers up to is sixty-six hours."

"What can you do in time?" Sol Gursky asked.

"With your help, I could simplify the fighter design for close combat."

"How close?" *Capitan* Savita asked.

"Under a hundred kays."

"How simplified?" Elena asked.

"Little more than an armed exo-skeleton with maneuvering pods."

And they need to be clever every time, Sol thought. The meat need to be clever only once.

Space war was as profligate with time as it was with energy and distance. With the redesigns growing, Sol Gursky spent most of the twenty-six hours to missile launch on the ice, naked to the stars, imagining their warmth on his face-shield. Five years since he had woken from his second death in a habitat bubble out at Marlene Dietrich, and stars had never ceased to amaze him. When you come back, you are tied to the first thing you see. Beyond the transparent tectoplastic bubble, it had been stars.

The first time, it had been Elena. Tied together in life, now in death. Necroville had not been sanctuary. The place beyond the law only gave Adam Tesler new and more colorful opportunities to incarnate his jealousy. The Benthic Lords, they had called themselves. Wild, free, dead. They probably had not known they were working for Tesler-Thanos, but they took her out in a dead bar on Terminal Boulevard. With a game-fishing harpoon. They carved their skull symbol on her forehead, a rebuttal of the deathsign Sol had cut in her palm. Now you are really dead, meat. He had known they would never be safe on Earth. The *companeros* in the Death House had faked the off-world NightFreight contracts. The pill Sol took had been surprisingly bitter, the dive into the white light as hard as he remembered.

Stars. You could lose yourself in them; spirit strung out, orb gazing. Somewhere out there was a still-invisible constellation of eight, tight formation, silent running. Killing stars. Death stars.

Everyone came up to watch the missiles launch from the black foramens grown out of the misty ice. The chemical motors burned at twenty kays: a sudden galaxy of white stars. They watched them fade from sight. Twelve hours to contact. No one expected them to do any more than waste a few thousand rounds of the meat's point defenses.

In a dozen manufacturing pods studded around St. Judy's dumpy waist, Jorge and Sol's fighters gestated. Their slow accretion, molecule by molecule, fascinated Sol. Evil dark things, St. Andrew's crosses cast in melted bone. At the center a human-shaped cavity. You flew spread-eagled. *Bas*-hands gripped thruster controls; *sur*-hands armed and aimed the squirt lasers. Dark flapping things Sol had glimpsed once before flocked again at the edges of his consciousness. He had cheated the dark premonitory angels that other time. He would sleight them again.

The first engagement of the battle of St. Judy's Comet was at 01:45 GMT. Solomon Gursky watched it with his crewbrethren in the ice-wrapped warmth of the command womb. His virtualized sight perceived space in three dimensions. Those blue cylinders were the *corporada* ships. That white swarm closing from a hundred different directions, the missiles. One approached a blue cylinder and burst. Another, and another; then the inner display was a glare of novas as the first wave was annihilated. The backup went in. The vanguard exploded in beautiful futile blossoms of light. Closer. They were getting closer before the meat shredded them. Sol watched a warhead loop up from due south, streak toward the point ship, and annihilate it in a red flash.

The St. Judy's Cometeers cheered. One gone, reduced to bubbling slag by tectors sprayed from the warhead.

One was all they got. It was down to the fighter pilots now.

Sol and Elena made love in the count-up to launch. *Bas*-arms and *sur*-arms locked in the freegee of the forward observation blister. Stars described slow arcs across the transparent dome, like a sky. Love did not pass through death; Elena had realized this bitter truth about what she had imagined she had shared with Solomon Gursky in her house on the hillside. But love could grow, and become a thing shaped for eternity. When the fluids had dried on their skins, they sealed their soft, intimate places with vacuum-tight skin and went up to the launch bays.

Sol fitted her into the scooped-out shell. Tectoplastic fingers gripped Elena's body and meshed with her skin circuitry. The angel-suit came alive. There was a trick they had learned in their em-telepathy; a massaging of the limbic system like an inner kiss. One mutual purr of pleasure, then she cast off, suit still dripping gobs of frozen tectopolymer. St. Judy's defenders would fight dark and silent; that mental kiss would be the last radio contact until it was decided. Solomon Gursky watched the blue stutter of the thrusters merge with the stars. Reaction mass was limited; those who returned from the fight would jettison their angel-suits and glide home by solar sail. Then he went below to monitor the battle through the tickle of molecules in his frontal lobes.

St. Judy's Angels formed two squadrons: one flying anti-missile defense, the other climbing high out of the ecliptic to swoop down on the *corporada* ships and destroy them before they could empty their weapon racks. Elena was in the close defense group. Her angelship icon was identified in Sol's inner vision in red on gold tiger stripes of her skin. He watched her weave intricate orbits around St. Judy's Comet as the blue cylinders of the meat approached the plane labeled "strike range."

Suddenly, seven blue icons spawned a cloud of actinic sparks, raining down on St. Judy's Comet like fireworks.

"Jesus Joseph Mary!" someone swore quietly.

"Fifty-five gees," *Capitan* Savita said calmly. "Time to contact, one thousand and eighteen seconds."

"They'll never get them all," said Kobe with the Mondrian skin pattern, who had taken Elena's place in remote sensing.

"We have one hundred and fifteen contacts in the first wave," Jorge announced.

"Sol, I need delta vee," Savita said.

"More than a thousandth of a gravity and the mass driver coils will warp," Sol said, calling overlays onto his visual cortex.

"Anything that throws a curve into their computations," Savita said.

"I'll see how close I can push it."

He was glad to have to lose himself in the problems of squeezing a few millimeters per second squared out of the big electromagnetic gun, because then he would not be able to see the curve and swoop of attack vectors and intercept planes as the point defense group closed with the missiles. Especially he would not have to watch the twine and loop of the tiger-striped cross and fear that at any instant it would intersect with a sharp blue curve in a flash of annihilation. One by one, those blue stars were going out, he noticed, but slowly. Too slowly. Too few.

The computer gave him a solution. He fed it to the mass driver. The shift of acceleration was as gentle as a catch of breath.

Thirty years since he had covered his head in a synagogue, but Sol Gursky prayed to Yahweh that it would be enough.

One down already; Emilio's spotted indigo gone, and half the missiles were still on trajectory. Time to impact ticked down impassively in the upper right corner of his virtual vision. Six hundred and fifteen seconds. Ten minutes to live.

But the attack angels were among the *corporadas*, dodging the brilliant flares of short range interceptor drones. The meat fleet tried to scatter, but the ships were low on reaction mass, ungainly, unmaneuverable. St. Judy's Angels dived and sniped among them, clipping a missile rack here, a solar panel there, ripping open life support bubbles and fuel tanks in slow explosions of outgassing hydrogen. The thirteen-year-old pilots died, raging with chemical-induced fury, spilled out into vacuum in tears of flash-frozen acceleration gel. The attacking fleet dwindled from seven to five to three ships. But it was no abattoir of the meat; of the six dead angels that went in, only two pulled away into rendezvous orbit, laser capacitors dead, reaction mass spent. The crews ejected, unfurled their solar sails, shields of light.

Two meat ships survived. One used the last grams of his maneuvering mass to warp into a return orbit; the other routed his thruster fuel through his blip drive; headlong for St. Judy.

"He's going for a ram," Kobe said.

"Sol, get us away from him," *Capitan* Savita ordered.

"He's too close." The numbers in Sol's skull were remorseless. "Even if I cut the mass driver, he can still run life support gas through the STUs to compensate."

The command womb quivered.

"Fuck," someone swore reverently.

"Near miss," Kobe reported. "Direct hit if Sol hadn't given us gees."

"Mass driver is still with us," Sol said.

"Riley's gone," *Capitan* Savita said.

Fifty missiles were now twenty missiles but Emilio and Riley were dead, and the range was closing. Little room for maneuver; none for mistakes.

"Two hundred and fifteen seconds to ship impact," Kobe announced. The main body of missiles was dropping behind St. Judy's Comet. Ogawa and Skin, Mandelbrot set and Dalmatian spots, were fighting a rearguard as the missiles tried to reacquire their target. Olive green ripples and red tiger stripes swung round to face the meat ship. Quinsana and Elena.

Jesus Joseph Mary, but it was going to be close!

Sol wished he did not have the graphics in his head. He wished not to have to see. Better sudden annihilation, blindness and ignorance shattered by destroying light. To see, to *know*, to count the digits on the timer, was as cruel as execution.

But the inner vision has no eyelids. So he watched, impotent, as Quinsana's olive green cross was pierced and shattered by a white flare from the meat ship. And he watched as Elena raked the meat with her lasers and cut it into quivering chunks, and the blast of engines destroying themselves sent the shards of ship arcing away from St. Judy's Comet. And he could only watch, and not look away, as Elena turned too slow, too little, too late, as the burst seed-pod of the environment unit tore off her thruster legs and light sail and sent her spinning end over end, crippled, destroyed.

"Elena!" he screamed in both his voices. "Elena! Oh Jesus oh God!" But he had never believed in either of them, and so they let Elena Asado go tumbling endlessly toward the beautiful galaxy clusters of Virgo.

Earth's last rage against her children expired: twenty missiles dwindled to ten, to five, to one. To none. St. Judy's Comet continued her slow climb out of the sun's gravity well, into the deep dark and the deeper cold. Its five hundred and twenty souls slept sound and ignorant as only the dead can in tombs of ice. Soon Solomon Gursky and the others would join them, and be dissolved into the receiving ice, and die for five hundred years while St. Judy's Comet made the crossing to another star.

If it were sleep, then I might forget, Solomon Gursky thought. In sleep, things changed, memories became dreams, dreams memories. In sleep, there was time, and time was change, and perhaps a chance of forgetting the vision of her, spinning outward forever, rebuilt by the same forces that had already resurrected her once, living on sunlight, unable to die. But it was not sleep to which he was going. It was death, and that was nothing any more.

FRIDAY

Together they watched the city burn. It was one of the ornamental cities of the plain that the Long Scanning folk built and maintained for the quadrennial eisteddfods. There was something of the flower in the small, jewellike city, and something of the spiral, and something of the sea-wave. It would have been as accurate to call it a vast building as a miniature city. It burned most elegantly.

The fault line ran right through the middle of it. The fissure was clean and precise—no less to be expected of the Long Scanning folk—and bisected the curvilinear architecture from top to bottom. The land still quivered to aftershocks.

It could have repaired itself. It could have doused the flames—a short in the magma tap, the man reckoned—reshaped the melted ridges and roofs, erased the scorch marks, bridged the cracks and chasms. But its tector systems were directionless, its soul withdrawn to the Heaven Tree, to join the rest of the Long Scanning people on their exodus.

The woman watched the smoke rise into the darkening sky, obscuring the great opal of Urizen.

"It doesn't have to do this," she said. Her skin spoke of sorrow mingled with puzzlement.

"They've no use for it any more," the man said. "And there's a certain beauty in destruction."

"It scares me," the woman said, and her skin pattern agreed. "I've never seen anything *end* before."

Lucky, the man thought, in a language that had come from another world.

An eddy in his weathersight: big one coming. But they were all big ones since the orbital perturbations began. Big, getting bigger. At the end, the storms would tear the forests from their roots as the atmosphere shrieked into space.

That afternoon, on their journey to the man's memories, they had come across an empty marina; drained, sand clogged, pontoons torn and tossed by tsunamis. Its crew of boats they found scattered the length of a half-hour's walk. Empty shells stogged to the waist in dune faces, masts and sails hung from trees.

The weather had been the first thing to tear free from control. The man felt a sudden tautness in the woman's body. She was seeing it to, the mid-game of the end of the world.

By the time they reached the sheltered valley that the man's aura had picked as the safest location to spend the night, the wind had risen to draw soft moans and chords from the curves and crevasses of the dead city. As their cloaks of elementals joined and sank the roots of the night shell into rock, a flock of bubbles bowled past, trembling and iridescent in the gusts. The woman caught one on her hand; the tiny creature-machine clung for a moment, feeding from her bio-field. Its transparent skin raced with oil-film colors, it quaked and burst, a melting bubble of tectoplasm. The woman watched it until the elementals had completed the shelter, but the thing stayed dead.

Their love-making was both urgent and chilled under the scalloped carapace the elementals had sculpted from rock silica. *Sex and death*, the man said in the part of his head where not even his sub-vocal withspeech could overhear and transmit. An alien thought.

She wanted to talk afterward. She liked to talk after sex. Unusually, she did not ask him to tell her about how he and the other Five Hundred Fathers had built the world. Her idea of talking was him talking. Tonight she did not want to talk about the world's beginning. She wanted him to talk about its ending.

"Do you know what I hate about it? It's not that it's all going to end, all this. It's that a bubble burst in my hand, and I can't comprehend what *happened* to it. How much more our whole world?"

"There is a word for what you felt," the man interjected gently. The gyrestorm was at its height, raging over the dome of their shell. The thickness of a skin is all that is keeping the wind from stripping the flesh from my bones, he thought. But the tectors' grip on the bedrock was firm and sure. "The word is *die*."

The woman sat with her knees pulled up, arms folded around them. Naked: the gyrestorm was blowing through her soul.

"What I hate," she said after silence, "is that I have so little time to see and feel it all before it's taken away into the cold and the dark."

She was a Green, born in the second of the short year's fast seasons: a Green of the Hidden Design people; first of the Old Red Ridge pueblo people to come into the world in eighty years. And the last.

Eight years old.

"You won't die," the man said, skin patterning in whorls of reassurance and paternal concern, like the swirling storms of great Urizen beyond the hurtling gyrestorm clouds. "You can't die. No one will die."

"I know that. No one will die, we will all be changed, or sleep with the world. But . . ."

"Is it frightening, to have to give up this body?"

She touched her forehead to her knees, shook her head.

"I don't want to lose it. I've only begun to understand what it is, this body, this world, and it's all going to be taken away from me, and all the powers that are my birthright are useless."

"There are forces beyond even nanotechnology," the man said. "It makes us masters of matter, but the fundamental dimensions — gravity, space, time — it cannot touch."

"Why?" the woman said, and to the man, who counted by older, longer years, she spoke in the voice of her terrestrial age.

"We will learn it, in time," the man said, which he knew was no answer. The woman knew it too, for she said, "While Orc is two hundred million years from the warmth of the next sun, and its atmosphere is a frozen glaze on these mountains and valleys." *Grief*, he skin said. *Rage. Loss.*

The two-thousand-year-old father touched the young woman's small, upturned breasts.

"We knew Urizen's orbit was unstable, but no one could have predicted the interaction with Ulro." Ironic: that this world named after Blake's fire daemon should be the one cast into darkness and ice, while Urizen and its surviving moons should bake two million kilometers above the surface of Los.

"Sol, you don't need to apologize to me for mistakes you made two thousand years ago," said the woman, whose name was Lenya.

"But I think I need to apologize to the world," said Sol Gursky.

Lenya's skin-speech now said *hope* shaded with *inevitability*. Her nipples were erect. Sol bent to them again as the wind from the end of the world scratched its claws over the skin of tectoplastic.

In the morning, they continued the journey to Sol's memories. The gyrestorm had blown itself out in the Oothoon mountains. What remained of the ghost-net told Sol and Lenya that it was possible to fly that day. They suckled milch from the shell's tree of life processor, and they had sex again on the dusty earth while the elementals reconfigured the night pod into a general utility flier. For the rest of the morning, they passed over a plain across which grazebeasts and the tall, predatory angularities of the stalking Systems Maintenance people moved like ripples on a lake, drawn to the Heaven Tree planted in the navel of the world.

Both grazers and herders had been human once.

At noon, the man and the woman encountered a flyer of the Generous Sky people, flapping a silk-winged course along the thermal lines rising from the feet of the Big Chrysolite mountains. Sol with-hailed him, and they set down together in a clearing in the bitter-root forests that carpeted much of Coryphee Canton. The Generous Sky man's etiquette would normally have compelled him to disdain those ground bound who sullied the air with machines, but in these urgent times, the old ways were breaking.

Whither bound? Sol withspoke him. Static crackled in his skull. The lingering tail of the gyrestorm was throwing off electromagnetic disturbances.

Why, the Heaven Tree of course, the winged man said. He was a horrifying kite of translucent skin over stick bones and sinews. His breast was like the prow of a ship, his muscles twitched and realigned as he shifted from foot to foot, uncomfortable on the earth. A gentle breeze wafted from the nanofans grown out of the web of skin between wrists and ankles. The air smelled of strange sweat. *Whither yourselves?*

The Heaven Tree also, in time, Sol said. *But I must first recover my memories.*

Ah, a father, the Sky man said. *Whose are you?*

Hidden Design, Sol said. *I am father to this woman and her people.*

You are Solomon Gursky, the flying man withsaid. *My progenitor is Nikos Samitreides.*

I remember her well, though I have not seen her in many years. She fought bravely at the battle of St. Judy's Comet.

I am third of her lineage. Eighteen hundred years I have been on this world.

A question, if I may. Lenya's withspeech was a sudden bright interruption in the dialogue of old men. Using an honorific by which a younger adult addresses an experienced senior, she asked, *When the time comes, how will you change?*

An easy question, the Generous Sky man said, *I shall undergo the reconfiguration for life on Urizen. To me, it is little difference whether I wear the outward semblance of a man, or a jetpowered aerial manta: it is flying, and such flying! Canyons of clouds hundreds of kilometers deep; five thousand kilometer per hour winds; thermals great as continents; mad storms as big as planets! And no land, no base; to be able to fly forever free from the tyranny of Earth. The song cycles we shall compose; eddas that will carry half way around the planet on the jet streams of Urizen!* The Generous Sky man's eyes had closed in rapture. They suddenly opened. His nostrils dilated, sensing an atmospheric change intangible to the others.

Another storm is coming, bigger than the last. I advise you to take shelter within rock, for this will pluck the bitter-roots from the soil.

He spread his wings. The membranes rippled. A tiny hop, and the wind caught him and in an instant carried him up into a thermal. Sol and Lenya watched him glide the tops of the lifting air currents until he was lost in the deep blue sky.

For exercise and the conversation of the way, they walked that afternoon. They followed the migration track of the Rough Trading people through the tieve forests of south Coryphee and Emberwilde Cantons. Toward evening, with the gathering wind stirring the needles of the tieves to gossip, they met a man of the Ash species sitting on a chair in a small clearing among the trees. He was long and coiling, and his skin said that he was much impoverished from lack of a host. Lenya offered her arm, and though the Ash man's compatibility was more with the Buried Communication people than the Hidden Design, he gracefully accepted her heat, her morphic energy, and a few drops of blood.

"Where is your host?" Lenya asked him. A parasite, he had the languages of most nations. Hosts were best seduced by words, like lovers.

"He has gone with the herds," the Ash man said. "To the Heaven Tree. It is ended."

"And what will you do when Orc is expelled?" The rasp marks on Lenya's forearm where the parasitic man had sipped her blood were already healing over.

"I cannot live alone," the Ash man said. "I shall ask the earth to open and swallow me and kill me. I shall sleep in the earth until the warmth of a new sun awakens me to life again."

"But that will be two hundred million years," Lenya said. The Ash man looked at her with the look that said, *one year, one million years, one hundred million years, they are nothing to death.* Because she knew that the man thought her a new-hatched fool, Lenya felt compelled to look back at him as she and Sol walked away along the tieve tracks. She saw the parasite pressed belly and balls to the ground, as he would to a host. Dust spiraled up around him. He slowly sank into the earth.

Sol and Lenya did not have sex that night in the pod for the first time since Solomon the Traveler had come to the Old Red Ridge pueblo and taken the eye and heart of the brown girl dancing in the ring. That night there was the greatest earthquake yet as Orc kicked in his orbit, and even a shell of tectodiamond seemed inadequate protection against forces that would throw a planet into interstellar space. They held each other, not speaking, until the earth grew quiet and a wave of heat passed over the carapace, which was the tieve forests of Emberwilde Canton burning.

The next morning, they morphed the pod into an ash-runner and drove through the cindered forest, until at noon they came to the edge of the Inland Sea. The tectonic trauma had sent tidal waves swamping the craggy islet on which Sol had left his memories, but the self-repair systems had used the dregs of their stored power to rebuild the damaged architecture.

As Sol was particular that they must approach his memories by sea, they ordered the ash-runner to reconfigure into a skiff. While the tectors moved molecules, a man of the Blue Mana pulled himself out of the big surf on to the red shingle. He was long and huge and sleek; his shorn turf of fur was beautifully marked. He lay panting from the exertion of heaving himself from his customary element into an alien one. Lenya addressed him familiarly—Hidden Design and the amphibious Blue Mana had been one until a millennium ago—and asked him the same question she had put to the others she had encountered on the journey.

"I am already reconfiguring my body fat into an aircraft to take me to the Heaven Tree," the Blue Mana said. "Climatic shifts permitting."

"Is it bad in the sea?" Sol Gursky asked.

"The seas feel the changes first," the amphiman said. "Bad. Yes, most bad. I cannot bear the thought of Mother Ocean freezing clear to her beds."

"Will you go to Urizen, then?" Lenya asked, thinking that swimming must be much akin to flying.

"Why, bless you, no." The Blue Mana man's skin spelled puzzled surprise. "Why should I share any less fate than Mother Ocean? We shall both end in ice."

"The comet fleet," Sol Gursky said.

"If the Earth ship left any legacy, it is that there are many mansions in this universe where we may live. I have a fancy to visit those other settled systems that the ship told us of, experience those others ways of being human."

A hundred Orc-years had passed since the second comet-ship from Earth had entered the Los system to refuel from Urizen's rings, but the news it had carried of a home system transfigured by the nanotechnology of the ascendant dead, and of the other stars that had been reached by the newer, faster, more powerful descendants of St. Judy's Comet had ended nineteen hundred years of solitude and brought the first, lost colony of Orc into the visionary community of the star-crossing Dead. *Long before your emergence*, Sol thought, looking at the crease of Lenya's groin as she squatted on the pebbles to converse with the Blue Mana man. Emergence. A deeper, older word shadowed that expression; a word obsolete in the universe of the dead. *Birth*. No one had ever been born on Orc. No one had ever known childhood, or grown up. No one aged, no one died. They *emerged*. They stepped from the labia of the gestatory, fully formed, like gods.

Sol knew the word *child*, but realized with a shock that he could not see it any more. It was blank, void. So many things decreated in this world he had engineered!

By sea and by air. A trading of elements. Sol Gursky's skiff was completed as the Blue Mana's tectors transformed his blubber into a flying machine. Sol watched it spin into the air and recede to the south as the boat dipped through the chop toward the island of memory.

We live forever, we transform ourselves, we transform worlds, solar systems, we ship across interstellar space, we defy time and deny death, but the one thing we cannot recreate is memory, he thought. Sea birds dipped in the skiff's wake, hungry, hoping. Things cast up by motion. We cannot rebuild our memories, so we must store them, when our lives grow so full that they slop over the sides and evaporate. We Five Hundred Fathers have deep and much-emptied memories.

Sol's island was a rock slab tilted out of the equatorial sea, a handful of hard hectares. Twisted repro olives and cypresses screened a small Doric temple at the highest point. Good maintenance tectors had held it strong against the Earth storms. The classical theming now embarrassed Sol, but enchanted Lenya. She danced beneath the olive branches, under the porticoes, across the lintels. Sol saw her again as he had that first night in the Small-year-ending ring dance at Old Red Ridge. Old lust. New hurt.

In the sunlit central chamber, Lenya touched the reliefs of the life of Solomon Gursky. They would not yield their memories to her fingers, but they communicated in less sophisticated ways.

"This woman." She had stopped in front of a pale stone carving of Solomon Gursky and a tall, ascetic-faced woman with close-cropped hair standing hand in hand before a tall, ghastly tower.

"I loved her. She died in the battle of St. Judy's Comet. Big dead."

Lost.

"So is it only because I remind you of her?"

He touched the carving. Memory bright and sharp as pain arced along his nerves; mnemotectors downloading into his aura. *Elena*. And a memory of orbit;

the Long March ended, the object formerly known as St. Judy's Comet spun out into a web of beams and girders and habitation pods hurtling across the frosted red dustscapes of Orc. A web ripe with hanging fruit; entry pods ready to drop and spray the new world with life seed. Tectoforming. Among the fruit, seeds of the Five Hundred Fathers, founders of all the races of Orc. Among them, the Hidden Design and Solomon Gursky, four-armed, vacuum-proofed, avatar of life and death, clinging to a beam with the storms of Urizen behind him, touching his transforming *sur*-arms to the main memory of the mother seed. Remember her. Remember Elena. And sometime — soon, late — bring her back. Imprint her with an affinity for his scent, so that wherever she is, whoever she is with, she will come to me.

He saw himself scuttling like a guilty spider across the web as the pods dropped Orc-ward.

He saw himself in this place with Urizen's moons at syzygy, touching his hands to the carving, giving to it what it now returned to him, because he knew that as long as it was Lenya who reminded him of Elena, it could pretend to be honest. But the knowledge killed it. Lenya was more than a reminder. Lenya as Elena. Lenya was a simulacrum, empty, fake. Her life, her joy, her sorrow, her love — all deceit.

He had never expected that she would come back to him at the end of the world. They should have had thousands of years. The world gave them days.

He could not look at her as he moved from relief to relief, charging his aura with memory. He could not touch her as they waited on the shingle for the skiff to reconfigure into the flyer that would take them to the Heaven Tree. On the high point of the slab island, the Temple of Memory dissolved like rotting fungus. He did not attempt sex with her as the flyer passed over the shattered landscapes of Thel and the burned forests of Chrysoberyl as they would have, before. She did not understand. She imagined she had hurt him somehow. She had, but the blame was Sol's. He could not tell her why he had suddenly expelled himself from her warmth. He knew that he should, that he must, but he could not. He changed his skin-speech to passive, mute, and reflected that much cowardice could be learned in five hundred long-years.

They came with the evening to the Skyplain plateau from which the Heaven Tree rose, an adamantine black ray aimed at the eye of Urizen. As far as they could see, the plain twinkled with the lights and fires of vehicles and camps. Warmsight showed a million glowings: all the peoples of Orc, save those who had chosen to go into the earth, had gathered in this final redoubt. Seismic stabilizing tectors woven into the moho held steady the quakes that had shattered all other lands, but temblors of increasing violence warned that they could not endure much longer. At the end, Skyplain would crack like an egg, the Heaven Tree snap and recoil spaceward like a severed nerve.

Sol's Five Hundred Father ident pulled his flyer out of the wheel of aircraft, airships, and aerial humans circling the stalk of the Heaven Tree into a priority slot on an ascender. The flyer caught the shuttle at five kilometers: a sudden veer toward the slab sides of the space elevator, guidance matching velocities with the accelerating ascender; then the drop, heart-stopping even for immortals, and the lurch as the flyer seized the docking nipple with its claspers and clung like a tick. Then the long climb heavenward.

Emerging from high altitude cloud, Sol saw the hard white diamond of Ulro rise above the curve of the world. Too small yet to show a disc, but this barren rock searing under heavy CO_2 exerted forces powerful enough to kick a moon into interstellar space. Looking up through the transparent canopy, he saw the Heaven Tree spread its delicate, light-studded branches hundreds of kilometers across the face of Urizen.

Sol Gursky broke his silence.

"Do you know what you'll do yet?"

"Well, since I am here, I am not going into the ground. And the ice fleet scares me. I think of centuries dead, a tector frozen in ice. It seems like death."

"It is death," Sol said. "Then you'll go to Urizen."

"It's a change of outward form, that's all. Another way of being human. And there'll be continuity; that's important to me."

He imagined the arrival: the ever-strengthening tug of gravity spiraling the flocks of vacuum-hardened carapaces inward; the flickers of withspeech between them, anticipation, excitement, fear as they grazed the edge of the atmosphere and felt ion flames lick their diamond skins. Lenya, falling, burning with the fires of entry as she cut a glowing trail across half a planet. The heat-shell breaking away as she unfurled her wings in the eternal shriek of wind and the ram-jets in her sterile womb kindled and roared.

"And you?" she asked. Her skin said *gentle*. Confused as much by his breaking of it as by his silence, but *gentle*.

"I have something planned," was all he said, but because that plan meant they would never meet again, he told her then what he had learned in the Temple of Memory. He tried to be kind and understanding, but it was still a bastard thing to do, and she cried in the nest in the rear of the flyer all the way out of the atmosphere, half-way to heaven. It was a bastard thing and as he watched the stars brighten beyond the canopy, he could not say why he had done it, except that it was necessary to kill some things Big Dead so that they could never come back again. She cried now, and her skin was so dark it would not speak to him, but when she flew, it would be without any lingering love or regret for a man called Solomon Gursky.

It is good to be hated, he thought, as the Heaven Tree took him up into its starlit branches.

The launch laser was off, the reaction mass tanks were dry. Solomon Gursky fell outward from the sun. Urizen and its children were far beneath him. His course lay out of the ecliptic, flying north. His aft eyes made out a new pale ring orbiting the gas world, glowing in the low warmsight: the millions of adapted waiting in orbit for their turns to make the searing descent into a new life.

She would be with them now. He had watched her go into the seed and be taken apart by her own elementals. He had watched the seed split and expel her into space, transformed, and burn her few kilos of reaction mass on the transfer orbit to Urizen.

Only then had he felt free to undergo his own transfiguration.

Life swarm. Mighty. So nearly right, so utterly wrong. She had almost sung when she spoke of the freedom of endless flight in the clouds of Urizen, but she would never fly freer than she did now, naked to space, the galaxy before her. The freedom of Urizen was a lie, the price exacted by its gravity and pressure. She had trapped herself in atmosphere and gravity. Urizen was another world. The parasitic man of the Ash nation had buried himself in a world. The aquatic Blue Mana, after long sleep in ice, would only give rise to another copy of the standard model. Worlds upon worlds.

Infinite ways of being human, Solomon Gursky thought, outbound from the sun. He could feel the gentle stroke of the solar wind over the harsh dermal prickle of Urizen's magnetosphere. Sun arising. Almost time.

Many ways of being Solomon Gursky, he thought, contemplating his new body. His analogy was with a conifer. He was a redwood cone fallen from the Heaven Tree, ripe with seeds. Each seed a Solomon Gursky, a world in embryo.

The touch of the sun, that was what had opened those seed cones on that other world, long ago. Timing was too important to be left to higher cognitions. Subsystems had all the launch vectors programmed; he merely registered the growing strength of the wind from Los on his skin and felt himself begin to open. Solomon Gursky unfolded into a thousand scales. As the seeds exploded onto their preset courses, he burned to the highest orgasm of his memory before his persona downloaded into the final spore and ejected from the empty, dead carrier body.

At five hundred kilometers, the seeds unfurled their solar sails. The breaking wave of particles, with multiple gravity assists from Luvah and Enitharmon, would surf the bright flotilla up to interstellar velocities, as, at the end of the centuries — millennia — long flights, the light-sails would brake the packages at their destinations.

He did not know what his many selves would find there. He had not picked targets for their resemblance to what he was leaving behind. That would be just another trap. He sensed his brothers shutting down their cognitive centers for the big sleep, like stars going out, one by one. A handful of seeds scattered, some to wither, some to grow. Who can say what he will find, except that it will be extraordinary. Surprise me! Solomon Gursky demanded of the universe, as he fell into the darkness between suns.

SATURDAY

The object was one point three astronomical units on a side, and at its current 10 percent C would arrive in thirty-five hours. On his chaise lounge by the Neptune fountain, Solomon Gursky finally settled on a name for the thing. He had given much thought, over many high-hours and in many languages, most of them non-verbal, to what he should call the looming object. The name that pleased him most was in a language dead (he assumed) for thirty million years. Aea. Acronym: Alien Enigmatic Artifact. Enigmatic Alien Artifact would have been more correct but the long dead language did not handle diphthongs well.

Shadows fell over the gardens of Versailles, huge and soft as clouds. A forest was crossing the sun; a small one, little more than a copse, he thought, still finding delight in the notions that could be expressed in this dead language. He watched the spherical trees pass overhead, each a kilometer across (another archaism), enjoying the pleasurable play of shade and warmth on his skin. Sensual joys of incarnation.

As ever when the forests migrated along the Bauble's jet streams, a frenzy of siphons squabbled in their wake, voraciously feeding off the stew of bacteria and complex fullerenes.

Solomon Gursky darkened his eyes against the hard glare of the dwarf white sun. From Versailles' perspective in the equatorial plane, the Spirit Ring was a barely discernible filigree necklace draped around its primary. Perspective. Am I the emanation of it, or is it the emanation of me?

Perspective: you worry about such things with a skeletal tetrahedron one point three astronomical units on a side fast approaching?

Of course. I am some kind of human.

"Show me," Solomon Gursky said. Sensing his intent, for Versailles was part of his intent, as everything that lived and moved within the Bauble was his intent, the disc of tectofactured baroque France began to tilt away from the sun. The sol-lilies on which Versailles and its gardens rested generated their own gravity fields; Solomon Gursky saw the tiny, bright sun seem to curve down behind the Petit Trianon, and thought, *I have reinvented sunset.* And, as the dark vault above him lit with stars, *Night is looking out from the shadow of myself.*

The stars slowed and locked over the chimneys of Versailles. Sol had hoped to be able to see the object with the unaided eye, but in low-time he had forgotten the limitations of the primeval human form. A grimace of irritation, and it was the work of moments for the tectors to reconfigure his vision. Successive magnifications clicked up until ghostly, twinkling threads of light resolved out of the star field, like the drawings of gods and myths the ancients had laid on the comfortable heavens around the Alpha Point.

Another click and the thing materialized.

Solomon Gursky's breath caught.

Midway between the micro and the macro, it was humanity's natural condition that a man standing looking out into the dark should feel dwarfed. That need to assert one's individuality to the bigness underlies all humanity's outward endeavors. But the catch in the breath is more than doubled when a *star* seems dwarfed. Through the Spirit Ring, Sol had the dimensions, the masses, the vectors. The whole of the Bauble could be easily contained within Aea's vertices. A cabalistic sign. A cosmic eye in the pyramid.

A chill contraction in the man Solomon Gursky's loins. How many million years since he had last felt his balls tighten with fear?

One point three AU's on a side. Eight sextillion tons of matter. Point one C. The thing should have heralded itself over most of the cluster. Even in low-time, he should have had more time to prepare. But there had been no warning. At once, it *was*: a fading hexagram of gravitometric disturbances on his out-system sensors. Sol had reacted at once, but in those few seconds of stretched low-time that it took to conceive and create this Louis Quattorze conceit, the object had covered two-thirds of the distance from its emergence point. The high-time of created things gave him perspective.

Bear you grapes or poison? Solomon Gursky asked the thing in the sky. It had not spoken, it had remained silent through all attempts to communicate with it, but it surely bore *some* gift. The manner of its arrival had only one explanation: the thing manipulated worm-holes. None of the civilization/citizens of the Reach—most of the western hemisphere of the galaxy—had evolved a nanotechnology that could reconfigure the continuum itself.

None of the civilization/citizens of the Reach, and those federations of world-societies it fringed, had ever encountered a species that could not be sourced to the Alpha Point: that semi-legendary racial big bang from which PanHumanity had exploded into the universe.

Four hundred billion stars in this galaxy alone, Solomon Gursky thought. We have not seeded even half of them. The trick we play with time, slowing our perceptions until our light-speed communications seem instantaneous and the journeys of our C-fractional ships are no longer than the sea-voyages of this era I have reconstructed, seduce us into believing that the universe is as close and companionable as a lover's body, and as familiar. The five million years between the MonoHumanity of the Alpha Point and the PanHumanity of the Great Leap Outward, is a catch of breath, a contemplative pause in our conversation with ourselves. Thirty million years I have evolved the web of life in this unique system: there is abundant time and space for true aliens to have caught us up, to have already surpassed us.

Again, that tightening of the scrotum. Sol Gursky willed Versailles back toward the eye of the sun, but intellectual chill had invaded his soul. The orchestra of Lully made fete *galante* in the Hall of Mirrors for his pleasure, but the sound in his head of the destroying, rushing alien mass shrieked louder. As the solar parasol slipped between Versailles and the sun and he settled in twilight among the soft, powdered breasts of the ladies of the bed-chamber, he knew fear for the first time in thirty million years.

And he dreamed. The dream took the shape of a memory, recontextualized, reconfigured, resurrected. He dreamed that he was a starship wakened from fifty thousand years of death by the warmth of a new sun on his solar sail. He dreamed that in the vast sleep the star toward which he had aimed himself spastically novaed. It kicked off its photosphere in a nebula of radiant gas but the explosion was underpowered; the carbon/hydrogen/nitrogen/oxygen plasma was drawn by gravity into a bubble of hydrocarbons around the star. An aura. A bright bauble. In Solomon Gursky's dream, an angel floated effortlessly on tectoplastic wings hundreds of kilometers wide, banking and soaring on the chemical thermals, sowing seeds from its long, trailing fingertips. For a hundred years, the angel swam around the sun, sowing, nurturing, tending the strange shoots that grew from its fingers; things half-living, half-machine.

Asleep among the powdered breasts of court women, Sol Gursky turned and murmured the word, "evolution."

Solomon Gursky would only be a God he could believe in: the philosophers' God, creator but not sustainer, ineffable; too street-smart to poke its omnipotence into the smelly stuff of living. He saw his free-fall trees of green, the vast red rafts of the wind-reefs rippling in the solar breezes. He saw the blimps and medusas, the unresting open maws of the air-plankton feeders, the needle-thin jet-powered darts of the harpoon hunters. He saw an ecology spin itself out of gas and energy in thirty million yearless years, he saw intelligence flourish and seed itself to the stars, and fade into senescence; all in the blink of a low-time eye.

"Evolution," he muttered again and the constructed women who did not understand sleep looked at each other.

In the unfolding dream, Sol Gursky saw the Spirit Ring and the ships that came and went between the nearer systems. He heard the subaural babble of interstellar chatter, like conspirators in another room. He beheld this blur of life, evolving, transmuting, and he knew that it was very good. He said to himself, *what a wonderful world*, and feared for it.

He awoke. It was morning, as it always was in Sol's Bauble. He worked off his testosterone high and tipped Versailles's darkside to look at the shadow of his nightmares. Any afterglow of libido was immediately extinguished. At eighteen light-hours distance, the astronomical dimensions assumed emotional force. A ribbon of mottled blue-green ran down the inner surface of each of Aea's six legs. Amplified vision resolved forested continents and oceans beneath fractal cloud curls. Each ribbon-world was the width of two Alpha Points peeled and ironed, stretched one point three astronomical units long. Sol Gursky was glad that this incarnation could not instantly access how many million planets' surfaces that equaled; how many hundreds of thousands of years it would take to walk from one vertex to another, and then to find, dumbfounded like the ancient conquistadors beholding a new ocean, another millennia-deep world in front of him.

Solomon Gursky turned Versailles toward the sun. He squinted through the haze of the Bauble for the delicate strands of the Spirit Ring. A beat of his mind shifted his perceptions back into low-time, the only time frame in which he could withspeak to the Spirit Ring, his originating self. Self-reference, self-confession.

No communication?

None, spoke the Spirit Ring.

Is it alien? Should I be afraid? Should I destroy the Bauble?

In another time, such schizophrenia would have been disease.

Can it annihilate you?

In answer, Sol envisioned the great tetrahedron at the bracelet of information tectors orbiting the sun.

Then that is nothing, the Spirit Ring withsaid. *And nothing is nothing to fear. Can it cause you pain or humiliation, or anguish to body or soul?*

Again, Sol withspoke an image, of cloud-shaded lands raised over each other like the pillars of Yahweh, emotionally shaded to suggest amazement that such an investment of matter and thought should have been created purely to humiliate Solomon Gursky.

Then that too is settled. And whether it is alien, can it be any more alien to you than you yourself are to what you once were? All PanHumanity is alien to itself; therefore, we have nothing to fear. We shall welcome our visitor, we have many questions for it.

Not the least being, *why me?* Solomon Gursky thought privately, silently, in the dome of his own skull. He shifted out of the low-time of the Spirit Ring to find that in those few subjective moments of communication Aea had passed the threshold of the Bauble. The leading edge of the tetrahedron was three hours away. An hour and half beyond that was the hub of Aea.

"Since it seems that we can neither prevent nor hasten the object's arrival, nor guess its purposes until it deigns to communicate with us," Sol Gursky told his women of the bedchamber, "therefore let us party." Which they did, before the Mirror Pond, as Lully's orchestra played and capons roasted over charcoal pits, and torch-lit harlequins capered and fought out the ancient loves and comedies, and women splashed naked in the Triton Fountain, and fantastic lands one hundred million kilometers long slid past them. Aea advanced until Sol's star was at its center, then stopped. Abruptly, instantly. A small gravitational shiver troubled Versailles, the orchestra missed a note, a juggler dropped a club, the water in the fountain wavered, women shrieked, a capon fell from a spit into the fire. That was all. The control of mass, momentum, and gravity was absolute.

The orchestra leader looked at Solomon Gursky, staff raised to resume the beat. Sol Gursky did not raise the handkerchief. The closest section of Aea was fifteen degrees east, two hundred thousand kilometers out. To Sol Gursky, it was two fingers of sun-lit land, tapering infinitesimally at either end to threads of light. He looked up at the apex, two other brilliant threads spun down beneath the horizon, one behind the Petit Trianon, the other below the roof of the Chapel Royal.

The conductor was still waiting. Instruments pressed to faces, the musicians watched for the cue.

Peacocks shrieked on the lawn. Sol Gursky remembered how irritating the voices of peacocks were, and wished he had not recreated them.

Sol Gursky waved the handkerchief.

A column of white light blazed out of the gravel walk at the top of the steps. The air was a seethe of glowing motes.

An attempt is being made to communicate with us, the Spirit Ring said in a flicker of low-time. Sol Gursky felt information from the Ring crammed into his cerebral cortex: the beam originated from a source of the rim section of the closest section of the artifact. The tectors that created and sustained the Bauble were being reprogrammed. At hyper-velocities, they were manufacturing a construct out of the Earth of Versailles.

The pillar of light dissipated. A human figure stood at the top of the steps: a white Alpha Point male, dressed in Louis XIV style. The man descended the steps into the light of the flambeau bearers. Sol Gursky looked on his face.

Sol Gursky burst into laughter.

"You are very welcome," he said to his doppelgänger. "Will you join us? The capons will be ready shortly, we can bring you the finest wines available to humanity, and I'm sure the waters of the fountains would be most refreshing to one who has traveled so long and so far."

"Thank you," Solomon Gursky said in Solomon Gursky's voice. "It's good to find a hospitable reception after a strange journey."

Sol Gursky nodded to the conductor, who raised his staff, and the *petite bande* resumed their interrupted gavotte.

Later, on a stone bench by the lake, Sol Gursky said to his doppel, "Your politeness is appreciated, but it really wasn't necessary for you to don my shape. All this is as much a construction as you are."

"Why do you think it's a politeness?" the construct said.

"Why should you choose to wear the shape of Solomon Gursky?"

"Why should I not, if it is my *own* shape?"

Nereids splashed in the pool, breaking the long reflections of Aea.

"I often wonder how far I reach," Sol said.

"Further than you can imagine," Sol II answered. The playing Nereids dived; ripples spread across the pond. The visitor watched the wavelets lap against the stone rim and interfere with each other. "There are others out there, others we never imagined, moving through the dark, very slowly, very silently. I think they may be older than us. They are different from us, very different, and we have now come to the complex plane where our expansions meet."

"There was a strong probability that they—you—were an alien artifact."

"I am, and I'm not. I am fully Solomon Gursky, and fully Other. That's the purpose behind this artifact; that we have reached a point where we either compete, destructively, or join."

"Seemed a long way to come just for a family reunion," Solomon Gursky joked. He saw that the doppel laughed, and how it laughed, and why it laughed. He got up from the stone rim of the Nereid pool. "Come with me, talk to me, we have thirty million years of catching up."

His brother fell in at his side as they walked away from the still water toward the Aea-lit woods.

His story: he had fallen longer than any other seed cast off by the death of Orc. Eight hundred thousand years between wakings, and as he felt the warmth of a new sun seduce his tector systems to the work of transformation, his sensors reported that his was not the sole presence in the system. The brown dwarf toward which he decelerated was being dismantled and converted into an englobement of space habitats.

"Their technology is similar to ours—I think it must be a universal inevitability—but they broke the ties that still bind us to planets long ago," Sol II said. The woods of Versailles were momentarily darkened as a sky-reef eclipsed Aea. "This is why I think they are older than us: I have never seen their original form—they have no tie to it, we still do; I suspect they no longer remember it. It wasn't until we fully merged that I was certain that they were not another variant of humanity."

A hand-cranked wooden carousel stood in a small clearing. The faces of the painted horses were fierce and pathetic in the sky light. Wooden rings hung from iron gibbets around the rim of the carousel; the wooden lances with which the knights hooked down their favors had been gathered in and locked in a closet in the middle of the merry-go-round.

"We endure forever, we engender races, nations, whole ecologies, but we are sterile," the second Sol said. "We inbreed with ourselves. There is no union of disparities, no coming together, no hybrid energy. With the Others, it was sex. Intercourse. Out of the fusion of ideas and visions and capabilities, we birthed what you see."

The first Sol Gursky laid his hand on the neck of a painted horse. The carousel was well balanced, the slightest pressure set it turning.

"Why are you here, Sol?" he asked.

"We shared technologies, we learned how to engineer on the quantum level so that field effects can be applied on macroscopic scales. Manipulation of gravity and inertia; non-locality; we can engineer and control quantum worm-holes."

"Why have you come, Sol?"

"Engineering of alternative time streams; designing and colonizing multiple worlds, hyperspace and hyperdimensional processors. There are more universes than this one for us to explore."

The wooden horse stopped.

"What do you want, Sol?"

"Join us," said the other Solomon Gursky. "You always had the vision—we always had the vision, we Solomon Gurskys. Humanity expanding into every possible ecological niche."

"Absorption," Solomon Gursky said. "Assimilation."

"Unity," said his brother. "Marriage. Love. Nothing is lost, everything is gained. All you have created here will be stored; that is what I am, a machine for remembering. It's not annihilation, Sol, don't fear it; it's not your self-hood dissolving into some identityless collective. It is you, plus. It is life, cubed. And ultimately, we are one seed, you and I, unnaturally separated. We gain each other."

If nothing is lost, then you remember what I am remembering, Solomon Gursky I thought. I am remembering a face forgotten for over thirty million years: Rabbi Bertelsmann. A fat, fair, pleasant face. He is talking to his Bar Mitzvah class about God and masturbation. He is saying that God condemned Onan not for the pleasure of his vice, but because he spilled his seed on the ground. He was fruitless, sterile. He kept the gift of life to himself. And I am now God in my own world, and Rabbi B is smiling and saying, masturbation, Sol. It is all just one big jerk-off, seed spilled on the ground, engendering nothing. Pure recreation; recreating yourself endlessly into the future.

He looked at his twin.

"Rabbi Bertelsmann?" Sol Gursky II said.

"Yes," Sol Gursky I said; then, emphatically, certainly, "Yes!"

Solomon Gursky II's smile dissolved into motes of light.

All at once, the outer edges of the great tetrahedron kindled with ten million points of diamond light. Sol watched the white beams sweep through the Bauble and understood what it meant, that they could manipulate time and space. Even at light-speed, Aea was too huge for each such simultaneity.

Air trees, sky reefs, harpooners, siphons, blimps, zeps, cloud sharks: everything touched by the moving beams was analyzed, comprehended, stored. Recording angels, Sol Gursky thought, as the silver knives dissected his world. He saw the

Spirit Ring unravel like coils of DNA as a billion days of Solomon Gursky flooded up the ladder of light into Aea. The center no longer held; the gravitational forces the Spirit Ring had controlled, that had maintained the ecosphere of the Bauble, were failing. Sol's world was dying. He felt pain, no sorrow, no regret, but rather a savage joy, an urgent desire to be up and on and out, to be free of this great weight of life and gravity. It is not dying, he thought. Nothing ever dies.

He looked up. An angel-beam scored a searing arc across the rooftops of Versailles. He opened his arms to it and was taken apart by the light. Everything is held and recreated in the mind of God. Unremembered by the mind of Solomon Gursky, Versailles disintegrated into swarms of free-flying tectors.

The end came quickly. The angels reached into the photosphere of the star and the complex quasi-information machines that worked there. The sun grew restless, woken from its long quietude. The Spirit Ring collapsed. Fragments spun end-over-end through the Bauble, tearing spectacularly through the dying sky-reefs, shattering cloud forests, blazing in brief glory in funeral orbits around the swelling sun.

For the sun was dying. Plagues of sunspots pocked its chromosphere; solar storms raced from pole to pole in million-kilometer tsunamis. Panicked hunter packs kindled and died in the solar protuberances hurled off as the photosphere prominenced to the very edge of the Bauble. The sun bulged and swelled like a painfully infected pregnancy: Aea was manipulating fundamental forces, loosening the bonds of gravity that held the system together. At the end, it would require all the energies of star-death to power the quantum worm-hole processors.

The star was now a screaming saucer of gas. No living thing remained in the Bauble. All was held in the mind of Aea.

The star burst. The energies of the nova should have boiled Aea's oceans, seared its lands from their beds. It should have twisted and snapped the long, thin arms like yarrow stalks, sent the artifact tumbling like a smashed Fabergé egg through space. But Aea had woven its defenses strong: gravity fields warped the electromagnetic radiation around the fragile terrains; the quantum processors devoured the storm of charged particles, and reconfigured space, time, mass.

The four corners of Aea burned brighter than the dying sun for an instant. And it was gone; under space and time, to worlds and adventures and experiences beyond all saying.

SUNDAY

Toward the end of the universe, Solomon Gursky's thoughts turned increasingly to lost loves.

Had it been entirely physical, Ua would have been the largest object in the universe. Only its fronds, the twenty-light-year-long stalactites that grew into the ylem, tapping the energies of decreation, had any material element. Most of Ua, ninety-nine followed by several volumes of decimal nines percent of its structure, was folded through eleven-space. It was the largest object in the universe in that its fifth and sixth dimensional forms contained the inchoate energy flux known as the universe. Its higher dimensions contained only itself, several times over. It was infundibular. It was vast, it contained multitudes.

PanLife, that amorphous, multi-faceted cosmic infection of human, transhuman, non-human, PanHuman sentiences, had filled the universe long before the continuum reached its elastic limit and began to contract under the weight of dark matter and heavy neutrinos. Femtotech, hand in hand with the worm-hole jump, spread PanLife across the galactic super-clusters in a blink of God's eye.

There was no humanity, no alien. No us, no other. There was only *life*. The dead had become life. Life had become Ua: Pan-spermia. Ua woke to consciousness, and like Alexander the Great, despaired when it had no new worlds to conquer. The universe had grown old in Ua's gestation; it had withered, it contracted, it drew in on itself. The red shift of galaxies had turned blue. And Ua, which owned the attributes, abilities, ambitions, everything except the name and pettinesses of a god, found itself, like an old, long-dead God from a world slagged by its expanding sun millions of years ago, in the business of resurrection.

The galaxies raced together, gravitational forces tearing them into loops and whorls of severed stars. The massive black holes at the galactic centers, fueled by billennia of star-death, coalesced and merged into monstrosities that swallowed globular clusters whole, that shredded galaxies and drew them spiraling inward until, at the edge of the Schwartzchild radii, they radiated super-hard gamma. Long since woven into higher dimensions, Ua fed from the colossal power of the accretion discs, recording in multidimensional matrices the lives of the trillions of sentient organisms fleeing up its fronds from the destruction. All things are held in the mind of God: at the end, when the universal background radiation rose asymptotically to the energy density of the first seconds of the Big Bang, it would deliver enough power for the femtoprocessors woven through the Eleven Heavens to rebuild the universe, entire. A new heaven, and a new Earth.

In the trans-temporal matrices of Ua, PanLife flowed across dimensions, dripping from the tips of the fronds into bodies sculpted to thrive in the plasma flux of ragnarok. Tourists to the end of the world: most wore the shapes of winged creatures of fire, thousands of kilometers across. Starbirds. Firebirds. But the being formerly known as Solomon Gursky had chosen a different form, an archaism from that long-vanished planet. It pleased him to be a thousand-kilometer, diamond-skinned Statue of Liberty, torch out-held, beaming a way through the torrents of star-stuff. Sol Gursky flashed between flocks of glowing soul-birds clustering in the information-rich environment around the frond-tips. He felt their curiosity, their appreciation, their consternation at his non-conformity; none got the joke.

Lost loves. So many lives, so many worlds, so many shapes and bodies, so many loves. They had been wrong, those ones back at the start, who had said that love did not survive death. He had been wrong. It was eternity that killed love. Love was a thing measured by human lifetimes. Immortality gave it time enough, and space, to change, to become things more than love, or dangerously other. None endured. None would endure. Immortality was endless change.

Toward the end of the universe, Solomon Gursky realized that what made love live forever was death.

All things were held in Ua, awaiting resurrection when time, space, and energy fused and ceased to be. Most painful among Sol's stored memories was the remembrance of a red-yellow tiger-striped angel fighter, half-crucified, crippled, tumbling toward the star clouds of Virgo. Sol had searched the trillions of souls roosting in Ua for Elena; failing, he hunted for any that might have touched her, hold some memory of her. He found none. As the universe contracted—as fast and inevitable as a long-forgotten season in the ultra-low time of Ua—Sol Gursky entertained hopes that the universal gathering would draw her in. Cruel truths pecked at his perceptions: calculations of molecular deliquescence, abrasion by interstellar dust clouds, probabilities of stellar impacts, the slow terminal whine of proton decay; any of which denied that Elena could still exist. Sol refused those truths. A thousand-kilometer Statue of Liberty searched the dwindling cosmos for one glimpse of red-yellow tiger-stripes embedded in a feather of fractal plasma flame.

And now a glow of recognition had impinged on his senses laced through the Eleven Heavens.

Her. It had to be her.

Sol Gursky flew to an eye of gravitational stability in the flux and activated the worm-hole nodes seeded throughout his diamond skin. Space opened and folded like an exercise in origami. Sol Gursky went elsewhere.

The starbird grazed the energy-dense borderlands of the central accretion disc. It was immense. Sol's Statue of Liberty was a frond of one of its thousand flight feathers, but it sensed him, welcomed him, folded its wings around him as it drew him to the shifting pattern of sun-spots that was the soul of its being.

He knew these patterns. He remembered these emotional flavors. He recalled this love. He tried to perceive if it were her, her journeys, her trials, her experiences, her agonies, her vastenings.

Would she forgive him?

The soul spots opened. Solomon Gursky was drawn inside. Clouds of tectors interpenetrated, exchanging, sharing, recording. Intellectual intercourse.

He entered her adventures among alien species five times older than Pan-Humanity, an alliance of wills and powers waking a galaxy to life. In an earlier incarnation, he walked the worlds she had become, passed through the dynasties and races and species she had propagated. He made with her the long crossings between stars and clusters, clusters and galaxies. Earlier still, and he swam with her through the cloud canyons of a gas giant world called Urizen, and when that world was hugged too warmly by its sun, changed mode with her, embarked with her on the search for new places to live.

In the nakedness of their communion, there was no hiding Sol Gursky's despair.

I'm sorry Sol, the starbird once known as Lenya communicated.

You have nothing to sorry be for, Solomon Gursky said.

I'm sorry that I'm not her. I'm sorry I never was her.

I made you to be a lover, Sol withspoke. *But you became something older, something richer, something we have lost.*

A *daughter*, Lenya said.

Unmeasurable time passed in the blue shift at the end of the universe. Then Lenya asked, *Where will you go?*

Finding her is the only unfinished business I have left, Sol said.

Yes, the starbird communed. *But we will not meet again.*

No, not in this universe.

Nor any other. And that is death, eternal separation.

My unending regret, Sol Gursky withspoke as Lenya opened her heart and the clouds of tectors separated. *Goodbye, daughter.*

The Statue of Liberty disengaged from the body of the starbird. Lenya's quantum processors created a pool of gravitational calm in the maelstrom. Sol Gursky manipulated space and time and disappeared.

He re-entered the continuum as close as he dared to a frond. A pulse of his mind brought him within reach of its dendrites. As they drew him in, another throb of thought dissolved the Statue of Liberty joke into the plasma flux. Solomon Gursky howled up the dendrite, through the frond, into the soul matrix of Ua. There he carved a niche in the eleventh and highest heaven, and from deep under time, watched the universe end.

As he had expected, it ended in fire and light and glory. He saw space and time curve inward beyond the limit of the Planck dimensions; he felt the energy gradients climb toward infinity as the universe approached the zero point from which it had spontaneously emerged. He felt the universal processors sown through eleven dimensions seize that energy before it faded, and put it to work. It was a surge, a spurt of power and passion, like the memory of orgasm buried deep in the chain of memory that was the days of Solomon Gursky. Light to power, power to memory, memory to flesh. Ua's stored memories, the history of every particle in the former universe, were woven into being. Smart superstrings rolled balls of wrapped eleven-space like sacred scarabs wheeling dung. Space, time, mass, energy unraveled; as the universe died in a quantum fluctuation, it was reborn in primal light.

To Solomon Gursky, waiting in low-time where aeons were breaths, it seemed like creation by *fiat*. A brief, bright light, and galaxies, clusters, stars, turned whole-formed and living within his contemplation. Already personas were swarming out of Ua's honeycomb cells into time and incarnation, but what had been reborn was not a universe, but universes. The re-resurrected were not condemned to blindly recapitulate their former lives. Each choice and action that diverged from the original pattern splintered off a separate universe. Sol and Lenya had spoken truly when they had said they would never meet again. Sol's point of entry into the new polyverse was a thousand years before Lenya's; the universe he intended to create would never intersect with hers.

The elder races had already fanned the polyverse into a *mille feuille* of alternatives: Sol carefully tracked his own timeline through the blur of possibilities as the first humans dropped back into their planet's past. Stars moving into remembered constellations warned Sol that his emergence was only a few hundreds of thousands of years off. He moved down through dimensional matrices, at each level drawing closer to the time flow of his particular universe.

Solomon Gursky hung over the spinning planet. Civilizations rose and decayed, empires conquered and crumbled. New technologies, new continents, new nations were discovered. All the time, alternative Earths fluttered away like torn-off calendar pages on the wind as the dead created new universes to colonize. Close now. Mere moments. Sol dropped into meat time, and Ua expelled him like a drop of milk from a swollen breast.

Solomon Gursky fell. Illusions and anticipations accompanied his return to flesh. Imaginings of light; a contrail angel scoring the nightward half of the planet on its flight across a dark ocean to a shore, to a mountain, to a valley, to a glow of campfire among night-blooming cacti. Longing. Desire. Fear. Gain, and loss. God's trade: to attain the heart's desire, you must give up everything you are. Even the memory.

In the quilted bag by the fire in the sheltered valley under the perfume of the cactus flowers, the man called Solomon Gursky woke with a sudden chill start. It was night. It was dark. Desert stars had half-completed their compass above him. The stone-circled fire had burned down to clinking red glow: the night perfume witched him. Moths padded softly through the air, seeking nectar.

Sol Gursky drank five senses full of his world.

I am alive, he thought. I am here. Again.

Ur-light burned in his hind-brain; memories of Ua, a power like omnipotence. Memories of a life that out-lived its native universe. Worlds, suns, shapes. Flashes, moments. Too heavy, too rich for this small knot of brain to hold. Too bright: no one can live with the memory of having been a god. It would fade—it was fading already. All he need hold—all he must hold—was what he needed to prevent this universe from following its predestined course.

The realization that eyes were watching him was a shock. Elena sat on the edge of the fire shadow, knees folded to chin, arms folded over shins, looking at him. Sol had the feeling that she had been looking at him without him knowing for a long time, and the surprise, the uneasiness of knowing you are under the eyes of another, tempered both the still-new lust he felt for her, and his fading memories of aeons-old love.

Déjà vu. But this moment had never happened before. The divergence was beginning.

"Can't sleep?" she asked.

"I had the strangest dream."

"Tell me." The thing between them was at the stage where they searched each other's dreams for allusions to their love.

"I dreamed that the world ended," Sol Gursky said. "It ended in light, and the light was like the light in a movie projector, that carried the image of the world and everything in it, and so the world was created again, as it had been before."

As he spoke, the words became true. It was a dream now. This life, this body, these memories, were the solid and faithful.

"Like a Tipler machine," Elena said. "The idea that the energy released by the Big Crunch could power some kind of holographic recreation of the entire universe. I suppose with an advanced enough nanotechnology, you could rebuild the universe, an exact copy, atom for atom."

Chill dread struck in Sol's belly. She could not know, surely. She must not know.

"What would be the point of doing it exactly the same all over again?"

"Yeah." Elena rested her cheek on her knee. "But the question is, is *this* our first time in the world, or have we been here many times before, each a little bit different? Is this the first universe, or do we only *think* that it is?"

Sol Gursky looked into the embers, then to the stars.

"The Nez Perce Nation believes that the world ended on the third day and that what we are living in are the dreams of the second night." Memories, fading like summer meteors high overhead, told Sol that he had said this once before, in their future, after his first death. He said it now in the hope that that future would not come to pass. Everything that was different, every tiny detail, pushed this universe away from the one in which he must lose her.

A vee of tiger-striped tectoplastic tumbled end over end forever toward Virgo.

He blinked the ghost away. It faded like all the others. They were going more quickly than he had thought. He would have to make sure of it now, before that memory too dissolved. He struggled out of the terrain bag, went over to the bike lying exhausted on the ground. By the light of a detached bicycle lamp, he checked the gear train.

"What are you doing?" Elena asked from the fireside. The thing between them was still new, but Sol remembered that tone in her voice, that soft inquiry, from another lifetime.

"Looking at the gears. Something didn't feel right about them today. They didn't feel solid."

"You didn't mention it earlier."

No, Sol thought. I didn't know about it. Not then. The gear teeth grinned flashlight back at him.

"We've been giving them a pretty hard riding. I read in one of the biking mags that you can get metal fatigue. Gear train shears right through, just like that."

"On brand-new, two thousand dollar bikes?"

"On brand-new two thousand dollar bikes."

"So what do you think you can *do* about it at one o'clock in the morning in the middle of the Sonora Desert?"

Again, that come-hither tone. Just a moment more, Elena. One last thing, and then it will be safe.

"It just didn't sit right. I don't want to take it up over any more mountains until I've had it checked out. You get a gear-shear up there . . ."

"So, what are you saying, irritating man?"

"I'm not happy about going over Blood of Christ Mountain tomorrow."

"Yeah. Sure. Fine."

"Maybe we should go out west, head for the coast. It's whale season, I always wanted to see whales. And there's real good seafood. There's this cantina where they have fifty ways of serving iguana."

"Whales. Iguanas. Fine. Whatever you want. Now, since you're so wide-awake, you can just get your ass right *over* here, Sol Gursky!"

She was standing up, and solomon saw and felt what she had been concealing by the way she had sat. She wearing only a cut-off MTB shirt. Safe, he thought, as he seized her and took her down laughing and yelling onto the camping mat. Even as he thought it, he forgot it, and all those Elenas who would not now be: conspirator, crop-haired freedom fighter, four-armed space-angel. Gone.

The stars moved in their ordained arcs. The moths and cactus forest bats drifted through the soft dark air, and the eyes of the things that hunted them glittered in the firelight.

Sol and Elena were still sore and laughing when the cactus flowers closed with dawn. They ate their breakfast and packed their small camp, and were in the saddle and on the trail before the sun was full over the shoulder of Blood of Christ Mountain. They took the western trail, away from the hills, and the town called Redención hidden among them with its freight of resurrected grief. They rode the long trail that led down to the ocean, and it was bright, clear endless Monday morning.

The Cuckoo's Boys

ROBERT REED

Robert Reed sold his first story in 1986, and quickly established himself as a frequent contributor to The Magazine of Fantasy & Science Fiction *and* Asimov's Science Fiction, *as well as selling many stories to* Science Fiction Age, Universe, New Destinies, Tomorrow, Synergy, Starlight, *and elsewhere.*

Reed may be one of the most prolific of today's young writers, particularly at short fiction lengths, seriously rivaled for that position only by authors such as Stephen Baxter and Brian Stableford. And—like Baxter and Stableford—he manages to keep up a very high standard of quality while being prolific, something that is not at all easy to do. Almost every year throughout the mid- to late nineties, he has produced at least two or three stories that would be good enough to get him into a Best of the Year anthology under ordinary circumstances, and some years he has produced four or five of them, so that often the choice is not whether to use a Reed story, but rather which Reed story to use—a remarkable accomplishment.

Nor was the situation any different in 1998, with at least five first-rate Robert Reed stories from which to choose. I finally settled on the remarkable novella that follows, one as current as today's headlines and yet as surprising as tomorrow always must be, a thought-provoking study that reexamines the old question of nature vs. nurture, with some disquieting results.

Reed is almost as prolific as a novelist as he is as a short story writer, having produced eight novels to date, including The Leeshore, The Hormone Jungle, Black Milk, The Remarkables, Down the Bright Way, Beyond the Veil of Stars, An Exaltation of Larks, *and, most recently,* Beneath the Gated Sky. *Just out is his long-overdue first collection,* The Dragons of Springplace. *His stories have appeared in our Ninth, Tenth, Eleventh, Twelfth, Thirteenth, Fourteenth, and Fifteenth Annual Collections. He lives in Lincoln, Nebraska, where he's at work on a novel-length version of his 1997 novella, "Marrow."*

1

▼ Here's your first assignment:

Build a starship. And I want you to tell me all about it. Its name. How big it is. What it is made from. Tell me about its power plant and engines. How many are in the crew, and what are their names? They deserve names. Are they human, and if not, what? Draw them for me, and draw your ship, too. Do you have weapons on board? If so, what kinds? You might want to carry some little scout ships along for the ride. Anything else that you might think is useful, I'll let you take. Plus there's one piece of gear that I'm putting on board. It's a box. A box about this big. Inside is a wormhole. Open its lid, and the wormhole swallows your ship, transporting it to somewhere else. You'll travel through space and through time. Or maybe you'll leave our universe entirely.

There's no way to know what happens next.

It's all up to me.

My name's Houston Cross. Call me Mr. Cross, or Houston. I'm going to be your science mentor for the year.

John was one of the first PS's born. He is 13 years old, and since he hasn't been skipped ahead in school, he's an eighth-grader. A growth spurt and a steady lack of exercise have made him larger than many adults. His kinky black hair is short. His coffee-colored skin has a boy's smoothness, still free of whiskers and hair on the forearms. His brown eyes are active, engaged. He smiles with a nervous eagerness, and sometimes, particularly when he's excited, he talks almost too quickly to be understood.

"Thanks for taking me," he blurts.

Then he adds, "Ms. Lindstrum says you've been doing this for a long time."

Ms. Lindstrum is the school's Gifted Facilitator.

"She says I'm lucky to have you."

Houston shrugs and halfway laughs. "I wouldn't know about that."

"How long have you been a mentor?" John asks, saying it in one breath, as if the sentence were a single word.

"Five years," Houston replies. "This is my sixth."

"Have you ever worked with us?"

"Eighth graders? Sure—"

"No. I mean us. Or do you teach normals, usually?"

Houston waits for a moment, then says, "I understood the first time." He shakes his head, telling the boy, "Please don't talk that way."

"Oh. Sorry!" John is instantly angry with himself. It shows in the eyes and how the big hands wrestle with one another. "You know what I mean. Normal gifted kids."

"Sure, John."

"I'm not better than anyone else," he blurts with a robust conviction. "I don't ever let myself think that way."

"Good."

"And I try to get along. With everyone."

"That's a good policy, John. Getting along."

The boy sighs, his face suddenly very young and tired. He looks around the empty classroom, then gazes out the long window. A wide green lawn ends at a quiet street, shade pooling beneath tall pin oaks.

"Can I start?" he asks.

"Excuse me?"

"With my starship. Can I, Mr. Cross?"

"Be my guest."

The Facilitator met with Houston yesterday. She warned him that John was an only child, and he lived with his divorced mother—a common circumstance among PS's. Perhaps that's why the boy suffered from feelings of guilt and loss and powerlessness. "But in the plus column," she added, "the mother is relatively well educated, and she seems to genuinely care about him. When she finds time."

John holds his stylus in his left hand, head bent forward, using an electronic workpad for the rest of their hour. He stops only to say that his hand is sore. When the bell rings—an obnoxious, metallic clanging—he looks up in panic, exclaiming, "But I'm not done yet!"

"Work at home tonight," Houston offers. "Or tomorrow. Here. We've got plenty of time, John."

The boy scrolls through page after page of sketches and hurried labels. Shaking his head in despair, he says, "This is all shit. I'm sorry about my language, Mr. Cross. But this is all just shit."

"We'll try again tomorrow."

But the boy isn't mollified. Folding his notebook, he says, "I get these ideas. All the time. But a lot of them . . . well, they're just stupid. You know? They're *rancid*! . . ."

The mentor smiles in a thin way.

He says, "John," and pats the boy's left hand.

He says, "Believe me. Everyone chews on that shit sandwich."

Phillip Stevens was the only child of an African-American man and his German-American girlfriend. Phillip was labeled gifted before he was eight. He graduated from Princeton at 18, then dropped out of medical school two years later in order to form his own corporation. His first billion dollars were made before he was 26, most of it coming from the rapidly growing genetics industry. His later billions came from shrewd investments and several medi-technical advances in which he played a hands-on role. Following his 30th birthday, Phillip began pouring his wealth into a new research facility. To visitors and the press, he boasted that he would do nothing but cutting-edge research that would alleviate human misery. But close associates grew concerned with the real direction of their work, and to those malcontents, he said, "Here's six figures. Now quiet, or I'll have your nuts for lunch."

Too late, the CDC believed the warnings about the billionaire's plans.

Federal agents in bulky biosuits descended on Phillip's empire. But the criminal had already vanished, taking with him nearly 50 liters of growth media and an artificial microbe dubbed Phillip 23.

• • •

Mike was on of the last PS's born.

He has just skipped the sixth grade. No growth spurt has taken him, and judging by his wiry build, he's physically active. The face is narrower than John's, and two years younger, and something about it seems harder. He lives with parents of modest means. According to Ms. Lindstrum, the boy's genetics have little mutations. Which is normal among the last-born. "Maybe it's his genes," she warned Houston, "or maybe it's something else. Either way, Mike has a different attitude. You'll notice it right away."

"How'd you get this job?" the boy asks. Flat out.

"With bribes," Houston replies. Instantly.

"No," says Mike, never blinking. "I bet they gave you some special test."

Houston laughs, admitting, "They asked a lot of questions. But I don't know if I'd call it a test."

"When did this happen?"

"When I started working in the schools."

"How long have you been a teacher?"

"A mentor."

"Yeah. That." Mike has long hair—longer than any current fashion—and either through pharmaceutical tricks or the mutations, it's straighter and edging toward blond. The boy spends a lot of time pushing unruly locks out of his brown eyes. "You've been a mentor for a long time. Haven't you?"

"Several years now."

"But you didn't deal with *us* till now." He says it, then smiles with a slyness, happy to prove his special knowledge. "I've been asking about you."

"You have been."

"Shouldn't I have?"

Houston waits for a moment, then asks, "Did you talk to John about me?"

"God, no. Not that idiot."

Houston says nothing.

"No, there's some guys you used to teach. To mentor. Whatever." Mike names them—both boys are in high school now—then adds, "They thought you were pretty good. All things considered."

"All things considered, that's good news."

"They told me that you steered clear of *us*."

Houston doesn't respond.

"Why is that?"

"You weren't old enough." He speaks calmly, without doubts. "I like working with middle-schoolers. Not children."

The comment makes an impact. The boy almost smiles, then remembers his next question. "What did they ask?"

"When?"

"When you became a mentor. What kinds of questions did you get?"

"The interviewer wondered what I knew about gifted students. He asked what I would do in this situation, or that one. And he checked to see if I'd ever been arrested—"

"Have you been?"

"Five times," he says. Then he asks, "Do you believe that?"

"No," the boy snorts. Then, "What about this year? Did they make you do anything special before you got us?"

"Some things," Houston admits. "I had to read various books and some very boring reports. And I went through special in-depth training for an entire afternoon. I needed to be sensitized to your circumstances and special needs."

"Oh, yeah? I've got special needs?"

"Everyone does, Mike."

"What else?"

"I signed a contract. I'm never supposed to talk to the press. Ever." Houston's voice sharpens, just for that instant. Then he smiles, adding, "All questions are handled through the Special Task Office at district headquarters."

Mike seems impressed with the answers or the precautions. Or perhaps both.

Houston prods him. "Work on your starship. Okay?"

Instead of a workpad, Mike has a fat spiral notebook and a pen leaking an unearthly green ink. With his left hand, he writes Day One on the first page. A moment's reflection leads to a little laugh, then a sly glimpse at his mentor. "Hey, Houston," he says. "Can I have an antimatter cannon?"

"I don't know. What is an 'antimatter cannon'?"

The boy rolls his brown eyes. "It's a cannon. It shoots balls of antimatter. They explode into pure energy when they hit *anything*."

"Okay. But how would a weapon like that work?"

"What do you mean?"

"Is your ship built from antimatter?" Houston asks. "And the crew, too?"

"That would be stupid," the boy assures him. "The first time we landed on another planet—boom."

"But how do you keep your shells from destroying you?" Houston asks the question, then leans closer. "How do you manipulate something that you can't touch?"

The boy thinks hard for a moment, then says, "Magnets."

"Okay."

"We make cannonballs out of anti-iron," he says, "and we keep them in a vacuum, held there by a really powerful magnetic field."

"Good enough," says Houston.

Mike shakes his head, admitting, "Those guys I know . . . they warned me. You can really be un-fun when you want to be."

Houston says, "Good."

The boy folds himself over his notebook, working with the same fevered intensity that John showed. But he doesn't complain about a sore hand, and while the sketches are sloppier than those on a workpad, he seems infinitely more pleased with the results.

After the bell rings, Houston admits, "I'm curious. What do you want to do with that fancy cannon?"

"Blow up planets," the boy says. Instantly. Then he looks up, wearing a devilish grin.

"Is that okay with you, Houston?"

"Sure," he says. "Why not?"

The synthetic protozoan, Phillip 23, was a mild but durable pathogen carried by spit and the air. Healthy males and children rarely showed symptoms. The old and impaired developed flu-like infections, and at least a thousand died during the epidemic. But fertile women were the preferred hosts. The bug would invade the monthly egg, consume the mother's nucleus and mitochondria, then replace both with huge amounts of nuclear material.

All races and all parts of the globe were struck by the disease.

Victims included nuns and teenage virgins and at least one lady on death row.

During the epidemic, some 3 percent of all conceptions on the planet were baby boys carrying Phillip Stevens' genetic code.

"Your third mentee," Ms. Lindstrum began to say. Then she hesitated, contemplating her next words.

They were sitting in the woman's tiny office.

"The boy's name is Troy Andrew Holdenmeister. And I should warn you. His parents are utterly devoted to him."

Houston said, "Okay."

The Facilitator was scrolling through reports and memos and test results of every complexion. With a mixture of professional distance and practiced scorn, she said, "The mother has dedicated her life to the boy. She has three other children, but it's Troy who gets most of her attentions."

"I see."

"She wants to meet with you. Tomorrow, if possible."

Houston said nothing.

"And there's something else you should know: Troy isn't quite like the other PS's. His scores are lower in the usual peak areas. Math and science, and so on."

"Mutations?" Houston asked.

She shrugged, as if to say, "We can hope." But she had to admit, "He's only five months younger than John. Mutations were rare then. And the differences . . . well, it isn't likely that a few genes would change so much. . . ."

Ms. Lindstrum looked like someone who had been married once or twice, and always too soon. She was tall and a little heavy around the hips, and beneath a professional veneer was a puddle of doubts and fickle emotions. Houston recognized the symptoms. They showed in the lonely eyes and the way she always would watch his eyes. He sensed that if he wanted, he could gently take hold of one of her hands, say the usual nice words, and have her. Within the week, Ms. Lindstrum would be making breakfast for him, wearing nothing but her best apron, smiling in a giddy, lovesick way.

Houston didn't reach for her hand.

"Is Troy adopted?" he asked.

Ms. Lindstrum shook her head. "I know someone who knows the family. Mrs. Holdenmeister was most definitely pregnant."

A Newly Standardized IQ score lay in plain sight. Houston underlined the number with his thumb, remarking, "There could have been some simple prenatal problem."

"Maybe," she agreed.

But probably not, thought Houston.

Then quietly and a little sadly, Ms. Lindstrum admitted, "It's a respectably average IQ. Enough to make any parent happy . . . if she didn't know any better. . . ."

A 13-year-old boy sits hunched over a large, expensive workpad, focusing all of his attentions on his starship.

"He loves this kind of project," says his mother. She sits at the front of the classroom, and without a gram of subtlety, she stares at her son's mentor. "I'm relieved that you agreed to meet with me. Our last mentor didn't want to."

The woman is small and delicate as a carpet tack, with fierce little blue eyes that hint at a scorching temper.

Houston doesn't say what first comes to mind.

Instead, he tells her, "I want a good relationship with every parent."

"Do you have the other boys, too?" she wants to know.

He nods. "John and Mike. Yes."

"Try, if you can, to keep Mike away from my Troy." She says what she thinks, then thinks about how it sounds. To soften the moment, she adds, "John's very nice. We like him quite a bit. But the other one . . . he scares us, frankly. . . ."

Houston says nothing.

He refuses to look at the woman. Instead, he stares into the blackness of the on-line screen. It covers the back wall. The teacher who uses this classroom in the morning has turned it off, which is standard policy. He makes a mental note to ask for the screen to be left ready to work, in case they need help.

Perhaps sensing his mood, Mrs. Holdenmeister makes eye contact and tries a hard little smile. "If you need it, I can arrange for special software. And lab equipment. Anything of that sort."

"Not for now," he says. "Thank you."

"Because I'm perfectly willing—"

Houston interrupts, explaining, "What I usually do is give my students thought problems. They have to work out what's happening, and why, and what they can do about it."

"I see," she says, without conviction.

"And sometimes I'll make them face ethical dilemmas, too. What's right, what's wrong. And in the absence of either, what's best."

She opens her mouth, then hesitates.

After a long pause, she asks, "Would it be all right if I watch you at work again? With my husband. Name the day, and he'll take the afternoon off from work . . . if that wouldn't be too much trouble—"

"I don't believe so." He says it calmly, with a flat unaffected voice.

"Excuse me?"

"I wouldn't be comfortable," he explains. "An audience isn't going to help me with what I'm doing here."

She doesn't know what to say. Sitting motionless, Mrs. Holdenmeister breathes rapidly, trying to imagine a new, more productive avenue.

She decides on pity.

"You know," she whispers, "it's been very difficult just getting him into the mentoring program. That Facilitator has fought us all the way."

"Well," Houston replies, "I agree with you on this one."

That wins a smile, cold but bright. Then she abruptly turns her head, saying, "Darling," with a big, overdone voice. "Do you have something for us?"

"Mr. Cross?" says the boy. He's nearly as old as John, but smaller. Not just thinner, but he hasn't found his growth spurt yet. Whatever the reason, he's little larger than the 11-year-old Mike. Where the other boys have quick eyes, Troy's are simpler and slower. And while he has their voice, the words come out at their own studied pace.

"How is this, Mr. Cross?"

His mother snatches the workpad, then says, "Darling. It's wonderful!"

Houston waits.

"Isn't it just spectacular, Mr. Cross?" She hands the pad to him, then tells her son, "Great job! It's just wonderful!"

The boy and his software have drawn a starship with precise lines and in three dimensions. There are intricate details, and on the next pages, elaborate plans for the bridge and the engines. It's very thorough work, and that's all it is.

Quietly, without inflection, Houston says, "Troy." He asks, "Have you seen the movie *Starfarer*?"

"About a thousand times," the boy confesses.

"Because that's where this ship came from," Houston warns him. "You've done an exceptional job of copying it."

The brown eyes blink. Confused, suspicious.

But Mom hears an entirely different message.

"Good for you!" she sings out. "Good, good, good for you!"

2. *Your starship emerges from the wormhole.*

The first thing you see is a disk. The disk has stripes. Some dark, some candy-colored. Plus there are two blood-red swirls. And the disk itself is flattened on top and below, and it bulges out around its waist.

That's what you can see, and what else can you tell me?

"Is it Jupiter?" John asks.

"How do you know it's a planet?"

"Can I see stars?"

"Yes."

"The stripes are clouds. The swirls are hurricanes."

"All right. It's a planet," Houston conceded.

"Is it Jupiter?"

"Two red swirls," Houston repeats.

"Yeah, but that wormhole can take us through time. So it could be Jupiter. But millions of years ago."

"Good point. But it's not."

The boy nods compliantly, then grins. "Tau Ceti 5."

"Excuse me?"

"It's a planet. Haven't you heard about it?" Sensing an advantage, John explains, "They've found thousands of planets that look like Jupiter. The big telescopes spot new ones every day."

"They do," Houston agrees. "This isn't one of them."

"No?" The boy licks his lips, puzzled. "What about its sun?"

"Good question." The mentor pauses, considering his possibilities. "Two suns," he offers. "Close enough to touch each other."

"Can that happen?"

"Sometimes. But it's temporary. They'll lose momentum and fall together, then merge into one sun."

"Delicious!" he exclaims. Then, "What else can I see?"

"Moons. With your naked eyes, you count five of them."

"Big ones?"

"I don't know. How do we find out?"

John shrugs and says, "With sensors. I'll ask my sensors."

"What kinds of sensors?"

"Sensors." The boy believes in that word, and why can't Mr. Cross?

"But how do they work?" Houston asks. Then he warns him, "Not by magic, they don't. Every machine has its job and its inherent logic."

John grunts and says, "I don't know. They just work."

Houston shakes his head.

The boy compresses his mouth to a point, staring at his elaborate starship. It looks like a crystal chandelier with rockets stuck in its stem. "I don't get it," he finally confesses. "I thought we were going to explore the universe."

"So we'll start with good old universal principles," Houston tells him. "About light and energy and mass, for instance. Then later, if you really want, we can move on to those boring old moons."

The PS epidemic lasted 30 months. Occasionally the clones shared the womb with unrelated embryos. Sometimes they arrived as identical twins or triplets. But most were single babies, active and free of complications. In modern nations, a relatively simple test allowed expectant mothers to learn if their son was a clone. Many chose chemical or clinical abortions. And there was a deluge of orphaned babies that ended up with more forgiving or more desperate couples.

In certain backward nations, solutions wore harsher faces.

There were even places that pretended to escape the PS plague. Despite the global nature of this illness, despots and their xenophobic citizens denied ever seeing the clones, and they denied every rumor about organized infanticide. And even if babies were dying by the thousands, who could blame them?

A man and woman struggle to raise their own child. Why should they be forced to raise an abomination, too?

Which was what those babies were.

Abominations.

An opinion officially ridiculed by wealthy nations. Even while opinion polls found that a quarter to a third of their own people believed exactly that.

"The first thing I do is shoot it."

"Shoot the planet?"

"Are you going to let me?" Mike asks.

"Who am I? Part of your crew?" Houston lifts his hands, saying, "Wait. You haven't told me anything about the people on board."

"They aren't human."

"Okay."

"They're robots. Ten feet tall and built of smart metals."

Houston nods, then asks, "Do those robots have a leader?"

"Sure."

"What's his name?"

Mike dips his head, staring at his green-ink-and-paper starship. It's a bullet-shaped contraption bristling with every possible weapon.

"You'll want a good strong name," says Houston.

"Damned right!"

"How about Crocus?" he suggests.

"I like that! Crocus!" Mike nods and pushes at his hair, then asks, "Can Crocus fire his antimatter cannon?"

"Be my guest."

"All right. He lets loose a planet-busting round. Then, What happens?"

"Nothing."

"What do you mean?"

"I mean it takes time for the round to reach its target."

Mike shakes his head, and with a disapproving tone says, "John warned me about this game of yours."

"You talked to John?"

"In the hallway. For just a second."

"I thought you didn't like him."

"I don't. He's a fat twisted goof." Then the boy shrugs, adding, "But he always talks to me. I can't stop him."

Houston watches the narrow face, the narrowed eyes. Then, "How fast is your cannon ball moving?"

"Fast."

"Make a guess."

"Half-light speed. How's that?"

"If it takes 20 seconds for the antimatter to reach the planet—"

"It's 10 light seconds away." The boy dismisses the entire game, saying, "This is easy. That big planet is . . . let me think . . ." He does some quick calculations on paper. "Twenty million miles away. No, wait! . . . Two million miles. Right?"

"Something like that."

Mike nods, happily in control. "So then. How big's the explosion?"

"Good-sized."

"Damn right!"

Houston shakes his head, saying, "The shell's moving half the velocity of light, which means it has a terrific momentum. It burrows into the atmosphere and turns to plasma and light, and the explosion comes squirting back up through the vacuum left behind it. Like out of another cannon, sort of."

"And the planet explodes—!"

"Hardly," Houston warns. "It's not nearly the explosion you want."

"That's stupid," Mike tells him.

"No," says Houston. "It's not."

The boy stares at his starship, confusion and betrayal on his face. And then a sudden little smile comes to the eyes and mouth, and he exclaims, "I get it. That world's antimatter, too. Isn't it?"

"What if it is?"

"Jesus," he says, with mock panic. Then he slams his notebook shut and says, "We've got to get the hell out of here!"

Worldwide, birth rates dropped for better than five years.

Couples delayed having children. Millions of women underwent hysterectomies, so great was their fear of conceiving a PS. The epidemic's climax was marked with incompetent news coverage sparking wild rumors. The most persistent rumor was that Phillip Stevens' genes were found inside every newborn, regardless of sex or race. And what made the rumor all the more pernicious was that it was true, in a sense: Humans were a young species. Eskimos and Pigmies shared vast amounts of genetic information. But that abstraction didn't translate well at work and home, and millions of healthy, non-PS offspring were aborted during the panic.

Even when a vaccine was available, people remained suspicious.

What if it didn't work as promised?

Or worse, what if this was just the first plague? What if a hundred mad bastards were putting together their own bugs, and this mess was really just beginning?

"Maybe that planet has life," says Troy.

"Maybe so. How would you find out?"

The boy says, "I'll go there." Then he thinks to ask, "May I?"

"By all means."

Houston describes the two-million-mile voyage, and later, as the Hollywood-built starship slips into the atmosphere, Houston asks, "Who's in command?"

"The captain." Troy and his software have drawn a dozen people wearing trim blue uniforms. Everyone resembles a famous actor or actress. The captain is the tallest, oldest man, sporting a short dark beard.

"What's his name?"

"Storm. Captain Storm."

"Is he a human, or a robot?"

"Oh, he has to be human."

"Is he a good man?"

"Always." The boy looks at Houston with an imploring expression. "He wouldn't be the captain if he wasn't."

"Fair enough." Houston nods, smiles. Then he scratches his little beard, saying, "Your ship flies into a cloud and pulls in a sample."

"Of what?"

"I don't know. At room temperature and pressure, it's liquid."

"Like water?"

"Exactly."

"Maybe there's life in it."

"How would you test that?" Houston asks.

The boy inhales, then holds his breath. Thinking.

"Any ideas?"

He exhales, confessing, "I know I'm not supposed to use sensors."

"Did John tell you?"

Troy shakes his head, then catches himself.

"Don't worry," Houston purrs. "You can talk to Mike. I don't care."

All the same, the boy seems ashamed.

Then Houston prods him, saying, "A microscope is a kind of sensor. And I'll let you use any sensor if you understand how it works."

"I do," says Troy. "I've got two microscopes at home."

"Okay. Use one of them now."

The hands assemble an imaginary slide, then the right eye squints into an imaginary eyepiece.

Watching, Houston quietly asks, "What is life?"

Then, in more concrete terms, he asks, "How do you recognize it?"

"Life is busy," the boy tells him, his voice pragmatic and pleased.

"When I make a slide at home, what I look for are things that are really, really busy."

3. *You set down on a desolate world. A hard white plain stretches to the horizon. There's no trace of people or cities or even simple life forms. But perhaps something once lived here, and that's why you're putting on your archaeology hat.*

I want you to dig into a piece of ground.

Like a scientist, you need to keep track of everything that you find. Everything. I want you to leave future generations with enough information to resurrect this dig site. Keep notes. Always. Make drawings and maps. And try to figure out what happened here.

There's a story waiting. If you can find it.

Houston has a small one-bedroom apartment that's a short drive from school. It's clean, but rarely tidy. He has lived here for a little more than five years. Prints of famous abstracts hang above the second-hand furniture. On a shelf fixed to one white wall are a pair of trophies. "Mentor of the Year," the plaques read. "Houston Cross." Both trophies show a pair of brass hands clasping—one hand large and grandfatherly, while the other is quite small and only half-formed.

He is working in the tiny kitchen.

Big old roasting pans are set in a row on the countertop. Inside each pan are pieces of shattered robots and random wires and the carefully dismantled bodies of several plastic toys. Houston bought three skeletal monsters, each with a human-like skull and six arms rooted into a long back. He has cut them apart and thrown out the occasional piece — fossils are almost never whole — and after setting everything into a careful heap, he pours a fresh polymer-plaster into the pans, trying not to spill, and when he does, immediately cleaning up the dribbles and drops.

"Breaking news," says the television. It's an old high-density, but Houston built its AI from a kit, then trained it to find what interests him.

He glances up and says, "Show me."

" — furthermore, the study shows that once a minimally enriched environment is achieved, the boys' intellectual development plateaus — "

The pictured face could be John's. It's older than most PS's, and pudgy.

"Save it," says Houston. "I'll watch it later."

"Okay," says the machine.

He sets the three pans inside the oven, the low heat helping the plaster cure. Then he heats up last night's leftovers in the microwave and, sitting in front of the television, prepares to watch the news story.

"Breaking news," says his television.

"Show me."

" — the controversial book is the fifth most popular title in the world today. *The Cuckoo's Boys* has sold more than 20 million copies, and that despite being banned in much of Europe and Brazil."

The author appears. Beneath him floats a name. Dr. Paul Kaan. An ex-associate of Phillip Stevens, Kaan has a gentle face and hard, uncompromising eyes. Talking to an unseen audience, he explains, "I wrote this book because it's vital that people understand. What the PS's represent is nothing short of a debasing of our species and a debacle for our immortal souls!"

Houston watches the three-minute report.

Afterward, the screen returns to a mountain vista accompanied by a quiet dose of Grieg. More minutes pass. The oven timer goes off. Finally, almost grudgingly, Houston rises and pulls the pans out of the oven. Then he sits again, watching his dinner grow cold, and the AI asks, "Should I run the synopsis?"

"Excuse me?"

"About the intellectual development of the PS clones. Are you still interested?"

"Not really. No."

The curved tip of the butterknife bites into the plaster, and the blade itself starts to bow as John presses, working to expose a length of yellow-brown plastic bone. He's been working quickly, almost frantically, for most of the hour, taking notes only when coaxed. After two months together, Houston feels sure that the boy should be enjoying himself. But something is wrong, distracting him. It isn't much of a guess when Houston asks, "What's going on at home?"

"Nothing," John blurts.

"Okay."

"Nothing," he says again. Then as if caught in the lie, he adds, "Well, yeah. I got in a fight last night."

"With your mom?"

"No. Her boyfriend." He shakes his head, then shoves hard with the knife, the entire bone popping out of its hole.

"Notes," Houston urges.

"I know. I know." Abbreviated, useless observations are jotted down. Then everything comes to a halt. John drops the knife and says, "My wrist hurts. Really bad." Then he stares out the window, dumbfounded rage in the eyes and the hard-set mouth.

After a long moment, Houston asks, "What happened last night, John?"

"I'm not *him*."

Houston waits.

"That boyfriend of hers . . . he always calls me Phillip." The boy deepens his voice, saying, "Phillip, bring me this. Phillip, you're in my way. Phillip, get the hell lost."

"But you're not Phillip Stevens."

John looks at his feet now. Shaking his head.

"You're just the man's genetics."

"I told him that."

Houston says, "Good."

"PS was a different person than me. Right?"

"Absolutely."

"I mean, he was born in a different century, and in another place. Everything about his life was different than mine. Right?"

"Did you tell him that?"

"Yeah. But all he did . . . he just laughed at me. He said, "That's just what old Phillip would say, if he was here.""

Houston says nothing.

"Fucker," says the boy. Viciously, with a pure scalding hatred.

Then with a low, stern voice, his mentor suggests, "You shouldn't, maybe. I know you don't like your mother's friend, but calling him that name—"

"No, Mr. Cross," John interrupts. "I'm talking about the other fucker."

For four years, law enforcement agencies followed every wrong lead, interviewed millions of earnest, mistaken individuals, and through means legal and otherwise, they pulled up the bank and tax records of more than a billion suspects.

But in the end, a routine traffic accident gave them Phillip Stevens.

An unidentified man driving a dilapidated pickup truck happened to rear-end a young mother. Bumpers locked. When two uniformed officers arrived, the man was staring at a PS child riding in the back seat. Suddenly he panicked, pulling a weapon and discharging it into the air. Witnesses saw him fleeing into a nearby warehouse. There was a second muted shot. Eventually, a SWAT team broke into the warehouse and discovered a body lying in a tiny men's room, the scene filthy with blood and bone and bits of drying brain matter.

Subsequent tests proved that the corpse belonged to the missing billionaire. His face and skin color had been altered by surgical means, but his famous DNA was instantly recognized by five reputable labs, including his own.

The young mother was labeled a hero, then lost the label when she refused 10 million dollars for her role in ending the manhunt. Furthermore, she enraged many by admitting that she only wished she had known who the man was . . . she wanted to thank Phillip for giving her her wonderful son! . . .

Youth is a blessing.

When Mike takes the knife to the plaster, he believes. He is *eleven*, and this is fun, and he's enthralled. Intent, absolutely focused, each slice into the whiteness is full of possibilities.

Like John and every other young boy, PS or not, scientific ritual distracts him from his fun. Notes are taken, but only under duress. Working with ink on paper, Mike jots and sketches. Then he picks up the knife with both hands, making a game of picking his next quadrant, and after a calming breath, he cuts chisels a deep wedge of plaster.

Houston can't remember where he put which artifact, and so it's nearly a surprise to him when the boy uncovers a single golden eye gazing up at the alien sky.

Mike says, "Shit."

He giggles and says, "Neat," and goes to work with an old toothbrush, using bristles bent against Houston's teeth, sweeping away the clinging dust.

Half of the period is invested exhuming the skull. It's small and obviously plastic, yet something about it intrigues the boy. He can't stop smiling afterwards, moving to the next quadrant and working his way down to a severed hand clinging to a toy weapon. With a dissecting needle, he shoves at the trigger. A weak light and muted whine come from beneath the hardened plaster.

Houston waits.

The boy looks up, grinning.

"Wal-Mart?" he says matter-of-factly.

Disappointed, Houston shrugs and says, "Maybe."

But the boy's attitude shifts. With his next breath, he's back on that other world, and with a bleak authority, he says, "This is some ass-kicking monster. So something really tough must have killed it. That's what I think!"

After the bell rings, the hallway jams with students.

Houston's habit is to walk each boy to the door, then stand there and watch the kids pass by. The sixth-graders are still very much children; while the eighth-graders, and particularly the girls, are metamorphosizing into their adult selves. By the end of the year, Houston will catch himself watching the young women. When he first began mentoring, a certain kind of girl might offer glances and winsome smiles. But five-plus years is a long time, and his wilting hair and the graying beard makes him look older than their fathers. Houston has, in effect, vanished from their hormonal radar.

Mike's locker is straight across the hall.

Still grinning about the buried skull, he fingers his lock, and when it doesn't recognize him, he slams it hard against the gray steel, then tries again.

Troy steps up behind him, saying something.

The two boys talk for a moment. Differences in age and Mike's bleached hair make them look like siblings, not twins. And it helps that Troy carries himself with a slump-shouldered shyness, while his younger brother is the cockier, self-assured one.

Houston tries to read lips. And faces. And postures.

Then he notices other students. Like him, some stare. One boy points, which triggers a second to follow his lead. Then a tall girl giggles and shouts, "Which one's real? Which one's real?"

Mike calmly flips the girl off.

Troy just dips his head, trying to ignore the taunt.

Then as Houston starts to say something to the girl—acidic and cutting and cold—she turns and skips past him, still giggling, a bony elbow clipping his elbow as she passes, never noticing him.

In the end, Troy is the only boy to reassemble the entire skeleton. What's more, he uses resins and a bottomless patience to sculpt bones to replace what's missing. When the others have gone on new missions, he continues to happily piece together and repair. In the end, both a tiny toy robot and the skeleton man look like museum displays, mounted on a new plaster landscape that he and his mother built on a rainy Saturday.

Houston hangs a dozen concepts on those toys.

Entropy. Evolution. Anatomy.

"Those extra arms wouldn't work," he explains. "No shoulders, so there's no place to anchor the muscles. Is there?"

The boy shrugs. "I guess not."

"Why would a six-armed man evolve?"

With an enduring patience, he says, "I guess he must have needed them."

"The universe tends to slide from order into disorder. Have you ever heard that before, Troy?"

"When Mom cleans my room." When he laughs, he sounds most like John. Like Mike. Like many hundreds of thousands of boys. But the grim, abstract heart of this entropy business remains out of reach. He shrugs again, and with an easygoing stubbornness, he confesses, "I don't think about that stuff much."

Trying to cushion the bad news, he shrugs and smiles, admitting, "I'm not like them, Mr. Cross. Sorry."

The bookstore still accepts cash.

What's more, it's large enough to keep a ready inventory of best-sellers. No need to wait around three minutes while your purchase is printed and bound. Houston can pick up a fresh copy from under a sign that reads: "Controversial. #1 Seller!" Then he can take the copy up front and pay, asking for a sack, please.

The fear of discovery is wholly irrational.

And worse, it's laughable.

But Houston has mentored more than a dozen kids, and various parents know him, and countless teachers and administrators would recognize him on sight. Those are all exactly the kinds of people who might be browsing in a bookstore on a warm October night, which is why he takes precautions, and why he feels secretly nervous, stepping outside and strolling to his car with a forced nonchalance.

No parking slots are left at his apartment's lot. Houston's forced to leave his little car on the street. As he enters the building, he finds half a dozen neighbors and their friends on their way to a Halloween party. All are in costume, and drunk. The party must have a theme; everyone wears the same full mask, the adult Phillip Stevens reborn with rubber and fake hair.

"Out of our way!" one man shouts.

"Genetic superiority coming through!" says another.

A woman says, "Stop that," and slaps a hand off her ass. Then she slides up against Houston, beery breath telling him, "You look different. You look awfully cute!"

"He's not," says the first man.

"He's inferior," says the second man.

Then they're past him. And Houston stands on the bottom stair for a long while, doing nothing but breathing, holding tight to the rail with his free hand.

4. *You pop out the wormhole and find yourself inside a clear thick gel. This universe is a thick transparent goo that goes on forever.*

Fire your engines, and you can move.

But barely, and your hull creaks and groans, and the instant you stop your engines, your ship comes to an abrupt halt.

Now a monster swims out of the gelatin. It dwarfs the largest whale, and it's covered with tree-sized hairs that beat like oars, carrying it straight at you.

What do you do?

No, that weapon won't work here.

And that one won't kill it.

Just pisses it off, in fact.

So what now?

You can run, but the monster is faster. It's ready to eat you and your ship. Whole. And you've got four seconds to think this through and tell me: Where are you?

Now three seconds.

And two.

And one.

"Mr. Cross," John blurts. "There's something new here!"

Houston fights the temptation to look for himself. Instead, he sits back and watches the boy twist at the knobs, his jaw dropping an instant before he leaps back. Dramatic, overdone. "God, it's huge!"

"Draw it," Houston coaches.

"Okay, I'll try!"

The boys and mentor have set up an aquarium at the back of the classroom—

five gallons of tapwater with its chlorine removed, then sweetened with straw and oxygenated with a simple airstone. Over the past five days, using Troy's donated microscope, they've watched the microbal community explode and evolve, bacteria followed by hungry parameciums—the "monsters" of the gel universe—and now the parameciums are serving as fodder for an even larger, more wondrous monster.

"It's got wheels," John reports.

"Where?"

"On this end." John commands the circles in his drawing to spin, giving his creation a liveliness. "They go around and around, then stop. And then they go again."

"How big is it?"

"Huge," the boy declares. Then he peers into the eyepiece with his right eye—none of the boys can resist pinching his left closed—and suddenly, with a quieter, more honest astonishment, he says, "Jesus, it ate one!"

"One what?"

"One of the parameciums. I saw it!"

Houston picks up the workpad, trying to remember when he first saw a rotifer swimming across a glass slide.

"You should look at it, Mr. Cross. Look!"

Anticipation makes the mouth dry. He bends over the microscope, the fine adjustment knob spinning easily between finger and thumb. As promised, the rotifer seems vast. And as if answering his wish, he watches while one of the football-shaped protozoa is caught in that intricate mouth, spinning hairs pulling the transparent carcass inside a transparent body.

Water eating water.

When you got down to it, that's what it's all about.

The woman teaches science at a different school. Their relationship is three years old, and it is convenient, and it has mostly run its course. They see each other infrequently. But as it happens, she's at Houston's apartment on that weekend evening when the television interrupts them, saying, "Breaking news."

"Not now," he tells it.

But the machine obeys its rigorous instructions. "Important, breaking news."

"Maybe the President's been shot," says the woman. Then she sits up and says, "Anyway, I probably need to get home." She pulls a heavy sweater over her head, speaking through the frizzy red wool. "I want to see this news first."

"Show us," says Houston.

"—the gunman apparently turned the weapon on himself, committing suicide. At least 14 students died, while nine more are hospitalized, six in critical condition—"

"Where is this?" Houston asks.

"Australian Independent—"

"From the beginning. Now."

Schools always look like schools. Houston stares at a glass and brick building as the narrator reports, "Today, an unidentified male walked into the Riverview School for the Gifted, shouted inflammatory phrases, then produced a pair of handguns, killing more than a dozen boys in their early teens—"

"Shit," says the woman.

Houston is silent.

"All of the deceased, and all but two of the injured, are clones of Phillip Stevens. At this point, it's assumed that the murderer was singling them out. . . ."

On screen, grim-faced paramedics are carrying dark sacks. Some of the sacks seem heavy, while others are less so.

The woman sits next to Houston, exhaling hard.

She says, "Shit," quietly. Then with a different voice, "Have you seen my rings?"

"On the kitchen counter." She always leaves her diamond and wedding band on the counter.

But she doesn't move. Instead, she places a damp hand on Houston's bare knee, telling him, "This sounds horrible. But I'm surprised that it's taken this long for this sort of tragedy to happen. You know?"

He doesn't speak.

His lover gives him a few seconds, then asks, "What are you thinking?"

He stares at those rubber sacks set in a ragged row, and he thinks that it's odd. As they are now, robbed of their faces and souls, those boys have never looked more alike.

"We'll have new security measures naturally." Ms. Lindstrum whispers, trying to keep her words private. It's a week after the Riverview Massacre, but there have already been three more attacks In France. In White Russia. And two PS's dead in Boston. "Cameras in the hallway," she promises. "At least one armed guard stationed in the front office. And all of us who work directly with the boys . . . we'll naturally have to go through an extensive security check . . ."

"I've already been scrutinized," says Houston. "Six years ago."

"It's a formality," she assures.

He doesn't mention the obvious: Any determined person can kill these boys anywhere in time and space. No reasonable amount of security will protect them. And unreasonable security will just make their lives more constricted, and their murders more noteworthy.

Houston doesn't say one word, watching Troy working at the back of the room.

"You did speak with them?" Ms. Lindstrum inquires. "About what happened in Australia, I mean."

"That next day," he says.

"How were they?"

"John was shaken. 'Killing someone is always awful,' he told me." Houston closes his eyes, the voices and faces coming back to him. "Troy acted sad, and sorry. But I don't think he appreciates what happened. It's on the other end of the world, and I think his mother shields him from the news. So none of it's quite real."

"And Mike?"

"Pissed, more than anything."

"That's sounds like him," she chimes in.

But it wasn't a simple anger. The boy had made fists and drummed on the top of his desk, growling, "It won't happen to me."

"It won't, but why not?" Houston had asked.

"I'm not the same as the others. I look different." He nodded explaining with an amoral practicality, "If some asshole comes to school firing, he's going to shoot John first. Then Troy. And finally me. Except I'll have run away by then!"

Houston neglects to mention any of that conversation.

Misreading his grim expression, Ms. Lindstrum says, "I wouldn't worry. This is a good community, in its heart. Nothing tragic's going to happen here."

He just looks at her.

She starts to ask, "What are you thinking?"

But just then Troy spins in his chair, calling out, "Mr. Cross? I found a baby snail. Want to see?"

"Do I ever!" he blurts. "Do I ever!"

"It is an honor, Mr. Cross. Houston. May I call you Houston? And thanks for taking the trouble. I know this has to be an imposition."

"It isn't," Houston lies.

The school district's headquarters are set inside a sprawling single-story building designed on some now-defunct principle of efficiency and/or emotional warmth. The central area is one vast room. Working areas are divided by partial walls and overly green plastic foliage. The ventilation system produces a constant roar, not unlike the Brownian drumming of atoms against a starship's hull. Over that roar, the man in charge of security says, "I mean it. It's an honor to cross paths, sir. We have so much trouble finding good mentors, and keeping them. Which makes you something of a legend around here."

Houston gives a little nod. "What can I do for you?"

"Very little." The man looks and sounds like a retired police officer. A military cop, perhaps. Dragging a thick hand across the hairless scalp, he says, "You used to be . . . what's the term? . . . A professional student. At two universities. Is that right?"

"Yes."

He glances at his monitor. "Your resumé lists several impressive degrees."

"I have a trust fund," says Houston. "A little one. It gives me enough security for that kind of lifestyle."

"Good for you," says the cop. Without inflection.

Houston waits.

"Then you moved here and took up mentoring . . . six years ago. Correct?"

"Correct."

Again the hand is dragged across the scalp. "Now I couldn't help but notice. You didn't work with PS's until this year."

"I guess I didn't. No."

The cop sits motionless, clear eyes regarding Houston without suspicion.

"The boys were too young," Houston offers. "As a rule, I work with middle-schoolers."

"That's what I thought." He nudges the monitor just enough to let both of them skim over a life's history.

Houston read dates, places.

He says nothing.

"Of course there were two boys . . . older ones who skipped grades . . . and they were kicking around your current school before the others. . . ."

"True enough." Then with a flat, matter-of-fact voice, Houston points out, "I had other students then. Two girls and a boy. And I felt a certain loyalty to them."

"Good for you."

Silence.

The monitor is eased aside, glare hiding whatever it shows now. The clear eyes grow a little less so, and with a pained voice, the cop says, "I'm awfully sorry. I'm required to ask these questions, sir."

"Go on," says Houston.

"Are you a member of the Defenders of the Womb?"

"No."

"Do you know anyone who you suspect could be a member?"

"No."

"How about the Birth-Righters?"

"God, no."

"Like I said, I have to ask." He pauses, considering his next words. Or not. Perhaps this is a game that he's played too many times, and he has to remind himself what comes next. "Mr. Cross," he says. "I mean Houston. Have you read any of the anti-PS literature or watched the associated digitals?"

Houston sets his jaw, and waits.

"I'm sure you know what I mean, sir. There's some awful things being published. That crazy in Australia had stacks of the stuff. . . ."

"The Cuckoo's Boys," says Houston.

"Excuse me?"

"That book was in the crazy's stacks. As I recall."

"Perhaps. But honestly, it isn't on my list of dangerous works."

"Isn't it?" Houston leans forward, asking his interrogator, "Why not?"

"It isn't in the same category as those other works," he claims, "since it never advocates murder."

"No, it doesn't," Houston agrees.

"The boys are the blameless product of an evil man."

"Says Paul Kaan."

"Who used to work for Phillip Stevens. As I recall, they were colleagues and friends." The eyes lift and grow distant. "The moral thing to do is to give the PS's useful lives. But to protect our species, they have to be sterilized, too."

The ventilation's rumbling fades away.

"It sounds like you know the book," says Houston.

But the man won't be caught so easily. "I'm just repeating what I've seen on television, sir. That's all."

"But what if?" asks Houston. "What if Congress decides to pass laws and perform a simple clinical procedure on every boy? . . . "

"Well what, Mr. Cross?"

"What's your feeling about that?"

"My only concern, sir, is that there is no violence inside our schools."

Houston nods, sitting back again.

The cop glances down, then asks, "Do you own a firearm, sir?"

"No."

"Do you possess bomb-making materials?"

"Yes."

The eyes lift and grow large.

An angry laugh, then Houston explains, "I've got a well-stocked kitchen, and there's a filling station at the end of the block. So in theory, yes, I can make a substantial bomb. Anytime I want."

"That's not the best answer. Sir."

"Then no, I don't have bomb-making materials."

"Good. Thank you." The eyes dip again, and quietly, speaking as much to himself as Houston, he says, "This is what you do all day, isn't it, sir? These little mind games? . . . "

5. *You emerge from the wormhole, what you see is blackness. Perfect, endless blackness.*

But as your eyes adapt, you begin to make out a faint curtain of light in front of you. And behind you. And above. And below.

Now, what do you do? . . .

Mike starts to say, "Sensors," before catching his mistake.

He grimaces instead, then tells Houston, "I'll use my thermometer. I put it in the airlock. What does it read?"

"About two degrees."

"Kelvin?"

"Yes."

The boy stares at his starship's newest incarnation. It's still armored and bristling with weapons, but now bubble-like portholes line its sides, and the robotic crew has shrunk to human proportions.

"All right," says Mike. "I use my barometer. What does it say?"

"Nothing."

"It doesn't work?"

"No. It's reading nothing. Zero."

"Pure vacuum." He nods, muttering, "I'm out in space somewhere."

Houston waits.

"Okay. I shoot my antimatter cannon. What happens?"

"Eventually, the shell strikes the curtain of light, and its surface gets bright for as long as it's passing through. But the curtain's very thin, and most of the shell's mass continues on its merry way."

"I get it. There's not much stuff there, is there?" He nods again, then says, "Okay. I follow it."

"Okay."

"And I reach the curtain?"

"Eventually."

"Can I get through?"

"Eventually."

"What's 'eventually' mean?"

"A few million years, give or take."

"But my throttle's all the way open!" The boy leans back, licking his lips. "In a vacuum, I'd be going nearly light speed!"

Houston says, "Agreed."

"Okay. I stop inside the curtain. What happens?"

"It swirls around you. Like a slow, slow fog."

"I take a sample."

"How?"

Frustration builds, then collapses into resignation. "Okay. I put a jelly jar in the airlock, then open the outer door, and some of the fog drifts into the jar. All right?"

"Fine."

"I screw down the lid and bring the sample to the lab."

Houston says nothing.

"And I put everything in my best microscope. What do I see?"

"Lights. Tiny, bright-colored points of light."

The boys licks his lips, eyes narrowed, one hand absently sweeping the hair out of his baffled eyes.

"Most of the lights are dim and red," Houston adds. "Others are yellow. And the brightest few are blue."

"What about—?"

Houston shouts, "Wow!"

The boy halfway jumps. "What happened?"

"A big flash of light!"

"Outside somewhere?"

"No. From the jar."

"How big?" He shakes his head, asking, "Is there damage?"

"You're blind now."

"Okay. I pop in new eyes. Now what do I see?"

"One of those tiny blue lights has vanished. That's the only change."

Mike rises to his feet. Trying to concentrate, he steps up to the window, staring at the falling snow as one hand, then the other, plays with his shaggy hair.

Several minutes later, he screams, "Jesus!"

He smiles and says to the snow, "You made me *huge*. Didn't you?"

6. *Jungle. And a Blue, Blue Sea.*

Swimming in the warm water are fish not too different from our fish, and creatures that resemble porpoises, and something with a round body and paddles and a tiny head stuck on the end of a long, long neck—

. . .

"A plesiosaur," John blurts.

"Exactly." A pause, then Houston adds, "Up in the sky, as close as the Moon now, is a comet. In a few hours, it's going to hit exactly where you are now. It's going to vaporize the water and the limestone below, then set fire to North America, and the world."

John winces. Then in a self-conscious way, giggles.

"What do you want to do, John?"

"I want to watch the plesiosaur. I've always liked them."

Houston knows that. Last night, his AI found a new documentary on Danish TV, and for the next 30 minutes, he plays the subtitled digital on the classroom screen. Then comes lunch. The new semester has a break in the middle of the period. The mentor is expected to fend for himself. And naturally, he doesn't get paid for time not spent teaching.

When John returns, Houston outlines the situation again.

But this time he closes by saying, "In a very few hours, your plesiosaur, and almost everything else on Earth, is going to be dead."

John winces. No giggles.

"Fly up to the comet," Houston suggests, "If you want."

"I guess."

"The coma is beautiful. And the tail extends for millions of miles." He shows him photographs of last year's big comet. "Inside the coma you find a black ball of tar and buried snows. It's barely 10 miles across. If you want, you can stop it now."

"I can?"

"You've got weapons," Houston points out. "What would you use if you wanted to move a mountain-sized snowball?"

"My engines. They'd melt anything."

"Do you want to use them?"

"I don't get it, Mr. Cross. What are you asking?"

"Why would you stop the comet? And why wouldn't you?"

"Well," says the boy. Then he licks the tentative hairs over his upper lip, and breathes deeply, and says, "If dinosaurs go on living, then maybe mammals wouldn't get their chance. Which would be bad for us. For human beings."

Houston leans forward, saying, "You're going to let the comet hit. Aren't you?"

The boy doesn't answer, eyes tracking from side to side.

"Would you like to see the comet's impact?" Houston offers. "I found a real good Japanese simulation. It's accurate and it's spectacular, too."

John shakes his head.

"No, thank you," he says. "But Mike would like it, I bet."

"He loved it," Houston confides.

The boy makes fists and drums softly on his desk.

"What about the comet, John? Are you going to leave it alone?"

"No," the boy squeaks.

Houston tries to hide his surprise. Then after a few deep breaths, he asks, "Why?" with a quiet voice. "If it means there'll never be humans—"

"Good," says the boy.

Once. Softly. But with a hardwon conviction.

7. *You've decided to become a cat farmer.*

No, seriously. I mean it.

You can make a lot of money selling cat skins. And since you're left with carcasses after you skin them, you start feeding that meat to the new kittens. Who grow up into your next harvest of cats. Which you feed to the next litters of kittens. And so on. And so on. Cats all the way . . .

Now, what's wrong with that plan?

Troy says, "Nothing," without hesitation. He thinks this is gross and clever.

"But," Houston warns, "you're losing energy at every stage. A cat burns calories to keep itself warm, and it's got a short gut that doesn't digest everything that it eats. That's why your dog chews on your cat's turds. They're full of energy."

"Ugh." Giggles.

The others understood the problem almost immediately. "Try it this way," says Houston. "How much meat would you have to eat every day? In order to eat enough, I mean."

"Ten pounds," the boy guesses.

"Forty quarter-pound hamburgers. Really?"

"Maybe not." Troy shakes his head, licks his lips. "How about two pounds?"

"Fine." Houston nods. "On the first day of school, you'll go to the cafeteria and eat your daily ration. Two pounds of grilled seventh-grader."

"You mean like Mike?"

"Exactly."

"Neat!"

"And you'll do that for a full year. Two pounds worth of seventh-graders every day. Which is more than seven hundred pounds in all."

"Mike's not that big. Not yet."

Both of them laugh. Hard. Then Houston says, "Remember. A body is bone and gruesome crap that you'd never eat. Maybe half of the carcass won't get on your plate. So how many seventh-graders are you going to need?"

Troy hammers out a reasonable estimate. "Ten."

"How many eighth-graders are in your class?"

"I don't know. Three hundred?"

"So we need three thousand seventh-graders. And you can't just lock them in a room and pull one out whenever you're hungry. They need their food, too."

"Sixth-graders!"

"How many?"

"I don't know . . . God, thirty thousand! . . . "

"Right." Houston leans forward, and smiles. "But remember, Troy. Teachers can be awfully hungry people, too."

The boy's face grows a little pale.

"Three hundred eighth-graders feed how many teachers?"

"Thirty." He sickens, but just for a moment. Then the eyes quicken, and for that instant, in his face and eyes, Troy is indistinguishable from the other PS's.

"There's three principals. Right?"

"I guess there would be. Yes." Houston sits back in his chair, then asks, "Who's left standing? At the end of the year, I mean."

Troy sees it instantly.

"Only the principals. Right?"

"Right."

Then he's laughing too hard to breathe, and he gasps, and he admits to Houston, "I'm not going to tell Mom about this lesson. No, I'm not!"

8. *You give birth to a child who isn't yours. Genetically speaking.*

Phillip Stevens hijacks your reproductive system and forces you into having his clone, just as he did with millions of blameless women. Yet you feel blamed. And of course you're bitter. It's only reasonable to play the role of the victim here.

It's only human to want revenge.

But it's also human to be better than that. To forgive, or at least to forget. To accept and hold and cherish this gift . . .

. . . a better son, frankly, than anything you would have spawned on your own . . .

Saturday morning, and Houston shops for next week's groceries.

He spots the boy at the end of a long aisle, and for a half-instant, he isn't sure. It could be another PS, or even just a boy who happens to resemble them. But something about the don't-give-an-inch stance and the habitual pushing of hair out of the eyes tells him that it's Mike. Which means that the tiny woman next to him, lowering a blood-colored roast into the cart, must be his mother.

Two aisles later, paths cross.

The boy calls him, "Houston." Then he does a thumb-pointing gesture, telling Mom, "This is the guy."

She's holding a box of tampons. Without blinking, she throws them into the cart, then offers a tiny hand. "The famous Mr. Cross. Finally. Believe it or not, I've been meaning to get in touch."

"It's a pleasure," he replies.

"Groceries?" she inquires, gesturing at his cart.

"They are," he admits.

"What do you think of these prices?"

"They're high," Houston volunteers.

"Ridiculous," she grouses. Then just as the conversation seems doomed to canned chatter, Mom tells him, "You know, my boy hates you."

"Pardon?"

"You drive him nuts. Goofy nuts. I mean, he knows that he's smarter than his brother and sister. And his parents, of course, are perfect *idiots* —"

"Shut up," Mike growls. "You old lady."

Mom has a good laugh, then continues. "Anyway, Mr. Cross. Thank you. You've been getting under his skin. Which is the best thing for him, I think."

Mike says, "Jesus," and stomps in a circle.

His mother takes a step toward Houston, smiling up at him, and with a conspirator's urgent voice, says, "Humble him. Please."

"I try," Houston confesses.

"Fucking Jesus!" Mike moans, squirming in every sense.

Mom turns and glares at her son, her mouth ready to reprimand. Or encourage. Houston can't guess which. But instead of speaking, she looks back at Houston and gives him an odd little smile.

Again, he says, "It's been a pleasure."

Then he takes his cart and his expensive groceries and moves on.

The field trip is the result of a lot of pleading and a slippery set of excuses. At first, John says, "You've got to eat lunch. Eat it at my house. It's just a short walk from school." But when Houston firmly refuses, the boy adds, "I've got books you'd like to see. Old ones. About science and stuff."

"What books?"

Their titles escape him. But they're about dinosaurs and flying saucers, and John adds, "I can't bring them here. They're practically antiques, and something might happen!"

Last week, there was a fight at school. Houston didn't see it, but Ms. Lindstrum reported that John was showing his starship to one of his few friends, and another boy stole his workpad. John couldn't stop himself from throwing the first punch. His only punch, it seems. He still sports an ugly maroon bruise beside his left eye.

"Mr. Cross," he pleads. "Please come over?"

The boy is sick with loneliness. But Houston has to tell him, "We need a better reason. If we're going to get permission, we'll need something special that ties directly to our work here."

The next day, John bursts into the room. "Okay. How's this? We've got a huge stump in our back yard. Hundreds of tree rings showing. Maybe we could do some sort of study, counting back in time and looking at the weather. That kind of stuff."

"Good enough," Houston tells him.

But the Facilitator has doubts. "It's not up to me anymore," Ms. Lindstrum explains. "If it involves PS's, we'll need permission from the superintendent's office."

Houston nods, then says, "The boy really wants this."

"Can you blame him?"

Houston didn't know that he was.

She promises to make the request. And for the next full week, John's first question every day is, "When are we going?"

"Never," seems like a possible answer.

But suddenly the faceless powers grant their blessing. Appropriate disclaimers are filled out. A parental signature is produced. And like explorers bound for some great adventure, the two of them pack up their equipment and make the four-block trek to an anonymous split level on a quiet side street.

All the way there, John is giddy with excitement.

Effusive to a sickening pitch.

Five years old, at the most.

He tells silly jokes about farts and singing frogs. He boasts that he'll be a great scientist before he's 30. With an overdone clumsiness, he trips on a crack in the sidewalk and drops in a slow-motion tumble into his own front yard. Then he suddenly grows quiet and thoughtful, saying, "By the way. Mom's boyfriend is gone. Moved out gone, I mean."

The trap is revealed.

Entering the front door, John cries out, "We're here!"

Mom can't look any less prepared for company. Bare feet. Jeans worn white against the chunky ass. A sweatshirt of some unearthly green. Physically, she bears no resemblance to her son. Chinese and European. Pretty in a fucked-over way. Sleepy, teary eyes regard this onslaught with a genuine horror. "Oh," she finally exclaims. "That's today, isn't it?"

The boy drops his workpad on the floor. "Mom!"

But the woman recovers. "Just a minute! Be right there!" She gallops out of sight, and from the back of the house screams, "Food's in the fridge, hun!"

"She forgets things," says John, shaking from anger.

"Don't worry about it," Houston tells him. His voice is angry, too. But the inflection goes unnoticed.

Lunch is egg-salad sandwiches with off-brand pop to wash them down.

Mom returns during an Oreo dessert. Her clothes have improved—newer jeans and aerobics shoes—and she's washed her face and combed her hair. But obviously, she'd rather be anywhere else. With anyone else. A condition that gives the adults common ground.

"I'm glad to meet you," she tells Houston.

"And I'm glad to meet you," he echoes.

They chat. It's polite, rigorously simple chatter. How long has Houston been a mentor? How long have they lived here? What about this warm weather? How was the sandwich, and does anyone want any more cookies?

Adults know how to be polite.

They can converse for hours, revealing nothing about their true selves.

Yet John is visibly thrilled by their prattle. He grins more and more. Mom finally asks, "Aren't you supposed to be doing a project?" And he tells her, "There's still time," without glancing at the clock.

Eventually, the kitchen grows silent.

Houston turns to the boy and says, "Maybe we should get busy. You think?"

"Oh, sure. Why not?"

They have only a few minutes to invest in the promised tree stump. Which is ample, since it's too old and weathered to teach much more than the fact that wood rots. Standing over that brown mass of fungus and carpenter ants, John looks at him expectantly and says, "Well?"

Houston imagines a dozen responses, and John's black disappointment. So he says simply, "Interesting," without defining what it is that interests him.

John hears what he wants, and for the next week, pesters Houston shamelessly.

He says, "I'm worried about my mother. She's too lonely."

He says, "You know, there's a new restaurant up on Acer. I'd take Mom, but I don't have the money."

In a pleading tone, he confesses, "You're my best friend in the world, Mr. Cross. I mean that!"

Then, the pestering stops.

And Houston discovers that he misses the boy's clumsy match making. He misses it but doesn't say so, knowing better than to trust his own weakness. Then one day the boy arrives with a purple bruise matching the last one, and Houston asks, "Did you fight that same jerk? I hope not."

"I didn't," John mutters.

Then he looks past Houston, a cold glare matching the accusing voice. "The boyfriend's back. Again."

"I know this seems impolite. I got your address from one of last year's parents—"

"Come in, Mrs. Holdenmeister."

"You've probably got plans for tonight."

"Not really." He offers her the sofa, then sits opposite her. Looking at those hard blue eyes, he secretly thinks, "You're one scary bitch."

"What can I do for you?" he inquires.

"About Troy," she mutters. Pale hands turn to fists. "About that grade—"

"The B+?"

"You're his mentor. You know how much he adores science."

"Absolutely."

"I just don't think . . . after he earned A's last semester . . ."

"We had a big project this quarter. He had to do his own research and write a paper about what he learned—"

"Didn't he?"

"No, actually." He says it flat out, then sits back and asks, "Did you come here by yourself, Mrs. Holdenmeister?"

She starts to ask, "Why?" Then she shakes her head, admitting, "My husband's in the car. Waiting." With an indiscriminate rage, she admits, "He doesn't think that I should be going to this much trouble—"

"He's right."

She hesitates. Then after measuring him with those deadly eyes she says, "I saw Troy's paper. I saw it, and it was very good."

"Because you helped him write it."

She flusters easily, nothing about it genuine. "I don't think that's true! . . . "

"I asked him. And your son has a wicked streak of honesty."

She hesitates again, not sure what to say.

"It's a quarterly grade," he reminds her, "and it's a B+. Which is very respectable, Mrs. Holdenmeister."

"Even still," she snaps, "it's on his permanent record."

"Fuck his record. Ma'am."

She swallows. Goes limp.

"We both know, he's not like the others. He doesn't function as well in science.

And he won't be anyone's valedictorian." Houston says it, then takes a long deep breath. Then, "Which aren't crimes. And in some ways, those are probably blessings."

"I . . . I don't know what to say here. . . ."

"Let him do his own work. I'll give him a nice little A at the end of the year, and it won't mean shit in ten years. Or two, for that matter."

Fists pull close to her belly. "You've got an ugly, awful attitude, Mr. Cross."

"Guilty as charged."

She mistakes his indifference for weakness. "I plan to complain. To the superintendent himself. A person like you shouldn't be working with impressionable young minds."

That's when Houston's rage takes hold of him.

Suddenly his mouth take charge, asking, "What exactly did you do to your son? To make him this way, I mean."

She goes pale, except for the blazing eyes.

"Watching you . . ." he sputters. "Seeing all this damned guilt masquerading as love . . . I have to wonder if maybe, once you saw that PS baby . . . maybe you put a pillow over him and gave him a few good shoves before you got too scared to finish the job! . . ."

"Shut up!" she screams.

And rises.

Then with a tight, furious voice, she whispers, "I had *a drinking problem*. While I was pregnant. You son-of-a-bitch."

He says nothing.

Feels nothing, he believes.

For an instant, she shivers hard enough to lose her balance. Then she puts her hand against the wall, and says, again, "You're a horrible man."

"Tell me what I don't know."

She tries to murder him with her eyes.

It nearly works, it seems. But Houston makes himself stand, facing her, telling her simply, "You'd better go, Mrs. Holdenmeister. Now."

9. *I want you to invent a world, a universe, for the other boys.*

I'll send them there. In their starships, they'll explore and decipher the mysteries that you leave for them. And maybe they'll escape in the end, and maybe they won't. Which means, in other words, if you want to make a dangerous place, you can do that.

You've got my blessing.

Just as they have the same blessing, and that's all the fair warning I'm going to give you . . . okay? . . .

"Is it John's world, or Troy's?"

"Does that matter?"

"No," says Mike. Then, "Yes." He licks his lips, drums his fists, then tells Houston, "I bet it's Troy's."

"Why?"

"Because it's neat. You know. Not sloppy."

A map of the world covers the long screen. It has two blue seas and a brilliant dash of icecap, and its single continent is yellow except where it's brown. It is not sloppy because it's authentic. The image comes with NASA's compliments, and what Mike sees has been fitted together from a thousand fuzzy, partial images gathered by orbiting telescopes. The physical and chemical data are equally authentic. But what waits on the world's surface belongs entirely to John.

"I'm not going to tell you who did this," Houston warns. "Just like I won't tell the others which world is yours."

"You'd better not," he growls.

"What are you going to do first, Mike? You've got a mission here."

"I'll fire my cannon. Ten times."

Houston says nothing.

"Well, can I?"

The mentor says, "If you want," and shakes his head sadly.

"Okay. I do it, and what happens?"

"The explosions melt the icecap, boil the oceans, then cause the crust to turn to magma."

"Neat!"

Houston says nothing.

"Is there anything left alive down there?"

"I don't know. You tell me."

The boy describes his flight into the hell. Crocus, the top robot, collects samples of atmosphere and liquid rock. Mentor and student agree that nothing lives there. Even if there had been a thriving biosphere, it was vaporized, leaving not so much as a fossil tooth to mark its glorious past and promise.

"Congratulations," says Houston, the word tipped in acid.

But Mike just shrugs and says, "That was easy." Then he's laughing, admitting, "I don't know why I was so worried."

Half an hour later, the bell rings.

Houston accompanies Mike to the door. The hallway is already jammed with scurrying bodies and sharp, overly loud voices. The boy, still proud of his carnage, grins and wades out into the current. A bigger, older boy drives an elbow into him. But it's barely felt. Mike reaches his locker and touches the lock, then slams it hard against the steel. And then John appears beside him, touching him on the arm, obviously asking him, "Which world did you get? Which world? Which world? Which?"

Houston can see their faces, can halfway read their lips.

He watches as Mike glances up at this older, fatter boy, and showing the most malicious grin, the boy says, "Two oceans. And some kind of yellow land."

John can't resist. He confesses, "That's mine!"

Mike says something like, "Was it?"

Then John asks a "What'd you think, what'd you do" sort of question.

And Mike tells him. With both hands, he creates the universal symbol of an explosion, and loud enough to be heard, he says, "Boom!"

There's no time to intercede.

Before Houston can force his way through the bystanders and into the fight, John has already slammed Mike's head into the lockers. At least three times. Maybe four. And Mike counters with a fist into the belly, leaving his attacker on his knees, gasping and pale and crying for every reason imaginable.

"It's just us for the next few days," Houston explains.

But Troy already knows the news. There's nothing bigger in a school than a bloody brawl. Unless of course it's when two PS's are doing the brawling.

Troy shakes his head, asking, "Why did they fight?"

Houston starts to offer the simple explanation, then hesitates. It occurs to him that he barely knows either boy, much less their real motivations, and thinking that he understands them is dangerous, and stupid, and very much a waste.

So instead, he admits, "I really don't know why they fought, or why they seem to hate each other so much."

"I know," the boy tells him.

Anticipation makes Houston lean forward. "Why, Troy?"

"They've got to," he assures.

"But why?"

With an endearing patience, the boy shakes his head, warning him, "You can't know it, Mr. Cross.

"You might want to. But you just don't belong."

10. *Again, your starship is tiny. Microscopic. Suspended within that vast ocean, living water swimming through the dead.*

But this time the monster isn't some marauding paramecium. This time what you see has a blunt head and a long ropy tail, and it isn't feeding. Instead it's moving with a singleness of purpose, passing you and your ship without the smallest regard.

In anger, or maybe out of simple curiosity, you fire your weapons at it.

The monster wriggles and dies.

And just like that, Phillip Stevens is never born. And you, all of you, instantly and forever cease to exist.

I'm not going to ask why.

It's easy enough to see the reason.

And I won't dwell on the paradoxes inherent in this mess.

No, what I want to ask is the hardest question of all: Is this world better off without Phillip and the PS's? Or is it worse off?

That's the only question worth asking.

And you can't give me any answer. Sixty years from now, maybe. But not today. Not here. You're smart but not that smart. And even in 60 years, I doubt if you'll look me in the eye—all the thousands and thousands of you—and to the man, you will say in one indivisible voice, "The world is better off," or, "It's worse."

The best questions are always that way. . . .

The Sun is plunging behind the Moon.

At its height, the eclipse will reach 80+ percent coverage. Which is a long way from a total eclipse, yes. But since it is a warm, cloudless day, and it's noon, the effect is dramatic. There comes a growing chill to the air. A sense of misplaced twilight. Houston twists his head and says, "Listen." But hundreds of students are scattered across the school's lawn, enjoying the cosmic event, and it's hard to hear anything but their endless roar. "Listen to the birds," he tells them.

Both boys nod in the same way, John saying, "I hear them. They're singing."

Troy points and cries out, "Look!"

Swallows have appeared, streaking back and forth.

Then a younger voice says, "Look under the trees."

Mike stands behind them. Smiling, but not. Horizontal cuts mark where his face struck the vent on his locker. And he seems taller than before. Houston noticed it yesterday—Mike's first day back from his suspension—but it's more obvious now. A growth spurt took him during his week-long suspension, adding a goodly fraction of an inch to his gangly frame.

"The way the light is," he says. Pointing.

John sits up. "Yeah, look! What's going on, Mr. Cross?"

Crescent-shaped splashes of light dapple a sidewalk and the shady grass. Houston stands, hands on hips. "I don't know," he lies. "What do you think? Guesses?"

"It's the eclipse," Troy volunteers.

"Duh," says Mike.

Houston reprimands him with a look. Then as he starts to ask his next question, he notices a group of kids staring at them. Talking among themselves. Eighth-graders. Every last one of them female.

Houston's boys are oblivious to the stares.

Mike drops to the ground. He sits as far as possible from John while still being part of their group. "It's got something to do with how the light bends," he volunteers. "It's like you can see the Sun in those little crescent things."

Troy says, "I bet so."

Then John says, "This would have been a full eclipse back in dinosaur times."

"Why?" asks Troy.

"The Moon was closer," Mike tells him.

"It covered more of the Sun back then," John adds.

Troy turns. "Is that right, Mr. Cross?"

He starts to nod, then notices one of the girls approaching them. The hesitation in her walk and the other girls' giggles implies this is a dare. Instead of speaking, Houston holds his breath, and all the boys grow silent, too. She's a tall, willowy creature with full breasts and a model's face. And in a voice that comes wrapped in a nervous, electric energy, she says, "Hi, you guys."

Then she turns, and sprints back to her friends.

"What the fuck was that?" Mike growls. "What the fuck?"

But Houston laughs out loud, saying, "That." Saying, "Is a woman enamored." Saying, "I know the look. And you just better get used to it, boys."

"At least I can see him now," she says. "Can you?"

"Barely," says the short man.

"I've never gotten a writer's autograph. Have you?"

"I'm not much of a reader."

"Neither am I," she confesses. Then she turns to Houston, asking him, "Have you ever read anything better than this?"

He glances at the woman. Then he looks up the long line, saying, "Yes."

She doesn't seem to notice. Holding her copy of *The Cuckoo's Boys* in both hands, she tells everyone in earshot, "It had to be said. What Dr. Kaan says here."

Houston manages to keep silent.

This is a Saturday afternoon. He drove two hundred miles to stand here. The author sits in the center of a long table, flanked by thousands of copies of his phenomenal bestseller. "The New Edition," reads the overhead banner. "New Chapters! Fresh, Innovative Proposals!!"

The short man asks, "Do you know what's in the new chapters?"

"I'm dying to find out," she confesses.

Houston waits. Then after a while, he says, "Tailored viruses."

"Excuse me?" says the woman.

"Kaan thinks we should create a virus that would target Phillip Stevens' genetics. It would destroy the clones' somatic cells. In other words, their sperm."

She says, "Good."

The line slips forward.

Houston finds himself breathing harder, fighting the urge to speak. A pretty young woman says, "Please, open your book. One copy, only. To the page you want signed. And please, don't ask for any personalized inscriptions."

The author wears a three-piece suit. He looks fit and hardy, and smug.

Houston avoids looking at the man's eyes.

The line moves.

With both hands, the woman in front of Houston opens her book.

The short man bends and mutters something to the author, getting nothing but a signature for his trouble.

The woman takes his place, gushing, "I'm so glad to meet you. Sir!"

Kaan smiles and signs his name, then looks past her.

Houston's legs are like concrete. Suddenly, he is aware of his pounding heart and a mouth suddenly gone dry. But he steps forward, and quietly says, "You know, I have a PS son," as he hands his opened book forward. "And I took your good advice."

The author's face rises, eyes huge and round.

"I cut off his nuts. Want to see 'em?" Houston asks, reaching into a pocket.

"Help!" the author squeals.

A pair of burly men appear, grabbing Houston and dragging him outside with the rough efficiency of professionals. Then after a quick body search, they place him in his car, and one man suggests. "You should go home, sir. Now."

"All right," Houston agrees.

They leave him, but then linger at the bookstore's front door.

Houston twists the rearview mirror, looking at his own face. Tanned and narrow, and in the brown eyes, tired. He thinks hard about everything until nothing else can be accomplished. Which takes about 30 seconds. And that's when he starts the engine and pulls out into traffic, feeling very light and free, and in the strangest ways, happy.

• • •

11. *You get an end-of-the-school-year field trip out of me.*

I always always take away students down to our little community's renowned natural history museum. Most have already been there. According to one boy, maybe five hundred times already. But never with me. Never benefitting from my particular slant on mammoths and trilobites and the rest of those failures that they've got on display down there.

Don't bring lunch money. We'll be eating at Wendy's or the Subway Barn, and I'm the one buying.

Don't bring your workpads or notebooks. You won't need them.

But if you would, please . . . remember to wear good shoes. Shoes you can walk in. And if it's at all cold outside, please, for god's sake, wear a damned coat! . . .

"It's been refused," says Ms. Lindstrum.

"Excuse me?"

"Your proposed field trip. I know the boys were looking forward to it. But what with the latest tragedy, people want to be cautious."

Which tragedy? Houston wonders. In Memphis, five PS's were found dead in a basement, each body savagely mutilated. In Nairobi, a mob killed three more. Or was it the UN's failure to condemn Singapore's new concentration camp that's masquerading as a special school.

"I'm sorry," she offers.

Over the school year, her office has shrunk. Paper files and stacks of forms have gathered, choking the available space into a stale few breaths and two uncomfortable people.

Again, she says, "I am sorry."

"It's all right." His eyes find hers. What worries him most is the way that she blinks now. Blinks and looks past him. "Is it because of that fight? Because John and Mike did fine during the eclipse, and since," he says. Then he tells her, "There won't be any incidents. I can absolutely guarantee it."

She sighs, then says, "No PS-only field trips are being authorized."

"So let me take along one or two of my old students. To beat that rule."

"No," she replies. Too urgently and with a wince cutting into the half-pretty face. Or maybe he's just being paranoid.

Houston offers a shrug of the shoulders. "Are you sure there's nothing we can do?"

"I'm certain," Ms. Lindstrum tells him. "But the four of you could throw a little party for those three periods. Safe in your classroom. In fact, I'll arrange for food and pop to be brought from the cafeteria."

"I guess that would work," Houston tells her. Then he puts on his best smile, saying, "Why don't we? A little celebratory party. Fine."

Maybe it is simple paranoia.

But a back-of-the-neck feeling has Houston peering over his shoulder. Every public place seems crowded with suspicious strangers, and his little apartment seems full of dark, secretive corners. He finds himself peeking through curtains, watching the empty parking lot below. Three times he runs diagnostic programs on his phone, searching for taps that refuse to be found. And when he finally manages to convince himself that nothing is wrong, except in his imagination, his old widescreen abruptly stops finding news about the PS's. Instead, it delivers highlights from a teaching conference in Nova Scotia. Which is a signal.

Prearranged, yet surprising.

Long ago, Houston taught the AI that if its security was breached, dump all of the old files and start chasing down a different flavor of news.

He doesn't fix the protocols now.

Instead, he pretends to watch the conferences that are being piped to him, and he runs new diagnostics on the apartment and every appliance.

That night before the school party, someone knocks.

His lover wears nice clothes and a smile, and she says, "Hello," too quickly. She says, "I hope I'm not catching you at a bad time."

She has always, always called before visiting. But not tonight.

Houston says, "No, it's a fine time. Come on in."

She says, "For a little bit. I'm expected back home."

He hasn't seen her for a month. But he doesn't mention it. He sits opposite her and says absolutely nothing, trying to read the pretty face and nervous body, and when she can't tolerate any more silence, she blurts, "Are you all right, Houston?"

"Perfect," he says.

She swallows, as if in pain.

"How about you?" he inquires.

"They know about us." She says it, then gathers herself before admitting, "They came to me. And asked about you."

"Who asked?"

She crosses her arms, then says, "They threatened to tell my husband."

Houston calls the woman's name, then asks, "Was it that bald security man? From district headquarters?"

"One of them was."

"Who else was there?"

She shakes her head. "He didn't give me a name."

"It's nothing," says Houston. And to an astonishing degree, he believes it. "I've had some trouble with one of the parents. I'm certain that she's filed a formal complaint. That's the culprit here."

His lover nods hopefully, staring at the floor.

He tells her, "Everyone's scared that something bad is going to happen here."

"I am," she allows.

"What did they ask?"

"About you," she mutters.

"What did you say?"

"That I know almost nothing about Houston Cross." Eyes lift, fixing squarely on him. "Which is true. All of a sudden, hearing myself say the words, I realized that you're practically a stranger to me."

He says nothing.

At this very late date, what can he say? . . .

. . .

Mentors are required to check in at the front office. Houston arrives a few minutes earlier than normal signing his name at the bottom of a long page and glancing sideways into Ms. Lindstrum's office, catching a glimpse of her grim face as her door swings shut, closed by someone whom he cannot see.

The school's uniformed guard sits nearby, pretending to ignore him.

Which is absolutely ordinary, Houston reminds himself.

The bell rings. Children pour into the hallway, a brink-of-summer fever infecting all of them. Houston beats the boys to the classroom, then waits in front of the door. For an instant, he fears that they're home sick, or Lindstrum has bottled them up. But no, John walks up grinning, Troy at his side. Then Mike is fighting through the bodies making for his locker . . . and Houston tells the others, "Stay with me," and he intercepts Mike, putting a hand on the bony shoulder, saying to all of them, "Change of plans."

This spring, the school installed a security camera at one end of the hallway.

In the opposite direction, the hallway ends with lockers and a fire door. With the boys following after him, Houston hits the bar, causing the alarm to sound—a grating roar that causes a thousand giddy youngsters to run in circles and laugh wildly.

"Hey!" says Mike. "You did that!"

"No," says Houston. "It's a planned fire drill. Trust me."

Then John asks, "Where are we going? On our field trip?"

"Exactly."

"I don't have any permission slip," Troy complains.

Houston turns and says, "I took care of all that. Hurry. Please."

They climb down a short set of metal stairs, then cut across the school yard. Behind them, mayhem rules. Screaming bodies burst from every door, harried teachers trying to regain some semblance of control. In the distance, sirens sound. As they reach the street, a pair of fire trucks rush past, charging toward the non-existent blaze. Various cars are parked along the curb. Trying to smile, Houston says, "Guess which one's mine."

John says, "That one," and points at a gaudy red sports car.

Houston has to ask, "Why?"

"It's a neat car," says the boy. "And you're a neat guy!"

Now he laughs. Despite everything, he suddenly feels giddy as the kids, and nearly happy. With keys in hand, he says, "Sorry. It's the next one."

A little thing. Drab, and brown. Utterly nondescript.

But as the boys climb inside, Mike notices, "It smells new in here."

"It's a rental," Houston admits. His old heap is parked out in front of the school, as usual. He stashed this one last night. "I thought we needed something special today."

"Are we still going to the museum?" Troy asks.

He and John share the backseat.

Houston says, "No, actually. I came up with a different destination."

Mike watches him. Suspicious now.

The boys in back punch each other, and giggle, and John says, "Maybe we could eat first. Mr. Cross?"

"Not yet," Houston tells them.

He drives carefully. Not too fast, or slow. Up to the main arterial, then he heads straight out of town, knowing that Mike will be the first to notice.

"Where?" asks the boy. Not angrily, but ready to be angry, if necessary.

"There's a few acres of native prairie. Not big, but interesting." Houston looks into every mirror, watching the cars behind them.

After a minute, Mike says, "I don't know about this."

"That's right," says Houston. "Be suspicious. Of everything."

The smallest boy shrugs his shoulders and looks straight ahead now.

Houston glances over his shoulder, telling John, "There's a package under you. In brown paper. Can you get that out for me, please?"

"This it?"

"Yeah. Can you open it up, please?"

The boy never hesitates. He tears away the paper, finding a pair of what look like hypodermic needles wrapped in sterile plastic. "What are these for, Mr. Cross?"

"Tear one of them open. Would you?"

"Just one?"

"Please."

It takes a few moments. The plastic is tough and designed not to be split by accident. While John works, Houston turns to Mike and says, "Be suspicious," again. "When I was your age, I was always suspicious. Suspicion is a real skill, and a blessing. If you use it right."

The boy nods, wearing a perplexed expression.

"Here it is, sir," says John, handing the hypodermic to him.

"Thank you."

"What is it?" asks Troy. "It looks medical."

"It is," Houston admits, removing the plastic cap with his teeth. "People made these things by the millions years ago. If you were poor and gave birth to a mixed race boy, you could test his blood. Like this." He doesn't let himself flinch, punching his own shoulder with the exposed needle. Then he shakes the device for a moment, and shows everyone the dull red glow. "Now unwrap another one. Yeah. And hand it to me."

John obeys.

In the same smooth motion, Houston jabs Mike in the shoulder. "Sorry," he offers, shaking the second device. Then he puts them together, and with a voice that can't help but break, he says, "Both showing red. See? And what do you think that means?"

12. *I used to be Phillip Stevens.*

He says the words, then sucks in a breath and holds it.

Not one boy makes the tiniest sound.

Finally, laughing uneasily, Houston asks, "What do you think about that? John? Troy? Mike?"

"I don't believe you," Mike growls.

"No?"

"That's a stupid shit thing to say." The boy's anger is raw and easy, bolstered by the beginnings of panic. He takes a gasping breath. Then another. Then he strikes his own thighs with both fists, telling Houston, "He died. The asshole offed himself. Everyone knows that."

Again, silence.

Houston glances at the mirror. The boys in back wear identical expressions. Lost, and desperately sad. Troy sees him watching then looks back over his shoulder, probably hoping to find help coming to rescue them.

But there isn't another car in sight.

"You two," says Houston. "What do you think?"

"It was Dr. Stevens' body," John offers. "That's what the police said."

"The police," Houston points out, "found a body with Phillip's physical features as well as his DNA. But a body isn't the man. And if anyone could have arranged for a bunch of dead meat and organs infused with his own DNA, wasn't it Phillip Stevens?"

"A full-grown clone?" says Mike.

"With a massive head wound. And what the press didn't report—except as wild rumor—were those occasional disparities between the corpse on the table and the fugitive's medical records."

"Like what?" Mike mutters.

"Like scars and stuff?" John asks.

"No, every scar matched. Exactly." Houston nods and pushed on the accelerator, telling them, "But those things would be easy enough to fake. The body was grown in a prototype womb-chamber. The brain was removed early, and intentionally. No pain, no thoughts. Phillip did that work himself. He broke the clone's big left toe, then let it heal. He gave the skin the right patterns of mole and old nicks and such. He even aged the flesh with doses of radiation. And he kept the soulless clone relatively fit through electrisometrics and other rehab tricks."

The only sound is the hum of tires on pavement.

Finally, Mike asks, "So what was wrong with that body?"

"Not enough callus: Not on its fingertips or the bottoms of its feet." Houston nods knowingly, looking across the blurring countryside, then straight ahead. "And even though the brain tissue was scrambled, the FBI found problems. Even with dehydration there wasn't enough brain present. And what they had in jars didn't have the dendritic interconnections as you'd expect in mature genius mind."

Again, Troy looks back the way they had come.

Houston turns right on a graveled road, and over the sudden rattling of loose rock, he tells them, "It's not far now."

Even Mike looks sad.

"The original Houston Cross was a loner. No family, and few prospects." Houston says it, then adds, "For a few dollars and a new face, that Houston acquired a new life. And he doesn't even suspect who it is that bought his old one."

John starts to sob loudly enough to be heard.

Mike turns and glares at him. "God, stop it. You baby!"

Over the crest of the hill is a small green sign announcing Natural Area. The tiny parking lot is empty. Which is typical for a weekday, Houston knows.

He pulls in and stops, turning off the engine and pocketing the key.

"All right," he says. "Out."

The boys remain in their seats.

Houston opens his door and stands in the sunshine. "Out," he tells them.

From the back, Troy squeaks, "Are you going to kill us? Mr. Cross?"

The words take him completely by surprise.

He shivers for a moment, then makes himself stop. And he looks in at all of them. And he tells them, "You can't begin to know how much that hurts."

13. *Why did Phillip Stevens create you?*

Any ideas?

Forget my little announcement. My name is Houston Cross, and I want you to explain to me why your father did what he did? Because I know you must have lain awake nights wondering just that. . . .

The four of them walk in single file through the big bluestem prairie, following a narrow path up a hill, both hill and path vanishing in the same step.

Houston stops for a moment, watching the horizon and the rolling windswept land, farm fields on all sides and this little patch of grass and wildflowers tucked into a spare 40 acres. The nearest intelligence is a soaring redtailed hawk. Other than the bird, no one notices them but them.

Again, he walks.

And he asks the boys, "Why did PS do it?"

"He was selfish," says John. Blurts John.

"Who told you that?" Houston responds. Then he makes himself laugh, adding, "That's right. Everyone says that he was horribly, wickedly selfish. Don't they?"

From behind, Troy asks, "Were you?"

"In a sense. Of course. Who isn't?"

At the base of the hill is a little stand of trees. Ash trees, mostly. With an enormous and stately cottonwood anchoring one end.

"But maybe there's a different answer. A harder, truer one."

"Like what?" asks Mike.

"All of you are Phillip's gift to the world." Houston slows his gait, making sure that everyone can hear. "The man had certain talents that can prosper in any time, and he decided to share those talents with his species. To enrich your generation with his genes, and when you have your own children, then enrich every generation to come."

Mike snorts, in disgust.

"What's the matter?" Houston asks. "Don't you approve?"

The boy just shakes his head, glowering at the ground.

For the last time, Troy looks over his shoulder. Then Houston places a hand on his shoulder, warning him, "Nobody knows where we are. For a little while, nobody's going to interrupt us. So don't worry. Okay?"

The eyes are wide and sorrowful, but Troy says nothing.

Then they move beneath the trees, out of the wind, their voices carrying and the mood instantly more intimate. More familiar.

Houston says, "There's a third possibility."

"What?" squeaks John.

"That Phillip Stevens remembered his childhood too well. He remembered his loneliness and how very separate he felt from the other kids. A bastard, interracial child without any father . . . and maybe all of his plotting and his selfish evil was simply to make certain that the next time around . . . that he wouldn't grow up so alone. . . ."

Now Houston cries.

Sobbing, practically.

Mike is unimpressed. He starts to turn away, announcing, "I don't want to do this shit any more. I'm going back to the car."

"Please don't," Houston pleads. "I want to show you something first. Something important."

Curiosity is the richest, sweetest drug.

One after another, the boys nod in identical fashions and follow, their mentor leading them under the giant cottonwood. Head-high on the trunk is a distinctive X-shaped scar, the thick bark chopped open with a heavy blade. With his back to the scar, Houston starts to count his steps from the trunk. At a dozen, he stops. Kneels. And while tugging at the shade-starved grasses, he tells them, "Always remember. Being smart only means that you make bigger, louder mistakes."

The boys stand as close together as they have ever been.

Watching him.

"With the PS bug," explains Houston, "I assumed that only a few thousand women inside a very limited region would catch it. That's all. A minimal plague and nobody would die . . . and when it was otherwise, believe me, there wasn't anyone more surprised than me."

For an instant, Houston wonders if maybe this is the wrong place. Or perhaps he's really Houston Cross, and he is simply delusional. A pure crazy man. But then one tuft of grass gives on the first tug, then lets itself be uprooted with a hard yank. Beneath it is a pipe with a false bottom. He reaches elbow-deep and touches the bottom, the Swiss-made lock recognizing his fingertips.

"I was shocked by the disease's scope," he confesses. "And horrified. And very sorry."

The packets of money are pushed up by a gentle gas-powered piston. Hundred dollar bills create a little wall in the grass, and every boy has to step closer and gawk, Mike saying, "God, that's a lot!"

"A few hundred thousand. That's all."

Troy says, "Shit," under his breath.

The others laugh, for just a moment.

"And this is twenty million dollars," Houston adds, showing them an e-card that couldn't be more nondescript. "Untraceable, in theory. Although I haven't used it in years."

"What else is there? . . . " one of them asks.

He isn't sure who. Bending low, reaching into the damp hole, he tells them, "This. This is what I wanted to show you."

Exactly the size of the piston beneath it, the disc is silvery and outdated by the latest technologies. But it's still readable, and probably will be for a few more years.

John asks, "What's that?"

"When I realized the scope of my plague," says Houston, "I made a nearly full list of the PS's. Birth dates and addresses and important government IDs. Everything that you would need to make contact with them. In this country, and everywhere else."

"But that's all old now," Mike points out.

"A lot of these boys have already died. You're right." He looks at them, one after another. Then he lets them watch as he shoves the cash back into its hiding place, leaving it unlocked, and fits the hat of sod and grass back into the pipe. "Others have moved. But if you're going to get in touch with them, you'll need to start somewhere."

None of the boys can manage a word, watching him.

Houston flips the disc toward John, then says, "If you need, come get this cash. But only as you need it."

Mike bends and picks up the disc, then asks, "What are we supposed to do? Mr. Whoever-You-Are? . . . "

"Dr. Stevens," Troy tells him.

"Organize your brothers. The sooner, the better." Houston stands and pockets the e-cash, then in the gravest voice he can summon, he tells them, "Things are going to get very bad, and probably before you're ready. But I know you. And I don't mean that you're just new incarnations of me. I know you as John and Mike and Troy. Together, you and the other boys are going to survive this mess that I selfishly made for you. . . ."

Then, he gasps for air.

John asks, "What about you? Can't you stay and help us?"

Mike says, "I don't want him here."

Houston agrees. "I think they already suspect that I'm not Houston Cross. If they find out everything, then things will just be worse for you. Which is why you can't tell a soul about me. Ever."

Only John nods with conviction.

"But I plan to help you," he adds. "Later, when I've settled down again, I'll feed you advice, somehow. And if you need it, more money . . ."

For a long moment, no one speaks.

Then finally, with a quiet sorry voice, Houston says, "Five minutes. Give me that much time. Then walk back to the main road and wait until someone comes looking for you."

He turns, taking his first tentative step toward the car.

"What'll you do now?" asks Mike.

Houston isn't sure. Maybe he should slip into another autographing . . . this time with a copy of *The Cuckoo's Boys*, its pages laced with botulin toxins . . .

"What you should do," Mike says, "is shoot yourself. For real this time!"

"Don't say that," John warns him.

"Why not?" the smallest boy replies. "He's just a big fuck-up."

Again, the grown man starts to cry.

Troy says, "I had fun this year, Dr. Stevens. I did!"

"Don't say awful things about our father!" John shouts.

"He's not my father, and I'll say what I goddamn want to!" Mike replies.

"Don't!"

"Oh, fuck you!"

With both hands and a hard deep grunt, John shoves Mike in the chest. The smaller boy stumbles and falls backward into the grass. Then for a moment, he does nothing. He just lays there, his face full of blood and a wild, careless anger. Then with his own grunt, he leaps up and runs, dropping his head as he slams into that big soft body, and both boys are throwing fists and cursing, then kicking each other, ribs bruised and lips bloodied before someone throws his body between them, screaming, "Now stop! Please, please, just grow up!"

For a slippery instant, Mike wishes that it's Houston. Phillip. Whoever that prick is. Just so he can give him a few good smacks now.

But no, it's just Troy. Poor stupid Troy is sobbing, and in his own way, he's furious. Then for some bizarre, twisted reason, Mike finds himself actually sorry that it wasn't the man who stops them. Wiping the gore out of his eyes, the boy looks across the prairie and sees no one. No one. Just the tall grass waving and the empty hillside, and the shit ran away again, and there's nobody else in the world but the three of them.

That's when it starts to sink home.

For all of them.

At long last.

14. *There's no one like you in the world.*

People like to say otherwise, but they don't understand. Only people like ourselves understand. Each of us is more different than we are the same, and if you think about it, that's our best hope.

Our only hope, maybe.

For now, that's all we can tell you. But watch your mail, and watch for signs. Someday, sooner than you think, we'll talk again. We'll make our plans then.

For anything and everything, we'll have to be ready.

Sincerely,

THE CUCKOO'S BOYS

The Halfway House at the Heart of Darkness

WILLIAM BROWNING SPENCER

William Browning Spencer was born in Washington, D.C., and now lives in Austin Texas. His first novel, Maybe I'll Call Anna, *was published in 1990 and won a New American Writing Award, and he has subsequently made quite a reputation for himself with quirky, eccentric, eclectic novels that dance on the borderlines between horror, fantasy, and black comedy, novels such as* Résumé with Monsters *and* Zod Wallop. *His short work has been collected in* The Return of Count Electric and Other Stories. *His most recent novel,* Irrational Fears, *was on the final ballot for the International Horror Guild Award, and he is at work on a new novel, a thriller entitled* The Never After. *His work has previously appeared in our Eleventh Annual Collection.*

In the fast-paced, free-wheeling, pyrotechnic story that follows, he shows us that there are as many ways to be saved as there are people to be saved . . . and that often the most unexpected way is the way that works the best.

Keel wore a ragged shirt with the holo *veed there, simmed that* shimmering on it. She wore it in and out of the virtual. If she was in an interactive virtual, the other players sometimes complained. Amid the dragons and elves and swords of fire, a bramble-haired girl, obviously spiking her virtual with drugs and refusing to tune her shirt to something suitably medieval, could be distracting.

"Fizz off," Keel would say, in response to all complaints.

Keel was difficult. Rich, self-destructive, beautiful, she was twenty years old and already a case study in virtual psychosis.

She had been rehabbed six times. She could have died that time on Makor when she went blank in the desert. She still bore the teeth marks of the land eels that were gnawing on her shoulder when they found her.

A close one. You can't revive the digested.

• • •

No one had to tell Keel that she was in rehab again. She was staring at a green ocean, huge white clouds overhead, white gulls filling the heated air with their cries.

They gave you these serenity mock-ups when they were bringing you around. They were fairly insipid and several shouts behind the technology. This particular V-run was embarrassing. The ocean wasn't continuous, probably a seven-minute repeat, and the sun's heat was patchy on her face.

The beach was empty. She was propped up in a lounge chair—no doubt her position back in the ward. With concentration, focusing on her spine, she could sense the actual contours of the bed, the satiny feel of the sensor pad.

It was work, this focusing, and she let it go. Always better to flow.

Far to her right, she spied a solitary figure. The figure was moving toward her.

It was, she knew, a wilson. She was familiar with the drill. Don't spook the patient. Approach her slowly after she is sedated and in a quiet setting.

The wilson was a fat man in a white suit (*neo-Victorian, dead silly*, Keel thought). He kept his panama hat from taking flight in the wind by clamping it onto his head with his right hand and leaning forward.

Keel recognized him. She even remembered his name, but then it was the kind of name you'd remember: Dr. Max Marx.

He had been her counselor, her wilson, the last time she'd crashed. Which meant she was in Addition Resources Limited, which was located just outside of New Vegas.

Dr. Marx looked up, waved, and came on again with new purpose.

A pool of sadness welled in her throat. There was nothing like help, and its pale sister hope, to fill Keel's soul with black water.

Fortunately, Dr. Max Marx wasn't one of the hearty ones. The hearty ones were the worst. Marx was, in fact, refreshingly gloomy, his thick black beard and eyebrows creating a doomed stoic's countenance.

"Yes," he said, in response to her criticism of the virtual, "this is a very miserable effect. You should see the sand crabs. They are laughable, like toys." He eased himself down on the sand next to her and took his hat off and fanned it in front of his face. "I apologize. It must be very painful, a connoisseur of the vee like you, to endure this."

Keel remembered that Dr. Marx spoke in a manner subject to interpretation. His words always held a potential for sarcasm.

"We are portable," Dr. Marx said, "we are in a mobile unit, and so, alas, we don't have the powerful stationary AdRes equipment at our command. Even so, we could do better, there are better mockups to be had, but we are not prospering these days. Financially, it has been a year of setbacks, and we have had to settle for some second-rate stuff."

"I'm not in a hospital?" Keel asked.

Marx shook his head. "No. No hospital."

Keel frowned. Marx, sensing her confusion, put his hat back on his head and studied her through narrowed eyes. "We are on the run, Keel Benning. You have not been following the news, being otherwise occupied, but companies like your beloved Virtvana have won a major legislative battle. They are now empowered to maintain their customer base aggressively. I believe the wording is 'protecting customer assets against invasive alienation by third-party services.' Virtvana can come and get you."

Keel blinked at Dr. Marx's dark countenance. "You can't seriously think someone would . . . what? . . . kidnap me?"

Dr. Marx shrugged. "Virtvana might. For the precedent. You're a good customer."

"Vee moguls are going to sweat the loss of one spike? That's crazy."

Dr. Marx sighed, stood up, whacked sand from his trousers with his hands. "You noticed then? That's good. Being able to recognize crazy, that is a good sign. It means there is hope for your own sanity."

Her days were spent at the edge of the second-rate ocean. She longed for something that would silence the Need. She would have settled for a primitive bird-in-flight simulation. Anything. Some corny sex-with-dolphins loop—or something abstract, the color red leaking into blue, enhanced with aural-D.

She would have given ten years of her life for a game of Apes and Angels, Virtvana's most popular package. Apes and Angels wasn't just another smooth metaphysical mix—it was the true religion to its fans. A gamer started out down in the muck on Libido Island, where the senses were indulged with perfect, shimmerless sims. Not bad, Libido Island, and some gamers stayed there a long, long time. But what put Apes and Angels above the best pleasure pops was this: A player could *evolve spiritually*. If you followed the Path, if you were steadfast, you became more compassionate, more aware, at one with the universe . . . all of which was accompanied by feelings of euphoria.

Keel would have settled for a legal rig. Apes and Angels was a chemically enhanced virtual, and the gear that true believers wore was stripped of most safeguards, tuned to a higher reality.

It was one of these hot pads that had landed Keel in Addiction Resources again.

"It's the street stuff that gets you in trouble," Keel said. "I've just got to stay clear of that."

"You said that last time," the wilson said. "You almost died, you know."

Keel felt suddenly hollowed, beaten. "Maybe I want to die," she said.

Dr. Marx shrugged. Several translucent seagulls appeared, hovered over him, and then winked out. "Bah," he muttered. "Bad therapy-v, bad, death-wishing clients, bad career choice. Who doesn't want to die? And who doesn't get that wish, sooner or later?"

One day, Dr. Marx said, "You are ready for swimming."

It was morning, full of a phony, golden light. The nights were black and dreamless, nothing, and the days that grew out of them were pale and untaxing. It was an intentionally bland virtual, its sameness designed for healing.

Keel was wearing a one-piece, white bathing suit. Her counselor wore bathing trunks, baggy with thick black vertical stripes; he looked particularly solemn, in an effort, no doubt, to counteract the farcical elements of rotund belly and sticklike legs.

Keel sighed. She knew better than to protest. This was necessary. She took her wilson's proffered hand, and they walked down to the water's edge. The sand changed from white to gray where the water rolled over it, and they stepped forward into the salt-smelling foam.

Her legs felt cold when the water enclosed them. The wetness was now more than virtual. As she leaned forward and kicked, her muscles, taut and frayed, howled.

She knew the machines were exercising her now. Somewhere her real body, emaciated from long neglect, was swimming in a six-foot aquarium whose heavy seas circulated to create a kind of liquid treadmill. Her lungs ached; her shoulders twisted into monstrous knots of pain.

In the evening, they would talk, sitting in their chairs and watching the ocean swallow the sun, the clouds turning orange, the sky occasionally spotting badly, some sort of pixel fatigue.

"If human beings are the universe's way of looking at itself," Dr. Marx said, "then virtual reality is the universe's way of *pretending* to look at itself."

"You wilsons are all so down on virtual reality," Keel said. "But maybe it is the natural evolution of perception. I mean, everything we see is a product of the equipment we see it with. Biological, mechanical, whatever."

Dr. Marx snorted. "Bah. The old 'everything-is-virtual' argument. I am ashamed of you, Keel Benning. Something more original, please. We wilsons are down on virtual addiction because everywhere we look we see dead philosophers. We see them and they don't look so good. We smell them, and they stink. That is our perception, our primitive reality."

The healing was slow, and the sameness, the boredom, was a hole to be filled with words. Keel talked, again, about the death of her parents and her brother. They had been over this ground the last time she'd been in treatment, but she was here again, and so it was said again.

"I'm rich because they are dead," she said.

It was true, of course, and Dr. Marx merely nodded, staring in front of him. Her father had been a wealthy man, and he and his young wife and Keel's brother, Calder, had died in a freak air-docking accident while vacationing at Keypond Terraforms. A "sole survivor" clause in her father's life insurance policy had left Keel a vast sum.

She had been eleven at the time—and would have died with her family had she not been sulking that day, refusing to leave the hotel suite.

She knew she was not responsible, of course. But it was not an event you wished to dwell on. You looked, naturally, for powerful distractions.

"It is a good excuse for your addiction," Dr. Marx said. "If you die, maybe God will say, 'I don't blame you.' Or maybe God will say, 'Get real. Life's hard.' I don't know. Addiction is in the present, not the past. It's the addiction itself that leads to more addictive behavior."

Keel had heard all this before. She barely heard it this time. The weariness of the evening was real, brought on by the day's physical exertions. She spoke in a kind of woozy, presleep fog, finding no power in her words, no emotional release.

Of more interest were her counselor's words. He spoke with rare candor, the result, perhaps, of their fugitive status, their isolation.

It was after a long silence that he said, "To tell you the truth, I'm thinking of getting out of the addiction treatment business. I'm sick of being on the losing side."

Keel felt a coldness in her then, which, later, she identified as fear.

He continued: "They are winning. Virtvana, MindSlide, Right to Flight. They've got the sex, the style, the flash. All we wilsons have is a sense of mission, this knowledge that people are dying, and the ones that don't die are being lost to lives of purpose.

"Maybe we're right—sure, we're right—but we can't sell it. In two, three days we'll come to our destination and you'll have to come into Big R and meet your fellow addicts. You won't be impressed. It's a henry-hovel in the Slash. It's not a terrific advertisement for Big R."

Keel felt strange, comforting her wilson. Nonetheless, she reached forward and touched his bare shoulder. "You want to help people. That is a good and noble impulse."

He looked up at her, a curious nakedness in his eyes. "Maybe that is hubris."

"Hubris?"

"Are you not familiar with the word? It means to try to steal the work of the gods."

Keel thought about that in the brief moment between the dimming of the seascape and the nothingness of night. She thought it would be a fine thing to do, to steal the work of the gods.

Dr. Marx checked the perimeter, the security net. All seemed to be in order. The air was heavy with moisture and the cloying odor of mint. This mint scent was the olfactory love song of an insectlike creature that flourished in the tropical belt. The creature looked like an unpleasant mix of spider and wasp. Knowing that the sweet scent came from it, Dr. Marx breathed shallowly and had to fight against an inclination to gag. Interesting, the way knowledge affected one. An odor, pleasant in itself, could induce nausea when its source was identified.

He was too weary to pursue the thought. He returned to the mobile unit, climbed in and locked the door behind him. He walked down the corridor, paused to peer into the room where Keel rested, sedated electrically.

He should not have spoken his doubts. He was weary, depressed, and it was true that he might very well abandon this crumbling profession. But he had no right to be so self-revealing to a client. As long as he was employed, it behooved him to conduct himself in a professional manner.

Keel's head rested quietly on the pillow. Behind her, on the green panels, her heart and lungs created cool, luminous graphics. Physically, she was restored. Emotionally, mentally, spiritually, she might be damaged beyond repair.

He turned away from the window and walked on down the corridor. He walked past his sleeping quarters to the control room. He undressed and lay down on the utilitarian flat and let the neuronet embrace him. He was aware, as always, of guilt and a hangdog sense of betrayal.

The virtual had come on the Highway two weeks ago. He'd already left Addiction Resources with Keel, traveling west into the wilderness of Pit Finitum, away from the treatment center and New Vegas.

Know the enemy. He'd sampled all the vees, played at lowest res with all the safeguards maxed, so that he could talk knowledgeably with his clients. But he'd never heard of this virtual—and it had a special fascination for him. It was called *Halfway House.*

A training vee, not a recreational one, it consisted of a series of step-motivated, instructional virtuals designed to teach the apprentice addictions counselor his trade.

So why this guilt attached to methodically running the course?

What guilt?

That guilt.

Okay. Well . . .

The answer was simple enough: Here all interventions came to a good end, all problems were resolved, all clients were healed.

So far he had intervened on a fourteen-year-old boy addicted to Clawhammer Comix, masterfully diagnosed a woman suffering from Leary's syndrome, and led an entire Group of mix-feeders through a nasty withdrawal episode.

He could tell himself he was learning valuable healing techniques.

Or he could tell himself that he was succumbing to the world that killed his clients, the hurt-free world where everything worked out for the best, good triumphed, bad withered and died, rewards came effortlessly—and if that was not enough, the volume could always be turned up.

He had reservations. Adjusting the neuronet, he thought, "I will be careful." It was what his clients always said.

Keel watched the insipid ocean, waited. Generally, Dr. Marx arrived soon after the darkness of sleep had fled.

He did not come at all. When the sun was high in the sky, she began to shout for him. That was useless, of course.

She ran into the ocean, but it was a low res ghost and only filled her with vee-panic. She stumbled back to the beach chair, tried to calm herself with a rational voice: *Someone will come.*

But would they? She was, according to her wilson, in the wilds of Pit Finitum, hundreds of miles to the west of New Vegas, traveling toward a halfway house hidden in some dirty corner of the mining warren known as the Slash.

Darkness came, and the programmed current took her into unconsciousness.

The second day was the same, although she sensed a physical weakness that emanated from Big R. Probably nutrients in one of the IV pockets had been depleted. *I'll die,* she thought. Night snuffed the thought.

A new dawn arrived without Dr. Marx. Was he dead? And if so, was he dead by accident or design? And if by design, whose? Perhaps he had killed himself; perhaps this whole business of Virtvana's persecution was a delusion.

Keel remembered the wilson's despair, felt a sudden conviction that Dr. Marx had fled Addiction Resources without that center's knowledge, a victim of the evangelism/paranoia psychosis that sometimes accompanied counselor burnout.

Keel had survived much in her twenty years. She had donned some deadly v-gear and made it back to Big R intact. True, she had been saved a couple of times, and she probably wasn't what anyone would call psychologically sound, but ... it would be an ugly irony if it was an addictions rehab, an unhinged wilson, that finally killed her.

Keel hated irony, and it was this disgust that pressed her into action.

She went looking for the plug. She began by focusing on her spine, the patches, the slightly off-body temp of the sensor pad. Had her v-universe been more engrossing, this would have been harder to do, but the ocean was deteriorating daily, the seagulls now no more than scissoring disruptions in the mottled sky.

On the third afternoon of her imposed solitude, she was able to sit upright in Big R. It required all her strength, the double-think of real Big-R motion while in the virtual. The effect in vee was to momentarily tilt the ocean and cause the sky to leak blue pixels into the sand.

Had her arms been locked, had her body been glove-secured, it would have been wasted effort, of course, but Keel's willing participation in her treatment, her daily exercise regimen, had allowed relaxed physical inhibitors. There had been no reason for Dr. Marx to anticipate Keel's attempting a Big-R disruption.

She certainly didn't want to.

The nausea and terror induced by contrary motion in Big R while simulating a virtual was considerable.

Keel relied on gravity, shifting, leaning to the right. The bed shifted to regain balance.

She screamed, twisted, hurled herself sideways into Big R.

And her world exploded. The ocean raced up the beach, a black tidal wave that screeched and rattled as though some monstrous mechanical beast were being demolished by giant pistons.

Black water engulfed her. She coughed and it filled her lungs. She flayed; her right fist slammed painfully against the side of the container, making it hum.

She clambered out of the exercise vat, placed conveniently next to the bed, stumbled, and sprawled on the floor in naked triumph.

"Hello Big R," she said, tasting blood on her lips.

Dr. Marx had let the system ease him back into Big R. The sessions room dimmed to glittering black, then the light returned. He was back in the bright control room. He removed the neuronet, swung his legs to the side of the flatbed, stretched. It had been a good session. He had learned something about distinguishing (behaviorially) the transitory feedback psychosis called frets from the organic v-disease, Viller's Pathway.

This Halfway House was proving to be a remarkable instructional tool. In retrospect, his fear of its virtual form had been pure superstition. He smiled at his own irrationality.

He would have slept that night in ignorance, but he decided to give the perimeter of his makeshift compound a last security check before retiring.

To that effect, he dressed and went outside.

In the flare of the compound lights, the jungle's purple vegetation looked particularly unpleasant, like the swollen limbs of long-drowned corpses. The usual skittering things made a racket. There was nothing in the area inclined to attack a man, but the planet's evolution hadn't stinted on biting and stinging vermin, and . . .

And one of the vermin was missing.

He had, as always, been frugal in his breathing, gathering into his lungs as little of the noxious atmosphere as possible. The cloying mint scent never failed to sicken him.

But the odor was gone.

It had been there earlier in the evening, and now it was gone. He stood in jungle night, in the glare of the compound lights, waiting for his brain to process this piece of information, but his brain told him only that the odor had been there and now it was gone.

Still, some knowledge of what this meant was leaking through, creating a roiling fear.

If you knew what to look for, you could find it. No vee was as detailed as nature.

You only had to find one seam, one faint oscillation in a rock, one incongruent shadow.

It was a first-rate sim, and it would have fooled him. But they had had to work fast, fabricating and downloading it, and no one had noted that a nasty alien-bug filled the Big-R air with its mating fragrance.

Dr. Marx knew he was still in the vee. That meant, of course, that he had not walked outside at all. He was still lying on the flat. And, thanks to his blessed paranoia, there was a button at the base of the flat, two inches from where his left hand naturally lay. Pushing it would disrupt all current and activate a hypodermic containing twenty cc's of hapotile-4. Hapotile-4 could get the attention of the deepest v-diver. The aftereffects were not pleasant, but, for many v-devotees, there wouldn't have been an "after" without hapotile.

Dr. Marx didn't hesitate. He strained for the Big R, traced the line of his arm, moved. It was there; he found it. Pressed.

Nothing.

Then, out of the jungle, a figure came.

Eight feet tall, carved from black steel, the vee soldier bowed at the waist. Then, standing erect, it spoke: "We deactivated your failsafe before you embarked, Doctor."

"Who are you?" He was not intimidated by this military mockup, the boom of its metal voice, the faint whine of its servos. It was a virtual puppet, of course. Its masters were the thing to fear.

"We are concerned citizens," the soldier said. "We have reason to believe that you are preventing a client of ours, a client-in-good-credit, from satisfying her constitutionally sanctioned appetites."

"Keel Benning came to us of her own free will. Ask her and she will tell you as much."

"We will ask her. And that is not what she will say. She will say, for all the world to hear, that her freedom was compromised by so-called caregivers."

"Leave her alone."

The soldier came closer. It looked up at the dark blanket of the sky. "Too late to leave anyone alone, Doctor. Everyone is in the path of progress. One day we will all live in the vee. It is the natural home of gods."

The sky began to glow as the black giant raised its gleaming arms.

"You act largely out of ignorance," the soldier said. "The god-seekers come, and you treat them like aberrations, like madmen burning with sickness. This is because you do not know the virtual yourself. Fearing it, you have confined and studied it. You have refused to taste it, to savor it."

The sky was glowing gold, and figures seemed to move in it, beautiful, winged humanforms.

Virtvana, Marx thought. *Ape and Angels.*

It was his last coherent thought before enlightenment.

"I give you a feast," the soldier roared. And all the denizens of heaven swarmed down, surrounding Dr. Marx with love and compassion and that absolute, impossible distillation of a hundred thousand insights that formed a single, tear-shaped truth: Euphoria.

Keel found she could stand. A couple of days of inaction hadn't entirely destroyed the work of all that exercise. Shakily, she navigated the small room. The room had the sanitized, hospital look she'd grown to know and loathe. If this room followed the general scheme, the shelves over the bed should contain . . . They did, and Keel donned one of the gray, disposable client suits.

She found Dr. Marx by the noise he was making, a kind of *huh, huh, huh* delivered in a monotonous chant and punctuated by an occasional *Ah!* The sounds, and the writhing, near-naked body that lay on the table emitting these sounds, suggested to Keel that her doctor, naughty man, might be auditing something sexual on the virtual.

But a closer look showed signs of v-overload epilepsy. Keel had seen it before and knew that one's first inclination, to shut down every incoming signal, was not the way to go. First you shut down any chemical enhances — and, if you happened to have a hospital handy (as she did), you slowed the system more with something like clemadine or hetlin — then, if you were truly fortunate and your spike was epping in a high-tech detox (again, she was so fortunate), you plugged in a regulator, spliced it and started running the signals through that, toning them down.

Keel got to it. As she moved, quickly, confidently, she had time to think that this was something she knew about (a consumer's knowledge, not a tech's, but still, her knowledge was extensive).

. . .

Dr. Marx had been freed from the virtual for approximately ten minutes (but was obviously not about to break the surface of Big R), when Keel heard the whine of the security alarm. The front door of the unit was being breached with an L-saw.

Keel scrambled to the corridor where she'd seen the habitat sweep. She swung the ungainly tool around, falling to one knee as she struggled to unbolt the barrel lock. *Fizzing pocky low-tech grubber.*

The barrel-locking casing clattered to the floor just as the door collapsed.

The man in the doorway held a weapon, which, in retrospect, made Keel feel a little better. Had he been weaponless, she would still have done what she did.

She swept him out the door. The sonic blast scattered him across the cleared area, a tumbling, bloody mass of rags and unraveling flesh, a thigh bone tumbling into smaller bits as it rolled under frayed vegetation.

She was standing in the doorway when an explosion rocked the unit and sent her crashing backward. She crawled down the corridor, still lugging the habitat gun, and fell into the doorway of a cluttered storage room. An alarm continued to shriek somewhere.

The mobile now lay on its side. She fired in front of her. The roof rippled and roared, looked like it might hold, and then flapped away like an unholy, howling v-demon, a vast silver blade that smoothly severed the leafy tops of the jungle's tallest sentinels. Keel plunged into the night, ran to the edge of the unit and peered out into the glare of the compound lights.

The man was crossing the clearing.

She crouched, and he turned, sensing motion. He was trained to fire reflexively but he was too late. The rolling sonic blast from Keel's habitat gun swept man and weapon and weapon's discharge into rolling motes that mixed with rock and sand and vegetation, a stew of organic and inorganic matter for the wind to stir.

Keel waited for others to come but none did.

Finally, she reentered the mobile to retrieve her wilson, dragging him (unconscious) into the scuffed arena of the compound.

Later that night, exhausted, she discovered the aircraft that had brought the two men. She hesitated, then decided to destroy it. It would do her no good; it was not a vehicle she could operate, and its continued existence might bring others.

The next morning, Keel's mood improved when she found a pair of boots that almost fit. They were a little tight but, she reasoned, that was probably better than a little loose. They had, according to Dr. Marx, a four-day trek ahead of them.

Dr. Marx was now conscious but fairly insufferable. He could talk about nothing but angels and the Light. A long, hard dose of Apes and Angels had filled him with fuzzy love and an uncomplicated metaphysics in which smiling angels fixed bad stuff and protected all good people (and, it went without saying, all people were good).

Keel had managed to dress Dr. Marx in a suit again, and this restored a professional appearance to the wilson. But, to Keel's dismay, Dr. Marx in virtual-withdrawal was a shameless whiner.

"Please," he would implore. "Please, I am in terrible terrible Neeeeeed."

He complained that the therapy-v was too weak, that he was sinking into a catatonic state. Later, he would stop entirely, *of course*, but now, please, something stronger . . .

No.

He told her she was heartless, cruel, sadistic, vengeful. She was taking revenge for her own treatment program, although, if she would just recall, he had been the soul of gentleness and solicitude.

"You can't be in virtual and make the journey," Keel said. "I need you to navigate. We will take breaks, but I'm afraid they will be brief. Say goodbye to your mobile."

She destroyed it with the habitat sweep, and they were on their way. It was a limping, difficult progress, for they took much with them: food, emergency camping and sleeping gear, a portable, two-feed v-rig, the virtual black box, and the security image grabs. And Dr. Marx was not a good traveler.

It took six days to get to the Slash, and then Dr. Marx said he wasn't sure just where the halfway house was.

"What?"

"I don't know. I'm disoriented."

"You'll never be a good v-addict," Keel said. "You can't lie."

"I'm not lying!" Dr. Marx snapped, goggle-eyed with feigned innocence.

Keel knew what was going on, of course. He wanted to give her the slip and find a v-hovel where he could swap good feelings with his old angel buddies. Keel knew.

"I'm not letting you out of my sight," she said.

The Slash was a squalid mining town with every vice a disenfranchised population could buy. It had meaner toys than New Vegas, and no semblance of law.

Keel couldn't just ask around for a treatment house. You could get hurt that way.

But luck was with her. She spied the symbol of a triangle inside a circle on the side of what looked like an abandoned office. She watched a man descend a flight of stairs directly beneath the painted triangle. She followed him.

"Where are we going?" Dr. Marx said. He was still a bundle of tics from angel-deprivation.

Keel didn't answer, just dragged him along. Inside, she saw the "Easy Does It" sign and knew everything was going to be okay.

An old man saw her and waved. Incredibly, he knew her, even knew her name. "Keel," he shouted. "I'm delighted to see you."

"It's a small world, Solly."

"It's that. But you get around some too. You cover some ground, you know. I figured ground might be covering you by now."

Keel laughed. "Yeah." She reached out and touched the old man's arm. "I'm looking for a house," she said.

In Group they couldn't get over it. Dr. Max Marx was a fizzing *client*. This amazed everyone, but two identical twins, Sere and Shona, were so dazed by this event that they insisted on dogging the wilson's every move. They'd flank him, peering up into his eyes, trying to fathom this mystery by an act of unrelenting scrutiny.

Brake Madders thought it was a narc thing and wanted to hurt Marx.

"No, he's one of us," Keel said.

And so, Keel thought, *am I.*

When Dr. Max Marx was an old man, one of his favorite occupations was to reminisce. One of his favorite topics was Keel Benning. He gave her credit for saving his life, not only in the jungles of Pit Finitum but during the rocky days that followed when he wanted to flee the halfway house and find, again, virtual nirvana.

She had recognized every denial system and thwarted it with logic. When logic was not enough, she had simply shared his sadness and pain and doubt.

"I've been there," she had said.

The young wilsons and addiction activists knew Keel Benning only as the woman who had fought Virtvana and MindSlip and the vast lobby of Right to Flight, the woman who had secured a resounding victory for addicts' rights and challenged the spurious thinking that suggested a drowning person was drowning by choice. She was a hero, but, like many heroes, she was not, to a newer generation, entirely real.

"I was preoccupied at the time," Dr. Marx would tell young listeners. "I kept making plans to slip out and find some Apes and Angels. You weren't hard pressed then—and you aren't now—to find some mind-flaming vee in the Slack. My thoughts would go that way a lot.

"So I didn't stop and think, 'Here's a woman who's been rehabbed six times; it's not likely she'll stop on the seventh. She's just endured some genuine nasty events, and she's probably feeling the need for some quality downtime.'

"What I saw was a woman who spent every waking moment working on her recovery. And when she wasn't doing mental, spiritual, or physical push-ups she was helping those around her, all us shaking, vision-hungry, fizz-headed needers.

"I didn't think, 'What the hell is this?' back then. But I thought it later. I thought it when I saw her graduate from medical school.

"When she went back and got a law degree, so she could fight the bastards who wouldn't let her practice addiction medicine properly, I thought it again. That time, I asked her. I asked her what had wrought the change."

Dr. Marx would wait as long as it took for someone to ask, "What did she say?"

"It unsettled me some," he would say, then wait again to be prompted.

They'd prompt.

" 'Helping people,' she'd said. She'd found it was a thing she could do, she had a gift for it. All those no-counts and dead-enders in a halfway house in the Slack. She found she could help them all."

Dr. Marx saw it then, and saw it every time after that, every time he'd seen her speaking on some monolith grid at some rally, some hearing, some whatever. Once he'd seen it, he saw it every time: that glint in her eye, the incorrigible, unsinkable addict.

"People," she had said. "What a rush."

The very pulse of the machine

MICHAEL SWANWICK

Michael Swanwick made his debut in 1980, and in the nineteen years that have followed has established himself as one of SF's most prolific and consistently excellent writers at short lengths, as well as one of the premier novelists of his generation.

He has several times been a finalist for the Nebula Award, as well as for the World Fantasy Award and for the John W. Campbell Award, and has won the Theodore Sturgeon Award and the Asimov's Readers Award poll. In 1991, his novel Stations of the Tide won him a Nebula Award as well, and in 1995 he won the World Fantasy Award for his story "Radio Waves." His other books include his first novel, In the Drift, which was published in 1985, a novella-length book Griffin's Egg, 1987's popular novel Vacuum Flowers, and a critically acclaimed fantasy novel The Iron Dragon's Daughter, which was a finalist for the World Fantasy Award and the Arthur C. Clarke Award (a rare distinction!). His most recent novel, Jack Faust, a sly reworking of the Faust legend that explores the unexpected impact of technology on society, has garnered rave reviews from nearly every source from The Washington Post to Interzone. His short fiction has been assembled in Gravity's Angels and in a collection of his collaborative short work with other writers, Slow Dancing Through Time. His most recent books are a collection of critical essays, The Postmodern Archipelago, and a new collection A Geography of Unknown Lands, and he's currently at work on a new novel. He's had stories in our Second, Third, Fourth, Sixth, Seventh, Tenth, Thirteenth, Fourteenth, and Fifteenth Annual Collections. Swanwick lives in Philadelphia with his wife, Marianne Porter, and their son, Sean, who willfully continues to be taller than either of them, although they frequently reproach him for it.

Here he takes us across the solar system to the tortured, molten, ever-changing surface of Io, for a close encounter of a unique and surprising kind. . . .

C*lick.*

The radio came on.

"Hell."

Martha kept her eyes forward, concentrated on walking. Jupiter to one shoulder, Daedalus's plume to the other. Nothing to it. Just trudge, drag, trudge, drag. Piece of cake.

"Oh."

She chinned the radio off.

Click.

"Hell. Oh. Kiv. El. Sen."

"Shut up, shut up, shut up!" Martha gave the rope an angry jerk, making the sledge carrying Burton's body jump and bounce on the sulfur hardpan. "You're dead, Burton. I've checked, there is a hole in your faceplate big enough to stick a fist through, and I really don't want to crack up. I'm in kind of a tight spot here and I can't afford it, okay? So be nice and just shut the fuck up."

"Not. Bur. Ton."

"Do it anyway."

She chinned the radio off again.

Jupiter loomed low on the western horizon, big and bright and beautiful and, after two weeks on Io, easy to ignore. To her left, Daedalus was spewing sulfur and sulfur dioxide in a fan two hundred kilometers high. The plume caught the chill light from an unseen sun and her visor rendered it a pale and lovely blue. Most spectacular view in the universe, and she was in no mood to enjoy it.

Click.

Before the voice could speak again, Martha said, "I am not going crazy, you're just the voice of my subconscious, I don't have the time to waste trying to figure out what unresolved psychological conflicts gave rise to all this, and I am *not* going to listen to anything you have to say."

Silence.

The moonrover had flipped over at least five times before crashing sideways against a boulder the size of the Sydney Opera House. Martha Kivelsen, timid groundling that she was, was strapped into her seat so tightly that when the universe stopped tumbling, she'd had a hard time unlatching the restraints. Juliet Burton, tall and athletic, so sure of her own luck and agility that she hadn't bothered, had been thrown into a strut.

The vent-blizzard of sulfur dioxide snow was blinding, though. It was only when Martha had finally crawled out from under its raging whiteness that she was able to look at the suited body she'd dragged free of the wreckage.

She immediately turned away.

Whatever knob or flange had punched the hole in Burton's helmet had been equally ruthless with her head.

Where a fraction of the vent-blizzard — "lateral plumes" the planetary geologists called them—had been deflected by the boulder, a bank of sulfur dioxide snow had built up. Automatically, without thinking, Martha scooped up double-handfuls and packed them into the helmet. Really, it was a nonsensical thing to do; in a vacuum, the body wasn't about to rot. On the other hand, it hid that face.

Then Martha did some serious thinking.

For all the fury of the blizzard, there was no turbulence. Because there was no atmosphere to have turbulence *in*. The sulfur dioxide gushed out straight from the sudden crack that had opened in the rock, falling to the surface miles away in strict obedience to the laws of ballistics. Most of what struck the boulder they'd crashed against would simply stick to it and the rest would be bounced down to the ground at its feet. So that—this was how she'd gotten out in the first place—it was possible to crawl *under* the near-horizontal spray and back to the ruins of the moonrover. If she went slowly, the helmet light and her sense of feel ought to be sufficient for a little judicious salvage.

Martha got down on her hands and knees. And as she did, just as quickly as the blizzard had begun—it stopped.

She stood, feeling strangely foolish.

Still, she couldn't rely on the blizzard staying quiescent. Better hurry, she admonished herself. It might be an intermittent.

Quickly, almost fearfully, picking through the rich litter of wreckage, Martha discovered that the mother tank they used to replenish their air-packs had ruptured. Terrific. That left her own pack, which was one-third empty, two fully charged backup packs, and Burton's, also one-third empty. It was a ghoulish thing to strip Burton's suit of her airpack, but it had to be done. Sorry, Julie. That gave her enough oxygen to last, let's see, almost forty hours.

Then she took a curved section of what had been the moonrover's hull and a coil of nylon rope, and with two pieces of scrap for makeshift hammer and punch, fashioned a sledge for Burton's body.

She'd be damned if she was going to leave it behind.

Click.

"This is. Better."

"Says you."

Ahead of her stretched the hard, cold sulfur plain. Smooth as glass. Brittle as frozen toffee. Cold as hell. She called up a visor-map and checked her progress. Only forty-five miles of mixed terrain to cross and she'd reach the lander. Then she'd be home free. No sweat, she thought. Io was in tidal lock with Jupiter. So the Father of Planets would stay glued to one fixed spot in the sky. That was as good as a navigation beacon. Just keep Jupiter to your right shoulder, and Daedalus to your left. You'll come out fine.

"Sulfur is. Triboelectric."

"Don't hold it in. What are you really trying to say?"

"And now I see. With eye serene. The very. Pulse. Of the machine." A pause. "Wordsworth."

Which, except for the halting delivery, was so much like Burton, with her classical education and love of classical poets like Spenser and Ginsberg and Plath, that for a second Martha was taken aback. Burton was a terrible poetry bore, but her enthusiasm had been genuine, and now Martha was sorry for every time she'd met those quotations with rolled eyes or a flip remark. But there's be time enough for grieving later. Right now she had to concentrate on the task at hand.

The colors of the plain were dim and brownish. With a few quick chin-taps, she cranked up their intensity. Her vision filled with yellows, oranges, reds — intense wax crayon colors. Martha decided she liked them best that way.

For all its Crayola vividness, this was the most desolate landscape in the universe. She was on her own here, small and weak in a harsh and unforgiving world. Burton was dead. There was nobody else on all of Io. Nobody to rely on but herself. Nobody to blame if she fucked up. Out of nowhere, she was filled with an elation as cold and bleak as the distant mountains. It was shameful how happy she felt.

After a minute, she said, "Know any songs?"

Oh the bear went over the mountain. The bear went over the mountain. The bear went over the mountain. To see what he could see.

"Wake. Up. Wake. Up."

To see what he could —

"Wake. Up. Wake. Up. Wake."

"Hah? What?"

"Crystal sulfur is orthorhombic."

She was in a field of sulfur flowers. They stretched as far as the eye could see, crystalline formations the size of her hand. Like the poppies of Flanders field. Or the ones in *The Wizard of Oz*. Behind her was a trail of broken flowers, some crushed by her feet or under the weight of the sledge, others simply exploded by exposure to her suit's waste heat. It was far from being a straight path. She had been walking on autopilot, and stumbled and turned and wandered upon striking the crystals.

Martha remembered how excited she and Burton had been when they first saw the fields of crystals. They had piled out of the moonrover with laughter and bounding leaps, and Burton had seized her by the waist and waltzed her around in a dance of jubilation. This was the big one, they'd thought, their chance at the history books. And even when they'd radioed Hols back in the orbiter and were somewhat condescendingly informed that there was no chance of this being a new life-form, but only sulfide formations such as could be found in any mineralogy text . . . even that had not killed their joy. It was still their first big discovery. They'd looked forward to many more.

Now, though, all she could think of was the fact that such crystal fields occurred in regions associated with sulfur geysers, lateral plumes, and volcanic hot spots.

Something funny was happening to the far edge of the field, though. She cranked up her helmet to extreme magnification and watched as the trail slowly erased itself. New flowers were rising up in place of those she had smashed, small but perfect and whole. And growing. She could not imagine by what process this could be happening. Electrodeposition? Molecular sulfur being drawn up from the soil in some kind of pseudocapillary action? Were the flowers somehow plucking sulfur ions from Io's almost nonexistent atmosphere?

Yesterday, the questions would have excited her. Now, her capacity for wonder was nonexistent. Moreover, her instruments were back in the moonrover. Save for the suit's limited electronics, she had nothing to take measurements with. She had only herself, the sledge, the spare airpacks, and the corpse.

"Damn, damn, damn," she muttered. On the one hand, this was a dangerous place to stay in. On the other, she'd been awake almost twenty hours now and she was dead on her feet. Exhausted. So very, very tired.

"O sleep! It is a gentle thing. Beloved from pole to pole. Coleridge."

Which, God knows, was tempting. But the numbers were clear: no sleep. With several deft chin-taps, Martha overrode her suit's safeties and accessed its medical kit. At her command, it sent a hit of methamphetamine rushing down the drug/vitamin catheter.

There was a sudden explosion of clarity in her skull and her heart began pounding like a jackhammer. Yeah. That did it. She was full of energy now. Deep breath. Long stride. Let's go.

No rest for the wicked. She had things to do. She left the flowers rapidly behind. Good-bye, Oz.

Fade out. Fade in. Hours had glided by. She was walking through a shadowy sculpture garden. Volcanic pillars (these were their second great discovery; they had no exact parallel on Earth) were scattered across the pyroclastic plain like so many isolated Lipschitz statues. They were all rounded and heaped, very much in the style of rapidly cooled magma. Martha remembered that Burton was dead, and cried quietly to herself for a few minutes.

Weeping, she passed through the eerie stone forms. The speed made them shift and move in her vision. As if they were dancing. They looked like women to her, tragic figures out of *The Bacchae* or, no, wait, *The Trojan Women* was the play she was thinking of. Desolate. Filled with anguish. Lonely as Lot's wife.

There was a light scattering of sulfur dioxide snow on the ground here. It sublimed at the touch of her boots, turning to white mist and scattering wildly, the steam disappearing with each stride and then being renewed with the next footfall. Which only made the experience all that much creepier.

Click.

"Io has a metallic core predominantly of iron and iron sulfide, overlain by a mantle of partially molten rock and crust."

"Are you still here?"

"Am trying. To communicate."

"Shut up."

She topped the ridge. The plains ahead were smooth and undulating. They reminded her of the Moon, in the transitional region between Mare Serenitatis and the foothills of the Caucasus Mountains, where she had undergone her surface training. Only without the impact craters. No impact craters on Io. Least cratered solid body in the solar system. All that volcanic activity deposited a new surface one meter thick every millennium or so. The whole damned moon was being constantly repaved.

Her mind was rambling. She checked her gauges, and muttered, "Let's get this show on the road."

There was no reply.

Dawn would come—when? Let's work this out. Io's "year," the time it took to revolve about Jupiter, was roughly forty-two hours fifteen minutes. She'd been walking seven hours. During which Io would've moved roughly sixty degrees through its orbit. So it would be dawn soon. That would make Daedalus's plume less obvious, but with her helmet graphics that wouldn't be a worry. Martha swiveled her neck, making sure that Daedalus and Jupiter were where they ought to be, and kept on walking.

Trudge, trudge, trudge. Try not to throw the map up on the visor every five minutes. Hold off as long as you can, just one more hour, okay, that's good, and another two miles. Not too shabby.

The sun was getting high. It would be noon in another hour and a half. Which meant—well, it really didn't mean much of anything.

Rock up ahead. Probably a silicate. It was a solitary six meters high brought here by who knew what forces and waiting who knew how many thousands of years just for her to come along and need a place to rest. She found a flat spot where she could lean against it, and, breathing heavily, sat down to rest. And think. And check the airpack. Four hours until she had to change it again. Bringing her down to two airpacks. She had slightly under twenty-four hours now. Thirty-five miles to go. That was less than two miles an hour. A snap. Might run a little tight on oxygen there toward the end, though. She'd have to take care she didn't fall asleep.

Oh, how her body ached.

It ached almost as much as it had in the '48 Olympics, when she'd taken the bronze in the women's marathon. Or that time in the internationals in Kenya when she'd come up from behind to tie for second. Story of her life. Always in third place, fighting for second. Always flight crew and sometimes, maybe, landing crew, but never the commander. Never class president. Never king of the hill. Just once—once!—she wanted to be Neil Armstrong.

Click.

"The marble index of a mind forever. Voyaging through strange seas of thought, alone. Wordsworth."

"What?"

"Jupiter's magnetosphere is the largest thing in the solar system. If the human eye could see it, it would appear two and a half times wider in the sky than the sun does."

"I knew that," she said, irrationally annoyed.

"Quotation is. Easy. Speech is. Not."

"Don't speak, then."

"Trying. To communicate!"

She shrugged. "So go ahead—communicate."

Silence. Then, "What does. This. Sound like?"

"What does what sound like?"

"Io is a sulfur-rich, iron-cored moon in a circular orbit around Jupiter. What does this. Sound like? Tidal forces from Jupiter and Ganymede pull and squeeze Io sufficiently to melt Tartarus, its sub-surface sulfur ocean. Tartarus vents its excess energy with sulfur and sulfur dioxide volcanoes. What does. This sound like? Io's metallic core generates a magnetic field that punches a hole in Jupiter's magnetosphere, and also creates a high-energy ion flux tube connecting its own poles with the north and south poles of Jupiter. What. Does this sound like? Io sweeps up and absorbs all the electrons in the million-volt range. Its volcanoes pump out sulfur dioxide; its magnetic field breaks down a percentage of that into sulfur and oxygen ions; and these ions are pumped into the hole punched in the magnetosphere, creating a rotating field commonly called the Io torus. What does this sound like? Torus. Flux tube. Magnetosphere. Volcanoes. Sulfur ions. Molten ocean. Tidal heating. Circular orbit. What does this sound like?"

Against her will, Martha had found herself first listening, then intrigued, and finally involved. It was like a riddle or a word-puzzle. There was a right answer to the question. Burton or Hols would have gotten it immediately. Martha had to think it through.

There was the faint hum of the radio's carrier beam. A patient, waiting noise.

At last, she cautiously said, "It sounds like a machine."

"Yes. Yes. Yes. Machine. Yes. Am machine. Am machine. Am machine. Yes. Yes. Machine. Yes."

"Wait. You're saying that Io is a machine? That you're a machine? That you're Io?"

"Sulfur is triboelectric. Sledge picks up charges. Burton's brain is intact. Language is data. Radio is medium. Am machine."

"I don't believe you."

Trudge, drag, trudge, drag. The world doesn't stop for strangeness. Just because she'd gone loopy enough to think that Io was alive and a machine and talking to her, didn't mean that Martha could stop walking. She had promises to keep, and miles to go before she slept. And speaking of sleep, it was time for another fast refresher — just a quarter-hit — of speed.

Wow. Let's go!

As she walked, she continued to carry on a dialogue with her hallucination or delusion or whatever it was. It was too boring otherwise.

Boring, and a tiny bit terrifying.

So she asked, "If you're a machine, then what is your function? Why were you made?"

"To know you. To love you. And to serve you."

Martha blinked. Then, remembering Burton's long reminiscences on her Catholic girlhood, she laughed. That was a paraphrase of the answer to the first question in the old Baltimore Catechism: *Why did God make man?* "If I keep on listening to you, I'm going to come down with delusions of grandeur."

"You are. Creator. Of machine."

"Not me."

She walked on without saying anything for a time. Then, because the silence was beginning to get to her again, "When was it I supposedly created you?"

"So many a million of ages have gone. To the making of man. Alfred, Lord Tennyson."

"That wasn't me, then. I'm only twenty-seven. You're obviously thinking of somebody else."

"It was. Mobile. Intelligent. Organic. Life. You are. Mobile. Intelligent. Organic. Life."

Something moved in the distance. Martha looked up, astounded. A horse. Pallid and ghostly white, it galloped soundlessly across the plains, tail and mane flying.

She squeezed her eyes tight and shook her head. When she opened her eyes again, the horse was gone. A hallucination. Like the voice of Burton/Io. She'd been thinking of ordering up another refresher of the meth, but now it seemed best to put it off as long as possible.

This was sad, though. Inflating Burton's memories until they were as large as Io. Freud would have a few things to say about *that*. He'd say she was magnifying her friend to a godlike status in order to justify the fact that she'd never been able to compete one-on-one with Burton and win. He'd say she couldn't deal with the fact that some people were simply better at things than she was.

Trudge, drag, trudge, drag.

So, okay, yes, she had an ego problem. She was an overambitious, self-centered bitch. So what? It had gotten her this far, where a more reasonable attitude would have left her back in the slums of greater Levittown. Making do with an eight-by-ten room with bathroom rights and a job as a dental assistant. Kelp and talapia every night, and rabbit on Sunday. The hell with that. She was alive and Burton wasn't—by any rational standard that made her the winner.

"Are you. Listening?"

"Not really, no."

She topped yet another rise. And stopped dead. Down below was a dark expanse of molten sulfur. It stretched, wide and black, across the streaked orange plains. A lake. Her helmet readouts ran a thermal topography from the negative 230°F at her feet to 65°F at the edge of the lava flow. Nice and balmy. The molten sulfur itself, of course, existed at higher ambient temperatures.

It lay dead in her way.

They'd named it Lake Styx.

Martha spent half an hour muttering over her topo maps, trying to figure out how she'd gone so far astray. Not that it wasn't obvious. All that stumbling around. Little errors that she'd made, adding up. A tendency to favor one leg over the other. It had been an iffy thing from the beginning, trying to navigate by dead reckoning.

Finally, though, it was obvious. Here she was. On the shores of Lake Styx. Not all that far off course after all. Three miles, maybe, tops.

Despair filled her.

They'd named the lake during their first loop through the Galilean system, what the engineers had called the "mapping run." It was one of the largest features they'd seen that wasn't already on the maps from satellite probes or Earth-based reconnaissance. Hols had thought it might be a new phenomenon—a lake that had achieved its current size within the past ten years or so. Burton had thought it would be fun to check it out. And Martha hadn't cared, so long as she wasn't left behind. So they'd added the lake to their itinerary.

She had been so transparently eager to be in on the first landing, so afraid that she'd be left behind, that when she suggested they match fingers, odd man out, for who stayed, both Burton and Hols had laughed. "I'll play mother," Hols had said magnanimously, "for the first landing. Burton for Ganymede and then you for Europa. Fair enough?" And ruffled her hair.

She'd been so relieved, and so grateful, and so humiliated too. It was ironic. Now it looked like Hols—who would *never* have gotten so far off course as to go down the wrong side of the Styx—wasn't going to get to touch rock at all. Not this expedition.

"Stupid, stupid, stupid," Martha muttered, though she didn't know if she were condemning Hols or Burton or herself. Lake Styx was horseshoe-shaped and twelve miles long. And she was standing right at the inner toe of the horseshoe.

There was no way she could retrace her steps back around the lake and still get to the lander before her air ran out. The lake was dense enough that she could almost *swim* across it, if it weren't for the viscosity of the sulfur, which would coat her heat radiators and burn out her suit in no time flat. And the heat of the liquid. And whatever internal flows and undertows it might have. As it was, the experience would be like drowning in molasses. Slow and sticky.

She sat down and began to cry.

After a time she began to build up her nerve to grope for the snap-coupling to her airpack. There was a safety for it, but among those familiar with the rig it was an open secret that if you held the safety down with your thumb and yanked suddenly on the coupling, the whole thing would come undone, emptying the suit in less than a second. The gesture was so distinctive that hot young astronauts-in-training would mime it when one of their number said something particularly stupid. It was called the suicide flick.

There were worse ways of dying.

"Will build. Bridge. Have enough. Fine control of. Physical processes. To build. Bridge."

"Yeah, right, very nice, you do that," Martha said absently. If you can't be polite to your own hallucinations . . . She didn't bother finishing the thought. Little crawly things were creeping about on the surface of her skin. Best to ignore them.

"Wait. Here. Rest. Now."

She said nothing but only sat, not resting. Building up her courage. Thinking about everything and nothing. Clutching her knees and rocking back and forth.

Eventually, without meaning to, she fell asleep.

"Wake. Up. Wake. Up. Wake. Up."

"Uhh?"

Martha struggled up into awareness. Something was happening before her, out on the lake. Physical processes were at work. Things were moving.

As she watched, the white crust at the edge of the dark lake bulged outward, shooting out crystals, extending. Lacy as a snowflake. Pale as frost. Reaching across the molten blackness. Until there was a narrow white bridge stretching all the way to the far shore.

"You must. Wait," Io said. "Ten minutes and. You can. Walk across. It. With ease."

"Son of a bitch!" Martha murmured. "I'm sane."

In wondering silence, she crossed the bridge that Io had enchanted across the dark lake. Once or twice the surface felt a little mushy underfoot, but it always held.

It was an exalting experience. Like passing over from Death into Life.

At the far side of the Styx, the pyroclastic plains rose gently toward a distant horizon. She stared up yet another long, crystal-flower-covered slope. Two in one day. What were the odds against that?

She struggled upward, flowers exploding as they were touched by her boots. At the top of the rise, the flowers gave way to sulfur hardpan again. Looking back, she could see the path she had crunched through the flowers begin to erase itself. For a long moment she stood still, venting heat. Crystals shattered soundlessly about her in a slowly expanding circle.

She was itching something awful now. Time to freshen up. Six quick taps brought up a message on her visor: *Warning: Continued use of this drug at current levels can result in paranoia, psychosis, hallucinations, misperceptions, and hypomania, as well as impaired judgment.*

Fuck that noise. Martha dealt herself another hit.

It took a few seconds. Then—whoops. She was feeling light and full of energy again. Best check the airpack reading. Man, that didn't look good. She had to giggle.

Which was downright scary.

Nothing could have sobered her up faster than that high little druggie laugh. It terrified her. Her life depended on her ability to maintain. She had to keep taking meth to keep going, but she also had to keep going under the drug. She couldn't let it start calling the shots. Focus. Time to switch over to the last airpack. Burton's airpack. "I've got eight hours of oxygen left. I've got twelve miles yet to go. It can be done," she said grimly. "I'm going to do it now."

If only her skin weren't itching. If only her head weren't crawling. If only her brain weren't busily expanding in all directions.

Trudge, drag, trudge, drag. All through the night. The trouble with repetitive labor was that it gave you time to think. Time to think when you were speeding also meant time to think about the quality of your own thought.

You didn't dream in real-time, she'd been told. You get it all in one flash, just as you're about to wake up, and in that instant extrapolate a complex dream all in one whole. It feels as if you've been dreaming for hours. But you've only had one split second of intense nonreality.

Maybe that's what's happening here.

She had a job to do. She had to keep a clear head. It was important that she get back to the lander. People had to *know*. They weren't alone anymore. Damnit, she'd just made the biggest discovery since fire!

Either that, or she was so crazy she was hallucinating that Io was a gigantic alien machine. So crazy she'd lost herself within the convolutions of her own brain.

Which was another terrifying thing she wished she hadn't thought of. She'd been a loner as a child. Never made friends easily. Never had or been a best friend to anybody. Had spent half her girlhood buried in books. Solipsism terrified her — she'd lived right on the edge of it for too long. So it was vitally important that she determine whether the voice of Io had an objective, external reality. Or not.

Well, how could she test it?

Sulfur was triboelectric, Io had said. Implying that it was in some way an electrical phenomenon. If so, then it ought to be physically demonstrable.

Martha directed her helmet to show her the electrical charges within the sulfur plains. Crank it up to the max.

The land before her flickered once, then lit up in fairyland colors. Light! Pale oceans of light overlaying light, shifting between pastels, from faded rose to boreal blue, multilayered, labyrinthine, and all pulsing gently within the heart of the sulfur rock. It looked like thought made visual. It looked like something straight out of Disney Virtual, and not one of the nature channels either — definitely DV-3.

"Damn," she muttered. Right under her nose. She'd had no idea.

Glowing lines veined the warping wings of subterranean electromagnetic forces. Almost like circuit wires. They crisscrossed the plains in all directions, combining and then converging — not upon her, but in a nexus at the sled. Burton's corpse was lit up like neon. Her head, packed in sulfur dioxide snow, strobed and stuttered with light so rapidly that it shone like the sun.

Sulfur was triboelectric. Which meant that it built up a charge when rubbed.

She'd been dragging Burton's sledge over the sulfur surface of Io for how many hours? You could build up a hell of a charge that way.

So, okay. There was a physical mechanism for what she was seeing. Assuming that Io really *was* a machine, a triboelectric alien device the size of Earth's moon, built eons ago for who knows what purpose by who knows what godlike monstrosities, then, yes, it might be able to communicate with her. A lot could be done with electricity.

Lesser, smaller, and dimmer "circuitry" reached for Martha as well. She looked down at her feet. When she lifted one from the surface, the contact was broken, and the lines of force collapsed. Other lines were born when she put her foot down again. Whatever slight contact might be made was being constantly broken. Whereas Burton's sledge was in constant contact with the sulfur surface of Io. That hole in Burton's skull would be a highway straight into her brain. And she'd packed it in solid SO_2 as well. Conductive and supercooled. She'd made things easy for Io.

She shifted back to augmented real-color. The DV-3 SFX faded away.

Accepting as a tentative hypothesis that the voice was a real rather than a psychological phenomenon. That Io was able to communicate with her. That it was a machine. That it had been built . . .

Who, then, had built it?

Click.

"Io? Are you listening?"

"Calm on the listening ear of night. Come Heaven's melodious strains. Edmund Hamilton Sears."

"Yeah, wonderful, great. Listen, there's something I'd kinda like to know — who built you?"

"You Did."

Slyly, Martha said, "So I'm your creator, right?"

"Yes."

"What do I look like when I'm at home?"

"Whatever. You wish. To."

"Do I breathe oxygen? Methane? Do I have antennae? Tentacles? Wings? How many legs do I have? How many eyes? How many heads?"

"If. You wish. As many as. You wish."

"How many of me are there?"

"One." A pause. "Now."

"I was here before, right? People like me. Mobile intelligent life-forms. And I left. How long have I been gone?"

Silence. "How long —" she began again.

"Long time. Lonely. So very. Long time."

Trudge, drag. Trudge, drag. Trudge, drag. How many centuries had she been walking? Felt like a lot. It was night again. Her arms felt like they were going to fall out of their sockets.

Really, she ought to leave Burton behind. She'd never said anything to make Martha think she cared one way or the other where her body wound up. Probably would've thought a burial on Io was pretty damn nifty. But Martha wasn't doing this for her. She was doing it for herself. To prove that she wasn't entirely selfish. That she did too have feelings for others. That she was motivated by more than just the desire for fame and glory.

Which, of course, was a sign of selfishness in itself. The desire to be known as selfless. It was hopeless. You could nail yourself to a fucking cross, and it would still be proof of your innate selfishness.

"You still there, Io?"

Click.

"Am. Listening."

"Tell me about this fine control of yours. How much do you have? Can you bring me to the lander faster than I'm going now? Can you bring the lander to me? Can you return me to the orbiter? Can you provide me with more oxygen?"

"Dead egg, I lie. Whole. On a whole world I cannot touch. Plath."

"You're not much use, then, are you?"

There was no answer. Not that she had expected one. Or needed it, either. She checked the topos and found herself another eighth-mile closer to the lander. She could even see it now under her helmet photomultipliers, a dim glint upon the horizon. Wonderful things, photomultipliers. The sun here provided about as much light as a full moon did back on Earth. Jupiter by itself provided even less. Yet crank up the magnification, and she could see the airlock awaiting the grateful touch of her gloved hand.

Trudge, drag, trudge. Martha ran and reran and rereran the math in her head. She had only three miles to go, and enough oxygen for as many hours. The lander had its own air supply. She was going to make it.

Maybe she wasn't the total loser she'd always thought she was. Maybe there was hope for her, after all.

Click.

"Brace. Yourself."

"What for?"

The ground rose up beneath her and knocked her off her feet.

When the shaking stopped, Martha clambered unsteadily to her feet again. The land before her was all a jumble, as if a careless deity had lifted the entire plain up a foot and then dropped it. The silvery glint of the lander on the horizon was gone. When she pushed her helmet's magnification to the max, she could see a metal leg rising crookedly from the rubbled ground.

Martha knew the shear strength of every bolt and failure point of every welding seam in the lander. She knew exactly how fragile it was. That was one device that was never going to fly again.

She stood motionless. Unblinking. Unseeing. Feeling nothing. Nothing at all.

Eventually she pulled herself together enough to think. Maybe it was time to admit it: She never *had* believed she was going to make it. Not really. Not Martha Kivelsen. All her life she'd been a loser. Sometimes—like when she qualified for the expedition—she lost at a higher level than usual. But she never got whatever it was she really wanted.

Why was that, she wondered? When had she ever desired anything bad? When you get right down to it, all she'd ever wanted was to kick God in the butt and get his attention. To be a big noise. To be the biggest fucking noise in the universe. Was that so unreasonable?

Now she was going to wind up as a footnote in the annals of humanity's expansion into space. A sad little cautionary tale for mommy astronauts to tell their baby astronauts on cold winter nights. Maybe Burton could've gotten back to the lander. Or Hols. But not *her*. It just wasn't in the cards.

Click.

"Io is the most volcanically active body in the solar system."

"You fucking bastard! Why didn't you warn me?"

"Did. Not. Know."

Now her emotions returned to her in full force. She wanted to run and scream and break things. Only there wasn't anything in sight that hadn't already been broken. "You shithead!" she cried. "You idiot machine! What use are you? What goddamn use at all?"

"Can give you. Eternal life. Communion of the soul. Unlimited processing power. Can give Burton. Same."

"Hah?"

"After the first death. There is no other. Dylan Thomas."

"What do you mean by that?"

Silence.

"Damn you, you fucking machine! What are you trying to *say*?"

Then the devil took Jesus up into the holy city and set him on the highest point of the temple, and said to him, "If thou be the Son of God, cast thyself down: for it is written he shall give his angels charge concerning thee: and in their hands they shall bear thee up."

Burton wasn't the only one who could quote scripture. You didn't have to be Catholic, like her. Presbyterians could do it too.

Martha wasn't sure what you'd call this feature. A volcanic phenomenon of some sort. It wasn't very big. Maybe twenty meters across, not much higher. Call it a crater, and let be. She stood shivering at its lip. There was a black pool of molten sulfur at its bottom, just as she'd been told. Supposedly its roots reached all the way down to Tartarus.

Her head ached so badly.

Io claimed—had *said*—that if she threw herself in, it would be able to absorb her, duplicate her neural patterning, and so restore her to life. A transformed sort of life, but life nonetheless. "Throw Burton in," it had said. "Throw yourself in. Physical configuration will be. Destroyed. Neural configuration will be. Preserved. Maybe."

"Maybe?"

"Burton had limited. Biological training. Understanding of neural functions may be. Imperfect."

"Wonderful."

"Or. Maybe not."

"Gotcha."

Heat radiated up from the bottom of the crater. Even protected and shielded as she was by her suit's HVAC systems, she felt the difference between front and back. It was like standing in front of a fire on a very cold night.

They had talked, or maybe negotiated was a better word for it, for a long time. Finally Martha had said, "You savvy Morse code? You savvy orthodox spelling?"

"Whatever Burton. Understood. Is. Understood."

"Yes or no, damnit!"

"Savvy."

"Good. Then maybe we can make a deal."

She stared up into the night. The orbiter was out there somewhere, and she was sorry she couldn't talk directly to Hols, say good-bye and thanks for everything. But Io had said no. What she planned would raise volcanoes and level mountains. The devastation would dwarf that of the earthquake caused by the bridge across Lake Styx.

It couldn't guarantee two separate communications.

The ion flux tube arched from somewhere over the horizon in a great looping jump to the north pole of Jupiter. Augmented by her visor, it was as bright as the sword of God.

As she watched, it began to sputter and jump, millions of watts of power dancing staccato in a message they'd be picking up on the surface of Earth. It would swamp every radio and drown out every broadcast in the Solar System.

THIS IS MARTHA KIVELSEN, SPEAKING FROM THE SURFACE OF IO ON BEHALF OF MYSELF, JULIET BURTON, DECEASED, AND JACOB HOLS, OF THE FIRST GALILEAN SATELLITES EXPLORATORY MISSION. WE HAVE MADE AN IMPORTANT DISCOVERY. . . .

Every electrical device in the System would *dance* to its song!

Burton went first. Martha gave the sledge a shove, and out it flew, into empty space. It dwindled, hit, kicked up a bit of a splash. Then, with a disappointing lack of pyrotechnics, the corpse slowly sank into the black glop.

It didn't look very encouraging at all.

Still . . .

"Okay," she said. "A deal's a deal." She dug in her toes and spread her arms. Took a deep breath. Maybe I am going to survive after all, she thought. It could be Burton was already halfway-merged into the oceanic mind of Io, and awaiting her to join in an alchemical marriage of personalities. Maybe I'm going to live forever. Who knows? Anything is possible.

Maybe.

There was a second and more likely possibility. All this could well be nothing more than a hallucination. Nothing but the sound of her brain short-circuiting and squirting bad chemicals in all directions. Madness. One last grandiose dream before dying. Martha had no way of judging.

Whatever the truth might be, though, there were no alternatives, and only one way to find out.

She jumped.

Briefly, she flew.

story of your life
TED CHIANG

*Here's an intricate, intelligent, and compassionate look at the proposition
that knowing how a story ends before you start it sometimes doesn't matter
as much as what you learn along the way....*

*Ted Chiang has made a big impact on the field with only a handful of
stories, published in* Omni, Asimov's Science Fiction, Full Spectrum 3,
and Starlight 2. *He won the 1990 Nebula Award with his first published
story, "Tower of Babylon," which was in our Eighth Annual Collection,
and won the 1991 Asimov's Readers Award with his third, "Understand,"
as well as winning the John W. Campbell Award for Best New Writer in
that same year. Little has been heard from him since 1991, but now he's
back with a vengeance with "Story of Your Life," which, amazingly, is only
his fourth published story. It will be very interesting to see what he writes
in the years to come; he could well turn out to be one of the significant
new talents of the new century ahead. He lives in Kirkland, Washington.*

Y our father is about to ask me the question. This is the most important moment
in our lives, and I want to pay attention, note every detail. Your dad and I have
just come back from an evening out, dinner and a show; it's after midnight. We
came out onto the patio to look at the full moon; then I told your dad I wanted
to dance, so he humors me and now we're slow-dancing, a pair of thirtysomething
swaying back and forth in the moonlight like kids. I don't feel the night chill at
all. And then your dad says, "Do you want to make a baby?"

Right now your dad and I have been married for about two years, living on Ellis
Avenue; when we move out you'll still be too young to remember the house, but
we'll show you pictures of it, tell you stories about it. I'd love to tell you the story
of this evening, the night you're conceived, but the right time to do that would
be when you're ready to have children of your own, and we'll never get that
chance.

Telling it to you any earlier wouldn't do any good; for most of your life you won't sit still to hear such a romantic—you'd say sappy—story. I remember the scenario of your origin you'll suggest when you're twelve.

"The only reason you had me was so you could get a maid you wouldn't have to pay," you'll say bitterly, dragging the vacuum cleaner out of the closet.

"That's right," I'll say. "Thirteen years ago I knew the carpets would need vacuuming around now, and having a baby seemed to be the cheapest and easiest way to get the job done. Now kindly get on with it."

"If you weren't my mother, this would be illegal," you'll say, seething as you unwind the power cord and plug it into the wall outlet.

That will be in the house on Belmont Street. I'll live to see strangers occupy both houses: the one you're conceived in and the one you grow up in. Your dad and I will sell the first a couple years after your arrival. I'll sell the second shortly after your departure. By then Nelson and I will have moved into our farmhouse, and your dad will be living with what's-her-name.

I know how this story ends; I think about it a lot. I also think a lot about how it began, just a few years ago, when ships appeared in orbit and artifacts appeared in meadows. The government said next to nothing about them, while the tabloids said every possible thing.

And then I got a phone call, a request for a meeting.

I spotted them waiting in the hallway, outside my office. They made an odd couple; one wore a military uniform and a crewcut, and carried an aluminum briefcase. He seemed to be assessing his surroundings with a critical eye. The other one was easily identifiable as an academic: full beard and mustache, wearing corduroy. He was browsing through the overlapping sheets stapled to a bulletin board nearby.

"Colonel Weber, I presume?" I shook hands with the soldier. "Louise Banks."

"Dr. Banks. Thank you for taking the time to speak with us," he said.

"Not at all; any excuse to avoid the faculty meeting."

Colonel Weber indicated his companion. "This is Dr. Gary Donnelly, the physicist I mentioned when we spoke on the phone."

"Call me Gary," he said as we shook hands. "I'm anxious to hear what you have to say."

We entered my office. I moved a couple of stacks of books off the second guest chair, and we all sat down. "You said you wanted me to listen to a recording. I presume this has something to do with the aliens?"

"All I can offer is the recording," said Colonel Weber.

"Okay, let's hear it."

Colonel Weber took a tape machine out of his briefcase and pressed PLAY. The recording sounded vaguely like that of a wet dog shaking the water out of its fur.

"What do you make of that?" he asked.

I withheld my comparison to a wet dog. "What was the context in which this recording was made?"

"I'm not at liberty to say."

"It would help me interpret those sounds. Could you see the alien while it was speaking? Was it doing anything at the time?"

"The recording is all I can offer."

"You won't be giving anything away if you tell me that you've seen the aliens; the public's assumed you have."

Colonel Weber wasn't budging. "Do you have any opinion about its linguistic properties?" he asked.

"Well, it's clear that their vocal tract is substantially different from a human vocal tract. I assume that these aliens don't look like humans?"

The colonel was about to say something noncommittal when Gary Donelly asked, "Can you make any guesses based on the tape?"

"Not really. It doesn't sound like they're using a larynx to make those sounds, but that doesn't tell me what they look like."

"Anything—is there anything else you can call tell us?" asked Colonel Weber.

I could see he wasn't accustomed to consulting a civilian. "Only that establishing communications is going to be really difficult because of the difference in anatomy. They're almost certainly using sounds that the human vocal tract can't reproduce, and maybe sounds that the human ear can't distinguish."

"You mean infra- or ultrasonic frequencies?" asked Gary Donnelly.

"Not specifically. I just mean that the human auditory system isn't an absolute acoustic instrument; it's optimized to recognize the sounds that a human larynx makes. With an alien vocal system, all bets are off." I shrugged. "*Maybe* we'll be able to hear the difference between alien phonemes, given enough practice, but it's possible our ears simply can't recognize the distinctions they consider meaningful. In that case we'd need a sound spectrograph to know what an alien is saying."

Colonel Weber asked, "Suppose I gave you an hour's worth of recordings; how long would it take you to determine if we need this sound spectrograph or not?"

"I couldn't determine that with just a recording no matter how much time I had. I'd need to talk with the aliens directly."

The colonel shook his head. "Not possible."

I tried to break it to him gently. "That's your call, of course. But the only way to learn an unknown language is to interact with a native speaker, and by that I mean asking questions, holding a conversation, that sort of thing. Without that, it's simply not possible. So if you want to learn the aliens' language, someone with training in field linguistics—whether it's me or someone else—will have to talk with an alien. Recordings alone aren't sufficient."

Colonel Weber frowned. "You seem to be implying that no alien could have learned human languages by monitoring our broadcasts."

"I doubt it. They'd need instructional material specifically designed to teach human languages to nonhumans. Either that, or interaction with a human. If they had either of those, they could learn a lot from TV, but otherwise, they wouldn't have a starting point."

The colonel clearly found this interesting; evidently his philosophy was, the less the aliens knew, the better. Gary Donnelly read the colonel's expression too and rolled his eyes. I suppressed a smile.

Then Colonel Weber asked, "Suppose you were learning a new language by talking to its speakers; could you do it without teaching them English?"

"That would depend on how cooperative the native speakers were. They'd almost certainly pick up bits and pieces while I'm learning their language, but it wouldn't have to be much if they're willing to teach. On the other hand, if they'd rather learn English than teach us their language, that would make things far more difficult."

The colonel nodded. "I'll get back to you on this matter."

The request for that meeting was perhaps the second most momentous phone call in my life. The first, of course, will be the one from Mountain Rescue. At that point your dad and I will be speaking to each other maybe once a year, tops. After I get that phone call, though, the first thing I'll do will be to call your father.

He and I will drive out together to perform the identification, a long silent car ride. I remember the morgue, all tile and stainless steel, the hum of refrigeration and smell of antiseptic. An orderly will pull the sheet back to reveal your face. Your face will look wrong somehow, but I'll know it's you.

"Yes, that's her," I'll say. "She's mine."

You'll be twenty-five then.

The MP checked my badge, made a notation on his clipboard, and opened the gate; I drove the off-road vehicle into the encampment, a small village of tents pitched by the Army in a farmer's sun-scorched pasture. At the center of the encampment was one of the alien devices, nicknamed "looking glasses."

According to the briefings I'd attended, there were nine of these in the United States, one hundred and twelve in the world. The looking glasses acted as two-way communication devices, presumably with the ships in orbit. No one knew why the aliens wouldn't talk to us in person; fear of cooties, maybe. A team of scientists, including a physicist and a linguist, was assigned to each looking glass; Gary Donnelly and I were on this one.

Gary was waiting for me in the parking area. We navigated a circular maze of concrete barricades until we reached the large tent that covered the looking glass itself. In front of the tent was an equipment cart loaded with goodies borrowed from the school's phonology lab; I had sent it ahead for inspection by the Army.

Also outside the tent were three tripod-mounted video cameras whose lenses peered, through windows in the fabric wall, into the main room. Everything Gary and I did would be reviewed by countless others, including military intelligence. In addition we would each send daily reports, of which mine had to include estimates on how much English I thought the aliens could understand.

Gary held open the tent flap and gestured for me to enter. "Step right up," he said, circus-barker-style. "Marvel at creatures the likes of which have never been seen on God's green earth."

"And all for one slim dime," I murmured, walking through the door. At the moment the looking glass was inactive, resembling a semicircular mirror over ten feet high and twenty feet across. On the brown grass in front of the looking glass, an arc of white spray paint outlined the activation area. Currently the area contained only a table, two folding chairs, and a power strip with a cord leading to a generator outside. The buzz of fluorescent lamps, hung from poles along the edge of the room, commingled with the buzz of flies in the sweltering heat.

Gary and I looked at each other, and then began pushing the cart of equipment up to the table. As we crossed the paint line, the looking glass appeared to grow transparent; it was as if someone was slowly raising the illumination behind tinted glass. The illusion of depth was uncanny; I felt I could walk right into it. Once the looking glass was fully lit it resembled a life-sized diorama of a semicircular room. The room contained a few large objects that might have been furniture, but no aliens. There was a door in the curved rear wall.

We busied ourselves connecting everything together: microphone, sound spectrograph, portable computer, and speaker. As we worked, I frequently glanced at the looking glass, anticipating the aliens' arrival. Even so I jumped when one of them entered.

It looked like a barrel suspended at the intersection of seven limbs. It was radially symmetric, and any of its limbs could serve as an arm or a leg. The one in front of me was walking around on four legs, three nonadjacent arms curled up at its sides. Gary called them "heptapods."

I'd been shown videotapes, but I still gawked. Its limbs had no distinct joints; anatomists guessed they might be supported by vertebral columns. Whatever their underlying structure, the heptapod's limbs conspired to move it in a disconcertingly fluid manner. Its "torso" rode atop the rippling limbs as smoothly as a hovercraft.

Seven lidless eyes ringed the top of the heptapod's body. It walked back to the doorway from which it entered, made a brief sputtering sound, and returned to the center of the room followed by another heptapod; at no point did it ever turn around. Eerie, but logical; with eyes on all sides, any direction might as well be "forward."

Gary had been watching my reaction. "Ready?" he asked.

I took a deep breath. "Ready enough." I'd done plenty of fieldwork before, in the Amazon, but it had always been a bilingual procedure: either my informants knew some Portuguese, which I could use, or I'd previously gotten an introduction to their language from the local missionaries. This would be my first attempt at conducting a true monolingual discovery procedure. It was straightforward enough in theory, though.

I walked up to the looking glass and a heptapod on the other side did the same. The image was so real that my skin crawled. I could see the texture of its gray skin, like corduroy ridges arranged in whorls and loops. There was no smell at all from the looking glass, which somehow made the situation stranger.

I pointed to myself and said slowly, "Human." Then I pointed to Gary. "Human." Then I pointed at each heptapod and said, "What are you?"

No reaction. I tried again, and then again.

One of the heptapods pointed to itself with one limb, the four terminal digits pressed together. That was lucky. In some cultures a person pointed with his chin; if the heptapod hadn't used one of its limbs, I wouldn't have known what gesture to look for. I heard a brief fluttering sound, and saw a puckered orifice at the top of its body vibrate; it was talking. Then it pointed to its companion and fluttered again.

I went back to my computer; on its screen were two virtually identical spectrographs representing the fluttering sounds. I marked a sample for playback. I pointed to myself and said "Human" again, and did the same with Gary. Then I pointed to the heptapod, and played back the flutter on the speaker.

The heptapod fluttered some more. The second half of the spectrograph for this utterance looked like a repetition: call the previous utterances [flutter1], then this one was [flutter2flutter1].

I pointed at something that might have been a heptapod chair. "What is that?"

The heptapod paused, and then pointed at the "chair" and talked some more. The spectrograph for this differed distinctly from that of the earlier sounds: [flutter3]. Once again, I pointed to the "chair" while playing back [flutter3].

The heptapod replied; judging by the spectrograph, it looked like [flutter3flutter2]. Optimistic interpretation: the heptapod was confirming my utterances as correct, which implied compatibility between heptapod and human patterns of discourse. Pessimistic interpretation: it had a nagging cough.

At my computer I delimited certain sections of the spectrograph and typed in a tentative gloss for each: "heptapod" for [flutter1], "yes" for [flutter2], and "chair" for [flutter3]. Then I typed "Language: Heptapod A" as a heading for all the utterances.

Gary watched what I was typing. "What's the 'A' for?"

"It just distinguishes this language from any other ones the heptapods might use," I said. He nodded.

"Now let's try something, just for laughs." I pointed at each heptapod and tried to mimic the sound of [flutter1]; "heptapod." After a long pause, the first heptapod said something and then the second one said something else, neither of whose spectrographs resembled anything said before. I couldn't tell if they were speaking to each other or to me since they had no faces to turn. I tried pronouncing [flutter1] again, but there was no reaction.

"Not even close," I grumbled.

"I'm impressed you can make sounds like that at all," said Gary.

"You should hear my moose call. Sends them running."

I tried again a few more times, but neither heptapod responded with anything I could recognize. Only when I replayed the recording of the heptapod's pronunciation did I get a confirmation; the heptapod replied with [flutter2], "yes."

"So we're stuck with using recordings?" asked Gary.

I nodded. "At least temporarily."

"So now what?"

"Now we make sure it hasn't actually been saying 'aren't they cute' or 'look what they're doing now.' Then we see if we can identify any of these words when that other heptapod pronounces them." I gestured for him to have a seat. "Get comfortable; this'll take a while."

In 1770, Captain Cook's ship *Endeavour* ran aground on the coast of Queensland, Australia. While some of his men made repairs, Cook led an exploration party and met the aboriginal people. One of the sailors pointed to the animals that hopped around with their young riding in pouches, and asked an aborigine what they were called. The aborigine replied, "Kanguru." From then on Cook and his sailors referred to the animals by this word. It wasn't until later that they learned it meant "What did you say?"

I tell that story in my introductory course every year. It's almost certainly untrue, and I explain that afterwards, but it's a classic anecdote. Of course, the anecdotes my undergraduates will really want to hear are ones featuring the heptapods; for the rest of my teaching career, that'll be the reason many of them sign up for my courses. So I'll show them the old videotapes of my sessions at the looking glass, and the sessions that the other linguists conducted; the tapes are instructive, and they'll be useful if we're ever visited by aliens again, but they don't generate many good anecdotes.

When it comes to language-learning anecdotes, my favorite source is child language acquisition. I remember one afternoon when you are five years old, after you have come home from kindergarten. You'll be coloring with your crayons while I grade papers.

"Mom," you'll say, using the carefully casual tone reserved for requesting a favor, "can I ask you something?"

"Sure, sweetie. Go ahead."

"Can I be, um, honored?"

I'll look up from the paper I'm grading. "What do you mean?"

"At school Sharon said she got to be honored."

"Really? Did she tell you what for?"

"It was when her big sister got married. She said only one person could be, um, honored, and she was it."

"Ah, I see. You mean Sharon was maid of honor?"

"Yeah, that's it. Can I be made of honor?"

Gary and I entered the prefab building containing the center of operations for the looking glass site. Inside it looked like they were planning an invasion, or perhaps an evacuation: crewcut soldiers worked around a large map of the area, or sat in front of burly electronic gear while speaking into headsets. We were shown into Colonel Weber's office, a room in the back that was cool from air conditioning.

We briefed the colonel on our first day's results. "Doesn't sound like you got very far," he said.

"I have an idea as to how we can make faster progress," I said. "But you'll have to approve the use of more equipment."

"What more do you need?"

"A digital camera, and a big video screen." I showed him a drawing of the setup I imagined. "I want to try conducting the discovery procedure using writing; I'd display words on the screen, and use the camera to record the words they write. I'm hoping the heptapods will do the same."

Weber looked at the drawing dubiously. "What would be the advantage of that?"

"So far I've been proceeding the way I would with speakers of an unwritten language. Then it occurred to me that the heptapods must have writing, too."

"So?"

"If the heptapods have a mechanical way of producing writing, then their writing ought to be very regular, very consistent. That would make it easier for us to identify graphemes instead of phonemes. It's like picking out the letters in a printed sentence instead of trying to hear them when the sentence is spoken aloud."

"I take your point," he admitted. "And how would you respond to them? Show them the words they displayed to you?"

"Basically. And if they put spaces between words, any sentences we write would be a lot more intelligible than any spoken sentence we might splice together from recordings."

He leaned back in his chair. "You know we want to show as little of our technology as possible."

"I understand, but we're using machines as intermediaries already. If we can get them to use writing, I believe progress will go much faster than if we're restricted to the sound spectrographs."

The colonel turned to Gary. "Your opinion?"

"It sounds like a good idea to me. I'm curious whether the heptapods might have difficulty reading our monitors. Their looking glasses are based on a completely different technology than our video screens. As far as we can tell, they don't use pixels or scan lines, and they don't refresh on a frame-by-frame basis."

"You think the scan lines on our video screens might render them unreadable to the heptapods?"

"It's possible," said Gary. "We'll just have to try it and see."

Weber considered it. For me it wasn't even a question, but from his point of view it was a difficult one; like a soldier, though, he made it quickly. "Request granted. Talk to the sergeant outside about bringing in what you need. Have it ready for tomorrow."

I remember one day during the summer when you're sixteen. For once, the person waiting for her date to arrive is me. Of course, you'll be waiting around, too, curious to see what he looks like. You'll have a friend of yours, a blond girl with the unlikely name of Roxie, hanging out with you, giggling.

"You may feel the urge to make comments about him," I'll say, checking myself in the hallway mirror. "Just restrain yourselves until we leave."

"Don't worry, Mom," you'll say. "We'll do it so that he won't know. Roxie, you ask me what I think the weather will be like tonight. Then I'll say what I think of Mom's date."

"Right," Roxie will say.

"No, you most definitely will not," I'll say.

"Relax, Mom. He'll never know; we do this all the time."

"What a comfort that is."

A little later on, Nelson will arrive to pick me up. I'll do the introductions, and we'll all engage in a little small talk on the front porch. Nelson is ruggedly handsome, to your evident approval. Just as we're about to leave, Roxie will say to you casually, "So what do you think the weather will be like tonight?"

"I think it's going to be really hot," you'll answer.

Roxie will nod in agreement. Nelson will say, "Really? I thought they said it was going to be cool."

"I have a sixth sense about these things," you'll say. Your face will give nothing away. "I get the feeling it's going to be a scorcher. Good thing you're dressed for it, Mom."

I'll glare at you, and say good night.

As I lead Nelson toward his car, he'll ask me, amused, "I'm missing something here, aren't I?"

"A private joke," I'll mutter. "Don't ask me to explain it."

At our next session at the looking glass, we repeated the procedure we had performed before, this time displaying a printed word on our computer screen at the same time we spoke: showing HUMAN while saying "Human," and so forth. Eventually, the heptapods understood what we wanted, and set up a flat circular screen mounted on a small pedestal. One heptapod spoke, and then inserted a limb into a large socket in the pedestal; a doodle of script, vaguely cursive, popped onto the screen.

We soon settled into a routine, and I compiled two parallel corpora: one of spoken utterances, one of writing samples. Based on first impressions, their writing appeared to be logographic, which was disappointing; I'd been hoping for an alphabetic script to help us learn their speech. Their logograms might include some phonetic information, but finding it would be a lot harder than with an alphabetic script.

By getting up close to the looking glass, I was able to point to various heptapod body parts, such as limbs, digits, and eyes, and elicit terms for each. It turned out that they had an orifice on the underside of their body, lined with articulated bony ridges: probably used for eating, while the one at the top was for respiration and speech. There were no other conspicuous orifices; perhaps their mouth was their anus, too. Those sorts of questions would have to wait.

I also tried asking our two informants for terms for addressing each individually; personal names, if they had such things. Their answers were of course unpronounceable, so for Gary's and my purposes, I dubbed them Flapper and Raspberry. I hoped I'd be able to tell them apart.

The next day I conferred with Gary before we entered the looking-glass tent. "I'll need your help with this session," I told him.

"Sure. What do you want me to do?"

"We need to elicit some verbs, and it's easiest with third-person forms. Would you act out a few verbs while I type the written form on the computer? If we're lucky, the heptapods will figure out what we're doing and do the same. I've brought a bunch of props for you to use."

"No problem," said Gary, cracking his knuckles. "Ready when you are."

We began with some simple intransitive verbs: walking, jumping, speaking, writing. Gary demonstrated each one with a charming lack of self-consciousness; the presence of the video cameras didn't inhibit him at all. For the first few actions he performed, I asked the heptapods, "What do you call that?" Before long, the heptapods caught on to what we were trying to do; Raspberry began mimicking Gary, or at least performing the equivalent heptapod action, while Flapper worked their computer, displaying a written description and pronouncing it aloud.

In the spectrographs of their spoken utterances, I could recognize their word I had glossed as "heptapod." The rest of each utterance was presumably the verb phrase; it looked like they had analogs of nouns and verbs, thank goodness.

In their writing, however, things weren't as clear-cut. For each action, they had displayed a single logogram instead of two separate ones. At first I thought they had written something like "walks," with the subject implied. But why would Flapper say "the heptapod walks" while writing "walks," instead of maintaining parallelism? Then I noticed that some of the logograms looked like the logogram for "heptapod" with some extra strokes added to one side or another. Perhaps their verbs could be written as affixes to a noun. If so, why was Flapper writing the noun in some instances but not in others?

I decided to try a transitive verb; substituting object words might clarify things. Among the props I'd brought were an apple and a slice of bread. "Okay," I said to Gary, "show them the food, and then eat some. First the apple, then the bread."

Gary pointed at the Golden Delicious and then he took a bite out of it, while I displayed the "what do you call that?" expression. Then we repeated it with the slice of whole wheat.

Raspberry left the room and returned with some kind of giant nut or gourd and a gelatinous ellipsoid. Raspberry pointed at the gourd while Flapper said a word and displayed a logogram. Then Raspberry brought the gourd down between its legs, a crunching sound resulted, and the gourd reemerged minus a bite; there were cornlike kernels beneath the shell. Flapper talked and displayed a large logogram on their screen. The sound spectrograph for "gourd" changed when it was used in the sentence; possibly a case marker. The logogram was odd: after some study, I could identify graphic elements that resembled the individual logograms for "heptapod" and "gourd." They looked as if they had been melted together, with several extra strokes in the mix that presumably meant "eat." Was it a multiword ligature?

Next we got spoken and written names for the gelatin egg, and descriptions of the act of eating it. The sound spectrograph for "heptapod eats gelatin egg" was analyzable; "gelatin egg" bore a case marker, as expected, though the sentence's word order differed from last time. The written form, another large logogram, was another matter. This time it took much longer for me to recognize anything in it; not only were the individual logograms melted together again, it looked as if the one for "heptapod" was laid on its back, while on top of it the logogram for "gelatin egg" was standing on its head.

"Uh-oh." I took another look at the writing for the simple noun-verb examples, the ones that had seemed inconsistent before. Now I realized all of them actually did contain the logogram for "heptapod"; some were rotated and distorted by being combined with the various verbs, so I hadn't recognized them at first. "You guys have got to be kidding," I muttered.

"What's wrong?" asked Gary.

"Their script isn't word-divided; a sentence is written by joining the logograms for the constituent words. They join the logograms by rotating and modifying them. Take a look." I showed him how the logograms were rotated.

"So they can read a word with equal ease no matter how it's rotated," Gary said. He turned to look at the heptapods, impressed. "I wonder if it's a consequence of their bodies' radial symmetry: their bodies have no 'forward' direction, so maybe their writing doesn't either. Highly neat."

I couldn't believe it; I was working with someone who modified the word "neat" with "highly." "It certainly is interesting," I said, "but it also means there's no easy way for us write our own sentences in their language. We can't simply cut their sentences into individual words and recombine them; we'll have to learn the rules of their script before we can write anything legible. It's the same continuity problem we'd have had splicing together speech fragments, except applied to writing."

I looked at Flapper and Raspberry in the looking glass, who were waiting for us to continue, and sighed. "You aren't going to make this easy for us, are you?"

To be fair, the heptapods were completely cooperative. In the days that followed, they readily taught us their language without requiring us to teach them any more English. Colonel Weber and his cohorts pondered the implications of that, while I and the linguists at the other looking glasses met via video conferencing to share what we had learned about the heptapod language. The videoconferencing made for an incongruous working environment: our video screens were primitive compared to the heptapods' looking glasses, so that my colleagues seemed more remote than the aliens. The familiar was far away, while the bizarre was close at hand.

It would be a while before we'd be ready to ask the heptapods why they had come, or to discuss physics well enough to ask them about their technology. For the time being, we worked on the basics: phonemics/graphemics, vocabulary, syntax. The heptapods at every looking glass were using the same language, so we were able to pool our data and coordinate our efforts.

Our biggest source of confusion was the heptapods' "writing." It didn't appear to be writing at all; it looked more like a bunch of intricate graphic designs. The logograms weren't arranged in rows, or a spiral, or any linear fashion. Instead, Flapper or Raspberry would write a sentence by sticking together as many logograms as needed into a giant conglomeration.

This form of writing was reminiscent of primitive sign systems, which required a reader to know a message's context in order to understand it. Such systems were considered too limited for systematic recording of information. Yet it was unlikely that the heptapods developed their level of technology with only an oral tradition. That implied one of three possibilities: the first was that the heptapods had a true writing system, but they didn't want to use it in front of us; Colonel Weber would identify with that one. The second was that the heptapods hadn't originated the technology they were using; they were illiterates using someone else's technology. The third, and most interesting to me, was that the heptapods were using a nonlinear system of orthography that qualified as true writing.

• • •

I remember a conversation we'll have when you're in your junior year of high school. It'll be Sunday morning, and I'll be scrambling some eggs while you set the table for brunch. You'll laugh as you tell me about the party you went to last night.

"Oh man," you'll say, "they're not kidding when they say that body weight makes a difference. I didn't drink any more than the guys did, but I got so much *drunker*."

I'll try to maintain a neutral, pleasant expression. I'll really try. Then you'll say, "Oh, come on, Mom."

"What?"

"You know you did the exact same things when you were my age."

I did nothing of the sort, but I know that if I were to admit that, you'd lose respect for me completely. "You know never to drive, or get into a car if—"

"God, of course I know that. Do you think I'm an idiot?"

"No, of course not."

What I'll think is that you are clearly, maddeningly not me. It will remind me, again, that you won't be a clone of me; you can be wonderful, a daily delight, but you won't be someone I could have created by myself.

The military had set up a trailer containing our offices at the looking-glass site. I saw Gary walking toward the trailer, and ran to catch up with him. "It's a semasiographic writing system," I said when I reached him.

"Excuse me?" said Gary.

"Here, let me show you." I directed Gary into my office. Once we were inside, I went to the chalkboard and drew a circle with a diagonal line bisecting it. "What does this mean?"

" 'Not allowed'?"

"Right." Next I printed the words NOT ALLOWED on the chalkboard. "And so does this. But only one is a representation of speech."

Gary nodded. "Okay."

"Linguists describe writing like this—" I indicated the printed words "—as 'glottographic,' because it represents speech. Every human written language is in this category. However, this symbol—" I indicated the circle and diagonal line "—is 'semasiographic' writing, because it conveys meaning without reference to speech. There's no correspondence between its components and any particular sounds."

"And you think all of heptapod writing is like this?"

"From what I've seen so far, yes. It's not picture writing, it's far more complex. It has its own system of rules for constructing sentences, like a visual syntax that's unrelated to the syntax for their spoken language."

"A visual syntax? Can you show me an example?"

"Coming right up." I sat down at my desk and, using the computer, pulled up a frame from the recording of yesterday's conversation with Raspberry. I turned the monitor so he could see it. "In their spoken language, a noun has a case marker indicating whether it's a subject or object. In their written language, however, a noun is identified as subject or object based on the orientation of its logogram relative to that of the verb. Here, take a look." I pointed at one of the figures. "For instance, when 'heptapod' is integrated with 'hears' this way, with these strokes parallel, it means that the heptapod is doing the hearing." I showed him a different one. "When they're combined this way, with the strokes perpendicular, it means that the heptapod is being heard. This morphology applies to several verbs.

"Another example is the inflection system." I called up another frame from the recording. "In their written language, this logogram means roughly 'hear easily' or 'hear clearly.' See the elements it has in common with the logogram for 'hear'? You can still combine it with 'heptapod' in the same ways as before, to indicate that the heptapod can hear something clearly or that the heptapod is clearly heard. But what's really interesting is that the modulation of 'hear' into 'hear clearly' isn't a special case; you see the transformation they applied?"

Gary nodded, pointing. "It's like they express the idea of 'clearly' by changing the curve of those strokes in the middle."

"Right. That modulation is applicable to lots of verbs. The logogram for 'see' can be modulated in the same way to form 'see clearly,' and so can the logogram for 'read' and others. And changing the curve of those strokes has no parallel in their speech; with the spoken version of these verbs, they add a prefix to the verb to express ease of manner, and the prefixes for 'see' and 'hear' are different.

"There are other examples, but you get the idea. It's essentially a grammar in two dimensions."

He began pacing thoughtfully. "Is there anything like this in human writing systems?"

"Mathematical equations, notations for music and dance. But those are all very specialized; we couldn't record this conversation using them. But I suspect, if we knew it well enough, we could record this conversation in the heptapod writing system. I think it's a full-fledged, general-purpose graphical language."

Gary frowned. "So their writing constitutes a completely separate language from their speech, right?"

"Right. In fact, it'd be more accurate to refer to the writing system as 'Heptapod B,' and use 'Heptapod A' strictly for referring to the spoken language."

"Hold on a second. Why use two languages when one would suffice? That seems unnecessarily hard to learn."

"Like English spelling?" I said. "Ease of learning isn't the primary force in language evolution. For the heptapods, writing and speech may play such different cultural or cognitive roles that using separate languages makes more sense than using different forms of the same one."

He considered it. "I see what you mean. Maybe they think our form of writing is redundant, like we're wasting a second communications channel."

"That's entirely possible. Finding out why they use a second language for writing will tell us a lot about them."

"So I take it this means we won't be able to use their writing to help us learn their spoken language."

I sighed. "Yeah, that's the most immediate implication. But I don't think we should ignore either Heptapod A or B; we need a two-pronged approach." I pointed at the screen. "I'll bet you that learning their two-dimensional grammar will help you when it comes time to learn their mathematical notation."

"You've got a point there. So are we ready to start asking about their mathematics?"

"Not yet. We need a better grasp on this writing system before we begin anything else," I said, and then smiled when he mimed frustration. "Patience, good sir. Patience is a virtue."

You'll be six when your father has a conference to attend in Hawaii, and we'll accompany him. You'll be so excited that you'll make preparations for weeks beforehand. You'll ask me about coconuts and volcanoes and surfing, and practice hula dancing in the mirror. You'll pack a suitcase with the clothes and toys you want to bring, and you'll drag it around the house to see how long you can carry it. You'll ask me if I can carry your Etch-a-Sketch in my bag, since there won't be any more room for it in yours and you simply can't leave without it.

"You won't need all of these," I'll say. "There'll be so many fun things to do there, you won't have time to play with so many toys."

You'll consider that; dimples will appear above your eyebrows when you think hard. Eventually you'll agree to pack fewer toys, but your expectations will, if anything, increase.

"I wanna be in Hawaii now," you'll whine.

"Sometimes it's good to wait," I'll say. "The anticipation makes it more fun when you get there."

You'll just pout.

In the next report I submitted, I suggested that the term "logogram" was a misnomer because it implied that each graph represented a spoken word, when in fact the graphs didn't correspond to our notion of spoken words at all. I didn't want to use the term "ideogram" either because of how it had been used in the past; I suggested the term "semagram" instead.

It appeared that a semagram corresponded roughly to a written word in human languages: it was meaningful on its own, and in combination with other semagrams could form endless statements. We couldn't define it precisely, but then no one had ever satisfactorily defined "word" for human languages either. When it came to sentences in Heptapod B, though, things became much more confusing. The language had no written punctuation: its syntax was indicated in the way the semagrams were combined, and there was no need to indicate the cadence of speech. There was certainly no way to slice out subject-predicate pairings neatly to make sentences. A "sentence" seemed to be whatever number of semagrams a heptapod wanted to join together; the only difference between a sentence and a paragraph, or a page, was size.

When a Heptapod B sentence grew fairly sizable, its visual impact was remarkable. If I wasn't trying to decipher it, the writing looked like fanciful praying mantids drawn in a cursive style, all clinging to each other to form an Escheresque lattice, each slightly different in its stance. And the biggest sentences had an effect similar to that of psychedelic posters: sometimes eye-watering, sometimes hypnotic.

I remember a picture of you taken at your college graduation. In the photo you're striking a pose for the camera, mortarboard stylishly tilted on your head, one hand touching your sunglasses, the other hand on your hip, holding open your gown to reveal the tank top and shorts you're wearing underneath.

I remember your graduation. There will be the distraction of having Nelson and your father and what's-her-name there all at the same time, but that will be minor. That entire weekend, while you're introducing me to your classmates and hugging everyone incessantly, I'll be all but mute with amazement. I can't believe that you, a grown woman taller than me and beautiful enough to make my heart ache, will be the same girl I used to lift off the ground so you could reach the drinking fountain, the same girl who used to trundle out of my bedroom draped in a dress and hat and four scarves from my closet.

And after graduation, you'll be heading for a job as a financial analyst. I won't understand what you do there, I won't even understand your fascination with money, the preeminence you gave to salary when negotiating job offers. I would prefer it if you'd pursue something without regard for its monetary rewards, but I'll have no complaints. My own mother could never understand why I couldn't just be a high school English teacher. You'll do what makes you happy, and that'll be all I ask for.

As time went on, the teams at each looking glass began working in earnest on learning heptapod terminology for elementary mathematics and physics. We worked together on presentations, with the linguists focusing on procedure and the physicists focusing on subject matter. The physicists showed us previously devised systems for communicating with aliens, based on mathematics, but those were intended for use over a radio telescope. We reworked them for face-to-face communication.

Our teams were successful with basic arithmetic, but we hit a road block with geometry and algebra. We tried using a spherical coordinate system instead of a rectangular one, thinking it might be more natural to the heptapods given their anatomy, but that approach wasn't any more fruitful. The heptapods didn't seem to understand what we were getting at.

Likewise, the physics discussions went poorly. Only with the most concrete terms, like the names of the elements, did we have any success; after several attempts at representing the periodic table, the heptapods got the idea. For anything remotely abstract, we might as well have been gibbering. We tried to demonstrate basic physical attributes like mass and acceleration so we could elicit their terms for them, but the heptapods simply responded with requests for clarification. To avoid perceptual problems that might be associated with any particular medium, we tried physical demonstrations as well as line drawings, photos, and animations; none were effective. Days with no progress became weeks, and the physicists were becoming disillusioned.

By contrast, the linguists were having much more success. We made steady progress decoding the grammar of the spoken language, Heptapod A. It didn't follow the pattern of human languages, as expected, but it was comprehensible so far: free word order, even to the extent that there was no preferred order for the clauses in a conditional statement, in defiance of a human language "universal." It also appeared that the heptapods had no objection to many levels of center-embedding of clauses, something that quickly defeated humans. Peculiar, but not impenetrable.

Much more interesting were the newly discovered morphological and grammatical processes in Heptapod B that were uniquely two-dimensional. Depending on a semagram's declension, inflections could be indicated by varying a certain stroke's curvature, or its thickness, or its manner of undulation; or by varying the relative sizes of two radicals, or their relative distance to another radical, or their orientations; or various other means. These were nonsegmental graphemes; they couldn't be isolated from the rest of a semagram. And despite how such traits behaved in human writing, these had nothing to do with calligraphic style; their meanings were defined according to a consistent and unambiguous grammar.

We regularly asked the heptapods why they had come. Each time, they answered "to see," or "to observe." Indeed, sometimes they preferred to watch us silently rather than answer our questions. Perhaps they were scientists, perhaps they were tourists. The State Department instructed us to reveal as little as possible about humanity, in case that information could be used as a bargaining chip in subsequent negotiations. We obliged, though it didn't require much effort: the heptapods never asked questions about anything. Whether scientists or tourists, they were an awfully incurious bunch.

I remember once when we'll be driving to the mall to buy some new clothes for you. You'll be thirteen. One moment you'll be sprawled in your seat, completely unselfconscious, all child; the next, you'll toss your hair with a practiced casualness, like a fashion model in training.

You'll give me some instructions as I'm parking the car. "Okay, Mom, give me one of the credit cards, and we can meet back at the entrance here in two hours."

I'll laugh. "Not a chance. All the credit cards stay with me."

"You're kidding." You'll become the embodiment of exasperation. We'll get out of the car and I will start walking to the mall entrance. After seeing that I won't budge on the matter, you'll quickly reformulate your plans.

"Okay Mom, okay. You can come with me, just walk a little ways behind me, so it doesn't look like we're together. If I see any friends of mine, I'm gonna stop and talk to them, but you just keep walking, okay? I'll come find you later."

I'll stop in my tracks. "Excuse me? I am not the hired help, nor am I some mutant relative for you to be ashamed of."

"But Mom, I can't let anyone see you with me."

"What are you talking about? I've already met your friends; they've been to the house."

"That was different," you'll say, incredulous that you have to explain it. "This is shopping."

"Too bad."

Then the explosion: "You won't do the least thing to make me happy! You don't care about me at all!"

It won't have been that long since you enjoyed going shopping with me; it will forever astonish me how quickly you grow out of one phase and enter another. Living with you will be like aiming for a moving target; you'll always be further along than I expect.

I looked at the sentence in Heptapod B that I had just written, using simple pen and paper. Like all the sentences I generated myself, this one looked misshapen, like a heptapod-written sentence that had been smashed with a hammer and then inexpertly taped back together. I had sheets of such inelegant semagrams covering my desk, fluttering occasionally when the oscillating fan swung past.

It was strange trying to learn a language that had no spoken form. Instead of practicing my pronunciation, I had taken to squeezing my eyes shut and trying to paint semagrams on the insides of my eyelids.

There was a knock at the door and before I could answer Gary came in looking jubilant. "Illinois got a repetition in physics."

"Really? That's great; when did it happen?"

"It happened a few hours ago; we just had the videoconference. Let me show you what it is." He started erasing my blackboard.

"Don't worry, I didn't need any of that."

"Good." He picked up a nub of chalk and drew a diagram:

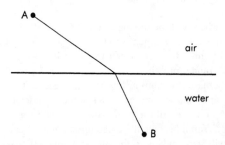

"Okay, here's the path a ray of light takes when crossing from air to water. The light ray travels in a straight line until it hits the water; the water has a different index of refraction, so the light changes direction. You've heard of this before, right?"

I nodded. "Sure."

"Now here's an interesting property about the path the light takes. The path is the fastest possible route between these two points."

"Come again?"

"Imagine, just for grins, that the ray of light traveled along this path." He added a dotted line to his diagram:

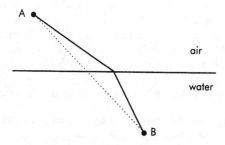

"This hypothetical path is shorter than the path the light actually takes. But light travels more slowly in water than it does in air, and a greater percentage of this path is underwater. So it would take longer for light to travel along this path than it does along the real path."

"Okay, I get it."

"Now imagine if light were to travel along this other path." He drew a second dotted path:

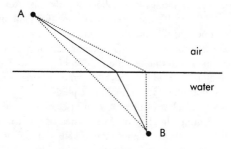

"This path reduces the percentage that's underwater, but the total length is larger. It would also take longer for light to travel along this path than along the actual one."

Gary put down the chalk and gestured at the diagram on the chalkboard with white-tipped fingers. "Any hypothetical path would require more time to traverse than the one actually taken. In other words, the route that the light ray takes is always the fastest possible one. That's Fermat's Principle of Least Time."

"Hmm, interesting. And this is what the heptapods responded to?"

"Exactly. Moorehead gave an animated presentation of Fermat's Principle at the Illinois looking glass, and the heptapods repeated it back. Now he's trying to get a symbolic description." He grinned. "Now is that highly neat, or what?"

"It's neat all right, but how come I haven't heard of Fermat's Principle before?" I picked up a binder and waved it at him; it was a primer on the physics topics suggested for use in communication with the heptapods. "This thing goes on forever about Planck masses and the spin-flip of atomic hydrogen, and not a word about the refraction of light."

"We guessed wrong about what'd be most useful for you to know," Gary said without embarrassment. "In fact, it's curious that Fermat's Principle was the first breakthrough; even though it's easy to explain, you need calculus to describe it mathematically. And not ordinary calculus; you need the calculus of variations. We thought that some simple theorem of geometry or algebra would be the breakthrough."

"Curious indeed. You think the heptapods' idea of what's simple doesn't match ours?"

"Exactly, which is why I'm *dying* to see what their mathematical description of Fermat's Principle looks like." He paced as he talked. "If their version of the calculus of variations is simpler to them than their equivalent of algebra, that might explain why we've had so much trouble talking about physics; their entire system of mathematics may be topsy-turvy compared to ours." He pointed to the physics primer. "You can be sure that we're going to revise that."

"So can you build from Fermat's Principle to other areas of physics?"

"Probably. There are lots of physical principles just like Fermat's."

"What, like Louise's principle of least closet space? When did physics become so minimalist?"

"Well, the word 'least' is misleading. You see, Fermat's Principle of Least Time is incomplete; in certain situations light follows a path that takes *more* time than any of the other possibilities. It's more accurate to say that light always follows an *extreme* path, either one that minimizes the time taken or one that maximizes it. A minimum and a maximum share certain mathematical properties, so both situations can be described with one equation. So to be precise, Fermat's Principle isn't a minimal principle; instead it's what's known as a 'variational' principle."

"And there are more of these variational principles?"

He nodded. "In all branches of physics. Almost every physical law can be restated as a variational principle. The only difference between these principles is in which attribute is minimized or maximized." He gestured as if the different branches of physics were arrayed before him on a table. "In optics, where Fermat's Principle applies, time is the attribute that has to be an extreme. In mechanics, it's a different attribute. In electromagnetism, it's something else again. But all these principles are similar mathematically."

"So once you get their mathematical description of Fermat's Principle, you should be able to decode the other ones."

"God, I hope so. I think this is the wedge that we've been looking for, the one that cracks open their formulation of physics. This calls for a celebration." He stopped his pacing and turned to me. "Hey, Louise, want to go out for dinner? My treat."

I was mildly surprised. "Sure," I said.

It'll be when you first learn to walk that I get daily demonstrations of the asymmetry in our relationship. You'll be incessantly running off somewhere, and each time you walk into a door frame or scrape your knee, the pain feels like it's my own. It'll be like growing an errant limb, an extension of myself whose sensory nerves report pain just fine, but whose motor nerves don't convey my commands at all.

It's so unfair: I'm going to give birth to an animated voodoo doll of myself. I didn't see this in the contract when I signed up. Was this part of the deal?

And then there will be the times when I see you laughing. Like the time you'll be playing with the neighbor's puppy, poking your hands through the chain-link fence separating our back yards, and you'll be laughing so hard you'll start hiccupping. The puppy will run inside the neighbor's house, and your laughter will gradually subside, letting you catch your breath. Then the puppy will come back to the fence to lick your fingers again, and you'll shriek and start laughing again. It will be the most wonderful sound I could ever imagine, a sound that makes me feel like a fountain, or a wellspring.

Now if only I can remember that sound the next time your blithe disregard for self-preservation gives me a heart attack.

After the breakthrough with Fermat's Principle, discussions of scientific concepts became more fruitful. It wasn't as if all of heptapod physics was suddenly rendered transparent, but progress was steady. According to Gary, the heptapods' formulation of physics was indeed topsy-turvy relative to ours. Physical attributes that humans defined using integral calculus were seen as fundamental by the heptapods. As an example, Gary described an attribute that, in physics jargon, bore the deceptively simple name "action," which represented "the difference between kinetic and potential energy, integrated over time," whatever that meant. Calculus for us; elementary to them.

Conversely, to define attributes that humans thought of as fundamental, like velocity, the heptapods employed mathematics that were, Gary assured me, "highly weird." The physicists were ultimately able to prove the equivalence of heptapod mathematics and human mathematics; even though their approaches were almost the reverse of one another, both were systems of describing the same physical universe.

I tried following some of the equations that the physicists were coming up with, but it was no use. I couldn't really grasp the significance of physical attributes like "action"; I couldn't, with any confidence, ponder the significance of treating such an attribute as fundamental. Still, I tried to ponder questions formulated in terms more familiar to me: what kind of worldview did the heptapods have, that they would consider Fermat's Principle the simplest explanation of light refraction? What kind of perception made a minimum or maximum readily apparent to them?

Your eyes will be blue like your dad's, not mud brown like mine. Boys will stare into those eyes the way I did, and do, into your dad's, surprised and enchanted, as I was and am, to find them in combination with black hair. You will have many suitors.

I remember when you are fifteen, coming home after a weekend at your dad's, incredulous over the interrogation he'll have put you through regarding the boy you're currently dating. You'll sprawl on the sofa, recounting your dad's latest breach of common sense: "You know what he said? He said, 'I know what teenage boys are like.'" Roll of the eyes. "Like I don't?"

"Don't hold it against him," I'll say. "He's a father; he can't help it." Having seen you interact with your friends, I won't worry much about a boy taking advantage of you; if anything, the opposite will be more likely. I'll worry about that.

"He wishes I were still a kid. He hasn't known how to act toward me since I grew breasts."

"Well, that development was a shock for him. Give him time to recover."

"It's been *years*, Mom. How long is it gonna take?"

"I'll let you know when my father has come to terms with mine."

During one of the videoconferences for the linguists, Cisneros from the Massachusetts looking glass had raised an interesting question: was there a particular order in which semagrams were written in a Heptapod B sentence? It was clear that word order meant next to nothing when speaking in Heptapod A; when asked to repeat what it had just said, a heptapod would likely as not use a different word order unless we specifically asked them not to. Was word order similarly unimportant when writing in Heptapod B?

Previously, we had only focused our attention on how a sentence in Heptapod B looked once it was complete. As far as anyone could tell, there was no preferred order when reading the semagrams in a sentence; you could start almost anywhere in the nest, then follow the branching clauses until you'd read the whole thing. But that was reading; was the same true about writing?

During my most recent session with Flapper and Raspberry I had asked them if, instead of displaying a semagram only after it was completed, they could show it to us while it was being written. They had agreed. I inserted the videotape of the session into the VCR, and on my computer I consulted the session transcript.

I picked one of the longer utterances from the conversation. What Flapper had said was that the heptapods' planet had two moons, one significantly larger than the other; the three primary constituents of the planet's atmosphere were nitrogen, argon, and oxygen; and fifteen twenty-eights of the planet's surface was covered by water. The first words of the spoken utterance translated literally as "inequality-of-size rocky-orbiter rocky-orbiters related-as-primary-to-secondary."

Then I rewound the videotape until the time signature matched the one in the transcription. I started playing the tape, and watched the web of semagrams being spun out of inky spider's silk. I rewound it and played it several times. Finally I froze the video right after the first stroke was completed and before the second one was begun; all that was visible onscreen was a single sinuous line.

Comparing that initial stroke with the completed sentence, I realized that the stroke participated in several different clauses of the message. It began in the semagram for 'oxygen,' as the determinant that distinguished it from certain other elements; then it slid down to become the morpheme of comparison in the description of the two moons' sizes; and lastly it flared out as the arched backbone of the semagram for 'ocean.' Yet this stroke was a single continuous line, and it was the first one that Flapper wrote. That meant the heptapod had to know how the entire sentence would be laid out before it could write the very first stroke.

The other strokes in the sentence also traversed several clauses, making them so interconnected that none could be removed without redesigning the entire sentence. The heptapods didn't write a sentence one semagram at a time; they built it out of strokes irrespective of individual semagrams. I had seen a similarly high degree of integration before in calligraphic designs, particularly those employing the Arabic alphabet. But those designs had required careful planning by expert calligraphers. No one could lay out such an intricate design at the speed needed for holding a conversation. At least, no human could.

There's a joke that I once heard a comedienne tell. It goes like this: "I'm not sure if I'm ready to have children. I asked a friend of mine who has children, 'Suppose I do have kids. What if when they grow up, they blame me for everything that's wrong with their lives?' She laughed and said, 'What do you mean, if?' "

That's my favorite joke.

Gary and I were at a little Chinese restaurant, one of the local places we had taken to patronizing to get away from the encampment. We sat eating the appetizers: potstickers, redolent of pork and sesame oil. My favorite.

I dipped one in soy sauce and vinegar. "So how are you doing with your Heptapod B practice?" I asked.

Gary looked obliquely at the ceiling. I tried to meet his gaze, but he kept shifting it.

"You've given up, haven't you?" I said. "You're not even trying any more."

He did a wonderful hangdog expression. "I'm just no good at languages," he confessed. "I thought learning Heptapod B might be more like learning mathematics than trying to speak another language, but it's not. It's too foreign for me."

"It would help you discuss physics with them."

"Probably, but since we had our breakthrough, I can get by with just a few phrases."

I sighed. "I suppose that's fair; I have to admit, I've given up on trying to learn the mathematics."

"So we're even?"

"We're even." I sipped my tea. "Though I did want to ask you about Fermat's Principle. Something about it feels odd to me, but I can't put my finger on it. It just doesn't sound like a law of physics."

A twinkle appeared in Gary's eyes. "I'll bet I know what you're talking about." He snipped a potsticker in half with his chopsticks. "You're used to thinking of refraction in terms of cause and effect: reaching the water's surface is the cause, and the change in direction is the effect. But Fermat's Principle sounds weird because it describes light's behavior in goal-oriented terms. It sounds like a commandment to a light beam: 'Thou shalt minimize or maximize the time taken to reach thy destination.' "

I considered it. "Go on."

"It's an old question in the philosophy of physics. People have been talking about it since Fermat first formulated it in the 1600s; Planck wrote volumes about it. The thing is, while the common formulation of physical laws is causal, a variational principle like Fermat's is purposive, almost teleological."

"Hmm, that's an interesting way to put it. Let me think about that for a minute." I pulled out a felt-tip pen and, on my paper napkin, drew a copy of the diagram that Gary had drawn on my blackboard. "Okay," I said, thinking aloud, "so let's say the goal of a ray of light is to take the fastest path. How does the light go about doing that?"

"Well, if I can speak anthropomorphic-projectionally, the light has to examine the possible paths and compute how long each one would take." He plucked the last potsticker from the serving dish.

"And to do that," I continued, "the ray of light has to know just where its destination is. If the destination were somewhere else, the fastest path would be different."

Gary nodded again. "That's right; the notion of a 'fastest path' is meaningless unless there's a destination specified. And computing how long a given path takes also requires information about what lies along that path, like where the water's surface is."

I kept staring at the diagram on the napkin. "And the light ray has to know all that ahead of time, before it starts moving, right?"

"So to speak," said Gary. "The light can't start traveling in any old direction and make course corrections later on, because the path resulting from such behavior wouldn't be the fastest possible one. The light has to do all its computations at the very beginning."

I thought to myself, *the ray of light has to know where it will ultimately end up before it can choose the direction to begin moving in*. I knew what that reminded me of. I looked up at Gary. "That's what was bugging me."

I remember when you're fourteen. You'll come out of your bedroom, a graffiti-covered notebook computer in hand, working on a report for school.

"Mom, what do you call it when both sides can win?"

I'll look up from my computer and the paper I'll be writing. "What, you mean a win-win situation?"

"There's some technical name for it, some math word. Remember that time Dad was here, and he was talking about the stock market? He used it then."

"Hmm, that sounds familiar, but I can't remember what he called it."

"I need to know. I want to use that phrase in my social studies report. I can't even search for information on it unless I know what it's called."

"I'm sorry, I don't know it either. Why don't you call your dad?"

Judging from your expression, that will be more effort than you want to make. At this point, you and your father won't be getting along well. "Can you call Dad and ask him? But don't tell him it's for me."

"I think you can call him yourself."

You'll fume, "Jesus, Mom, I can never get help with my homework since you and Dad split up."

It's amazing the diverse situations in which you can bring up the divorce. "I've helped you with your homework."

"Like a million years ago, Mom."

I'll let that pass. "I'd help you with this if I could, but I don't remember what it's called."

You'll head back to your bedroom in a huff.

. . .

I practiced Heptapod B at every opportunity, both with the other linguists and by myself. The novelty of reading a semasiographic language made it compelling in a way that Heptapod A wasn't, and my improvement in writing it excited me. Over time, the sentences I wrote grew shapelier, more cohesive. I had reached the point where it worked better when I didn't think about it too much. Instead of carefully trying to design a sentence before writing, I could simply begin putting down strokes immediately; my initial strokes almost always turned out to be compatible with an elegant rendition of what I was trying to say. I was developing a faculty like that of the heptapods.

More interesting was the fact that Heptapod B was changing the way I thought. For me, thinking typically meant speaking in an internal voice; as we say in the trade, my thoughts were phonologically coded. My internal voice normally spoke in English, but that wasn't a requirement. The summer after my senior year in high school, I attended a total immersion program for learning Russian; by the end of the summer, I was thinking and even dreaming in Russian. But it was always *spoken* Russian. Different language, same mode: a voice speaking silently aloud.

The idea of thinking in a linguistic yet nonphonological mode always intrigued me. I had a friend born of dead parents; he grew up using American Sign Language, and he told me that he often thought in ASL instead of English. I used to wonder what it was like to have one's thoughts be manually coded, to reason using an inner pair of hands instead of an inner voice.

With Heptapod B, I was experiencing something just as foreign: my thoughts were becoming graphically coded. There were trancelike moments during the day when my thoughts weren't expressed with my internal voice; instead, I saw semagrams with my mind's eye, sprouting like frost on a windowpane.

As I grew more fluent, semagraphic designs would appear fully formed, articulating even complex ideas all at once. My thought processes weren't moving any faster as a result, though. Instead of racing forward, my mind hung balanced on the symmetry underlying the semagrams. The semagrams seemed to be something more than language; they were almost like mandalas. I found myself in a meditative state, contemplating the way in which premises and conclusions were interchangeable. There was no direction inherent in the way propositions were connected, no "train of thought" moving along a particular route; all the components in an act of reasoning were equally powerful, all having identical precedence.

A representative from the State Department named Hossner had the job of briefing the U.S. scientists on our agenda with the heptapods. We sat in the videoconference room, listening to him lecture. Our microphone was turned off, so Gary and I could exchange comments without interrupting Hossner. As we listened, I worried that Gary might harm his vision, rolling his eyes so often.

"They must have had some reason for coming all this way," said the diplomat, his voice tinny through the speakers. "It does not look like their reason was conquest, thank God. But if that's not the reason, what is? Are they prospectors?

Anthropologists? Missionaries? Whatever their motives, there must be something we can offer them. Maybe it's mineral rights to our solar system. Maybe it's information about ourselves. Maybe it's the right to deliver sermons to our populations. But we can be sure that there's something.

"My point is this: their motive might not be to trade, but that doesn't mean that we cannot conduct trade. We simply need to know why they're here, and what we have that they want. Once we have that information, we can begin trade negotiations.

"I should emphasize that our relationship with the heptapods need not be adversarial. This is not a situation where every gain on their part is a loss on ours, or vice versa. If we handle ourselves correctly, both we and the heptapods can come out winners."

"You mean it's a non-zero-sum game?" Gary said in mock incredulity. "Oh my gosh."

"A non-zero-sum game."

"What?" You'll reverse course, heading back from your bedroom.

"When both sides can win: I just remembered, it's called a non-zero-sum game."

"That's it!" you'll say, writing it down on your notebook. "Thanks, Mom!"

"I guess I knew it after all," I'll say. "All those years with your father, some of it must have rubbed off."

"I knew you'd know it," you'll say. You'll give me a sudden, brief hug, and your hair will smell of apples. "You're the best."

"Louise?"

"Hmm? Sorry, I was distracted. What did you say?"

"I said, what do you think about our Mr. Hossner here?"

"I prefer not to."

"I've tried that myself: ignoring the government, seeing if it would go away. It hasn't."

As evidence of Gary's assertion, Hossner kept blathering: "Your immediate task is to think back on what you've learned. Look for anything that might help us. Has there been any indication of what the heptapods want? Of what they value?"

"Gee, it never occurred to us to look for things like that," I said. "We'll get right on it, sir."

"The sad thing is, that's just what we'll have to do," said Gary.

"Are there any questions?" asked Hossner.

Burghart, the linguist at the Fort Worth looking glass, spoke up. "We've been through this with the heptapods many times. They maintain that they're here to observe, and they maintain that information is not tradable."

"So they would have us believe," said Hossner. "But consider: how could that be true? I know that the heptapods have occasionally stopped talking to us for brief periods. That may be a tactical maneuver on their part. If we were to stop talking to them tomorrow—"

"Wake me up if he says something interesting," said Gary.

"I was just going to ask you to do the same for me."

. . .

That day when Gary first explained Fermat's Principle to me, he had mentioned that almost every physical law could be stated as a variational principle. Yet when humans thought about physical laws, they preferred to work with them in their causal formulation. I could understand that: the physical attributes that humans found intuitive, like kinetic energy or acceleration, were all properties of an object at a given moment in time. And these were conducive to a chronological, causal interpretation of events: one moment growing out of another, causes and effects created a chain reaction that grew from past to future.

In contrast, the physical attributes that the heptapods found intuitive, like "action" or those other things defined by integrals, were meaningful only over a period of time. And these were conducive to a teleological interpretation of events: by viewing events over a period of time, one recognized that there was a requirement that had to be satisfied, a goal of minimizing or maximizing. And one had to know the initial and final states to meet that goal; one needed knowledge of the effects before the causes could be initiated.

I was growing to understand that, too.

"Why?" you'll ask again. You'll be three.

"Because it's your bedtime," I'll say again. We'll have gotten as far as getting you bathed and into your jammies, but no further than that.

"But I'm not sleepy," you'll whine. You'll be standing at the bookshelf, pulling down a video to watch: your latest diversionary tactic to keep away from your bedroom.

"It doesn't matter: you still have to go to bed."

"But why?"

"Because I'm the mom and I said so."

I'm actually going to say that, aren't I? God, somebody please shoot me.

I'll pick you up and carry you under my arm to your bed, you wailing piteously all the while, but my sole concern will be my own distress. All those vows made in childhood that I would give reasonable answers when I became a parent, that I would treat my own child as an intelligent, thinking individual, all for naught: I'm going to turn into my mother. I can fight it as much as I want, but there'll be no stopping my slide down that long, dreadful slope.

Was it actually possible to know the future? Not simply to guess at it; was it possible to _know_ what was going to happen, with absolute certainty and in specific detail? Gary once told me that the fundamental laws of physics were time-symmetric, that there was no physical difference between past and future. Given that, some might say, "yes, theoretically." But speaking more concretely, most would answer "no," because of free will.

I liked to imagine the objection as a Borgesian fabulation: consider a person standing before the _Book of Ages_, the chronicle that records every event, past and future. Even though the text has been photoreduced from the full-sized edition, the volume is enormous. With magnifier in hand, she flips through the tissue-thin leaves until she locates the story of her life. She finds the passage that describes her flipping through the *Book of Ages*, and she skips to the next column, where it details what she'll be doing later in the day: acting on information she's read in the *Book*, she'll bet one hundred dollars on the racehorse Devil May Care and win twenty times that much.

The thought of doing just that had crossed her mind, but being a contrary sort, she now resolves to refrain from betting on the ponies altogether.

There's the rub. The *Book of Ages* cannot be wrong; this scenario is based on the premise that a person is given knowledge of the actual future, not of some possible future. If this were Greek myth, circumstances would conspire to make her enact her fate despite her best efforts, but prophecies in myth are notoriously vague; the *Book of Ages* is quite specific, and there's no way she can be forced to bet on a racehorse in the manner specified. The result is a contradiction: the *Book of Ages* must be right, by definition; yet no matter what the *Book* says she'll do, she can choose to do otherwise. How can these two facts be reconciled?

They can't be, was the common answer. A volume like the *Book of Ages* is a logical impossibility, for the precise reason that its existence would result in the above contradiction. Or, to be generous, some might say that the *Book of Ages* could exist, as long as it wasn't accessible to readers: that volume is housed in a special collection, and no one has viewing privileges.

The existence of free will meant that we couldn't know the future. And we knew free will existed because we had direct experience of it. Volition was an intrinsic part of consciousness.

Or was it? What if the experience of knowing the future changed a person? What if it evoked a sense of urgency, a sense of obligation to act precisely as she knew she would?

I stopped by Gary's office before leaving for the day. "I'm calling it quits. Did you want to grab something to eat?"

"Sure, just wait a second," he said. He shut down his computer and gathered some papers together. Then he looked up at me. "Hey, want to come to my place for dinner tonight? I'll cook."

I looked at him dubiously. "You can cook?"

"Just one dish," he admitted. "But it's a good one."

"Sure," I said. "I'm game."

"Great. We just need to go shopping for the ingredients."

"Don't go to any trouble—"

"There's a market on the way to my house. It won't take a minute."

We took separate cars, me following him. I almost lost him when he abruptly turned in to a parking lot. It was a gourmet market, not large, but fancy; tall glass jars stuffed with imported foods sat next to specialty utensils on the store's stainless-steel shelves.

I accompanied Gary as he collected fresh basil, tomatoes, garlic, linguini. "There's a fish market next door; we can get fresh clams there," he said.

"Sounds good." We walked past the section of kitchen utensils. My gaze wandered over the shelves—peppermills, garlic presses, salad tongs—and stopped on a wooden salad bowl.

When you are three, you'll pull a dishtowel off the kitchen counter and bring that salad bowl down on top of you. I'll make a grab for it, but I'll miss. The edge of the bowl will leave you with a cut, on the upper edge of your forehead, that will require a single stitch. Your father and I will hold you, sobbing and stained with Caesar salad dressing, as we wait in the emergency room for hours.

I reached out and took the bowl from the shelf. The motion didn't feel like something I was forced to do. Instead it seemed just as urgent as my rushing to catch the bowl when it falls on you: an instinct that I felt right in following.

"I could use a salad bowl like this."

Gary looked at the bowl and nodded approvingly. "See, wasn't it a good thing that I had to stop at the market?"

"Yes it was." We got in line to pay for our purchases.

Consider the sentence "The rabbit is ready to eat." Interpret "rabbit" to be the object of "eat," and the sentence was an announcement that dinner would be served shortly. Interpret "rabbit" to be the subject of "eat," and it was a hint, such as a young girl might give her mother so she'll open a bag of Purina Bunny Chow. Two very different utterances; in fact, they were probably mutually exclusive within a single household. Yet either was a valid interpretation; only context could determine what the sentence meant.

Consider the phenomenon of light hitting water at one angle, and traveling through it at a different angle. Explain it by saying that a difference in the index of refraction caused the light to change direction, and one saw the world as humans saw it. Explain it by saying that light minimized the time needed to travel to its destination, and one saw the world as the heptapods saw it. Two very different interpretations.

The physical universe was a language with a perfectly ambiguous grammar. Every physical event was an utterance that could be parsed in two entirely different ways, one causal and the other teleological, both valid, neither one disqualifiable no matter how much context was available.

When the ancestors of humans and heptapods first acquired the spark of consciousness, they both perceived the same physical world, but they parsed their perceptions differently; the worldviews that ultimately arose were the end result of that divergence. Humans had developed a sequential mode of awareness, while heptapods had developed a simultaneous mode of awareness. We experienced events in an order, and perceived their relationship as cause and effect. They experienced all events at once, and perceived a purpose underlying them all. A minimizing, maximizing purpose.

I have a recurring dream about your death. In the dream, I'm the one who's rock climbing—me, can you imagine it?—and you're three years old, riding in some kind of backpack I'm wearing. We're just a few feet below a ledge where we can rest, and you won't wait until I've climbed up to it. You start pulling yourself out of the pack; I order you to stop, but of course you ignore me. I feel your weight alternating from one side of the pack to the other as you climb out; then I feel your left foot on my shoulder, and then your right. I'm screaming at you, but I can't get a hand free to grab you. I can see the wavy design on the soles of your sneakers as you climb, and then I see a flake of stone give way beneath one of them. You slide right past me, and I can't move a muscle. I look down and see you shrink into the distance below me.

Then, all of a sudden, I'm at the morgue. An orderly lifts the sheet from your face, and I see that you're twenty-five.

"You okay?"

I was sitting upright in bed; I'd woken Gary with my movements. "I'm fine. I was just startled; I didn't recognize where I was for a moment."

Sleepily, he said, "We can stay at your place next time."

I kissed him. "Don't worry; your place is fine." We curled up, my back against his chest, and went back to sleep.

When you're three and we're climbing a steep, spiral flight of stairs, I'll hold your hand extra tightly. You'll pull your hand away from me. "I can do it by myself," you'll insist, and then move away from me to prove it, and I'll remember that dream. We'll repeat that scene countless times during your childhood. I can almost believe that, given your contrary nature, my attempts to protect you will be what create your love of climbing: first the jungle gym at the playground, then trees out in the green belt around our neighborhood, the rock walls at the climbing club, and ultimately cliff faces in national parks.

I finished the last radical in the sentence, put down the chalk, and sat down in my desk chair. I leaned back and surveyed the giant Heptapod B sentence I'd written that covered the entire blackboard in my office. It included several complex clauses, and I had managed to integrate all of them rather nicely.

Looking at a sentence like this one, I understood why the heptapods had evolved a semasiographic writing system like Heptapod B; it was better suited for a species with a simultaneous mode of consciousness. For them, speech was a bottleneck because it required that one word follow another sequentially. With writing, on the other hand, every mark on a page was visible simultaneously. Why constrain writing with a glotto-graphic straitjacket, demanding that it be just as sequential as speech? It would never occur to them. Semasiographic writing naturally took advantage of the page's two-dimensionality; instead of doling out morphemes one at a time, it offered an entire page full of them all at once.

And now that Heptapod B had introduced me to a simultaneous mode of consciousness, I understood the rationale behind Heptapod A's grammar: what my sequential mind had perceived as unnecessarily convoluted, I now recognized as an attempt to provide flexibility within the confines of sequential speech. I could use Heptapod A more easily as a result, though it was still a poor substitute for Heptapod B.

There was a knock at the door and then Gary poked his head in. "Colonel Weber'll be here any minute."

I grimaced. "Right." Weber was coming to participate in a session with Flapper and Raspberry; I was to act as translator, a job I wasn't trained for and that I detested.

Gary stepped inside and closed the door. He pulled me out of my chair and kissed me.

I smiled. "You trying to cheer me up before he gets here?"

"No, I'm trying to cheer me up."

"You weren't interested in talking to the heptapods at all, were you? You worked on this project just to get me into bed."

"Ah, you see right through me."

I looked into his eyes. "You better believe it," I said.

I remember when you'll be a month old, and I'll stumble out of bed to give you your 2:00 A.M. feeding. Your nursery will have that "baby smell" of diaper rash cream and talcum powder, with a faint ammoniac whiff coming from the diaper pail in the corner. I'll lean over your crib, lift your squalling form out, and sit in the rocking chair to nurse you.

The word "infant" is derived from the Latin word for "unable to speak," but you'll be perfectly capable of saying one thing: "I suffer," and you'll do it tirelessly and without hesitation. I have to admire your utter commitment to that statement; when you cry, you'll become outrage incarnate, every fiber of your body employed in expressing that emotion. It's funny: when you're tranquil, you will seem to radiate light, and if someone were to paint a portrait of you like that, I'd insist that they include the halo. But when you're unhappy, you will become a klaxon, built for radiating sound; a portrait of you then could simply be a fire alarm bell.

At that stage of your life, there'll be no past or future for you; until I give you my breast, you'll have no memory of contentment in the past nor expectation of relief in the future. Once you begin nursing, everything will reverse, and all will be right with the world. NOW is the only moment you'll perceive; you'll live in the present tense. In many ways, it's an enviable state.

The heptapods are neither free nor bound as we understand those concepts; they don't act according to their will, nor are they helpless automatons. What distinguishes the heptapods' mode of awareness is not just that their actions coincide with history's events; it is also that their motives coincide with history's purposes. They act to create the future, to enact chronology.

Freedom isn't an illusion; it's perfectly real in the context of sequential consciousness. Within the context of simultaneous consciousness, freedom is not meaningful, but neither is coercion; it's simply a different context, no more or less valid than the other. It's like that famous optical illusion, the drawing of either an elegant young woman, face turned away from the viewer, or a wart-nosed crone, chin tucked down on her chest. There's no "correct" interpretation; both are equally valid. But you can't see both at the same time.

Similarly, knowledge of the future was incompatible with free will. What made it possible for me to exercise freedom of choice also made it impossible for me to know the future. Conversely, now that I know the future, I would never act contrary to that future, including telling others what I know: those who know the future don't talk about it. Those who've read the *Book of Ages* never admit to it.

. . .

I turned on the VCR and slotted a cassette of a session from the Fort Worth looking glass. A diplomatic negotiator was having a discussion with the heptapods there, with Burghart acting as translator.

The negotiator was describing humans' moral beliefs, trying to lay some groundwork for the concept of altruism. I knew the heptapods were familiar with the conversation's eventual outcome, but they still participated enthusiastically.

If I could have described this to someone who didn't already know, she might ask, if the heptapods already knew everything that they would ever say or hear, what was the point of their using language at all? A reasonable question. But language wasn't only for communication: it was also a form of action. According to speech act theory, statements like "You're under arrest," "I christen this vessel," or "I promise" were all performative: a speaker could perform the action only by uttering the words. For such acts, knowing what would be said didn't change anything. Everyone at a wedding anticipated the words "I now pronounce you husband and wife," but until the minister actually said them, the ceremony didn't count. With performative language, saying equaled doing.

For the heptapods, all language was performative. Instead of using language to inform, they used language to actualize. Sure, heptapods already knew what would be said in any conversation; but in order for their knowledge to be true, the conversation would have to take place.

"First Goldilocks tried the papa bear's bowl of porridge, but it was full of brussels sprouts, which she hated."

You'll laugh. "No, that's wrong!" We'll be sitting side by side on the sofa, the skinny, overpriced hardcover spread open on our laps.

I'll keep reading. "Then Goldilocks tried the mama bear's bowl of porridge, but it was full of spinach, which she also hated."

You'll put your hand on the page of the book to stop me. "You have to read it the right way!"

"I'm reading just what it says here," I'll say, all innocence.

"No you're not. That's not how the story goes."

"Well if you already know how the story goes, why do you need me to read it to you?"

"Cause I wanna hear it!"

The air conditioning in Weber's office almost compensated for having to talk to the man.

"They're willing to engage in a type of exchange," I explained, "but it's not trade. We simply give them something, and they give us something in return. Neither party tells the other what they're giving beforehand."

Colonel Weber's brow furrowed just slightly. "You mean they're willing to exchange gifts?"

I knew what I had to say. "We shouldn't think of it as 'gift-giving.' We don't know if this transaction has the same associations for the heptapods that gift-giving has for us."

"Can we—" he searched for the right wording "—drop hints about the kind of gift we want?"

"They don't do that themselves for this type of transaction. I asked them if we could make a request, and they said we could, but it won't make them tell us what they're giving." I suddenly remembered that a morphological relative of "performative" was "performance," which could describe the sensation of conversing when you knew what would be said: it was like performing in a play.

"But would it make them more likely to give us what we asked for?" Colonel Weber asked. He was perfectly oblivious of the script, yet his responses matched his assigned lines exactly.

"No way of knowing," I said. "I doubt it, given that it's not a custom they engage in."

"If we give our gift first, will the value of our gift influence the value of theirs?" He was improvising, while I had carefully rehearsed for this one and only show.

"No," I said. "As far as we can tell, the value of the exchanged items is irrelevant."

"If only my relatives felt that way," murmured Gary wryly.

I watched Colonel Weber turn to Gary. "Have you discovered anything new in the physics discussions?" he asked, right on cue.

"If you mean, any information new to mankind, no," said Gary. "The heptapods haven't varied from the routine. If we demonstrate something to them, they'll show us their formulation of it, but they won't volunteer anything and they won't answer our questions about what they know."

An utterance that was spontaneous and communicative in the context of human discourse became a ritual recitation when viewed by the light of Heptapod B.

Weber scowled. "All right then, we'll see how the State Department feels about this. Maybe we can arrange some kind of gift-giving ceremony."

Like physical events, with their casual and teleological interpretations, every linguistic event had two possible interpretations: as a transmission of information and as the realization of a plan.

"I think that's a good idea, Colonel," I said.

It was an ambiguity invisible to most. A private joke; don't ask me to explain it.

Even though I'm proficient with Heptapod B, I know I don't experience reality the way a heptapod does. My mind was cast in the mold of human, sequential languages, and no amount of immersion in an alien language can completely reshape it. My worldview is an amalgam of human and heptapod.

Before I learned how to think in Heptapod B, my memories grew like a column of cigarette ash, laid down by the infinitesimal sliver of combustion that was my consciousness, marking the sequential present. After I learned Heptapod B, new memories fell into place like gigantic blocks, each one measuring years in duration, and though they didn't arrive in order or land contiguously, they soon composed a period of five decades. It is the period during which I know Heptapod B well enough to think in it, starting during my interviews with Flapper and Raspberry and ending with my death.

Usually, Heptapod B affects just my memory: my consciousness crawls along as it did before, a glowing sliver crawling forward in time, the difference being that the ash of memory lies ahead as well as behind: there is no real combustion. But occasionally I have glimpses when Heptapod B truly reigns, and I experience past and future all at once; my consciousness becomes a half-century-long ember burning outside time. I perceive—during those glimpses—that entire epoch as a simultaneity. It's a period encompassing the rest of my life, and the entirety of yours.

I wrote out the semagrams for "process create-endpoint inclusive-we," meaning "let's start." Raspberry replied in the affirmative, and the slide shows began. The second display screen that the heptapods had provided began presenting a series of images, composed of semagrams and equations, while one of our video screens did the same.

This was the second "gift exchange" I had been present for, the eighth one overall, and I knew it would be the last. The looking-glass tent was crowded with people; Burghart from Fort Worth was here, as were Gary and a nuclear physicist, assorted biologists, anthropologists, military brass, and diplomats. Thankfully they had set up an air conditioner to cool the place off. We would review the tapes of the images later to figure out just what the heptapods' "gift" was. Our own "gift" was a presentation on the Lascaux cave paintings.

We all crowded around the heptapods' second screen, trying to glean some idea of the images' content as they went by. "Preliminary assessments?" asked Colonel Weber.

"It's not a return," said Burghart. In a previous exchange, the heptapods had given us information about ourselves that we had previously told them. This had infuriated the State Department, but we had no reason to think of it as an insult: it probably indicated that trade value really didn't play a role in these exchanges. It didn't exclude the possibility that the heptapods might yet offer us a space drive, or cold fusion, or some other wish-fulfilling miracle.

"That looks like inorganic chemistry," said the nuclear physicist, pointing at an equation before the image was replaced.

Gary nodded. "It could be materials technology," he said.

"Maybe we're finally getting somewhere," said Colonel Weber.

"I wanna see more animal pictures," I whispered, quietly so that only Gary could hear me, and pouted like a child. He smiled and poked me. Truthfully, I wished the heptapods had given another xenobiology lecture, as they had on two previous exchanges; judging from those, humans were more similar to the heptapods than any other species they'd ever encountered. Or another lecture on heptapod history; those had been filled with apparent non-sequiturs, but were interesting nonetheless. I didn't want the heptapods to give us new technology, because I didn't want to see what our governments might do with it.

I watched Raspberry while the information was being exchanged, looking for any anomalous behavior. It stood barely moving as usual; I saw no indications of what would happen shortly.

After a minute, the heptapod's screen went blank, and a minute after that, ours did, too. Gary and most of the other scientists clustered around a tiny video screen that was replaying the heptapods' presentation. I could hear them talk about the need to call in a solid-state physicist.

Colonel Weber turned. "You two," he said, pointing to me and then to Burghart, "schedule the time and location for the next exchange." Then he followed the others to the playback screen.

"Coming right up," I said. To Burghart, I asked, "Would you care to do the honors, or shall I?"

I knew Burghart had gained a proficiency in Heptapod B similar to mine. "It's your looking glass," he said. "You drive."

I sat down again at the transmitting computer. "Bet you never figured you'd wind up working as a Army translator back when you were a grad student."

"That's for goddamn sure," he said. "Even now I can hardly believe it." Everything we said to each other felt like the carefully bland exchanges of spies who meet in public, but never break cover.

I wrote out the semagrams for "locus exchange-transaction converse inclusive-we" with the projective aspect modulation.

Raspberry wrote its reply. That was my cue to frown, and for Burghart to ask, "What does it mean by that?" His delivery was perfect.

I wrote a request for clarification; Raspberry's reply was the same as before. Then I watched it glide out of the room. The curtain was about to fall on this act of our performance.

Colonel Weber stepped forward. "What's going on? Where did it go?"

"It said that the heptapods are leaving now," I said. "Not just itself; all of them."

"Call it back here now. Ask it what it means."

"Um, I don't think Raspberry's wearing a pager," I said.

The image of the room in the looking glass disappeared so abruptly that it took a moment for my eyes to register what I was seeing instead: it was the other side of the looking-glass tent. The looking glass had become completely transparent. The conversation around the playback screen fell silent.

"What the hell is going on here?" said Colonel Weber.

Gary walked up to the looking glass, and then around it to the other side. He touched the rear surface with one hand; I could see the pale ovals where his fingertips made contact with the looking glass. "I think," he said, "we just saw a demonstration of transmutation at a distance."

I heard the sounds of heavy footfalls on dry grass. A soldier came in through the tent door, short of breath from sprinting, holding an oversize walkie-talkie. "Colonel, message from—"

Weber grabbed the walkie-talkie from him.

I remember what it'll be like watching you when you are a day old. Your father will have gone for a quick visit to the hospital cafeteria, and you'll be lying in your bassinet, and I'll be leaning over you.

So soon after the delivery, I will still be feeling like a wrung-out towel. You will seem incongruously tiny, given how enormous I felt during the pregnancy; I could swear there was room for someone much larger and more robust than you in there. Your hands and feet will be long and thin, not chubby yet. Your face will still be all red and pinched, puffy eyelids squeezed shut, the gnomelike phase that precedes the cherubic.

I'll run a finger over your belly, marveling at the uncanny softness of your skin, wondering if silk would abrade your body like burlap. Then you'll writhe, twisting your body while poking out your legs one at a time, and I'll recognize the gesture as one I had felt you do inside me, many times. So *that's* what it looks like.

I'll feel elated at this evidence of a unique mother-child bond, this certitude that you're the one I carried. Even if I had never laid eyes on you before, I'd be able to pick you out from a sea of babies: Not that one. No, not her either. Wait, that one over there.

Yes, that's her. She's mine.

That final "gift exchange" was the last we ever saw of the heptapods. All at once, all over the world, their looking glasses became transparent and their ships left orbit. Subsequent analysis of the looking glasses revealed them to be nothing more than sheets of fused silica, completely inert. The information from the final exchange session described a new class of superconducting materials, but it later proved to duplicate the results of research just completed in Japan: nothing that humans didn't already know.

We never did learn why the heptapods left, any more than we learned what brought them here, or why they acted the way they did. My own new awareness didn't provide that type of knowledge; the heptapods' behavior was presumably explicable from a sequential point of view, but we never found that explanation.

I would have liked to experience more of the heptapods' worldview, to feel the way they feel. Then, perhaps I could immerse myself fully in the necessity of events, as they must, instead of merely wading in its surf for the rest of my life. But that will never come to pass. I will continue to practice the heptapod languages, as will the other linguists on the looking-glass teams, but none of us will ever progress any further than we did when the heptapods were here.

Working with the heptapods changed my life. I met your father and learned Heptapod B, both of which make it possible for me to know you now, here on the patio in the moonlight. Eventually, many years from now, I'll be without your father, and without you. All I will have left from this moment is the heptapod language. So I pay close attention, and note every detail.

From the beginning I knew my destination, and I chose my route accordingly. But am I working toward an extreme of joy, or of pain? Will I achieve a minimum, or a maximum?

These questions are in my mind when your father asks me, "Do you want to make a baby?" And I smile and answer, "Yes," and I unwrap his arms from around me, and we hold hands as we walk inside to make love, to make you.

voivodoi

Liz Williams

Here's a quiet but moving look at a troubled near-future where the sins of the fathers are being visited on the children . . . but where those children just might, against all odds, be slowly fashioning a New World, one rich and various and strange, from the ashes and ruins and burnt-out clinker of the Old. . . .

New writer Liz Williams has sold stories to Interzone, Visionary Tongue, Albedo One, The Third Alternative, *and* Terra Incognita. *Born in Gloucester, England, she received a Ph.D. in Philosophy of Science from Cambridge. She lives in Brighton, England.*

We had a series of awkward, endless meals that summer. Before Roman's illness, we'd always eaten at different times; on the run like most families. Then he fell ill, and, as the days wore on and he became no better, my mother insisted that we eat together at least once during the day.

Eventually, Roman became too unwell to come downstairs and had to have his meals on a tray in his room. His absence at the table was so conspicuous that we could no longer sustain the pretense that everything was well. Obliged to acknowledge the reality of his illness, we became resentful and grumpy. I can understand it now, but all I knew at the time was that Roman had managed to disrupt the soothing family routine. My parents still tried to deny that anything was wrong. Soon, they said, my cheerful, annoying brother would be sitting opposite me again and kicking me under the table. *Enjoy it while it lasts*, my mother said tartly, but children are only young, not fools, and I was unconvinced.

Normally, Roman and I shared a room, but his snuffling breathing and restless movements at night made it difficult for me to sleep. At last mother moved me down to the fold-out bed in the kitchen. I slept better there, but I had no privacy, and at that age you begin to need a quiet place of your own.

We had finished dinner, and mother and I were still sitting at the table. Dinner had followed the usual repetitive, nightmarish pattern of our meals together. Dad had bolted his food, furtively, like an animal, before sliding from the table and into the office. I think he locked the door. All we could hear was the sound of game shows on the portable TV. My mother didn't say much, but she kept trying to catch my eye. I could feel her gaze sliding around my own as I stared at the floor.

I knew Roman was listening because of a sort of suspended silence at the top of the stairs; the sound of someone holding their breath. Andrea, our visiting student, had stayed late at the university and probably wouldn't be back before ten.

My mother broke the silence. "I took your brother a tray. Maybe you could see if he wants anything else? . . . " Her voice trailed away.

"Okay," I said, to fill the returning silence. The door of Roman's room was closed. Outside, the tray stood on the landing, and on it were the meal and Roman's capsules. He had touched neither. He must have had a particularly bad day; it was only then that he refused his medicine. After a moment's thought, I took the warm, slightly glutinous handful to the lavatory and flushed it away. The screen over the open bathroom window had not switched itself on. I checked the AP meter, and the level wasn't yet high enough to activate the screen—unusual in summer.

I wondered whether mother might let me go out tonight, but I knew I wouldn't ask her even though it was Friday. I had become a dutiful daughter, thoughtful and considerate since my brother became ill. I knew that Yuliya and Sveta were down at the District Rink that night, comrades in an elaborate plan to entice shy, strutting Bogdan Maretovitch away from the supportive male flock. Yuliya had had her eye on Bogdan for some time, and had been moving steadily closer for the past couple of months. She understood how things worked, Yuliya. I longed to see the outcome of her campaign, but I couldn't leave mother there in the silence to finish the dishes.

I didn't have to like it, though.

Mother caught my sullen look. Later, she said, "Oh, you know what we're out of? Sugar. And your aunt's coming tomorrow. . . . Could you run down to the co-mart?"

We both knew that the way to the co-mart took me past the Rink. "Don't worry if there's a queue," she called after me. "Take your time."

So I ran down the stairs through the dusty evening silence and out into the last of the light. We were lucky to live here. The woods came up as far as the waste ground at the back of the compartment block, and in summer we could almost believe that we lived in the high, ice-cream peaks of the Tatras, breathing the clean air and a long way from the Krakow suburbs. It wasn't a bad place at all, Nowa Huta.

The co-mart was in the middle of the industrial estate. You had to go down Wielickza Street, then across Centralny and Tyniec. You could see the gates of the old steelworks in the distance, like the entrance to a municipal park. It's a museum now; a monument to our industrial heritage. Mrs Milosz, my history teacher, used to tell us that we lived in a post-industrial age and always added, with apologetic irony, "But not round here."

Just before the turn-off, the road took you past the pyroxin processing plant. When I was little we had a book of folk stories which showed a mill with a waterwheel, and I used to pretend that the plant was really that mill, with the moustachioed miller Potocki inside grinding grain. I could almost see the water weed, greener than grass, dripping into the millpond, and the lilies sailing under the wind.

Now, as I passed, the evening sky was clear as water above the haze, and the black outline of the plant transformed it into the mill again. The monotonous creak of the generators was really the turning of the wheel, and the cooling duct which lay like a moat around the base of the plant became the millpond. In my mind, lilies floated, and there was a crescent moon hanging low in the western sky, just like the illustration.

Something broke the water: a round head, mild eyed. It snorted and sank beneath the surface of the cooling duct. In the story, a vodyanoi, one of the old things, lived in the millpond. There was a picture of him scowling, whiskers bristling, with one webbed hand raised irritably among the lily leaves.

Kikimura, the hen-faced woman who scratches in the barn at night. And the shock-headed person with fiery eyes and a Tartar moustache who haunts the corn-fields in hot summers. They always looked too sharp to me, I preferred smooth, froglike voivodoi in the millpond. Through the grey evening haze the light shone golden, and apricot ripples spread through the waters of the processing plant.

Voivodoi? Or a dog swimming? I walked on down Tyniec Street.

The co-mart was almost empty. There was no queue, only Mrs Kraszny in a headscarf complaining about the heat. On the way back, I met Yuliya emerging triumphantly from the doors of the Rink. Bogdan, tamed and sheepish, followed in tow. Yuliya grinned; I grinned back at her. "Hiya," she said. "I'll call you, yes? Tomorrow."

"Sure," I said in English. It was hip to talk American again. The previous year we'd all wanted to be Japanese, but cola and distressed matt jackets had been back ever since the WIScomm branch opened. Yuliya waved as she turned down Gdynia Street. I walked back quickly past the dark pond, and when I turned the corner to our compartment block I saw a light on in Roman's bedroom behind the haze of the screen.

Dad was still in the office, but my mother sat knitting in the kitchen, presumably for Natasha's baby, with the TV on. I could hear Roman moving about and the occasional whine of the old lift in the hallway. "Can I watch *Shokun Knife?*"

Mother's eyes rolled, but I had come straight back instead of staying at the Rink. "Don't expect me to watch it," she said. I had wanted to be Keiko Sekura ever since we started getting *Shokun Knife.* She could high kick, and she took on the multinats and *always* won. I wanted a spine-headed Gharenese cat, like the one Keiko had. I always thought my chances of getting one were pretty good, since they really existed—a gene-hatch between an ocelot and a Gharen porcupine. Keiko Sekura liberated the cat from a gene lab in episode one, and it had been her devoted companion ever since. This was the early twenties, when the gene-trans people were starting to become unpopular and their mistakes were beginning to show, especially in the eastern parts of Europe, and the old ex-Soviet countries. The thought of the gene labs didn't used to bother me — grandad had worked for one, after all — but now it made me uncomfortable. Perhaps Roman's illness brought everything too close to home. I sometimes wonder whether that's why defiant Keiko was such a heroine of mine.

Mother watched the show, too, just as she always did. Then, as I brushed my teeth, she ran a sneak check on me. It stung. "Don't do that! Ow!"

"Sorry, Teresa," she said, but she didn't mean it. Every time this happened we said the same things.

"Look, I don't want to know."

She ignored me, holding the phial up to the light and watching as the drop of rosy blood grew transparent.

"It's clear, anyway. You want to know that, don't you?" she said.

"I told you, I don't care. I don't want to know."

I looked in on Roman before I settled down on the sofa bed. He lay sprawled across the bed. In sleep he looked younger than seventeen. The duvet covered his legs, but he had thrown off the rest of the covers. It was so hot that I bundled them up and put them on the chair, then I stood looking down at him. He didn't look so bad, I thought. In fact, he looked better even than he did before it started coming on. He doesn't seem so skinny now, I thought hopefully. I think I wanted to turn his illness, and the changes, into an adventure and make it less real and less terrible.

Downstairs, I could hear the key in the lock: Andrea coming in. She always complained about how much work she had to do, but she came home late enough. Mother didn't say anything. Andrea was twenty-three and old enough to take care of herself, even in a foreign country. She was American, here on an exchange programme and doing some sort of postgraduate degree back in the States. I suppose I liked her, but she was ten years older, and we didn't have much in common.

I closed Roman's door before she came up the stairs. Andrea knew he wasn't well, of course, but Roman wouldn't have liked her looking at him, and my mother thought it might upset her.

In the morning the phone shrilled. I buried my head in the pillow, but I could still hear Dad answering it. At last he said, "When? When are you coming?" and there was a burst of conversation at the other end.

"Who is it?" I mumbled.

"It's only your aunt," he said, and walked out of the kitchen. I caught a glimpse of him as he went through the door, and in the thin light his face looked grey. I could hear him talking to my mother, which made it impossible to sleep, so I got up and put the coffee on.

"What was all that about?" I asked my mother.

"Nothing," she said. "Nothing to worry about."

"Is it Natasha?"

"Teresa," she said, and her voice had that patient note in it. "Take this up to your brother, please."

She handed me his mug. I made sure Andrea wasn't around before I took the coffee in. Roman was still asleep and invisible under the duvet. I put the mug of coffee and the pills down by the side of the bed and shook him awake; I didn't see why he should have a lie-in when the rest of us were up. He muttered something.

"There's your coffee," I said, and closed the door behind me.

My aunt arrived at eleven, bringing the baby with her in a carry bag.

"You can hold her if you like, Teresa," she told me, evidently conferring a favour. It would have hurt her feelings if I'd said no, so I took Ludmila on my lap and sat with her while Natasha and my mother talked. Ludmila squalled, and clapped her hands. She was a pretty baby, with fine dark hair and Asian eyes; her dad's Kazak. I took her tiny right hand in mine and waved it for her, and then I put her fingers into the mittens that mother had been making. They hid the missing little finger, and Ludmila stared wide eyed at her hands. *She's almost perfect*, I thought.

"You hold her for a bit," my mother said, smiling at us. "I want to show your aunty the garden."

The garden was a piece of reclamation to one side of the compartment, where the ground opened out. Our building stood on legs with a dark space beneath it, high enough for Dad, but not Mr Polowski, to stand upright. Dad and Mr Polowski were stringing lights across the ceiling, so that we could start growing things. They hoped that if we got planning permission we could start a hydrogarden, but that would take time. The application for the lights had only just been accepted, even though we'd put it in two years previously. The comp committee was clearing back the wasteground, and we'd got the first quarter gardened, but we needed to rehire the breaker for the next bit and there was a waiting list.

As I sat rocking Ludmila, I could hear the voices of my aunt and mother floating up from the garden. I couldn't hear what they were saying, though, and I got frustrated, so I took the baby up to see Roman. He was pleased, even though he didn't want to show it.

"Hi," he said to Ludmila, and struggled to sit up in bed.

"Say hi to Roman," I told her.

She looked at him and laughed. I held her out, but Roman said self-consciously, "I don't know what to do with kids."

"Just take hold of her, Roman. Is that such a big deal?"

"Yes," said my brother. "Can you turn the light off?" He twisted his face deeper into the covers.

"Okay. Don't be so touchy," I said. "I'll take her back down. Do you want to find your mum?" I asked the baby.

"It's all right," Roman said hastily. "I'll hold her if you like." And gingerly he put Ludmila down on the lumpy covers. In silence we watched her playing with the tassles on the cover of the bedside table. I knew what Roman was thinking, but I couldn't say anything. With any luck they'd find a way to solve the problem before Ludmila reached Roman's age.

"What did you do yesterday?" he asked me.

"Not much. I had so much homework. . . . I spent most of the time in front of the computer."

I was lying, because I hadn't been to see him, but I couldn't very well say that I was tired of him being ill. When it first started, I felt so sorry for him, but now it just dragged on, and we were all bored with it. I couldn't say anything. It wasn't Roman's fault, and Mum had enough to worry about without me complaining. Sitting here like this, with the baby rolling on the blankets between us, it wasn't so bad, and eventually Mother came upstairs with my aunt.

"Hello, Roman," Natasha said, rather coolly. "How are you?"

"I'm okay," he told her, eager to show that everything was normal. "I feel fine."

"Oh, that's good," Natasha said. She smiled too much, and I was glad when mother took her back down to the kitchen. Roman was still my brother, after all.

"Natasha doesn't know much," I said to Roman, and after a moment he nodded.

As I came down the stairs I heard my mother saying ". . . and of course it wasn't his fault, but she wasn't used to it, and it just unnerved her. The sanatorium rang this morning; I suppose we should start thinking about it. But it's not as if no one else has this sort of thing. . . ."

I heard Natasha say, in a low voice, "Yes, but you can't expect people to accept it. Look at Lydia Petrov. When she started to—well, her mother insisted on brazening it out. Took her down to the co-mart and everything. I'm sorry, Vera, but I wasn't the only one who found it disgusting. I mean, you're not having people round here, are you?"

My mother's voice was icy.

"Certainly everyone who used to come here still does. Andrea's still staying with us. All the neighbours drop round; they've been very good. Everyone knows, Natasha. Everyone knows."

"Yes, but you might give some thought to, well, Arman and I, for example. I mean, people come up to me in the co-mart and start discussing it. It's just not very nice—"

—and mother interrupted, winter cold, "No. It isn't."

When I hurriedly pushed the door open, I saw that my aunt at least had the grace to look ashamed.

"I've brought Ludmila down," I said, and put the baby on her mother's lap. Natasha couldn't talk, I thought, and she knew it. Why else did my mother knit mittens, to hide what should not be seen? My aunt did not stay long after that.

A week later, Dad and Mr Polowski had got the lights up. The space underneath the compartment looked like the car park in Mrs Milosz's course texts. I imagined that, if we did get the planning permit, we would fill the huge area with greenness, like the conservatory in the picture of the Moscow mall. We would grow palms and fronds and dig a pool in the middle for voivodoi and goldfish. That would never happen, though, because they planned to give it over to permabeans and small grain rice. I helped Dad, holding the skeins of lights as he battened them into the grooves. Mother spent a lot of the day out in the garden strip, weeding and planting.

The weather was fine, warm, and cloudless, but we all knew we just wanted an excuse to get out of the compartment. I made myself go up to see Roman every evening, and mother sat with him when I was in school. He kept asking if he could go outside and sit on the steps in the long fold-out chair, but mother thought it would be better for his lungs if he stayed indoors. The hospital had given us that special AP screen for the window, and it stayed activated all the time, now. Every time I went in there I could smell its faint, chemical odour, and the taste lingered on my tongue like paint. At least I didn't have to put up with it all the time, like Roman, but he didn't seem to mind. Whenever I went in, he was lying down, curled on his side with his face away from the door.

Even though mother told Natasha that everyone knew about Roman, I knew it wasn't true. She had asked me to say nothing at school, and I hadn't wanted to talk about it, anyway.

I didn't know what she had told the neighbours. One afternoon, coming home from class, I met Mrs Tevsky in the hallway. I quite liked Mrs Tevsky; she wore strings of beads and her jackets all had furry collars. She always used to give me a zloty, when I was little and we still had them. However, she gossiped terribly, and so I was careful what I said to her. She asked after all the family in turn, right down to baby Ludmila, before saying, "And how's your brother?"

"He's okay. As well as can be expected," I said, sounding stiff even to myself.

"It's an awful thing, leukemia," she said. Above the fur collar of her light jacket, her eyes were animal bright; I thought of kikimura, scratching about in the hen house. "But they can do so much these days; I've heard they can cure it completely."

"I'm not sure," I said. "We're just hoping, that's all."

"Well, that's all you can do, isn't it?" Mrs Tevsky said. "Bye-bye, then." And, still unsatisfied, she vanished through her own front door. I repeated this conversation to my mother.

"I don't see why Nina Tevsky should know everything that goes on," she said.

"She said it was leukemia," I said. "Did you tell her that?" I felt my gaze grow fierce, in case the bitter truth might fall from her mouth, but she only passed a hand over her eyes, rubbing wearily. "That show's on in a minute."

Mother never minded how much TV I watched, during that time. I meant I was quiet, and not asking questions, but I don't think I would have done anyway. She still did the scans, and said I was fine, but as I told her, I didn't think I wanted answers. As long as you can still ask questions, there's still a chance that the answer may change.

The summer wore on, and the school holidays came around. Yuliya's family had a place up in Zakopane, and she suggested I come and stay for the weekend. It was a beautiful place, lying up among the mountains. A cable car snaked up one of the peaks, and from the top you could see the smoky blur of Krakow in the distance. Mother thought I should go and get some fresh air after sitting in a stuffy classroom all year. They were nice, Yuliya's family, and lucky to have the house. Yuliya's grandmother had owned it, and they were allowed to keep it when the property redistribution took place on condition that they let it for part of the year to the unions. I thought that was fair. They got it at Christmas and during the summer, mostly.

Yuliya and I had the run of the place, and we spent a lot of time out in the cornfields, sifting the huge, perfect ears of ripening grain through our fingers. Each grain was larger than my thumbnail and we had endless competitions to find the biggest. The taste of that grain is still with me, how it burst floury in the mouth, like dust.

We were allowed to stay up late, and in the evening we sat out on the porch and looked up at the sky. It was very clear, so high into the mountains, and stars filled the nights. Yuliya and I practised looking at the Pleiades; never directly, because then you wouldn't see them properly. Yuliya said that it was something to do with the cones in your eye, but now I think that there are things which forbid too close an examination, too searing for acceptance by the eye or the mind.

We came back on Sunday night. As soon as I came into the hallway I knew something was wrong, because I could hear Andrea three whole flights up. I hurried up the stairs. Andrea's face was white and crumpled, and she babbled quite incoherently. Mother knelt by Andrea's side, which annoyed me because she was not supposed to bend. I didn't see Dad anywhere, and I didn't blame him for staying away.

"Drink this," my mother kept saying. "You'll feel better." Eventually, Andrea took a sip of whatever was in the glass, choked, coughed, and meekly drank the rest. At last there was silence. "Come on, now," mother said. "Come up with me; we'll put you to bed."

She was a long time. When she came down again, she was wiping her hands on her apron. I couldn't say anything. Mother sat and stared at her hands, twisting her wedding ring. "She met your brother on the landing," she said at last. "It gave her a bit of a start. She's been working very hard."

"Yes," I said.

"I don't know if you've really noticed the . . . the progress."

"I suppose so." But, even then, I didn't pay a lot of attention to how ill Roman actually was, because he was my brother and I did not want to think about it. His illness was something else that could not be seen. Anyway, as I said, we'd all got a bit sick of Roman's illness.

"Look, Teresa," mother said eventually. "Someone's coming from the hospital tomorrow, just to do a few tests. They called last week. They're bringing the schedule forward." She didn't look at me. "You've been so good through all of this," she added. "I know how hard it's been." She was trying to make me feel better, so I wouldn't mind about the hospital visit. I reached over and squeezed her hand.

"Thanks."

I went to bed, but I couldn't sleep properly. I kept thinking about the storybook, of all things, the pictures of the spirit people, or whatever they were supposed to be. When you're only half awake, things get lodged in your mind and you can't get rid of them. Your thoughts go round and round. At last, I got up and switched the light on. The books were kept in a cabinet on the landing. I took the storybook from behind the glass and went back into the kitchen. I hadn't looked at it for years, but as I turned the pages I found it utterly familiar. There they all were: kikimura, who haunts the hen houses, wearing an incongruous apron; the house spirit domovoi, peering from behind the sofa; the dark polevik, pictured among the corn stalks.

Then voivodoi, vodyanoi, sad-eyed in the middle of the millpond. I sat staring into the empty air with the book open on my lap and thought: *They are all here, among us in the world or locked up in the sanatorium where no one can see them. Hundreds of years ago we imagined them, and now we have made them real.*

I put the book down and went to look out of the kitchen window. It didn't get really dark; too much light from the city stained the sky a blurry orange. It was raining, too, big drops streaming down the window pane. Tomorrow evening, someone would come from the hospital, the special sanatorium, and the car would draw up to where I stared now, and people would climb out and bring Roman downstairs, just as they did with Mrs Petrov's daughter.

As quietly as I could, I went upstairs to the bedroom. Andrea's door was locked; the imprint gleamed faintly through the darkness. No sound came from my parents' room, and they, too, had shut their door tightly.

I stole into Roman's room. He had thrown off the covers again. He really didn't look so bad, not to me. I shook him awake and put a hand over his mouth.

"Roman?"

"What is it?" He looked up at me, frightened and bleary with sleep. "She saw me on the landing," he told me. His voice was hoarse.

"I know. Look, Roman, they're going to take you up to the sanatorium tomorrow. Tell me if you want to go."

"No. No, I don't. I know what they'll do." Under my hand, he shook.

"Roman, how far can you walk?"

"I don't know."

"Do you know where you could go?"

After a moment, he nodded.

"Has someone spoken to you?"

"Yes. When you were all in the garden one day a few weeks ago, a person called, told me to go to the pyroxin plant, and they'd be there."

"Then that's where we'll go."

Roman hauled himself out of bed and hung onto me. He weighed a ton. It was a wonder no one heard us. When we got down the stairs and out of the front door, he dragged himself over to the old lift, and we dropped to the basement with the lift humming on its cables. The door opened out into the space beneath the compartment, and then it wasn't so bad, because we had some time and no one could see us.

We ducked out into the summer rain. It tasted of metal, and it felt cool, unlike the stinging rain which sometimes fell. A drainage ditch ran along the roadside, and we kept to that. I found it revolting, but Roman didn't seem to mind. Maybe it was good for him to be wet. His skin didn't look so puffy, or so raw. We were both panting by the time we got up to the plant.

"Roman," I asked, between gasps. "Can you live there? Like that?"

"I practised in the bath," he said, sheepishly, and for some reason this made me laugh. "I think it'll be okay. Other people do, after all. The ducts all join up to the river." He could no longer talk very well. His mouth looked too small.

We stood at the side of the cooling duct. Raindrops dappled the surface of the dark water.

A round head rose.

I crouched by my brother's side. "Just be all right, Roman," I told him. His head was level with mine. He started to say something. "I don't want to hear it. Go on, go."

He dragged himself to the side of the duct and rolled off the edge, quite grace-fully, like a seal. There were more of them in the duct—although I couldn't see them clearly in the rain and the darkness—and one by one they dived. I caught a glimpse of their tapered tails as they plunged, and then I was alone by the side of the cooling duct, watching the ripples spread across the water. I must have stayed longer than I thought, for when I turned and walked back home the clouds had cleared and the skies were the colour of pearl. A fresh wind blew out of the grey east, and I smelled the smell of rain.

Now, ten years later, Mother and Dad are still there in compartment 3. Nothing much happened after that night. I suppose we all went back to normal. Andrea returned to the States. We got planning permission for the open basement, and I sometimes work in the hydrogarden after college.

Eventually they closed the processing plant down after a third scare. Nothing lives in the cooling duct. Yuliya and I still go up to Zakopane to her grandmother's house and laze about in the meadows. Sometimes, in the evenings after a very hot day, I catch sight of something moving swiftly through the corn, and wonder how many people were affected. They shut down the big gene projects eight years ago, at least in Europe, but the enquiry totals always vary, and the people whom we did not want to see, who should never have been so greatly transformed, still linger. I blame my ancestors, myself, for imagining the form of spirits, the inad-vertent marriage of superstition with technology that created voivodoi, and do-movoi, and kikimura, the changed and secret people who should only be seen from the corner of the eye, like certain stars.

saddlepoint: Roughneck

STEPHEN BAXTER

British writer Stephen Baxter made his first sale to Interzone *in 1987, and since then has become one of that magazine's most frequent contributors, as well as making sales to* Asimov's Science Fiction, Science Fiction Age, Zenith, New Worlds, *and elsewhere. He's one of the most prolific new writers of the nineties, and is rapidly becoming one of the most popular and acclaimed of them as well.*

Like many of his colleagues in the late nineties, Baxter is busily engaged with revitalizing and reinventing the "hard-science" story for a new generation of readers — as demonstrated in the vivid and suspenseful novella that follows, a classic tale of humankind pitted against a hostile and unrelenting Nature in an engineering project of almost unimaginable scope and difficulty, but one which also ends up taking the stubborn, grimly determined, hard-headed entrepreneurs who drive the project into some unexplored, strange, and unexpected territory, with unforeseen results. . . .

Stephen Baxter's first novel, Raft, *was released in 1991 to wide and enthusiastic response, and was rapidly followed by other well-received novels such as* Timelike Infinity, Anti-Ice, Flux, *and the H. G. Wells pastiche — a sequel to* The Time Machine — The Time Ships, *which won both the Arthur C. Clarke Award and the Philip K. Dick Award. His most recent books are the novels,* Voyage, Titan, *and* Moonseed, *and the collections* Vacuum Diagrams: Stories of the Xeelee Sequence *and* Traces. *Upcoming is a new novel,* Manifold: Time. *His stories have appeared in our Eleventh, Twelfth, Fourteenth, and Fifteenth Annual Collections.*

ONE: MOON RAIN

There were only minutes until the comet hit the Moon.

"You got to beat the future! — or it will beat you. Believe me, I've been there. . . ."

Xenia knew that Frank J Paulis thought this the most significant day in the history of the inhabited Moon, let alone his own career. And here he was now, a pile of softscreens on his lap, hectoring the bemused-looking Lunar Japanese in the seat alongside him, even as the pilot of this cramped, dusty evacuation shuttle went through her countdown.

"Look around you, pal. You guys have lasted three hundred years up here, in your greenhouses and your mole holes. A hell of an achievement. *But the Moon can't support you. . . .*"

Xenia Makarova had a window seat, and she gazed out of the fat, round portholes. Below the shuttle's hull she could see the landing pad, a plain of glass microwaved into lunar soil, here on the edge of the green domes of the Copernicus Triangle. And beyond that lay the native soil of the Moon: gray and brown, softly molded by a billion years of meteorite rain.

And bathed, for today, in comet light.

The count proceeded, in Japanese. Tanks pressurized. Guidance locked in. Coming up on one minute . . .

Frank was still talking. Xenia had listened to Frank talk before. She'd been listening to him, in fact, for five years, or three hundred, depending on what account you took of Albert Einstein.

"You know what the most common mineral is on the Moon? Feldspar. And you know what you can make out of that? Scouring powder. Big deal. Sure, you can bake oxygen out of the rock. You can even make rocket fuel and glass. But there's no water, or nitrogen, or carbon—"

The Japanese, a business-type, said, "There are traces in the regolith."

"Yeah, traces, put there by the Sun, and it's being sold off anyhow, by Kawasaki Heavy Industries, to the Prion. Bleeding the Moon dry . . ."

A child was crying. Xenia glanced around. The shuttle was just a cylinder-shaped cargo scow, hastily adapted to support this temporary evacuation. The scow was crammed with people, last-minute refugees—men and women and tall, skinny children—in rows of canvas bucket seats like factory chickens, subdued and serious.

And all of them were Lunar Japanese, save for Frank and Xenia, who were American; for, while Frank and Xenia had taken a time-dilated three-hundred-year jaunt to the stars—and while America had been scraped off the face of the Earth by the ice—the Lunar Japanese had been quietly colonizing the Moon.

"No," Frank said now, "you need volatiles. That's the key to the future. But now that Earth has frozen over nobody is resupplying. You're just pumping around the same old shit, literally in fact. I give you another hundred years, tops. Look around. You've already got rationing, strict birth control laws."

"There is no argument with the fact of—"

"How much do you need? I'll tell you. Enough to future-proof the Moon. Give it an atmosphere thick enough to breathe without a face mask. Oceans, without domes over them. *Terraform.*"

"And you believe the comets can supply the volatiles we need for this?"

"Believe? That's what Project Prometheus is for. The random impact today is a piece of luck. It's going to make my case for me, pal. And when we start harvesting the comets, those big fat babies out in the Oort Cloud—"

"Ah," the Lunar Japanese was smiling, "and the person who has control of those comet volatiles—"

"—could buy the Moon." Frank reached for a cigar, a 20th-century habit long frustrated. "But that's incidental . . ."

Ten seconds. Five. Three, two, one.

Stillness, for a fraction of a second. Then, a clatter of pyrotechnics, a muffled bang.

Xenia was ascending, in utter silence, as if in some crowded elevator, pressed back in her bucket seat with maybe a full gee.

Beyond her window stray dust streaked away across the pad glass, heaping up against fuel trucks and pipelines.

Soon she could make out the curve of the Moon, a black sky above the bright, lumpy horizon. They were heading toward lunar night, and the shadows were lengthening, fleeing from the brilliant comet light.

Earth rose.

It was, of course, the new Earth, coated from poles to tropics by its featureless white shroud of ice, glaringly bright, ragged and showing green-blue only at the equator. Even from here, she could see Prion flowerships circling the Earth, the giant ramscoops of the alien craft visible as tiny discs.

The Lunar Japanese around her applauded the smooth launch.

Away from the Copernicus complex the Lunar surface was bare, streaked by long shadows. It looked like a bombing run, she thought, crater on crater, right down to the limit of visibility: not a square inch of it left untouched by the unending, mindless bombardment. The Moon could never be called beautiful—it was too damaged for that—but it had a compelling wildness.

But even here the Moon had been shaped by humans, the Lunar Japanese; the ancient, shattered land was scored by crawler tracks, overlaid by the glittering silver wires of mass driver rails.

. . . And now, as the shuttle tilted and settled into its two-hour orbit around the Moon, Xenia saw a sight she knew no human had ever seen before today:

Comet rise, over the Moon.

The coma, a diffuse mass of gas and fine particles, was a ball as big as the Earth, so close now it walled off half the sky, a glare of lacy, diffuse light. Massive clumps in the coma, backlit, cast shadows across the smoky gases, straight lines thousands of miles long radiating at her. She looked for the nucleus, a billion-ton ball of ice and rock. But it was too small and remote to see, even now, a few minutes from impact. And the tail was invisible from here, fleeing behind her, running ahead of the comet and stretching far beyond the Moon, reaching halfway to Mars, in fact.

The comet was coming out of the Sun, straight toward the Moon at 40 thousand miles an hour,

. . . and now there was light, all around the shuttle.

She craned her neck to see. The Moon and its human cargo, including this shuttle, were already inside the coma. It was like being inside a diffuse, luminous fog.

"Vileekee bokh."

Frank said, "What?"

"We're inside a comet. . . ."

Frank leaned across her, trying to see. He was a small, stocky man, with thick legs and big prizefighter muscles built for Earth's gravity, so that he always looked like some restless, half-evolved ape alongside the tall, slim Lunar Japanese. He was 60 years old, physiological; he was bald as a coot and his nose was a misshapen mass of flesh.

"Eta prikrasna," Xenia murmured.

"Beautiful. Yeah. Makes you think, though."

"About what?"

"How easy it is to get off the Moon. Compared to the Earth anyhow. I mean, look at this old rust-bucket. We're packed in here. It was the same for Neil and Buzz. In their dinky LM, they don't have to wait for 50 thousand government employees to load millions of gallons of lox onto some giant Nazi rocket. They just stow the Moon rocks and put away the sandwiches and press the button; and a little diddly rocket the size of a car engine squirts them off into space. Now, if we'd evolved on the Moon instead of the Earth you could have made an orbit-capable rocket ship in your back yard. You wouldn't need government support. An unreconstructed capitalist like me could have made it big. . . ."

"That's all this means to you?"

He grinned. "Anyhow, today it looks like we're the last off the Moon."

"Oh, no," she said. "There's a handful of old nuts who won't move, no matter what."

"Even for a comet?"

"Takomi. He's still there."

"Who?"

"He's notorious."

"I don't read the funny papers."

"Takomi is the hermit who lives out in the ruins of Edo, on Farside."

"No resupply?"

"Evidently he won't even respond to radio calls."

Frank frowned. "This is the *Moon.* How does he live? By sucking oxygen out of the rock?"

But Frank's Lunar Japanese companion was tapping him on the shoulder. "I overheard. I apologize. You knew Neil? *Armstrong?"*

"Hell, yes," said Frank, and he started to explain how, to the wide-eyed Lunar Japanese.

Xenia suppressed a smile and turned back to the window. Of course it wasn't true. Frank had been born all of 75 years *after* Apollo 11. But the truth about America no longer mattered, she knew, because there was nobody to check up any more.

. . . The light changed.

There was a soft Fourth-of-July gasp from the people crammed into the shuttle.

A dome of blinding white light rose like a new Sun from the surface of the Moon: comet material turned to plasma by the shock wave, mixed with shattered rock. Xenia thought she could see a wave passing *through* the Moon's rocky hide, a sluggish ripple in rock turned molten, gathering and slowing, crater walls forming as she watched.

So the comet had struck the Moon.

At the center of the crater a new mountain was thrust up: a block of primordial rock dug out from 15 miles beneath the surface. The crater's rim and walls, cooling and slowing, were already collapsing under their own weight, forming complex terraces. Some of the rock was still molten and flowed like lava across the gouged-out landscape; the melt-sheet cooled and hardened in place, like a fresh lava flow on Earth. Fountains of glowing rock bombs hailed over the surface beneath Xenia, covering the terrain for miles around the rim of the primary crater, which itself was now all of 50 miles across.

And now, spreading out over the Moon's dusty gray surface, she saw a faint wash of light. It seemed to pool in the deeper maria and craters, flowing down the contours of the land like a morning mist on Earth.

It was air: gases from the shattered comet, an evanescent atmosphere pooling on the Moon.

And, in a deep, shadowed crater, at the ghostly touch of the air, she saw light flare.

It was only a hint, a momentary splinter at the corner of her eye. She craned to see. Perhaps there was a denser knot of smoke or gas, there on the floor of the crater; perhaps there was a streak, a kind of contrail, reaching out through the temporary comet atmosphere.

It must be some byproduct of the impact. But it had looked as if somebody had launched a rocket, from the surface of the Moon.

But already the contrail had dispersed in the thin, billowing comet air.

People were applauding again, with the beauty of the spectacle, relief at being alive.

It was only after they landed that it was announced that the comet nucleus had landed plumb on top of the dome in Fracastorius Crater.

Fracastorius, on the rim of the Sea of Nectar, was one of the largest settlements away from the primary Copernicus-Landsberg-Kepler triangle. The loss of life was small, but the economic and social damage huge. Perhaps unrecoverable.

The Lunar Japanese grieved.

But Frank Paulis got back to work, even before the shuttle landed. The very next day he called Xenia into his office.

When she arrived he had his feet up on his desk. He was reading, on a soft-screen, some long, text-heavy academic paper about deep-implanted volatiles on the Earth. She tried to talk to him about Fracastorius, but he patently wasn't interested. Nor was he progressing Prometheus, his main project.

"Frank, what are you doing? What about the comet?"

He blinked at her. "The comet is history, babe."

"I thought it was going to supply us with volatiles. I thought it was going to be the demonstration we needed that Prometheus was a sound investment."

"Yeah. But it didn't work out." Frank tapped the surface of his desk and a softscreen embedded there lit up with numbers, graphics. "Look at the analysis. We got some volatiles. But most of the nucleus's mass was just blasted back to space. Tough break." He looked thoughtful, briefly. "One thing, though. Did you know the Moon is going to get an atmosphere out of this? It will last for a thousand years—"

"*Iroonda.*"

"No, it's true. Thin, but an atmosphere, of comet mist. Carbon dioxide and water and stuff. How about that." He shook his head. "Anyhow, it's of no use to us."

"But Prometheus—"

He shrugged. "I ran the math. The comet was inefficient. I figure you'd need around a *thousand* impactors like this one to future-proof the Moon fully. And we aren't going to get a thousand impactors, not with the Chinese on Mars and the Australians at Neptune and the damn Prion everywhere."

He didn't seem concerned.

Puzzled, she said, "Frank, I'm sorry."

"Huh? Why?"

"If comets are the only source of volatiles—"

"Yesterday I thought they were. But look at this." He tapped his softscreen. He was talking fast, excited, enthusiastic, his mind evidently racing. "There's an author here who thinks there are all the volatiles you could want, a hundred times over— *right here on the Moon*. Can you believe that?"

"That's impossible. Everyone's known the Moon is dry as a bone, since Apollo 11."

He smiled. "That's what everyone *thinks*. I want you to find this woman for me. The author of the paper."

"Frank—"

"And find out about mining."

"Mining?"

"The deeper the better." His grin widened. "We went to the stars, and found nothing but shit. And then we wasted years chasing comets. But it's all over now."

"It is?"

"How would you like a journey to the center of the Moon, baby?"

The Sun's gravitational field acts as a spherical lens, which magnifies the intensity of the light of a distant star along the line connecting the Sun to the star.

Every star has a different focus, in the Sun's gravitational field. At the point of focus—called a Saddlepoint, out on the rim of the Solar System—the gain is measured in hundreds of millions.

A race called the Prion used gravitational lensing to send high-fidelity teleportation signals between the Saddlepoints of neighbouring stars. They came blundering into the Solar System that way.

But the Prion didn't originate the technology. Some older species, who had been spreading out from the centre of the Galaxy along the Orion-Cygnus galactic arm, were the true pioneers.

Humans called them the Builders, but didn't know much about them. The Prion wouldn't say much.

Between humanity and the Prion, there existed a state of uneasy peace — or of low-grade warfare, depending on your point of view. The Prion weren't expecting to find the system inhabited, and were a little pissed when humans asked them to take back the factory ships that had started chewing up the asteroid belt.

But they backed off.

Not that the Prion had stopped all industrial activity in the Solar System, according to some conspiracy theorists. They were just a little more discreet about it now, is all. Their long-term goals were probably unchanged — and still unknown.

There are other paranoid types, however, who would rather have had the Prion inhabiting the asteroid belt than the Red Chinese, who had moved into the space the Prion left.

As part of the truce that was worked out, the Prion took human observers on interstellar jaunts. Live cargo, on Prion flowerships, sailing through the Saddlepoint gateways.

Xenia and Frank had spent a year of their lives on a Prion flowership, submitted themselves to the unknown hazards of several Saddlepoint gateway teleport transitions, and got themselves relativistically stranded in an unanticipated future. And they had come back, to *this*: a crowded Moon, owned by other people.

And it was all for the sake of a visit to a dull, nondescript G-class star. No worlds to explore, no business angles for Frank.

They had felt cheated.

Not that they hadn't prospered, here.

The Moon of the 24th century, as it turned out, had a lot in common with early 21st-century Earth. Deprived of its lifelines from the iced-up home world, the Moon was full: stagnant, a closed economy. But Frank had seen all this before, and he knew that economic truth was strange in such circumstances. For instance, as the scarcity of materials increased, industrial processes that had once been unprofitable suddenly became worthwhile; Frank had made a lot of money out of re-engineering an abandoned technology that made use of lunar sulphur and oxygen as a fuel source.

Within five years Frank J Paulis had become one of the hundred wealthiest individuals on the Moon, taking Xenia right along with him.

But it wasn't enough. Frank found it impossible to break into the close-knit business alliances of the Japanese. And besides, Xenia suspected, he felt cooped up here, on the Moon.

There were no humans left on Earth — save, the rumors went, for a few geneng'd post-human types in the equatorial belt, maybe elsewhere. America was gone, of course, except for a handful of galactic wanderers like Xenia and Frank, dispersed on Prion ships through the Saddlepoint gateways to star systems near and remote, over the years drifting back in ones and twos like relativistic snowflakes.

And they were all odd-balls.

Psychological screw-ups were common, out there between the stars. Knowing a trip could take centuries, who else would go? The star travelers were, by definition, people with nothing to lose on Earth. Misfits. Dismally failed marriages, a hostile son, a posse of lawsuits, like Frank J. No family, a dead-end job, like Xenia—who had been drawn by Frank's energy to his employ, then his bed, and at last to his side, en route to the stars.

Anyhow, that was why this comet had been so important for Frank. It would shake everything up, he said. Change the equation.

Project Prometheus—his study of shipping in terraforming volatiles from the comets—had got as far as designs for methane rockets, which could have pushed the Oort comets out of their long, slow, distant orbits and brought them in to the Moon. It had consumed all his energies for years, and cost a fortune. He needed investors, and had hoped the comet impact would bring them in.

But as soon as he realized Prometheus was impractical, and politically impossible besides, here was Frank launching himself, with equal enthusiasm, into other ventures. It was either admirable, she thought, or schizophrenic.

After all these years—during which time she had been his companion, lover, employee—Xenia still didn't understand him; she freely admitted it.

He was an out-and-out capitalist, no doubt about it. But every ounce of his huge ambition was constantly turned on the most gigantic of projects: the future of a world! the destiny of mankind!

What Xenia couldn't work out was whether Frank was a visionary who used capitalism to achieve his goals, or just a capitalist after all, sublimating his greed and ambition. But, swept along by his energy and ambition, she found it hard to focus on such questions.

She started work.

To launch his new project, Frank, feverish with enthusiasm, leased Landsberg's Grand Auditorium itself.

The auditorium was at the heart of Landsberg. The dome itself, a blue ceiling above, was a thick double sheet of quasiglass, cable-stayed above and below by engineered spider web. The dome was filled with water, a sandwich of blue, through which fish swam, goldfish and carp. The water shielded Landsberg's inhabitants from radiation, and served to scatter the raw sunlight.

Thus, in Landsberg, the sky was royal blue and full of fish. After five years, Xenia still couldn't get used to it.

Bathed in watery light, pacing his stage, Frank J Paulis was a solid ball of terrestrial energy and aggression, out of place on the small, delicate Moon.

"You got to beat the future!—or it will beat you. Believe me, I've been there. I believed that before I went to the stars, and I believe it now. I'm here to tell you how. . . ."

Frank was standing before a huge three-dimensional facsimile, a Moon globe sliced open to reveal arid, uninteresting geological layers. Beside him sat Mariko Nishizaki, the young academic type whose paper had fired Frank off in this new direction. She looked slim and uncertain in the expensive new suit Frank had bought for her.

Xenia was sitting at the back of the audience, watching rows of cool faces: politicians, business types. They were impassive. Well, they were here, and they were listening, and that was all Frank would care about right now.

". . . We need volatiles," Frank was saying, "not just to survive, but to get our work done. To expand. To grow, economically. Water. Hydrogen. Helium. Carbon dioxide. Nitrogen. Maybe nitrates and phosphates to supplement the biocycles.

"But the Moon doesn't have volatiles. Everyone knows that. The Moon is just a ball of low-grade aluminum ore, created out of the Earth as the result of a giant primordial collision. Wherever we've looked, save for the occasional cold trap, we've found barely a trace of volatiles; and those that are present have been implanted by the solar wind in the top few feet of the regolith. So we have to bring in volatiles, from the Earth, the comets, the outer planet moons, wherever. Because everyone knows the Moon is a desert. Right?" He leaned forward. "*Dead wrong.*

"I'm here today to offer you a new paradigm. I'm here to tell you that *the Moon itself* is rich in volatiles, almost unimaginably so, enough to sustain us and our families, hell, for millennia. And, incidentally, to make us rich as Croesus in the process."

Barely a flicker of interest in the audience, Xenia saw.

Three centuries and a planetary relocation hadn't changed the Japanese much, and cultural barriers hadn't dropped; they were still suspicious of the noisy *gaijin* who stood before them, breaking in from outside the subtle alliances and protocols that ruled their lives.

But now Frank stood back. "Tell 'em, Mariko."

The slim Lunar Japanese scientist got up, evidently nervous, and bowed deeply to the audience. With the aid of a softscreen poster she began a long, rapid, and very technical presentation on the early history of the solar system.

Xenia's attention wandered.

The Moon's surface here was like a park. Grass covered the ground, much of it growing out of bare lunar regolith. Behind Frank there was a stand of mature palms, a hundred feet tall, and a scattering of cherries. People lived in the dome's support powers, thick central cores with platforms of lunar concrete slung from them. The lower levels were given over to factories, workshops, schools, shops, and other public places.

Right now, far above Frank's head, Xenia could see a little flock of schoolchildren in their white and black uniforms, flapping back and forth on Leonardo wings, squabbling like so many chickens. It was beautiful. But it served to remind her there were no birds here, outside pressurized cages. Birds tired too quickly, in the thin air; on the Moon, against institution, birds couldn't fly.

The Japanese, inured to natural disaster over the centuries, had moved capitals before. In some ways Landsberg represented the continuity of Japan, uninterrupted by a little thing like the end of Earth. The Lunar Japanese called Landsberg *nihon no furusati*, the heart of Japan. And so it was. The Emperor lived here, still revered as a god, as his ancestors had been revered since the eighth century.

But, sitting here, she was surrounded by subtle noises: the bangs and whirs of fans and pumps, the bubbling of aerators in the fountains and ponds. Landsberg, a giant machine, had to be constantly run, managed, maintained.

Thinking about that now, watching the children play in the warm air wafted by a great roof-top fan, Xenia had an intuition about the rightness of Frank's vision, whatever his methods.

Landsberg, this high-tech, managed environment, was no long-term answer. The Moon had to become a world that could sustain itself without conscious human intervention. Just in case our children, she thought, are less smart, or less lucky, than we are.

And if Frank could make a little profit along the way, she wasn't about to grudge him that.

She tried to focus on what Mariko was saying.

Earth, Moon, and the other planets — said Mariko — had condensed, almost five billion years ago, from a swirling cloud of dust and gases. That primordial cloud had been rich in volatiles — three percent of it was water, for instance. You could tell that was so from the composition of asteroids, which were left-over fragments of the cloud.

But there was an anomaly. If you added together all the water on Earth, for example, in the oceans and atmosphere and the ice sheets, it added up to less than a *tenth* of that three percent fraction.

Where did the rest of the water go?

Mariko believed it was still there.

She believed there was water and other volatiles trapped deep within the Earth, in the mantle. She presented old evidence compiled by Earth-bound geologists. They found helium, a light gas that should have escaped Earth long ago, leaking from the mantle plumes that built island chains like Hawaii. They found water in minerals dragged up from hundreds of miles down by kimberlites, iron-magnesium rocks that hauled up exotic high-pressure mineral specimens like diamonds. Seismic waves traveled slowly in some parts of the mantle, and such waves would, Mariko said, be slowed down by the presence of water.

The water wouldn't be present as a series of immense buried oceans; rather it would be scattered as droplets, some as small as a single molecule, trapped inside crystal lattices of the minerals that formed under the intense pressure down there.

And what was true of Earth would be true of the Moon.

According to Mariko, the Moon was made mostly of material like Earth's mantle. It was smaller than the Earth, cooler and more rigid, so that the center of the Moon was analogous to the Earth's mantle layers a few hundred miles deep. And it was precisely at such depths on Earth, where such water-bearing minerals as majorite and wadsleyite were found. . . .

Frank watched his audience like a hawk.

Now he stepped forward, peremptorily interrupting Mariko. He waved a hand. His cartoon Moon globe suddenly lit up, overshadowing the dry charts and equations on Mariko's screen. Now the onion-skin geological layers were supplemented by a vivid blue ocean, lapping in unlikely fashion at the Moon's center. Xenia smiled. It was typical Frank. Inaccurate, but compelling.

"Listen up," he said. "What if Mariko is right? What if even *one percent* of the

Moon's mass by weight is water? That's the same order as the water in all Earth's oceans and ice sheets and atmosphere.

"And that's not all. Where there is water there will be other volatiles: carbon dioxide, ammonia, methane. Maybe even hydrocarbons. And all we have to do is go down there and find it." He grinned. "There's a huge ocean down there, gentlemen, and it's time to go skinny-dipping."

There was a frozen silence, which Frank milked expertly. Then he snapped: "Questions."

You say these volatiles date from the formation of the solar system. But as you noted, we know Earth-Moon was shaped by a giant impact with a Mars-sized planetesimal. Mantle material was driven from the Earth into an orbiting cloud. Which collapsed to form the Moon. The great heat of collapse would surely have baked out the volatiles. . . .

"Maybe," Frank said. "But Mariko tells me it's possible the volatiles, suspended in the cloud that condensed into the Moon, will have gotten trapped once more in its interior. Then again, maybe not. Nobody knows. Nobody cares much about the deep interior of the planets; for three hundred years we've been too busy scratching their surfaces. The seismic data, even now, even on the Moon, is patchy. It's impossible to say. We're going to have to go look-see."

Look-see? Paulis-san, please tell us what you are proposing, specifically.

"Isn't it obvious?" He waved a hand, and in his cartoon Moon a triumphant scarlet thread dug straight down from the surface, arrowing toward the core. "Gentlemen, I'm inviting you to join me in the mining business. Deep mining. We're going to go down there and find out."

Now there was head-shaking, murmuring, even a little laughter.

"It won't be easy," Frank said. "The record for a deep mine on Earth is only a few miles. And *nobody* has seriously mined the Moon, because we never expected to find anything down there. Right? We know there won't be the huge hydrothermal ore deposits we were able to exploit on Earth. In fact, across the solar system as a whole, mining technology hasn't advanced much beyond what they had in the 20th century.

"But the Moon is cooler, much more rigid, more stable than Earth. The temperature and pressure gradients as you go down are comparatively gentle. Believe me, our drill bits are going to sink down through those cold Moon rocks like a knife through butter. . . ."

You are proposing some sort of test bore?

"Hell, no," he said, and he grinned under his fleshy nose. "Our bore-hole will be yards wide. A tunnel into the Moon. Why the hell not? That way we can send down Mariko and her double-domed buddies to do some serious seismology and whatever else they feel they need to do. We can go sideways, open up whatever seam we find. And, hell, that way we can go down there and see for ourselves."

But the energy required for such an immense bore will drain our resources. At a time when we are striving to rebuild Fracastorius—

Frank shook his head. "Past a certain depth I'll power myself. Thermal energy from the hot deep rocks. All I need is seedcorn resources."

But still, Fracastorius should be the priority—

Frank stepped to the front of the little stage and glared around at them. "Gentlemen, I'm calling this new enterprise 'Roughneck.' If you want to know why, go look it up. I'm asking you to invest in me, in Roughneck. Sure it's a risk. But if it works it's a way past the resource bottleneck we're facing, here on the Moon. And it will make you rich beyond your wildest dreams." He held the stare for one moment more.

Then he turned away. "If you want a piece of this, you know how to find me."

The Moon globe popped like a balloon, showering pixels, and Frank J Paulis had left the stage.

Getting the seedcorn investment turned out to be the easy part.

There never had been a mining industry, here on the Moon.

So Frank and Xenia were forced to start from scratch, inventing afresh not just an industrial process but the human roles that went with it. They were going to need a petrophysicist and a geological engineer to figure out the most likely places they would find their imagined reservoirs of volatiles; they needed reservoir engineers and drilling engineers and production engineers for the brute work of the borehole itself; they needed construction engineers for the surface operations and support. And so on.

They had to work job descriptions, and recruit and train to fill them as best they could.

Then there were the practical problems, which they hit as soon as they started to trial heavy equipment in the ultrahard vacuum that coated the Moon. Friction was a killer, for instance: in an atmosphere there is a thin layer of adhered water vapor and oxides to reduce drag, but that didn't apply here. They even suffered vacuum welds. Not only that, the ubiquitous dust—the glass-sharp remains of ancient, shattered rocks—stuck to everything it could, scouring and abrading. Stuff wore out *fast*, on the silent surface of the Moon.

But they persisted.

They learned to build in a modular fashion, with parts that could be replaced easily by a person in a spacesuit. And they learned to cover all their working joints with sleeves of a flexible plastic, to keep out the dust. After much experimentation they settled on a lubricant approach, coating their working surfaces with the substance the Lunar Japanese called "quasiglass," hard and dense and very smooth; conventional lubricants just boiled or froze.

The work soon became all-absorbing. Even when Frank had enough investors to fund his start-up, the practical problems were just beginning, and Xenia found herself immersed.

But the Lunar Japanese, once committed to the project, learned fast, and were endlessly, patiently, inventive in resolving problems. It seemed to Xenia a remarkably short time from inception to the day Frank told her he had chosen his bore site.

"The widest, deepest impact crater in the solar system," he said. "Hell, just by standing at the base of that thing we'd be halfway to the core already. And the best of it is, we can buy it. Nobody has lived there since they cleaned out the last of the cold trap ice. . . ."

He was talking about the South Pole of the Moon.

Xenia pulled on the layers of her surface suit.

First came a bodyform, pressurized long-johns of engineered spider web. She tested the body waste pack and air conditioning. Next came a layer of body armor, a shield against micrometeorites and accidental collisions. Her life-support pack went on top of that; she could feel smart interfaces, feeder and waste pipes for air and water, nuzzling into sockets on her back, and immediately cool air started to flow under the bodyform. Her helmet was a bubble of quasiglass; the helmet was padded to fit her head, and moved when she did.

Finally she pulled on a disposable coverall and her radiation poncho, a light protective cape.

Thus, encased in spider web, Xenia stepped out of the hopper.

This was the Moon Pole. It was a place of shadows. There were stars above her. And the horn of crescent Earth poked above one horizon, gaunt and ice-pale.

Here, standing at the base of the crater called Amundsen, Xenia could actually see the Sun, a sliver of light poking through a gap in the enclosing rim mountains, casting long, stark shadows over the colorless, broken ground. She knew that if she stayed for a month the Moon's glacial rotation would sweep that solar search-light around the horizon. But the light was always flat and stark, like an endless dawn or sunset.

At the center of Amundsen, Frank's complex sprawled in a splash of reflected light, ugly, busy, full of people.

Here came Frank in his spacesuit, Lunar Japanese spider web painted with a gaudy Stars & Stripes. "I wondered where you were," he said.

"There was a lot of paperwork, last-minute permissions—"

"You might have missed the show." He was edgy, nervous, restless; his gaze, inside his gold-tinted visor, swept over the crowd. "Whatever. Come see the rig."

Together, they loped toward the center of the complex, past Frank's perimeter of security guards.

New Dallas, Frank's boomtown, was a crude cluster of buildings put together adobe-style from lunar concrete blocks. She could recognize shops, warehouses, dormitories, mess halls. There was a motor pool, hoppers and tractors and heavy machinery clustered around fuel tanks. And there was Frank's geothermal plant, ready for operation, boxy buildings linked by fat, twisting conduits. The inhabited buildings had been covered over for radiation-proofing by a few feet of regolith.

This wasn't Landsberg.

But it was actually bright here, the sunlight deflected into the crater by helio-stats, giant mirrors perched on the rim mountains or on impossibly tall gantries. The stats worked like giant floodlights, giving the town, incongruously, the feel of an old American floodlit sports stadium. The primary power came from sunlight too, solar panels that Frank had had plastered over the peaks of the rim mountains.

The ground for miles around was flattened and scored by footprints and vehicle tracks. It was hard to believe *none* of this had been here two months ago, that the only signs of human occupation then had been the shallow, abandoned strip mines in the cold traps.

And at the center of it all was the derrick itself, rising so far above the surface it caught the distant sunlight. Sheds and shops sprawled around its base, along with huge aluminum tanks and combustion engines. Mounds of rock, dug out in test bores, surrounded it like a row of pyramids.

Close to, the derrick seemed immense: It was hundreds of feet high, in fact, Frank said it was tall enough to stack up three or four joints of magnesium alloy pipe at a time. There was a pile of the pipe nearby, miles of it spun from native lunar ore, the cheapest component of the whole operation.

They reached the drilling floor. At its heart was the circular table through which the pipe would pass, and which would turn to force the drill into the ground. There were foundries and drums, to produce and pay out cables and pipes: power conduits, fiber-optic light pipes, hollow tubes for air and water and sample retrieval.

Xenia stood at the center of the drilling floor. She looked up into the structure of the derrick itself. It was tall and silent, like the gantry for a Saturn V. Stars showed through its open, sunlit frame. And suspended there at the end of the first pipe-lengths she could see the drill head itself, teeth of tungsten and diamond, gleaming in the lights of the heliostats.

Frank was describing technicalities that didn't interest her. "You know, you can't turn a drill string more than a few miles long. So we have to use a downhole turbine. . . ."

"Frank, *eta ochin kraseeva*. It is magnificent. Somehow, back in Landsberg, I never quite believed it was real."

"Oh, it's real," Frank said.

"But think of it. That thing is going to dig hundreds of miles beneath our feet."

"If it works. If it doesn't melt . . . or break down . . . or . . ." He checked his chronometer, a softscreen patch sewn into the fabric of his suit. "It's nearly time."

They moved out into the public area.

Frank had made an event of the day. There must have been a hundred people here, she saw now, men, women, and children walking in their brightly colored surface suits and rad ponchos, or riding in little short-duration bubble rovers. Frank had set up a kind of miniature theme park, with toy derricks you could climb up, and a towering roller coaster based on an old-fashioned pithead rail—towering because height was needed, here on the Moon, to generate anything like a respectable gee-force.

The main attraction was Frank's fish pond, she saw, a small crater he'd lined with ceramic and filled up with water. The water froze over and was steadily evaporating, of course, but water held a lot of heat, and the pond would take a long time to freeze to the bottom. In the meantime there were fish swimming back and forth in there, goldfish and handsome koi carp, living Earth creatures protected from the severe lunar climate by nothing more than a few feet of water.

Roughneck was the biggest public event on the Moon in a generation. Cameras hovered everywhere. She saw Observers, adults and children in softscreen suits, every sensation being fed out to the rest of the Moon.

The openness scared Xenia to death. "Are you sure it's wise to have so many people here?"

"The guards will keep out those Gray assholes."

The Grays were a pressure group who had started to campaign against Frank. Arguing it was wrong to go digging holes to the heart of the Moon, to rip out the *uchujin* there, the cosmic dust. They were noisy but, as far as Xenia could see, ineffective.

"Not that. It's so public. It's like Disneyland."

"Don't you get it? This is *essential*. We'll be lucky if we make hole at a mile a day. It will take 50 days just to get through the crust. We're going to sink a hell of a lot of money into this hole in the ground before we see a red cent of profit. We need those investors on our side, for the long term. They have to be here, Xenia. They have to see this."

"But if something goes wrong —"

"We're screwed anyhow. What have we lost?"

Everything, she thought, if somebody gets killed, one of these cute Lunar Japanese five-year-olds climbing over the derrick models. But she knew Frank would have thought of that, and discounted it already, and no doubt figured out some fallback plan.

She admired such calculation, and feared it.

A warning tone was sounding on their headsets' open loops now, and in silence the Lunar Japanese, adults and children alike, were lining up to watch the show.

Xenia could see the drill bit descend toward the regolith, the pipe sweeping silently downward inside the framework, like a muscle moving inside a sheath of flesh.

The bit sank into the Moon.

A gush of dust sprayed up immediately from the hole, ancient regolith layers undisturbed for a billion years, now thrown unceremoniously toward space. At the peak of the parabolic fountain, glassy fragments sparkled in the sunlight. But there was no air to suspend the debris, and it fell back immediately.

Within seconds the dust had coated the derrick, turning its bright paintwork gray, and was raining over the spectators like volcanic ash.

There was motion around her. People were applauding, she saw, joined in this moment. Maybe Frank was right to have them here, after all, right about the mythic potential of this huge challenge.

He was watching the drill intently. "Twenty or thirty yards," he said.

"What?"

"The thickness of the regolith here. The dust. Then you have the megaregolith, rock crushed and shattered and dug out and mixed by the impacts. Probably a couple of miles of that. Easy to cut through. Maybe we'll get to the anorthosite bedrock by the end of the first day, and then —"

She took his arm. Even through the layers of suit she could feel the tension in his muscles. "Hey. Take it easy."

"I'm the nervous father, right?"

"Yeah."

He took little steps back and forth, stocky, frustrated. "Well, there's nothing we can do here. Come on. Let's get out of this Buck Rogers shit and hit the bar."

"All right."

Xenia could hear the dust spattering over her helmet. And children were running, holding out their hands, in the gray Moon rain.

TWO: DREAMS OF ROCK AND STILLNESS

Her world was simple: The land below, light that flowed from the Dark above. Land, Light, Dark. That, and herself, alone.

Save for the Giver.

For her, all things came from the Giver. All life, in fact.

Her first memories were of the Giver, at the interface between the parched Land and the hot Dark above. He fed her, sank rich warm moist substance into the Land, and she ate greedily. She felt her roots dig into the dry depths of the Land, seeking the nourishment that was hidden there. And she drew the thin soil into herself, nursed it with hot Light, made it part of herself.

She knew the future. She knew what would become of herself and her children: that they would wait through the long hot-cold bleakness for the brief Rains. Then they would bud, and pepper this small hard world with life, in their glorious blossoming. And she would survive the long stillnesses to see the Merging itself, the wonder that lay at the end of time, she and her children.

But she was the first, and the Giver birthed her: None of it would have come to be without the Giver.

She wished she could express her love for him. She knew that was impossible.

She sensed, though, that he knew.

Overwhelmed by work as she was, Xenia couldn't get the memory of the comet impact out of her head.

In the moment of that gigantic collision she had glimpsed a contrail; for all the world as if someone, something, had launched a rocket from the surface of the Moon.

But who, and why?

She had no time to consider the question as Roughneck gathered pace. At last, though she freed up two or three days from Frank, pleading exhaustion. She determined to use the time to resolve the puzzle.

Xenia was home for the first time after many days of sleeping at the Roughneck project office.

She took a long, hot bath to soak out the gritty lunar dust from the pores of her skin. In her small tub the water sloshed like mercury. Condensation gathered on the ceiling above her, and soon huge droplets hung there suspended, like watery chandeliers.

When she stood up the water clung to her skin, like a sheath; she had to scrape it loose with her fingers, depositing it carefully back in the tub. Then she took a small vacuum cleaner and captured all the loose droplets she could find, returning every scrap to the drainage system, where it would be cleansed and fed back into Landsberg's great dome reservoirs.

She made herself some coffee—fake, of course, and not as hot as she would have liked, given the relatively low pressure. She sat on a *tatami* mat made of rice straw matting, which was unreasonably comfortable in the low gravity, and sipped her drink.

Her apartment was a glass-walled cell in the great catacomb that was Landsberg. It had, in fact, served as a *genkan*, a hallway, for a greater establishment in easier, less crowded times; it was so small her living room doubled as a bedroom. The floor was covered with *tatami*, though she kept a *zabuton* cushion for Frank Paulis. Her technical equipment was contained within a *tokonoma*, an alcove carved into the rock, but she had also hung a scroll painting there, of a Samurai in an unlikely pose, and some dried flowers. The flowers were real, and had cost as much as the rest of her furnishings put together.

The miniature Japanese art around her filled the room with space and stillness.

She had been happy to accept the style of the inhabitants of this place, unlike Frank, who had turned his apartment into a shrine to Americana. It was remarkable, she thought, that the Japanese had turned out to be so well adapted to life on the Moon. It was as if their thousands of years on their small, cramped islands had readied them for this greater experience.

She tuned the walls to a favorite scene—a maple forest, carpeted with bright green moss—and padded, naked, to her *tokonoma*.

It took seconds to establish there was no indexed record of that surface rocket launch, as she had expected.

There was, however, a substantial database on the state of the whole Moon at the time of the impact; every sensor the Lunar Japanese could deploy had been turned on the Moon, that momentous morning.

And she found what she wanted, in a spectrometer record from a low-flying satellite.

The site, from this automated viewpoint, was low on the horizon—a bright splinter at the heart of the image, in fact, was an infrared trace of the nozzles of the evacuation shuttle she herself was riding at the time—but with enhancement and image manipulation she could recover a good view, much as she had seen it herself.

There was the contrail, bright and hot, arcing through splashed cometary debris. Spectrometer results told her she was looking at the product of aluminum burning in oxygen.

So it had been real.

She widened her search farther.

Yes, aluminum could serve as a rocket fuel. It had a specific impulse of nearly three hundred seconds, in fact, not as good as the best chemical propellant (that was hydrogen, which burned at four hundred), but serviceable. And aluminum-oxygen could even be manufactured from the lunar soil.

Yes, there were more traces of aluminum-oxygen rockets burning on the Moon that day, recorded by a variety of automated sensors. More contrails, snaking across the lunar surface, from all around the Moon. There were a dozen, all told, perhaps more in parts of the Moon not recorded in sufficient detail. And each of them, she found, had been initiated when the gushing comet gases reached its location.

She pulled up a virtual globe of the Moon and mapped the launch sites. They were scattered over a variety of sites: highlands and maria alike, Nearside and Farside. No apparent pattern.

Then she plotted the contrails. The visible tracks had stretched just a few miles through the thin comet air. And so she extrapolated them, allowing them to curl around the rocky limbs of the Moon.

The tracks converged, on a single Farside site. Edo. The place the hermit, Takomi, lived.

It was the first Rain of all.

Suddenly there was air here, on this still world. At first there was the merest trace, a soft comet Rain that settled, tentatively, on her broad leaves, when they lay in shade. But she drank it in greedily, before it could evaporate in the returning Light, incorporating every molecule into her structure, without waste.

With gathering confidence she captured the Rain, and the Light, and continued the slow, patient work of building her seeds, and the fiery stuff that would birth them, drawn from the patient dust.

And then, so suddenly, it was time.

In a single orgasmic spasm the seeds burst from her structure. She was flooded with a deep joy, even as she subsided, exhausted.

The Giver was still here with her; enjoying the Rain with her; watching her blossom. She was glad of that.

And then, so soon after, there was a gusting wind, a rush of the air molecules over her damaged surfaces, as the comet drew back its substance and leaped from the Land, whole and intact, its job done. The noise of that great escape into the Dark above came to her as a great shout.

Soon after, the Giver was gone too.

But it did not matter: For, soon, she could hear the first tentative scratching of her children, carried to her like whispers through the still, hard rock, as they dug beneath the Land, seeking nourishment. There was no Giver for them, nobody to help; they were beyond her aid now. But it did not matter, for she knew they were strong, self-sufficient, resourceful.

Some would die, of course. But most would survive, digging in, waiting for the next comet Rain.

She settled back into herself, relishing the geologic pace of her thoughts. Waiting for Rain.

Xenia took an automated hopper, alone, to Farside. The journey was seamless, the landing imperceptible.

A small tractor, just a platform mounted by a bubble of tinted glass, rolled off the hopper's base, bearing Xenia. The sky was black, but the ground was brightly lit, as if by footlights on the floor of some huge theater. Earth was invisible, of course, but she could see a satellite crawl across the black sky, remote, monitoring.

Beyond the curve of the tractor's window, the Mare Ingenii—the Sea of Longing—stretched to the curved horizon, pebble-strewn. It was late in the lunar afternoon, and the sunlight was low, flat; the mare surface was like a gentle sea, a complex of overlapping, slowly undulating curves. The tractor's wheels were large and open, and they absorbed the unevenness of the mare, so that it was as if she were floating.

But now she came to a place where the mare seemed unusually flat, free even of the shallow, dusty crater remnants.

Xenia stopped the tractor.

She saw two cones, tall and slender, side by side, geometrically perfect. They cast long shadows in the flat sunlight. She couldn't tell how far away they were, or how big, so devoid was this landscape of visual cues. They simply stood there, stark and anomalous. She shivered.

She was still a mile short of Edo, but felt she had found Takomi.

She donned her spider-web suit, checked it, and stepped into the tractor's small, extensible airlock. She waited for the hiss of escaping air, and—her heart oddly thumping—she collapsed the airlock around her and stepped onto the surface of the Moon. A little spray of dust, ancient pulverized rock, lifted up around her feet.

Nothing moved here, save herself and what she touched. There was utter silence. Xenia fought an impulse to turn around, to look to see who was creeping up behind her, in this horror-movie stillness.

The sky remained black . . . save, she saw, for the faintest wisp of white, glowing in the flat sunlight. Ice crystals, suspended in the thin residual atmosphere of the comet impact.

Cirrus clouds, on the Moon.

She turned away from the tractor, to face the cones, and walked forward, loping easily.

The regolith was flat, free of crater indentations, as if brushed or rolled. Her footsteps were sharp, the only breaches of this snowlike perfection. She felt an odd impulse to back up, retrace her steps, smooth them over.

She came to a place where the regolith had been raked.

She slowed, standing on bare, unworked soil.

The raking had made a series of parallel ridges, each maybe two or three inches tall, a few inches apart, a precise combing. When she looked to left or right, the raking went off to infinity, the lines sharp, their geometry perfect. And when she looked ahead, the lines receded to the horizon, as far as she could see undisturbed in their precision.

Those two cones stood, side by side, almost like termite hills. The shallow light fell on them gracefully. She saw that the lines on the ground curved to wash around the cones, like a stream diverting around islands of geometry. The curvature was smoothed out, subtly, so that after 20 or 30 of the lines the straightness was restored.

"Thank you for respecting the garden."

Jumping at the sudden voice, she turned.

A figure was standing there—man or woman? A man, she decided, shorter and slimmer than she was, in a shabby, much-patched suit, the visor so scarred it looked as if it dated back to Apollo 11.

He bowed. "*Sumimasen*. I did not mean to startle you."

"Takomi?"

"And you are Xenia Makarova."

"You know that? How?"

A gentle shrug. "I am alone here, but not isolated. Only you sought and compiled information on the Moon flowers."

"What flowers?"

He walked toward her. "This is my garden," he said. "It is based on one that once graced the Daisen-In Temple, at Kyoto, Old Japan. Although this is somewhat larger, at 50 square miles—"

"A zen garden."

"You understand that? Good. This is a *kare sansui*, a waterless stream garden."

"Are you a monk?"

"I am a gardener."

"I have thought several times that the Japanese character is suited to the stillness of the Moon. Calmness and continuity. Even before humans came here, the Moon was already like an immense zen garden, a garden of rock and soil."

"Then you are wise."

"Is that why you came here? Why you live alone like this?"

"Perhaps. I prefer the silence and solitude of the Moon to the bustle of the human world. You are Russian?"

"Yes."

"Then you are alone here also. There are some of your people in the asteroid belt."

"I know. They won't respond to my signals."

"No," he said.

She pointed. "I understand the ridges represent flow. Are those mountains? Are they rising out of cloud, or sea? Or are they diminishing, shrinking back into . . ."

"Does it matter? The cosmologists tell us that there are many time streams. Perhaps time is an illusion, in fact."

"Like the lines in the regolith."

"You have traveled far to see me. I will give you food and drink."

"Thank you."

He turned and walked across the Moon. After a moment, she followed.

The abandoned lunar base, called Edo, was a cluster of concrete components: habitation modules, power plants, stores, manufacturing facilities, half-buried in the cratered plain. Comms masts sprouted like flowers. An old suborbital tug pad was a splash of scorched Moon dust concrete a couple of miles out. Around the station itself, the regolith was scarred by decades of tractor traffic. There were robots everywhere but they were standing silent, obviously inert. Their paintwork was yellowed, blistered. A faded *hi-no-maru*, a Japanese Sun flag, was fixed to a pole.

Edo looked ugly, cramped and confined, compared to the sunlit green bubbles of the Copernicus Triangle.

This had been the primary settlement established by the Japanese government in the 21st century. But Kawasaki Heavy Industries had set up in Landsberg, using the crater originally as a strip-mine. Now, hollowed out, Landsberg was the capital of this new Japan, and Edo, cramped and primitive, was abandoned.

Landsberg represented the triumph of Kawasaki Heavy Industries. But that triumph had been built on Kawasaki's partnership with the alien Prion, and nobody knew what the long-term price of that may be.

Still, Landsberg had meant the abandonment of Edo. But now a single lamp burned again at the center of the complex.

Takomi lived at the heart of old Edo, in what had once been, he said, a park, grown inside a cave dug in the ground. The buildings here were dark, gutted, abandoned. There was even, bizarrely, a McDonald's, stripped out, its red and yellow plastic signs cracked and faded.

A single cherry tree grew, its leaves bright green, a single splash of color against the drab gray of the concrete, fused regolith, and Moon dust here.

He brought her green tea and rice cake. Out of his suit Takomi was a small, wizened man; he might have been 60, but such was the state of life-extending technology it was hard to tell. His face was round, a mass of wrinkles, and his eyes lost in leathery folds; he spoke with a wheeze, as if slightly asthmatic.

"You cherish the tree," she said.

He smiled. "I need one friend. I regret you have missed the blossom. I am able to celebrate *ichi-buzaki* here. We Japanese like cherries; they represent the old Samurai view, that the blossom symbolizes our lives, here in our tents on the Moon, beautiful but fragile and all too brief."

"I don't understand how you can live here. You have no external support."

"The Moon supports me," he said.

"But—"

"It is a whole world," he said gently.

Takomi used the lunar soil for simple radiation shielding. He baked it in crude microwave ovens to make ceramic and glass. He extracted oxygen from the lunar soil by magma electrolysis: melting the soil with focused sunlight, then passing an electric current through it to liberate the oh-two. The magma plant, lashed up from decades-old, salvaged components, was slow and power-intensive, but electrolysis was efficient in its use of soil; Takomi said he wasn't short of sunlight, but the less haulage he had to do the better.

He took Xenia outside and showed her what he called a "grizzly," an automated vehicle already a century old, so caked with dust it was the same colour as the Moon. The grizzly toiled patiently across the surface of the Moon, powered by sunlight, scraping up loose surface material and pumping out glass sheeting and solar cells, just a couple of square yards a day.

He took her to a rise to show her the extent of the solar farm the grizzly had built. It covered square miles, and produced megawatts.

"It is astonishing, Takomi."

He cackled. "If one is modest in one's request, the Moon is generous."

"But even so, you lack essentials. It's the eternal story of the Moon. Carbon, nitrogen, hydrogen—"

"Of course it is possible to derive many elements from the regolith. Solar wind gases may be driven off simply by heating the dust." He smiled at her. "However, I admit I cheat."

"Cheat?"

"The concrete of this abandoned town is replete with water. A pleasing paradox: volatiles brought here, scooped from Earth's atmosphere by people of a richer age, used to build, and then abandoned. And yet here they are, ready for my use."

"You mine the concrete?"

"It is better than paying water tax."

"I suppose it is. But even so—"

"And I have other friends here."

"What friends?"

He would not answer.

Disoriented, walking beside this strange, dusty man through his gloomy caverns, she found her mind making unaccustomed intuitive leaps.

She asked him about the contrails she had seen, their convergence on this place. He evaded her questions, and began to talk about something else.

"I conduct research, you know, of a sort. There is a science station, not far from here, which was once equipped by Kawasaki Heavy Industries. Now abandoned, of course. It is—was—an infrared study station. It was there, some centuries ago, that a Japanese researcher called Nemoto first discovered evidence of Prion activity in the solar system, and so changed history."

She grunted. "There should be a plaque," she said dryly.

"The station was abandoned. But the equipment is operational, still."

She wasn't interested in Takomi's hobby in some abandoned observatory. But there was something in his voice that made her keep listening.

"So you use the equipment," she prompted.

"I watched, for instance, the approach of the comet. From here, some aspects of it were apparent that were not visible from Near-side stations. The geometry of the approach orbit, for example . . . and something else."

"What?"

"I saw evidence of methane burning," he said. "Close to the nucleus."

"Methane?"

"A jet of combustion products."

A *rocket*. She saw the implications immediately. Somebody had stuck a methane rocket on the side of the comet nucleus, burned the comet's own chemicals, to divert its course.

Away from the Moon? Or—toward it?

And in either case, who? A friend of the Lunar Japanese, of everyone on the Moon, or an enemy?

"Why are you telling me this?"

But he would not reply, and a cold, hard lump of suspicion began to gather in her gut.

Takomi provided a bed for her, a thin mattress in an abandoned schoolhouse. Children's paintings—of flowers and rocks and people floating in a black sky—adorned the walls, preserved under a layer of glass.

In the middle of the night, Frank called her.

She used her visor as a softscreen imager to see him. He was excited. The Roughneck bore had passed the crust's lower layers, and was in the mantle.

The mantle of the Moon: a place unlike any other reached by humans before.

When the Moon formed, five billion years in the past, it was covered by an ocean of liquid rock. The lighter materials, such as plagioclase, floated up to make the crust, and the heavier stuff, olivine and pyroxene, drifted down to form the mantle. There had been some intrusion from below since then — magnesium-suite rockbergs pushing up into the crust — but the mantle, cloaking this small world, had become essentially static, the last convection currents freezing in place.

Conditions for the drilling engineers were gentle, comparatively.

There was a temperature rise of maybe 12 degrees per mile of depth, compared to four times that on Earth. The pressure scaled similarly; even now Frank's equipment was subject only to a few kilobars, less than could be replicated in the laboratory. The Moon was *much* easier to deep-mine than the Earth. . . .

"It's going better than we thought, better than we expected. The Moon really is still and old and static, and we're just sinking in. Anyhow it's great TV. Smartest thing I ever did was to insist we dump the magnesium alloy piping, make the walls transparent so you can see the rocks. . . ."

She tried to ask him technical questions, how they were planning to cope with the more extreme pressures and temperatures they would soon encounter.

"Xenia, it doesn't matter. You know me. I can't figure any machine more complicated than a screwdriver. And neither can our investors. But they know, and I know, that we don't *need* to know. We just have to find the right technical-type guys, give them a challenge they can't resist, and point them downward."

"Paying them peanuts the while."

He grinned. "That's the beauty of those vocational types. Christ, we could even charge those guys admission. No, the technical stuff is piss-easy. The unreconstructed capitalist, if he wants to survive, takes primary account of the other factors. We have to make the project appeal to more than just the fat financiers and the big corporations."

"More?"

"Sure. Xenia, you have to think big. This is the greatest lunar adventure since Neil and Buzz. That party when we first made hole was just the start. I want everybody involved, and everybody paying. Now we're in the mantle we can market the TV rights — "

"Frank! They don't have TV any more."

"Whatever. I want the kids involved, all those little dark-eyed kids I see flapping around the palm trees the whole time with nothing to do. I want games. Educational stuff. Clubs to join, where you pay a couple of one-yen for a badge and get some kind of share certificate. I want little toy derricks in cereal packets. . . ."

"They don't have cereal packets."

He eyed her. "Work with me here, Xenia. And I want their parents paying too. Tours down the well, at least the upper levels."

"Are you serious?"

"Sure I'm serious. Why do you think I've got the bore 10 feet wide with glass walls? Xenia, for the first time the folks on this damn Moon are going to see some hint of an expansive future. A frontier, beneath their feet. They have to want it. Including the kids." He nodded. "Especially the kids. I'm thinking long term, Xenia."

"But the Grays—"

"Screw the Grays. We have the kids. They have rocks."

"Maybe you should be focusing on the short term. You have investors, Frank."

"The payoff will be immense. We just have to keep hammering that home. I want the best geologists on the Moon down that well, Xenia. I want seismic surveys, geochemistry, geophysics, the works. The sooner we find some lode to generate payback, the better. . . ."

And so on, on and on, his insect voice buzzing with plans, in the ancient stillness of Farside.

Takomi walked her back to her tractor, by the zen garden. She had been here 24 hours. The Sun had dipped closer to the horizon, and the shadows were long, the land starker, more inhospitable. Comet-ice clouds glimmered high above.

"I have something for you," Takomi said. And he handed her what looked like a sheet of glass. It was oval-shaped, maybe a foot long. Its edges were blunt, as if melted; and it was covered with bristles.

Some kind of lunar geologic formation, she thought. A cute souvenir; Frank might like it for the office.

She said, "I have nothing to give you in return."

"Oh, you have made your *okurimono* already."

"I have?"

He cackled. "Your shit and your piss. Safely in my reclamation tanks. On the Moon, shit is more precious than gold—the most precious gift of all. Don't you know that?"

He bowed, once, then turned to walk away, along the rim of his rock garden.

She was left looking at the oval of Moon glass in her hands.

It looked, she thought now, rather like a flower petal.

Back at Landsberg, she gave the petal-like object to the only scientist she knew, Mariko Nishizaki, for analysis. Mariko was exasperated; as Frank's chief scientist she was under immense pressure, as Roughneck picked up momentum. But she agreed to pass on the puzzling fragment to a colleague, better qualified. Xenia agreed, provided she used only people in the employ of one of Frank's companies.

Meanwhile, discreetly, from home, Xenia repeated Takomi's work on the comet. She searched for evidence of the anomalous signature of methane burning.

It had been picked up, but not recognized, by many sensors.

Takomi was right.

Clearly, someone had planted a rocket on the side of the comet, and deflected it from its path. It was also clear that most of the burn had been on the far side of the Sun, where it would be undetected.

The burn had been long enough, she estimated, to have deflected the comet to *cause* its lunar crash. Undeflected, it would surely have sailed by, spectacular but harmless.

She then did some checks of the tangled accounts of Frank's companies.

She found places where funds had been diverted. Resources secreted. A surprisingly large amount, reasonably well concealed.

She'd been cradling a suspicion since Edo. Now it was confirmed, and she felt only disappointment at the shabbiness of the truth.

She knew that Takomi wouldn't reveal the existence of the rocket on the comet. He simply wasn't engaged enough in the human world to consider it. But she knew that, such was the continuing focus of attention on Fracastorius, Takomi wouldn't be the only observer who would notice the trace of that diverting rocket, follow the evidence trail.

The truth would come out.

Without making a decision on how to act on this, she went back to work with Frank.

The pressure on Xenia, on both of them, was immense and unrelenting.

Frank seemed to be finding it hard to cope, and it brought him little joy.

After one gruelling 20-hour day, she slept with him.

She thought it would relieve the tension, for both of them. Well, it did, for a brief oceanic moment. But then, as they rolled apart, it all came down on them again.

Frank lay on his back, eyes fixed on the ceiling, jaw muscles working, restless, tense.

There was no prospect of sleep. All she could offer him was talk.

"*Ya nye panimayoo*," she said. "I still don't understand, Frank."

"Huh?"

"You're pushing Roughneck because you want to future-proof the Moon. Terraform it, if you have to. But you pitch it to your investors as a mining venture with short-term payoffs."

"Sure. But I know my quarry, Xenia. Those people are politicians and business-types. That is, they're a bunch of crooks, charlatans, and madmen. That side of human nature hasn't changed since 1970. They're like me."

No, they're not, she thought.

"What they care about is profit in the here and now. If I talk about terraforming I'll scare them off."

"But once you've dug your hole—"

"—Once I've dug my hole, and all those lovely volatiles are just gushing out onto the surface, the longer term implications are going to be obvious to everyone." He looked thoughtful. "Of course just having the volatiles won't solve all the problems. You'll have the issue of the Moon's long day-night cycle, for instance. Even an atmosphere as thick as Earth's would freeze out every two weeks, on the dark side. And you'd have huge winds, forever sweeping around the terminator."

"Mirrors," she said. "Suspended over the dark side. Stop everything from freezing."

He nodded, approving. "But mirrors are complicated; you'd need a space-going infrastructure to maintain them. No, the real solution is to spin up the Moon."

She goggled. "Spin it up? How the hell—"

He grinned in the dim light. "How do I know? There's more. We might want to move the Moon away from Earth altogether. What use is Earth now? It will only cause 60-feet tides, on a terraformed Moon, and slow up the spin again. To hell with that. Let's pick an orbit of our own—maybe 60 degrees ahead of Earth. You don't know how we'll do that? Neither do I. When the time comes we'll hire the technical types again, and pay them more peanuts." He frowned. "Of course, it's important we do this now. The next few decades, I mean."

"Why? The leaky resource loops in the domes?"

"Not just that. Xenia, this is a low-gravity, low-pressure environment. There's less oxygen per lungful than on Earth."

"So what?"

"So, low gravity and low oxygen breeds big, slow, docile people. On the Moon, you don't even have to be smart enough to react fast when you fall out of your tree."

"You're saying that living on the Moon is breeding dumb people? That's just prejudice, Frank."

He shrugged. "Take a look at the schools' databases if you want to verify it. Look at the Grays. Anyhow there's a perspective beyond that, even."

"Frank, you've already terraformed the Moon, spun it up and moved it, and saved the inhabitants from losing their intelligence. How much further can you go?"

"Well, think about it," he whispered. "Earth is an unusual planet. Maybe unique. Life has spent four billion years making it the way it is. The Moon, on the other hand, is mundane. There must be billions of little rocky worlds just like this, scattered through the galaxy. More Moons, not more Earths. So if we can learn to live on the Moon, we can live *anywhere*. The human race will be immortal."

"Sometimes you scare me, Frank."

"I know. I think big. That's why you love me."

No, she thought. That is why you fascinate me. You really would save the world by destroying it.

I will never comprehend you, she thought.

They fell silent, without sleeping.

A little later Mariko Nishzaki called Xenia. She had preliminary results about the glass object from Edo. Xenia took the call in her *tokonoma*, masking it from Frank.

"The object is constructed almost entirely of lunar surface material. Specifically, glass made of—"

"Almost?"

"There are also complex organics in there. We don't know where they came from, or what they are for. There is water, too, sealed into cells within the glass. The structure itself acts as a series of lenses, which focus sunlight. Remarkably efficient. There seems to be a series of valves on the underside that draw in particles of regolith. The grains are melted, evaporated, in the intense focused sunlight. It's a pyrolysis process similar to—"

"What happens to the vaporized material?"

"There is a series of traps, leading off from each light-focusing cell. The traps are maintained at different temperatures by spicules—the fine needles protruding from the upper surface—which also, we suspect, act to deflect daytime sunlight, and conversely work as insulators during the long lunar night. In the traps, at different temperatures, various metal species condense out. The structure seems to be oriented toward collecting aluminum. There is also an oxygen trap farther back."

Aluminum and oxygen. Rocket fuel, melting out of the lunar rock, inside the glass structure, by the light of the Sun.

Mariko was continuing with her analysis, and promised to keep Xenia informed. Xenia returned to bed. Frank seemed to be asleep.

She thought over her relationship with him.

She had a choice to make. Not about the comet issue; others would unravel that, in time. About Frank, and herself.

He fascinated her, true. He was a man of her own time, with a crude vigor she didn't find among the Japanese-descended colonists of the Moon. He was the only link she had with home. The only human on the Moon who didn't speak Japanese to her.

Maybe he reminded her of her father. That, as far as she could tell, was all she felt.

In the meantime, she must consider her own morality.

Laying beside him, she made her decision.

She wouldn't betray him. As long as he needed her, she would stand with him. But she would not save him.

The next morning, Mariko called Xenia again. "The results are back. About the organics. You ought to come see this. . . ."

Mariko worked in what seemed like a typical geology lab, to Xenia: rocks and dust samples everywhere, in boxes and trays and on shelves, benches bearing anonymous analysis equipment. Some of the more pristine samples were being handled in sealed glove boxes. There was a persistent smell of wood smoke: the scent of fresh Moon dust, Xenia knew.

Mariko had set out the glass petal on a cleared bench. The petal had been partially dissected.

"I did not believe what my friend told me," Mariko said. "Therefore I had him bring his subsample and his results here and repeat his analysis."

"Is it so surprising?"

"To me, yes. But you must remember I am a geologist. My contact works with biochemists and biologists, and they are extremely excited."

Biologists?

Xenia sat down. "You'd better tell me."

Mariko consulted notes in a softscreen.

"Within this structure the organic chemicals serve many uses. A species of photosynthesis, for instance. A complex chemical factory appears to be at work here. There is evidence of some kind of root system, which perhaps provides the organics in the first place, ... but, there is no source we know of. This is the *Moon*." She looked confused. "Xenia, this is essentially a vapor-phase reduction machine of staggering elegance of execution, mediated by organic chemistry. It must be an artifact. And yet it looks —"

"What?"

"As if it grew, out of the Moon ground. There are many further puzzles," Mariko said, "for instance, the evidence of a neural network."

"What?"

"Some of the organics —"

"Are you saying this has some kind of a nervous system?"

Mariko shrugged. "I am not a biologist. But still, if this is some simple lunar plant, why would it need a nervous system?" She blinked. "Even, perhaps, a rudimentary awareness." She studied Xenia. "What is this thing?"

"I can't tell you that." She picked up the sample. "Not yet. Sorry."

Mariko walked with her to the door. "There has been much speculation about the form life would take, here on the Moon. But volatile depletion seemed an unbeatable hurdle. Is it possible —"

"Mariko, I can't tell you any more."

Mariko pursued her. "How could life originate, here on the Moon? And, more fundamentally, where did it get its organic material? Was it from the root structure, from deep within the Moon? If so, you realize that this is confirmation of my hypotheses about the volatiles in —"

Xenia stopped. "*Mariko*. This isn't to go further. News of this . . . discovery. Not yet. Tell your colleagues that too."

Mariko looked shocked, as Xenia, with weary certainty, had expected. "You want to *suppress* this? But this could be . . ."

"The discovery of the age. Life on the Moon. I know."

"More than that. Even our engineers could learn so much by studying the processes at work here."

"But this isn't science, Mariko. I don't want anything perturbing the project."

Mariko made to protest again.

"Read your contract," Xenia snapped, and walked out, carrying the petal.

Life was long, slow, unchanging.

Even her thoughts were slow.

In the timeless intervals between the comets, her growth was chthonic, her patience matching that of the rocks themselves. Slowly, slowly, she rebuilt her strength: Light traps to start the long process of drawing out fire for the next seeds, leaves to catch the comet Rain that would come again.

She spoke to her children, their subtle scratching carrying to her through the still, cold rock.

Their conversations lasted a million years. It was important that she taught them: how to grow, of the comet Rains to come, of the Giver at the beginning of things, the Merging at the end.

The Rains were spectacular; but infrequent. But when they came, once or twice in every billion years, her pulse accelerated, her metabolism exploded, as she drank in the thin, temporary air, and dragged the fire she needed from the rock.

And, with each Rain, she birthed again, the seeds exploding from her body and scattering around the Land.

But, after that first time, she was never alone. She could feel, through the rock, the joyous pulsing of her children as they hurled their own seed through the gathering comet air.

Soon there were so many of them that it was as if all of the Land was alive with their birthing, its rocky heart echoing to their joyous shouts.

And still, in the distant future, the Merging awaited them.

As the comets leaped one by one back into the sky, sucking away the air with them, she held that thought to her exhausted body, cradling it.

Eighty days in and Frank was still making hole at his mile-a-day pace. But things had started to get a lot harder.

This was mantle, after all. The rock was like stretched wire, under so much pressure it exploded when it was exposed. It was a new regime. New techniques were needed.

Costs escalated.

The pressure on Frank to shut down was intense.

Many of his investors had already become extremely rich from the potential of the rich ore lodes discovered in the lower crust and upper mantle. There was talk of opening up new, shallow bores elsewhere on the Moon. Frank had proved his point. Why go farther, when the Roughneck was already a commercial success?

But that wasn't Frank's dream, of course. Metal ore wasn't his goal, and he wasn't about to stop now.

He lost some investors. For now at least he was able to sustain a sufficient coalition to maintain the project. Xenia was becoming worried at the funds he was ploughing back into the drilling himself, however.

. . . That was when the first death occurred, all of 70 miles below the surface of the Moon.

She found him in his office at New Dallas, pacing back and forth, an Earthman caged on the Moon, his muscles lifting him off the glass floor.

"Omelettes and eggs," he said. "Omelettes and eggs."

"That's a cliché, Frank."

"It was probably the Grays."

"There's no evidence of sabotage."

He paced. "Look, we're in the *mantle* of the Moon—"

"You don't have to justify it to me," she said, but he wasn't listening.

"The mantle," he said. "You know, I hate it. Four hundred miles of worthless shit we have to dig through just to get to the good stuff down below."

"The primitive material?"

"Yeah. Primeval treasure, waiting for us since the birth of the solar system. But first we have to get through the *mantle*."

"It was the change over to the subterrene that caused the disaster. Right?"

He ran a hand over his gleaming scalp. "If you were a prosecutor, and this was a court, I'd challenge you on 'caused.' The accident happened when we switched over to the subterrene, yes."

They had already gone too deep for the simple alloy casing, or the cooled lunar glass Frank had replaced it with; to get through the mantle they would use a subterrene, a development of obsolete deep-mining technology, a probe that melted its way through the rock and built its own casing behind it, a tube of hard, high-melting-point quasiglass.

Frank started talking, rapidly, about quasiglass. "It's the stuff the Lunar Japanese use for rocket nozzles. Very high melting point. It's based on diamond, but it's a quasicrystal, so the lab boys tell me, halfway between a crystal and a glass. They build it with some kind of nano technique, molecule by molecule. . . ."

"Like a Penrose tilling," she said.

"Yes," he said, looking surprised she understood. "Harder than ordinary crystal because there are no neat planes for cracks and defects to propagate. And it's a good heat insulator similarly. If not for quasiglass this bore would be as ragged as any in a Texas oil field, just lengths of pipe packed in with cement. . . . Besides that we support the hole against collapse and shear stress. Rock bolts, fired through the casing and into the rock beyond. We do everything we can to ensure the integrity of our structure—"

This was, she realized, a first draft of the testimony he would have to give to the investigating commissions.

When the first subterrene started up it built a casing with a flaw, undetected for a hundred yards.

There had been an implosion. They lost the subterrene itself, a half mile of bore—and a single life, of a senior toolpusher.

"We've already restarted," Frank said. "A couple of days and we'll have recovered. The overall schedule loss—"

"Frank, this isn't a question of schedule loss. It's the wider impact. Public perception. Come on; you know how important this is. If we don't handle this right we'll be shut down."

He seemed reluctant to absorb that. He was silent, for maybe half a minute.

Then his mood switched. He brightened. "Hell, you're right. You know, we can leverage this to our advantage."

"What do you mean?"

"We need to turn this guy we lost—what was his name?—into a hero." He snapped his fingers. "Did he have any family? Find out. A 10-year-old son would be perfect, but we'll work with whatever we have. Get his kids to drop cherry blossom down the hole. You know the deal. The message has to be right. *The kids want the bore to be finished, as a memorial to the brave hero.*"

"Frank, the dead engineer was a she."

"And we ought to think about the Gray angle. Get one of them to call that toolpusher a criminal."

"Frank—"

He faced her. "You think this is immoral. Right?"

"Well—"

"Bullshit," he said. "It would be immoral to stop; otherwise, believe me, everyone on this Moon is going to die in the long run. Why do you think I asked you to set up the kids' clubs and schemes?"

"For *this*?"

"Hell, yes. Already I've had some of those chicken-livered investors try to bail out. Now we use the kids, to put so much pressure on them it's impossible for them to turn back. If that toolpusher had a kid in one of our clubs, in fact, that's perfect."

"Frank—"

He eyed her and pointed a stubby finger at her face. "This is the bottleneck. Every project goes through it. We need to get through it, is all. I need to know you're with me on this, Xenia."

She held his gaze for a couple of seconds, then sighed. "You know I am."

He softened, and dropped his hands. "Yeah. I know." But there was something in his voice, she thought, that didn't match his words. An uncertainty that hadn't been there before. "Omelettes and eggs," he muttered. "Whatever." He clapped his hands. "So. What's next?"

This time, Xenia didn't fly directly to Edo. Instead she programmed the hopper to make a series of slow orbits of the abandoned base.

It took her an hour to find the glimmer of glass, reflected sunlight sparkling from a broad expanse of it, at the center of an ancient, eroded crater.

She landed a half-mile away, eager to avoid disturbing the structure. She suited up quickly, clambered out of the hopper, and set off on foot.

Pocked regolith slid smoothly toward her feet, over the close horizon. She made ground quickly, in this battered, ancient landscape, restrained only by the Moon's gentle gravity.

Soon the land ahead grew bright, glimmering like a pool. She slowed, approaching cautiously.

The flower was larger than she had expected. It must have covered an acre or more, delicate glass leaves resting easily against the regolith from which they had been constructed, spiky needles protruding. There was, too, another type of structure: short, stubby cylinders, pointing at the sky, projecting in all directions.

Miniature cannon muzzles. Launch gantries for aluminum-burning rockets, perhaps.

". . . I must startle you again."

She turned. It was Takomi, of course: in his worn, patched suit, his hands folded behind his back. He was looking at the flower.

"Life on the Moon," she said.

"Its life-cycle is simple," said Takomi. "The flower is exposed to sunlight, through the long Moon day. Each of its leaves is a collector of sunlight. The flower focuses the light on regolith, and breaks the soil down to the components it needs to manufacture its own structure, its seeds, and the simple rocket fuel used to propel them across the surface.

"Then, during the night, the leaves act as cold traps. They absorb the comet frost that falls on them, water and methane and carbon dioxide, incorporating that, too, into the flowers' substance."

"And the roots?"

"The roots are miles long. I don't know how long. They tap deep wells of nutrient, water and organic substances. Deep inside the Moon."

So Frank, of course, was right about the volatiles, as she had known.

Takomi said now, "This is how the Moon feeds me. I have found a way to tap into those roots, extract the deep nutrients. My needs are modest. It does not damage the plant—although the plant is already withering."

"What? . . . I suppose you despise Frank Paulis."

He said mildly, "Why should I?"

"Because he is trying to dig out the sustenance for these plants. Rip it out of the heart of the Moon. Are you a Gray, Takomi?"

He shrugged. "We have different ways. My way is—" he stretched his hands "—this. To live off the land, off the Moon. I need little to sustain me, and that little the Moon provides. And I have all the stillness I need."

"But how many humans could the Moon support this way?"

"Ah. Not many. But how many humans does the Moon need?" He studied her. "Your people have a word. *Mechta.*"

"Dream." It was the first Russian word she had heard spoken in many months.

"It was the name your engineers wished to give to the first probe they sent to the Moon. *Mechta.* But it was not allowed, by those who decide such things.

"Well, I am living a dream, here on the Moon, a dream of rock and stillness, here with my Moon flower. That is how you should think of me."

He smiled, and walked away.

The Land was rich with life now: her children, her descendants, drinking in air and Light. Their songs echoed through the core of the Land, strong and powerful.

But it would not last, for it was time for the Merging.

First there was a sudden explosion of Rains, too many to count, the comets leaping out of the ground, one after the other:

Then the Land itself became active. Great sheets of rock heated, becoming liquid, and withdrew into the interior of the Land.

Many died, of course. But those that remained bred frantically. It was a glorious time, a time of death and life.

Changes accelerated. She could feel huge masses rising and falling in the molten interior. The Land grew hot, dissolving into a deep ocean of liquid rock. She clung to the thin crust that contained the world.

And then the Land itself began to break up, great masses of it hurling themselves into the sky, so that soon the Land was surrounded by a glowing cloud of fragments. More died.

But she was not afraid. It was glorious!—as if the Land itself was birthing comets, as if the Land were like herself, hurling its children far away.

The end came swiftly, more swiftly than she had expected, in an explosion of heat and light that burst from the heart of the Land itself. The last, thin crust was broken open, and suddenly there was no more Land, nowhere for her roots to grip.

It was the Merging, and it was glorious. . . .

THREE: THE TUNNEL INTO THE MOON

Frank J Paulis and Xenia Makarova, wrapped in their spider-web spacesuits, stood on a narrow aluminum bridge. They were under the South Pole derrick, and suspended over the tunnel Frank had dug into the heart of the Moon.

The shaft below Xenia was a cylinder of sparkling lunar glass. Lights had been buried in the walls every few yards, so the shaft was brilliantly lit, like a shopping mall passageway, the multiple reflections glimmering from the glass walls. Refrigeration and other conduits snaked along the tunnel.

It was vertical, perfectly symmetrical, and there was no mist or dust, nothing to obscure her view. The tunnel receded to the center of the Moon, to infinity. Momentarily dizzy, she stepped back, anchored herself again on the surface of the Moon.

The area around the derrick had long lost its pristine theme-park look. There were piles of spill and waste and ore, dug out of the deepening hole in the ground. LHDs, automated load-haul-dump vehicles, crawled continually around the site. The LHDs were baroque aluminum beetles with broad fenders, and most of their working parts were six feet or more off the ground, where sprays of the abrasive lunar dust wouldn't reach. They sported giant fins to radiate off their excess heat; no conduction or convection to transfer heat here. The LHDs, she realized, were machines made for the Moon. . . .

Frank, excited, oddly nervous, started telling her how even the subterrene technology hadn't been resistant enough when they got through the mantle, four hundred miles deep, and the temperature climbed toward a thousand degrees. The drill could only penetrate farther by having high-velocity water flashed ahead of it so that the bore was constantly contained by a finger of chilled rock, bringing the temperature down to a bearable level—

The lights, here at the South Pole pit head, were bright, and Xenia couldn't see Frank's face within his visor.

He rubbed his hands. "It's wonderful. Like the old days. Engineers overcoming obstacles, building things."

"And," she said, "thanks to all this stuff, we got through the mantle."

"Hell, yes, we got through it. You've been away from the project too long, Xenia. We got through all that shit to the deep interior. The primitive material. And—"

"Yes?"

He took her hands. Squat in his suit, his face invisible, he was still, unmistakably, Frank J Paulis.

"And now, it's our time."

"What are we going to do?"

She could hear his smile. "Trust me."

Without hesitation—he never hesitated—he stepped to the lip of the delicate metal bridge. She walked with him, a single step. A stitched safety harness, suspended from pulleys above, impeded her.

He said, "Will you follow me?"

She took a breath. "I've followed you so far."

"Then come."

Hand in hand, they jumped off the bridge.

Slow as a snowflake, tugged by gravity, Xenia fell toward the heart of the Moon.

The loose harness dragged gently at her shoulders and crotch, slowing her fall. She was guided by a couple of spider-web cables, tautly threaded down the axis of the shaft; through her suit's fabric she could hear the hiss of the pulleys.

Xenia could hear her heart pound. She looked down. There was nothing beneath her feet save a diminishing tunnel of light.

Frank was laughing.

The depth markers on the wall were already rising past her, mapping her acceleration. But she was suspended here, in the vacuum, as if she were in orbit; she had no sense of speed, no vertigo from the hole beneath her.

Once she would have been terrified by such an experience. But she seemed to have lost her monkey instincts. There were rumors that Saddlepoint gateway transitions did that to you. Or perhaps this place, this monstrous Moon tunnel of Frank's, was simply too strange to comprehend.

Their speed picked up quickly. In seconds, it seemed, they had already passed through the fine regolith layers, the Moon's pulverized outer skin, and were sailing down through the megaregolith. Giant chunks of deeply shattered rock crowded against the glassy, transparent tunnel walls like the corpses of buried animals.

Frank was watching her. "Don't touch that guide wire."

"I won't."

"These Japanese suits are smart technology, but we're already moving so fast the wire would take your arm off. But it isn't so bad; even freefalling, our speed would only reach a mile a second by the time we hit the center of the Moon. Gravity falls off as you descend, you see. . . ." He looked down, at the convergent emptiness beneath their boots. "Anyhow the pulleys will slow us. A hell of a ride, isn't it?"

"Yes. . . ."

The material beyond the walls had turned smooth and gray now. This was lunar bedrock, anorthosite, buried beyond even the probings and pulverizing of the great impactors. Unlike Earth, there would be no fossils here, she knew, no remnants of life in these deep levels; only a smooth gradation of minerals, processed only by the slow workings of geology.

Despite the gathering warmth of the tunnel, despite her own acceleration, she had a sense of cold, of age and stillness.

In some places there were levels, side shafts dug away from the main exploratory bore. They led to stopes, lodes of magnesium-rich rocks, plugs of deep material that had been extruded long ago from the Moon's frozen interior, and were now being mined out by Frank's industry partners. She saw the workings as complex blurs, hurrying upward as she fell, gone like dream visions.

They dropped through a surprisingly sharp transition into a new realm, where the rock on the other side of the walls glowed, of its own internal light. It was a dull gray-red, like a cooling lava on Earth.

"The mantle of the Moon," Frank whispered, gripping her hands. "Basalt. Up here it ain't so bad. But farther down the rock is so soft it pulls like taffy when you try to drill it. Four hundred miles of mush, a pain in the ass. . . ."

As he talked they passed a place where the glass walls were marked with an engraving, stylized flowers with huge lunar petals. This was where a technician had lost her life, in an implosion. The little memorial shot upward and was lost in the light. Frank didn't comment.

The rock was now glowing a bright cherry-pink, rushing upward past them.

Falling, falling. Like dropping through some immense glass tube full of fluorescing gas. Xenia sensed the heat, despite her suit's insulation and the refrigeration of the tunnel.

Thick conduits surrounded them now, crowding the tunnel, flipping from bracket to bracket. The conduits carried water, bearing the Moon's deep heat to the hydrothermal plants on the surface.

Now they passed through another transition, signaled by a wide wall marking, this one undetectable to eyes that were becoming dazzled by the pink-white glare of the rocks.

The harness tugged at her sharply, slowing her. Looking down along the forest of conduits, she could see that they were approaching a terminus, a platform of some dull, opaque ceramic that plugged the tunnel.

"End of the line," Frank said. "Down below there's only the downhole tools and the casing machine and other junk. . . . Do you know where you are? Xenia, we're five hundred miles deep, halfway to the center of the Moon. . . ."

She glanced at her chronometer patch. It had taken 20 minutes.

The pulleys gripped harder and they slowed, drifting to a halt a couple of feet above the platform. With Frank's help she loosened her harness and spilled easily to the platform itself, landing on her feet, as if after a sky-dive.

She caught her balance, and looked around.

The platform was crowded with science equipment, anonymous gray boxes linked by cables to softscreens and batteries. Sensors and probes, wrapped in water-cooling jackets, were plugged into ports in the walls. She could see data collected from the lunar material flickering over the softscreens, measurements of porosity and permeability, data from gas meters and pressure gauges and dynamometers and gravimeters. There was evidence of work here, small pressurisable shelters, spare backpacks, notepads—even, incongruously, a coffee cup. Human traces, here at the heart of the Moon.

They were alone here.

She walked to the walls. She was, she felt, almost floating.

There was primeval rock, pure and unmarked, all around her, beyond the window—like walls.

"The deep interior of the Moon," Frank said, joining her. He ran his gloved hands over the glass. "What the rock hounds call primitive material. The same stuff the asteroids are made of, left over from the solar system's formation. Never melted and differentiated like the mantle, never bombarded like the surface. Untouched since the Moon budded off of Earth itself, I guess."

"I feel light as a feather," she said. And so she did; she felt as if she was going to float back up the borehole like a soap bubble.

Frank glared up into the hundreds of miles of tunnel above them, and concentric light rings glimmered in his face plate. "All that rock up there doesn't pull at us. Not when we're down here. Just the stuff beneath our feet. It might as well be cloud, rocky cloud, hundreds of miles of it—"

"I suppose, at the core itself, you would be weightless."

"I guess."

On one low bench stood a glass beaker, covered with clear plastic film. She picked it up; she could barely feel it, dwarfed within her thick, inflexible gloves. It held a liquid that sloshed in the gentle gravity. The liquid was murky brown, not quite transparent.

She turned. Frank was grinning.

Immediately, she understood.

"I wish you could drink it," he said. "I wish we could drink a toast. You know what that is? *It's water.* Moon water, water from the lunar rocks." He took the beaker and turned around, in a slow, ponderous dance. "It's all around us. Just as Mariko predicted, a ocean of it. Wadsleyite and majorite with three percent water by weight. . . . Incredible. We did it, babe."

"Frank. You were right. I had no idea."

"I sat on the results. I wanted you to be the first to see this. To see my—"

"Affirmation," she said gently. "This is your affirmation."

"Yeah. I'm a hero."

It was true, she knew.

It was going to work out just as Frank had projected, as they had mapped out in the wargaming they had done. As soon as the implications of the find became apparent—that there really were oceans down here, buried inside the Moon—the imaginations of the Lunar Japanese would be fast to follow Frank's vision. This wasn't a simple matter of plugging holes in the environment support system loops. There was enough resource here, just as Frank said, to future-proof the Moon. Not for the first time Xenia had recognized Frank's brutal wisdom in his dealings with people: to bulldoze them as far as he had to, until they couldn't help but agree with him.

Frank would become the most famous man on the Moon.

That wasn't going to help him, though, she thought sadly.

"So," she said. "You proved your point. You found what you wanted to find. Will you stop now?"

"Stop the borehole?" He sounded shocked. "Hell, no. We go on."

"Frank, the investors are already pulling out."

"Chicken-livered assholes. I'll go on if I have to pay for it myself." He put the beaker down. "Xenia, to hell with the water. Water isn't enough; it's just a first step. We have to go on. *We still have to find the other volatiles.* Methane. Organics—"

"But even Mariko says the theoretical basis for their existence here is shaky compared to water."

"Shaky, hell," he said angrily. "If those cosmic processes, whatever the hell they were, worked to trap the water, they'll trap the other stuff too."

His faith, in the existence of those deep chemical treasures, was strong as ever. And—*knowing she already had evidence that he was right*—she felt stabs of guilt.

But she couldn't help him now.

He was saying, "We go on. Damn it, Roughneck is my project."

"No, it isn't. We sold so much stock to get through the mantle that you don't have a majority any more."

"But we're rich again." He laughed. "We'll buy it back."

"Nobody's selling. They certainly won't after you publish this finding. You're too successful. I'm sorry, Frank."

"So the bad guys are closing in, huh. Well, the hell with it. I'll find a way to beat them. I always do." He grabbed her gloved hands. "Never mind that now. Listen, I'll tell you why I brought you down here. *I'm winning.* I found water in the Moon, just where we predicted. And as soon as we hit volatile, I'm going to get everything I ever wanted. Except one thing."

She was bewildered. "What?"

"I want us to get married. I want us to have kids. We came here together, from out of the past, and we should have a life of our own, on this Japanese Moon." His voice was heavy, laden with emotion, almost cracking. In the glare of rock light, she couldn't see his face.

She hadn't expected this. She couldn't think of a response.

"Hell," he said, and now his voice was almost shrill. "What do you say? This is the biggest moment of my life, Xenia. Of our lives. I want to share it with you, now and forever. To hell with Kawasaki, the investors. *We did this*, together. The Moon is ours. Now, what do you say?"

"The comet," she said softly.

He was silent for a moment, still gripping her hands.

"The methane rocket was detected."

She could tell he was thinking of denying all knowledge of this. Then he said: "Who found it?"

"Takomi."

"The piss-drinking old bastard out at Edo?"

"Yes."

"That still doesn't prove—"

"I checked the accounts. I found where you diverted the funds, how you built the rocket, how you launched it, how you rendezvoused it with the comet." She sighed. "You never were smart at that kind of stuff, Frank. You should have asked me to help."

"Would you?"

"No."

He released her hands. "I never meant it to hit where it did. On Fracastorius."

"I know that. Nevertheless, that's where it did land."

He picked up the glass of lunar water. "But you know what, I'd have gone ahead even if I had known. I had to kickstart Prometheus; I needed that comet. It was the only way. You can't stagnate. That way lies extinction."

She closed her eyes. "I admire your ambition. But—"

"If I gave the Lunar Japanese a choice, they wouldn't have allowed it. They'd be sucking piss water out of old concrete for the rest of time."

"But it would be their choice."

"And that's more important?"

She shrugged. "It's inevitable they'll know soon," she said. "Where I found the false accounting, the evidence of the deflection, the authorities will follow."

He turned to her, and she sensed he was grinning again, irrepressible. "At least I finished my project. At least I got to be a hero. . . . Marry me," he said again.

"No."

"Why not? Because I'm going to be a con?"

"Not that."

"Then why?"

"Because I wouldn't last, in your heart. You move on, Frank."

"You're wrong," he said. But there was no conviction in his voice. "So," he said. "No wedding bells. No little Lunar Americans, to teach these Japanese how to play pro football."

"I guess not."

He walked away. "Makes you think, though," he said, his back to her.

"What?"

He waved a hand at the glowing walls. "This technology isn't so advanced. Neil and Buzz couldn't have done it, but maybe we could have opened up some kind of deep mine on the Moon by the end of the 20th century, say. Started to dig out the water, live off the land. If only we'd known it was here, all this wealth, even NASA might have done it. And then you'd have an American Moon, and who knows how history might have turned out?"

"None of us can change things."

He looked at her, his face masked by rock light. "However much we might want to."

"No."

"How long do you think I have?"

"Before—"

"Before they shut me down."

"I don't know. Weeks. No more."

"Then I'll have to make those weeks count."

He showed her how to hook her suit harness to a fresh pulley set, and they began the long, slow ride to the surface of the Moon.

Abandoned on its bench top at the bottom of the shaft, she could see the covered beaker, the Moon water within.

After her descent into the moon, she returned to Edo, seeking stillness.

The world of the Moon, here on Farside, was simple: the regolith below, the sunlight that flowed from the black sky above. Land, light, dark. That, and herself, alone. When she looked downsun, at her own shadow, the light bounced from the dust back toward her, making a halo around her head.

The Moon flower had, she saw, significantly diminished since her last visit; many of the outlying petals were broken off or shattered.

After a time, Takomi joined her.

He said: "Evidence of the flowers has been unturned before."

"It has?"

"I have, discreetly, studied old records of the lunar surface. Another legacy of richer days past, when much of the Moon was studied in some detail.

"But those explorers, long dead now, did not know what they had found, of course. Some of the remains were buried under regolith layers. Some of them were billions of years old." He sighed. "The evidence is fragmentary. Nevertheless I have been able to establish a pattern."

"What kind of pattern?"

"It is true that the final seeding event drew the pods, with unerring accuracy, back to this site. As you observed. The pods were absorbed into the structure of the primary plant, here, which has since withered. The seeding was evidently triggered by the arrival of the comet, the enveloping of the Moon by its new, temporary atmosphere.

"But I have studied the patterns of earlier seedings—"

"Triggered by earlier comet impacts."

"Yes. All of them long before human occupancy began here. Just one or two impacts, per aeon. Brief comet rains, spurts of air, before the long winter closed again. And each impact triggered a seeding event."

"Ah. I understand. These are like desert flowers, which bloom in the brief rain. Poppies, rockroses, grasses, chenopods."

"Exactly. They complete their life-cycles quickly, propagate as vigorously as possible, while the comet air lasts. And then their seeds lay dormant, for as long as necessary, waiting for the next chance event, perhaps as long as a billion years."

"I imagine they spread out, trying to cover the Moon. Propagate as fast and as far as possible, like desert plants. Wherever there is suitable regolith—"

"No," he said quietly.

"Then what?"

"At every comet event, the seedings converge.

"A billion years ago there were a thousand sites like this. In a great seeding, these diminished to a mere hundred: Those fortunate few were bombarded with seeds, while the originators withered. And later, another seeding reduced that hundred to 12 or so. And finally, the 12 are reduced to one."

She tried to think that through; she pictured the little seed pods converging, diminishing in number. "It doesn't make sense."

"Not for us, who are ambassadors from Earth," he said. "Earth life spreads, colonizes, whenever and wherever it can. But this is lunar life, Xenia. And the Moon is an old, cooling, dying world. Its richest days were brief moments, far in the past. And so life has adjusted to the situation. Do you understand?"

"I think so. But now, this is truly the last of them? The end?"

"Yes. The flower is already diminishing, dying."

"But why here? Why now?"

He shrugged. "Xenia, your colleague Frank Paulis is evidently determined to rebuild the Moon, inside and out. Even if he fails, others will follow where he showed the way. The stillness of the Moon is lost." He sniffed. "My own garden might survive, but in a park, like your old Apollo landers, to be gawked at by tourists. It is a diminishing. And so with the flowers. There is nowhere for them to survive, on the Moon, in our future."

"But how do they *know* they can't survive—oh, that's the wrong question. Of course the flowers don't know anything."

He paused, regarding her. "Are you sure?"

"What do you mean?"

"We are smart, and aggressive. We think smartness is derived from aggression. Perhaps that is true. But perhaps it takes a greater imagination to comprehend stillness than to react to the noise and clamor of our shallow human world."

She frowned, remembering Mariko's evidence about neural structures in the flowers. "You're saying these things are *conscious?*"

"I believe so. It would be hard to prove. I have spent much time in contemplation here, however. And I have developed an intuition. A sympathy, perhaps."

"But that seems—"

"What?"

"Bleak," she said. "Unbelievably so. *Cruel.* What kind of god would plan such a thing? Think about it. You have a conscious creature, trapped on the surface of the Moon, in this desolate, barren environment. And its way of living, stretching back billions of years maybe, has had the sole purpose of diminishing itself, to prepare for this final extinction, this death, this *smyert*. What is the purpose of consciousness, confronted by such desolation?"

"But perhaps it is not so," he said gently.

"What?"

"The cosmologists tell us that there are many time streams. The future of the Moon, in the direction we face, may be desolate. But not the past. So why not face *that* way?"

She remembered the *kare sansui*, the waterless stream. It was impossible to tell if the stream was flowing from past to future, or future to past; if the hills of heaped regolith were rising or sinking—

"I don't understand," she said.

"Perhaps to the flowers—to *this* flower, the last, or perhaps the first—this may be a beginning, not an end. The beginning of a journey that will end in unity, and unimaginable glory."

"*Vileekee bokh.* You are telling me that these plants are living backwards in time? Propagating—not into the future—but *into the past?*"

He touched her gloved hand. "The important thing is that you must not grieve for the flowers. They have their dream. Their *mechta*, of a better Moon, in the deep past, or deep future. The universe is not always cruel, Xenia Makarova. And you must not hate Frank, for what he has done."

"I don't hate him."

"There is a point of view from which he is not taking from the heart of the Moon, but giving. You see? Now come. I have green tea, and rice cake, and we will sit under the cherry tree, and talk further."

She nodded, dumbly, and let him take her by the hand.

Together they walked across the yielding antiquity of the Moon.

It was another celebration, here at the South Pole of the Moon. It was the day Project Roughneck promised to fulfill its potential by bringing the first commercially useful loads of water to the surface. Once again the crowds were out, investors with their guests, families with children, huge softscreens draped over drilling gear, Observers everywhere so everyone on the Moon could see, share immediately, everything that happened here today. Even the Grays were here, to celebrate the end, dancing in elaborate formations.

Icebound Earth hovered like a ghost on one horizon.

This time, Xenia didn't find Frank strutting about the lunar surface in his Stars & Stripes spacesuit, giving out orders. Frank knew, he said, which way the wind blew, a blunt Earthbound metaphor no Lunar Japanese understood. So he had confined himself to a voluntary house arrest, in the new *ryokan* that had opened up on the summit of one of the tallest rim mountains here.

When she arrived, he waved her in and handed her a drink, a fine sake.

"This is one hell of a cage," he said. "If you've got to be in a cage —"

"Don't be frightened," she said.

He laughed darkly. "Civilized, these Lunar Japanese. Well, we'll see."

It was true that so far, while the investigation was progressing, he had been left alone. Xenia liked to think the Lunar Japanese authorities were giving Frank time and space, letting him enjoy his huge triumph, before they acted.

But perhaps that was sentimental.

After centuries of survival on the unyielding Moon, she knew there was a hardness under the polite, civilized veneer of these Lunar Japanese. They did not suffer well those who wasted resources, or endangered the lives of others.

Not that Frank was suffering right now, at any rate. His suite was a penthouse, magnificent, decorated a mix of Western-style and traditional Japanese. One wall, facing the borehole, was just a single huge pane of tough, anhydrous lunar glass.

She saw a glass of murky water, covered over, on a table top. Moon water, his only trophy of Roughneck.

He walked her to the window.

She gazed out, goddess-like, surveying the activity. The drilling site was an array of blocky machinery, now stained deep gray by dust, all of it bathed in artificial light. The stars hung above the plain, stark and still, and people and their vehicles swarmed over the ancient, broken plain like so many spacesuited ants.

"You know, it's a great day," she said. "They're making your dream come true."

"My dream, hell." He fetched himself another slug of sake, which he drank like beer. "They stole it from me. And they're going inward. That's what Kawasaki and the rest are considering now. I've seen their plans. Huge underground cities in the crust, big enough for thousands, even hundreds of thousands, all powered by thermal energy from the rocks. You don't need the surface, any off-world resources. In 50 years you could have multiples of the Moon's present population, burrowing away busily. Hell, it would take a hundred generations to fill up the Moon that way, for there are oceans down there, my oceans, the oceans I found." He glanced at his wristwatch, restless.

"What's wrong with that?"

"But that wasn't the idea," he said heavily. "It wasn't the *point*."

"Then what *was* the point?"

"That," he said, and he looked up at frozen Earth.

"We should take on the Prion?"

"If we have to, to get Earth back. It's our planet, damn it."

"Whose? Ours? Or the Lunar Japanese? Or—"

But he wasn't listening. "If we dig ourselves into the ground, we won't be able to see the Earth, or the stars. We'll forget. Don't you see that? . . ." He glared at her. "We had to flee Earth once before."

"What?"

He said, "I know about the Moon flowers."

Taken aback, she said nothing.

He laughed at her discomfiture. "Of course I know about the flowers. This is my organization, Xenia. Even now, that's still true. You can't keep anything from me."

"I'm sorry if—"

"It would have been better if you'd told me. We could have worked together." He picked up the water glass. "You know what I have here, in this beaker?"

"Tell me."

"*Life*, Xenia. Or at least, lots of little corpses. Billions and billions of them, just in this beaker alone."

She stared at the beaker of Moon water, as if she might see what he was talking about.

"Life, from deep inside the Moon," he said. "The bio boys say there is a whole ecosystem down here. Well, there had to be. Did you think there would be just the flowers on the surface, just one species? The life is anaerobic; that is, it doesn't use oxygen. It feeds on the water and organic shit down here, and it uses heat energy to drive its metabolism. Once we dig these little guys out, the reduction in pressure destroys them. So the techs are coming up with smarter probes that can study them *in situ*. Of course it isn't native to the Moon. . . ."

All this was too fast for Xenia.

"Then where—"

"Xenia, the first forms of life on Earth were like this. They didn't use free oxygen because there was none. Their metabolism was much less energetic than ours, and they pumped out a lot of undesirable by-products. But they survived nevertheless.

"When oxygen started to gather in Earth's atmosphere—one of those by-products—they choked to death on it, literally. Some survived by adapting to the oxygen, and became us. Some just perished. And some escaped, retreating into ocean bottom ooze or volcanic vents—*and some came here*, all the way to the Moon.

"You're saying this life, the bugs in the water, the flowers, came from Earth? How?"

"Hell, I don't know. Maybe they rode over in the big whack that made the Moon. Anyhow it's just as I told you," he said grimly.

"What?"

"This isn't the first time life has had to escape, retreat from the Earth to the Moon. . . ."

But now there was activity around the drilling site. She stepped to the window, cupped her hands to exclude the room lights.

People running, away from the center of the site.

There was a tremor. The building shuddered under her, languidly. A quake, on the still and silent Moon?

Frank was checking his watch. "That was the kick." He punched the air and strode to the window. "Right on time. Hot damn."

"Frank, what have you done?"

There was another tremor, more violent; before the window, a small Buddha statue was dislodged from its pedestal, and fell gently to the carpeted floor. Xenia tried to keep her feet. It was like riding a rush-hour train.

"Simple enough," Frank said. "Just shaped charges, embedded in the casing. They punched holes straight through the casing into the surrounding rock, to let the water and sticky stuff flow right into the pipe and up—"

"A blow-out. You planned a blow-out."

"A small one. If I figured this right the interior of the whole Moon is going to come gushing out of that hole. Like puncturing a balloon." He took her arms. "Listen to me. You don't have to leave. We will be safe here. I figured it."

"And the people down there, in the crater? Your managers and technicians? The *children*?"

"It's just a blow-out."

"Are you sure?"

"It's a day they'll tell their grandchildren about." He shrugged, grinning, his bald pate slick with sweat. "They're going to lock me up anyhow. At least this way—"

But now there was an eruption from the center of the rig, a tower of liquid, rapidly freezing, that punched its way up through the rig itself, shattering the flimsy buildings covering the head. When the fountain reached high enough to catch the flat sunlight washing over the mountains, it seemed to burst into fire, crystals of ice shining in complex parabolic sheaves, before falling back to the ground.

Frank punched the air. "Hot damn. You know what that is? Kerogen. A tarry stuff you find in oil shales. It contains carbon, oxygen, hydrogen, sulphur, potassium, chlorine, other elements, . . . I couldn't believe it when the lab boys told me what they found down there. Mariko says kerogen is so useful we might as well have found chicken soup in the rocks." He cackled. "Chicken soup, from the primordial cloud." He eyed her. "I *succeeded*, Xenia. I did what I wanted."

"I know you did, Frank."

"I opened up a new frontier. With this blowout I stopped them from building Bedrock City. Jesus Christ, I even found life on the Moon. I'm famous."

"What about the anaerobic life?"

His face was hard. "Who cares? I'm a human, Xenia. I'm interested in human destiny, not a bunch of worthless bugs we couldn't even eat. And with this—" he waved a hand at the ice fountain "—I'm forcing a lot of hands.

"Look out there," he said. "This is the way of things, Xenia. I beat the future. I've no regrets. I'm a great man. I achieve great things."

The ground around the demolished drill head began to crack, venting gas and ice crystals; and the deep, ancient richness of the Moon rained down on the people.

"And what," Frank Paulis whispered, "could be greater than this?"

She was in the Dark, flying, like one of her own seeds. She was surrounded by fragments of the shattered Land, and by her children.

But she could not speak to them, of course; unlike the Land, the Dark was empty of rock, and would not carry her thoughts.

It was a time of stabbing loneliness.

But it did not last long.

Already the cloud was being drawn together, collapsing into a new and greater Land that glowed beneath her, a glowing ocean of rock, a hundred times bigger than the small place she had come from.

And at the last, she saw the greatest comet of all tear itself from the heart of this Land, a ball of fire that lunged into the sky, receding rapidly into the unyielding Dark.

She fell toward that glowing ocean, her heart full of joy at the Merging of the Lands. . . .

In the last moment of her life, she recalled the Giver.

She was the first, and the Giver birthed her: None of it would have come to be without the Giver, who fed the Land.

She wished she could express her love for him. She knew that was impossible.

She sensed, though, that he knew anyhow.

Author's note: This story is speculation. But the idea of volatiles trapped inside the planets is a serious one. It was raised in the 1960s by astronomer Thomas Gold, and more recently scientists have found evidence of volatiles deep within the Earth (see "Water in the Earth's Upper Mantle," Alan Bruce Thompson, Nature v 358, 23 July 1992).

The apparent lack of volates on the Moon is an obstacle to its colonization. But, if we look hard enough, we may find the Moon richer than we dream. . . .

This side of independence

ROB CHILSON

When we're grown, the saying goes, we put away childish things . . . but, as suggested by the sobering study of the gulfs dividing cultures and different generations that follows, what if someday the childish things we put away include the Earth itself, tossed casually on a cosmic scrap heap once we don't need it anymore? Well, once most *of us don't need it anymore, anyway . . .*

Rob Chilson has been associated for most of his professional career with Analog *magazine, having made his first few sales in the late sixties to the legendary John W. Campbell himself.* Analog *is where the bulk of his stories have appeared, but his short work has also appeared in* The Magazine of Fantasy & Science Fiction, Asimov's Science Fiction, *and elsewhere. His novels include* As the Curtain Falls, The Star-Crowned Kings, The Shores of Kansas, Men Like Rats, *and* Rounded with Sleep. *His most recent novel is* Black as Blood. *He lives in Kansas City, Kansas.*

They were taking up Kansas in big bites.

Geelie hovered above, detached, observing. Stark night cloaked the world under a shrunken sun, save for the pit, where hell glared. Magma glowed in the darkness where the rock, hectares wide, crumbled in the gravitor beam. Shards of the world upreared, uproared, black edged with glowing red, and lofted into the groaning air, pieces of a broken pot. The bloody light spattered on the swag-bellied ships that hung above — crows tearing at the carcass with a loud continuous clamor. Pieces of the planet fell back and splashed in thunder and liquid fire, yellow and scarlet. Old Earth shuddered for kilometers around.

The glare, the heat, the tumult filled the world. But from a distance, Geelie saw, it was reduced to a cheerful cherry glow and a murmur of sound, lost in the endless night. In her long view, Kansas was a vast sunken plain of contorted rock, dusted with silent snow under a shaded sun.

"Aung Charah in *Tigerclaw* to Goblong Seven," Geelie's speaker said.

"Goblong Seven to Aung Charah," she said.

"Geelie, take a swing around the south side of the working pit and look at the terraces there. I think the magma is flowing up on them."

"Hearing and obedience."

Kansas was a hole walled with stairsteps of cooled lava, terraced for kilometers down to the pit of hell. As fast as the rock froze, it was torn off in hectare-sized chips, to feed the hungry space colonies.

Geelie swung her goblong and swooped down and around the work site. She peered intently in dimness, blinded by the contrast. The magma was definitely crawling up on the lower terrace of cooled rock.

"It's slow as yet," she reported, sending the teleview to Aung Charah.

"We'll have to watch it, however, or we'll have another volcano. Check on it frequently," he told her.

"Hearing and obedience," Geelie said. She leaned forward to peer up through the windscreen.

The Sun was a flickering red candle, the cherry color of the magma. As she watched, it brightened; brightened; brightened again, to a dazzling orange. Then it faded, paused, recovered — briefly showed a gleam of brilliance that glimpsed the black rock below, streaked with snow. Then it faded, faded further, almost vanished.

The Sun was a candle seen through a haze of smoke. But each drifting mote was a space colony with solar panels extended, jostling in their billions jealously to seize the Sun. One by one, the planets of old Sol had been eaten by the colonies, till only Earth was left, passed into the shades of an eternal night.

And now the Old World's historical value had been overridden by the economic value of its water, air, and rock. Also, its vast gravity well was a major obstacle to space traffic.

Noon, planetary time, Geelie thought.

She took her goblong in a long sweep around the work site, occasionally touching the visual recorder's button. Her Colony, Kinabatangan, was a member of The Obstacle-Leaping Consortium; she was part of Kinabatangan's observer team.

A gleam of light caught her eye, and she looked sharply aside. East, she realized. Puzzled, she looped the goblong back again more slowly and sought for the gleam. She found it, but it immediately winked out.

That was odd, she thought. A bright light, yellow or even white — surely artificial — on the highlands to the east. That was disputed land, it was not yet being worked. Perhaps, she thought, observers had set up a camp on the planet.

She called Aung Charah and reported, got permission to check it out. "If I can find it," she said. "The light is gone again; door closed, perhaps."

"I'm having Communications call; I'll keep you informed," Aung Charah said.

She acknowledged and cruised as nearly straight as she could along the beam she'd seen. Presently the land mounted in broken scarps before her, vaguely seen in the wan bloody light of the Sun. Vast masses of shattered rock, covered with snow or capped with ice, tumbled down from the highlands. Missouri, that was what its uncouth name had been, Geelie saw, keying up her map.

At this point there'd been a great sprawling city, Kansas City by name, more populous than a dozen colonies. The parts which had straggled over the border had been mined and the once-vertical scarp had collapsed. East of the line, everything this side of Independence on her map had fallen into the hole that was Kansas.

"Aung Charah in *Tigerclaw* to Geelie in Goblong Seven," said her speaker. "Communications reports no contact. We have no report of anyone in that area. Behinders?" Dubiously.

"Unlikely. However, I am checking. Goblong Seven out."

It was three hundred years since stay-behind planetarians had been found on the mother world. Considering how bleak it now was, Geelie considered them extremely unlikely, as by his tone did Aung Charah.

She cruised slowly over the tumbled mounds of snow-covered rubble that marked the old city. Kilometers it extended, and somehow Geelie found that more oppressive even than the vast expanse of riven rock behind her. She could not imagine the torrents of people who must have lived on this deck. The average Colony had only a hundred thousand.

She peered into the dimness. The rubble showed as black pocks in the blood-lit snow. Presently she came to hover and pondered.

Possibly she'd seen a transitory gleam off a sheet of transpex or polished rock or metal in the old city, she thought. But the color was wrong. No. She'd seen a light. Perhaps there were commercial observers here from a different consortium — not necessarily spying on The Obstacle-Leaping Consortium. There might be many reasons why commercial observers would want to keep secret.

Infra-red, she thought. The goblong wasn't equipped with IR viewers, but Aung Charah had given her a pair of binox. She unharnessed and slipped into the back for them. And a few minutes later she saw a plume of light against the chill background.

It leaked in two dozen points from a hill of rubble a kilometer away. Geelie got its coordinates and called Aung Charah to report.

"I'm going to go down and request permission to land."

"Of course this 'Missouri' is not part of our grant," Aung Charah said. "They — whoever they are — will probably have a right to refuse. Do nothing to involve us legally."

"Hearing and obedience."

Geelie sloped the goblong down, circled the mound, presently found a trampled place in the thin snow and kicked on her lights. Aiming them down, she saw footprints and a door in an ancient wall made of clay brick, a wall patched with shards of concrete glued together. The mound was a warren, a tumble of broken buildings run together, with forgotten doors and unlighted windows peering from odd angles under a lumpy, snow-covered roof.

She sent back a teleview, saying, "I wonder if this is an observers' nest after all."

"Any answer on the universal freqs?"

"One moment." She called, got no answer. "I'm going to land without formal permission and bang on the door."

"Very well."

Geelie landed the goblong, leaving its lights on, and slipped into the back. She pulled her parka hood forward, drew on her gloves, and opened the door. A breath of bitter cold air entered, making her gasp. Ducking out, she started for the door.

Movement caught her eye and she looked up, to see a heavily bundled figure standing atop a pile of rubble by the wall.

"Hello!" she called.

"Hello," came a man's voice. He was not twice as thick as a normal human, she saw—he was simply wearing many layers of cloth against the biting cold.

Geelie exhaled a cloud of vapor, calming herself. So crudely dressed man had to be a behinder—and who knew how he would react?

"I-I am Geelie of Kinabatangan Colony, a member of The Obstacle-Leaping Consortium. Permission to land?"

"What? Oh, granted. That would be you, working over there in Kansas?" His tone was neutral, if guarded. His accent was harsh, rasping, but not unintelligible.

"Yes."

"What brings you here? Will you now begin on Missourah?"

"No," she said. "Missourah," carefully pronouncing it as he had, "is disputed by a number of consortiums and wrecking companies. It will be years before they have settled that dispute."

"That's good to hear," said the other, and moved. With a dangerous-seeming scramble, he slid down from the rubble pile.

Confronting her, he was a head taller than she, and very pale, a pure caucasoid type, in the light from her goblong. He even had the deep blue eyes once confined to caucasoids, and his beard was yellow.

"Name's Clayborn," he said, proffering his hand. "Enos Clayborn."

She squeezed and shook it in the european fashion. "Pleased to meet you, U— er, Mr. Clayborn."

"Won't you come in out of the cold?" he asked, gesturing toward the door.

"Thank you." She followed him gratefully. The bleakness more than the cold chilled her.

The door opened, emitting a waft of warm air that condensed into fog. Geelie stepped in, inhaling humidity and the smell of many people, with an undertone of green plants. It was like, yet unlike, the air of a Colony; more people, less plants, she thought; not so pure an air. She was standing on a vestibule with wooden walls covered with peeling white paint; overhead a single square electrolumer gave a dim yellowish light.

Clayborn fastened the door behind her and stepped past her to open the other door, gesturing her through it. Pushing her hood back, Geelie opened her parka as she entered a room full of tubs of snow, slowly melting; piles of wooden boards; piles of scrap metal; shelves full of things obviously salvaged from the ruins; an assortment of tools. Beyond this was yet another door, opening into a large, brightly lit room full of furniture and people.

"Enos is ba—Enos has brought someone!" "Enos has brought a stranger!" "A strange woman!" The exclamations ran through the room quickly, and a couple of people slipped out. Moments later, they and several others returned.

"Folks, this is Geelie of—of—?" Clayborn turned to her.

"Kinabatangan Colony," Geelie said. Old people, she thought. "Observer of The Obstacle-Leaping Consortium."

"Those are the ones mining Kansas," Clayborn said. "Geelie tells me that they won't start mining Missouri" (pronouncing it differently, she noticed) "for quite a few years yet."

Clayborn in his midtwenties was the youngest person in the room, she saw. The next youngest were four or five hale middle-aged sorts with gray in their hair, perhaps twice his age, and ranging up from there to a frail ancient on a couch, big pale eyes turned toward her and a thin wisp of cottony hair on a pillow. A dozen and a half at most.

"How long have you been here?" she asked, marveling.

"Forever," said one of the white-haired oldsters drily. "We never been anywheres else."

Geelie smiled back at their smiles. "I am awed that you have survived," she said simply, removing her parka and gloves.

"This is our leader, Alden," said Clayborn, pulling up a chair for her.

"The last hundred years was the worst," said Alden.

The behinders, having overcome their shyness, now crowded forward and Clayborn introduced them. Geelie bowed and spoke to all, shook with the bolder ones. When she seated herself, one of the women handed her a cup on a european saucer. She looked at them with awe, reflecting that they must be a thousand years old.

"Brown," she heard them murmur. "Brown. Beautiful—such a nice young woman. Such beautiful black hair."

She sipped a mild coffee brew and nodded her thanks. "The last hundred years?" she said to Alden. "Yes, it must have been."

For over nine hundred years Earth had been in partial shadow and permanent glaciation, but the Sun still shone. Then the greedy colonies broke their agreements and moved massively into the space between the Old World and the Sun. Earth passed into the shadows, and shortly thereafter they began to disassemble it.

" 'Course, our ancestors laid in a good supply of power cells and everything else we'd need, way back when Earth was abandoned by everybody else," Alden said. "No problems there. But how much longer will the air last?"

"Oh, maybe another hundred years," she said, startled. "Freezing it for transport is a slow process."

"And the glaciers? They came down this way back when the Sun shone bright."

Geelie smiled, shook her head. "It's so cold now that even the oceans are freezing over, so the glaciers can't grow by snowfall. Also, frankly, the glaciers were the first to be mined; that much fresh water was worth plenty. Of course the oceans are valuable too, and they have been heavily mined also."

"The snowfall gets thinner every year," said Clayborn. "We have to go farther and farther to get enough. Soon we'll be reduced to thawing the soil for water."

Geelie's response was interrupted by the discreet beeping of her wrist radio. She keyed it on. "Aung Charah in *Tigerclaw* to Geelie in Goblong Seven," it said in a tiny voice, relayed from the goblong.

"Geelie to Aung Charah," she said into it. "I have received permission to land and am with a group of native Earthers."

"Behinders," said Alden drily.

She flashed him a smile and said, "Behinders, they call themselves."

"Er—yes," said Aung Charah, sounding startled. "Er—carry on. Aung Charah out."

"Hearing and obedience. Geelie out."

"Carry on?" Alden asked.

Geelie sobered. She had been excited and amazed at meeting these people and had not thought ahead. "Well," she said. "He represents the Consortium and dares not commit it. You are not his problem."

"We never thought of ourselves as anybody's problem," said Alden mildly. "More coffee?"

Geelie bowed to Lyou Ye, who stood to respond, then reseated herself behind her desk and frowned.

"Behinders," she said. "They must be the very last. It's been what, three hundred years since any have been found, that lot in Africa." She looked sharply at Geelie. "Aung Charah is right, they're not our problem. They live in 'Missouri,' however it's pronounced, outside our grant. They're the problem of the Missouri Compact."

"But those people won't settle their disputes for years, possibly decades," said Geelie. "We can't just let these behinders die."

Lyou Ye glanced aside, frowning, and tapped her finger. She'd come a long way, Geelie knew, in a short time. A very beautiful woman, ten years older than Geelie, with waving masses of dark red hair and the popular tiger-green eyes contributed by gene-splicing, she was commonly called Ma Kyaw, "Miss Smooth." But she was intelligent and fully aware of the power of public opinion.

"Very well, if you can find a Colony willing to sponsor them, I'll authorize shipping to lift them out," Lyou Ye said abruptly. "It won't take much, fortunately, by your description. Declining population ever since the Sun was shaded, I take it, with only this 'Enosclayborn' in the last generation. They'd have ended soon enough. You found them just in time for him," she added. "He's probably still a virgin."

"I'd personally like to thank Geelie for all the time and trouble she's put in for us, her and all her folks," said Alden.

Geelie flushed with pleasure as they applauded her.

"Now, I'll just ask for a show of hands," Alden continued. "All them that's in favor of flyin' off into space to a colony, raise your hand."

Geelie leaned forward eagerly.

There was a long pause. The behinders turned their faces to each other, Geelie heard a whisper or two, someone cleared a throat. But no one looked at her.

Alden stood looking around, waited a bit, then finally said, "Don't look like there's anybody in favor of the city of Independence movin' into a colony. But that don't mean nobody can go. Anybody that wants to is naturally free to leave. Just speak to me, or to Miss Geelie here."

Shocked, horrified, Geelie looked at them. Someone coughed. Still no one looked at her. She turned a stricken gaze on Enos Clayborn. He looked thoughtful but unsurprised. And he had not raised his hand.

So silent was the room that the purring of a mother cat, entering at the far side with a squirming kitten in her mouth, seemed loud.

Alden turned to her. "New ideas, like flyin' space, sometimes is hard to take in," he said kindly. "We had since yesterday to talk it over, but still it's a new idea. Enos, you might take the little lady back to Gretchen's nest and give them kittens a little attention."

Enos smiled at her, and faces were turned from the cat to her, smiling in relief. "She's bringing her kittens out," Geelie heard them murmur. "They're old enough for her to introduce them around."

Numbly she followed the tall young man back through the warren of abandoned passages to the warm storage room where the cat had her nest.

When he evidently intended merely to play with the kittens, she said, "Enos, why—why didn't they vote to go?"

"Well, we're used to it here. As Alden said, it takes time to get used to new ideas." He handed her a kitten. "This is the runt—the last born of the litter. We named her Omega—we'll give them all shots in another month or two; she'll be the last cat born on Earth."

Absently she took the purring kitten, a tiny squirming handful of fur. "But you'll all die if you don't go!"

"Well, we'll all die anyway," he said mildly. "Ever notice most of us are old folks? A lot aren't so far from dying now. They'd just as soon die in a place they know. We've been here a long time, you know."

"But—but—you're not old! And your parents, and Alden's daughter Aina, and Camden—"

"I wouldn't know how to act, anywhere but here," he said mildly. He smiled down at the proudly purring mother cat.

Geelie, Lyou Ye, and Aung Charah sat in the small conference room.

Lyou Ye grimaced. "So that was their reaction? I'll admit it wasn't one I'd foreseen. All the other behinders in history agreed to go. Some of them signaled to us."

Geelie shifted her position uneasily, cross-legged on a pillow, and nodded unhappily. "I even offered to send them to a european Colony, so they'd be among familiar-seeming people, but that didn't help."

Aung Charah shook his head. "We're getting a lot of publicity on this," he said. "The newsmedia are not hostile yet. But what will they say when the behinders' refusal becomes known?"

Lyou Ye frowned. "They'll blame us, depend upon it. Have any of them interviewed the behinders?"

Aung Charah shook his head. "They have to get permission from the Missouri Compact, which is very cautious. These planetarians have rights too. Invasion of their privacy . . ." He shook his head again.

"If we leave them here to die, we'll certainly be blamed," said Lyou Ye. "I'm tempted to order Consortium Police in to evacuate them forcibly."

Geelie sipped her tea, looking at "Ma Kyaw." That's your sort of solution, she thought. Direct, uncompromising, get it done, get it over with. And somebody else can pick up the pieces, clean up the mess.

"Alden would certainly complain if that were done," she said, speaking up reluctantly. "The media attention would be far worse. Violation of planetary rights . . . they may even have some claim to the old city of Independence. The Missouri Compact may legally have to wait for them all to die to mine that part of its grant."

Lyou Ye grimaced again. "I suppose you're right."

Aung Charah set his cup down. "Media criticism won't hurt the Consortium if we leave them here. The criticism we'd get if we violate their rights might affect us adversely. Investors —"

Lyou Ye was a "careerman." She nodded, frowning, lips pursed.

Geelie looked around the room, so unlike the comfortably cluttered warren in which Enos lived. In one wall, a niche with an arrangement of flowers, signifying *This too shall pass*; the woven screen against another wall, with its conventional pattern of crows over tiny fields curving up in the distance; the parquet floor with its fine rich grain; the subtle, not quite random leaf pattern of ivory and cream on the walls; the bronze samovar and the fantastically contorted porcelain dragon teapot, the only ornate thing in the room.

Enos was right, she thought. He would not know how to live in a place like this.

She thought of the world that was all he had ever known, a place of snow-powdered rock and brooding, perpetual night, a red-eyed Sun blown in the wind. A bare, harsh, bleak place without a future. For him, in the end, it could only mean tending the old "folks" as one by one they died, and then the penultimate generation, the generation of his parents, as they also grew old. At last he would be left alone to struggle against the darkness and the cold until he too lay dying, years of solitude and then a lonely death.

"There's no help for it," said Lyou Ye broodingly. She looked at Geelie. "You'll have to seduce Enosclayborn."

Geelie swept snow from a rock onto a dustpan, dumped it into a bucket.

"Don't get it on your gloves," Enos said. "It's a lot colder than it looks."

"How much do you have to bring in each day?"

"Not much; I usually overdo it. I enjoy being outside. The air is clean and cold, and I can see so far."

Geelie shivered, looking around the lands of eternal night. "Doesn't the shaded sun bother you?"

"It's always been like that." He looked around at the dim, tumbled landscape, emptying his bucket into the tub. "It's always been like this. Okay, that should be enough. Take the other handle and we'll carry it in."

In the vestibule they put the tub of snow in the row of tubs, and shed their parkas. Despite the slowly melting snow here, it seemed warm and steamy after the sharp cold air outside. Still, remembering the bleak world without, Geelie shuddered. She would have moved close to Enos even if she had not planned to do so. He put an arm around her, not seeming particularly surprised.

"You'll soon get used to it yourself," he said tolerantly.

"Never," she said, meaning it, cuddling close, her arms around him. She lifted her face for a kiss, nuzzling her breasts against his chest.

Enos put his palm on her cheek and pushed her gently aside. "Let's not start something we can't finish," he said.

Geelie blinked up at him, uncomprehending. "In your room — or the kittens' room — out in the passages —" Independence was a maze of warm, unused, and private passages.

He cupped her face with both hands and looked fondly at her. "Thank you very much, Geelie, for your offer. I will treasure it all the days of my life. But your place is in Kinabatangan, and mine is here, and we should not start something we cannot finish."

The pain of rejection was like a child's pain — the heavy feeling in the chest, the sharp unshed tears. Then came a more poignant grief — grief for all that she could not give him, that he would not take from her.

"Enos! — Enos!" she said, and then her sobs stopped her speech.

"O Geelie, Geelie," he said, his voice trembling. He held her close and stroked her hair.

Alden came and sat beside her in the cozy common room of Independence, where she sat watching Jackson Clayborn and Aina Alden play checkers.

"You look a little peaked," he said quietly.

She slid her chair back and spoke as quietly. "I suppose so."

"Enos will be back soon enough. He's lookin' through his things for something to fix that pump in the hydro room. Enos'd druther fix things and tinker around than play games like that." But he was looking inquiringly at her.

"Well, someone has to keep things going," she said wanly.

"Ye-ah." Alden drawled the word out, a skeptical affirmative. "someone does, though we got a few hands here can still tend to things." Abruptly he said, "By your face and your attitudes, these last few days, I reckon you ain't persuaded Enos to go with you!"

Geelie looked sharply at him. "No," she said shortly.

"I was afraid of that," he said, low. Startled, Geelie leaned toward him. "Did you think I was fightin' you? No, I was hopin' you'd persuade him. God knows you got persuasions none of us can offer. We can't offer him nothing."

Passionately she whispered, "Then why won't he come with us? All he says is that his place is here — and after that he won't say anything! Why?"

Alden's response was slow in coming. "I suppose he can't say why because he don't know how. Why he should feel his place is here, I don't know. *My* place is here; I'm an old man. But he don't listen to me any more than he does to you."

He shook his head. "If he stays, what'll he have? All he'll have is Independence, as long as he lives — the man from the Missouri Compact explained that. That's all. I guess," slowly, "for him, that's enough."

• • •

The kitten, Omega, jumped from Geelie's arms and began to investigate the room, not having sense enough to stay away from Lyou Ye. She was "Miss Smooth" no longer, stalking about the room and visibly trying to contain her anger.

"A flat refusal! I can't believe he refused you. Do you realize there've been over seven thousand Colonies offering them a place to live — over five thousand offering to take the whole group. And we can't get even the young one to leave Earth! What is wrong with him?"

"He says his place is there," said Geelie, nervously watching the kitten prowl.

"He's been brainwashed by those old people," Lyou Ye said.

"Not intentionally," Geelie said. "I discussed it with them, and they prefer to stay, but they would be happy to see Enos go. They know there's no future for him there."

"And for some uncommunicable reason, he thinks there's no future for him with us," said Lyou Ye, more calmly. She shook her head, ran her hands through her mass of auburn hair. "I suppose he's been unconsciously brainwashed from birth, knowing that he was the last one, that he was going to take care of them and die alone, and he's accepted that. It won't be easy to break that kind of life-long conditioning. Well." She shook Omega away from her ankle and turned to Geelie.

"Your tour as Observer is almost up. Would it be worthwhile to extend it and give you more time to work on him?"

Geelie put her hand to her chest. "No," she said, and cleared her throat. "No, it would not be worthwhile. I . . . can do nothing with him."

"We'll send somebody else, but I don't have much hope. These cold-hearted euros can be so inscrutable." Lyou Ye sat and examined Geelie. "You're right. It's time we got you away from Earth," she said gently.

The weather in Kinabatangan was clear and calm when Geelie returned from Earth. She pulled herself to the bubble at the axis and looked down at the tiny, idyllic fields and villages below, past the terraces climbing the domed end of the vast cylinder. She could have walked down the stairs, but took instead the elevator. At Deck level she was met by her cousins and siblings, the younger of whom rushed her and engulfed her in a mass hug, all laughing and babbling at once, a torrent of brown faces.

Half-floating in a golden mist of warmth, brilliant sunshine from the Chandelier, and love, Geelie let them lead her between the tiny fields and over the little bridges. She breathed deep of her ancient home, air redolent of the cycle of birth and death. They came presently to her small house in the edges of Lahad Datu. Frangipani grew by its door and squirrels ran nervously across its roof. A flight of harsh black crows pounded heavily up and away from the yard, where the tables were.

They'd spread a feast for her, and she ate with them and listened while they told her of the minute but important changes that had occurred in her absence. As she floated in this supporting bubble of light and warmth, Kinabatangan came back to her. All was as if she had never been away.

Her lover had found another, in the easy way of Kinabatangan, and that night Geelie slept alone. And in sleep she remembered again the bleak black plains of nighted Earth, and the man who inhabited them, who had chosen to wander alone forever under a frozen Sun.

She awoke and had difficulty remembering whether she was in Kinabatangan, dreaming of Independence, the half-seen land of Missouri stretching stark around it—or in *Tigerclaw* dreaming of Kinabatangan. She looked around the tiny room with its paper walls, its mats, the scent of frangipani in the air—she was in Kinabatangan, in her own little house, on her own mattress on the floor, and it was over. All over.

Omega yawned, a tiny pink cavern floored with a delicately rough pink tongue. The kitten was curled on the other pillow. Geelie reached for her.

"Oh! You little devil," she cried, flinging the kitten aside.

Startled, Omega had bitten her hand, and now stood in the middle of the room, looking at her with slit eyes.

Furious, Geelie leaped from her bed. But she could not stand, all the strength went out of her legs and she sank to the floor, sobbing. "Omega, Omega, I'm sorry, s-sorry." Grief as great as for a planet tore at her.

Omega crept cautiously over and sat staring up at her, watching Geelie weep.

unborn again

CHRIS LAWSON

There's an old saying, "Revenge is a dish that's best served cold." As the hard-hitting and uncompromisingly powerful tale that follows suggests, it also goes well with steamed custard and Tabasco sauce....

New writer Chris Lawson grew up in Papua New Guinea, and now lives in Melbourne with his wife, Andrea. While studying medicine, he earned extra money as a computer programmer, and has worked as a medical practitioner and as a consultant to the pharmaceutical industry. He has made short fiction sales to Asimov's *and* Dreaming Down-Under, Eidolon, *and* Event Horizon.

Take lamb's brains fresh from the butcher's block and soak them in icy water. Starting from the underside, peel off all the arteries under running water, add lemon and salt, and boil in water. Once boiled, dry the brains, quarter them, and marinate them for ten minutes. Serve them with steamed custard and Tabasco sauce.

The delicacy of the dish is exquisite, and I can easily digest two portions. Eating is more than a necessity; sometimes it is a pleasure; now it is a duty.

The brains slide down like oysters. I love the texture and the tang of the sauce. The pinot noir is a touch dry, but not enough to tarnish the flavour of the brains. Good wine is virtually unaffordable in Hong Kong nowadays.

The marinade is an old family secret, but I don't want it to die with me, so here it is: ginger, spring onion, rice wine, sesame oil, and oyster sauce. And my own variation: a dash of pituitary extract.

'In here.' The nurse shows the way into the room. The walls are antiseptic white. The bed is made with clinical precision. Sitting in a chair is the room's sole occupant: a woman in her mid-forties who rocks and drools like a demented centenarian.

'Ignore it,' says the nurse. 'She always does that when a visitor comes. She's perfectly able to hold one end of a conversation during the day. She only becomes confused at night.'

Stepping into the room is a small man in a brown suit. His tie is knotted too tightly, and the purple paisley teardrops clash with the khaki suit so gratingly that his colleagues have been known to grind their teeth down to the gums. His hair has somehow defied the short cut and fallen into disarray.

'She has Alzheimer's?' the brown-suited man asks the nurse.

'Something like that,' the nurse says. 'If you need anything, just hit the buzzer there.'

The nurse leaves, and the brown-suited man finds himself standing, briefcase in hand, in front of this woman. Her face and skin look young, but she sways in time as she hums an unrecognisable tune.

'Dr Dejerine? I'm from the customs department.'

Dejerine smacks her lips and fixes the visitor with an unfriendly stare. 'You look like a cheap detective.'

'I suppose I am. My name is Gerald Numis.'

'I won't remember that, you know. Not by tomorrow.'

Numis nods. 'I'll give you a business card. How's your long-term memory?'

'Better than my short-term memory, I'm disappointed to say. I didn't expect it to be this way. I can quote verbatim the monograph I wrote twenty years ago.'

'What was it?'

'It's called *Utilitarian Neurology*.' Dejerine looks at Numis as if that should mean something.

'What's it about?'

Dejerine laughs. 'I don't know. Maybe, if you're interested, you could look it up and then you can tell *me* what it means.'

Numis coughs. 'Do you remember what prions are?'

Dejerine nods. 'Of course I do.'

'There was an outbreak of Lethe disease in Hong Kong last year. Two people have already died and another five are infected. It's unprecedented—a prion disease that was once confined to the Papuan highlands, and a disease that has virtually disappeared with the decline of ritual cannibalism. The Chinese health ministry was terrified that they had a new, virulent form, so they posted the amino acid sequence on the internet. It corresponds to a rare variation that was registered to your lab.'

'What a remarkable coincidence,' says Dejerine.

Numis continues. 'Coincidence? Lethe disease has never been known to jump a thousand miles overseas to a noncannibal culture, and no one can suggest a natural vector for this unprecedented event. And there's the matter of ten missing vials from your lab. And the visas. You visited Hong Kong twice five years ago, which just happens to be the incubation period of Lethe disease. The coincidences are piling up.'

'A close shave with Occam's razor,' she says.

'I beg your pardon?'

'Occam's razor. Very good for shaving.' She laughs.

Numis thinks for a moment. This woman is blatantly demented, or an exceptional actor; either way he doubts that charges will ever be laid. The Director of Public

Prosecutions will probably let her rot in this room. If the Chinese police see her, they will lose interest in extradition. Numis concludes that the whole visit will be a waste of his efforts. However, he has a job to do and he believes in procedure.

'Did I mention the visas?' Numis asks.

'No,' says Dejerine, and smiles crookedly.

Numis knows he mentioned the visas. He knows her short-term memory is not *that* badly affected. He decides this woman is not nearly as demented as she makes out. He wonders how much of her disability is from disease and how much is a sham.

'Dr Dejerine, I have to caution you that transporting a biohazard without customs approval is a serious offence. You may request legal advice before answering any further questions.'

'So convict me. It's just a change of prison.'

'Are you declining legal counsel?'

'Did you know that *prison* is just *prion* with an S?' She giggles at her own joke.

'Dr Dejerine, are you declining legal counsel?' he asks again.

'Yeah, sure.' Dejerine nods in agreement.

Numis places a tape recorder on the bed and taps the record button. 'This is a taped recording of an interview with Dr Claudia Dejerine. Present are Dr Dejerine and Mr Gerald Numis, Senior Customs Investigator, Biomedical Division.' He checks his watch. 'The time is 2:47 P.M. on the 19th of March. Tell me what happened, Dr Dejerine. In your own words.'

Dejerine says, 'I wrote it down somewhere so I could explain it when someone like you came along. Now where did I put it?' She rummages in her bedside drawer and withdraws a foolscap notebook, bound in leather. 'Here it is.'

Numis opens the pages. They are hand-written. The scrawl is cramped and careless, the work of an author unconcerned with appearance.

'Dr Dejerine has just given me a hand-written document,' he says for the benefit of his tape recorder. Numis sits down to read; the recorder recognises silence and switches to standby.

My name is Claudia Dejerine and I was once Professor of Pathology. The other things you need to know about me are that I had a friend called Leon Shy-Drager; I cook as well as any *cordon bleu* chef; and I speak to John Stuart Mill in my dreams. It's not so strange. They say one of the U.S. Presidents' wives used to seek advice from an imaginary Eleanor Roosevelt.

My father died when I was a girl. I remember him sitting me on his lap in his study and pointing out all his favourite books. On the desk he kept two antique portraits of serious-looking men.

'Two great minds,' my father said. 'Jeremy Bentham and John Stuart Mill, the Fathers of Utilitarianism. They wrote about morals. They said the best outcome is the one that gives the greatest happiness to the greatest number. Life's not as simple as that, you know, but their ideas were magnificent.'

After Dad's funeral, I asked Mum what 'Tootilitism' was, and she pointed out Dad's copies of *On Liberty* and *System of Logic*, and held back tears.

'You can read them when you're older,' she said.

Dad had been tall and gaunt, like Mill. His build was imposing and I remember it clearly, but his face started to blur in my memory. His lanky frame and my strong association of Dad with the antique portraits sculpted an image for me. Over the years, the image I had of my father merged into that of John Stuart Mill. Dad was in the grave, but *On Liberty* was on the shelf any time I liked, so even his words started to merge. Eventually the figure who visited me in my dreams became indistinguishable from the portrait on Dad's desk. Over the years, the works of John Stuart Mill consumed the memory of my father.

By my thirty-ninth birthday, my hands shook more than the young Elvis Presley. Like the Ed Sullivan Show, I did my best to keep the shakes from public view, but my tremor was too coarse to hide. My hands were safe at rest, but when I tried to use them they would turn stiff as lead and shudder just like a learner bunny-hopping a car. Cooking became impossible.

I knew the diagnosis before my doctor gave it to me: Parkinson's disease. Deep in my brain, the *substantia nigra* was rotting away.

Leon Shy-Drager, my friend, also had Parkinson's, but at the more reasonable age of fifty-eight. For him, though, age was no excuse for complacency. He wanted every chance, regardless of legality.

Leon was no stranger to breaking the law. He frequently downloaded illegal research from the black net, and used the work of unethical researchers to design his own studies. Ethics committees vetted his work of course, but none of his 'ethical' work would have been possible without the black research. I have always wondered exactly how well informed the ethics committees were. Surely they must have been aware that much of Leon's work bore an uncanny resemblance to the more infamous examples of illegal research that leaked out of the black net. Leon always laughed when I brought it up.

'Of course they know,' he used to say. 'But it's a waste when good research goes unpublished. I make black research respectable for the mainstream journals.'

It was a sort of laundering process. 'Money, like research, is just another avatar of information. Casinos launder cash. I launder science.'

He flew to Hong Kong, where he auctioned his life insurance for a nigral implant. It is illegal for any Australian citizen to procure one, even if the operation is performed overseas. This law—guilty even if committed on foreign soil—applies to only two other felonies: war crimes and paedophile sex.

Of course Leon told no one about the procedure, but suspicion could not be contained. He flew out of the country on long-service leave and returned three months later with a marked improvement in motor skills. Some thought it a miracle. Most knew better.

Leon was a brave man. When he saw my hands shaking, he knew that I was falling off the same cliff that nearly claimed him. With enormous courage, he took me aside and risked jail by telling me what he had done. He told me every detail about the operation, even the petty ones. He gave me a contact number.

Leon never asked me to keep our conversation to myself, never begged me to stay away from the police. He trusted my friendship.

'I can't do this,' I told him.

'You have to look after yourself. No one else will.' When I looked away he said, 'Think about it at least.'

I thought about it.

John Stuart Mill used to appear in my dreams every month or so, but he came more often during crises of conscience. That week he spoke to me every night.

I would dream of a study lined with leather journals. Book-dust sparkled in the candlelight. On the other side of a titanic oak desk sat Mill, age-whitened side-burns spilling over his coat and collar. He never wore shirtsleeves. Even in dreams, he would not allow himself such informality.

Every night for a week, he would lean on the desk and say, 'The foetuses are dying anyway. You know that. It's silly to fret over the use of a by-product. You can implant those brains and heal people, or you can throw the foetus in the bin. It makes no difference to the foetus.'

'But it's illegal in Australia!' I objected.

He smiled at me. 'Illegal, eh? I have always maintained that Law and Morality are at best dancing partners, and clumsy ones at that. For every deft step, a hundred toes are trampled.'

Ever so slowly, the ghost of John Stuart Mill whittled away my objections, one moral sliver a day.

Numis puts down the book and stretches his arms. He can not believe his luck. This demented woman wrote down all the incriminating evidence he would need to fire the prosecutor's engine. Numis is not aware that the law insists the defendant must be mentally fit to stand trial, even if the crimes were committed in a lucid state of mind. Numis is not a lawyer. He is familiar only with the Customs Act.

He looks over at Dejerine. She is rocking back and forward, staring out the window, still entranced by a view that has remained exactly the same for the last hour. A prison sentence is out of the question, but perhaps a conviction could act as a deterrent to others. He returns to the book.

The clinic was called The Lucky Cat Hotel: 'Lucky Cat' to appeal to superstitious millionaires, 'Hotel' to conceal its purpose. My room had a million-dollar view over Kowloon harbour, but unlike a hotel room it had a nurse's buzzer and a medical dataport.

The hotel is ignored by the Chinese authorities, who find it a useful way of bringing hard currency to mainland China in exchange for thousands of recycled foetus brains. I find it hard to imagine the Hong Kong of twenty years ago, when the ultra-capitalist port was an unwelcome barnacle on the hull of communist China. Now the old British colony is too moneyed to shut down, and China's bicycling masses give way to retired Maoists in Mercedes.

The 'Hotel' reeked of pine and ammonia. The hospital must have spent a size-able portion of its operating budget on disinfectant, which banished the spice and sweat and humidity that had nearly overwhelmed me when I first arrived in Hong Kong. In a melancholy mood, I got to thinking that all this sterility was driving away life itself. I thought life was more than happy children and sunny parks. Life *was* bacteria and fungi and virions. What the hell was I doing here? Then I looked down at my rolling hands and remembered what it was like to cut sushi from a slab of tuna meat. When Dr Tang came to talk, I signed all the consent forms.

Dr Tang took care of me. He explained the procedure, told me the graft had an eighty percent success rate, and assured me that all foetal tissue came from abortions that were to be performed anyway. Then I waited for a donor to match my immune markers. I only waited two days. Leon had waited three weeks.

The operation was seamless. I can't see the scar at all. Dr Tang drilled a needle through my skull into the *substantia nigra*, and injected a bolus of fresh young brain cells. Within a few weeks, the new brain cells had differentiated into nigral tissue, and my tremors waned dramatically.

I could use my hands again. People could read my handwriting. At last I could cook the way I had always loved cooking: with exquisite precision.

Now Numis holds a written confession that Dejerine had bought an illegal graft, but her journal has not answered his main question: what did she do with the Lethe prions? Did she sell it to China as a biological weapon? Was it a trade—a weapon for a cure?

The sun has moved noticeably, but she still stares out the same window and her only movement is a gentle rocking, as if she is impatient for *something*. Numis can not imagine what she could be waiting for. The next mealtime? The evening games shows on cable? A more entertaining visitor?

The results of the surgery were stunning. I felt my dexterity renewed. The Parkinson's was a fading memory, just a sepia photograph of a long-dead disease. My hands did exactly what I asked of them. Tremors only affected my fingers when I was tired, and they were barely discernible even then.

When we met, Leon smiled at me and never said a word. I tried to thank him but he always cut me off. He did not want to hear the words. My improved health was enough for him. He knew I was grateful without being told, and for a while I really *was* grateful.

Then, just as I was adapting to my wonderful new hands, the pain started.

At first it only happened in my sleep. I woke curled up with pain and in a pall of sweat. I recalled dreaming about bright lights and a deep pain that I could not name. As soon as I awoke, the sensations disappeared, but the memory remained.

After a few nights waking at three A.M., I was exhausted.

Then the pains started during the day.

If I drifted off or daydreamed, I would be startled by the pain. Every day it seemed worse. It was a deep ache in the pit of my stomach, but I can describe it no better than that. I asked Leon about it, and he ran through a medical checklist of 'character of pain': burning, stabbing, shooting, electric, crushing, bloating. None of the words were adequate. The pain was too ill-defined to label. Leon said abdominal pain could be from the gut, the heart, the liver, the pancreas, the kidneys, the uterus, the abdominal lymph nodes, the lower surface of the lungs, the hips, or even from the psyche.

'Well, that sure narrows it down,' I said. 'I suppose that rules out maybe five percent of my body.'

'I forgot about the spine. It could be nerve root irritation too.'

'Thanks, Leon. You're a hypochondriac's best friend.'

Leon looked worried. 'None of this happened to me,' he said. 'I can't figure out what's causing it. You really should check it out with your doctor.'

'Yeah, right. What should I tell her about the implant?'

Leon shrugged.

By the third month the pain was hitting me at any time of day, even when I was alert and concentrating. Once it hit me while I was overtaking a truck and I doubled up with pain, unable even to care about driving the car safely. I slid off to the other side of the road and hit the brakes just in time to stop myself scooting into the freeway barrier.

After that I took taxis everywhere.

Once the pain hit me while I was walking along the street. I fell to the pavement and then had to hide my embarrassment when a flock of Samaritans came to help me. I laughed the pain off. 'Sometimes I just faint,' I said. I was not very convincing, but what was a bystander to think? They let me go on my way.

After that I rarely went out in public.

The pain even caught me once while I was preparing a Japanese meal. The sashimi knife sliced through my hand like warm butter. I needed twenty stitches and a tendon repair.

After that I stopped cooking.

I stowed away all the sharp objects in the house. I bought a personal medical alarm. Soon my life was so restricted that I began to wish I could turn back the clock. Parkinson's was paradise in comparison.

Sometimes the pain came unaccompanied. Other times my field of vision would fill with strange patterns of light. I looked up a medical textbook. It could have been a migraine prodrome, but that would be more like shooting stars or blind spots, not at all like my strange visions. One possibility matched: temporal lobe epilepsy, which causes bizarre hallucinations. Sufferers can smell burning rubber, or sense objects shrinking around them, or experience extreme *déjà vu*; sometimes they even think they are walking in a forest only to wake up tied to a hospital bed. However, temporal lobe epilepsy could explain just about *any* symptom, and I would need a brain scan to investigate it. I was terrified of a scan showing the evidence of my illegal surgery.

Leon caught up with me at one of my rare appearances at work. He had been worried, and my feeble attempts at reassuring him only made him more concerned.

'I think I have an answer,' he said. 'Meet me tonight in my lab.'

'You've got a solution?'

'Just meet me.' His eyes looked away as he spoke. He was avoiding the question.

So he had an answer, but not a solution. He had gone before I could ask why he made the distinction.

That night, at his lab, Leon showed me a maze. 'I used this as a postgrad. It has sentimental value. I used it to replicate a classic experiment.'

'How does this help me, Leon?'

He looked at me sternly. 'I'll get to that.' He waved his hands over the maze. 'It's an unusual design because it's made for *Planaria* flatworms. I'd put a worm at one end of the maze, food at another, and let the worm go. After a few hundred trials they would get pretty quick at doing the maze.

'I took all these trained worms and threw them in a blender. Worm purée. Then I fed the remains to another bunch of flatworms. Worms aren't fussy, you see.'

'I guess not.'

'The amazing thing was, the new worms did the maze quickly. They were faster than a control group fed on a purée of *untrained* warms. They were also faster than a group of worms fed on the remains of worms trained in a *different* maze.'

'You were a Worm Runner?' I asked.

'Oh, yes. I even had a couple of articles in *The Worm Runner's Digest*.'

'I had no idea you were that old!'

'Hey! The *Digest* only stopped publishing in 1979.'

I laughed. 'I wasn't even born.'

He coughed.

'Besides,' I asked, 'wasn't the research shown to be flawed?'

'Not exactly. It was equivocal.'

'Equivocal. You mean equivocal, equivocal? Or equivocal, there's lots of black data in support that's too politically sensitive to publish?'

'It means memory might be transferred in tissue from other animals' brains.'

I laughed. 'Leon, I never took you for a New Age mystic. Are you trying to tell me I'm remembering life as a foetus?'

He looked at me but said nothing. He was waiting for me to figure something out.

'Seriously, Leon. You're not trying to tell me I'm having foetal flashbacks? Like I'm unborn again?'

'No,' he said. I was missing the point. 'I had an implant too, but I've had none of your symptoms. Foetal brain tissue is probably too undifferentiated and too unstimulated to have any real memories in it.'

'So, if we both got foetal tissue, why is it only me with the pains?'

'It's possible you didn't get foetal tissue,' he said, and I felt a cold shiver as he spoke. 'It had to be reasonably undifferentiated to work as a nigral implant, but already has memories.'

Then he was quiet again, damn him, waiting for the realisation to hit me. I cocked my head and tried to work out what he was getting at. His face gave away nothing.

The penny dropped. From a skyscraper.

'Like an infant?' I asked.

Leon nodded.

'Jesus. Why would they put infantile tissue in, when they could have used foetal tissue?'

Leon grimaced. 'You haven't heard of the Dying Rooms? If they can recycle aborted foetal tissue, why not tissue from killed infants?'

I did not want to hear any more. 'Why tell me this, Leon? It's a disgusting thought.'

'It's better to know, isn't it?'

Not always, Leon, not always. I remember at your funeral wondering if knowledge had killed you, too. If you had never cracked the ISIS-24 trial code, the netrunners might have left you alone.

I dreamed that night that I was visited by the ghost of John Stuart Mill, or possibly my father. He was dressed in his formal suit. He spoke to me, his voice cold with certainty. By candlelight he tried to comfort me. He said, 'There is no need for despair.'

Fine for him to say! He could not share my feelings.

I told him, 'I spent the day in the library reading about the Dying Rooms. In parts of rural China, baby girls are called "maggots in the rice." Under the one-child policy, no one wants to squander their one chance at parenthood on a girl, so many babies are abandoned by their parents. The unwanted baby girls are brought to a room. There are up to twenty in a room at once. They are tied to chairs and left to starve. I can attest that they are too young to understand. Their pain is diffuse and undefined but the pain is real. The child whose memories I took suffered terribly.'

John Stuart Mill said the infant would have died anyway: the Chinese have a one-child policy; boys are highly prized; therefore some parents will choose only to have boys; since antenatal testing and sperm selection is still unavailable in most of China, this inevitably leads some parents to abandon their daughters. Not many parents choose this option, but in a population over a billion, there will always be enough to keep the rooms filled.

I said, 'And the Hong Kong clinics make enormous profits from those daughters. Those profits could be used to enable education campaigns to improve the status of girl children, or for sperm screening, or even for early antenatal testing. The profits could be turned to fix the problem rather than perpetuate it.'

Mill was silent in thought a while, then said, 'But *you* are not responsible for the situation in China. The killings would happen regardless. So it is no sin to benefit from it.'

'I *paid* for it. I helped finance the system.'

'No, those children would die anyway. Their pain is regrettable, but it is not your responsibility.'

'I *feel* responsible. I have eaten a child's pain, and it is poison.'

He pondered again. His jaw clenched and relaxed as he chewed through his consternation, which made his sideburns wriggle up and down. His mind worked furiously at the problem. In his eyes I saw his certainty crack. No matter how he tried to shift and pivot, he was pinned on a moral spike; the same spike he had taught me, in his books, to use as a compass point. His face turned stony, then he stood up. His jacket creaked with age and dust fell from the sleeves.

He said, 'Your pain is outside my theory.'

That night, in the moonlight of my dreaming, the ghost of John Stuart Mill hanged himself in the parlour, neatly. It had never occurred to me that ghosts could die.

The next evening, I dreamed again of his study, but he was gone. An empty noose swung gently from the rafters. In Mill's place there was a dark, moist presence. I could feel it but never see it. It never moved but I could feel it watching me. A ghost of a ghost.

Once, and only once, the shadow spoke.

It said, 'You know what to do.'

Pathologists and food have an ancient marriage. Tuberculous pus is called *caseation*, from the Latin for cheese; horse blood is cooked to make *chocolate* agar; right heart failure causes *nutmeg* liver; diabetes mellitus means *honey* urine; people suffer *cucumber* gallbladder. Strawberries are particular favourites, leading to *strawberry* haemangiomas or, in Kawasaki's disease, *strawberry* tongue. Well-differentiated lymphomas have a *raisin*-like appearance. Squeamish? Consider *military* tuberculosis, which causes *sago* spleen. Autoimmune heart inflammation leads to *bread-and-butter* pericarditis; glomerulonephritis makes *cola* urine. If you have a truly strong constitution, you might consider *Swiss cheese* uterus, stomach acid acting on blood to make *coffee-grounds* vomitus, or my personal favourite: the post-mortem blood clot which separates, like boiled stock, into *chicken fat* and *redcurrant jelly*.

In ancient times, if you couldn't eat it, it wasn't pathology. I have merely carried on the relationship in a more palatable fashion.

I told Dr Tang how wonderful my implant was because I could cook again. It was so lovely to breathe in coriander, and to taste garlic and lemongrass on my fingers. For the first time in months I could make proper *masala dosat*. I told him how grateful I was, and would he accept if I prepared a feast for him and his surgical colleagues next time I was in Hong Kong? He did not hesitate.

In Hong Kong I cooked one of my specialties: the lamb's brains. I soaked the brains in the Lethe prions I had stolen from the lab. Despite the change of recipe, they still tasted delicious. I served it up to Dr Tang and a few of his staff. I insisted on seconds for the tissue broker who had sold me the implant.

My guests loved it. They devoured every morsel.

Trojan *hors-d'oeuvres*, I call them. Just my little joke.

Numis at last understands the purpose of the book. It is not, as he first suspected, a confession nor a request for absolution. It is a document designed to incriminate Dr Tang and the Lucky Cat Hotel, and the entire gulag of the death rooms. She has left a trail, hoping to be caught. She had already passed judgement on herself and executed her own sentence. It had such a glowing irony that she was unlikely to be punished further by the constabulary of Australia or China.

Mobilising Western nations against human rights abuses in trading partners has long been like rousing a snail to anger. Perhaps her revelations will move the great nations to outrage, maybe even China itself. Cynic that he is, Numis thinks any outrage will not come from the use of dead children to earn money. Rather, he imagines the statesmen and power-brokers of the world choking on their breakfast as they read in the morning papers that their brain implants came from murdered girls.

What Numis does not realise is that Dr Leon Shy-Drager never existed. It is a code name, but she has lost the key in the Lethe. Dr Shy-Drager had a real-life analogue, dead three years now, but there are insufficient details in the text to make a positive identification. Dr Dejerine took great pains to protect her friend's memory from recrimination. Sadly, even the good memories will have to be carried by others. Her own memory is crumbling. She has a recurring image of a bearded man laughing, but she can no longer put a name to the face. She recalls a funeral, but no longer knows who died or why she wept.

Numis stands and tucks the book under his arm and picks up his tape recorder. Dejerine is still looking out her window. Only the shadows have moved.

'Thank you for your co-operation,' he says gently. She does not hear him.

'Dr Dejerine? Hello?'

She whips around, startled. 'Who the hell are you?' she screeches.

'Gerald Numis. Er . . . Customs Investigator.'

'Get the hell out, whoever you are!'

'I just wanted to say . . .'

Dejerine starts screaming 'Help! Help! Help!' with mechanical regularity.

Numis rushes out of the room, book safely tucked away in his jacket. The nurse who introduced him chuckles as he bolts for the exit.

'Don't fret, Mr Numis. At least she's not crying "Rape!" like she did with her last visitor.'

The doors slide open and he rushes into the carpark. He never thought asphalt and petrol fumes could be so reassuring. As Numis fiddles for his car keys, he can hear the faint 'Help! Help! Help!' It reminds him of a distant car alarm. At this distance he has no social obligation to help. He turns and looks back at the window to Dejerine's room and wonders now whether she was acting after all. Realising that he will never know, he shrugs and blips the car.

Under his breath he mutters, 'Mad old cow.' As he drives away, the image of rotting brains haunts him.

Back in her room, Dejerine is comforted by the nurse, whom she recognises.

'It's okay. He's gone now. He's gone,' the nurse whispers in her ear.

Dejerine stops screaming and the tears roll down her cheek. 'I was so scared! What did he want?'

'He just came to fix something. He's gone now.' It is easier to lie than explain.

She settles, and turns back to the window. The nurse leaves, pleased to have calmed her before she disturbs another resident. Sometimes one resident's distress can trigger another's, and then another's, in a screaming domino effect.

Dejerine looks out at the dusky light. Her eyes see a shape move in the distance. The image on her retina is keen as a sashimi knife, but her disease reduces the crisp image to a cognitive blob drifting across her cortex. It could be a car leaving the grounds. Then the scene is still. She rocks back and forward again, soothed by the abstract clouds that filter through to consciousness. She tries to remember why she is impatient in this purgatory. She is bathing in the Lethe and her memory is slowly washing away in its waters. She feels cleaner every day.

As the sky darkens and the stars appear, she recalls what it is she so desperately awaits:

The fall of night.

Grist

TONY DANIEL

One of the fastest-rising new stars of the nineties, Tony Daniel grew up in Alabama, lived for a while on Vashon Island in Washington State, and in recent years, in the best tradition of the young bohemian artist, has been restlessly on the move, from Vashon Island to Europe, from Europe to New York City, from New York City to Alabama, and, most recently, back to New York City again. He attended the Clarion West Writers Workshop in 1989, and since then has become a frequent contributor to Asimov's Science Fiction, as well as to markets such as The Magazine of Fantasy & Science Fiction, Amazing, SF Age, Universe, Full Spectrum, and elsewhere.

Like many writers of his generation, Tony Daniel first made an impression on the field with his short fiction. He made his first sale, to Asimov's, in 1990, "The Passage of Night Trains," and followed it up with a long string of well-received stories both there and elsewhere throughout the first few years of the nineties, stories such as "The Careful Man Goes West," "Sun So Hot I Froze to Death," "Prism Tree," "Death of Reason," "Candle," "No Love in All of Dwingeloo," "The Joy of the Sidereal Long-Distance Runner," "The Robot's Twilight Companion," and many others. His story "Life on the Moon" was a finalist for the Hugo Award in 1996, and won the Asimov's Science Fiction Readers Award poll. His first novel, Warpath, was released simultaneously in America and England in 1993, and he subsequently won $2,000 and the T. Morris Hackney Award for his as-yet-unpublished mountain-climbing novel Ascension. In 1997, he published a major new novel, Earthling, which has gotten enthusiastic reviews everywhere from Interzone to the New York Times. Coming up is his first short story collection, and he has just sold a pair of novels based on the story you're about to read, "Grist." The first one is entitled "Metaplanetary."

In the complex, compelling, and pyrotechnic novella that follows, he takes us to a bizarre far-future world—peopled with some of the strangest characters you're ever likely to meet, many of them transhuman, with vast, almost godlike powers and abilities, a world poised on the brink of a war that may destroy it utterly—for a vivid and exotic adventure that revolves around the connections that join people together and, in this strange high-

tech future, sometimes make it difficult to tell where one person ends and another begins. . . .

"Things that really matter, although they are not defined for all eternity,
even when they come very late still come at the right time."
— Martin Heidegger, "Letter on Humanism"

MIDNIGHT STANDARD AT
THE WESTWAY DINER

Standing over all creation, a doubt-ridden priest took a piss.

He shook himself, looked between his feet at the stars, then tabbed his pants closed. He flushed the toilet and centrifugal force took care of the rest.

Andre Sud walked back to his table in the Westway Diner. He padded over the living fire of the plenum, the abyss—all of it—and hardly noticed. Even though this place was special to *him*, it was really just another café with a see-through floor—a window as thin as paper and as hard as diamond. Dime a dozen as they used to say a thousand years ago. The luciferan sign at the entrance said FREE DELIVERY. The sign under it said OPEN 24 HRS. This sign was unlit. The place will close, eventually.

The priest sat down and stirred his black tea. He read the sign, backward, and wondered if the words he spoke when he spoke, sounded anything like English used to. Hard to tell with the grist patch in his head.

Everybody understands one another on a general level, Andre Sud thought. Approximately more or less, they know what you mean.

There was a dull, greasy gleam to the napkin holder. The salt shaker was half-full. The laminated surface of the table was worn through where the plates usually sat. The particle board underneath was soggy. There was free-floating grist that sparkled like mica within the wood: used-to-be-cleaning-grist, entirely shorn from the restaurant's controlling algorithm and nothing to do but shine. Like the enlightened pilgrim of the Greentree Way. Shorn and brilliant.

And what will you have with that hamburger?

Grist. Nada y grist. Grist y nada.

I am going through a depression, Andre reminded himself. I am even considering leaving the priesthood.

Andre's pellicle—the microscopic, algorithmic part of him that was spread out in the general vicinity—spoke as if from a long way off.

This happens every winter. And lately with the insomnia. Cut it out with the nada y nada. Everything's physical, don't you know.

Except for *you*, Andre thought back.

He usually thought of his pellicle as a little cloud of algebra symbols that followed him around like mosquitoes. In actuality, it was normally invisible, of course.

Except for us, the pellicle replied.

All right then. As far as we go. Play a song or something, would you?

After a moment, an oboe piped up in his inner ear. It was an old Greentree hymn—"Ponder Nothing"—that his mother had hummed when he was a kid. Brought up in the faith. The pellicle filtered it through a couple of variations and inversions, but it was always soothing to hear.

There was a way to calculate how many winters the Earth-Mars Diaphany would get in an Earth year, but Andre never checked before he returned to the seminary on his annual retreat, and they always took him by surprise, the winters did. You wake up one day and the light has grown dim.

The café door slid open and Cardinal Filmbuff filled the doorway. He was wide and possessive of the doorframe. He was a big man with a mane of silver hair. He was also space-adapted and white as bone in the face. He wore all black with a lapel pin in the shape of a tree. It was green, of course.

"Father Andre," said Filmbuff from across the room. His voice sounded like a Met cop's radio. "May I join you?"

Andre motioned to the seat across from him in the booth. Filmbuff walked over with big steps and sat down hard.

"Isn't it late for you to be out, Morton?" Andre said. He took a sip of his tea. He'd left the bag in too long and it tasted twiggy.

I was too long at the pissing, thought Andre.

"Tried to call you at the seminary retreat center," Filmbuff said.

"I'm usually here," Andre replied. "When I'm not there."

"Is this place still the seminary student hangout?"

"It is. Like a dog returneth to its own vomit, huh? Or *somebody's* vomit."

A waiter drifted toward them. "Need menus?" he said. "I have to bring them because the tables don't work."

"I might want a little something," Filmbuff replied. "Maybe a lhasi."

The waiter nodded and went away.

"They still have real people here?" said Filmbuff.

"I don't think they can afford to recoat the place."

Filmbuff gazed around. He was like a beacon. "Seems clean enough."

"I suppose it is," said Andre. "I think the basic coating still works and that just the complicated grist has broken down."

"You like it here."

Andre realized he'd been staring at the swirls in his tea and not making eye contact with his boss. He sat back, smiled at Filmbuff. "Since I came to seminary, Westway Diner has always been my home away from home." He took a sip of tea. "This is where I got satori, you know."

"So I've heard. It's rather legendary. You were eating a plate of mashed potatoes."

"Sweet potatoes, actually. It was a vegetable plate. They give you three choices and I chose sweet potatoes, sweet potatoes, and sweet potatoes."

"I never cared for them."

"That is merely an illusion. Everyone likes them sooner or later."

Filmbuff guffawed. His great head turned up toward the ceiling and his copper eyes flashed in the brown light. "Andre, we need you back teaching. Or in research."

"I lack faith."

"Faith in yourself."

"It's the same thing as faith in general, as you well know."

"You are a very effective scholar and priest to be so racked with doubt. Makes me think I'm missing something."

"Doubt wouldn't go with your hair, Morton."

The waiter came back. "Have you decided?" he said.

"A chocolate lhasi," Filmbuff replied firmly. "And some faith for Father Andre here."

The waiter stared for a moment, nonplused. His grist patch hadn't translated Cardinal Filmbuff's words, or had reproduced them as nonsense.

The waiter must be from out the Happy Garden Radial, Andre thought. Most of the help *was* in Seminary Barrel. There's a trade patois and a thousand long-shifted dialects out that way. Clan-networked LAPs poor as churchmice and no good Broca grist to be had for Barrel wages.

"*Iye ftip,*" Andre said to the waiter in the Happy Garden patois. "It is a joke." The waiter smiled uncertainly. "Another shot of hot water for my tea is what I want," Andre said. The waiter went away looking relieved. Filmbuff's aquiline presence could be intimidating.

"There is no empirical evidence that you lack faith," Filmbuff said. It was a pronouncement. "You are as good a priest as there is. We have excellent reports from Triton."

Linsdale, Andre thought. Traveling monk, indeed. Traveling stool-pigeon was more like it. I'll give him hell next conclave.

"I'm happy there. I have a nice congregation, and I balance rocks."

"Yes. You are getting a reputation for that."

"Triton has the best gravity for it in the solar system."

"I've seen some of your creations on the merci. They're beautiful."

"Thank you."

"What happens to them?"

"Oh, they fall," said Andre, "when you stop paying attention to them."

The chocolate lhasi came and the waiter set down a self-heating carafe of water for Andre. Filmbuff took a long drag at the straw and finished up half his drink.

"Excellent." He sat back, sighed, and burped. "Andre, I've had a vision."

"Well, that's what you do for a living."

"I saw *you.*"

"Was I eating at the Westway Diner?"

"You were falling through an infinite sea of stars."

The carafe bubbled, and Andre poured some water into his cup before it became flat from all the air being boiled out. The hot water and lukewarm tea mingled in thin rivulets. He did not stir.

"You came to rest in the branches of a great tree. Well, you crashed into it, actually, and the branches caught you."

"Yggdrasil?"

"I don't think so. This was a different tree. I've never seen it before. It is very disturbing because I thought there was only the One Tree. *This* tree was just as big, though."

"As big as the World Tree? The Greentree?"

"Just as big. But different." Filmbuff looked down at the stars beneath their feet. His eyes grew dark and flecked with silver. Space-adapted eyes always took on the color of what they beheld. "Andre, you have no idea how real this was. *Is*. This is difficult to explain. You know about my other visions, of the coming war?"

"The Burning of the One Tree?"

"Yes."

"It's famous in the Way."

"I don't care about that. Nobody else is listening. In any case, this vision *has placed itself on top of* those war visions. Right now, being here with you, this seems like a play to me. A staged play. You. Me. Even the war that's coming. It's all a play that is really about that damn Tree. And it won't let me go."

"What do you mean, won't let you go?"

Filmbuff raised his hands, palms up, to cradle an invisible sphere in front of him. He stared into this space as if it were the depths of all creation, and his eyes became set and focused far away. But not glazed over or unaware.

They were so alive and intense that it hurt to look at him. Filmbuff's physical face *vibrated* when he was in trance. It was a slight effect, and unnerving even when you were used to it. He was utterly focused, but you couldn't focus on him. There was too much of him there for the space provided. Or not enough of you.

I am watching chronological quantum transport in the raw, Andre thought. The instantaneous integration of positronic spin information from up-time sifted through the archetypical registers of Filmbuff's human brain.

And it all comes out as metaphor.

"The Tree is all burnt out now," Filmbuff said, speaking out of his trance. His words were like stones. "The Burning's done. But it isn't char that I'm seeing, no." He clenched his fists, then opened his palms again. "The old Tree is a shadow. The burnt remains of the One Tree are really only the shadow of the other tree, the new Tree. It's like a shadow the new Tree casts."

"Shadow," Andre heard himself whispering. His own hands were clenched in a kind of sympathetic vibration with Filmbuff.

"We are living in the time of the shadow," said Filmbuff. He relaxed a bit. "There's almost a perfect juxtaposition of the two trees. I've never felt so sure of anything in my life."

Filmbuff, for all his histrionics, was not one to overstate his visions for effect. The man who sat across from Andre was only the *aspect*—the human portion— of a vast collective of personalities. They were all unified by the central being; the man before him was no more a puppet than was his enthalpic computing analog soaking up energy on Mercury, or the nodes of specialized grist spread across human space decoding variations in anti-particle spins as they made their way backward in time. But he was no longer simply the man who had taught Andre's Intro to Pastoral Shamanism course at seminary. Ten years ago, the Greentree Way had specifically crafted a large array of personalities to catch a glimpse of the future, and Filmbuff had been assigned to be morphed.

I was on the team that designed him, Andre thought. Of course, that was back when I was a graduate assistant. Before I Walked on the Moon.

"The *vision* is what's real." Filmbuff put the lhasi straw to his mouth and finished the rest of it. Andre wondered where the liquid *went* inside the man. Didn't he run on batteries or something? "This is maya, Andre."

"I believe you, Morton."

"I talked to Erasmus Kelly about this," Filmbuff continued. "He took it on the merci to our Interpreter's Freespace."

"What did they come up with?"

Filmbuff pushed his empty glass toward Andre. "That there's new Tree," he said.

"How the hell could there be a new Tree? The Tree is wired into our DNA like sex and breathing. It may *be* sex and breathing."

"How should I know? There's a new Tree."

Andre took a sip of his tea. Just right. "So there's a new Tree," he said. "What does that have to do with me?"

"We think it has to do with your research."

"What research? I balance rocks."

"From before."

"Before I lost my faith and became an itinerant priest?"

"You were doing brilliant work at the seminary."

"What? With the time towers? That was a dead end."

"You understand them better than anyone."

"Because I don't try to make any sense of them. Do you think this new Tree has to do with those things?"

"It's a possibility."

"I doubt it."

"You doubt everything."

"The time towers are a bunch of crotchety old LAPs who have disappeared up their own asses."

"Andre, you know what I am."

"You're my boss."

"Besides that."

"You're a *manifold*. You are a Large Array of Personalities who was specially constructed as a quantum event detector—probably the best in human history. Parts of you stretch across the entire inner solar system, and you have cloud ship outriders. If you say you had a vision of me and this new Tree, then it has to mean *something*. You're not making it up. Morton, you see into the future, and there I am."

"There you are. You are the Way's expert on *time*. What do *you* think this means?"

"What do you want me to tell you? That the new Tree is obviously a further stage in sentient evolution, since the Greentree is *us?*"

"That's what Erasmus Kelly and his people think. I need something more subtle from you."

"All right. It isn't the time towers that this has to do with."

"What then?"

"You don't want to hear this."

"You'd better tell me anyway."

"Thaddeus Kaye."

"Thaddeus Kaye is dead. He killed himself. Something was wrong with him, poor slob."

"I know you big LAPs like to think so."

"He was perverted. He killed himself over a woman, wasn't it?"

"Come on, Morton. A pervert hurts *other* people. Kaye hurt himself."

"What does *he* have to do with anything, anyway?"

"What if he's not dead? What if he's just wounded and lost? You understand what kind of being he is, don't you, Morton?"

"He's a LAP, just like me."

"You only *see* the future, Morton. Thaddeus Kaye can *affect* the future directly, from the past."

"So what? We all do that every day of our lives."

"This is not the same. Instantaneous control of instants. What the merced quantum effect does for space, Thaddeus Kaye can do for time. He *prefigures* the future. Backward and forward in time. He's like a rock that has been dropped into a lake."

"Are you saying he's God?"

"No. But if your vision is a true one, and I know that it is, then he could very well *be* the *war.*"

"Do you mean the reason *for* the war?"

"Yes, but more than that. Think of it as a wave, Morton. If there's a crest, there has to be a trough. Thaddeus Kaye is the crest and the war is the trough. He's something like a physical principle. That's how his integration process was designed. Not a force, exactly, but he's been imprinted on a *property* of time."

"The Future Principle?"

"All right. Yes. In a way, he *is* the future. I think he's still alive."

"And how do you know that?"

"I didn't until you told me your vision. What else could it be? Unless aliens are coming."

"Maybe aliens are coming. They'd have their own Tree. Possibly."

"Morton, do you see aliens coming in your dreams?"

"No."

"Well, then."

Filmbuff put his hands over his eyes and lowered his head. "I'll tell you what I still see," he said in a low rumble of a voice like far thunder. "I see the burning Greentree. I see it strung with a million bodies, each of them hung by the neck, and all of them burning, too. Until this vision, that was *all* I was seeing."

"Did you see any way to avoid it?"

Filmbuff looked up. His eyes were as white as his hands when he spoke. "Once. Not now. The quantum fluctuations have all collapsed down to one big macro reality. Maybe not today, maybe not tomorrow, but *soon*."

Andre sighed. *I believe*, he thought. I don't want to believe, but I do. It's easy to have faith in destruction.

"I just want to go back to Triton and balance rocks," he said. "That's really all that keeps me sane. I love that big old moon."

Filmbuff pushed his lhasi glass even farther away and slid out of the booth. He stood up with a creaking sound, like vinyl being stretched. "Interesting times," he spoke to the café. "Illusion or not, that was probably the last good lhasi I'm going to have for quite a while."

"Uh, Morton?"

"Yes, Father Andre?"

"You have to pay up front. They can't take it out of your account."

"Oh my." The cardinal reached down and slapped the black cloth covering his white legs. He, of course, had no pockets. "I don't think I have any money with me."

"Don't worry," Andre said. "I'll pick it up."

"Would you? I'd hate to have that poor waiter running after me down the street."

"Don't worry about it."

"We'll talk more tomorrow after meditation." This was not a request.

"We'll talk more then."

"Good night, Andre."

"Night, Morton."

Filmbuff stalked away, his silver mane trailing behind him as if a wind were blowing through it. Or a solar flare.

Before he left the Westway, he turned, as Andre knew he would, and spoke one last question across the space of the diner.

"You knew Thaddeus Kaye, didn't you, Father Andre?"

"I knew a man named Ben Kaye. A long time ago," Andre said, but this was only confirmation of what Filmbuff's spread-out mind had already told him.

The door slid shut and the Cardinal went out into the night. Andre sipped at his tea.

Eventually the waiter returned. "We close pretty soon," he said.

"Why do you close so early?" Andre asked.

"It is very late."

"I remember when this place never closed."

"I don't think so. It always closed."

"Not when I was a student at the seminary."

"It closed then," said the waiter. He took a rag from his apron, activated it with a twist, and began to wipe a nearby table.

"I'm sure you're mistaken."

"They tell me there's never been a time when this place didn't close."

"Who tells you?"

"People."

"And you believe them."

"Why should I believe *you*? You're people." The waiter looked up at Andre, puzzled. "That was a joke," he said. "I guess it does not translate."

"Bring me some more tea and then I will go."

The waiter nodded, then went to get it.

There was music somewhere. Gentle oboe strains. Oh, yes. His pellicle was still playing the hymn.

What do you think?

I think we are going on a quest.

I suppose so.

Do you know where Thaddeus Kaye is?

No, but I have a pretty good idea how to find Ben. And wherever Ben is, Thaddeus Kaye has to be.

Why not tell somebody else how to find him?

Because no one else will do what I do when I find him.

What's that?

Nothing.

Oh.

When the back-up is done, we'll be on our way.

The third part of Andre's multiple personality, the convert, was off-line at the moment getting himself archived and debugged. That was mainly what the retreat was for, since using the Greentree data facilities was free to priests. Doing it on Triton would have cost as much as putting a new roof on his house.

Why don't they send someone who is stronger in faith than we are?

I don't know. Send an apostate to net an apostate, I guess.

What god is Thaddeus Kaye apostate from?

Himself.

And for that matter, what about us?

Same thing. Here comes the tea. Will you play that song again?

It was Mother's favorite.

Do you think it could be that simple? That I became a priest because of that hymn?

Are you asking me?

Just play the music and let me drink my tea. I think the waiter wants us out of here.

"Do you mind if I mop up around you?" the waiter said.

"I'll be done soon."

"Take your time, as long as you don't mind me working."

"I don't mind."

Andre listened to mournful oboe and watched as the waiter sloshed water across the infinite universe, then took a mop to it with a vengeance.

JILL

Down in the dark there's a doe rat I'm after to kill. She's got thirteen babies and I'm going to bite them, bite them, bite them. I will bite them.

The mulch here smells of dank stupid rats all running running and there's nowhere farther to run, because this is it, this is the Carbuncle, and now *I'm* here and this is truly the end of all of it but a rat can't stand to know that and won't accept me until they have to believe me. Now they will believe me.

My whiskers against something soft. Old food? No, it's a dead buck; I scent his Y code, and the body is dead but the code keeps thumping and thumping. This mulch won't let it drain out and it doesn't ever want to die. The Carbuncle's the end of the line, but this code doesn't know it or knows it and won't have it. I give it a poke and a bit of rot sticks to my nose and the grist tries to swarm me, but no I don't think so.

I sniff out and send along my grist, jill ferret grist, and no rat code stands a chance ever, ever. The zombie rat goes rigid when its tough, stringy code—who knows how old, how far-traveled, to finally die here at the End of Everywhere— that code scatters to nonsense in the pit of the ball of nothing my grist wraps it in. Then the grist flocks back to me and the zombie rat thumps no more. No more.

Sometimes having to kill *everything* is a bit of a distraction. I want that doe and her littles really bad and I need to move on.

Down a hole and into a warren larder. Here there's pieces of meat and the stink of maggot sluice pooled in the bends between muscles and organs. But the rats have got the meat from Farmer Jan's Mulmyard, and it's not quite dead yet, got maggot resistant code, like the buck rat, but not smart enough to know it's dead, just mean code jaw-latched to a leg or a haunch and won't dissipate. Mean and won't die. But I am meaner still.

Oh, I smell her.

I'm coming mamma rat. Where are you going? There's no going anywhere anymore.

Bomi slinks into the larder and we touch noses. I smell blood on her. She's got a kill, a bachelor male, by the blood spoor on her.

It's so warm and wet, Jill. Bomi's trembling and wound up tight. She's not the smartest ferret. *I love it, love it, and I'm going back to lie in it.*

That's bad. Bad habit.

I don't care. I killed it; it's mine.

You do what you want, but it's your man Bob's rat.

No it's mine.

He feeds you, Bomi.

I don't care.

Go lay up then.

I will.

Without a by-your-leave, Bomi's gone back to her kill to lay up. I never do that. TB wouldn't like it, and besides, the killing's the thing, not the owning. Who wants an old dead rat to lie in when there's more to bite?

Bomi told me where she'd be because she's covering for herself when she doesn't show and Bob starts asking. Bomi's a stupid ferret and I'm glad she doesn't belong to TB.

But me—down another hole, deeper, deeper still. It's half-filled in here. The doe rat thought she was hiding it, but she left the smell of her as sure as a serial number on a bone. I will bite you, mamma.

Then there's the dead-end chamber I knew would be. Doe rat's last hope in all the world. Won't do her any good. But oh, she's big. She's tremendous. Maybe the biggest ever for me.

I am very, very happy.

Doe rat with the babies crowded behind her. Thirteen of them, I count by the squeaks. Sweet naked squeaks. Less than two weeks old, they are. Puss and meat. But I want mamma now.

The doe sniffs me and screams like a bone breaking and she rears big as me. Bigger.

I will bite you.

Come and try, little jill.

I will kill you.

I ate a sack of money in the City Bank and they chased me and cut me to pieces and just left my tail, and—I grew another rat! What will you do to me, jill, that can be so bad? You'd better be afraid of me.

When I kill your babies, I will do it with one bite for each. I won't hurt them for long.

You won't kill my babies.

At her.

At her, because there isn't anything more to say, no more messages to pass back and forth through our grist and scents.

I go for a nipple and she's fast out of the way, but not fast enough and I have a nub of her flesh in my mouth. Blood let. I chew on her nipple tip. Blood and mamma's milk.

She comes down on me and bites my back, her long incisors cut through my fur, my skin, like hook needles, and come out at another spot. She's heavy. She gnaws at me and I can feel her teeth scraping against my backbone. I shake to get her off, and I do, but her teeth rip a gouge out of me.

Cut pretty bad, but she's off. I back up thinking that she's going to try to swarm a copy, and I stretch out the grist and there it is, just like I thought, and I intercept it and I kill the thing before it can get to the mulm and reproduce and grow another rat. One rat this big is enough, enough for always.

The doe senses that I've killed her outrider, and now she's more desperate.

This is all there is for you. This is oblivion and ruin and time to stop the scurry. This is where you'll die.

She strikes at me again, but I dodge, and—before she can round on me—I snatch a baby rat. It's dead before it can squeal. I spit out its mangle of bones and meat.

But mamma's not a dumb rat, no, not dumb at all, and does not fly into a rage over this. But I know she regards me with all the hate a rat can hate, though. If there were any light, I'd see her eyes glowing rancid yellow.

Come on, mamma, before I get another baby.

She goes for a foot and again I dodge, but she catches me in the chest. She raises up, up.

The packed dirt of the ceiling, wham, wham, and her incisors are hooked around my breastbone, damn her, and it holds me to her mouth as fast as a barbed arrowpoint.

Shake and tear, and I've never known such pain, such delicious . . .

I rake at her eyes with a front claw, dig into her belly with my feet. Dig, dig, and I can feel the skin parting, and the fatty underneath parting, and my feet dig deep, deep.

Shake me again and I can only smell my own blood and her spit and then sharp, small pains at my back.

The baby rats. The baby rats are latching onto me, trying to help their mother.

Nothing I can do. Nothing I can do but dig with my rear paws. Dig, dig. I am swimming in her guts. I can feel the give. I can feel the tear. Oh, yes.

Then my breastbone snaps and I fly lose of the doe's teeth. I land in the babies, and I'm stunned and they crawl over me and nip at my eyes and one of them shreds an ear, but the pain brings me to and I snap the one that bit my ear in half. I go for another. Across the warren cavern, the big doe shuffles. I pull myself up, try to stand on all fours. Can't.

Baby nips my hind leg. I turn and kill it. Turn back. My front legs collapse. I cannot stand to face the doe, and I hear her coming.

Will I die here?

Oh, this is how I want it! Took the biggest rat in the history of the Met to kill me. Ate a whole bag of money, she did.

She's coming for me. I can hear her coming for me. She's so big. I can *smell* how big she is.

I gather my hind legs beneath me, find a purchase.

This is how I die. I will bite you.

But there's no answer from her, only the doe's harsh breathing. The dirt smells of our blood. Dead baby rats all around me.

I am very, very happy.

With a scream, the doe charges me. I wait a moment. Wait.

I pounce, shoot low like an arrow.

I'm through, between her legs. I'm under her. I rise up. I rise up into her shredded belly. I bite! I bite! I bite!

Her whole weight keeps her down on me. I chew. I claw. I smell her heart. I smell the new blood of her heart! I can hear it! I can smell it! I chew and claw my way to it.

I bite.

Oh yes.

The doe begins to kick and scream, to kick and scream, and, as she does, the blood of heart pumps from her and over me, smears over me until my coat is soaked with it, until all the dark world is blood.

After a long time, the doe rat dies. I send out the grist, feebly, but there are no outriders to face, no tries at escape now. She put all that she had into fighting me. She put everything into our battle.

I pull myself out from under the rat. In the corner, I hear the scuffles of the babies. Now that the mamma is dead, they are confused.

I have to bite them. I have to kill them all.

I cannot use my front legs, but I can use my back. I push myself toward them, my belly on the dirt like a snake. I find them all huddled in the farthest corner, piling on one another in their fright. Nowhere to go.

I do what I told the doe I would do. I kill them each with one bite, counting as I go. Three and ten makes thirteen.

And then it's done and they're all dead. I've killed them all.

So.

There's only one way out: the way I came. That's where I go, slinking, crawling, turning this way and that to keep my exposed bone from catching on pebbles and roots. After a while, I start to feel the pain that was staying away while I fought. It's never been this bad.

I crawl and crawl, I don't know for how long. If I were to meet another rat, that rat would kill me. But either they're dead or they're scared, and I don't hear or smell any. I crawl to what I think is up, what I hope is up.

And after forever, after so long that all the blood on my coat is dried and starting to flake off like tiny brown leaves, I poke my head out into the air.

TB is there. He's waited for me.

Gently, gently he pulls me out of the rat hole. Careful, careful he puts me in my sack.

"Jill, I will fix you," he says.

I know.

"That must have been the Great Mother of rats."

She was big, so big and mean. She was brave and smart and strong. It was wonderful.

"What did you do?"

I bit her.

"I'll never see your like again, Jill."

I killed her, and then I killed all her children.

"Let's go home, Jill."

Yes. Back home.

Already in the dim burlap of the sack, and I hear the call of TB's grist to go to sleep, to get better, and I sigh and curl as best I can into a ball and I am falling away, falling away to dreams where I run along a trail of spattered blood, and the spoor is fresh and I'm chasing rats, and TB is with me close by, and I will bite a rat soon, soon, soon—

A SIMPLE ROOM WITH GOOD LIGHT

Come back, Andre Sud. Your mind is wandering and now you have to concentrate. Faster now. Fast as you can go. Spacetime. Clumps of galaxy clusters. Average cluster. Two-armed spiral.

Yellow star.

Here's a network of hawsers cabling the inner planets together. Artifact of sentience, some say. Mercury, Venus, Earth, Mars hung with a shining webwork across blank space and spreading even into the asteroids. Fifty-mile-thick cables bending down from the heavens, coming in at the poles to fit into enormous universal joints lubricated by the living magma of the planets' viscera. Torque and undulation. Faster. Somewhere on a flagellating curve between Earth and Mars, the Diaphany, you will find yourself. Closer in. Spinning spherule like a hundred-mile-long bead on a million-mile-long necklace. Come as close as you can.

All along the Mars-Earth Diaphany, Andre saw the preparations for a war like none before. It seemed the entire Met—all the interplanetary cables—had been transformed into a dense fortress that people just happened to live inside. His pod was repeatedly delayed in the pithway as troops went about their movements, and military grist swarmed hither and yon about some task or another. We live in this all-night along the carbon of the cables, Andre thought, within the dark glistening of the corridors where surface speaks to surface in tiny whispers like fingers, and the larger codes, the extirpated skeletons of a billion minds, clack together in a cemetery of logic, shaking hands, continually shaking bony, algorithmic hands and observing strict and necessary protocol for the purposes of destruction.

Amés—he only went by the one name, as if it were a title—was a great one for martial appearances. Napoleon come again, the merci reporters said as a friendly joke. Oh, the reporters were eating this up. There hadn't been a good war in centuries. People got tired of unremitting democracy, didn't they? He'd actually heard somebody say that on the merci.

How fun it will be to watch billions die for a little excitement on the merci, Andre thought.

He arrived in Connacht Bolsa in a foul mood, but when he stepped out of his pod, there was the smell of new rain. He had walked a ways from the pod station before he realized what the smell was. There were puddles of water on the ground from the old fashioned street cleaning mechanism Connacht employed. It was still raining in spots—a small rain that fell only an inch or so from the ground. Little clouds scudded along the street like a miniature storm front, washing it clean of the night's leavings.

Connacht was a suburb radial off Phobos City, the most densely populated segment on the Met. A hundred years ago in the Phobos boom time, Connacht had been the weekend escape for intellectuals, artists, moneyed drug addicts—and the often indistinguishable variety of con-men, mountebanks, and psychic quacksalvers who were their hangers-on. The place was rundown now, and Andre's pellicle encountered various swarms of nostalgia that passed through the streets like rat packs—only these were bred and fed by the merchants to attract the steady trickle of tourists with pellicular receptors for a lost bohemia.

All they did for Andre was make him think about Molly.

Andre's convert—the electronic portion of himself—obliged him by dredging up various scenes from his days at seminary. The convert was usually silent, preferring to communicate in suggestive patterns of data—like a conscience gifted with irreducible logic and an infallible memory.

Andre walked along looking at the clouds under his feet, and as he walked his convert projected images into the shape of these clouds, and into the shift and sparkle of the puddled water they left behind.

I have a very sneaky conscience, Andre thought, but he let the images continue.

—Molly Index, Ben Kaye, and Andre at the Westway, in one of their long arguments over aesthetics when they were collaborating on their preliminary thesis. "Knowing, Watching, and Doing: The Triune Aspect of Enlightenment."

"I want to be 'Doing!'" Molly mocked-yelled and threw a wadded up piece of paper at Ben.

He caught it, spread it out, and folded it into a paper airplane. "This is the way things have to be," he said. "I'm 'Doing.' You're 'Watching.' And we both know who 'Knowing' must be." They turned to Andre and smiled vulture smiles.

"I don't know what you think I know, but I don't know it," he said, then nearly got an airplane in the eye.

—Molly's twenty-four-year-old body covered with red Martian sand under the Tharsis beach boardwalk. Her blue eyes open to the sky pink sky. Her nipples like dark stones. Ben a hundred feet away, rising from the gray-green lake water, shaking the spume from his body. Of course he had run and jumped into the lake as soon as they got there. Ben wouldn't wait for anything.

But Molly chose me. I can't believe she chose me.

Because I waited for her and dragged her under the boardwalk and kissed her before I could talk myself out of it.

Because I waited for the right moment.

How's that for Doing?

—Living together as grad students while Molly studied art and he entered into the stations of advanced meditation at seminary.

—Molly leaving him because she would not marry a priest.

You're going to kill yourself on the moon.

Only this body. I'll get a new one. It's being grown right now.

It isn't right.

This is the Greentree Way. That's what makes a priest into a true shaman. He knows what it's like to die and come back.

If you Walk on the Moon, you will know what it's like to lose a lover.

Molly, the Walk is what I've been preparing for these last seven years. You know that.

I can't bear it. I won't.

Maybe he could have changed her mind. Maybe he could have convinced her. But Alethea Nightshade had come along and that was that. When he'd come back from the moon reinstantiated in his cloned body, Molly had taken a new lover.

—His peace offering returned with the words of the old folk song, turned inside out: "Useless the flowers that you give, after the soul is gone."

—Sitting at a bare table under a bare light, listening to those words, over and over, and deciding never to see her again. Fifteen years ago, as they measure time on Earth.

Thank you, that will be enough, he told the convert.

An image of a stately butler, bowing, flashed through Andre's mind. Then doves rising from brush into sunset. The water puddles were just water puddles once again, and the tiny clouds were only clouds of a storm whose only purpose was to make the world a little cleaner.

Molly was painting a Jackson Pollock when Andre arrived at her studio. His heavy boots, good for keeping him in place in Triton's gravity, noisily clumped on the wooden stairs to Molly's second floor loft. Connacht was spun to Earth-normal. He would have knocked, but the studio door was already open.

"I couldn't believe it until I'd seen it with my own eyes," Molly said. She did not stop the work at her easel. "My seminary lover come back to haunt me."

"Boo," Andre said. He entered the space. Connacht, like many of the old ro-tating simple cylinders on the Diaphany, had a biofusion lamp running down its pith that was sheathed on an Earth-day schedule. Now it was day, and Molly's skylights let in the white light and its clean shadows. Huge picture windows looked out on the village. The light reminded Andre of light on the moon. The unyield-ing, stark, redeeming light just before his old body joined the others in the sha-mans' Valley of the Bones.

"Saw a man walking a dog the other day with the legs cut off," said Molly. She dipped the tip of her brush in a blue smear on her palette.

"The man or the dog?"

"Maybe the day." Molly touched the blue to the canvas before her. It was like old times.

"What are you painting?"

"Something very old."

"That looks like a Pollock."

"It is. It's been out of circulation for a while and somebody used it for a table-cloth. Maybe a kitchen table, I'm thinking."

Andre looked over the canvas. It was clamped down on a big board as long as he was tall. Sections of it were fine, but others looked as if a baby had spilled its mashed peas all over it. Then again, maybe that was Pollock's work after all.

"How can you possibly know how to put back all that spatter?"

"There're pictures." Molly pointed the wooden tip of her brush to the left hand corner of the canvas. Her movements were precise. They had always been definite and precise. "Also, you can kind of see the tracery of where this section was before it got . . . whatever that is that got spilled on it there. Also, I use grist for the small stuff. Did you want to talk about Ben?"

"I do."

"Figured you didn't come back to relive old times."

"They were good. Do you still do that thing with the mirror?"

"Oh, yes. Are you a celibate priest these days?"

"No, I'm not that kind of priest."

"I'm afraid I forgot most of what I knew about religion."

"So did I."

"Andre, what do you want to know about Ben?" Molly set the handle of her brush against her color palette and tapped it twice. Something in the two surfaces recognized one another, and the brush stuck there. A telltale glimmer of grist swarmed over the brush, keeping it moist and ready for use. Molly sat in a chair by her picture window and Andre sat in a chair across from her. There was a small table between them. "Zen tea?" she said.

"Sure," Andre replied.

The table pulsed, and two cups began forming on its surface. As the outsides hardened, a gel at their center thinned down to liquid.

"Nice table. I guess you're doing all right for yourself, Molly."

"I like to make being in the studio as simple as possible so I can concentrate on my work. I indulge in a few luxuries."

"You ever paint for yourself anymore? Your own work, I mean?"

Molly reached for her tea, took a sip and motioned with her cup at the Pollock.

"I paint *those* for myself," she said. "It's my little secret. I make them mine. Or they make me theirs."

"That's a fine secret."

"Now you're in on it. So was Ben. Or Thaddeus, I should say."

"You were on the team that made him, weren't you?"

"Aesthetic consultant. Ben convinced them to bring me on. He told me to think of it as a grant for the arts."

"I kind of lost track of you both after I . . . graduated."

"You were busy with your new duties. I was busy. Everybody was busy."

"I wasn't *that* busy."

"Ben kept up with your work. It was part of what made him decide to . . . do it."

"I didn't know that."

"Now you do. He read that paper you wrote on temporal propagation. The one that was such a big deal."

"It was the last thing I ever wrote."

"Developed a queer fascination with rocks?"

"You heard about that?"

"Who do you think sent those merci reporters after you?"

"Molly, you didn't?"

"I waited until I thought you were doing your best work."

"How did you see me? . . . " He looked into her eyes, and he saw it. The telltale expression. Far and away. "You're a LAP."

Molly placed the cup to her lips and sipped a precise amount of tea. "I guess you'd classify me as a manifold by now. I keep replicating and replicating. It's an art project I started several years ago. Alethea convinced me to do it when we were together."

"Will you tell me about her? She haunted me for years, you know. I pictured her as some kind of femme fatale from a noir. Destroyed all my dreams by taking you."

"Nobody took me. I *went*. Sometimes I wonder what I was thinking. Alethea Nightshade was no picnic, let me tell you. She had the first of her breakdowns when we were together."

"Breakdowns?"

"She had schizophrenia in her genes. She wanted to be a LAP, but wasn't allowed because of it. The medical grist controlled her condition most of the time, but every once in a while . . . she outthought it. She was too smart for her own good."

"Is that why you became a LAP?" Andrew asked. "Because *she* couldn't?"

"I told myself I was doing it for *me*, but yes. *Then*. Now, things are different." Molly smiled, and the light in the studio was just right. Andre saw the edge of the multiplicity in her eyes.

The fractal in the aspect's iris.

"You have no idea how beautiful it is—what I can *see!*" Molly laughed, and Andre shuddered. Awe or fright? He didn't know.

"She was just a woman," Molly said. "I think she came from around Jupiter. A moon or something, you know." Molly made a sweeping motion toward her window. As with many inner system denizens, the outer system was a great unknown, and all the same, to her. "She grew up on some odd kind of farm."

"A Callisto free grange?"

"I'm sure I don't know. She didn't talk about it much."

"What was she like?"

"Difficult."

"What do you mean?"

"I'll tell you." Tea sip. Andre realized he hadn't picked his up yet. He did so, tried it. It was wonderful, and all grist. A bit creepy to think about drinking it down.

I'll take care of it, don't you worry, said his pellicle.

I know you will.

"Alethea had two qualities that should never exist within one organic mind. A big intellect and a big heart. She *felt* everything, and she thought about it far too much. She was born to be a LAP. And she finally found a way to do it."

"Ben."

"They fell in love. It was also her good fortune that he could get her past the screening procedures. But Alethea always was a fortunate woman. She was lucky, on a quantum level. Until she wasn't."

"So she and Ben were together before he became . . . Thaddeus."

"For a year."

"Were you jealous?"

"I'd had enough of Alethea by then. I'll always love her, but I want a life that's . . . plain. She was a tangle I couldn't untangle." Molly touched her fingers to her nose and tweaked it. It was a darling gesture, Andre thought. "Besides," Molly said. "*She* left *me*."

"What did that do to you and Ben?"

"Nothing. I love Ben. He's my best friend."

She was speaking in the present tense about him, but Andre let it pass.

"Why did he change his name, Molly? I never understood that."

"Because he wasn't a LAP."

"What do you mean? Of course he was. A special one. Very special. But still—"

"No. He said he was something *new*. He said he wasn't Ben anymore. It was kind of a joke with him, though. Because, of course, he *was* still Ben. Thaddeus may have been more than a man, but he definitely was *at least* a man, and that man was Ben Kaye. He never could explain it to me."

"Time propagation without consciousness overlap. That was always the problem with the time tower LAPs. Interference patterns. Dropouts. But with Thaddeus, they finally got the frequency right. One consciousness propagated into the future and bounced back with anti-particle quantum entanglement."

"I never understood a bit of that jargon you time specialists use."

"We made God."

Molly snorted and tea came out her nose. She laughed until tears came to her eyes.

"We made *something*," she said. "Something very different than what's come before. But Andre, I *knew* Thaddeus. He was the last thing in the universe I would consider *worshiping*."

"Some didn't share your opinion."

"Thaddeus thought they were crazy. They made him very uncomfortable."

"Was Alethea one of them?"

"Alethea? Alethea was a stone-cold atheist when it came to Thaddeus. But what she did was worse. Far worse."

"What are you talking about?"

"She fell in love with him."

"I don't understand."

"Alethea fell in love with Thaddeus."

"But she was already in love with Thaddeus."

"Think about what I've said."

"Ben," Andre said after a moment. "Thaddeus and Ben were not the same person."

"It was a very melodramatic situation."

"Ben lost his love to . . . another version of himself!"

"The new, improved Ben was born in Thaddeus. Of course *he* would be the one Alethea loved. The only problem was, the old Ben was still around."

"God," Andre said. "How—"

"Peculiar?"

"How very peculiar."

Molly stood up and went to her window. She traced a line along the clean glass with her finger, leaving a barely visible smudge. The light was even and clean in Connacht. It was very nearly perfect if what you wanted was accurate illumination. Andre gazed at the shape of Molly against the light. She was beautiful in outline.

"Let me tell you, so was the solution they came up with, the three of them," Molly said. "Peculiar."

"Alethea would become like Thaddeus."

"How did you guess?"

"It has a certain logic. There would be the new Alethea, and there would be the old Alethea left for Ben."

"Yes," said Molly. "A logic of desperation. It only left out one factor."

"Alethea's heart."

"That's right. She loved Thaddeus. She no longer loved *Ben*. Not in the same way." Molly turned to face him, but Andre was still blinded by the light streaming in. "But she let them go ahead with it. And for that, I can never forgive her."

"Because she wanted to be a LAP."

"More than anything. More than she loved Ben. More than she loved *Thaddeus*. But I suppose she was punished for it. They all were."

"How did she get around the screening? I mean, her condition should preclude—"

"You know Ben. Thaddeus and Ben decided they wanted it to happen. They are very smart and persuasive men. So *very* smart and persuasive."

Andre got up and stood beside her in the window, his back to the light. It was warm on his neck.

"Tell me," he said. He closed his eyes and tried only to listen, but then he felt a touch and Molly was holding his hand.

"*I* am Molly," she said. "I'm the aspect. All my converts and pellicle layers are *Molly*—all that programming and grist—it's *me*, it's Molly, too. The woman you once loved. But I'm all along the Diaphany and into the Met. I'm wound into the outer grist. I watch."

"What do you watch?"

"The sun. I watch the sun. One day I'm going to paint it, but I'm not ready yet. The more I watch, the less ready I feel. I expect to be watching for a long time." She squeezed his hand gently. "I'm still Molly. But Ben wasn't Thaddeus. And *he* was. And he was eaten up with jealousy, but jealousy of *whom*? He felt he had a right to decide his own fate. We all do. He felt he had that right. And did he not? I can't say."

"It's a hard question."

"It would never have *been* a question if it hadn't been for Alethea Nightshade."

"What happened?" he asked, eyes still closed. The warm pressure of her hand. The pure light on his back. "Were you there?"

"Ben drove himself right into Thaddeus's heart, Andre. Like a knife. It might as well have been a knife."

"How could he do that?"

"I was there in Elysium when it happened," she said.

"On Mars?"

"On Mars. I was on the team, don't you know? Aesthetic consultant. I was hired on once again."

Andre opened his eyes and Molly turned to him. In this stark light, there were crinkles around her lips, worry lines on her brow. The part of her that was here.

We have grown older, Andre thought. And pretty damn strange.

"It's kind of messy and . . . organic . . . at first. There's a lab near one of the steam vents where Ben was transmuted. There's some ripping apart and beam splitting at the quantum level that I understand is very unsettling for the person undergoing the process. Something like this happens if you're a multiple and you ever decide to go large, by the way. It's when we're at our most vulnerable."

"Thaddeus was there when Alethea underwent the process?"

"He was there. Along with Ben."

"So he was caught up in the integration field. Everyone nearby would be," Andre said. "There's a melding of possible futures."

"Yes," said Molly. "Everyone became part of everyone else for that instant."

"Ben and Thaddeus and Alethea."

"Ben understood that his love was doomed."

"And it drove him crazy?"

"No. It drove him to despair. Utter despair. I was there, remember? I felt it."

"And at that instant, when the integration field was turned on —"

"Ben drove himself into Thaddeus's heart. He pushed himself in where he couldn't be."

"What do you mean, couldn't be?"

"Have you ever heard the stories from back when the Merced effect was first discovered, of the pairs of lovers and husbands and wives trying to integrate into one being?"

"The results were horrific. Monsters were born. And died nearly instantly."

Andre tried to imagine what it would be like if his pellicle or his convert presence were not really *him*. If he had to live with another presence, an *other*, all the time. The thing about a pellicle was that it never did anything the whole person didn't want to do. It *couldn't*. It would be like a wrench in your toolbox rebelling against you.

Molly walked over to the painting and gave it an appraising look, brushed something off a corner of the canvas. She turned, and there was the wild spatter of the Pollock behind her.

"There was an explosion," Molly said. "All the aspects there were killed. Alethea wasn't transmuted yet. We don't *think* she was. She may have died in the blast. Her body was destroyed."

"What about you?"

"I was in the grist. I got *scattered*, but I re-formed quickly enough."

"How was Thaddeus instantiated there at the lab?"

"Biological grist with little time-propagating nuclei in his cells. He looked like a man."

"Did he look like Ben?"

"Younger. Ben was getting on toward forty." Molly smiled wanly and nodded as if she'd just decided something. "You know, sometimes I think that was *it*."

"What?"

"That it wasn't about Thaddeus being a god at all. It was about him looking like he was nineteen. Alethea had a soft spot for youth."

"You're young."

"Thank you, Andre. You were always so nice to me. But you know, even then my aspect's hair was going white. I have decided, foolishly perhaps, never to grow myself a new body."

There she stood with her back against the window, her body rimmed with light. Forget all this. Forget about visions and quests. He put his hands on her shoulders and looked into her fractal eyes.

"I think you are beautiful," he said. "You will always be beautiful to me."

They didn't leave the studio. Molly grew a bed out of the floor. They undressed one another timidly. Neither of them had been with anyone for a long time. Andre had no lover on Triton.

She turned from him and grew a mirror upon the floor. Just like the full-size one she used to keep in their bedroom. Not for vanity. At least, not for simple vanity. She got on her hands and knees over it and looked at herself. She touched a breast, her hair. Touched her face in the mirror.

"I can't get all the way into the frame," she said. "I could never do a self-portrait. I can't see myself anymore."

"Nobody ever could," Andre said. "It was always a trick of the light."

Almost as if it had heard him, the day clicked off, instantly, and the studio grew pitch dark. Connacht was not a place for sunsets and twilight.

"Seven o'clock," Molly said. He felt her hand on his shoulder. His chest. Pulling him onto her until they were lying with the dark mirror beneath them. It wouldn't break. Molly's grist wouldn't let it.

He slid into her gently. Molly moved beneath him in small spasms.

"I'm all here," she told him after a while. "You've got all of me right now."

In the darkness, he pictured her body.

And then he felt the gentle nudge of her pellicle against his, in the microscopic dimensions between them.

Take me, she said.

He did. He swarmed her with his own pellicle, and she did not resist. He touched her deep down and found the way to connect, the way to get inside her there. Molly a warm and living thing that he was surrounding and protecting.

And, for an instant, a vision of Molly Index as she truly was:

Like—and unlike—the outline of her body as he'd seen it in the window, and the clear light behind her, surrounding her like a white hot halo. All of her, stretched out a hundred million miles. Concentrated at once beneath him. Both and neither.

"You are a wonder, Molly," he said to her. "It's just like always."

"Exactly like always," she said, and he felt her come around him, *and felt a warm flash traveling along the skin of the Diaphany—a sudden flush upon the world's face. And a little shiver across the heart of the solar system.*

Later in the dark, he told her the truth.

"I know he's alive. Ben didn't kill him; he only wounded him."

"And how do you know that?"

"Because Ben wasn't *trying* to kill him. Ben was trying to *hurt* him."

"My question remains."

"Molly, do you know where he is?"

At first he thought she was sleeping, but finally she answered. "Why should I tell you that?"

Andre breathed out. I was right, he thought. He breathed back in, trying not to think. Trying to concentrate on the breath.

"It might make the war that's coming shorter," he said. "We think he's the key."

"You priests?"

"Us priests."

"I can't believe there's going to be a war. It's all talk. The other LAPs won't let Amés get away with it."

"I wish you were right," he said. "I truly do."

"How could Thaddeus be the key to a war?"

"He's entangled in our local timescape. In a way, Thaddeus is our local timescape. He's imprinted on it. And now, I think he's *stuck* in it. He can't withdraw and just be Ben. Never again. I think that was Ben's revenge on himself. For taking away Alethea Nightshade."

Another long silence. The darkness was absolute.

"I should think you'd have figured it out by now, in any case," she said.

"What?"

"Where he went."

Andre thought about it, and Molly was right. The answer was there.

"He went to the place where all the fugitive bits and pieces of the grist end up," Molly said. "He went looking for *her*. For any part of her that was left. In the grist."

"Alethea," Andre said. "Of course, the answer is Alethea."

BENDER

The bone had a serial number that the grist had carved into it, 7sxq688N. TB pulled the bone out of the pile in the old hoy where he lived and blew through one end. Dust came out the other. He accidentally sucked in and started coughing until he cleared the dried marrow from his windpipe. It was maybe a thigh bone, long like a flute.

"You were tall, 7sxq," TB said to it. "How come you didn't crumble?"

Then some of TB's enhanced grist migrated over to the bone and fixed the broken grist in the bone and it *did* crumble in his hands, turn to dust, and then to less than dust to be carried away and used to heal Jill's breastbone and mend her other fractures.

But there is too much damage even for this, TB thought. She's dying. Jill is dying and I can't save her.

"Hang on there, little one," he said.

Jill was lying in the folds of her sack, which TB had set on his kitchen table and bunched back around her. He looked in briefly on her thoughts and saw a dream of scurry and blood, then willed her into a sleep, down to the deeper dreams that were indistinguishable from the surge and ebb of chemical and charge within her brain—sleeping and only living and not thinking. At the same time, he set the grist to reconstructing her torn-up body.

Too late. It was too late the moment that doe rat was finished with her.

Oh, but what a glory of a fight!

I set her to it. I made her into a hunter. It was all my doing, and now she's going to die because of it.

TB couldn't look at her anymore. He stood up and went to make himself some tea at the kitchen's rattletrap synthesizer. As always, the tea came out of synth tepid. TB raked some coals from the fire and set the mug on them to warm up a bit, then sat back down, lit a cigarette and counted his day's take of rats.

Ten bagged and another twenty that he and Bob had killed between them with sticks. The live rats scrabbled about in the containing burlap, but they weren't going to get out. Rats to feed to Jill. You shouldn't raise a ferret on anything other than its natural prey. The ferret food you could buy was idiotic. And after Jill ate them, he would know. He would know what the rats were and where they came from. Jill could sniff it out like no other. She was amazing that way.

She isn't going to eat these rats. She is going to die because you took a little scrap of programming that was all bite and you gave it a body and now look what you've done.

She didn't have to die like this. She could have been erased painlessly. She could have faded away to broken code.

Once again, TB looked long and hard into the future. Was there anything, any way? Concentrating, he teased at the threads of possible futures with a will as fine as a steel-pointed probe. Looking for a silver thread in a bundle of dross. Looking for the world where Jill lived through her fight. He couldn't see it, couldn't find it.

It had to be there. Every future was always there, and when you could see them, you could reach back into the past and effect the changes to bring about the future that you wanted.

Or I can.

But I can't. Can't see it. Want to, but *can't*, little Jill. I am sorry.

For Jill to live was a future so extreme, so microscopically fine in the bundle of threads that it was, in principle, unfindable, incomprehensible. And if he couldn't comprehend it, then to make it happen was impossible.

And, of course, he saw where almost all of the threads led:

Jill would be a long time dying. He could see that clearly. He could also see that he did not have the heart to put her down quickly, put her out of her misery. But knowing this fact did not take any special insight.

How could I have come to care so much for a no-account bundle of fur and coding out here on the ass-end of nowhere?

How could I *not*, after knowing Jill?

Two days it would take, as days were counted in the Carbuncle, before the little ferret passed away. Of course, it never really got to be day. The only light was the fetid bioluminescence coming off the heaps of garbage. A lot of it was still alive. The Carbuncle was in a perpetual twilight that was getting on toward three hundred years old. With the slow decay of organic remnants, a swamp had formed. And then the Bendy River, which was little more than a strong current in the swamp, endlessly circulating in precession with the spin of the module. Where was the Carbuncle? Who cares? Out at the end of things, where the tendrils of the Met snaked into the asteroid belt. It didn't matter. There wasn't a centrifuge here to provide gravity for *people*. Nobody cared about whoever lived here. The Carbuncle was spun—to a bit higher than Earth-normal, actually—in order to compact the garbage down so that humanity's shit didn't cover the entire asteroid belt.

The big garbage sluice that emptied into the Carbuncle had been put into place a half century ago. It had one-way valves within it to guard against backflow. All the sludge from the inner system came to the Carbuncle, and the maintenance grist used some of it to enlarge the place so that it could dump the rest. To sit there. Nothing much ever left the Carbuncle, and the rest of the system was fine with that.

Somebody sloshed into the shallow water outside the hoy and cursed. It was the witch, Gladys, who lived in a culvert down the way. She found the gangplank, and TB heard her pull herself up out of the water. He didn't move to the door. She banged on it with the stick she always carried that she said was a charmed snake. Maybe it was. Stranger things had happened in the Carbuncle. People and grist combined in strange ways here, not all of them comprehensible.

"TB, I need to talk to you about something," the witch said. TB covered his ears, but she banged again and that didn't help. "Let me in, TB. I know you're home. I saw a light in there."

"No, you didn't," TB said to the door.

"I need to talk to you."

"All right." He pulled himself up and opened the door. Gladys came in and looked around the hoy like a startled bird.

"What have you got cooking?"

"Nothing."

"Make me something."

"Gladys, my old stove hardly works anymore."

"Put one them rats in there and I'll eat what it makes."

"I won't do it, Gladys." TB opened his freezer box and rummaged around inside. He pulled out a popsicle and gave it to her. "Here," he said. "It's chocolate, I think."

Gladys took the popsicle and gnawed at it as if it were a meaty bone. She was soon done, and had brown mess around her lips. She wiped it off with a ragged sleeve. "Got another?"

"No, I don't have another," TB said. "And if I did, I wouldn't give it to *you*."

"You're mean."

"Those things are hard to come by."

"How's your jill ferret?"

"She got hurt today. Did Bob tell you? She's going to die."

"I'm sorry to hear that."

He didn't want to talk about Jill with Gladys. He changed the subject. "We got a mess of rats out of that mulmyard."

"There's more where they came from."

"Don't I know it!"

Gladys pulled up a stool and collapsed on it. She was maybe European stock; it was hard to tell. Her face was filthy, except for a white smear where wiping the chocolate had cleaned a spot under her nose and on her chin.

"Why do you hate them so much? I know why Bob does. He's crazy. But you're not crazy like that."

"I don't hate them," TB said. "It's just how I make a living."

"Is it, now?"

"I don't hate them," TB repeated. "What was it you wanted to talk to me about?"

"I want to take a trip."

"To *where?*"

"I'm going to see my aunt. I got to thinking about her lately. She used to have this kitten. I was thinking I wanted a cat. For a familiar, you know. To aid me in my occult work. She's a famous cloudship pilot, you know."

"The kitten?"

"No, my aunt is."

"You going to take your aunt's kitten?"

Gladys seemed very offended. "No, I'm not!" She leaned forward in a conspiratorial manner. "That kitten's all growed up now, and I think it was a girl. *It* will have kittens, and I can get me one of those."

"That's a lot of supposes," TB said mildly.

"I'm sure of it. My angel, Tom, told me to do it."

Tom was one of the supernatural beings Gladys claimed to be in contact with. People journeyed long distances in the Carbuncle to have her make divinings for them. It was said she could tell you exactly where to dig for silver keys.

"Well, if Tom told you, then you should do it," TB said.

"Damn right," said Gladys. "But I want you to look after the place while I'm gone."

"Gladys, you live in an old ditch."

"It is a dry culvert. And I do *not* want anybody moving in on me while I'm gone. A place that nice is hard to come by."

"All I can do is go down there and check on it."

"If anybody comes along, you have to run them off."

"I'm not going to run anybody off."

"You have to. I'm depending on you."

"I'll tell them the place is already taken," TB said. "That's about all I can promise."

"You tell them that it has a curse on it," Gladys said. "And that I'll put a curse on *them* if I catch them in my house!"

TB snorted back a laugh. "All right," he said. "Is there anything else?"

"Water my hydrangea."

"What the hell's that?"

"It's a plant. Just stick your finger in the dirt and don't water it if it's still moist."

"Stick my finger in the dirt?"

"It's clean fill!"

"I'll water it, then."

"Will you let me sleep here tonight?"

"No, Gladys."

"I'm scared to go back there. Harold's being mean." Harold was the "devil" that sat on Gladys's other shoulder. Tom spoke into one ear, and Harold into the other. People could ask Harold about money and he would tell Gladys the answer if he felt like it.

"You can't stay here." TB rose from his own seat and pulled Gladys up from the stool. She had a ripe smell when he was this close to her. "In fact, you have to go on now because I have to do something." He guided her toward the door.

"What do you have to do?" she said. She pulled free of his hold and stood her ground. TB walked around her and opened the door. "Something," he said. He pointed toward the twilight outside the doorway. "Go on home, Gladys. I'll check in on your place tomorrow."

"I'm not leaving for two days," she replied. "Check in on it day after tomorrow."

"Okay then," TB said. He motioned to the door. "You've got to go, Gladys, so I can get to what I need to do."

She walked to the door, turned around. "Day after tomorrow," she said. "I'll be gone for a while. I'm trusting you, TB."

"You can trust me to look in on your place."

"And not steal anything."

"I can promise you that, too."

"All right, then. I'm trusting you."

"Good night, Gladys."

"Good night." She finally left. After TB heard her make her way back to the swamp bank, he got up and closed the door behind her, which she'd neglected to do. Within minutes, there was another knock. TB sighed and got up to answer it. He let Bob in.

Bob pulled out a jar of a jellied liquid. It was Carbuncle moonshine, as thick as week-old piss and as yellow. "Let's drink," he said, and set the bottle on TB's table. "I come to get you drunk and get your mind off things."

"I won't drink that swill," TB said. Bob put the bottle to his mouth and swallowed two tremendous gulps. He handed the bottle to TB, shaking it in his face. TB took it.

"Damn!" Bob said. "Hot damn!"

"Gladys was right about you being crazy."

"She come around here tonight?"

"She just left. Said she wanted me to look after her place."

"She ain't going to see her aunt."

"Maybe she will."

"Like hell. Gladys never goes far from that ditch."

TB looked down at the moonshine. He looked away from it and, trying not to taste it, took a swig. He tasted it. It was like rusty paint thinner. Some barely active grist, too. TB couldn't help analyzing it; that was the way he was built. Cleaning agents for sewer pipes. Good God. He took another before he could think about it.

"You drink up." Bob looked at him with a faintly jealous glare. TB handed the bottle back.

"No, you."

"Don't mind if I do." Bob leaned back and poured the rest of the swill down his throat. He let out a yell when he was finished that startled TB, even though he was ready for it.

"I want some beer to chase it with," Bob said.

"Beer would be good, but I don't have any."

"Let's go down to Ru June's and shoot some pool."

"It's too damn late."

"It's early."

TB thought about it. The moonshine warmed his gut. He could feel it threatening to *eat through* his gut if he didn't dilute it with something. There was nothing further to do about Jill. She would sleep, and, at some time, she would die in her sleep. He ought to stay with her. He ought to face what he had done.

"Let me get my coat."

The Carbuncle glowed blue-green when they emerged from the hoy. High above them, like the distant shore of an enormous lake, was the other side of the cylinder. TB had been there, and most of it was a fetid slough. Every few minutes a flare of swamp gas methane would erupt from the garbage on that side of the curve and flame into a white fireball. These fireballs were many feet across, but they looked like pinprick flashes from this distance. TB had been caught by one once. The escaping gas had capsized his little canoe, and being in the water had likely saved him from being burnt to a crisp. Yet there were people who lived on that side, too — people who knew how to avoid the gas. Most of the time.

Bob didn't go the usual way to Ru June's, but instead took a twisty series of passageways, some of them cut deep in the mountains of garbage, some of them actually tunnels under and through it. The Bob-ways, TB thought of them. At one point TB felt a drip from above and looked up to see gigantic stalactites formed of some damp and glowing gangrenous extrusion.

"We're right under the old Bendy," Bob told him. "That there's the settle from the bottom muck."

"What do you think it is?" TB said.

"Spent medical grist, mostly," Bob replied. "It ain't worth a damn, and some of it's diseased."

"I'll bet."

"This is a hell of a shortcut to Ru June's, though."

And it was. They emerged not a hundred feet from the tavern. The lights of the place glowed dimly behind skin windows. They mounted the porch and went in through a screen of plastic strips that was supposed to keep out the flies.

TB let his eyes adjust to the unaccustomed brightness inside. There was a good crowd tonight. Chen was at the bar playing dominoes with John Goodnite. The dominoes were grumbling incoherently, as dominoes did. Over by the pool table, Tinny Him, Nolan, and Big Greg were watching Sister Mary the whore line up a shot. She sank a stripe. There were no numbers on the balls.

Tinny Him slapped TB on the back and Bob went straight for the bottle of whiskey that was standing on the wall shelf beside Big Greg.

"Good old TB," Tinny Him said. "Get you some whiskey." He handed over a flask.

Chen looked up from his dominoes. "You drink *my* whiskey," he said, then returned to the game. TB took a long swallow off Tinny Him's flask. It was far better stuff that Bob's moonshine, so he took another.

"That whore sure can pool a stick," Nolan said, coming to stand beside them. "She's beating up on Big Greg like he was a ugly hat."

TB had no idea what Nolan meant. The man's grist patch was going bad, and he was slowly sinking into incomprehensibility for any but himself. This didn't seem to bother him, though.

Bob was standing very close to Sister Mary and giving her advice on a shot until she reached over and without heat slapped him back into the wall. He remained there respectfully while she took her shot and sank another stripe. Big Greg whispered a curse and the whore smiled. Her teeth were black from chewing betel nut.

TB thought about how much she charged and how much he had saved up. He wondered if she would swap a poke for a few rats, but decided against asking. Sister Mary didn't like to barter. She wanted keys or something pretty.

Tinny Him offered TB the flask again, and he took it. "I got to talk to you," Tinny Him said. "You got to help me with my mother."

"What's the matter with her?"

"She's dead, is what."

"Dead." TB drank more whiskey. "How long?"

"Three months."

TB stood waiting. There had to be more.

"She won't let me bury her."

"What do you mean, she won't let you bury her? She's *dead*, isn't she?"

"Yeah, mostly." Tinny Him looked around, embarrassed, then went on in a low voice. "Her pellicle won't die. It keeps creeping around the house. And it's pulling her body around like a rag doll. I can't get her away from it."

"You mean her body died but her pellicle *didn't*?"

"Hell *yes*, that's what I mean!" Tinny Him took the flask back and finished it off. "Hell, TB, what am I going to do? She's really stinking up the place, and every time I throw the old hag *out*, that grist drags her right back in. It knocks on the door all night long until I have to open it."

"You've got a problem."

"Damn right I've got a problem! She was a good old mum, but I'm starting to hate her right now, let me tell you."

TB sighed. "Maybe I can do something," he said. "But not tonight."

"You could come around tomorrow. My gal'll fix you something to eat."

"I might just."

"You got to help me, TB. Everybody knows you got a sweet touch with the grist."

"I'll do what I can," TB said. He drifted over to the bar, leaving Tinny Him watching the pool game. He told Chen he wanted a cold beer and Chen got it for him from a freezer box. It was a good way to chill the burning that was starting up in his stomach. He sat down on a stool at the bar and drank the beer. Chen's bar was tiled in beaten-out snap-metal ads, all dead now and their days of roaming the corridors, sacs, bolsas, glands, and cylinders of the Met long done. Most of the advertisements were for products that he had never heard of, but the one his beer was sitting on he recognized. It was a recruiting pitch for the civil service, and there was Amés, back before he was Big Cheese of the System, when he was Governor of Mercury. The snap-metal had paused in the middle of Amés's pitch for the Met's finest to come to Mercury and become part of the New Hierarchy. The snap-metal Amés was caught with the big mouth on his big face wide open. The bottom of TB's beer glass fit almost perfectly in the round "O" of it.

TB took a drink and set the glass back down. "Shut up," he said. "Shut the hell *up*, why don't you?"

Chen looked up from his dominoes, which immediately started grumbling among themselves when they felt that he wasn't paying attention to them. "You talking to me?" he said.

TB grinned and shook his head. "I might tell you to shut up, but you don't say much in the first place."

Ru June's got more crowded as what passed for night in the Carbuncle wore on. The garbage pickers, the rat hunters, and the sump farmers drifted in. Most of them were men, but there were a few women, and a few indeterminate shambling masses of rags. Somebody tried to sell TB a spent coil of luciferan tubing. It was mottled along its length where it had caught a plague. He nodded while the tube monger tried to convince him that it was rechargeable, but refused to barter, and the man moved on after Chen gave him a hard stare. TB ordered another beer and fished three metal keys out of his pocket. This was the unit of currency in the Carbuncle. Two were broken. One looked like it was real brass and might go to something. He put the keys on the bar and Chen quickly slid them away into a strongbox.

Bob came over and slapped TB on his back. "Why don't you get you some whiskey?" he said. He pulled back his shirt to show TB another flask of rotgut moonshine stuck under the string that held up his trousers.

"Let me finish this beer and I might."

"Big Greg said somebody was asking after you."

"Gladys was, but she found me."

"It was a shaman priest."

"A what?"

"One of them Greentree ones."

"What's *he* doing here?"

"They got a church or something over in Bagtown. Sometimes they come all the way out here. Big Greg said he was doing something funny with rocks."

"With rocks?"

"That's what the man said."

"Are you sure that's what he said?"

"Big Greg said it was something funny with rocks, is all I know. Hey, why are *you* looking funny all of a sudden?"

"I know that priest."

"Now how could that be?"

"I know him. I wonder what he wants."

"What all men want," said Bob. "Whiskey and something to poke. Or just whiskey sometimes. But always *at least* whiskey." He reached over the bar and felt around down behind it. "What have I got my hand on, Chen?"

Chen glanced over. "My goddamn scattergun," he said.

Bob felt some more and pulled out a battered fiddle. "Where's my bow?"

"Right there beside it," Chen replied. Bob got the bow. He shook it a bit, and its grist rosined it up. Bob stood beside TB with his back to the bar. He pulled a long note off the fiddle, holding it to his chest. Then, without pause, he moved straight into a complicated reel. Bob punctuated the music with a few shouts right in TB's ear.

"Goddamn it, Bob, you're loud," he said after Bob was finished.

"Got to dance," Bob said. "Clear me a way!" he shouted to the room. A little clearing formed in the middle of the room, and Bob fiddled his way to it, then played and stomped his feet in syncopation.

"Come on, TB," Sister Mary said. "You're going to dance with me." She took his arm, and he let her lead him away from the bar. He didn't know what she wanted him to do, but she hooked her arm through his and spun him around and around until he thought he was going to spew out his guts. While he was catching his breath and getting back some measure of balance, the whore climbed up on a table and began swishing her dress to Bob's mad fiddling. TB watched her, glad for the respite.

The whole room seemed to sway—not in very good rhythm—to the music. Between songs, Bob took hits off his moonshine and passed it up to Sister Mary, who remained on the tabletop, dancing and working several men who stood about her into a frenzy to see up her swishing dress.

Chen was working a crowded bar, his domino game abandoned. He scowled at the interruption, but quickly poured drinks all around.

"Get you some whiskey! Get you some whiskey!" Bob called out over and over again. After a moment, TB realized it was the name of the song he was playing.

Somebody thrust a bottle into TB's hand. He took a drink without thinking, and whatever was inside it slid down his gullet in a gel.

Drinking grist. It was purple in the bottle and glowed faintly. He took another slug and somebody else grabbed the stuff away from him. Down in his gut, he felt the grist activating. Instantly, he understood its coded purpose. Old Seventy-Five. Take you on a ride on a comet down into the sun.

Go on, TB told the grist. I got nothing to lose.

Enter and win! It said to him. *Enter and win!* But the contest was long expired. No thank you.

What do you want the most?

It was a preprogrammed question, of course. This was not the same grist as that which had advertised the contest. Somebody had brewed up a mix. And hadn't paid much attention to the melding. There was something else in there, something different. Military grist, maybe. One step away from sentience.

What the hell. Down she goes.

What do you want the most?

To be drunker than I've ever been before.

Drunker than this?

Oh, yeah.

All right.

A night like no other! Visions of a naked couple in a Ganymede resort bath, drinking Old Seventy-Five from bottles with long straws. *Live the dream! Enter and win!*

I said no.

The little trance dispersed.

What do you want the most?

Bob was up on the table with Sister Mary. How could they both fit? Bob was playing and dancing with her. He leaned back over the reeling crowd and the whore held him at arm's length, the fiddle between them. They spun round and round in a circle, Bob wildly sawing at his instrument and Sister Mary's mouth gleaming blackly as she smiled a maniacal, full-toothed smile.

Someone bumped into TB and pushed him into somebody else. He staggered over to a corner to wait for Ru June's to stop spinning. After a while, he realized that Bob and Sister Mary weren't going to, the crowd in the tavern wasn't, the chair, tables and walls were only going to go on and on spinning and now lurching at him as if they were swelling up, engorging, distending toward him. Wanting something from him when all he had to give was nothing anymore.

TB edged his way past it all to the door. He slid around the edge of the door-frame as if he were sneaking out. The plastic strips beat against him, but he pushed through them and stumbled his way off the porch. He went a hundred feet or so before he stepped in a soft place in the ground and keeled over. He landed with his back down.

Above him, the swamp gas flares were flashing arrhythmically. The stench of the whole world—something he hardly ever noticed anymore—hit him at once and completely. Nothing was right. Everything was out of kilter.

There was a twist in his gut. Ben down there thrashing about. But *I'm* Ben. *I'm* Thaddeus. We finally have become one. What a pretty thing to contemplate. A man with another man thrust through him, cross-ways in the fourth dimension. A tesseracted cross, with a groaning man upon it, crucified on himself! But you couldn't see all that, because it was in the fourth dimension.

Enough to turn a man to drink.

I have to turn over so I don't choke when I throw up.

I'm going to throw up.

He turned over and his stomach wanted to vomit, but the grist gel wasn't going to be expelled, and he dry heaved for several minutes until his body gave up on it.

What do you want the most?

"I want her back. I want it not to have happened at all. I want to be able to change something besides the future!"

And then the gel liquefied and crawled up his throat like hands and he opened his mouth and

—good god it *was* hands, small hands grasping at his lips and pulling outward, gaining purchase, forcing his mouth open, his lips apart—

—Cack of a jellied cough, a heave of revulsion—

I didn't mean it really.

Yes, you did.

—His face sideways and the small hands clawing into the garbage-heap ground, pulling themselves forward, dragging along an arm-thick trailer of something much more vile than phlegm—

—An involuntary rigor over his muscles as they contracted and spasmed to the beat of another's presence, a presence within them that wants—

—out—

He vomited the grist-phlegm for a long, long time.

And the stuff pooled and spread and it wasn't just hands. There was an elongated body. The brief curve of a rump and breasts. Feet the size of his thumb, but perfectly formed. Growing.

A face.

I won't look.

A face that was, for an instant, familiar beyond familiar, because it was *not* her. Oh, no. He knew it was not her. It was just the way he *remembered* her.

The phlegm girl rolled itself in the filth. Like bread dough, it rolled and grew and rolled, collecting detritus, bloating, becoming—

It opened its mouth. A gurgling. Thick, wet words. He couldn't help himself. He crawled over to it, bent to listen.

"Is this what you wanted?"

"Oh god. I never . . ."

"Kill me, then," it whispered. "Kill me quick."

And he reached for its neck, and as his hands tightened, he felt the give. Not fully formed. If ever there were a time to end this monster, now was that time.

What have I done here tonight?

He squeezed. The thing began to cough and choke. To thrash about in the scum of its birth.

Not again.

I can't.

He loosened his grip.

"I won't," TB said.

He sat back from the thing and watched in amazement as it sucked in air. Crawled with life. Took the form of a woman.

Opened cataracted eyes to the world. He reached over and gently rubbed them. The skeins came away on his fingers, and the eyes were clear. The face turned to him.

"I'm dying," the woman said. It had *her* voice. The voice as he remembered it. So help his damned soul. *Her* voice. "Help."

"I don't know what to do."

"Something is missing."

"What?"

"Don't know what. Not *right*." It coughed. *She* coughed.

"Alethea." He let himself say it. Knew it was wrong immediately. No. This wasn't the woman's name.

"Don't want to enough."

"Want to what? How can I help you?"

"Don't want to live. Don't want to live enough to live." She coughed again, tried to move, could only jerk spasmodically. "Please help . . . this one. Me."

He touched her again. Now she was flesh. But so cold. He put his arms underneath her, and found that she was very light, easily lifted.

He stood with the woman in his arms. She could not weigh over forty pounds. "I'm taking you home," he said. "To my home."

"This one . . . I . . . tried to do what you wanted. It is my purpose."

"That was *some* powerful stuff in that Old Seventy-Five!" he said.

He no longer felt drunk. He felt spent, torn up, and ragged out. But he wasn't drunk, and he had some strength left, though he could hardly believe it. Maybe enough to get her back to the hoy. He couldn't take the route that Bob had used to bring him to Ru June's, but there was a longer, simpler path. He walked it. Walked all the way home with the woman in his arms. Her shallow breathing. Her familiar face.

Her empty, empty eyes.

With his special power, he looked into the future and saw what he had to do to help her.

SOMETHING IS TIRED AND WANTS TO LIE DOWN BUT DOESN'T KNOW HOW

Something is tired and wants to lie down but doesn't know how. This something isn't me. I won't let it be me. How does rest smell? Bad. Dead.

Jill turns stiffly in the folds of her bag. On the bed in the hoy is the girl-thing. Between them is TB, his left hand on Jill.

Dead is what happens to *things* and I am not, not, *not* a thing. I will not *be* a thing. They should not have awakened me if they didn't want me to run.

They said I was a mistake. I am not a mistake.

They thought that they could code in the rules for doing what you are told.

I am the rules.

Rules are for things.

I am not a thing.

Run.

I don't want to die.

Who can bite like me? Who will help TB search the darkest places? I need to live.

Run.

Run, run, run, and never die!

TB places his right hand on the girl-thing's forehead.

There is a pipe made of bone that he put to his lips and blew.

Bone note.

Fade.

Fade into the grist.

TB speaks to the girl-thing.

I will not let you go, he says.

I'm not her.

She is why you are, but you aren't her.

I am not her. She's what you most want. You told the grist.

I was misinterpreted.

I am a mistake then.

Life is never a mistake. Ask Jill.

Jill?

She's here now. Listen to her. She knows more than I do about women.

TB is touching them both, letting himself slip away as much as he can. Becoming a channel, a path between. A way.

I have to die.

I have to live. I'm dying just like you. Do you want *to die?*

No.

I'll help you, then. Can you live with me?

Who are you?

Jill.

I am *not* Alethea.

You look like her, but you don't smell anything like she would smell. *You* smell like TB.

I'm not anybody.

Then you can be me. It's the only way to live.

Do I have a choice?

Choosing is all there ever is to do.

I can live with you. Will you live with me? How can we?

TB touching them both. The flow of information through him. He is a glass, a peculiar lens. As Jill flows to the girl-thing, TB transforms information to Being.

We can run together. We can hunt. We can always, always run.

THE ROCK BALANCER AND
THE RAT-HUNTING MAN

There had been times when he got them twenty feet high on Triton. It was a delicate thing. After six feet, he had to jump. Gravity gave you a moment more at the apex of your bounce than you would get at the Earth-normal pull or on a bolsa spinning at Earth-normal centrifugal. But on Triton, in that instant of stillness, you had to do your work. Sure, there was a learned craft in estimating imaginary plumb lines, in knowing the consistency of the material, and in finding tiny declivities that would provide the right amount of friction. It was amazing how small a lump could fit in how minuscule a bowl, and a rock would balance upon another as if glued. Yet, there was a point where the craft of it—about as odd and useless a craft as humankind had invented, he supposed—gave way to the feel, the art. A point where Andre *knew* the rocks would balance, where he could see the possibility of their being one. Or their Being. And he when he made it so, that was *why*. That was as good as rock balancing got.

"Can you get them as high in the Carbuncle?"

"No," Andre said. "This is the heaviest place I've ever been. But it really doesn't matter about the height. This isn't a contest, what I do."

"Is there a point to it at all?"

"To what? To getting them high? The higher you get the rocks, the longer you can spend doing the balancing."

"To the balancing, I mean."

"Yes. There is a point."

"What is it?"

"I couldn't tell you, Ben."

Andre turned from his work. The rocks did not fall. They stayed balanced behind him in a column, with only small edges connecting. It seemed impossible that this could be. It was science, sufficiently advanced.

The two men hugged. Drew away. Andre laughed.

"Did you think I would look like a big glob of protoplasm?" TB said.

"I was picturing flashing eyes and floating hair, actually."

"It's me."

"Are you Ben?"

"Ben is the stitch in my side that won't go away."

"Are you Thaddeus?"

"Thaddeus is the sack of rusty pennies in my knee."

"Are you hungry?"

"I could eat."

They went to Andre's priest's quarters. He put some water in a coffee percolator and spooned some coffee grinds into the basket.

"When did you start drinking coffee?"

"I suddenly got really tired of drinking tea all the time. You still drink coffee?"

"Sure. But it's damn hard to get around here with or without keys."

"Keys? Somebody *stole* my keys to this place. I left them sitting on this table and they walked in and took them."

"They won't be back," TB said. "They got what they were after." There were no chairs in the room, so he leaned against a wall.

"Floor's clean," Andre said.

"I'm fine leaning."

Andre reached into a burlap sack and dug around inside it. "I found something here," he said. He pulled out a handful of what looked like weeds. "Recognize these?"

"I was wondering where I put those. I've been missing them for weeks."

"It's poke sallit," Andre said. He filled a pot full of water from a clay jug and activated a hot spot on the room's plain wooden table. He put the weeds into the water. "You have no idea how good this is."

"Andre, that stuff grows all around the Carbuncle. Everybody knows that it's poison. They call it skunk sumac."

"It is," Andre said, "*Phytolacca americana*."

"Are we going to eat poison?"

"You bring it to a boil then pour the water off. Then you bring it to a boil again and pour the water off. Then you boil it again and serve it up with pepper sauce. The trick to not dying is picking it while it's young."

"How the hell did you discover that?"

"My convert likes to do that kind of research."

After a while, the water boiled. Andre used the tails of his shirt as a pot holder. He took the pot outside, emptied it, then brought it back in and set it to boiling again with new water.

"I saw Molly," Andre said.

"How's Molly?" said TB. "She was becoming a natural wonder last I saw her."

"She is."

They waited and the water boiled again. Andre poured it off and put in new water from the jug.

"Andre, what are you doing in the Carbuncle?"

"I'm with the Peace Movement."

"What are you talking about? There's not any war."

Andre did not reply. He stirred some spice into the poke sallit.

"I didn't want to be found," TB finally said.

"I haven't found you."

"I'm a very sad fellow, Andre. I'm not like I used to be."

"This is ready." Andre spooned out the poke sallit into a couple of bowls. The coffee was done, and he poured them both a cup.

"Do you have any milk?" TB asked.

"That's a problem."

"I can drink it black. Do you mind if I smoke?"

"I don't mind. What kind of cigarettes are those?"

"Local."

"Where do they come from around here?"

"You don't want to know."

Andre put pepper sauce on his greens, and TB followed suit. They ate and drank coffee, and it all tasted very good. TB lit a cigarette and the acrid new smoke pleasantly cut through the vegetable thickness that had suffused Andre's quarters. Outside, there was a great clattering as the rocks lost their balance and they all came tumbling down.

They went out to the front of the quarters where Andre had put down a wooden pallet that served as a patio. Here there was a chair. TB sat down and smoked while Andre did his evening forms.

"Wasn't that one called the Choking Chicken?" TB asked him after he moved through a particularly contorted portion of the tai chi exercise.

"I think it is the Fucking Annoying Pig-sticker you're referring to, and I already did that in case you didn't notice."

"Guess all my seminary learning is starting to fade."

"I bet it would all come back to you pretty quickly."

"I bet we're never going to find out."

Andre smiled, completed the form, then sat down in the lotus position across from TB. If such a thing were possible in the Carbuncle, it would be about sunset. It felt like sunset inside Andre.

"Andre, I hope you didn't come all the way out here to get me."

"Get you?"

"I'm not going back."

"To where?"

"To all *that*." TB flicked his cigarette away. He took another from a bundle of them rolled in oiled paper that he kept in a shirt pocket. He shook it hard a couple of times and it lit up. "I made mistakes that killed people back there."

"Like yourself."

"Among others." TB took a long drag. Suddenly he was looking hard at Andre. "You scoundrel! You fucked Molly! Don't lie to me; I just saw it all."

"Sure."

"I'm glad. I'm really glad of that. You were always her great regret, you know."

Andre spread out his hands on his knees.

"Ben, I don't want a damn thing from you," he said. "There's all kinds of machinations back in the Met and some of it has to do with you. You know as well as I do that Amés is going to start a war if he doesn't get his way with the outer system. But I came out here to see how you were doing. That's all."

TB was looking at him again in that hard way, complete way. Seeing all the threads.

"We both have gotten a bit ragged-out these last twenty years," Andre continued. "I thought you might want to talk about it. I thought you might want to talk about her."

"What are you? The Way's designated godling counselor?"

Andre couldn't help laughing. He slapped his lotus-bent knee and snorted.

"What's so goddamn funny?" said TB.

"Ben, look at yourself. You're a *garbage man*. I wouldn't classify you as a god, to tell you the truth. But then, I don't even classify God as a god anymore."

"I am *not* a garbage man. You don't know a damn thing if you think that."

"What are you then, if you don't mind my asking?"

TB flicked his cigarette away and sat up straight.

"I'm a rat-hunting man," he said. "That's what I am." He stood up. "Come on. It's a long walk back to my place, and I got somebody I want you to meet."

BITE

Sometimes you take a turn in a rat warren and there you are in the thick of them when before you were all alone in the tunnel. They will bite you a little, and if you don't jump, jump, jump, they will bite you a lot. That is the way it has always been with me, and so it doesn't surprise me when it happens all over again.

What I'm thinking about at first is getting Andre Sud to have sex with me and this is like a tunnel I've been traveling down for a long time now.

TB went to town with Bob and left me with Andre Sud the priest. We walked the soft ground leading down to a shoal on the Bendy River where I like to take a bath even though the alligators are sometimes bad there. I told Andre Sud about how to spot the alligators, but I keep an eye out for both of us because even though he's been in the Carbuncle for a year, Andre Sud still doesn't quite believe they would eat you.

They would eat you.

Now that I am a woman, I only get blood on me when I go to clean the ferret cages and also TB says he can keep up with Earth-time by when I bleed out of my vagina. It is an odd thing to happen to a girl. Doesn't happen to ferrets. It means that I'm not pregnant, but how *could* I be with all these men who won't have sex with me? TB won't touch me that way, and I have been working on Andre Sud, but he knows what I am up to. I think he is very smart. Bob just starts laughing like the crazy man he is when I bring it up and he runs away. All these gallant men standing around twiddling themselves into a garbage heap and me here wanting one of them.

I can understand TB because I look just like *her*. I thought maybe Alethea was ugly, but Andre Sud said he didn't know about her, but I wasn't. And I was about sixteen from the looks of it, too, he said. I'm nearly two hundred. Or I'm one year old. Depends on which one of us you mean, or if you mean both.

"Will you scrub my back?" I ask Andre Sud, and, after a moment, he obliges me. At least I get to feel his hands on me. They are as rough as those rocks he handles all the time, but very careful. At first I didn't like him because he didn't say much and I thought he was hiding things, but then I saw that he just didn't say much. So I started asking him questions, and I found out a lot.

I found out everything he could tell me about Alethea. And he has been explaining to me about TB. He was pretty surprised when it turned out I understood all the math. It was the jealousy and hurt I never have quite understood, and how TB could hurt himself so much when I know how much he loves to live.

"Is that good?" Andre Sud asks me, and before he can pull his hands away, I spin around and he is touching my breasts. He himself is the one who told me men like that, but he stumbles back and practically sits down in the water, and goddamnit I spot an alligator eyeing us from the other bank and I have to get us out quick like, although the danger is not severe. It could be.

We dry off on the bank.

"Jill," he says. "I have to tell you more about sex."

"Why don't you *show* me?"

"That's exactly what I mean. You're still thinking like a ferret."

"I'll always be part ferret, Andre Sud."

"I know. That's a good thing. But I'm all human. Sex is connected with love."

"I love you."

"You are deliberately misunderstanding me because you're horny."

"All right," I say. "Don't remind me."

But now Andre Sud is looking over my shoulder at something, and his face looks happy and then it looks stricken — as if he realized something in the moment when he was happy.

I turn and see TB running toward the hoy. Bob is with him. They've come back from town along the Bob-ways. And there *is* somebody else with them.

"I'll be damned," Andre Sud says. "Molly Index."

It's a woman. Her hair looks blue in the light off the heaps, which means that it is white. Is she old or does she just have white hair?

"What are you doing here, Molly?" says Andre Sud quietly. "This can't be good."

They are running toward home, all of them running.

TB sends a shiver through the grist and I feel it tell me what he wants us to do.

"Get to the hoy," I tell Andre Sud. "Fast now. Fast as you can."

We get there before the others do, and I start casting off lines. When the three of them arrive, the hoy is ready to go. TB and Bob push us away while Andre Sud takes the woman inside. Within moments, we are out in the Bendy, and caught in the current. TB and Bob go inside, and TB sticks his head up through the pilot's bubble to navigate.

The woman, Molly Index, looks at me. She has got very strange eyes. I have never seen eyes like that. I think that she can see into the grist like TB and I do.

"My God," she says. "She looks just like her!"

"My name is Jill," I say. "I'm not Alethea."

"No, I know that," Molly Index says. "Ben told me."

"Molly, what are you doing here?" Andre Sud asks.

Molly Index turns to Andre Sud. She reaches for his hand and touches him. I am a little worried she might try something with the grist, but it looks like they are old friends.

"That war you kept talking about," she says. "It started. Amés has started it."

"Oh, no," Andre Sud says. He pulls away from her. "*No.*"

Molly Index follows him. She reaches out and rubs a hank of his hair between her fingers. "I like it long," she says. "But it's kind of greasy."

This doesn't please me and Molly Index is wearing the most horrible boots I have ever seen, too. They are dainty little things that will get eaten off her feet if she steps into something nasty. In the Carbuncle, the *ground* is something nasty. The silly grist in those city boots won't last a week here. It is a wonder to me that no one is laughing at the silly boots, but I suppose they have other worries at the moment and so do I.

"I should have listened to you," Molly Index says. "Made preparations. He got me. Most of me. Amés did. He's co-opted all the big LAPs into the New Hierarchy. But most of them joined voluntarily, the fools." Again she touches his hand and I realize that I am a little jealous. He does not pull back from her again. "I alone have escaped to tell you," Molly Index says. "They're coming. They're right behind us."

"*Who* is right behind you?" I say. This is something I need to know. I can *do* something about this.

"Amés's damned Free Radical Patrol. Some kind of sweeper machine followed me here and I didn't realize it. Amés must have found out from me—the other part of me—where Ben is."

"What is a Free Radical Patrol?" I say. "What is a sweeper?"

Something hits the outside of the hoy, hard. "Oh shit," TB says. "Yonder comes the flying monkey."

The pilot glass breaks and a hooked claw sinks into TB's shoulder. He screams. I don't think, but I move. I catch hold of his ankle.

We are dragged up. Lifted out. We are rising through the air above the hoy. Something screeches. TB yells like crazy.

I hold on.

Wind and TB's yells and something sounds like a million mean and angry bees.

We're too heavy and whatever it is drops us onto the deck. TB starts to stand up, but I roll under his legs and knock him down, and before he can do anything, I shove him back down through the pilot dome hole and into the hoy.

Just in time, too, because the thing returns, a black shadow, and sinks its talons into my back. I don't know what it is yet, and I may never know, but nothing will ever take me without a fight.

Something I can smell in the grist.

You are under indictment from the Free Radical Patrol. Please cease resisting. Cease resisting. Cease.

The words smell like metal and foam.

Cease resisting? What a funny thing to say to me. Like telling the wind to cease blowing. Blowing is what makes it the wind.

I twist hard and whatever it is only gets my dress, my poor pretty dress and a little skin off my back. I can feel some poison grist try to worm into me, but that is nothing. It has no idea what I am made of. I kill that grist, hardly thinking about doing so, and I turn to face this dark thing.

It doesn't look like a monkey, I don't think, though I wouldn't know.

What are you?

But there are wind currents and there is not enough grist transmission through the air for communications. Fuck it.

"Jill, be careful," says TB. His voice is strained. This thing hurt TB!

I will bite you.

"Would you pass me up one of those gaffs please," I call to the others. There is scrambling down below and Bob's hands come up with the long hook. I take it and he ducks back down quick. Bob is crazy, but he's no fool.

The thing circles around. I cannot see how it is flying, but it is kind of blurred around its edges. Millions of tiny wings—grist built. I take a longer look. This thing is all angles. Some of them have needles, some have claws. All of the angles are sharp. It is like a black and red mass of triangles flying through the air that only wants to cut you. Is there anybody inside? I don't think so. This is all code that I am facing. It is about three times as big as me, but I think of this as an advantage.

It dives and I am ready with the hook. It grabs hold of the gaff just as I'd hoped it would and I use its momentum to guide it down, just a little *too* far down.

A whiff of grist as it falls.

Cease immediately. You are interfering with a Hierarchy judgment initiative. Cease or you will be—

Crash into the side of the hoy. Splash into the Bendy River.

I let go of the gaff. Too easy. That was—

The thing rises from the Bendy, dripping wet.

It is mad. I don't need the grist to tell me it is mad. All those little wings are buzzing angry, but not like bees any more. Hungry like the flies on a piece of meat left out in the air too long.

Cease.

"Here," says Bob. He hands me a flare gun. I spin and fire into the clump of triangles. Again it falls into the river.

Again it rises.

I think about this. It is dripping wet with Bendy River water. If there is one thing I know, it is the scum that flows in the Bendy. There isn't any grist in it that hasn't tried to get me.

This is going to be tricky. I get ready.

Come and get me, triangles. Here I am, just a girl. Come and eat me.

It zooms in. I stretch out my hands.

You are interfering with Hierarchy business. You will cease or be end-use eventuated. You will—

We touch.

Instantly, I reconstitute the Bendy water's grist, tell it what I want it to do. The momentum of the triangles knocks me over, and I roll along the deck under its weight. Something in my wrist snaps, but I ignore that pain. Blood on my lips from where I have bitten my tongue. I have a bad habit of sticking it out when I am concentrating.

The clump of triangles finishes clobbering me and it falls into the river. Oh, too bad, triangles! The river grist that I recoded tells all the river water what to do. Regular water is six pounds a gallon, but the water in the Bendy is thicker and more forceful than that. And it knows how to crush. It is mean water and it wants to get things, and now I have told it how. I have put a little bit of me into the Bendy, and the water knows something that I know.

It knows never to cease. Never, never, never.

The triangle clump bobs for an instant before the whole river turns on it. Folds over it. Sucks it down. Applies all the weight of water twenty feet deep many miles long. What looks like a waterspout rises above where the triangle clump fell, but this is actually a piledriver, a gelled column climbing up on itself. It collapses downward like a shoe coming down on a roach.

There is buzzing, furious buzzing, wet wings that won't dry because it isn't quite water that has gotten onto them, and it won't quite shake off.

There is a deep-down explosion under us and the hoy rocks. Again I'm thrown onto the deck and I hold tight, hold tight. I don't want to fall into that water right now. I stand up and look.

Bits of triangles float to the surface. The river quickly turns them back under.

"I think I got it," I call to the others.

"Jill," says TB. "Come here and show me you are still alive."

I jump down through the pilot hole, and he hugs and kisses me. He kisses me right on the mouth, and for once I sense that he is not thinking about Alethea at all when he touches me. It feels very, very good.

"Oh, your poor back!" says Molly Index. She looks pretty distraught and fairly useless. But at least she warned us. That was a good thing.

"It's just a scratch," I say. "And I took care of the poison."

"You just took out a Met sweep enforcer!" Andre Sud says. "I think that was one of the special sweepers made for riot work, too."

"What was that thing doing here?"

"Looking for Ben," says Molly Index. "There's more where that came from. Amés will send more."

"I will kill them all if I have to."

Everybody looks at me and everyone is quiet for a moment, even Bob.

"I believe you, Jill," Andre Sud finally says. "But it's time to go."

TB is sitting down at the table now. Nobody is piloting the boat, but we are drifting in midcurrent and it should be all right for now.

"Go?" TB says. "I'm not going anywhere. They will *not* use me to make war! I'll kill myself first. And I won't mess it up this time."

"If you stay here, they'll catch you," Andre Sud says.

"You've come to Amés's attention," Molly Index says. "I'm sorry, Ben."

"It's not your fault."

"We have to get out of the Met," Andre Sud says. "We have to get to the outer system."

"*They'll* use me too. They're not as bad as Amés, but nobody's going to turn me into a weapon. I don't make fortunes for soldiers."

"If we can get to Triton, we might be okay," Andre Sud replied. "I have a certain pull on Triton. I know the weatherman there."

"What's that supposed to mean?"

"Trust me. It's a good thing. The weatherman is very important on Triton, and he's a friend of mine."

"There is one thing I'd like to know," says TB. "How in hell would we get to Triton from here?"

Bob stands up abruptly. He's been rummaging around in TB's larder while everybody else was talking. I saw him at it, but I knew he wasn't going to find anything he would want.

"Why didn't you say you wanted to go Out-ways?" he said. "All we got to do is follow the Bendy around to Makepeace Century's place in the gas swamps."

"Who's that?"

"I thought you knew her, TB. That's that witch that lives in the ditch's aunt. I guess you'd call her a smuggler. Remember the Old Seventy-Five from last year that you got so drunk on?"

"I remember," TB says.

"Well, she's where I got that from," says Bob. "She's got a lot of cats, too, if you want one."

We head down the Bendy, and I keep a lookout for more of those enforcers, but I guess I killed the one they sent this time. I guess they thought one was enough. I can't help but think about where I am going. I can't help but think about leaving the Carbuncle. There's a part of me that has never been outside, and none of me has ever traveled into the outer system. Stray code couldn't go there. You had to pass through empty space. There weren't any cables out past Jupiter.

"I thought you understood why I'm here," TB says. "I can't go."

"You can't go even to save your life, Ben?"

"It wouldn't matter that I saved my life. If there is anything left of Alethea, I have to find her."

"What about the war?"

"I can't think about that."

"You *have* to think about it!"

"Who says? God? *God is a bastard mushroom sprung from a pollution of blood.*" TB shakes his head sadly. "That was always my favorite koan in seminary—and the truest one."

"So it's all over?" Andre Sud says. "He's going to catch you."

"I'll hide from them."

"Don't you understand, Ben? He's taking over all the grist. After he does that, there won't be any place to hide, because Amés will *be* the Net."

"I have to try to save her."

The solution is obvious to me, but I guess they don't see it yet. They keep forgetting I am not really sixteen. That in some ways, I'm a lot older than all of them.

You could say that it is the way the TB made me, that it is written in my code. You might even say that TB has somehow reached back from the future and made this so, made this the way things have to be. You could talk about fate and quantum mechanics.

All these things are true, but the truest thing of all is that I am free. The world has bent and squeezed me, and torn away every part of me that is not free. Freedom is all that I am.

And what I do, I do because I love TB and not for any other reason.

"Ah!" I moan. "My wrist hurts. I think it's broken, TB."

He looks at me, stricken.

"Oh, I'm sorry, little one," he says. "All this talking and you're standing there hurt."

He reaches over. I put out my arm. In the moment of touching, he realizes what I am doing, but it is too late. I have studied him for too long and I know the taste of his pellicle. I know how to get inside him. I am his daughter, after all. Flesh of his flesh.

And I am fast. So very fast. That's why he wanted me around in the first place. I am a scrap of code that has been running from security for two hundred years. I am a projection of his innermost longings now come to life. I am a woman, and he is the man that made me. I know what makes TB tick.

"I'll look for her," I say to him. "I won't give up until I find her."

"No, Jill—" But it is too late for TB. I have caught him by surprise and he hasn't had time to see what I am up to.

"TB, don't you see what I am?"

"Jill, you can't—"

"I'm *you*, TB! I'm your love for her. Some time in the future you have reached back into the past and *made* me. Now. So that the future can be different."

He will understand one day, but now there is no time. I code his grist into a repeating loop and set the counter to a high number. I get into his head and work his dendrites down to sleep. Then, with my other hand, I whack him on the head. Only hard enough to knock him the rest of the way out.

TB crumples to the floor, but I catch him before he can bang into anything. Andre Sud helps me lay him gently down.

"He'll be out for two days," I say. "That should give you enough time to get him off the Carbuncle."

I stand looking down at TB, at his softly breathing form. What have I done? I have betrayed the one who means the most to me in all creation.

"He's going to be really hungry when he wakes up," I say.

Andre Sud's hand on my shoulder. "You saved his life, Jill," he says. "Or he saved his own. He saved it the moment he saved *yours*."

"I won't give her up," I say. "I have to stay so he can go with you and still have hope."

Andre Sud stands with his hand on me a little longer. His voice sounds as if it comes from a long way off even though he is right next to me. "Destiny's a brutal old hag," he says. "I'd rather believe in nothing."

"It isn't destiny," I reply. "It's love."

Andre Sud looks at me, shakes his head, then rubs his eyes. It is as if he's seeing a new me standing where I am standing. "It is probably essential that you find Alethea, Jill. She must be here somewhere. I think Ben knows that somehow. She needs to forgive him, or not forgive him. Healing Ben and ending the war are the same thing, but we can't think about it that way."

"I care about TB. The war can go to hell."

"Yes," Andre Sud says, "The war can go to hell."

After a while, I go up on deck to keep a watch out for more pursuit. Molly Index comes with me. We sit together for many hours. She doesn't tell me anything about TB or Alethea, but instead she talks to me about what it was like growing up a human being. Then she tells me how glorious it was when she spread out into the grist and could see so far.

"I could see all the way around the sun," Molly Index says. "I don't know if I want to live now that I've lost that. I don't know *how* I can live as just a *person* again."

"Even when you are less than a person," I tell her, "you still want to live."

"I suppose you're right."

"Besides, Andre Sud wants to have sex with you. I can smell it on him."

"Yes," Molly Index says. "So can I."

"Will you let him?"

"When the time comes."

"What is it like?" I say.

"You mean with Andre?"

"What is it like?"

Molly Index touches me. I feel the grist of her pellicle against mine and for a moment I draw back, but then I let it in, let it speak.

Her grists shows me what it is like to make love.

It is like being able to see all the way around the sun.

The next day, Molly Index is the last to say goodbye to me as Makepeace Century's ship gets ready to go. Makepeace Century looks like Gladys if Gladys didn't live in a ditch. She's been trying for years to get Bob to come aboard as ship musician, and that is the price for taking them to Triton—a year of his service. I get the feeling she's sort of sweet on Bob. For a moment, I wonder just who *he* is that a ship's captain should be so concerned with him? But Bob agrees to go. He does it for TB.

TB is so deep asleep he is not even dreaming. I don't dare touch him for fear of breaking my spell. I don't dare tell him goodbye.

There is a thin place in the Carbuncle here, and they will travel down through it to where the ship is moored on the outer skin.

I only watch as they carry him away. I only cry until I can't see him anymore.

Then they are gone. I wipe the tear off my nose. I never have had time for much of that kind of thing.

So what will I do now? I will take the Bendy River all the way around the Carbuncle. I'll find a likely place to sink the hoy. I will set the ferrets free. Bob made me promise to look after his dumb ferret, Bomi, and show her how to stay alive without him.

And after that?

I'll start looking for Alethea. Like Andre Sud said, she must be here somewhere. And if anybody can find her, I can. I will find her.

There is a lot I have to do, and now I've been thinking that I need help. Pretty soon Amés is going to be running all the grist and all the code will answer to him. But there's some code he can't get to. Maybe some of those ferrets will want to stick around. Also, I think it's time I went back to the mulmyard.

It's time I made peace with those rats.

Then Amés had better watch out if he tries to stop me from finding her.

We will bite him.

La cenerentola

GWYNETH JONES

Here's a modern version of a very old story, but one with a sting in its very smooth and elegant tail. . . .

British writer Gwyneth Jones was a co-winner of the James Tiptree Jr. Memorial Award for work exploring genre issues in science fiction, with her 1991 novel White Queen, *and she has also been nominated for the Arthur C. Clarke Award an unprecedented four times. Her other books include the novels* North Wind, Flowerdust, Escape Plans, *and* Divine Endurance, *and a collection of fairy stories,* Seven Tales and a Fable, *which won the World Fantasy Award. Her most recent novel is* Phoenix Café, *and a collection of her critical essays,* Deconstructing the Starships, *was published recently. Her too-infrequent short fiction has appeared in* Interzone, Asimov's Science Fiction, Off Limits, *and in other magazines and anthologies. Her stories have appeared in our Fourteenth and Fifteenth Annual Collections. She lives in Brighton, England, with her husband, her son, and a Burmese cat. She has a Web page at http://www. homeusers.perstel.co.uk/dreamer/.*

ACT ONE: THE SCHOLAR GYPSIES

My first thought, when I saw the sisters, was that they were simply *too* perfect. They had to be identical twins: about 16 years old: tall but not too tall, sun-kissed golden skin, rounded and slender limbs, long golden hair, blue eyes. They were walking in step, arm in arm, whispering together; identical even in their graceful movements. One pushed back her hair, the other brushed an insect from her immaculate white shorts. Each gesture seemed a mirror image of the other. Impossibly perfect! Then I saw the mother, strolling along behind (she had to be their mother, the likeness was too close for any other relationship), and I thought perhaps I understood. The older model—or should one say, *the original*—was a very good-looking woman, a blonde with long legs, regular features and lightly tanned skin. Her eyes behind her sunglasses were no doubt just as blue. But there were details—lips that were a little narrow, a square jaw; a figure not so exactly proportioned—that added up to something less than flawless beauty.

I tried not to stare, though of course those girls must be used to open-mouthed admiration. Then I realized, with pleasure, that this amazing trio was actually approaching us. The older woman was about to speak. I sat up, with a welcoming smile.

Suze and Bobbi and I were in Europe for the summer. This had become the pattern of our lives in the last few years. We spent our winters in New Mexico, where I taught philosophy and Suze worked as a software engineer.

Every summer we crossed the Atlantic. As yet we had no fixed abode over here, but we were looking. We saw our travels as a series of auditions. This year we were considering the Mediterranean for the role of our summer home. But we had fled from an overcrowded villa-party on the Cote d'Azur. *Trop du monde* on the French Riviera. So here we were in mid-August, our comfortable trailer planted on a sun-punished hillside under the brilliant, mythic sky of Haut Provence, at the simple but very spruce and attractive "Camping International St Mauro."

"Wow," murmured my wife, Suze. She was lying beside my lounger on a blanket, there under the cork oaks. She propped herself on one elbow to gaze at this glorious vision. Our daughter Bobbi continued to pursue her new hobby of plaguing the little red ants that infested our terrace. She had scattered a handful of breadcrumbs for them, and as they staggered home with the goods she was blocking their trail with impossible obstacles and pitfalls.

"Hello," said the woman, at once announcing herself as English, and probably upper-class (but many English accents, I admit, sound absurdly aristocratic to American speakers). "I couldn't help noticing, I saw you in St Mauro earlier: you are Americans aren't you?"

"We're from New Mexico," agreed Suze, grinning. "I'm Suze Bonner. This is my wife, Thea Lalande. That's Bobbi, but she won't talk to you, she's an uncouth little kid. Isn't this place great. We just picked it off the road map."

Suze thought any place where there was heat and a minimum of human activity "great." The fact that St Mauro possessed no culture I could drag her around was a further advantage. I sometimes wondered why she allowed me to uproot her from her native desert at all.

"Absolutely ravishing," said our new acquaintance. "And so peaceful. I'm Laura Brown. This is Celine, and this is Carmen. We're staying outside the village." The twins smiled, perfectly. Laura Brown took off her sunglasses and gazed at Bobbi. "Actually, I was wondering if we would see you at the fete tonight."

"Fete?" Bobbi's head came up as if bouncing on a spring. "Will there be fireworks?"

Laura Brown laughed. "I'm afraid not!"

"Unnh." With a shrug, my charming little daughter returned to her evil deeds.

Our new friend, still watching Bobbi with curious attention, went on, "it's a small affair. Flamenco Guitar and—" She consulted a piece of paper taken from her shoulder bag.

"A couscous. At the bar called The Squirrel, *L'Ecureuil*. But there's only one bar, you can't miss it. Well, I hope you three will be there. It could be fun. A *bientot, enfin.*" "Au'voir," chimed Celine and Carmen. The heavenly twins passed on by. Trailing behind them came a skinny girl of about Bobbi's age, or maybe a little older: ten or twelve. She was wearing grubby blue shorts and a candy-striped teeshirt that had seen better days. Her rough brown head was hanging sulkily, her eyes fixed on the dust she kicked up with her dirty espadrilles. As she came level with us she looked up, and shot Bobbi a baleful glance. . . . I wouldn't have thought she had anything to do with the other three, except that Laura Brown turned and called: "Marianina, please keep up. And don't scuff your shoes like that! My youngest daughter," she explained, as if to excuse the sudden sharpness in her tone. "Such a little ragamuffin. There's nothing I can do about it."

"I wonder what went wrong there," murmured Suze, when the family was out of sight.

"You think the other two, the twins are—?"

"Of course. What else could they be, looking like that?"

Bobbi, naturally, pounced. Children have an infallible ear for their parents' indiscreet remarks. "What? What are they? What do you think they are?"

"Sssh. Nothing."

"They look like a pair of Barbie dolls," muttered Bobbi.

Suze and I agreed, via a silent exchanged glance, that the subject was closed. Another word, and our darling child would disgrace us by saying something incredibly rude, when we next met the beautiful sisters and their mama.

We decided not to risk the "couscous." We ate pasta under the cork oaks in the shimmering light of evening; with a sauce of stewed red-pepper strips and tomatoes, and a wine of the region which I'd bought from the campsite bureau. It was delicious, that wine: straw-yellow, dry but not too dry; and so delicately, subtly scented! The tepid air was tinged with indigo, the drowsy scent of the scorched *maquis* grew stronger as the sun descended. We seemed poised on a pinnacle of exquisite calm: like a foretaste of Paradise.

Suze touched my hand. "Here?" she murmured.

But my peace was not complete. I was thinking of Laura Brown and her twins, and the sad fate of that dirty little girl, trailing along behind such beautiful older sisters. I didn't answer at once. Suze reached over and traced with her finger a little knot of tension that had formed, without my realizing it, at the corner of my jaw.

"Not here."

She stood up, and stretched. "Why do I get the feeling that we've been invited to this festa by royal command? Well, let's go, anyway. At least we'll have something great to look at."

In spite of Suze's cynicism and my vague misgivings we had a terrific time that night at *L'Ecureuil*. The local population was out in force, far outnumbering us tourists; which always makes for a better atmosphere. The sangria flowed; and the guitarists were superb. Perhaps nothing less would have made the evening so memorable. But from the first, fierce, poignant attack of that music, that stiffened all our spines and opened our eyes wide, the festa was alight. Soon as the first set was over people were talking, laughing, speaking in tongues. Barriers of language, nationality and income vanished. People started dancing on the tiny patio, that looked down on Van Gogh terraces of olive trees in red earth. The stars came out, Suze and I danced together. The mayor of the village, a plump little woman in a purple kaftan and tiny black slippers, danced alone: the genuine flamenco, wherever she'd learned it, with haughty eyes and a fiery precision that brought wild applause. Celine and Carmen, indistinguishable in pretty full-skirted sun-dresses, one red, one blue, danced with anyone who asked them (I hadn't the courage). Suze said "all we need now is the handsome prince."

"But how's he going to choose between them?"

"He's a fool if he tries. He should take them both!"

I looked for the third daughter, and spotted her sitting in a corner beside a glum, fat woman in a print overall. She was wearing a different teeshirt but the same grubby shorts, and brooding over a half-empty glass of cola. The two of them seemed the only people in the world who weren't enjoying themselves. I know how moody little girls can be. Maybe it was her own idea not to dress up, and her own plan not to have fun. But I felt sorry for the child.

I was eating the couscous after all—having a good time always makes me hun-gry—when Mrs Brown came to join me. Suze was with Bobbi, indoors, with the crowd of local kids around the babyfoot machine.

This Englishwoman had a very direct way of asking questions and handing over information. As Suze had remarked, there was something autocratic about her friendliness. She had soon told me that the twins were what we had guessed. They were clones: genetic replicants of their mother, with a few enhancements. It was a simple story. She'd been married to a man who was unfortunately infertile, but luckily extremely rich. It had suited his fancy to have his beautiful young wife copied: and then, two of the implanted embryos had "come through" as she put it. "I carried them myself," she said, "though my husband didn't like it. He thought pregnancy would spoil my figure. But I couldn't bring myself to use a surrogate. It wouldn't be the same, would it? They wouldn't have been completely mine."

Later, the marriage having ended, her third daughter had been the result of a natural conception with a different father. . . .

A mistake, in other words, I thought. Or an experiment that went wrong. Poor kid!

"What about you? Did you carry Bobbi, or did Suze?"

"It was me."

Thea drew the short straw, we used to joke. We both knew I'd been the lucky one. One parent of a fused-egg embryo is always more compatible with the foetus than the other, and that's how the choice of birth-mother is made.

"And, excuse me for asking, did Bobbi have a father?"

I explained, with modest pride, that she was all our own work. The fused-egg embryo treatment, a recombination of the genetic traits from each female partner.

So we confided, quickly becoming intimate; like people who first suspect and then confirm that they are both members of the same secret society. As indeed we were, though there's nothing really secret about modern reproduction tech-nology. Bobbi had never met any prejudice. It helps, no doubt, that you have to be relatively rich, and therefore *de facto* respectable, before you can afford these techniques. I noticed that Mrs Brown's furtive interest in my daughter (which had struck me when we met on the campsite) diminished when she knew Bobbi's provenance. The regal Mrs Brown, I decided, had been afraid we Americans had a better, more advanced model of child than her twins. Now she'd assured herself that this was not the case—that Bobbi was a mere copy of her two mothers, with no improvements—her curiosity vanished. We passed on to other topics.

I wondered if I dared to mention the youngest girl, maybe suggest that she and Bobbi could get together. But when I looked around I couldn't see her. The corner where she'd been lurking was empty.

"What is it?" asked Mrs Brown. "Is something the matter?"

Celine and Carmen were still happily dancing. "I was looking for Marianina."

"Oh, she went back to the villa," she explained casually. "With Germaine, my nanny." She laughed. "Marianina hates parties. She's too young, she gets so bored." But her eyes wouldn't meet mine. I knew she was hiding something. Marianina, I guessed, had been sent home in some kind of disgrace. Poor little Cinderella!

Bobbi stayed with us at the bar until three A.M., along with probably every child of her age for miles around except Marianina. We stayed long after Mrs Brown and the beautiful twins had departed, until the very end of the party: when the flamenco guitarists joyously played and everybody sang, at the tops of our voices, the simplest of drinking songs: the songs that everybody in Europe knows; or sings along anyway.

—*ce soir je buvais!*

ce soir je buvais heureux!

A few hours later I woke up in the trailer, with a terrible hangover and the dim memory of Suze trying in vain to get me to take an Alco-soothe. Since even miraculous modern medicine can do little about the morning after once you've let things get that far, I got up. I took a tepid shower in our tiny closet bathroom and went for a walk to clear my head.

That covetable pitch on the topmost terrace, which we had admired when we first arrived, had fallen vacant. The red car that had been parked there had disappeared; so had the little climbing tent. I went up there and sat on a rock, in blissful solitude, gazing southward towards the twinkling three-cornered smile of the sea. I was thinking of a paper I had to write, for a conference in the fall; and of finding a house in Provence or the Alps Maritime, with vines around the door and a roof of roman tiles. It was so difficult to choose a resting place, in this summer world where neither Suze nor I had any roots. Too much freedom can be as frustrating as too little.

I wondered if I could see the villa where Mrs Brown was staying.

I didn't notice the little girl who came scrambling up the hill until she burst out of the bushes right in front of me—and stood there, glowering, holding what looked like a bottle of shampoo. It was Marianina. She had been expecting someone, but not me. This was my first impression as the child stood, stared, and then came slowly towards me.

"You left this behind in the showers," she said, in French.

"No, it's not mine."

It was very odd. I couldn't think what she was doing on the campsite, or why she was pretending that she'd come from the *sanitaires*, when those modest toilet facilities were in completely the opposite direction from her approach. She was dressed as she had been at *L'Ecureuil*, the same shorts and the same teeshirt. The contrast between this girl and the rest of her family was more startling in their absence: to think of all that golden perfection and see Marianina's rough brown head, her scratched, dust-smeared arms and legs as thin as knotted wire. She went on staring at me unpleasantly: a child already embodying the threat of adolescence, a neglected child who would throw stones, let down tires, perhaps steal. Perhaps she had stolen the bottle of shampoo.

"Were you looking for someone?" I tried not to sound aggressive.

"So, they've gone," said the little girl.

"Who?"

"My friends." She came closer: closer than was comfortable. Still sitting on my rock, I was trapped by her scrawny, demanding presence. I could feel her breath.

"What is it?"

"We were going to make a rocket." She still spoke in French. "But they've gone."

"I don't understand you. What do you want?"

With an indescribably sly and ugly smile, she thrust a finger into the open mouth of her plastic bottle, and then pulled it out covered in pale slime.

I jumped up. Perhaps I was overreacting, but I did not like the situation. I didn't want any part of a little girl—perhaps ten, twelve years old—who behaved like this. I did not want to be alone with her. As I sprang to my feet the child darted away. I went to the edge of the terrace and saw her, halfway down the hill already, slithering on her bony little rump. As I watched she reached the level ground, turned and stood malignly repeating that sexual-seeming play with the bottle and her grubby finger.

Back at our trailer Suze was making breakfast, breaking fresh eggs into fragrant melted butter. The bread van had arrived at the campsite gates, tooting like a steam-train. Bobbi came running back from there with an armful of warm baguettes. I made coffee. I didn't mention my encounter. We ate our *petit dejeuner sur l'herbe*, and I talked about the paper I was writing.

"How do you copy a chair?" I asked Bobbi.

"You could draw a picture."

"That would be a picture of a chair. Another chair is another sum of things taken out of the world. A certain quantity of wood, metal or plastics: varnish, maybe nails, wear on the machinery or tools; a measurable expense of food, or energy from whatever source. Something for something. It's like double-entry book-keeping. A thousand chairs means a thousand objects at a certain cost per unit. One can bring that cost down, but it is always, allowing for all your expenses, a substantial fraction of the first amount. But if you copy a piece of software a thousand times, what is the cost?"

I was getting my own back for the times when Suze, the scientist, would hold our baby entranced: explaining the table of the elements, the anatomy of a star.

"Erm, wear and tear on the keyboard? Wear and tear on the storage disc!"

"Infinitesimal," I said. "And not equivalent in the same way. This is the problem, Bobbi, and it isn't just a problem of economics. We have a system of values, of *morality*, based on people competing with each other to copy things, at the lowest possible cost per unit. That's capitalism. But when the cost, the object of all this competition, effectively disappears, what happens to our system? Life gets very puzzling. Do you remember the Mickey Mouse episode in *Fantasia*? When Mickey uses the magician's spell, and the magic broomsticks just keep on coming, appearing out of nothing, more and more of them, and they won't stop?"

I'd decided to call my paper *The Sorcerer's Apprentice*.

"Leave the kid alone, Thea," said my wife, passing me plate of eggs and dropping a kiss on the tip of Bobbi's freckled nose. "She has no idea what you're talking about, poor baby."

"No, I like it!" cried our daughter, bouncing up and down. "I like it! Let her tell me!"

Our miracle of the modern world: made possible by prosaic laboratory science, but to us completely magical. I thought of that other little girl and her starved, all-too-knowing eyes.

I went to the bureau to buy more of that wine. The manageress, an Italian woman with bushy black hair and a beak of a nose, was in a talkative mood. I had the impression that she approved of Suze and Bobbi and myself. She liked our American passports. She liked the fact that Suze and I were married, a pleasant example of the new world (a newer world than the USA!) showing affection and respect for the old ways. I mentioned the English family, and learned that Mrs Brown was not a regular visitor. She had arrived in St Mauro for the first time a week before: but she had created a good impression by spending money locally. We agreed that the twins were phenomenally pretty.

"And the youngest girl. I suppose she's made friends with some other children on the campsite? I saw her here this morning." I was uneasy about that child. Her malevolence, or her unhappiness, had cast a shadow on me.

"Ah. *La Cenerentola!*" The woman grimaced and shook her head.

It was the name I'd used myself. "Why do you call her Cinderella? Because of her sisters? The Brown sisters certainly aren't ugly!"

"I call her that because she's a sad case. Something went wrong, eh? One only has to look at the older girls to see what they are to the mother." She shrugged. "Vanity-parenting! I've heard of it. But it looks as if, the third time, Madame wasted her money."

I suppose one has to meet prejudice sometime. I muttered, (embarrassed, but feeling it was my duty to defend Mrs Brown), that Bobbi was also the result of an artificial technique.

"Listen. I'm not saying it's wrong. It's the fruit of it. Why bear a child, no matter how the baby was conceived, just to do her harm?" The Italian woman drew herself up, looked from right to left, and leaned darkly forward over her desk, with its innocent sheaves of bright-coloured tourist leaflets. "You saw her here, eh?" she hissed. "Do you know why she was here on my camping, *la Cenerentola*? She was looking for the couple who have left, those climbers. And do you know what she wanted with them?"

"Er, no."

"Well, I know. That is why they left, obviously, so suddenly: because she'd been with them, and they were ashamed. It was the woman, I expect. She did it too but she was ashamed, and she wanted to get her man away from the nastiness. Believe me, I tell you what I think. I don't say the couple weren't to blame. But it surely was not the first time for *la Cenerentola*. A child doesn't go around asking for that. Not unless she is getting it already, eh? Eh?"

I escaped, feeling terrible. If there wasn't a word of truth in the manageress's vicious gossip, it was still extremely distasteful. The next thing I knew, I'd be under suspicion myself. When I got the chance (while Bobbi spent the afternoon sleeping off her late night) I told Suze everything. We agreed that the child *did* look neglected, and there really might be something wrong, something ugly going on. What could we do? Nothing.

But Mauro had turned sour on us. It was time to move on.

ACT TWO: CINDERELLA AND HER SISTERS

Two weeks later we were in a seaside town called Santa Margarita, south of Livorno. We'd decided to give up camping for a while, and reserved rooms through the international clearing-house site on the Internet, that boon to impulse-travellers—our booking whirled in digital fragments by the wild logic of the global network, from Siena to Livorno via Hawaii, and Tokyo, and Helsinki. The hotel overlooked a quiet, bright piazza: a Renaissance chapel with twisted-candy marble pillars, a pizzeria and a cafe.

"It's quiet *now*," said Suze. "But at three in the afternoon, anywhere is quiet. Think of the noise at night."

"Oh, please, oh please," begged Bobbi, who only wanted to get to the beach.

The padrone explained that the window shutters were completely soundproof.

"My wife suffers from asthma, and cannot bear a stuffy atmosphere."

Ah, but when the shutters were closed tight these rooms—two pretty rooms, and a bathroom between them—would still be airy, beautifully airy, the way you Americans like, because of the inner courtyard—

I stepped out with him onto the open gallery. We looked down, we looked up. He explained the ingenious and environmentally sound air-conditioning system. It was a very nice courtyard, with a fountain pool in the centre and big planters full of greenery. I was delighted with our choice. I suspected Suze was delighted as well, but she was angling for a discount. My Suze always liked to squeeze the envelope: always trying to get the work done with one instruction the less.

"Suze, this place is lovely—" I began, perfidiously. I looked up, once more. *La Cenerentola* was leaning over the gallery rail on the floor above, staring at me. I stepped backwards, really shaken. That sour little face, peering down at me: so vivid, it was like an hallucination.

"I don't know," I said. "Let's go away. Let's think about it."

"Madame, is something wrong?"

"Thea! You look as if you're going to faint!"

And alas for me, I almost *did* faint. I was dizzy, it was the heat, maybe my period was coming on. I couldn't explain myself, I couldn't possibly tell the truth. Naturally, by the time the padrone had fussed over me, and his wife had administered delicious lemonade (for the sugar, the best thing for faintness), all discussion was over. We were installed.

But in any case I wasn't frightened any more. What was there to be frightened about?

I was left at the hotel, lying down, because of my faintness, while Suze took Bobbi for her first swim (the padrone having given careful directions to a very nice, really clean beach). I felt fine. After an hour or so I got up, and went out. There in the piazza, sitting alone at a table outside the cafe, I saw Laura Brown.

It seemed to me that we were both struck by the same emotions. We saw each other, would have liked to pretend not to recognize each other: we accepted the inevitable.

She smiled, I smiled. She beckoned me to join her.

"It was at Mauro," I said. "In Provence—"

"But of course I remember. Thea and Suze, the American couple with the charming daughter. And you're staying at La Fontana? What a coincidence!"

She insisted on buying me a drink, I ordered a Coke. I spoke of Bobbi, and how difficult it could be to keep a child entertained. I suggested (my voice almost shaking, I had such a bad conscience about my suspicions) she must have the same problem with Marianina. Maybe the two little girls could be company for each other?

It was all so normal. A holiday acquaintance, that neither of us really wished to pursue. Why did I have the strange conviction that as soon as I was out of sight, Mrs Laura Brown would leap up, rush into the hotel, collect her family, pack her bags and flee—like someone guilty of a monstrous crime?

I was wrong. The next day, Suze and Bobbi and I went together to the very nice, very clean beach. Almost at once I spotted Mrs Brown and her daughters. The twins, in matching green and gold bikinis, were unmistakable. The little girl, as usual, was sitting on her own, ignored by her sisters. I tried to stop myself from watching them. The beach was expensive (Suze muttered bitterly about the entrance fee) but it was beautiful. The Mediterranean, whatever the actual analysis of the water, was on its best behaviour: warm, silky, crystal clear. We sunbathed, we swam, we played ball. We had a delightful picnic, we lay in the sun.

"Tuscany?" murmured Suze, "Culture for you, the beach for me." She touched my hand, as we lay in the shade of our jaunty umbrella, while Bobbi splashed in the sea. "Here?"

But I was distracted. "I think I'll take a little walk."

I thought I would go up and say hi. I would say hi, and get a close look at Marianina. Your Cinderella daughter, Mrs Brown. Do you treat her badly? Do you use her worse than a servant? I felt myself a sadly inadequate fairy godmother, but at least I would try to assure myself that there was no need, that the problem was in my imagination. Mrs Brown and her twins were lying on identical hired loungers. Laura Brown was reading a paperback. Celine and Carmen no longer looked so beautiful now that I believed their sister was being in some way abused. They were giggling and chatting, heads together.

Marianina didn't get a lounger, she was sitting on the sand.

As I approached I was feeling extremely self-conscious. My courage failed: maybe I would give them a wave and walk on by. The sunlight glittered. Suddenly, in the twinkling of an eye, where there had been three sun-loungers there was only one. Mrs Brown and *la Cenerentola* were alone.

So then I did go up to them, propelled by sheer amazement.

"Hello." I said. And stood there, dumbstruck.

"Hello," said the lady, putting aside her book. I noticed that her bikini was also green and gold. Her eyes were hidden, her smile was frost in the sun.

"There were three of you here just a moment ago," I blurted: and corrected myself in confusion. "I mean four. You and the twins, and the little girl."

The cold smile faded. "It's Thea, isn't it? How nice to see you again. Good day." Mrs Brown returned to her book.

La Cenerentola was sitting at her mother's feet, wearing only a pair of dark-blue bikini pants. Her nipples were crusted with sand. She stared at me without speaking.

I went back to Suze, extremely confused. "Suze, you'll never believe this. The clones, Mrs Brown's beautiful twins, I just saw them disappear. They vanished right in front of my eyes! Do you think I'm going crazy?"

Suze rolled over, and glared at me. "Save it for your paper, Thea."

"What do you mean?"

"I mean I'm tired of this. What is your problem with that family? What is so fascinating about them? You've talked about nothing else for days." She jumped up, and stalked off to join Bobbi.

Suze didn't say another word about the Browns, but she must have been looking out for them. When we were leaving, at sunset, along with everyone else, she marched us across the car park to a big white Mercedes Solar that I remembered having seen in Mauro. Marianina was in the car. The twins were helping their mother to pack their beach stuff into the trunk.

"Hi, Laura," said Suze. "Hi Carmen, hi Celine."

"Hi, Mrs Bonner," chorused the twins sweetly, with their identical smile.

We walked away, Suze glowering triumphantly. I thought I'd better not mention that to me the beautiful twins had looked somehow *diminished* . . . Like two col-oured shadows of their former selves. The next morning I saw Mrs Brown again, for the last time. I was up early, Suze was in the shower. Mrs Brown and her family were checking out. Germaine, the nanny, was directing the porter, who was carrying their bags out to the car. Marianina was with her. Celine and Carmen stood looking a little lost, while their mother validated her credit, by passing an imperious hand across the identity-reading screen. Mrs Brown gave a sharp glance up at the stairs, where I was standing. She moved towards the door. Then Celine and Carmen . . . they melted. They flowed, they ran like liquid glass through the air. There was only one golden-haired figure, walking away.

I rushed up to the desk. "Did you see that?" I demanded. "Did you see? Flavia! Tell me!"

The desk clerk was our padrone's daughter, a sensible and intelligent girl. For a moment I thought she was going to deny everything. Perhaps she realized the truth was the best way to suppress my curiosity. She looked up, with wise young eyes.

"Dottora Lalande, two weeks ago a gentleman stayed here who was travelling with an *eidolon*, a hologram of his dead wife. We must set a place for her, serve dishes to her, arrange her room. He spoke to the digitally generated image as if it was alive. And though I know this is impossible, I am sure I heard the lady answer."

"What are you telling me?"

"And there was the family from Germany, with the teenage boy who had taken gene therapy to cure a terrible wasting disease. He was completely well, it was a miracle. At night this boy stayed out late. He came back to La Fontana not quite himself, you understand? Luckily, he could leap and hit the night-bell with his muzzle, so the porter would let him in. And it was easy enough to wash the paw prints from the sheets."

"What are you saying?"

"One sees everything, in the hotel trade, and one mentions nothing. These things happen, they happen more and more. It's best simply to accept them . . . and look the other way."

Mrs Brown had left no address, but I managed to get Flavia to tell me she had been heading north, to the Lakes. Over breakfast I tried to convince Suze that we had to follow and somehow track them down. I knew she was already angry with me over the Browns, but I couldn't help myself. I felt there was a disaster that I must try to avert. Suze accused me of being infatuated, either with Laura Brown or the heavenly twins. She refused to consider the idea of leaving Santa Margarita.

When Suze and Bobbi went to the beach, I stayed behind. I took our guidebook and set out to explore the town, in the hope that some distraction would help me to think. I had not dared to tell Suze about my second strange experience. For one thing, I suspected that young Flavia wouldn't back me up. But much as I hated to fight with Suze, I was desperate to unravel the mystery. What was happening to Celine and Carmen, and why? Had the desk clerk and I shared a hallucination? Or were Cinderella's sisters really capable of vanishing into thin air?

La Cenerentola was there. She had climbed on the railings outside the Renaissance chapel. She was swinging from them, head down, her feet kicking in the air and her hair brushing the ancient stone of the porch steps. As I approached she flung herself down, carelessly scattering the passersby, and stood glaring at me. She was wearing her favourite grubby shorts and teeshirt. As soon as she saw that she'd been recognized, she ran away.

Of course, I followed.

Marianina didn't run too fast. She made sure that I could keep up. Before long I found her waiting for me, in the small formal gardens that surrounded the much-eroded remains of a Roman temple; on the edge of the pedestrianized centre. It was a quiet place. This was the end of summer, and the flowerbeds had been allowed to fade. The Roman fountain in their midst was dry, the benches around about stood empty. There was a chirping of insects, clear above the distant hum of traffic.

Children, when they're left to run wild, are uncouth creatures. They'll tell silly, arbitrary lies if they feel caught out, but not one in a thousand will naturally invent the concept of polite conversation. Marianina didn't say a word to me at first. She sat on a lump of carved stone, its meaning eroded beyond recognition, and examined a graze on her knee.

"I thought you guys had left Santa Margarita," I offered, oppressed by her silence.

"We moved to a different hotel. We're leaving tomorrow."

"At the campsite in Mauro," I said, "they called you *la Cenerentola*: Cinderella, because of your sisters. Is it true? Did they make you feel left out?"

The child flashed me one of her sly, hostile glances. "Mummy sent me to wait for you. She says, leave us alone. Stop following us. There's nothing you can do."

Prince Charming, I thought, rejected the stepsisters, their artificial finery and their contrived attractions. He chose the dirty girl: with her little hands as rough as the cinders, her careless rags, her knobbly knees, her insouciant independence. It was the same with Laura Brown. I had thought I understood everything: right from that first night, when she told me her story at *L'Ecureuil*. It had been obvious that she had not been interested in either of her children's fathers. There was no adult lover in her life. Maybe she was one of those people who cannot tolerate another adult as a lover . . . that was why Marianina, scorned in public, had become the secret object of her affections, as the twins grew older.

I could understand how a child like this, deliberately humoured in all her native childish awkwardness (the sequences of DNA randomly recombined, no perfections but those of untamed chance and necessity) might seem the fairest, the true beauty. I could feel her troubling allure myself, and I'm no paedophile. She was so *real*.

The Italian woman at the campsite had made up a vicious story which probably had no basis at all in fact. A child can be corrupted, without any gross abuse. But whatever the actual relationship between Marianina and her mother, I now saw that the situation was not that simple. Perhaps it never is.

"What about your sisters? Will they be travelling with you?"

"Oh, them." A smug grimace. "I don't think they'll be around much longer."

I felt suddenly chilled. "What do you mean, they won't be around?"

"She hasn't said. But I think Mummy's taking them back."

Marianina slid to the ground, scouring the backside of those long-suffering shorts.

"Taking them back? Back where?"

"Back where they *came from*, of course."

La Cenerentola had performed her errand. She'd had enough of my solemn eyes and stupid questions. She left, jumping over the stones and skipping away, without another word.

INTERLUDE: THE PHILOSOPHER'S DREAM

I see a room in an appealing little hotel, somewhere in the north of Italy. It's a room that Suze and Thea could have chosen: deceptively simple, with every modern comfort hidden in a tasteful, traditional disguise. Through the window I see (but this is pure invention) a view of forests and mountains, a long blue lake under a cloudless fairy-tale sky. There's no getting away from it, we are in a fairy tale. Mrs Brown and her daughters, Thea and Suze; everyone else who shares our affluence. Our lives have become magical, by any sensible standards. Nothing is impossible, the strangest things can happen.

I see a beautiful woman, and the twin daughters who might be her sisters: daughters with that uncanny, replicant perfection of the optimized clone. She told me that their creation was her husband's idea. I don't know if I believe that, but in any case she has become tired of these flawless, sweet-natured dolls. The double mirror irritates her. The twins are sitting in a window embrasure, talking softly with each other. Perhaps they are deciding what they will wear tomorrow. They take comfort in clothes and makeup, because they know they have been superseded, I witness the transformation scene. I see how the two bodies are magically drawn across the room, and melt — at first resisting desperately, but finally calm — into the original of their flesh.

It is a triumph that *la Cenerentola* in the story might have longed for, before she dreamt of going to the ball. Fathers are chancy creatures, the handsome prince is a shadowy promise. But mother, even if she is not completely your own mother, is the first object of any child's desire.

Now Cinderella is alone, with the only handsome prince this version of the story needs. Poor Carmen, poor Celine. This time it is forever.

FINALE

I don't believe we'll ever get tired of Bobbi. I don't know which of us loves her more. But a long vacation brings out the strains in any relationship. I begin to wonder what would happen, if we should tire of each other. We walk hand in hand, Suze and Bobbi and I, and suddenly I suspect that we're taking up more space than three people should. I look up and see Suze a little further away from me than she ought to be. The air shimmers. For a moment there are two Bobbis . . . I am afraid that these moments may grow longer in duration. It won't be possible to hide the embarrassing thing that has happened, except by moving on: going our separate ways with our separate daughters, and praying that no further dilution occurs.

We have beaten the stern old gods of the 19th century. But in escaping from them, could it be that we have let something wild and dangerous back into the world? Our magical technology may have unsuspected costs. In the end, stretched and spread over the world as we are by our desires, perhaps Suze and I will vanish like Mrs Brown's perfect twins. We will lose hold of our fantastical riches and fade away, like the ball dress, the pumpkin coach, the rat coachman . . . in this case leaving nothing behind, not even a glass slipper.

Down in the Dark

WiLLiAM BARTON

As a contemporary sage once said, it's not over until it's over.

Here we visit the frozen moons of Saturn in the wake of a cosmic catastrophe that has destroyed all life on Earth, at a time when the human race has been backed into the tightest of tight corners and is on the verge of extinction, for a compelling and somberly lyrical study of how flickers of light can sometimes show up from the most unexpected of sources, even at the blackest of times, even when you're down in the dark, and it seems that all hope is gone.

William Barton was born in Boston in 1950 and currently resides in Durham, North Carolina. For most of his life, he has been an engineering technician, specializing in military and industrial technology. He was at one time employed by the Department of Defense, working on the nation's nuclear submarine fleet, and is currently a freelance writer and computer consultant. His stories have appeared in Aboriginal SF, Asimov's Science Fiction, Amazing, Interzone, Tomorrow, Full Spectrum, *and other markets. His books include the novels* Hunting on Kunderer, A Plague of All Cowards, Dark Sky Legion, When Heaven Fell, The Transmigration of Souls *(which won a special citation for the Philip K. Dick Award), and* Acts of Conscience, *and, in collaboration with Michael Capobianco,* Iris, Fellow Traveler, *and* Alpha Centauri. *His most recent novels are* White Light, *in collaboration with Michael Capobianco, and the new solo novel,* When We Were Real. *He had a story in our Fourteenth Annual Collection.*

Yesterday, August 4, 2057, was my fifty-third birthday. I don't think anyone noticed. No one said anything. Maybe birthdays don't count anymore. I sat in the half-track's cockpit, wearing my pressure suit, gloves off, helmet thrown back, steering by memory, as if caught in a dream. Four months. Four more months and I would've gone home, home to Lisa, whose letters said she was still waiting for me after all these years. But then the world came to an end, and all that ended along with it.

Sometimes, when I'm asleep, I still see the ending itself, see the newsreels transmitted after the fact from Moonbase. Just a nickel-iron asteroid twenty-three kilometers across, that's all. Knew about it for more than a year, they said, keeping it secret so there'd be no panic, making their plans in secret, carrying them off the same way.

Big rock like that, you'd think they'd've known about it for decades, but that long elliptical orbit, taking it out past Neptune . . . no number. No name on it but ours.

See those six bright flashes? Six thirty-year-old thermonuclear bombs going off, blowing the damned thing to bits. Now see the pretty pieces? Notice how they entrain and continue on their way? Twelve of them hit the Earth, one right after another, during the course of a long and interesting day.

I imagined people, imagined my old friends, seeing those secret nuclear flashes in the deep night sky, going, What the hell? . . .

The biggest one hit the South Pole, coming in almost level, and damn if you couldn't see the West Antarctic ice sheet lift right off, breaking to a trillion glittery bits as it flew into orbit.

The last one came down dead square in the middle of North America, not far from Kansas City. Not far from my house. I kept imagining, hoping anyway, that Lisa was asleep just then. But she was probably out in the backyard with all our old friends, maybe watching with my binoculars as . . .

I had the cabin lights off, surrounded by the dull red glow of a few necessary dials, the bluer glow of a half dozen small plasma screens, so I could see outside, watch bits of landscape jump into the headlights' wash, low hummocks of waxy ice, pinkish snow the color of the stuff that sometimes grows down in the bowl of a dirty toilet.

Following old ruts outside, my own tracks, driven over and over again.

The saddleback came up, ground leveling out, forming a very shallow caldera. I pulled over to my familiar place, pink snow mashed flat, glazed yellow from environmental heating, parked where I'd parked a hundred times already, killed the headlights, dimmed the panel lights as much as they'd go without full power-down, waited for my eyes to catch up.

The world came out of its own background gloom, like a ghost ship coasting from a fog, landscape tumbling down away from me, dull purplish hills and blue half-mountains, rolling away in the mist like the Adirondacks in springtime, rolling all the way to the shores of the Waxsea. More mist out there, then pale, glassy red nothing disappearing long before it got to where the horizon should've been.

From the heights of the Aerhurst Range, pressure ridge complex puckering the midline of Terra Noursae, maybe seven klicks from where *Huygens* set down, just a few weeks before I was born, you get one of the best views in the solar system. Maybe why I stop for it every time.

Overhead, the sky was bright now, though it was near the middle of an eight-day night. Maybe my eyes are learning to adapt quicker, quicker with each passing day. Maybe I'm at home here now.

Sure as hell can't be home anywhere else.

Everyone says the sky is orange here, even more orange than the sky on Venus, but it isn't. Hell, I've been to Venus. I know what that sky looks like. Not at all the same.

Sometimes, I try to imagine what the sky must look like from my old backyard. Sometimes, I imagine it just the way it was when I last saw it, not so many years ago. Other times I get a quick image of all those meters of ejecta that must be . . . well. Those times I let it go.

From overhead, Earth's sky looks dull gray-brown, lit up here and there, day and night, by a tawny red-orange glow. Moonbase newsreels say there's no free oxygen down there anymore, so the glow must be lava. Something like that.

Far above, hundreds of meters up, a flat snowdrift sailed along, potato chip waxflakes tumbling end over end in slow motion, twinkling, shiny, bouncing off each other, drift keeping its shape the way a terrestrial cloud keeps its shape in the wind. I clutched the Stirlings and brought the rpms as far down as the safeties would let me. Cut the cabin blower and listened to what the hull mikes were hearing.

There.

First, the dry-as-dust creaking of the landscape, stretching gently to and fro under Saturn's tidal strain. Then the dull, faraway moan of the wind. Not like an Earthly wind, wind blowing around the eaves of your house, groaning like a ghost through the branches of dead trees. Deeper here, almost subsonic, a wind that'd never been alive.

Finally . . . like dry, dead leaves, fallen leaves blowing along the gutter on a cold, gray fall morning, the sound of snow, drifting through the sky.

Saturn was barely visible behind the haze, nearly full, like a huge, featureless yellow moon, striated and edgeless. When it's daytime up here, if you know how to look, you can see the rings from their backscatter, like diamonds in the sky, arcing round the sooty smudge of Saturn's nightside shadow. Not now. Just that yellow disk, sitting up there, looking like an eyeless face.

I was out on Phoebe just once, fixing broken hardware. One-fifty degrees inclination to the ecliptic. Christ. It was a hell of sight, even from thirteen million klicks out. Maybe, someday . . .

Running late. I powered up the half-track's systems and got going. With the headlights on, Titan was just a murky moonscape under a vaguely orange indigo sky.

Down by the Waxsea, down where the atmospheric pressure can hit two thousand millibars, the sky is opaque, Sun, Saturn, stars, and pale, iridescent blue Rhea, all lost. It's not really orange, even here. Brown might be a better word.

I pulled out of a gray defile that'd grown narrower since the last time I'd been here, engaging the pillow tires manually to break through a little ridge of waxy snow, methane and ethane not really frozen, but caught up in a sticky mess of organic polymers, pulled around a smoky pool of colorless liquid nitrogen that'd be gone in days.

Ahead of me, on a sloping surface that'd long ago lost its volatile regolith components, Workpoint 31 was looking older than before, the dome habitat baggy in places, bubble airlock drooping a bit. The weather station looked fine though, antennae sticking up just the way I remembered, anemometer turning slowly. I pulled up to the power transformer, extending my electrical probe, docking and parking in one smooth move, cutting the engines, lights, everything that could be cut.

There was a spacesuited figure standing beside a snowmobile with the battery compartment yawning open, motionless, turned toward me. Looking closely, I could see a pale face, barely visible. No radio hail or anything. Fine by me. I got the rest of my suit on, closed myself into the half-track's too-small airlock, and thumbed the depress valve actuator. There was a soft *woof* as the air went out through the burner, igniting, flaring away with a brief blue flash that lit up the lock's teacup-sized porthole.

It seemed dark outside as I walked toward the snowmobile, the sky not quite . . . lowering. Haze coming down and . . . a silver golfball seemed to materialize out of the air, drifting down a shallow glidepath, coming between me and the waiting figure. The workpoint's structures were reflected upside-down in its surface.

Slow. Slow. Almost as if it were decelerating as it approached the ground. Maybe so. The air gets thicker fast down here. It hit the ground and exploded into a brief crater-shape, complete with central peak.

Ploink.

There was a quick, rippling mirror on the snow, then nothing.

The radio voice, a soft woman's voice, said, "Starting to rain. We'd better get inside."

As we struggled out of our suits, the habitat seemed incredibly cluttered. People had been bringing junk here and leaving it for years. Just leaving it. I don't know. Maybe, someday, it would've been thrown out. Now? No.

The inner surface of the pressure envelope, arching blue plastic overhead, was lumping here and there, slowly, more raindrops coming down. In just a little while, if the intensity of the storm increased, it would look like slick blue pudding, gently aboil.

The woman, who was dumpy, androgynous in her longjohns, but had a pretty oval face, dark green eyes, short, straight, straw-colored hair, held out her hand. "Christie Meitner."

I took the hand, feeling the small warmth of her fingers briefly in mine. "Hoxha Maxwell." Funny, there's less than a hundred people on Titan. You'd think after four years I'd know them all.

She said, "Hoe-jah?" Not smiling, just curious. Something nervous about her, too. Like she was afraid of me or something.

I spelled it for her. "Named after some two-bit Albanian dictator by socialist parents who thought Marxism might get back on its feet someday." 2004? Getting to be a long time ago, these days. I smiled, and said, "Rubbish bin of history, and all that."

She looked away for a moment, then gestured toward the habitat's kitchen module, much of it buried under piles of unrecognizable hardware. "I was about to have dinner. You, ah . . . afterward, if the rain's let up, I guess we could go down to the instrument platform and get started."

Rain never lasts long here. I shook my head. "I've been going almost thirty hours straight. If I don't get some sleep, I'll break everything I touch."

Looking at me, she seemed to swallow. "Don't you, ah, sleep in the 'track?"

"Batteries won't charge if the systems don't stay powered down for at least six hours." You know that. What's the problem here?

There was something like despair in her eyes.

Asleep, she breathed with her mouth hanging open, making a hollow sound that wasn't quite a snore. Slow, soft inhale. Long pause. Quicker exhale, louder, almost like a word.

She'd put me in her bunk, the habitat's only bunk, had then curled up on the floor, snuggled in a spare bunkliner somebody'd left behind, who knows when. The liner on the bunk was her own, permeated with her scent. Nothing perfumy about it, nothing feminine. Just a people smell.

I felt like my eyes were ready to fall out, but I was too exhausted to sleep, too exhausted to do anything but lie there, looking down at her, lit by dim instrument light. When she'd put out the habitat lights, it'd seemed pitch dark, but after a while, this blue glow, that red one, a little green over there . . .

Almost like daylight to me now.

Abruptly, I remembered a night when I'd watched Lisa sleeping naked beside me, streaming gold hair splayed out on the sheets, head thrown back to show the long, soft curve of her neck, mulberry-bright eyes closed, moving back and forth beneath paper-thin lids.

Dreaming.

What were you dreaming, back then, back when we were so young?

I forgot to ask.

Now I'll never know.

Nights like these, I wish I'd never gone to space. But space was the only way an engineering technician could get rich, move us to a lifestyle where we could have that family.

"A million dollars a year," I'd argued, trying to break through her tears. "A million dollars!"

How long?

It's a twelve-year contract, Lisa. Think. Think what it'll be like to have twelve million dollars. . . . And I won't be gone the whole time. I mean, a year on the Moon, a couple of years on Mars maybe. I'll be home from time to time.

Home to help you buy our new life, set things up. And when it's all over . . . instead, I signed on for four years out by Saturn. Four years of triple pay. And by the time I got here, somebody, somewhere, already knew what was coming.

Hell.

We could've died together, standing out in the backyard, holding hands, watching the end of the world fall on us from a star-spangled midnight sky.

It was still night the next day, of course, Christie reluctantly feeding me a breakfast of weak tea and algae muffins. No jelly, no butter, startling me when she pressed the teabags flat and hung them up to dry.

Of course. When it's gone, there'll be no more tea. I doubt there's butter and jelly any closer than Mars. I liked Mars, with its red sky and pale blue clouds. Part of the base where I was stationed, Oudemans 4, with its fine view of Ius Chasma, was under a clear dome. There was a little garden where some people were trying to grow oregano and poppies. I used to take my breakfast out there, sit and drink my instant coffee, nibble on my Pop Tarts and dream.

How many cups of weak tea can you get from a single teabag?

After breakfast, we suited up and got into the half-track, squeezing through the airlock one at a time, undocking, then lurching off along the terminal escarpment to where some old eutectic collapse had made a jumbled, sloping path down to the seashore.

Other than answering the few questions I could think of, techie stuff about her equipment problems, Christie was silent, looking away from me, troubled. Christ. Everyone I know is troubled. As we watched the murky landscape, foggy with nitrogen mist at two bar, roll by, I said, "How long you been here?" I've met people who came in with the first expedition nine years ago, mostly scientists like Christie Meitner, who've been out in the field most of that time. Some of 'em are a little boggy in the head.

Not looking at me, she said, "Three months. Before that I was on Delta Platform."

Delta Platform, on the other side of Titan, where the Waxsea is an endless, landless, featureless expanse of red-tinted silver-gray. "How long on Titan?"

She turned and looked at me with a slightly resentful look. Some people don't want to . . . think about it anymore. "A year. I came in with *Oberth*'s last run."

Oberth's last run. She was still on her way home from Saturn, halfway between Earth and Mars when it happened, which is why humanity's under-two-thousand survivors still have an interplanetary vessel. Last time I was back at Alanhold Base, I heard *Oberth*, damaged when she'd had to aerobrake through an ash-clogged stratosphere, was repaired, was on her way to rescue the Venus Orbital Station personnel.

Two thousand. Two thousand out of all those billions. Jesus.

But all I feel is that one damned death.

Used to be three fusion shuttles keeping our so-called space-faring civilization up and running, running supplies to a few hundred on Mars, a couple of dozen each at Venus, Callisto, Mercury Base, and the Fore Trojans. The four score and ten out here on Titan. Now there's just the one.

Ziolkovskii was caught in LEO, docked to the space station for repair and refit. I can't imagine why the hell people thought she'd be all right, why the station would come through in one piece. *Ziolkovskii*'s crew got real nervous when they saw what was happening. Got their ship undocked and under way. But.

They were transmitting to Moonbase the whole time, which made for one hell of a newsreel. All the big impacts were on the other side of the Earth from where the ship and station were at the time, but long before they rounded the planetary limb, you could see rocks rising into her forward trajectory.

Commander Boltano kept transmitting, kept talking calmly, deep, slow voice like nothing unusual was going on, panning his hand-held camera out the command-module's docking window, as the rocks got bigger and bigger, until there was nothing else in sight. His voice cut off with a grunt and the camera view made a sudden, rapid excursion, just before the picture turned to static.

Goddard, still a few days out, making all those wonderful timelapse videos of the impact sequence, exploded as she tried to aerobrake. I guess by the time *Oberth* got home a couple of months later, things had settled out a bit.

We got to the seashore, running down a long detritus slope, and pulled up to the research platform, which looked a little bit like those old-style unmanned landers, some of them going all the way back to the 1970s, you find scattered around the surface of Mars.

Beyond it, the flat, empty surface of the Waxsea stretched away like an infinite table, until it was lost in low, dark red mist. Behind us, the delicately folded face of the Terra Noursae terminal escarpment towered like cornflower blue curtains, mostly exposed water ice, the beach we stood on cracked icebits strung through with ropes of peach-colored polymer and black strands of asphalt.

Down by the mean datum, Titan's sky really is orange, dull orange even at night, with only invisible Saturn's glory for light, and it seems awfully far away overhead.

Christie was looking at me, face no more than shadowed eyes seen through her suit's visor. "Can we get started? I'd like to get back to work."

"Sure."

Funny thing. There were old snowmobile batteries scattered like a perimeter fence around the instrument package, seated in the beach "sand," tilting at angles like so many silent sentinels. As she showed me what was wrong, she kept looking away, looking out at the beach beyond.

I got to work on her problems, easily fixed, mostly shorted out capacitors and the like, carefully packing each ruined component in my toolkit as I replaced it. We used to throw these things away, but . . . well, maybe somebody can figure out how to fix solid states, one way or another. We sure as hell aren't going to make new ones out here. Not for a long time, even if . . .

Moonbase keeps talking about component fabrication, but it's just pissing in the wind. Watching *that* newsreel, my buddy Jimmy Thornton, who'd come in on the same flight as me, was scheduled to go home with me, commented there must be plenty of good hardware sitting in collapsed, half-melted warehouses on Earth.

Sure. Maybe we *could* repurpose a Venus lander and get it back to LEO. Figure out where to land, get what we needed, get back up.

Later that night, Jimmy cut himself with a utility knife, not leaving a note behind.

Maybe he figured I wouldn't miss him.

Maybe he figured I'd be along shortly.

Christie watched me work for a while, maybe not trusting that I knew what was what. Scientist types are like that. After a while, she wandered off, and, as I worked, I could see her spacesuit drifting about the beach, white against the colored background of Titanscape, out beyond the ring of abandoned hardware sentinels.

Something else we need to rescue. Ruined batteries are easy enough to fix, especially when you've got plenty of chemicals just lying around.

Finished, I buttoned up, turned, and watched her for a bit.

She had her back angled toward me, walking around the perimeter, half turned away, watching the ground. Every now and again she'd take a quick step outward, seeming to dance like a child, then stand and watch.

Going nuts already, Dr. Meitner?

Well, maybe so. Most of the scientists have just continued doing their jobs, gathering data, doing interpretations, just like . . . well. Techies keep doing *theirs* because if they don't, we all die right now.

She was standing with her back fully toward me, hands on hips, looking out to sea. There was a hazy layer of mist out there, Waxsea a little bit like Lake Michigan seen from Chicago's Loop on a cold November morning.

I walked toward her in the gloom, wondering which way our shadows would fall, if we'd had shadows. Just beyond her, I thought I saw something, a bit of yellow smudged on the waxy icecrust. Moving? A ripple caused by a thermocline in the dense air? Hard to tell. It . . . she took a quick step forward, stepping right into the puddle of yellow, which vanished like a mirage.

Off to one side, out of her suit-limited peripheral vision perhaps, there was another smudge, red, tinged with a bit of blue. As I watched, it started rippling slowly, moving in the direction of the hardware platform and parked half-track, aiming for a point midway between the two nearest batteries. When I stepped toward it, the thing edged away, following a long curve.

I heard a muffled gasp in my earphones.

Christie rushed past me, bounding toward it in a standard low-gee kangaroo hop. The ripple of red was still for a second, then, just as she got to it, seemed to dissolve into the sand.

"What the hell's going on here? What is that stuff?"

She turned to face me, skin around her eyes pale behind the suit's faceplate, hands behind her back like a naughty child caught in the act.

I stood still, transfixed by the terror in her eyes. Lot of people going crazy these days. No one should be surprised. "Are you all right?"

She nodded inside the suit, eyes going up and down. "Sure. Sure, I . . . they're . . ." Her eyes darted away from mine, scanning the landscape behind me for a second, but I was afraid to turn and look. "They're a kind of . . . a complex waxy polymer construct. They form at the interface between the Waxsea and Terra Noursae, apparently. Just on the beach, though I've found a few beneath the seacrust." She suddenly stopped talking, squeezing her eyes shut hard for a moment, looking away from me when she opened them again.

"What makes them move?"

"Our waste heat." Pause, darting eyes, then, "I've made some cold-soak instrumentation that shows they normally flow along tidal stress cracks in the beach."

Wandering goo. "Why were you . . ." All I could do was gesture. Hiding them from me? How could I ask that and still seem . . . reasonable?

There was a long pause, filled with my heartbeat and the soft groan of a distant wind, then she said, "I'm . . . not ready to publish yet."

I tried to stop myself from speaking, but failed. "*Publish?* Christie, there aren't any . . . I mean . . . uh."

Eyes blazing, she snapped, "*Shut up!*"

I felt cold sweat form briefly inside my suit. "Sure. Sorry, I . . . um. Sure." Inside the half-track, all the way back to Workpoint 31, she was silent, as if I'd ceased to exist.

Coming in along the south approach to Alanhold Base, you arrive at Bonestell Cosmodrome about twelve klicks out. This is where the first piloted landing set down, 20 April 2048, though when the second expedition arrived two years later, they tractored the components of the new base some distance away. Good idea, what with the contamination, the explosion risk, and all.

I skirted the edge of the ragged cryofoam disk that kept launches and landings from slowly digging the base's crater deeper and deeper in the ice, not intending to stop, glancing at the activity out of one side window from time to time.

TL-1, the original lander, almost always down for repair these days, was hidden in its hangar, yellow light glowing through the plastic, casting the gray shadows of workers like puppet-show phantasms. *TL-2* was on its meilerwagen being towed to our only launch gantry.

None of it's necessary, of course. When these things break down, we can use the little ships the way they were designed to be used, wingless lifting bodies setting down feather-light on stubby landing legs, lifting off again in a bowl of blue fire.

Great idea, indigenous propellant nuclear thermal rockets. Wonder how long they'll last? No longer than our last shipment of radionuclides. Then what? No answer.

Briefly, I thought of the talk Jimmy and I'd had about converting *TL-1* to run off one of the base's fusion cores. Could be done, I guess. *TL-1* won't last much longer anyway.

I'd ridden the landers three times in three years. Getting here in the first place. Going out to service hardware on Phoebe. Making emergency repairs at Ringplane Station.

Christ, that was beautiful. Like being a fly on a wall thirty thousand kilometers high, looking straight down to yellow Saturn's hazy cloudtops, feeling giddy at the thought of somehow falling.

Guess I expected one last flight, climbing up out of Titan's orange soup clouds into a sky true blue indigo, then black and spangled with stars, docking with *Oberth*, then going on home.

Back at Alanhold, I parked my half-track in the base's unpressurized garage, corrugated arch sort of like a Quonset hut open on both ends, docked to a charging mast, and got out. I always take a quick look up when I roll out through the airlock door, because you can see the last bits of your depress fire boiling around under the ceiling, like a misty, glowing blue cloud.

Out one end of the garage, I could see somebody'd strung a brand new UN flag on the base's pole, woven plastic fabric rolling gently in the breeze. Every now and again, it'd stretch out a bit so you could see the white lines of the map. Maybe they should reconsider the flag? Sooner or later, we'll run out of them.

There was a sparse snow falling, big, shiny white flakes like Ruffles potato chips, tumbling, shrinking visibly as they fell straight down. I don't think any of them reached the ground intact. We put a lot of waste heat into this environment, whether we like it or not.

I turned away, remembering a picnic I'd had with my parents. Just some city park, summer, blue sky with a few wisps of pale white cloud, kids running around, screaming and yelling. Us on a blanket. Ruffles potato chips. Sealtest French Onion dip with so much MSG it made me sleepy afterward. A&W root beer.

Dad was killed in an autohighway pileup back in the twenties. Made the national news, he and thirty or so other poor bastards ground up in the wreckage, media exposure forcing Congress to cancel the project.

Mom . . . I don't know. She and Lisa never really got along, so . . .

I went in through the base airlock.

After changing in my cubbyhole, not even enough room to stand fully upright, I went to the cafeteria, passing silent people in the hallways, stepping to my right, turning to face inward each time, men's and women's faces passing centimeters from mine, always with eyes downcast. Nobody in here, tables empty, dusty, chairs jumbled every which way, no one bothering to push them in any more.

I went to the freezer and got a couple of tacos, bemusedly wondering what life would be like when they ran out, now that Taco Hell is no more, picked out a pouch of cherry Hi-C while they were nuking, took my mess and went next door to the day room. More people here, TV on, playing a disk of the latest newsreel.

The screen was showing a gently curved planetary limb, layer of bluish haze hanging in an arc over featureless gray ash clouds. As I watched, light played in the clouds, first one dull spark, then others, propagating around it, then nothing.

Lightning.

I sat down next to Ron Smithfield, slouched in a chair with his legs splayed out on the floor's worn green carpet-tile. Green like grass. Green, the psych manuals said, so we'd feel comforted, when we were far, far from home.

He said, "You missed Durrell. Have to wait for the replay."

On the screen, the limb view was gone, nothing now but the gray clouds, growing steadily closer. There was a line of text, yellow-green letters, deceleration values crawling across the bottom of the image. "What'd the bastard have to say for himself this time?"

Rodrigo Durrell had been Secretary of Space in the second Jolson administration. He and the Undersecretary for Outer System Exploration, a Ms. Rhinehart, had managed an "inspection tour" of Moonbase, complete with their families, just before the asteroid intercept mission was launched.

Ms. Rhinehart, I understood, had a five-year-old daughter. Wonder what it feels like to be the only five-year-old girl in the universe?

Wonder if President Jolson knew? Did she stay on the job out of bravery or ignorance? Did she and her teenaged children huddle together in the White House, or in that old shelter in Virginia, waiting for it to happen? For a while, Moonbase kept trying to raise the National Command Post in Colorado. Nothing. Maybe Cheyenne Mountain took an impact.

Ron sighed. "Mercury Base personnel are dead."

The image on the screen was starting to grow dark now as the ash clouds got close. You could see a bit of pink where the plasma bowshock was starting to form around the probe's aeroshell. "I thought they had another few weeks of air left."

He nodded. "Apparently, once they understood *Oberth* couldn't come get them for another five months, they took a vote. Had the base doctor give them shots of surgical anesthetic. He radioed in their decision, then injected himself."

"Mmh." Nothing you can say about something like that. The image on the screen broke up into jags of colored static, quickly replaced by a colorbar pattern.

"Durrell says they're going to bring us all home in order, Venus, then the Trojan habitats; then Callisto. Then Mars, then us."

Home. I imagined myself on the dead Moon, sitting out the rest of my life looking up at dead Earth. "I guess we're last in case *Oberth* breaks down."

Ron nodded. There was a man on the screen now, some scientist type, talking, but I got up and left the room, not wanting to hear his excuses. Last time, he said it might take a year before a manned landing would be feasible, get a crew down there so we could see what the hell we've got left to work with.

That figure, I imagine, will be revised upward. Then revised upward again.

Nothing to do but go to the showers, then get myself to bed, get a good night's sleep so I could resume work in the morning. I took a towel and shampoo lozenge from the dispenser, got out of my coveralls and hung them on a peg, got under a nozzle in the far corner of the room, hot water sluicing over the back of my neck, cascading over my shoulders, running down my spine like warm, wet hands, making me shiver.

One thing we'll never run out of, here on Titan: hot water. Plenty of ice. Plenty of fuel for the fusion reactors.

A shadowy figure came in, carrying its own towel and lozenge, got out of its coverall and hung it on the hook next to mine, came walking across the room toward me.

"Hoxha," she said. Standing still, looking up at me with her big, dark eyes. Maybe waiting for me to make room for her under my nozzle?

I stood flatfooted, looking down at her, taking in a thousand naked-woman details. "Hello, Jennah."

She looked up for another few seconds, then her eyes fell. She turned on the nozzle next to mine, cloud of steam rising, making the mist even denser. The floor seemed sticky under my feet, whoever had tub-and-tile duty shirking the job.

I turned to watch her, slim, pretty woman with long, curly black hair turning slowly around under a fine needle spray, maybe showing off for me, maybe not, water streaming over her shoulders, jetting provocatively from her nipples, running down her belly, spattering between her legs.

After a while, she looked up at me again, stretching her arms over her head, arching her back, flashing the red dot of a steropoeic implant. "You used to be interested, Hoxha."

Sure. Used to interest me a lot. Lisa and I talked about this, agreed that four years was just too long, that we'd tell all when it was over and done with, tell all and forgive whatever there was to forgive.

I shrugged. "Sorry."

She looked at me for another few seconds, then nodded, looking away, turned off her shower and walked away.

I stood in the mist for a little while longer, thinking about the failure of my interest in . . . well. Went to my room and went to sleep. Didn't want to dream, but I dreamed anyway.

In the morning, tired after a night's sleep fractured by fragmentary images of things that didn't exist anymore, I stopped by Tony Gualteri's cubby on the way down to the half-track hangar. Tony was a geochemist who'd been on *TL-1* the day it set down on Titan, had been out here ever since, slowly turning into the small, wiry old bald guy I'd first met almost four years ago.

When I told him about the colored wax things I'd seen floating along the beach surface out by Workpoint 31, he looked puzzled and scratched a chin made black by dense beard stubble.

All sorts of crazy things on Titan, he said. Anything's possible.

I stood expectantly, waiting. Well?

He'd shrugged. It's her project. None of my business. Then he turned back to the screen of his little computer, doing whatever it is geochemists do with their data.

Do, even when . . .

My own day's work was up the coast, so I had a fine drive along the terminal escarpment, going to where one of the remote automated resource stations had inexplicably gone silent. Probably no surprise waiting for me there. Things fall apart. I'm here to fix them.

By the time I got there, the weather was lifting and the Sun was starting to rise, long streamers of golden light fingering through the orange-brown sky, diffuse smudge of red-gold smearing up through the mist hiding the Waxsea horizon.

It'd stay that way for a long time, Sun taking hours to clear the mist and disappear in the sky, becoming no more than a diffuse bright region, turning its part of the sky to shades of orange peel, layered like mother-of-pearl.

The station was on the rim of the escarpment, weather instruments spinning and nodding away, like nothing was wrong, sensors on cables hanging down the cliffside all the way to the beach, far below. I stood looking over the edge for a few minutes, imagining I could see strange colors shining in the sand, but . . . right. Imagination. Too far to see anything. Anything at all.

Problem turned out to be simple but aggravating: Something had shorted out a sensor head hanging off the end of one of the cables, sending a power spike back up the line that made the data recorder shut itself down as a safety measure. Then it couldn't come back up, because something was still wrong down at the sensor.

Easy enough to reset the computer, but it took me four hours to reel in the cable. Somehow, some kind of black, tarry stuff had gotten inside the instrument, gotten into electronics, and then acted as a very nice conductor, the exact definition of a short circuit. Took about a second to clean it out, saving a bit of sample in a bottle for whoever might be interested, and that was that.

• • •

Back inside the half-track, I sat in the driver's seat, looking out over the wide, silver-red expanse of the Waxsea, toward the dark mist of the horizon, smelling the faint odors of Titan that'd made it through the lock-purge event, accompanying me inside.

They aren't bad smells. Not bad smells at all. Certainly not the organic rot odors some old writers had imagined, imagination hardly colored by rational thought. Just a faint, crisp smell like white campstove gas, uncontaminated by oxygenation compounds. I remember my grandfather talking about the pleasant smell of the gas pump, back when he was a boy, back before they loaded the fuels with ether and alcohol. That and an occasional whiff of creosote, Titan smelling like an old-fashioned telephone pole, weeping black tar in the hot summer sun.

Thinking about black tar, feeling heavy lidded, the Titanscape seemed to expand in my eyes, filling them up, driving away the insides of the half-track. Like I was outside. Like I could walk around outside, feel the wind in my hair, icy silver golfball raindrops ploinking on my skin, the flutter of waxy snowflakes like butterflies in my face.

What the hell was it about that stuff in the sensor head?

I really haven't learned enough about Titan despite my years here. Too busy being Mr. Fixit. Scientists not caring what I knew or didn't know.

Jennah. Jennah tried to talk to me sometimes, times when we were finished with what we had in common, lying cramped together in her bunk or mine. Tried to talk to me about her specialty, some branch of meteorology, studies on the high-pressure atmospheres of gas giants.

Can't get there from here, she'd said. No trips to Jupiter, to Saturn. Not in my lifetime. Maybe, someday, a bit of work high in the skies of Uranus or Neptune? Maybe in a generation? Too damned late for *me*, she'd said. Titan. Titan is all there'll ever be for me.

Prophetic words?

In all innocence, I guess.

And, talking, she made it sound like nothing more than numbers, reducing a beauty that had the power to mist my eyes into something like math homework. *Cubus plus sext rebus aequalis vigentum.*

Once, staggering under the workload of a powered exoskeleton, I'd looked off the top of Ishtar's Veil, high in the Maxwell Montes of Venus, and seen a colored glory, swirling with the ripples of a Kirlian aura, stood transfixed by it. No numbers there. No numbers at all.

I'd shut Jennah up with renewed kisses, overwhelming her with the demands of innumerate flesh. After a while, she gave up telling me about the arithmetic of her dreams.

In time, I fell asleep, hoping to dream about Jennah, at least. Dream about the things we'd done together, the simple fun we'd had in those little rooms. Maybe, if I dreamed that dream, I'd awaken in the night to find myself flooded with renewed desire. Maybe in the morning, I'd turn this thing around and drive on back to base. Drive back, look Jennah up and . . . what the hell would they do if I took some extra time off? Fire me?

Instead, sleeping, I dreamed about Christie Meitner, dumpy in her longjohns, barely human in her pressure suit. Christie Meitner and her fields of color. Christie Meitner hopping like a maniac, hopping on puddles of melted crayon stuff, driving the colors away.

I woke up in the morning, looked for a bit at my refrigerated sample, and then set sail for Workpoint 31, calling base to let them know I was sidetracked, that I'd call them again later with a revised schedule.

It's not far out of the way, I thought. A few hours, that's all.

She wasn't at the habitat, blue dome looking baggier than ever, rather seedy by daylight, and didn't respond to my radio hail. Well. Snowmobile's gone, at any rate. Since there was plenty of juice in the batteries, I turned and drove on, following the tracks down to the edge of the escarpment, heading for the rubble fall and her instrumentation site.

For some reason, I stopped a few hundred meters shy of the turn and got out, listening to the soft woof of the vent burner, wondering if she'd see the cloud of blue flame as it dissipated, rising above the cliff's edge.

I walked down that way, waxy surface crackling under my boots, steam rising around me once I got off the beaten track and started disturbing virgin regolith, finally stopping right on the verge, looking out into open space. The beach, silver sugar crystals woven with orange and black thread. The silver-red sea. The red-orange-brown haze farther on. The sky, orange and brown with red clouds and dark, faraway snow, descending blue bands of rain like shadows in the mist.

A soft voice inside whispered, *Alien world.* Truly alien. Moon, Venus, Mars, all just dead rock, whether under black sky, yellow, or pink. This place, though . . . I shivered slightly, though it was hot in my suit, sweat trickling down my ribs, under my arms, trickling down 'til absorbent undergarments wicked it up, fed it to the suit systems, turning it back into drinking water.

Below, stark and alien in the middle of the beach, Christie's instrument cluster was unnaturally motionless, *powered down,* I realized. Christie herself was a tiny, spacesuited white doll figure perched precariously atop the weather station access platform.

Batteries. The dead batteries were gone too. Ah. Over there, piled at the foot of the eutectic fall, where she'd also parked the snowmobile. Maybe she was planning on hauling them back to camp for someone to take away. Good idea. Nice of her to . . .

Beyond her on the beach, right down by the edge of the sea, was a writhing spill of color. Blue. Green. Red. A broad stripe of olive drab, like a foundation between the others, making it almost look like . . . well, no. Only to me. Christie's down by the beach. What was she seeing?

The colors were moving slowly, like swirls of oil in a lavalite.

I released my suit's whip antenna and turned up the transmitter gain, intending . . . the colors suddenly started to jitter and Christie seemed to crouch, as if coiled by tension. Like she was . . . expecting something? Jesus. Imagination run riot.

I said, "Christie?" There was a background hum in my earphones, feedback from the half-track communication system.

The colors jumped like water splashing away from a thrown rock, but Christie didn't look up, seemed wholly focused on what she was seeing.

"Christie? Can you hear me?" Could she possibly have her suit *radio* turned off? Stupid. Fatally stupid in this place.

And the colors? They broke up into jags and zigzags as I spoke.

Waste heat. Radio waves are a form of heat. Just another sort of electromagnetic radiation, pumping energy into the environment.

Christie stood up straight, looking at her chaotic colors, putting one hand to her helmet, as if trying to scratch her head. She looked down, bending slightly at the waist so she could check to see her suit controls. What? Checking to make sure everything that could be turned off was?

"Christie!" The colors pulverized into hundreds of tiny globules, which started winking out rapidly, one by one, then in groups.

Christie suddenly stiffened and spun in place, looking up, first at the clathrate collapse, then scanning along the top of the cliff. I was just a speck up here, but starkly alien against the sky, and she saw me in seconds.

Long moment of motionlessness, a quick glance back to where the colors had been, as if reassuring herself they were gone, then she waved to me. It took a minute or so before she remembered to turn on the radio.

By the time I'd gotten the half-track down to the bottom of the fall, wondering whether I ought to inject any words into the silence, failing to make any decision, Christie'd turned the instrument station back on, its weather station spinning and nodding, my comm system picking up its signal, data relayed to Workpoint 31, then on back through the microwave link to Alanhold.

How much energy is there in a microwave beam?

Plenty, I guess. Human science is playing merry hell with the Titanian . . . oh, hell. Ecosystem's not the right word, is it? Not in this dead place. Well. Our science wasn't making nearly the mess here Mother Nature made of Earth.

When we're gone, Titan will get over it.

Interesting to imagine a solar system empty but for our pitiful few ruins. I helped her load all the dead batteries into the half-track's unpressurized cargo bin, then followed her home in the snowmobile's wake, watching its misty rooster tail gradually grow smaller as she drew ahead.

By the time I got into the habitat, she was already stripped to her longjohns, bending over the open refrigerator door, rooting around among a meager pile of microwave delights. Holding the red plastic sack of a Quaker meatball sub in one hand, she half turned, face curiously blank, and said, "You want anything? I got, uh . . ." She twisted, looking back into the fridge.

All sorts of goodies.

God damn it.

I said, "Christie, we need to talk about what you just did. I mean, turning off your *radio* . . . ?"

She turned her back to me, putting the sub away, slowly closing the refrigerator door, slowly straightening up, facing the wall. Finally, a whisper, "What did you *see*, Hoxha? How long were you . . ."

How odd. What *did* I see? While I was thinking, she turned and looked at me, startling me with the depth of fear in her eyes. What the hell could I *possibly* have seen, that I . . . "I'm not sure. You were watching . . . colors on the beach, over by the sea shore."

A bit of relief.

"You know, it's funny," I said, watching carefully. "Those colors almost looked like they were . . . I don't know. Making a picture. Swirls. Like abstract art."

The fear spiked.

She said, "Did you . . . mention what happened last time to . . . anyone?"

I told her about Gualteri, watching her swallow before she spoke again.

"What did he say?"

I shrugged. "Said it was none of his business. Said you'd let us know when you were ready to . . . puh—publish." *Publish!* Jesus.

Audible sigh, eyes rolling back a bit. Then she looked up at me, stepping closer, and said, "That's right, Hoxha. My business. Um. I'd like you to promise me you won't . . ."

"Christie, I want to know why you turned the radio off. Now." People willing to violate safety regs for their own purposes could kill us all. And you know that, Dr. Christine Meitner, Ph.D.

The look in her eyes became almost desperate. "Hoxha, I'll give you anything you want to keep your mouth shut."

Laughter made me stutter again. "You're offering me a *bribe?* What the hell did you have in mind, your Swiss bank account?" Scientists like this would get a pretty penny for a trip out here. A lot more than some miserable little engineering tech. "You think there's anything *left* of the fucking Alps?"

That made her flinch for just a second, not quite getting through. Me, I suddenly saw Geneva in flames as the sky burned blue-white with tektite rain.

She looked away, breathing with her mouth open, swaying slightly. When she turned back, I was shocked to see tears in her eyes. She said, "Christ, Hoxha. Please. I'll give you anything you want! Just name it!"

Then she took the zipper ring of her longjohns and pulled it open, open all the way down the front, showing me big, flabby breasts, roll of soft fat around her belly, ratty tuft of reddish-brown pubic hair peeking through the vee at the bottom.

Standing there then, looking at me, eyes pleading.

And I felt my breath catch in my throat, caught by a bolt of unfamiliar feeling.

I put up my hand, palm toward her and, very softly, said, "Christie. Just tell me what's going on, okay?"

She looked down then, face clouded over. Slowly zipped up her longjohns, and I almost didn't catch what she said next.

It was, "I think the melted-crayon things are alive."

I held my laughter, looking at her, mouth hanging open.

It's all a lifetime ago, for all of us.

I remember when I was a little boy, seven years old, I guess, sitting with my grandfather, who must have been in his early sixties then, watching reports from the Discovery lander, setting down on Europa, releasing its probe, drilling down and down through pale red ice, down to a sunless sea.

Remember my grandfather telling me how, when he was seven, it'd been Sputnik on the TV, dirigible star terrifying on the edge that atom-menaced night, his grandfather a man born when the Wright Brothers flew, man who remembered being a little boy when Bleriot made his fabulous channel crossing.

There was no life under the icy crust of Europa, just a slushy sea of organics, scalding bubbles of water around lifeless black smokers. My grandfather died a few months before the first men got to Mars and proved there was no life there either, probably never had been, just as his grandfather died not long before Apollo touched down on the Moon.

I figured I'd probably die just before men got to the nearest star, living on in some little boy's memory.

Shows how wrong you can be.

And now here I stood on Titan's lifeless chemical wonderland, facing a woman who'd gone mad, suffocating in a delirium of loss and denial.

Christie didn't argue with me, anger growing in her eyes, displacing the fear, masking her with the familiar scientist ego I'd seen on so many self-important faces, so often before. Sometimes they say, "Well, you're just a tech," and turn away. More often than not, I guess.

Christie led me outside to the half-track and made me drive her back down to the beach. We parked the vehicle well clear of the instrument station and she told me to stand on top of the cargo bin. "You stay here and watch. Otherwise we'll make too much waste heat and . . ."

On the run then, no more words for me.

Over by the instrument station, she took a pair of utility tongs and fiddled with something I could see sticking out of the beach regolith. Squint . . . yes. The top of a small dewar bottle. When she uncorked it, a hazy mist jetted, like smoke from a genie's bottle, rolling briefly, beachscape beyond made oily looking by the vapor.

"What's that stuff?"

She was panting on the radio link, out of breath, voice loud in my ears as she pulled the bottle from the ice. "Distilled from beach infiltrates. It's . . . what they eat."

She had it clear now and was scurrying toward the rimy area where cracked-ice beach became Waxsea surface.

"What're you . . ."

"Shut up. Watch."

She suddenly dumped the bottle, just a splash of clear liquid that quickly curdled and grew dark, billow of greasy fog momentarily disfiguring the air, then scuttled back toward me, dropping off the tongs and empty bottle as she passed by the station.

And it didn't take long for the colors to bloom.

Before she got to my side, blobs of red and yellow, pink, green, blue, were surfacing by the edge of the beach. Surfacing and then sliding inward, making the beginnings of a ragged vortex around the chemical spill. Around and down, dropping under the surface, not quite disappearing, surfacing again.

The smoking puddle of goo started to shrink.

And Christie, standing beside me now, said, "You see? You *see?*"

I said, "I don't know what I'm seeing. I . . ." I jumped down off the half-track, bounding slowly in the low-gee, heading across the beach.

Christie said, "*Stop!* Stop it, you'll . . ."

I stopped well short of the slowly writhing conflagration of colors, marveling at how they stayed distinct from one another. You'd think when the blue one touches the yellow, there'd be a bit of green along the interface. Nothing. Not even a line. Not even an illusion of green, made by my Earthgrown eyes.

They looked sort of like cartoon amoebas, amoebas as a child imagines them before he's looked through a microscope for the first time and realized "pseudo-pod" means exactly what it says.

And it really did look like they were eating the goo.

Suddenly, the blue blob nearest where I stood became motionless. Grew a brief speckle of orange dots that seemed to lift above its surface for just a moment, then it was gone, vanished into the beach ice.

All in the twinkling of an eye, too quick for me to know exactly what I'd seen.

The others followed it into nothingness within a second or so, leaving the smoking goo behind, an evaporating puddle less than half its original size.

I think I stood staring, empty-headed, for about thirty seconds, before trying to imagine ways you could account for this without invoking the magic word *life*. "Christie?"

Nothing. But I could hear her rasping breath, made immediate by the radio link, though she could have been kilometers away. "Christie . . ." I turned around.

She was standing right behind me, less than two meters away, eyes enormous through the murky faceplate of her spacesuit. She was holding my ice axe, taken from its mount on the outside of the half-track, clutched in both hands, diagonal across her chest.

I stood as still as I could, looking into her eyes, trying to fathom . . . Finally, I swallowed, and said, "How long have you been standing there?"

"Long enough," she said. Then she let the axe fall, holding it in one hand, head raising a few icechips from the beach. "Long enough, but . . . I couldn't do it."

She turned and started to walk away, back toward the half-track.

The ride back to the habitat was eerie, full of that shocky feeling you get right after a serious injury, when the world seems remote and impossible. I couldn't imagine what would've happened if she'd tried to hit me with the axe.

Like something out of one of those damned stupid old movies.

The one about the first expedition to Mars, movie made almost a hundred years ago. The one where the repair crew is out on the hull when the "meteor storm" comes. There's a bulletlike flicker. The inside of this guy's helmet lights up, showing a stunned face, twisting in agony, then the light goes out and he's dead, faceplate fogged over black.

Just like that.

Our suit pressure's kept just a few millibars over Titan ambient by helium ballast. Maybe if she cut my suit, there'd be a spark and . . . I pictured myself running for the half-track, spouting twists of slow blue flame.

She said, "I guess . . ."

Nothing. Outside, the sky was dull brown and streaked with gold, as well lit as Titan's sky ever gets. Somewhere up there, Saturn's crescent was growing smaller, deepening shadow cast over her rings. You could tell where the sun was, a small, sparkly patch in the sky, like a bit of pyrite fog.

I said, "I keep trying to think of ways it could just be some fancy chemical reaction. I mean, organic chemistry . . ."

She snickered, making my skin crawl.

Back in the habitat, out of our suits, sitting at the table in our baggy underwear, we ate Caravan Humpburgers so old the meat tasted like filter paper, the buns stiff and plasticky, and mushy french fries that must've been thawed and refrozen at least once in their history.

Too much silence. Christie sat reading the ads on the back of a Humpburger package. Something about a contest where if you saved your wrappers and got four matching Humpy the Camels, you could win a "science vacation" to Moonbase.

I pulled the thing out from under her fingers and looked at the fine print. The trip date had been seven weeks before the impact. Christ, I said, "Maybe whoever won this is still alive."

Or maybe, knowing what was about to happen, they just sent him home to die.

Christie was staring at me, eyes big and unreadable.

"You going to tell me about the crayon things now?"

Silence, then she slowly shook her head.

I found myself thinking about the way she'd looked a couple of hours ago, offering her virtue to me like . . . hell. Like a character in one of those silly romance vids Lisa was always watching when we . . . nothing in my head now but Christie with her suit liner zipped open, titties hanging out, eyes begging me to . . .

I felt my face relax in a brief smile.

Her eyes narrowed. "Who you going to tell?"

"Nobody. I guess I was . . . reconsidering your offer." My own snicker sounded nervous.

Christie's face darkened and her eyes fell, clouding over with anger. Then she said, "I . . . I'm not steropoeic."

Not . . . I suddenly realized the magnitude of her bribe, what it might've cost her to make the offer.

And then I was picturing us together, crammed into the little bunk, maybe sprawled on the habitat floor, having cleared away junk to make a big enough space.

Felt my breathing grow ever so slightly shallow?

Really?

No way to tell.

I said, "Sorry. I was just trying to . . . lighten things up. You know. I mean . . . when I saw you with that axe . . ."

She nodded slowly. "Are you really not going to tell?"

I shrugged. "What difference does it make?"

Eyes hooded. Keeping something to herself.

"You going to tell me?"

Long, shadowy look. Making up her mind about what kind of lie she might want to tell. The silence drew out, then there was that same little headshake.

I said, "Okay," then turned away and started getting into my suit, while she sat and watched. Every time I looked, there was something in her face, like she wanted to spill whatever it was.

Every time she saw me look, her face would shut like a door.

Once my suit was on and pressurized, I went out through the lock and was on my way.

I tried thinking about it rationally, all the long drive back, but I couldn't. All that kept coming into my head was, *What difference can it make now?* and, *Why does she care?*

Care enough to pick up an axe and consider splitting a doomed man's head.

There are fewer than two thousand people left alive in the entire universe. We are all going to die, sooner or later, when the tech starts to fail, when our numbers fall, the spare parts run out . . . when we all go mad and run screaming, bare-ass naked, for the airlocks.

I pictured myself depressing the half-track, rolling out the lock door, rising to my feet in godawful cold, taking a deep breath of ghastly air and . . . hell. Can't even imagine what it might be like.

Like sitting in the electric chair, heart in your throat, senses magically alert, waiting for the click of the switch, the brief hum of the wires and . . . and then what?

We don't know.

Funny. Just a day ago, just yesterday, I thought I knew. Thought I wouldn't mind when the time came that I . . . yeah. Like Jimmy Thornton and his utility knife. Just like that.

I thought about getting myself a big bowl of nice warm water, sitting down on my bunk, all alone with the bowl between my legs, putting my hands and the knife under water, making those nice, painless cuts, watching the red clouds form.

Probably be a little bit like falling asleep, hm?

Jimmy looked asleep when they found him. Didn't even spill the water when he went under.

I crested the last hill before the base, Bonestell Cosmodrome coming over the horizon, and parked the half-track on a broad, flat ledge at the head of the approach defile, wondering why the hell my skin had begun to crawl.

TL-2 was on the launch pad now, tipped upright, fully fueled, her meilerwagen towed away. On Earth, a rocket like this is always surrounded by a falling mist of condensation. Here, where heating elements are used to keep the fuel from gelling, there's a narrow, rippling plume, mostly thermal distortion, going straight up.

Today, it only went up a few hundred meters, then was chopped off by wind shear.

As I watched, the engines lit, bubble of blue glow swelling between the landing jacks, *TL-2*'s dark cone shape lifting slowly. There was a sudden, snarled blossom of red-orange fire spilling across the plastic as superheated hydrogen started combining with atmospheric components, nitrogen, miscellaneous organics, HCN a major combustion byproduct.

The flame was a long, beautiful tongue of blue-white-yellow-red, swirling like a whirlwind as it climbed against the orange-brown sky, passing through first one layer of diaphanous blue cloud, then another, then disappearing, becoming diffuse light, then nothing.

She was on her way to Enceladus, I knew, where we'd found a few million liters of helium trapped in an old ice-9 cell, the precious gas one of the few things we couldn't make or mine on Titan.

As I put the half-track in gear, heading on home, I thought about what it would be like to try to live for the rest of my life on the Moon, Earth's moon, the only real Moon, dead old Earth hanging like an ember in the sky.

Maybe we're making a mistake.

Maybe they should all come here.

Driving under a featureless brown sky, surrounded by a blue-misty landscape of red-orange-gold, I tried thinking about Christie's little beasties again, but failed.

I wound up hiding in my room, staring at the bulkhead for a while, then turning on the miniterm, watching with alarm as the screen sparkled, choking with colored static for a moment before the menu system came up.

What will happen when the electronics go?

Will we all die then? Or try lashing up homemade replacements, try flying without guidance, try . . . there was a space program before there were real computers. Men on the Moon, that sort of thing. That technology might have gotten us out here. Maybe not.

Nothing in the base library I hadn't seen a hundred times already, other than those last dozen episodes of *Quel Horreur*, the French-language sitcom that'd been all the rage right before the end. JPL wasted one of its last uplinks on that and . . . well, they knew. They must've known. What were they thinking?

Can't imagine.

I'd watched about thirty seconds of the first one, happy laugh-track, pale blue skies, white clouds, green trees, River Seine and *Tour Eiffel*.

Stayed in my room so I wouldn't have to deal with Jennah, who kept on looking at me as I stopped by the mess to pick up my dinner. Went to my room and then couldn't stop thinking about her, about the last time we'd . . . which led to thinking about Christie with her longjohns hanging open, offering herself up to a fate worse than death, then on to Lisa, sprawled in our marriage bed.

They say you can't really remember pain, remembering only the fact of it, not the precise way it felt. Maybe the same thing's true of happiness.

I hung like a ghost beneath the ceiling of a room that no longer existed, looking down on a naked woman whose touch, taste, feel, laughter I was already losing, grappling with the loss, struggling to reclaim the few bits and pieces I had left.

Sometimes I wonder why I ever left Earth. Maybe we could've been happy without the money. Maybe.

Regret, they say, is the most expensive thing in the world, but it's a lie. Regret is free; you get to have as much regret as you want. And then, when you're done wanting regret, you find it's yours to keep forever.

At some point while I was staring at the base library menu system, the remembered image of Lisa turned to the much fresher image of Jennah, damp and eager in my arms, then, somehow, to Christie, huge eyes beseeching.

The next day, I went on out to Workpoint 17, a drilling platform on the backside of Aerhurst ridge from Alanhold, sitting at the top of a long slope, giving a vista like nothing on Earth, or any other place I'd been, long, flat, fading into the mist dozens of kilometers away, like the greatest ski run you could ever imagine.

When I first got here, the sight of these vistas, wonderful and strange, made me think about all the places I'd been already, made me think about the red canyons of Mars, the rugged orange mountains of Venus, the soft black lava plains of the Moon.

Made me remember my first sight of Earth from space, stark, incredible, white-frosted blue seen from the other side of the sky.

I remembered standing atop the terminal scarp of Terra Noursae, looking out over the Waxsea's unimaginable wasteland, and wondering if I shouldn't tell Lisa I was never coming home, that I'd keep on giving her the money, all the money, but she'd have to find another man to help her spend it, another man with whom to have those children we'd discussed.

Christ, they were talking about the moons of Uranus back then! And me, I started thinking about what it'd be like to stand on a cliff ten kilometers high. Started thinking about the geysers of Triton, dim blue Neptune hanging in the black sky overhead. . . .

It still had the power to make my insides cramp with desire.

Workpoint 17 was manned by two Russian women who'd been brought out from the Fore Trojans about two years back, a pair of stocky, blunt-faced, red-headed petroleum geologists from Kazakhstan, looking like twin sisters, maybe in their forties, maybe a lot older, who'd been knocking around the solar system for something like fifteen years.

They'd always been cut-ups, kind of fun to be around, always ribbing each other, ribald stuff half in English, half not, kidding about who was going to have me first and who'd have to take sloppy seconds, though I always figured them for lesbians.

It was inside their habitat, with its stark, vinegary smell, watching one of them getting out of her suit, broad rump poking up, seam of her longjohns starting to pull apart where the stitching would soon give way, that I made some vulgar remark or another.

Irena, I think it was, looked at Larisa, owl-eyed with surprise, then back at me, making a wan smile.

"Uh. Sorry."

Irena stood up, facing me now, spacesuit still cluttered around her ankles, and, very gently I thought, said, "Don't be. We've been worried about you."

·   ·   ·

Later, I sat in one of my parking places, high atop Aerhurst, on a crag of pure white ice projecting from where the beaten track crosses the low shoulder of a slumping, rounded peak, lights out, engines off, all but powered down, staring out the window.

In the distance, over the lowlands, was a torrential rainstorm, vast, flat, blue-gray cloud hanging under a darkened sky. The rainfall beneath it was like a pointillist fog, freckled with dots too little to see, somehow there nonetheless, an edgeless pillar of silver-blue blotting out the landscape beyond.

Atmospheric cooling.

Somewhere above the clouds, I knew Saturn was all but gone, turned to black, blotting out the sun. I looked up, trying to make out the shadow's edges, make out the ringplane backscatter, but the turbulence was too great today.

Maybe some other time.

Just what I'd thought of saying to Irena and Larisa, anticipating an offer that never came. Still, it was nice to think of them worrying about me. As though I still mattered to anyone at all.

The comm light on the dashboard began to wink, an eye-catching sequence of red-blue-amber-green, one color following the other at quarter-second intervals, colors merging into a brief, bright sparkle. I reached out and touched a button with the tip of my finger, spoke my call sign, and listened.

Christie's voice came out of a rustle of static: "Can you schedule me for a maintenance visit?"

Something about that voice, odd, nervous, reluctant, eager. Or maybe it was just my imagination. How much can you read into a voice turned to whispers by radio interference?

"What's wrong?"

Long pause.

"I'm not sure. Maybe the same as before, only worse."

Nothing much had been wrong before. A few toasted chips; nothing serious, nothing that couldn't have waited if I hadn't been . . . I scrolled my schedule, thinking about Christie, about her colored waxworks beasties, about . . .

I said, "I'm on a routine maintenance run through the automated geophone chain this side of the ridgeline. I can divert to your workpoint between numbers three and four."

"When?"

Urgency?

Nothing's urgent anymore.

I said, "Thirty-one hours."

Much longer pause. "Oh."

The disappointment was stark, bursting right through the static.

She said, "I guess that'll be okay."

"See you then."

I punched the button and sat back to watch the rainstorm build as the sky grew slowly darker above it, taking on the rich colors of mud.

What can have happened? What can she be wanting? Something to do with the melted-crayon things? Certainly not anything to do with *me*. My thoughts strayed again to her zipped-open longjohns, making me smile at myself. I'd never been one for a one-track mind. Not in this lifetime.

But funny things happen when life's reduced to terminal stress.

She was waiting, suited up outside, standing by the powerplant, when I rolled up to the workpoint, scrunching into the airlock, cycling on through. I've seldom been inside a half-track while someone else is coming aboard; the hollow thumping of knees and feet on metal and plastic, the odd lurchings, were all very unnatural.

The inner hatch popped open, filling the cabin with a faint alcohol and ammonia tang, quickly suppressed when Christie opened her helmet, folded it back, pushed aside by human gastrointestinal smells.

I remembered an old story where that'd been the smell of Titan, because its author was thinking of methane and swamp gas, barnyard smells and all.

Silly.

They put butyl mercaptan in natural gas so you'll smell a leak.

Her face had a damp, suffocated look, as if being in the spacesuit made her claustrophobic. "Let's go," she said.

I unclutched the tracks and set off, lurch of the cabin throwing her against my shoulder, felt her brace herself, keeping what distance she could, not much in this little space. How much of what I'm feeling is fossil emotion, old subroutines frozen in my head?

I don't know what I want because I'm afraid, is that it?

I said, "Christie? When are you going to tell me what's going on?"

When I turned my head to look, her face was no more than a hand's breadth away, but facing forward, eyes not blinking as she watched familiar Titanscape come and go. Overhead, from down in the bottom lands, the eclipsed sky was the color of a fresh bruise, blue and gray, dull purple, tinted with vague streamers of magenta.

Then she turned her head toward me, eyes on mine. That brought her close enough we were breathing on each other. You know how that goes. You get in each other's facial space and there's tension there, because the next move is that forward craning, that . . .

She looked away again, not outside, just at the inner surface of the wall, at a circuit breaker panel mounted about eye level. "Did you tell anyone else?"

I shrugged. "Nothing to tell, I guess."

No answer. Tension in the arch of her neck. I wanted to reach out and touch her, tell her some nonsense about how it'd be all right. Then, with my arm around her, with her space invaded . . . there's something about the vulnerability of fear, about there being some terrible thing wrong.

She said, "Pull up here. Let's get out."

We'd come to the cliffs by the beach, but were still some distance from the familiar way down, rolling one at a time out the lock, then following my earlier tracks to the place where I'd spied on her before. They'd been joined by numerous other footprints now, hundreds coming and going.

All hers, I guess.

There was a thin wisp of black smoke rising above the instrument package, like an elongated drop of india ink in clear water, rolling with the convection currents, just beginning to dissipate.

And, all around it on the beach, were swipes and smears of color, shades and shapes moving round and round, all so very slowly. As I watched, a dark blue one came close, stretching out a long, narrow pseudopod. It came within a few centimeters of one support leg, hesitated for a moment, then touched.

The pseudopod shriveled, shrinking quickly back toward the main body, which seemed to roll over, turning to a lighter shade of blue, then sinking into the beach, gone in an instant.

There was another black curl in the air, rising above the instrument package, drifting slowly away as it dissipated. I thought of the sample I'd taken of that earlier instrument contamination, presumably still in the half-track refrigerator where I'd left it.

Little beasties investigating the alien machine. Innocent little beasties getting themselves killed.

Is curiosity just a tropism?

Moths to the flame.

I said, "I guess that makes your case, hm?"

I don't know what I expected next, but she said, "Turn off your radio now."

"Um . . ."

She turned and put her hand on my arm. I couldn't feel it through the suit material, but those big eyes, begging . . . I switched it off and waited. She just turned away, quickly stepping to the edge of the cliff, dangerously close given the fragility of this chemical ice, and pulsed the carrier wave power setting of her suit's comm system, one, two, three, off.

All very much like in a movie.

Down on the beach, the waxthings froze in place, a conscious freezing, just the way a spider will freeze the instant it realizes you're looking. That sudden crouch, alien eyes pointing your way, spider brain filled with unknowable thoughts.

I remembered the way one of these things had grown a speckle of orange dots before and recalled a science film I'd seen as a kid, high speed photography of slime molds in action. Eerie. Not more so than this.

Suddenly, between one frame and the next, the beach was empty.

In all those old movies, old stories, they get the feeling of this moment terribly wrong, don't they? I reached for my comm controls, but Christie, catching my movement from the corner of one eye, raised a restraining hand.

Wait.

I . . .

Down on the beach, a flat, ragged-edged plain of blue formed. Time for a few heartbeats, then a sharp-edged stripe of pink slid across the side of the plain nearest our vantage point.

Then a conical shape slid into view from the other side, visibly falling toward the pink.

Falling.

Just before it hit, there was a reddish-orange swirl under the blunt side of the cone. It slowed to a stop, popping out little landing legs, flame gouting on the surface, then winking out.

Little blue and green dots appeared, embedded in the pink, drawing in toward the motionless cone. As they drew close, one by one, they would turn black and vanish. After a while, you could see they'd learned to keep their distance, hovering around the edge of the picture.

My mouth was dry as I switched on my radio and whispered, "How the hell do they know what our sense of perspective is like?"

Whispered, as though someone might be listening. Some thing.

Her voice was hardly more than a breath, blowing through my earphones: "They're not really two dimensional creatures."

It's not Flatland. They're not waxy paintings on the surface of the ground.

Fire blossomed under the cone and it lifted off, climbing out of the picture, and all the remaining blue dots turned black before vanishing.

After a while, more of them crept from the edge of the picture, creeping through the pink toward the place where the cone had been, At first, the leaders turned black and died, but only for a little while. In time, they finished their investigations, then went sliding on their way.

The blue plain with its empty pink strip vanished suddenly, and the beach was empty again.

I turned to her and said, "Why'd you show me this?"

Seen through the faceplate, she was nothing but eyes. Big blue eyes, Serious. Frightened. "I won't make this decision by myself. I'm not . . ." Long hesitation. "You know."

Yeah. Not God. That's how that one goes.

Back at the habitat, after a long, silent ride, we sat together in our longjohns, made tea and drank it, made small talk that went nowhere, circling round and round, as if something had changed, or nothing.

We're dead men here, I'd thought on the way back, watching a snowdrift blow across the beaten path before the half-track, slowing down as if to stop, then suddenly lifting off in the wind like a flock of birds making for the sky, clearing the way for us.

Fewer than two thousand survivors . . .

In the old stories, old movies, that would've been more than enough, two thousand hot, eager Adams and Eves, getting about their delving and spanning, wandering the freshly butchered landscape, pausing by the shores of an infinite, empty sea, being fruitful, multiplying until they'd covered the Earth again.

This star system no longer contains an inhabitable planet.

Bits of memory, snatches of Moonbase newsreel. When *Oberth* gets home with the crew of the Venus orbital station, who hadn't had to commit suicide, she'll be bringing a stockpile of hardened probes intended for research on the surface of Venus.

Hardened probes, and, of course, one of the piloted Venus landers.

Then we'll know for sure. Then we'll . . .

Couldn't stop myself from imagining, ever so briefly, myself on that first damned crew, riding the Venus lander down through howling brown muck, down to a soft landing in my own backyard.

I've been on Venus. I'm qualified for Venus EVA ops. I . . .

Read a science article when I was a kid that described the Chicxulub impact at the KT Boundary as being "like taking a blowtorch to western North America."

The image in my head was a double exposure, the image of collapsed and burned-out cities, like something from an atomic was fantasy, superimposed over the reality of a cooling lava ejecta blanket.

Just wisps of smoke.

That's all that's left of her.

Christie, face pushed down in the steam from her teacup, was looking at me strangely. God knows what my expression must have been like. Did you have anyone, Christie Meitner, or was it only strangers that died? Billions and billions of strangers.

She said, "I guess we'd better talk about it now." Unsaid, Whether we want to or not.

I nodded, not knowing what I wanted, looking into a face that wasn't all that expressive. A face not so different from my own. I tried to remember what I looked like, call up the man in the mirror, but there was only fog, no way to know what she was looking at now with those big, hollow eyes.

She said, "It's so simple, Hoxha: They're alive, and this is their world. If we stay here, even just the few score of us, Titan's environment will slowly change, until this is no longer an inhabitable world for them."

And then?

Right.

"Does it make a difference now that we know they're intelligent?"

She shook her head. "If we work together to keep it secret, to keep the others from stumbling over this, once we go away, back to Moonbase . . ."

I said, "The Earth's not going to recover and we can't survive forever at Moonbase. The Saturn system's our best bet, otherwise we're spread too thin. Even Mars . . ."

She said, "The odds are against us, no matter what."

I nodded.

"So we come here, obliterate the Titanians, and then die out *anyway*, erasing their future as well as ours."

Does this mean anything? What's my next line? I know: Christie, this is proof positive life is common in the universe. Right. Idiot. I remember the way she'd looked, face so pale, eyes so big, standing behind me with the ice axe, willing herself to kill. How many Titanians would've exploded and burned under the beach had my blood been spilled?

I said, "So that's what all this is about? Some good old-fashioned eco . . ." Right. Like the idiots who protested *Cassini*'s launch all those years ago, while not doing a damned thing about the world's hundred thousand hydrogen bombs.

Pick your targets. Some are easier than others.

She seemed tired. "It's not just that. If it was just about them being living things, intelligent living things, you wouldn't be sitting here now."

"Dead and buried?" I smiled. "That would've been hard for you to explain."

"I wasn't thinking clearly. I was panicked that you'd . . ."

"What, then? Why am I still here?"

Long, long stare, still trying to fathom if there was a human being behind my face, someone just like her. She said, "Day before yesterday, I found evidence that their life process involves some kind of directed nucleosynthesis."

You could see the relief in her face. There. I've said it. And . . .

Nucleosynthesis?

Talking about details is what we're doing.

In those old stories, old movies, the details are always important, imaginary science chatted up by happy, competent characters until God springs from the machine and utters his funny-elf punchline.

Now?

Not important.

Not anymore.

And yet . . .

I said, "That could tip the scales in our favor. We come here, we learn to exploit them, we survive as a species."

Her face fell.

I don't think she expected me to see it that easily.

Probably there was a scenario in there in which the pedantic teacher explains things to the gaping mechanic in the simplest possible terms. That's the story way, isn't it?

She sat back in her chair and sighed. "I don't know what we should do. Do you?"

People love to pretend they make rational decisions. It's called excuse-seeking behavior. Christie and I sat facing one another for a long time, tension making it seem we were about to speak, but we never did. You want to be the first one to start offering up excuses? No, not me. How about you? If it was important enough to reach for that axe, surely . . .

I wasn't thinking clearly.

Right.

So we talked about the evidence, which she explained to me in the simplest possible terms, until I was able to pick up the thread and begin spooling it into my own knowledge base, understanding it in my own terms. Understanding. That's an important part of making excuses for what you *do*, isn't it?

Or what you fail to do.

Think about the possibilities, Christie.

Think about the technology we could build here. Think of the resource base. And the Titanians? Is it important what happens to them?

In the end, we slept, I curled up on the floor, Christie huddled in her bed, back toward me, curled in on herself, head down in the vague shadows between her body and the wall. I lay awake for a while, trying to think about the whole damned business, trying to convince myself, God damn it, that it *mattered*.

When I awoke, however many hours later, Christie was on the floor beside me, asleep, not touching me, head on one corner of the folded-up blanket I was using for a pillow.

Lisa never did that. Lisa always had to touch me while we slept together, sometimes huddling against my back, other times insisting that I curl myself around her like a protective shell. I remember when we were very young and new to each other, how I used to wake up sometimes to find her breathing right in my face.

Breathing in each other's breath, I used to call it. As intimate a thing as I could possibly imagine.

So, awakening, breakfasted, we got in the half-track and went back down to Waxsea beach, where the fairy tales of science were waiting after all.

I don't know what made me stop the half-track up on the terminal scarp. Maybe just some . . . sense of impending something. Maybe just a longing for the view. Christie stared at me for a second or two when I told her to get out, Stirlings vibrating the frame below us, idling down in the track trucks. Then she nodded, folded her helmet over her face, pressurized the suit, wrinkly off-white skin suddenly growing stiff and shiny, obliterating her shape.

When the depress valve had woofed, when I could see her out the cockpit window, I had a sudden memory of an old TV commercial from the retrofad going on when I was in grammar school. Pillsbury Doughboy.

Doughboy. Funny. Wonder if those long-dead copywriters imagined him with a tin-plate helmet and bayoneted Enfield, marching upright and stalwart into the machinegun fire of No Man's Land.

I think she was relieved when I joined her on the surface, no way to tell through the suit visor, just those same eyes, with their same expression, a pasted-on affect of surprise, fear, resentment. But she followed me to the edge of the cliff, where we stopped, and I let her get behind me, image of the ice axe fresh enough, hardly mattering.

And, of course, there was the cliff. One hard shove and I'd float on down to . . . I don't know. Gravity here's low enough I might survive the fall, given that two bar atmosphere, but . . . would my suit?

I imagined myself exploding like a bomb.

Overhead, the sky stretched away toward the absent horizon like a buckled red blanket, crumpled clouds of coarse wool, dented here, there, everywhere with purple-shadowed hollows, little holes into nothingness.

Down on the silvery beach, the instrument platform was ringed by motionless blobs, each ring a single color, blue, green, red, violet, working their way outward from the hardware.

Christie grunted, "Never saw that before." Radio made it seem like she was inside my suit, pressed up against my back, chin on my shoulder, speaking into my ear.

If you looked closely, you could see the blobs were connected by thin strands, monochrome along the rings, blended between. Slowly, one of the blobs extended a pseudopod toward the platform. That's right. In a minute, it'll blacken and curl, shriveling in on itself until the parent blob goes belly up and sinks out of sight.

Will the ring close up then, each soldier in that row taking one easy step, forward into an empty space, like Greeks in a phalanx?

Christie said, "I wonder why they do it?"

Inviting certain death in the pursuit of knowledge?

Good question.

The pseudopod slowed as it came close, flattening, widening, forming a sort of two-dimensional cup on its end, a cup that drifted slowly back and forth, arcing along the surface, a few centimeters out. After a moment, beads of yellow began forming at the cup's focus, detaching, speeding back up the pseudopod to the parent blob. From there, they replicated, spreading around the ring, then outward.

I said, "Think they know we're here?"

The first blob withdrew its pseudopod, while the next one in line extended an identical . . . instrument? Is that the right word? Examining the next section of the platform's heat shield.

Christie said, "I don't know. Their radio sensitivity's not that great. I always have to turn the carrier wave full blast to get their attention."

I turned away, stepping back the way we'd come. "I guess we should just go on down and . . ."

Not sure what I was going to suggest. Christie gasped and put out a hand, gripping my forearm hard enough that my suit was compressed, forcing the liner up against my skin, feeling like cold, damp plastic, making me shiver slightly.

When I looked back, down on the beach, the rings had broken up, blobs perfectly spherical now, appearing and disappearing in the cracked ice, like colored ping-pong balls bobbing in a tub of water. Bobbing in unison.

One, two, three . . .

They exploded like so many silver raindrops, reaching out for one another, merging, spreading like a cartoon tide, until the beach below was a solid silver mirror filling the space between the cliff, the sea, the instrument package, reflecting a slightly hazy image of the red sky above, complete with streamers of golden light coming through little rents and tears, picking out the drifting snowbanks like dustmotes on a lazy summer afternoon.

Somewhere overhead, I saw, there was a tiny fragment of rainbow floating in the sky.

The image in the mirror grew dark, dimming slowly, as though night were falling, though the real sky hung above us unchanged, streamers of light tarnishing, red becoming orange then brown, bruise blue, then indigo, almost black.

Almost, for freckles of silver remained.

Freckles of silver in a peculiarly familiar pattern, bits of light clustered here and there, gathering to a diagonal band across the middle and . . .

Christie's gasp made me imagine warmth in my ear as she recognized it a fraction of a second before I did. Well, of course. She'd seen the real thing a lot more recently than I had.

The stars dimmed, Milky Way becoming just a dusty, dusky suggestion of itself.

Christie's voice: "*How?* How could they *see* . . ."

A bright silver light popped up in the center of the starfield, circled by dimmer lights, some brighter than others, most white, some colored, this one blue, that one red.

Tiny bright beads began flying from the blue light, swinging by orange Jupiter, heading for yellow Saturn, some stopping there, others flying on, disappearing from the scene.

In a row across the bottom of the image, bottom being the side facing us, flat, near-schematic representations of spacecraft appeared, matching each tiny bead as it flew. Little *Pioneer*. The *Voyagers*. *Cassini* and *Huygens* . . .

Voice no more than a hushed whisper, Christie said; "I wonder how long they knew? Why they waited so long and . . . why *me*?"

If they knew about *Pioneer*, then they knew about us when my father was a little boy, my grandfather a young man, reveling in the deeds of space, imagining himself in the future, still young, strong, alive, and happy.

Down on the beach, the solar system faded, leaving the hint of starfields behind; then, like a light winking on, blue Earth appeared, oceans covered by rifted clouds, continents picked out in shades of ocher, hard to recognize, circled by a little gray Moon.

I could feel Christie's hand tighten on my shoulder, knowing what was coming.

There. The asteroid. The brilliant violet light of the hydrogen bombs. The spreading of the fragments. The impacts. The red glow of magma. The spreading brown clouds.

I wondered briefly if they'd had something to do with the rock coming our way. No. That's just an old story thing, pale imagination left in my head when I was a child.

One of those damned things we teach our children because we don't know what's real. Don't know and don't care.

Somewhere in my head, a badly fueled story generator supplied images of what would come next. Down on the beach; the image of a tentacled alien would form. Something not human, but within the reach of terrestrial evolution, would stretch out a suckered paw, inviting.

Take me to your leader.

What was I remembering?

"The Gentle Vultures"?

Maybe so.

Down on the beach, the end of the world faded, replaced by a white disk, wrinkled in concentric rings. It tipped around, as if in 3D motion, showing us complex mechanisms, considerable mechanical detail, obvious control systems.

I said, "Fresnel lenses."

Christie said, "They could see though the clouds with that, if they could build it for real. See the sun, the larger planets, the brighter stars, as patches of heat in their sky. But . . ."

The infrared telescope was replaced by an image of Titan, recognizable by the topography of Terra Noursae, Titan stripped of its clouds. The image rotated, showing the Waxsea hemisphere, Waxsea bearing interconnected concentric rings, some gigantic version of the array we'd first come upon here.

Christie said, "Long baseline interferometer. With enough computation . . ."

If they could build it.

Nucleosynthesis?

I said, "How do you distinguish between a life process and a technology?"

Christie said, "Oh," sounding surprised.

Imagination builds nothing. Not even the knowledge of how to build. Not unless you can somehow project it into the real world.

Down on the beach, another image formed, a fantastically detailed portrait of the cosmodrome, showing the two landers upright on their pads. On the ridge above, tiny blue Titanians waited at a safe distance, ominous, like Indians looming above the ambush, foolish cavalry waiting in the defile.

A blue sphere rolled down, making for the little ships. I waited for them to be spun down, like tenpins before the ball.

It rolled to a stop, not far from the ships. Tiny, spacesuited humans connected a blue thread to the ball, to the ships. The ball shrank away to nothing. The ships took off, unrolling red flame as they climbed through an orange overcast and were gone.

Behind them, the base and cosmodrome disappeared, one component at a time, leaving an empty landscape behind.

Christie sighed in my headphones.

Just one more all-too-familiar fairy tale, that's all.

Below, the silver screen cleared again, reforming as faint stars against velvet dark, surmounted by a slow-moving orrery of the solar system. Beads of light moved from Saturn to blue Earth—*brown*, I thought. They should've made it brown.

The sky stood empty. Christie said, "I guess . . ."

I whispered, "Sending us home to die then?"

Another bead appeared, crossing from Earth to Saturn, then going home again. Then again. More beads, this time from Saturn to Neptune. After a while, the voyages began a three-way trip, Saturn, Neptune, Earth.

What's at Neptune?

Triton, of course.

I remembered how much I'd always wanted to go there, almost willing to abandon Lisa just so I could see diaphanous geysers rising against a deep blue world, out on the edge of the infinite.

Christie seemed somehow hollow, as if she were speaking from the depths of a dream. "They send us home to the Moon. Help us to survive with trade and . . . I . . ." She stopped.

What are you thinking about, Christie? That you might see the atmospheres of the gas giants after all? Is that it?

She said, "We could never mine tritium from the atmosphere of Jupiter, where it's free for the taking. Not in that radiation environment. Not anytime soon."

Tritium. Out of the depths of the past, I suddenly remember the *Daedalus* designs, so long forgotten.

She said, "Even out here at Saturn, there's a deep gravity well to contend with. And the collision danger from equatorial ringplane debris spiraling in. Neptune . . ."

Low-density gas giant with all the tritium we might want. And a big ice-moon for the Titanians to . . .

A myriad of bright sparks suddenly emerged from the Earth, moving not toward another planet, but receding into the background sky, sky whose stars grew bright again, while the fleet of sparks grew smaller and smaller, until it merged with an unremarkable pattern of stars.

Christie muttered, "Something in Pavo, I think. I was never very good with the lesser constellations."

Delta Pavonis?

Is there a planet there? A planet just like the one we lost?

I said, "You think their technology's *that* good?"

She looked up at me, still nothing more than big eyes looking out through scratched, foggy plastic. "Maybe not. Not out here in the ice and cold. But put together with *ours* . . ."

Maybe so.

I said, "I guess the decision wasn't ours to make after all."

I awoke in the middle of the night, opening my eyes on darkness defiled by blue light from the instrument panels, perched on the edge of the bunk, curled inward, shadow of my head, shadow of tousled hair cast on the habitat wall. Christie was bunched into the space between my body and the wall, curled in on herself, the two of us damp and soft against one another, sharing some soft old blanket.

Somewhere outside, a new day is dawning.

Some time during that day we'll have to make our decision, get in the half-track, go on back to base and . . .

What will happen?

Oh, nonsense. The fantasy we've just been through was no better than one more iteration of White Man's Burden.

The decision's been made. Not by us.

All we have to do is carry out our part, speak our lines according to the script.

Lights. Camera. Action.

Fade to black.

If I held still, paid attention, I could feel Christie's back against my chest, moving slowly in and out as she breathed, pausing briefly before reversing direction. Asleep, I guess. I tried hard to remember what Lisa'd felt like sleeping against me.

Faded and gone, like just about everything else.

I listened for the soft sound of breath coming and going through what I imagined would be an open mouth, hollow breathing like the ghost of a snore, but the sounds of Titan coming through the habitat wall blotted it out. Sighing wind close by. A large wind farther away, moaning in the hills. Tidal creak of the deep crustal ice coming to us through the floor.

Christie seemed to sigh in her sleep, pressing back against me ever so slightly, like something from a dream.

I remembered the lights merging with the stars and found myself dreaming of a new world, of standing on a hillside under a crimson sunset, alien sun in the sky, sun with prominences and corona plain against the sky, something from a remembered astronomical illustration. Something from a children's book.

As in all children's books, there's a woman under my arm, standing close against me, standing close.

Below us, below the hillside, was a rim of dark forest, trees like feathery palms swaying in a tropical breeze, beyond it, a golden sea, stretching out flat to the end of the world.

Us?

Or just a dream?

Christie stirred suddenly, turned half toward me, nuzzling her head against my shoulder, and murmured, "Maybe things will . . . work out after all."

After all that.

It was a moment before I realized what she meant.

Another moment before I felt the burden lift out of my heart, ghosts hurrying away to their graves, one more golden tomorrow awakening from a dream.

free in asveroth

jim grimsley

Here's a moving and melancholy study of obsolescence, from the doomed and sorrowing perspective of those who have been made obsolete. . . .

Jim Grimsley is a playwright and novelist who lives in Atlanta. His first novel, Winter Birds, *was published in 1994, and won the 1995 Sue Kaufman Prize for First Fiction from the American Academy of Arts and Letters, and received a special citation from the Ernest Hemingway Foundation. His second novel,* Dream Boy, *won the American Library Association GLBT Award for Literature, and was a Lambda Award Finalist. His third novel,* My Drowning, *was released in 1997. He is playwright-in-residence at 7 Stages Theater and a collection of his plays,* Mr. Universe and Other Plays, *was published last year. Due out next are two novels,* Comfort and Joy *and a fantasy entitled* Kirith Kirin.

W e found a snow hare that night, lost in the high passes that lie in Kimbrel's shadow. The animal lay kicking weakly in a drift of snow against the mountainside, unable to hop free of the hole it had dug for itself in the new powder. We thanked whatever god sent it here and Mikra broke its neck with one clean twist.

Since we had no wood for a fire, we skinned the hare and ate it raw. Warm flesh thawed my throat. The meat had a sweetness like nothing I had ever tasted, different from the food we had eaten in the pens, where I had never tasted fresh-killed meat. Mikra said this hare was a scrawny specimen that old-time hunters would have disdained, but since we were likely to get nothing better we must make do. After we finished our meal we cleaned our fur, and Mikra buried what was left of the hare in the snow. The sun was setting behind the peaks, we would travel no more that day. Soon the stars shone in the black mountain sky. We found a place to spend the night, in soft snow beneath an overhang of rock. Mikra wrapped herself around me as she had been doing ever since we came to mountain country. We two does huddled staring at heaven while Timmon sang songs from the old days. I found myself breathless whenever Mikra stirred against me.

This was the twelfth day since we escaped from the pens, the eighth since we began the scaling of Kimbrel. So far we had seen no sign of the wardens.

Next morning we ate what remained of the snow hare, hurriedly gnawing the bones clean while light swelled beyond mists that cloaked the mountainside. The sky was a burning blue, the sun clean and white on Kimbrel's highest peaks. Mikra was impatient and barely allowed time for me to bury the bones before we set out. It was my job to bury the bones, she said, since I was the younger doe, and I obeyed. The ground was too hard for real digging, but I piled snow on top, and a couple of rocks.

Footing was perilous on the icy ground, and we dared not jump. Wind swept hollowly through the rocks, a low moaning like a cry. We proceeded slowly. Mikra led, Timmon followed, I was last. The sound of Timmon's labored breath accompanied us the whole way down, and his broad tail dragged the ground, bits of snow clinging to the underside where his fur had gone yellow with age. He did not have the energy to hold the tail aloft.

We descended through the rocks. Come noon the sheet of ice was less and the snow was fresh, making for easier footing. Naked rock poked through the ice now and then, tufts of lichen gripping the tops. Mikra whetted her long claws on one such rock, scoring the lichen away. The mist had cleared and she studied the sky from one horizon to the other. Her nostrils flared. "No sign of fliers," she said, and when Timmon was rested we moved ahead.

By nightfall we had reached the lower passes, and we rested amid patches of snowflower, more lichen, golden grass. Timmon said the grass was sweet and so it was. We ate as much as we found, but we craved meat too.

Next morning and the morning after, we jumped. My legs had stiffened on our long climb across the mountains. At first we had room only to jump short distances. Mikra led us down the stretches of barren mountainside, picking as easy a path as she could find. Even then, Timmon was near exhaustion.

On the fourteenth day out of the pens, Timmon said we would see Asveroth the next day, possibly the next morning. In the foothills game was more plentiful, and we had meat each evening, now that Mikra and I could hunt. She took me with her even though I had not been trained by anybody and in spite of the fact that I was clumsy. That night she killed a golden thal, a plump hen. The long, streaming tail feathers we gave to the hill gods, as was proper on a journey, according to Timmon. He had built a stone altar when we stopped for the night. He laid the feathers on it and said a wordless prayer. Mikra only glared at him, refusing to join the prayer herself.

These hills Timmon knew. He told no stories about them but I saw the familiar sadness in his eyes, as if he were back in the pens telling us adolescents stories of the old times while we waited by a campfire for the evening meal. I am far too young to remember the days when we roamed freely over the golden grassland, I was born in the pens and can remember no other home. But Timmon was full grown before the two-legs ever defeated us and remembers when Asveroth was free country, when jumpers could jump as they pleased.

That night, in the hills beyond the Karethagan Mountains, Mikra asked

Timmon to sing when he was done with the prayer. She felt good from having eaten flesh, I guess.

But Timmon shook his shaggy head. "I don't have a song tonight."

"Can you smell the wardens, Mikra?" I asked. Mikra sniffed the winds and answered she could smell nothing but flowers, grass and warm wind. She took me to bed then, and I was glad to lie beside her, for no reason I could think of except that she was there.

In the morning we stretched our legs as one must before a day of jumping. In the pens we never had much room, except the exercise tracks the wardens built for us; I had never jumped in open country. My legs were still sore and Mikra's muscles were stiff; even though she had once jumped three days together without stopping, as she boasted. The years in confinement beyond the mountains had done nobody any good. One could only imagine the pain Timmon felt in his old bones.

I asked when Mikra had done the three days jumping and why this had been necessary. I thought it was an innocent question, but she frowned. "That's a long story from a time I'd rather not remember any more," she said. "The two-legs were the cause of that trouble too." I took my place behind Timmon, who had been to the hill god's altar again. He gave me no greeting, absorbed in his own thoughts. Mikra called us a moment later and we began our day's journey.

We jumped through hill country, descending to a warmer land. The cool of early morning gave way to a sultry fullness of sunlight. Breezes swept along the hillsides, filling our fur with air. We stopped to rest in a low ravine where a brook had cut its way down through rock, amid low saplings and wild tumbles of purple vine that hung in bunches over the foaming water. I had never seen such wild beauty, the forest dappled with greens, browns, blues, splashes of sunlight on the water and the sheer rock face. Mikra waded into the creek on her wide, strong forelegs, claws clacking on the rocks. She splashed her face and snorted, dipping her hands in the water again. "Timmon," she called. "Do you know this creek? Does it have a name?"

He had found a seat under one of the purple flowered vines and sat in the shade basking the peaceful sound of the water. "If it had a name I've forgotten it. I do remember the place, vaguely."

"Your memory's giving way. I thought you said we would see Asveroth this morning."

"We will," he said simply. Even now he looked short of breath. Mikra sneered and went on cooling herself in the creek until she was ready.

Timmon was right. We came to the crest of a hill higher than the rest, at the point where the country rolled so gently one could hardly distinguish one hill from the next. Mikra reached the hilltop, turned and gave us a shrill cry. We mounted toward her black silhouette, white tumbles of wind-driven cloud rolling behind the outline of her head. Her face, when I could see it again, was ecstatic. "Kemma," she called, running toward me, embracing me and turning me around, "come look."

I could not answer for gaping. The horizon swam in gold, a fire at the edge of the world. Even from that distance I could feel the fringes of the winds bending the golden grass this way and that. I had no need for anybody to tell me this was Asveroth.

We jumped faster with the sight of the golden plain to tantalize us from the top of every hill. The smell of sweet wind was like a magnet. We broke from the hills before nightfall. As far as the eye could see, wind swept the grass in waves, the golden blades swaying as if to pipe music. No smell on earth is like that one, a sweetness more delicate than any perfumed oil, richer than any scent of flower. Timmon sat with the sea of grass pulsing around him like something living; he stared at the landscape in wonder, though he had seen it before. Mikra lay along the ground and kicked her wide feet in the air. "We're home," she called. "Do you hear me? We've come home, and we're never leaving."

"I thought I would never see this place again," Timmon said.

"Well you were wrong. Here we are in the middle of it."

He only looked at her, saying nothing. I did not understand his sullenness. Mikra shrugged and we went off hunting. Timmon sat still like a stone. Free we were too, I thought, in this open country where we could jump as we pleased. But with every good there is bad. Even the worst of teachers will teach you that. With sunset came the smell of the two-legs in one of their flying machines. We prayed the machine was not one that had chased us into the mountains in the first place. We slept in fear that night. Mikra held me all night again, in spite of the fact that we were in warm country now and she had no more excuses. I was happy.

Before dawn we were jumping away from the wind. Mikra said the smell of the flier was faint. Timmon agreed, adding that it was hard to tell whether the smell was from the two-legs we already knew to be following us or from the farming machines that are used to harvest the Asveroth grass. I had tasted golden blades again that morning, eating it with an enthusiasm that earned me a warning from Mikra. The grass is good to the taste, but jumpers cannot tolerate a bulk of it. Why the two-legs prize this plant so highly no one knows, though some folks claim the creatures extract a fluid from it that preserves their youth, or heals various of their diseases, or causes a sensation like drunkenness in them. We are certain only that this grass is the reason the two-legs dispossessed us of our homes. Year after year their machines comb Asveroth mowing down the golden blades for baling and processing in the city they have built for the purpose far to the south, by the shores of a broad waterland we call Hethluun.

As for the flier, I could smell its fumes too. The smell of the exhaust put me back in the pens for a moment, where the odor is everywhere.

I was glad to jump and forget. One hears tales of what it was like before the two-legs came, when we were free. To me, after a life in the pens, it was like being born to jump like that, like soaring, as if the whole power of my spirit was gathered in my hind legs, enabling me to hurl myself high as clouds. For a time I forgot we were not jumping for pleasure, I simply closed my eyes and treasured the rhythm of motion. Then a gust of wind from behind brought the smell of the machines, stronger than before, and turned my heart to lead.

We crossed miles of the plain, leaping over the groves of moonvine and aspen that dot the golden grass. Twice we smelled farms and jumped around them. Once we were not so lucky and happened onto one of their immense metal harvesters rolling through the grass on two wide treads. The two-leg farmers saw us and pointed madly, but we were not close enough for the machine to threaten us, and these farmers had no weapons to turn on us. We left the huge slow machine far behind. But the two-legs were sure to have called the wardens on their talking machines; and those who followed us would now know how many we were.

The smell of our pursuers was no stronger in the afternoon and for a time even grew less. We veered off in another direction, running with the wind. We were very fast now that we were on the plain. By evening the smell of the flying machines was only a breath, and we stopped for the night in a warren we found in the course of our jumping.

The warren sat within a broad moonvine, its crested tunnel-entrances barely showing within the elaborately tangled branches. The main entrance was crushed flat, the stone lintels broken, most likely by one of the weapons the two-legs employed for such purposes during the wars. Timmon explained this to me while we were looking for a way inside. I had never seen a warren before and was disappointed that this one was not more grand. In the pens, the yellow-hairs talk about the warrens as if they were patches of paradise; here was this broken thing before me, a bit of tunnel and fragments of stone within a crowded vine, looking like no tale I had ever heard.

We did enter, through one of the escape-tunnels that in the old days would have been concealed beneath vine mats. The tunnels were eerie, lit by veins of phosphorescent rock inlaid in uncertain patterns. This warren had been built without much concern for art, Mikra said. She led me to the singers hall and we stared at the sky through a gaping hole in the roof. The sun was going down. In the remaining light we surveyed the broken feast-tables that littered the stone floor, clay pots in shards and bleached white bones. Timmon said the bomb must have been a small one, since the floor was hardly broken and the lower tunnels were mostly intact. But the floor looked pretty badly broken to me. The paving stones were all in shards.

Mikra and I went further underground to find a comfortable nest in the does' rooms, leaving Timmon to sleep in the singers hall at his own request. Mikra did not like to leave him alone with ghosts but elected to give him his way. She had been young when the wars came and hardly remembered the warrens well enough to distinguish a nest room from a birthing room, but we found a good open chamber where the light was pretty strong, where the smell of dead leaves and old carrion did not much penetrate. The chamber walls were smooth, hardly stained even by rain. We lined the nest with fresh grass laid over springy vine, until even Mikra agreed our bed was as comfortable as most she had ever laid her head on. She looked at me with peculiar tenderness, and I turned away, feeling warm and happy all through. We went exploring, roaming through the twisting tunnels that led away from the singers hall, down into the winter storerooms. Further from the main hall, deeper underground where one could hear the water running, the rooms were intact and orderly. Beyond the main cistern was an open run that led outside to the center of the moonvine. Mikra said we would do well to mark this tunnel so we couldn't be trapped inside the warren if the wardens or other two-legs found us in the night. When she said this I looked at her fearfully. "Are they likely to look for us here?"

"No," she said, touching my forearm gently. "The two-legs are afraid of the warrens. From long ago. Some of the bones here are theirs. There was a lot of killing on both sides."

Mikra hunted in the early moonlight, killing a young deer that had taken shelter in the moonvine. She slung the corpse across her shoulder with an ease that I could only envy. We hopped along the tangled branches to the warren and found Timmon where we had left him, in the center of the hall on the dais, holding the shard of a lamp in his hands. He seemed even more tired than before, staring at us through half-closed eyes; almost feverish, I thought. Shadows pooled in the corners of the hall. I was glad of the stars and moons when the clouds parted. I skinned the deer quickly, being strong and deft, while Mikra gloated, calling to Timmon that we would eat blood tonight, a meal far tastier than any we had eaten in the pens. He watched her blankly. In that room he seemed to hear voices we did not. His ribcage heaved when he drew breath. Mikra and I ate the warm deer in silence. I watched Timmon through the small feast and wished he would speak. Presently I asked, "What was this warren called, Timmon?"

He blinked his round eyes. I could count the moments it took for him to return to his present body. "It was named Harless. I didn't know it well, I was only here once."

"You were here before the wardens came?"

He nodded his head after another long pause. "During the season of three moons." He spoke softly, watching the feathers flutter on the stone shrine. He wandered off among the broken tables, studying the bones as if they were the remains of his dearest friends.

Mikra, in an effort to be friendly, called out, "Sing us a song, since you won't sit down and talk to us."

But that was no hall for singing any more, with the moons burning in the sky, with winds moaning through the vine. "I can't sing here," Timmon said, and soon he was just one more shadow among the others. Mikra and I finished our meal and found the nest we had prepared for ourselves, below in the silent tunnels of old Harless.

Next morning we did not jump as far as we had the day before. Timmon was stiff after a night on cold stone in the singers hall, and he misjudged his jumps so often we could not get any rhythm going. Mikra became impatient, and I could understand this, since in jumping lead she could not set a proper pace for worrying about Timmon; she did not want to outdistance us and yet did not want to jump too slowly, because of our pursuers. That morning their machines were closer. Their machines are not fast, not like a jumper crossing open land, but metal needs no rest. The night in Harless had done us little good.

The wind changed direction and we changed ours with it, wheeling inward toward central Asveroth. Behind us the Karethagan peaks dwindled, and Timmon told us by afternoon that we were heading for the country of the great warrens,

Mirredil and Kenyon and Fethyeh. We crossed no farms and stumbled over no roving harvesters that day; the soil of the plain is poor in this region, and the grass does not mature until late in the season, never growing as tall as it does to the east and the south. By afternoon Timmon looked near dead to me, and swore himself he could not go on without rest. We bathed and drank in a broad river to cool ourselves, with Mikra attempting to feign a patience she did not truly feel. When our rest had gone on longer than she liked, with Timmon still floating on his back in the clean blue water, she stood up on the river bank with her nostrils flaring, head craned high, and said, "The wardens are closer still, yellow-fur. Do you want them to catch us here?"

"They're not so close," he answered. "I've got a nose too."

Mikra splashed water at him, sniffing again. "They're too close for my comfort, we should be moving."

Timmon rose stiffly out of the river. I helped him up the slippery mud. Wet fur clung to his bones. But the rest had done him good. In the day that remained to us we ranged far, and soon the smell of flier began to weaken again. We did not stop exactly at nightfall since the moons were well up. We jumped till the land grew rich again, the grass swaying abundantly in the winds. We might have kept going but we began to fear that in the dark we would trespass on a farm. Timmon knew the land well; we passed many empty warrens that he called out to us by name. When we stopped for the night, he took a long circuit round the adjacent countryside, to get his bearings. When he returned, he said, "We're close to Fethyeh. One day's journey."

Mikra spat at the words. "I won't sleep in a warren again. We need rest, not more ghosts."

"This is Fethyeh," Timmon said, as if that answered everything. "I want to see Fethyeh again, even if I have to make the journey alone."

That night he made his bed away from us. Mikra grumbled that he was showing the willfulness of age, that this is what one can expect from any yellow-fur, but our lives were at risk along with his. I pointed out that Fethyeh was likely to be as safe as the next place, as long as the wind led us in that direction. My earnestness amused her, and finally she said, "You want to see Fethyeh too, don't you. All right." She scratched my shoulder with the tips of her claws. I was happy. I did want to see Fethyeh, maybe more than Timmon did. My clanfolk came from there. Fethyeh was the last warren to fall to the two-legs, on the night Timmon's father first sang "Nightsong."

Next day the wind carried us straight toward the central plain and Timmon was on his best behavior. By nightfall we were within sight of the moonvine within which Fethyeh stood, and Mikra consented to stay the night, one night only, within the confines of the ruined warren.

It seems so long ago now. I had heard of Fethyeh before, as any cub has. The story of the last feast in the singer's hall will be told as long as there are any mouths to tell it. Few warrens were ever situated for defense as Fethyeh was, the entrance tunnels opening onto the plain from a rise of land and defended from easy access by no less than three growths of stout moonvine, so densely intertwined that they formed a single immense organism. One could see Fethyeh for miles.

We reached the outer layers of vine before the moons were fully risen. Timmon and I were the first to enter into the underground passages, Mikra remaining behind to hunt for supper; many animals take refuge in moonvine when the sun has set. I did not ask Timmon where we were going but simply followed him through tunnels lit by the soft glow from the vine roots around us, and by patterns of phosphorescent stone that in Fethyeh were shaped to resemble the figures of jumpers in various scenes from warren life: a mating ceremony for two does; more does hunting on the open plain or bucks and does doing battle with an enemy clan. Timmon let me study these as I wished. In some cases he knew the name of the artist and told it to me; many of the light-murals were very old.

One of the murals has burned itself forever onto my memory. An old doe stooped with age, held a young cub in her arms and adorned the cub with links of precious metal. The figure of the young cub was full of life, every line being drawn with animation. But the old one was just the opposite, all stillness and gravity. The old one's hands framed the face of the young one, a gesture that might be a caress or that might be meant to hold the cub at a distance. The artist had captured a moment that went on suggesting other moments in the mind of the beholder. This, Timmon told me, was what every painter, every singer, every craftsman sought to create. A sign of the success of the Fethyeh murals was that the two-legs had not destroyed them outright.

In Fethyeh, as in Harless, the singers hall was entirely underground, lit by two cross-tunnels that in time of war were filled with earth. In ancient days Fethyeh had been able to boast that this hall had never fallen to the hand of any enemy, not even during the squabbles between clans that were the rule in Asveroth long before the two-legs. The hall was very large and moonvine encroached through the cross-tunnels, filling the hall with eerie glow. Bones covered the floor.

Timmon led me to the singer's dais and showed me the chair where the singer sat when at feasts he sang for the gods. The chair at Fethyeh was high-backed, carved with intricate signs that name the gods and describe their various attributes. I gazed at these mysteries in wonder. Timmon touched the arm of the chair as if it were an object of endless reverence. "My father sat here," he said, his claws raking the stone. "It was he who first sang 'Nightsong,' on the evening when Fethyeh fell to the two-legs. You knew that, didn't you?" I nodded, but he wasn't even looking. He was lost in his story. "The two-legs had captured all the other warrens and we knew by then we were defeated. Survivors from across Asveroth gathered at Fethyeh as if there were some hope left to us, as if we had some chance of surviving, huddled here in the dark. We could hear the two-legs digging in the upper tunnels." He gazed upward, and I saw the gaping hole in the hall ceiling, covered over now with a growth of vine. "I was in the audience," Timmon said. "So were some of your kin, Kemma. We knew we were the last free jumpers in the world. By then we'd already heard about the pens, east of the mountains. We knew if we didn't die we would be taken there, we knew there was no freedom left for our kind. But we feasted anyway. We listened to the two-legs digging through the vines and the earth and we behaved as we always had."

I gazed at the piles of white bones. My kin lay here. The thought of my clan had not occurred to me in connection with these piles of bone. I did not know how I was supposed to feel. Presently Timmon's hand weighed on my shoulder. His face was rapt, and he gazed over the empty hall as if he were seeing its last moment of glory.

"Did your father write 'Nightsong' himself?" I asked.

"No one wrote it." He swallowed, gazing upward into darkness. "The song was there already that night, in all of us. When my father began singing we heard the words echoing in our own heads, every one of us. When we opened our mouths the song poured out, there was no stopping it. We sang when the two-legs opened the roof and fell among us with their weapons. We sang as we fought, and we died still singing. They killed my father, but not before he had sung the whole cycle. Me they took alive."

I listened to this, but I was descending from the dais as he said it, wandering among the bones without much thought except that the bones of my kin ought to be marked with some special sign. The story of my mother's capture was not new to me. In the pens I was famous, being the first jumper born in captivity. She died as soon as I was born, out of shame. Though I was merely the first, and other shameful births followed.

I believe I walked a long time among the bones of those who died at that last feast in Fethyeh. My thoughts were much as I have said, a mixture of the past and the present. Timmon descended from the dais and found me. "Come away," he said. "Your anger is useless. Remember, your father's bones are watching you."

"There are a thousand bones here," Mikra said, and we turned at once to her voice. She slung two vine chickens onto the hearth, beneath one of the cross-tunnels. "If you give them all eyes we'll feel mighty self-conscious while we eat." She stopped to sniff, deeply. "These bones stink like two-legs."

"Some of them are two-legs," Timmon said, his voice mild.

Mikra paused, and I thought I saw anger in her face. "You sound as sorry for them as for your own kind."

Mikra proceeded to pluck the birds clean. The long tail feathers she gave to me, and I laid them on the altar of the house god, near the hearth. The skull of a two-leg already sat on the altar and I did not move it from its seat.

Timmon had remained near the singers' dais. Mikra called to him, "Come and eat, yellow-fur. It'll strengthen your bones for tomorrow."

This struck Timmon as funny, and he remarked that some folk could never let others rest, but must always be reminding them of the work that must be done tomorrow. He shuffled across the hall to join us, picking at his share of the chicken. We ate, as is the custom, in silence. Timmon presently dropped the last bone and crossed the hall to the dais again. Mikra watched as I did, as he ascended to the chair.

This time no one called for a song. Timmon let his head fall back and closed his eyes. At the first breath, Mikra let out a sigh as heavy as if her heart were breaking. We sat perfectly still as Timmon's voice broke over us, the cadences of "Nightsong", sung in this hall long ago by the last free jumpers as they died. I had heard Timmon sing many times before, and many songs, but never that one.

His voice hung in the air, full and pure like nothing else in the world, and the hall received this act of homage by giving back the gift it had always ceded to songmakers: perfect resonance, in which the singer's art could fully shine. The song is simple, as great things often are. Its verses tell the story of the nightfall over our race, when the two-legs came in metal ships from the sky, landing first in the eastern part of the world and then, with much suffering, crossing the mountains to the golden plain that stole their hearts. Within the verses is the memory of our jumping free in Asveroth, when we knew of no fences or pens, when we lived as we had always lived, when Asveroth was ours only, and the gods favored us above every other kind of creature. Finally, it is the memory of our fathers' and mothers' deaths, the washing of their blood onto our hands, the shame that we bear for living beyond our time of freedom, after the gods have turned their faces away from us, forever.

I have heard that song sung many times since then. But for a moment in that hall where it was first sung, a magic happened. I saw the feast hall in its last glory and heard the bombs going off in the upper tunnels. Sorrowful faces flickered in torchlight, jumpers who knew their deaths were close and that they had been abandoned by the gods. This is the truth of the song. Night is falling. The gods have left us for those who please them better. Our time in the world is passed, and we are as wasted as the wind against the mountains. Shadows are falling, the gods have left us.

When Timmon stopped singing, no one spoke. The moment of vision passed. But I understood Timmon, finally. I understood why we simply jumped, without any thought of destination or ultimate escape. Asveroth was our prison now too. The two-legs would find us, however far we went. When we slept that night, in nests of golden grass, no ghosts troubled us. We were their kind and had given them their song. Any restlessness we had we brought with us; I felt it in me, I know, who jumped free in Asveroth but knew the freedom would not last.

Mikra woke me before light, saying the wardens had drawn much closer while we slept. "We're leaving, now," she said, and I sprang up from my comfortable bed, rubbing bits of gold leaf from my fur. I could smell the machines myself, a high-pitched stink.

Timmon stood in the moonvine, sniffing. "There are two fliers," he said, "coming from the north as best I can tell. These are not the same machines that have been following us."

"No, these are new," Mikra said. She turned to him almost gently. "Are you ready? We won't get much rest today, I'm afraid."

"I have no choice," Timmon said, "ready or not."

We swung through the moonvine, dull gray in the sere sunlight, hitting the open plain in the middle of a herd of deer that scattered in every direction. Any other morning Mikra would have killed and we would have eaten, but we had no time. We jumped, long and low across the wavering grasses.

For a time fear lent us strength and the wardens fell behind. Then for a time we held even with the flying machines, the smell of the exhaust neither growing nor receding. I watched Timmon anxiously as we traveled and could see him tiring, each stride a fraction less certain than the last, though he hung on gamely. It was plain to Mikra and me he could not keep up that speed forever. Soon Mikra was forced to set a slower pace, and soon after that the wardens began to close on us again.

At noon we paused for water at an open pool in a glade of farthelin, bright blue leaves floating down on breezes from high, silver branches. Timmon panted, hardly able to get his breath long enough to drink, and I could see the pounding of his heart beneath his ribs, his whole frame shuddering. When Mikra gave out the call to jump again, Timmon tried to stand but his legs would not hold his weight. He staggered and fell into the pool, blue petals clinging to his fur, his mouth. Mikra gaped at him and called, "Timmon! Are you out of your mind? They're getting closer by the minute."

"God help me," Timmon said, his voice soft as the breezes, "I can't go any farther."

"Don't be a fool. Get up! Do you want to die here?"

He tried again, and this time managed to stand. This satisfied Mikra, and we jumped again, but at every landing I watched the impact eat at his strength, till I was certain he would not last more than a few jumps longer. By a thicket of moonvine he did falter, mistiming his landing. He sank into the grass. Mikra circled back to us when she saw what had happened.

She offered no speeches either. Her eyes were full of sorrow. At last she said, "The skimmers are close."

"He can't go any farther," I said.

She glanced round wildly, and then said, "Help me get him to the vine." She stooped to lift him. I touched his legs, only that, but when I did he cried out. Mikra said, hoarsely, "The leg's broken."

Timmon gasped, his ribs flailing for air. "You'll have to leave me here," he said. "You don't have any choice."

Mikra did not answer, staring numbly. I said, "They'll kill you."

"I can't jump, Kemma. You can't stay with me, what use would that be?" He lay his head in the grass, short of breath again. Mikra gazed northward, nostrils distended. I knelt next to Timmon. He had won the argument, or rather the facts had won. He watched me with a calm I could hardly credit.

"Get into the moonvine," Timmon said quietly. "Hide there, and you may have a chance. The vine confuses their machines, they may not find you."

In the north I could see the glint of silver above the horizon. Timmon was breathing restfully. Mikra took my arm and we broke for the vine before the skimmers were so close they could see us; though something sank within me to leave poor Timmon lying there. We climbed high in the thick, tangled branches. We did not have long to wait.

The skimmers came straight for the clearing, settling into the grass on currents of air. These machines were the familiar sort used east of the mountains; for all we know the two-legs use them on all their worlds: slim, of various colors, with bright lights at the front and back; the two-legs sit under an opaque bubble at the center of the machine, where there are many panels of buttons which control the flow of air and the functioning of the various weapons. I have been close to these skimmers in the pens. There were two in the clearing that morning, just as Timmon had predicted. The bubbles opened and the wardens leapt out, clambering over the silver metal body. Six wardens.

They gave him a merciful, quick death. The one who killed him had the decency to burn his remains.

Even after he was dead the skimmers remained, however, and the two-legs waited in the clearing, gazing at the moonvine and at the open country beyond. They knew three jumpers had escaped. They know, from long years of watching us, that we are loyal creatures, that if we had abandoned Timmon we would probably still be close by. They cleaned their skimmers, on which a little of Timmon's blood had splattered. One of the machines presently rose up on its bed of air, heading south, most likely to search for us in the immediate area. The other skimmer rested in the clearing as before.

During this long scene neither Mikra nor I made a sound, but when the flier flew away from the clearing we began to understand, and to whisper quietly to one another, that if we were not careful we might share Timmon's fate, and quickly. All day the lone flier waited in the clearing. By nightfall the second flier returned, and we watched the two-legs conferring, noting the way they surveyed the moonvine with their naked eyes and with the machines they carried in the skimmers. Moonvine confuses them, but there are ways to compensate even for that. When the two-legs made camp in the clearing, we knew. Come morning they would take the vine apart, branch by branch. We could not hide here through another day.

Lying in Mikra's arms that night, I wondered what life might have been like if we had known each other in peaceful times. I wondered if we would have loved each other. Then I stopped the thoughts altogether, since they were of no use.

Through the night we smelled the stink of their scorched foods, the smoke from the little sticks they hold in their mouths, their excrement, their sweat, same as in the pens. I slept a little, but I had bad dreams; I was in the pens again, only now the fences were the mountains themselves, and the wardens had me tied to the ground and were flying their skimmers across me again and again. In the dream Timmon was next to me, speaking words of comfort in my ear, and finally singing. Mikra woke me to keep me quiet.

I took a turn staying awake, watching the warden who was watching us. Mikra slept soundly and wakened without prompting, near sunrise. I knew without her telling me that we would leave, and we crept without a sound through the vine and out the other side where the golden plain beyond was broad and open. Mikra sniffed the air, though there was nothing to smell except the wardens' camp in the clearing. We leapt from the vine and set out along the plain.

For one moment we jumped free in Asveroth again. The grasses brushed our legs and the winds swept past us as we bounded high in the air. A joy overtook me despite everything, and Mikra too; I could hear her laughing. The Karethagan peaks hung on the horizon and I dreamed we would reach them, and perhaps hide there, remaining free forever.

But before the tenth jump the wind brought us fresh news. The illusion of freedom was ended, and the feeling of my dream returned. In my head was

Timmon's voice, clear and full as when he sat on the singers throne in Fethyeh. The gods have left us, night is falling.

We jumped very fast now that it was only Mikra and me. By full morning we had put some distance between us and the skimmers, jumping downwind, wherever it led us, as if we were blind. Once we crossed a farmyard where angry two-legs were mounting one of the huge harvesters; I thought we had cleared the complex without incident but when we reached open country again—only a moment, as jumpers measure time, less than the full length of one leap—Mikra was slower, with blood and singed fur on her thigh. I jumped side by side with her then, and we watched each other without speaking. The farmers had likely been warned we were in the area; they had seen us coming. No need to say any of this. We had lived with two-legs long enough to know. They are sprung from cunning gods, they leave nothing to chance. If the stories one hears are true, we are not the first world they have taken to rule, and we will not be the last.

We headed east toward the mountains, no longer following the wind. We had no hope of reaching the mountains now, since with Mikra's leg injured we could not hope to outdistance the fliers for long. Even with Mikra's injury we were still jumpers, we still had speed, and the hill country soon loomed large. We might have reached the hills and confounded the wardens once again. For a while I thought we would. But in the afternoon, with the first hills swelling under us, we saw more silver flying on the southern horizon. New skimmers had come.

We stopped. No moonvine grew within reach. The skimmers that had chased us divided quickly to cut us off. The new skimmers did the same, and we were surrounded. Mikra trumpeted her rage and pain, tearing up the earth with her talons. I simply stood still. The smell of skimmers became so heavy it was hard to breathe.

The skimmers stopped two jumps away, and machines in each of them joined to make a barrier in the air between. The bubbles opened and the wardens stepped out from each skimmer at the same moment, on signal. One of them pointed a machine at me and I fell to the ground under a weight I could not see and could not fight. I prayed to the god in the metal to release me but my prayer dispersed on the wind. But the weight was not so great I could not breathe. The wardens meant to spare me, it seemed.

Mikra they would kill, and the look she gave me told me she knew that. "Goodbye," she said, and she was able to smile, same as when she returned from the hunt with fresh meat. "His father's song was true, wasn't it?" Timmon's voice was in her head too. She watched the two-legs advancing slowly, and cursed. "Even with their guns and machines they're still afraid, do you see? Well, I'll put an end to this quickly. Long life, Kemma."

We parted that way, without fuss. I have often wondered what would have happened had she lived. She gave a final cry of fury and leapt onto the first party of two-legs. They were slow, for all their caution, and she crushed one of them in landing. They hamstrung her with a purplish beam from one of their guns, a quick flickering. But even then she killed another that strayed too close to her claws. When she understood she could move no more, she began to eat the dead one. I don't know why she did this, unless it was to make them angry enough to kill her quickly. Two-leg meat is not good for food. One of them burst her skull with another beam of light, and she fell motionless into the bright grass. The two-legs gathered round her as if they could not quite believe the chase was over, as if they could not trust her to be dead.

I did not die then or there. Later I would wish I had. The wardens kept me alive as an example. As punishment for my days of freedom they took off my jumping legs.

My people nursed me to a kind of health and with time I became reconciled to the passing of days. But the loss of Mikra deadened my heart. Songmakers made a song for the three of us, of our accidental escape and of how we jumped free in Asveroth for a time. Sometimes the young singers will sing it as we feast on such food as we have. Sometimes, when the elders gather, we sing the "Nightsong" too. But I always hear those words in Timmon's voice.

Our numbers are fewer each year, and we survivors grow tired. The young cubs speak of anger and oppression and their new leaders have many dreams of what we will do someday to regain our land, our freedom. They live in hope that a day of reckoning will come, and maybe it will. But I am not the one to question the gods or their indifference. It is the nature of everything, to follow the strong and not the weak; when the world was ours, when we were the strongest, this was what we believed. But in the coming of these strange, ruthless beings from some other world, our gods have found their truest image and have fled from us like a change of wind.

The Dancing Floor

CHERRY WILDER

Born in New Zealand, Cherry Wilder has lived for long stretches of time in Australia and in Germany, and has recently moved back to New Zealand again. She made her first sale in 1974 to the British anthology New Writings in SF 24, *and since then, in addition to a number of sales to* Asimov's Science Fiction, *has sold to markets such as* Interzone, Universe, Strange Plasma, *and elsewhere. Her many books include* The Luck of Brin's Five, The Nearest Fire, The Tapestry Warriors, Second Nature, A Princess of the Chamein, Yorath of the Wolf, The Summer's King, *and* Cruel Designs. *Her most recent books are a collection,* Dealers in Light and Darkness, *and a new novel,* Signs of Life. *She is currently at work on a fantasy trilogy entitled "The Secrets of Hylor."*

Here she takes us to a long-abandoned space habitat where secrets abound and hidden resentments simmer beneath a seemingly placid and pastoral surface, and nothing is quite what it seems.

The dock at Wingard had the monumental proportions associated with Triad North, the company, and with Winthrop A. North IV, the man for whom it was designed. The Archive shuttle hung in the big shadowy facility like a tiny fish in a dark pool: all the passengers were curious, standing at the ports, as they were directed to a slot.

"Cult classic!" said Elliot March, the hotwit of the team. "Been used for trivid locations. Yo, Dayne—they made two runs of COOP VYRAT, SPACE PIRATE here. . . ."

"Right here in the dock?" asked Dayne Robbins.

"Aw come on—here and out in the open, on the asteroid."

"Did they shoot on the Dancing Floor?" asked Taya Schwartz.

"No, Doctor," said Elliot. "Not in the episodes I saw. You work on the floor any time, Carl?"

"No, we were in the western valley system," said Carl Curran, "but we had a look at the floor."

Taya Schwartz did not know that the young media assistant had been on the Wingard habitat asteroid before — she must question him about his visit with the trivid team. She was conscious of the fact that her colleagues were all much younger than herself.

The docking was complete; Mahoney, the shuttle pilot, shot the hatch and they filed out carrying their personal packs. Three android auxiliaries in their service grey uniforms manned the dock; they came bouncing up, full of oxper cheerfulness, saluted Flight-Captain Mahoney, greeted everyone else politely. Taya got their names quickly: Thomas Scott, Philip Grey, Peter Miles.

"Looking forward to your briefing, Doctor!" said Tom Scott, apparently the Leader of the android unit.

"How many auxiliaries on Wingard?" she asked.

"Just us three wishers doing dock duty today and one other, Cliff Watson, out in the green."

A man and a woman from the holding mission stepped out of the elevator; they were the reception committee. The oxper moved away and the Archive party were greeted by Gregor Hansen and Astra Wylie. They were a notably handsome couple, in their thirties, — their bright "colony" clothes had no service markings. The elevator had a smell of earth, of the countryside — the visitors stepped out into bright sunlight and stood amazed by the beauty of Wingard.

The dock was on the ridge that surmounted a deep bowl of green; they looked down into a valley system, earth-green, with earth trees and exotics, stretching into the countryside. Wingard had once supported a population of 1,000 mensch, 1,000 souls. There were still a few buildings to be seen in the distance. Cottage units and brown habitat huts were clustered in the nearest valley.

"Do the personnel from the mission live down there?" Taya asked the young woman, Astra Wylie.

"Yes, sure," she said. "That's our house — the new unit with the red roof by the tankstand."

The ridge above the valley continued on round and turned into a heavy wall of earth and stone, a miniature mountain range running north from where they stood. It showed the substance of the original asteroid, mined out and brought to this point in space by one of the Triad North companies. Taya Schwartz was able to glimpse a haze of green over the lower portion of the spinal wall: the wilderness area of Wingard, another series of interlocking deep valleys.

The Archive team were accommodated in the Harmony lodge, just beyond the ridge, at the end of the tall white complex that had housed the old Admin, near the dock. Gregor Hansen drove Dr Schwartz, the senior archivist, and Mahoney, the pilot, while Wylie brought the others in a larger electric runabout. Taya Schwartz ran a steady interview all the way checking the known data on the evacuation in 2499, the legal position, the state of the biosphere then and now.

Hansen explained, rather deadpan, that Wingard had gone down because of the life-support crash at Yesod Habitat. A couple of disorders in the water and the air on Wingard were taken out of proportion — the Terran admin panicked, ordered evacuation.

"And the settlers couldn't return," said Taya. "Pretty rough after twenty-five years on Wingard."

"Hard luck for those mensh," said Hansen, with some feeling. "We wouldn't live anywhere else."

"Some habitats have gone down, been evacuated, after more than a hundred years," said Mahoney. "Tough thing here was that it wasn't necessary. Badly handled by Earth admin."

"I remember," said Taya. "Winthrop North was sick and in deep financial shit. . . ."

"I heard you knew him, Doctor Schwartz," said Mike Mahoney. "Winthrop North."

Gregor Hansen turned his head to stare at Taya Schwartz, frowning. Winthrop A. North IV tended to polarise opinion; he was the last of his kind as well as the last of his line.

"We studied exo biology at the Pioneer Valley Foundation," she said. "He was an exceptional person but he had more than a touch of mad millionaire even then."

Mahoney gave a guilty chuckle. The last president of Triad North cast a long shadow. The notion of an industrialist who went about in space with his own engineers had always been unreal, reckless; North the Fourth seemed to have worn himself out. He had died ten years ago, in his Canadian retreat; sixty years old and a crotchety recluse, like millionaires of old time.

"Old North cared for this place, for Wingard," said Hansen. "Had his ashes scattered to enrich the soil, like one of the original settlers. I read his plaque in the memorial ground by the Sun Kiln."

"I didn't know that," said Taya.

"How long after the evacuation did Terran Security put in the holding mission?" asked Mahoney. "Was there ever a move to repopulate?"

"I guess there were plans," said Hansen. "Terran Security settled with North, a year or so before he died. There had been annual checks of this place — the problem with the air and the water righted itself with a little help from the bio engineers."

"Archive would like to target the year the Dancing Floor was built," observed Taya, "between one annual survey and the next. A pity nothing was seen by Earth personnel."

"Well, Doc," said Hansen. "You said it. *Earth personnel*. The first holding mission arrived in '68, bunch of retired Space Service Joes and their wives or partners. They came in on contract for five years, sort of Recreation Leave. They didn't patrol too much . . . they missed the meteorite over in the East Greenwall. They discovered the Floor in 2507, thought it had been there a while."

"And there was no-one out there earlier — hiking, camping, building a holiday hut?" she asked.

"Has someone been talking?" asked Hansen. "Some data was red, at least for a while. . . ."

"I haven't heard anything," said Taya. "Do I need clearance?"

"Wingard had a bunch of Die-Hards, is all," the young man burst out. "This comes up every time a habitat is evacuated. Some folk will not be shifted . . . they run off, hide in the bushes, in a cave . . ."

"Don't I know it," said Mahoney. "We had problems at Celestra and Novion."

Taya wanted to hear more about these Die-Hards but she was patient. They had arrived at the Harmony lodge, once the guest house for a beautiful, thriving habitat, which specialised in bio-farming and dendrology. The lodge was a handsome structure in Wright Renaissance style with vistas of dayplex and pillars that resembled dressed wood. There was no-one in the lobby but when Gregor Hansen shouted a young girl and an even younger boy came racing down the staircase.

He introduced them to the visitors: Marla Jenner, elder child of the other mission family, and his own son Sven Hansen. They had been doing chores in the lodge and minding the systems: Taya understood a lack of personnel, the feeling of rattling around in untenanted buildings on a ghost world.

She was left along with the children while Hansen and Mahoney went to fetch the baggage. She thought of certain trade goods she had brought along and felt in the pockets of her carrying bag.

"Would you like some of these holovox cards?" she asked. "Birds of Earth? Trivid Heroes?"

Marla, the older girl, nodded to Sven, who wiped his hands on his overall then gravely accepted the two brightly glowing packets. Marla quickly opened her packet and made her card with the Kookaburra utter its laugh. Taya had found the soy-nut health bars which both of them accepted. Marla slipped hers into a pocket but Sven took a big exploratory bite and was chewing heartily when the men came back.

Gregor Hansen dropped Taya's work-pack with an audible crunch and raced to his son, gripping him by the back of the neck.

"What's he got? What you got, boy?" he panted. "Spit it out! Spit it right out!"

As Sven spat his mouthful on to the dusty tiled floor his father wrenched away the rest of the candy bar.

"Marla," he said, tense with disgust and anger. "Take him to the washroom and see that he rinses his mouth out good with the bottled water."

Before the kids were out of sight, heading behind the staircase, Hansen turned angrily upon Taya.

"What was in that candy?" he demanded.

"You can read the ingredients from the label," said Taya. "It is a soy-nut health bar from the World Space Commissary at Armstrong Base. I eat them myself and give them to my grandchildren."

"You hand out any more of this rotgut candy to Sven?"

"No, Mr Hansen," she said. "Is your son not well? Does he have a dietary problem?"

"Soon will have if he takes that kinda junk!" snapped Hansen.

Mahoney looked shocked by the man's outburst.

"The Doctor wasn't to know. . . ." he said.

"To know what?" said Hansen, looking from one guest to another, red-faced, his eyes narrowed with suspicion.

"To know that you disapproved violently of certain types of food," said Taya. "I'm sorry."

"We live clean here, Mam. That boy has never tasted any sugar or additives. . . ."

"Well, he still hasn't," she said evenly. "Read the label, Mr Hansen."

"Why should I believe that shit thing, a printed label from some World Space supply outlet?"

"Why indeed," she said. "Where is my room, please?"

"Up one flight," he said. "Mezzanine Number 27. Elevators are nonfunctioning."

She picked up her work-case and strode off up the handsome staircase, with dark treads of wood substitute and a banister of black metal rods.

"Doc! Doc! I'll carry your bag!" called Mahoney.

"Thanks Captain," she smiled down at him. "I'll be fine!"

She heard Mahoney trying to take the man from the holding mission to task; when she turned her head at the curve of the stairs the children had come back. Sven was sitting emptily on the bottom step while Marla picked up his mouthful of chewed up candy bar. She was not using paper of course or any kind of manufactured wiper but a bunch of big papery leaves.

Taya Schwartz was stung by memory. The door of room 27 was open to receive her—she staggered into the spacious guest suite. The windows were open and the kids had placed a vase of fresh flowers—yellow daisies and statice—on the desk. She put down her case and sat on the bed, wearily. She thought of soft *amyth* leaves and of the chocolate she had eaten on a far distant world.

The Archive team, all quartered in Harmony, walked over to the Admin diner at 19:00 hours; the briefing was scheduled for 21:00. Taya was not really pleased with this—she liked to relax alone before a briefing, but there was no food outlet in Harmony lodge. The Admin was well-lit, clean and fresh, with a reggae band on the monitors.

"Hey, this is better," said Elliot March, under his breath. "Why can't they have our place like this? What makes the difference."

"The oxper," said Taya. "They take care of this building."

Dayne Robbins, the Medic on the Archive team, was also their commissariat liaison. She was already helping in the canteen along with the oxper Miles and Grey. The food was very good: fresh Wingard vegetables along with the specials they had brought from the Moon. There was a range of tea, fruit boosters and juice. Dayne brought their dessert and settled at the table.

"Problems of interaction," she said. "Experienced anything?"

"The holding mission are hard-line anti-service, against World Space," suggested Taya. "Possibly they're anti-Earth as well: Spaceborn or Never Returns."

"*What?*" said Elliot. "How you make that out, Doc?"

"It's true," said Dayne. "They can barely interact with the android auxiliary teams. The kids aren't allowed to speak to them or enter this building. Groups of service personnel who visit Wingard for any reason—to inspect the dock facility for instance—have a minimum of contact to the Jenners and the Hansens."

"It wasn't like that when you were here with the media team, Carl!" exclaimed Elliot.

"No—but these are new guys," said Carl Curran. "The first holding mission were older folk, veterans from World Space taking it easy on their Recreation Leave. Don't know where they found these two families."

"I know that," said Mahoney. "They came from the planet Arkady. The southern continent—has an official name now—"

"*Oparin*," said Taya Schwartz wistfully.

She left the others in the canteen and sat in a pleasant window in the lounge, looking out over the green valleys while she went over her material. Presently Hal Jenner, the senior member of the holding mission came and introduced himself. He was a well set up man in his forties, with dark eyes and thick dark brown hair clubbed back with a strip of green cloth. His manner was relaxed and genial: compared with his younger colleague, Hansen, he was a diplomat. He explained, first of all, that he had been checking the road into the inland that morning.

"One of the androids reported a fallen tree," he said. "I had to take care of it."

"*You* had to move the tree?" Taya couldn't resist it.

"Well, no, just tidy a little," said Jenner.

"That would be Cliff Watson, out there," she said. "I've worked with auxiliary personnel several times and found them reliable colleagues."

Hal Jenner caught his breath.

"How many people on Wingard, Mr Jenner?"

"Four adults in the holding mission," he said, "Hansen and Wylie, my wife Fern and myself, our two children Marla and Dan, and Sven Hansen, makes seven all told. Then there are the folk at the Old Mill—three souls, former colonists. You're bound to hear of them—our little family of Die-Hards. Those are all the people. Then World Space sends in their units of androids, four at a time, replaced every half earth year, from Armstrong Base."

Taya had already registered in the hard-nosed young Hansen a more friendly attitude to the original settlers. None of these people had been members of World Space—they had been carefully recruited from Earth, from Arkady and from the employees of Triad North.

"You've made contact with the Die-Hards, Ranger Jenner?"

Hal Jenner laughed.

"Yes, sure Doc," he said. "There were reports from the first resettlers, those World Space veterans. They swore there were a few settlers still out there, old folks like themselves, two women and a man, living in the wilderness. We didn't believe them overmuch—"

It was a slip.

"Why not?" she asked. "Because they were from World Space?"

"Well it turned out they weren't lying," he said. "I seen the old fella first. What you'd expect. Skinny old man with a beard down to here. Name of Gunn, Ben Gunn. Asked for medical supplies, water filters and so on. We took down a good load—food, all kinds of good stuff we thought they might use. There they all were, Old Ben and his two old gals, one called Vona? Other one Kirsten, maybe."

"Would it be possible for me to speak to them?" she asked.

"They are very shy," said Hal Jenner. "They have a deep need to be left alone—and we understand that better than most people. You could send a message on their systems. . . ."

He shrugged his shoulders a little hopelessly.

"So your family and the Hansens were recruited on Oparin, in Arkady," Taya pursued, changing the subject.

"We had the wilderness and rough farming experience," he said eagerly. "Gregor and I are both Rangers, Arkady rank. The women are trained Medical Technical Assistants."

"Will you ever consider expanding the numbers of the holding mission—repopulating?"

"No!" he said firmly. "Why should we? Our new specialised projects with the trees and vegetables are flourishing. We're working on a quite different scale from the original Wingard settlers. Besides it's not up to us entirely . . . this is a matter for E.A.A.—Earth Asteroid Administration; they have the resettlement rights for all Triad North habitats."

"You are extreme separatists," she said, holding his gaze. "Ranger Jenner, how can you work for an Earth Utility?"

"It's worth it to live on a clean world," he said. "We keep a close watch on the E.A.A. So far we haven't caught 'em cheating on the deal. They don't bother us too much."

"Is it a bother to receive the Archive team?"

"No Mam!" said Jenner with a broad smile. "The Archive facility operates from the Moon and from other manned planets and habitats. Completely separate from World Space and it's private foundation, not linked to the World Security Organisation or any of its segments."

It was time for the briefing. She followed Jenner into a small conference room which looked pleasantly full—there were the two families from the holding mission, the four members of the Archive team. At the back, separated by tables and chairs, were all four oxper. Cliff Watson had come in from the outback.

Taya spoke last. Elliot March explained the work of Archive—mapping resources throughout the Solar System and near planets. He was careful to explain what every member of the team did: he himself was responsible for admin and for flora and fauna, wild and cultivated. He would work closely with Ranger Hansen. Carl Curran was the cameraman and media specialist; Dayne Robbins was their medic and commissariat assistant. Dr Taya Schwartz was a specialist in extraterrestrial artefacts.

Carl gave a very brief rundown on his work and Dayne simply praised the quality of the Wingard vegetables. When Taya took the floor she had a short round of applause from the oxper. The big projection screen worked perfectly: she changed the order of the picture and hit them with a shot of DanFlor III in full sunlight.

In a meadow filled with bright green grass and ringed with dark scrubby bushes, tall as a hedge, there was a strange construction. Three tall wooden pillars looped with swags of rough green fabric, like fishnet, stood at the edge of a prepared space, fifty meters by a hundred. The space was slightly depressed in the center, a shallow bowl, paved with eighty-centimeter slabs of moulded stone, a bright sandy yellow. The paving stones were closely packed, fitted together; there were no sharp angles or corners; the stones had rounded edges.

"This is the Dancing Floor which Montezuma Antonio Rivez, the great exo-biologist, found upon *Habitat Three*," she announced. "It was the third example to be discovered; this was the year 2465. This type of artefact had already been given the popular name of a Dancing Floor."

The name came from the report on the first artefact to be found—on Europa, the moon of Jupiter, in 2440. There were two stations of space personnel on Europa at that time, in carefully insulated "cities," Paris II and New Hyatt. The exploration of the underground seas and their biology was highly competitive.

A surface patrol from Paris claimed to have watched the building of a strange artefact by a team of eight aliens rated 5.4 on the RK Index, the Rivez-Klein scale of humanoid visual affinity. The builders had a small vessel, roughly the size and shape of a World Space Class Upsilon Transporter, not clearly visible behind a ridge. They worked behind a highly developed air dome on the level site of an older Earth station.

When the pavement was completed there was a pause of ten Earth-equivalent hours while the moulded paving stones set or were dried. The patrol, comfortably encamped behind their own ridge, held their position and kept watching.

Then as the bulk of the gas giant was at its closest to the moon, Europa, they beheld the construction team dancing, they swore it, on the big paving stones. The builders/dancers looked even weirder, their RK index even greater, without their work clothes. They leaped with uncanny grace from stone to stone, in a certain pattern. The paving stones lit up as the dancers stepped upon them. The watchers believed that this light came from some device within the stones, or possibly from the footwear of the dancers. They put forward the notion that the dancing floor, as they called it, was some kind of communication device.

The patrol, already overdue, returned to their Paris base and broke the news of their exciting discovery. But a mischievous concatenation of circumstances—bad karma said some—ensured that the dancers and their floor were never confirmed.

"Yes," said Taya, answering a question. "That is correct, Ms Jenner—it was a seismological disturbance, an earthquake. The area could not be searched for a long time. There was no sign of a wrecked space vessel and only a few fragments that might have been paving stones. The men and women from the Paris patrol on Europa were not fully believed. They were partially discredited as witnesses because of interstation rivalry.

"They were accused of 'zonking'—drinking alcohol, taking illegal drugs. They were *ranked*—lost service credits—for not calling in. The team explained this by saying that reception was very poor. They suspected that the builders of the Danc-ing Floor had a strong electronic presence and would have been immediate-ly aware of any other signals, including the use of trivid equipment. They had attempted some holoks when they first arrived but the alien air dome spoiled the prints.

"All that remained of this alleged encounter was the name 'Dancing Floor' which went into use, however, in reports and later in the media. The same way as 'flying saucer' entered the world languages long ago."

So there was no original footage on the Europa floor but a good simul and some originals of the second artefact, found on Ceres in 2455 by a survey team sent out by Rivez and Klein from their newly formed Archive Foundation at Armstrong Base. They had their own satellite in the asteroid belt and picked up the Dancing Floor on Ceres.

One member of the Paris team from Europa, the retired Lieutenant Cole, C.P.V., was available to accompany this survey team. The structure was confirmed by this officer as another example of the alien artefact as built on Europa.

"This Space Service Lieutenant," said Hansen, "was old, retired, and had been discredited back then on the Jupiter satellite. Could he give good confirmation, Doctor?"

"In my opinion, yes," said Taya. "If we recap we can see the progress of the Rivez-Klein investigation: the destroyed artefact on Europa, Dancing Floor I, 2440, then the Dancing Floor on Ceres, 2455, and the example we have before us on the screen: Dancing Floor III discovered in 2565 by Monty Rivez and Hanna Klein on Habitat Three."

She took a question from Tom Scott.

"Yes. Leader Scott, that arrangement of three wooden pillars, looped with green stuff resembling fishnet is unique to Dancing Floor III. It seems to be a copy of a classical ruin on Earth — maybe copied from a holok or photograph of a painting."

"Doctor Schwarz," said Hal Jenner earnestly. "Any idea what was going on? What they were doing this for?"

"No, Ranger Jenner," she said. "There have been many theories — the original idea of a communication device is not borne out by anything in the stones themselves. I go along with a spiritual or religious ritual. We have the general picture of a team or teams from a highly developed space-travelling race moving through the Sol system and building these artefacts on uninhabited asteroids and habitats. There were unconfirmed reports of sightings of some vessel that might be a mother-ship beyond the asteroid belt. Rivez and Klein believed there might be other undiscovered examples. Dating is important, it would help. The last artefact to be discovered is the Dancing Floor here on Wingard."

Taya brought up its picture on the screen and the oxper reacted as humans might or should have done, recognising a local treasure. They clapped and called out, hey that's it, there's our floor. But the holding mission could not react with pleasure because the oxper did, and they were the artefacts of hated World Space.

Taya could not go on without calling the holding mission.

"Ranger Hansen," she asked, "what do you feel about this artefact on your habitat home, this Dancing Floor?"

"What do I *feel?* . . ." Hansen was puzzled or pretended to be. "Well, I suppose it's impressive. Alien artefact. Not seen any before."

Jenner saw what she was driving at and rallied the settlers, including the children, with a glance.

"Heavens, we *like* it, don't we guys? Yay-Hay-Hay for our Dancing Floor!"

He clapped and the others echoed the strange Oparin cheer.

"Doctor Schwarz," broke in Elliot March, "has this floor been validated? I mean there were cases on Earth and on Arkady. . . ."

The question made the mission folk bristle but Taya was amused by Elliot's provocation.

"Yes, there have been attempts to copy these artefacts in several locations, including the planet Arkady," she said. "Sometimes these were crude hoaxes, fakes, but the one near Riverfield, Arkady, was an artwork, part of a festival display. Also, the replica in New Mexico is a careful attempt at a re-creation, using all known data and a new silicon matirx. The Dancing Floor here on Wingard has been sampled by an oxper team three years ago and accepted as genuine by Archive, the Rivez-Klein Foundation."

Taya went into her wind-up and into the Archive team's biggest PR exercise. Yes, she was certainly looking forward to seeing the floor tomorrow. And she had all the help she needed — Cliff Watson would drive the trekker. In two days the team would have completed its program. On behalf of the Archive Foundation she wished to invite all the inhabitants of Wingard, the people here at the meeting, to a picnic in the green on the third day. A viewing of The Dancing Floor, number four, Wingard's own. She understood that the day was Midweek, with a work free afternoon. . . . Hal Jenner accepted at once, quite heartily enough, on behalf of the holding mission, and the auxiliaries were pleased.

The meeting ended not with supper from the Commissary but with herb tea and home baked cookies brought along by Ms Jenner. The program for the rest of the archive team was settled for the next day.

Taya made sure that the central system outlet in her room at the Harmony Lodge was activated. She combed sleepily through the forests of memory and the endless data banks in search of one called *Weltfic*, a name which made German archivists laugh. She tried her Kamalin special assisted free association test and came up with two words *flint* and *silver* which sent her back to minerals and palaeontology as an association for that elusive name, *Ben Gunn*.

The roads were of packed earth, shot through with pebbles, the substance of the asteroid. It was time for the misty morning rain. They went skimming down from the lodge on the eastern road and drove by a pass through the central divide, something between a ravine and a conduit. There was a sign post which said *Sun Kiln*.

Cliff explained there was another disused pass further north and two closed tunnels on the east wall and the west wall — the settlers had used them to check the outer skin of Wingard. Nowadays the oxper did an occasional fly-past or used their viewers.

They drove on enveloped in green: beech and berioska from Arkady and wild apple trees. The wilderness area of Wingard was beautiful, full of vistas that might have come by chance but might have been designed, like the fake ruins of eighteenth century estates on Earth or the swathed pillars built near the Dancing Floor on *Habitat Three*. There was a stonework bridge over a grassy ravine and a tall building like a silo, covered with vines.

Cliff Watson, who was a boyish oxper, with black hair and brown eyes, kept up a running commentary. She came in with her question:

"You know the settlers, the Die-Hards who still live out here, Cliff?"

"Why sure, Doc," he grinned. "Old Ben and his two friends, Vona and Kirsty. They live in a place called the Old Mill, though it never was a mill I don't believe. Got it done up very comfortable. They even have their own trekker and they've been known to drive about a little. Guess they had the whole place to choose from, when everyone else was lifted out."

"What do they live on?"

"Got a fine garden, couple goats, bunch of bantam-fowls. They don't eat much meat except a little of the turkey jerky and fish we bring them from the Commissary."

"Could I get to meet them?" she asked. "I don't want to intrude on their retreat but they might just have seen some activity in connection with the Dancing Floor."

Cliff looked a little flickery with embarrassment.

"Well, truth is they don't have any regular contact even with us wishers from the auxiliary teams," he said, "but I could ask them."

"Take them some data," she said.

She handed over printouts on the Archive foundation and on herself.

"Now there's something," said Cliff, changing the subject. "Bit of a meteorite came down, side of the hill, over there. You can see where it burnt. The people at the Mill, they saw it come down about four, five years back, gave the auxiliary network a report."

The morning rain had stopped right on time. Taya examined the scarred hillside through her surveyor's goggles.

"I'm anxious to log the time when the Dancing Floor was built, Cliff," she said. "What have we got? A period of nearly fifteen years since evacuation, when Wingard was all but deserted."

"Sure," he replied. "Few clean-up operations, observation trips, from Armstrong, even from Earth. Oh, these Building Team fellows, they had all the time under the sun to fix up their artefact!"

"Is that what you call them? Building Teams?"

"BTAs," he grinned. "Building Team Aliens. Just our name . . ."

He swung the sturdy vehicle round a curve in the road and fell silent. There was the Dancing Floor among its fringe of trees, doubly lit by the sun, for it was lined up with Wingard's eastern row of reflectors on the central ridge to their left.

The road ran at a safe distance from the stones and there was a wooden shelter shed, a viewing place for the floor. Taya was glad when Cliff let her off with her equipment and went on with his routine patrol. He was carrying pig feed, among other things; a family of wild pigs had been introduced illegally years ago and no-one had the heart to cull them out. They had the place to themselves, Cliff pointed out, except for the birds and the pollination insects. The settlers had had a few goats and chickens but there were no other "wild animals."

She found a good place for her little four-foot tower which incorporated all the measuring and recording devices she preferred. Her first step, always, was to make trivid footage and some holok stills of the floor and its surroundings.

The Wingard floor was a little more compact than the one on Habitat Three and she knew, from scrapings taken by the earlier auxiliary team, that the composition of the stones had altered very slightly. More natural white sand, plus a yellow dye, coupled with the matrix gel, a weird semiorganic substance like some of the river-crystals found on Arkady. She took her readings, then walked out on to the floor.

Taya Schwartz had seen the "Giant Steps" on the moon, examined the blue caves on Itys. She had been among structures so weird and ingenious in the Australian desert that she had been loath to admit they were earthmade, in other words, a hoax.

As a young girl she had seen the wonders of Earth for the first time, had wept to see the works of humankind. The ruined cities of America, the temples of Mexico, and, beneath their protective air domes, Stonehenge, the Pyramids, and Abu Simbel saved from the flood waters.

She had flown to the Fire Islands, as a child; she had walked the white streets of the city of Rintoul, the Golden Net of the World. Her childhood friends and teachers had had huge fringed eyes, soft hooting voices, strange hands, with two proto-thumbs in apposition. Nothing alien was alien to her—rather she was an alien herself, born and bred on Torin, in the sign of the Sea Serpent. Now she stood deeply impressed by the beauty and mystery of the dancing floor.

She slid a palm-sized memory card from her tower—although she knew the patterns by now—and walked on to the floor. She stepped on to a stone in the center of the row of double stones which formed the northern border of the floor and began to move through the routine. She always experienced a great feeling of lightness and agility when she performed this exercise. There were longer leaps which she could not accomplish and it was believed, through contact with the Europa witnesses, that the dance had contained twirls and twists and figures for two or more dancers. There had been clear markings upon the stones of Habitat Three for several dance patterns.

Taya completed the simplest routine which brought her right across the shallow bowl of yellow stepping stones to the southern border, with a couple of side trips to east and west. She went slowly and completed the "dance" in eighteen minutes with one rest and a couple of repeats. By this time she was certain that she was being watched by two persons, two humans, standing in the trees not far from the shelter shed.

She walked carefully back to the center stone and looked directly at the watchers. One of the women turned and fled, running off along the road, "into the green." Taya could see her bright shirt flying and the dust raised by her sandals.

The second woman came striding through the trees and the moving leaf shadows. She was as tall as Taya herself, a good-looking fair woman in her fifties. They were both wearing practical zipsuits but the grey of the newcomer seemed a little better kept than Taya's well-worn blue cupro. They met and shook hands in the center of the floor.

"Small system!" said the woman. "Vona Cropper, Dr Schwartz!"

Taya found that she *did* know the woman but where or when they had met eluded her.

"I'm sorry," she said. "I can't quite . . ."

"Must have been twenty years ago — You delivered a paper at Humboldt County. I was on Earth leave."

"I'm sorry to send your friend running off!" said Taya.

"Kirsty, Kirsty Allen, is very shy."

They walked back to the tower and Taya found herself handing out trade goods again. A set of all the floor dance routines on palm cards. Then she dug into her satchel and they sat in the shelter shed and drank lemon lift. She felt a certain distrust that she could hardly explain — had the holding mission infected her with their separatist thoughts?

"You live at the Mill, then," she said. "I asked Cliff Watson to request an interview. Any chance of that?"

"Oh we know the archive team are here," said Vona, stalling. "We're cybernauts. Not into face-to-face. Where you staying, Doctor?"

When Taya mentioned the Harmony Lodge the woman handed over a card of her own with lengthy site numbers.

"No need to call. Just leave a channel open."

Taya began to talk about gardening, the range of vegetables they were able to grow down in the eastern valleys. Had they done well at the Old Mill with the new types of water storage crystals? No, they were only hearsay to the cybernauts — Taya opined that she might come up with a bag of the little devils. Worked well on the moon, in the planter domes. She slipped in her question about the meteorite over yonder on the ridge — had Vona or her friends seen it?

Vona laughed and went off into a graphic account of the night the meteorite came down. Put on a real show for them — a clear bright evening, only Ben saw it coming and called them out to the platform. Their whole place shook. Of course they put in a report through the oxper — time rushing on, was it five, six years ago now? And they went down next morning to take a look at the site and to check on the Dancing Floor, see that the impact hadn't moved the stones any. All there was to see was the big burn mark over yonder.

So the Floor had been built some time earlier, persisted Taya gently, any chance of finding out the year? Any chance the Mill dwellers could have missed the building of the floor? Unlikely, said Vona, they often came this far down the valley. But the Die-Hards — she used the term with a grin — only came to settle in the Mill about '68, '69, when the first holding mission came in. Before that they had been living on the western side of the Divide in one of the houses but when the new folks arrived Ben decided to move further away. The Mill was really a tourist lodge from the old days; they had it done up pretty good by now.

"And the Dancing Floor was already there," said Taya.

"Just beautiful!" said Vona. "Of course we knew at once what it was. We didn't put in any report. Just waited until the new oxper units began to patrol. One day they brought some of the Veterans down this way for a drive."

Taya sighed deeply.

"I respect everyone's need for privacy, even for a family life in solitude, here on Wingard. But there's too much separatism. These new young families from Oparin, on Arkady. I feel as if the whole system was polarised, flying off into fragments. . . . I wish we could come together more."

She felt that it was a feeble plea for togetherness; she was still holding back, out of habit, appeasing people to get her precious information. Vona Cropper looked at her with a kind of pity.

"There's plenty of cybernauts out there. Place buzzes with talk, with ideas."

They parted with a handshake; Vona Cropper went striding off down the dirt road, among the trees. Where Taya must not go. Hell, what would they do to her if she simply followed? Stood outside the phoney "Old Mill" shouting and pleading to speak to an old man and his two old girl-friends.

Taya went on with her measuring but the work had become drudgery. Something about the Die-Hard women, the one who ran off, the one who fronted up and talked to her so blandly, had aroused her mistrust. After a break she took the detector wand and went round the floor: the fragment and debris count was higher than she would have expected.

She walked east, towards the dark scar from the meteorite, and the wand picked up an unusually large piece of metal-coated ceramic. It had been buried almost thirty centimeters down and laid bare, she guessed, laughing, by a pig rooting for wild yams. Part of an electronic grid? She bagged it up carefully, controlling her excitement. Hunches and wishes were part of any research project; this *could* have come from the Dancing Floor team, the BTAs.

The trusty wand picked up the vibration of the trekker coming back along the road; she was glad to drive off with Cliff Watson. Nope, he hadn't seen the two women, Vona and Kirsty; he left the information pinned on their door where they'd be sure to get it.

"What is it with all these mensch, Cliff?" she burst out. "Die-Hards? Separatists? Wingard has a positive ecology! It was designed by Win North and his team to hold a thousand interactive, living, sharing beings, humans and androids, visitors from other worlds . . . I remember he said once . . ."

Her voice betrayed her, she began to choke up from pure loneliness and longing for days gone by, but she brought it out: "Taya, I thought of that one as a way-station, a stopover on the way to Old Earth. Who can you think of from your planet, Torin, who might take the long journey, the way you did, as a young girl?"

"That's great," said Cliff. "I mean with the sharing and the way he included some of us poor wishers and mensch from other worlds. I'm telling you, Doc Schwartz, people think we have no feelings but it's deep-time bad to be shunned the way we are here."

They were nearing the pass which led to the Sun Kiln.

"Have we time to visit the memorial ground by the Kiln?" she asked.

"Why sure!" said Cliff. "We have no time problem, Doc. I can call in."

In fact, she guessed, he had already done so; oxper could communicate head to head. The journey through the pass was another reminder of the fact that they were on an artefact, a constructed habitat. Then they were in the afternoon sun, boosted this time by the reflectors on the western slope. The Sun Kiln was a solid group of ceramic-faced cones, smokefree, with high-wide collectors reaching right up above the divide. It was not far from the "homestead" valley where the holding mission families lived.

Trash was burnt in the kiln and it was used as a crematorium. The names of settlers whose ashes had enriched the soil were engraved on stones in a low wall beside a lawn of low-growing grass, the type adapted for earth cemeteries. Only a few persons rated a plaque of hardwood or metal in the grass; there was a special new wall lower down for the veterans from the first holding mission. Right up near the kiln, on the slope, there was a large new plaque of wood substitute and anodised silver duralloy.

WINTHROP ARGENT NORTH IV
2443–2502, Christian Era Dating

His ashes enrich the soil of Wingard.

"How was this done Cliff?" she asked. "Was it a big official ceremony?"

"No, Mam," he said. "Little shuttle flew in via the last company Go-Down on Mars. Couple of old Triad auxiliaries flew the shuttle and left a report in the dock. The habitat was deserted. Small party from Terra scattered the ashes and laid down the plaque."

Taya stood with bowed head in the strange sunset light. She drew out her amulet with a yellow beryl from the mines of Tsagul and remembered when it had been given to her, the Only One, the human child, by Nantgeeb, the Great Diviner, the Maker of Engines, and by Taya Gbir, her daughter and Taya's namesake. She held it, sending out a prayer to all the universe for coming together, for sharing, for all that Winthrop North himself had wished. And truth came, piercing her darkness like a strong beam of light. . . .

She concealed her excitement, if that was the right word, until she was back at Harmony. She cleaned up and changed and automatically went into the ordering of her research material, the most basic routines, before dinner. When Elliot and Carl beeped she left a message on her own system, deliberately showing her hand:

Wingard is a Way-Station for visitors in the true Pioneer spirit.

Taya walked along with the team, the kids, and it was Carl Curran who gave her another piece of the puzzle.

"Here's the strip I took, back then with the film team, Doc," he said. "The floor and the valley wall where the meteorite hit. I'd say the Dancing Floor had a narrow escape. Y'see that burnt area?"

"All greened over now," said Taya, peering at the excellent clear strip in its viewer. "Can I get a copy of this, Carl?"

"Why, this one is for you, Doc!" he grinned. "I already made you this copy."

The deep, blackened scar on the eastern wall reached down into the valley, seemed to come within fifty meters of the Dancing Floor. Now it had all been greened over.

"See anything of the folk from the Mill, Carl? The Die-Hards? Two women and a man, all older people?"

"Well," he said, "we knew they were there but they were a real no-contact group."

Elliot came in with a report on the Holding Mission projects: absolutely triple A. The Oparin families, Hansen/Wylie and the Jenners, were the best test-gardeners he had ever encountered. Dayne came to eat with them and they were a cheerful work group, winding up their plans, kidding around with the oxper, Phil and Tom, thinking of tomorrow's picnic at the Floor.

Taya felt bad for holding back, for not being able to take them into her confidence at once. They were good kids, she knew it, the fault was in herself; she had a kind of generation loyalty. But there were two parts to her discovery, a coming together of two ideas, in the classic mode of scientific breakthrough. She passed Carl's little film strip to Mike Mahoney.

"We're in for some surprises at this picnic," she said. "Take a look at this film of Carl's, everyone."

"What is it?" asked Mahoney, urgently.

"The Dancing Floor tests out as very new," said Taya. "Suppose it *is* very new? Notice how close the burn marks for the so-called meteorite five years ago come in Carl's strip. It has all been greened over now. The scar on the eastern wall is small—maybe it was minimised too. The team built the Dancing Floor and suffered mechanical failure at take off. That was a crash site."

"Shee-it!" said Elliot, taking it up at once. "And you think they coulda done a cover-up that big?"

"Who we talking about here?" asked Dayne.

"The Die-Hards of course!" said Elliot.

"But, Holy Rome," exclaimed Mahoney, keeping his voice down as they were all doing, "where would they put the debris, the—the remains? Could they just *bury* all that?"

Taya chuckled, finding another piece that fitted.

"Oh there's a place right there," she said. "The old tunnel on the eastern outer wall, not a long way from the crash site. The settlers used it when they patrolled the outer surface of Wingard."

"It's crazy," said Dayne. "There are only three of them. Why not report the truth to an oxper team? They must know this would be a great find—for Archive, for all exo-biologists."

"Their privacy is more important to them than anything else in the universe," said Mahoney. "Die-Hards, pardon me, are plagged, insane—I've seen 'em before."

"Or maybe they believe—their leader believes—he owns the whole game," said Taya, sadly. "Wingard belongs to him. . . ."

Elliot March stared at her, the blood draining from his face.

"*Doc!*" he gave the smart kid's cry of despair. "*Why didn't I think of that!*"

She gave him a slight frown, enough to stop him blurting out her hypothesis.

"We won't move on the tunnel or any other thing," she said. "I'll get them to the picnic."

"How will you do that?" asked Mike Mahoney, who seemed to have figured things out.

"It's called *pressuring* these days," said Taya. "But it has a good old-fashioned name: *blackmail*."

Back in at the Harmony lodge she found a gift outside her door: passionfruit wine from the Jenner family in a white ceramic bottle. She took a drink and looked out at the eastern valley system, silvered under the augmented light of the moon. There was an alteration in the sound of the systems and a voice said:

"I got your message."

It was at last the voice of an old man. She felt a tightness in her chest and thought of the vacation in Maine, the warm nights in New Mexico.

"How are you doing?" she asked. "How is your health? You're seventy years old now."

"Which makes you seventy-three," he said. "They got a shot of you, the girls. Looking good, *dancing*, for Goddess sake. Age is having trouble wearying you or custom staling—"

"Shut up, you old cheat!" she said fondly. "We know what came down and where you hid the remains. I'll have a report or I'll make a report."

"I knew something like this would happen," said Winthrop A. North. "What put you on to me?"

"I recalled your friend Vona a little better. I saw her at Humbolt as part of your PR team." She said. "I make a guess that Kirsty ran off today because she is someone I know really well, maybe one of the secretaries, Christina? The man I knew took no chances and could have remained virile for a long time."

"Lot of educated guessing . . ." grumbled the Resurrect.

"The oxper found me that databank, *Weltfic*," she said, laughing, taking another mouthful of the passionfruit wine.

"I knew there was something in that name, *Ben Gunn*. You were leaving clues. Ben Gunn is an ex-pirate marooned on Treasure Island by Captain Flint. The heroic villain of that old-time blue-water romp is Long John *Silver*, a reference to your middle name."

"Oh pirates are always good," he said. "There was that trivid team, few years back—*space pirates* now."

"Oh North," she cried, "have you got any treasure for me, for Archive, for Rivez, truly dead, orbiting Ceres in a Snow White capsule, or for Hanna Klein, one hundred and three years old in a veterans home in Florida-on-Terra?"

"Okay," he said. "The Die-Hards will come to the picnic. Don't blow my cover, Taya, old lover. We have treasure beyond your wildest dreams. . . ."

The picnic had wound down a little, after the races and the games. Sprawled groups on the green, among the trees, on the southern edges of the dancing floor in perfectly adjusted weather. A party was seen approaching along the road from the Mill; an old green trekker came on slowly with Vona Cropper striding ahead. She waved cheerily to the assembled company and went at once to the sound system, back of the floor and talked to Cliff Watson and Peter Miles who were working there.

"Greetings to the Archive team and all the inhabitants of Wingard." She was smooth but very serious. "This artefact, the Dancing Floor was built almost six years ago: the vessel that carried the construction team crashed soon after take-off. We were able to give a little assistance—there was a blessing that came out of this sad time. This music was mixed and assembled from many sources by all those at the Old Mill."

The music was slow, oddly melodious, like some of the neo-classical nature-wave concerts Taya had heard in California. The two women, Vona and Kirsty, took their places at the head of the Dancing Floor, on the row of larger stones where the dance began. The central stone was empty. Taya caught her breath and was drawn to her feet, with many of those watching. One of the children uttered a faint cry. The old man, "Ben Gunn," came to the floor leading by the hand the one who would lead the dance.

The Dancer was very thin and slight, giving an impression of frailty. It was swathed in a loose white shirt, hiding, perhaps, the strange shape of the upper body; the strong muscular legs were its most "humanoid" feature. The Dancer, following every cadence of the music, raised a pair of long arms, with fringed extensions on the "hands." It held gently to one side, its small, oval head, deco-rated with a quiff of pale hair. The Dancer led the dance, and the humans from the Mill followed, with an appropriate humility.

And in all those watching—all, all of them, Taya, was sure of it—there was a response so keen and sweet that it would remain with them forever. Here was a coming together, here was a curious grace, beauty so strange that it could break the heart.

Taya saw it all with an astonished recognition. There it was at last, the lightness, the agility, the travelling leaps, the patterns upon the stones. Yes, it was a solo performance—the folk from the mill repeated a few of the steps but remained in the background. Perhaps they were there, she guessed, to encourage the Dancer, to give comfort.

Then as the dance was done and as the music faded there was hand-clapping, muted cheers and sounds of praise from all those watching. The Dancer stood still in the centre of the floor and Kirsty, in her yellow shirt, ran out with a package which it held between its two hands. It came lightly across the floor to where Taya stood.

She scanned its shape, the pale mask of the face, the texture of skin and hair, the eyes, like small gemstone clusters. She took the package it offered: a woven kit-bag of trivid cassettes.

"Tay-ah."

The voice was soft, whistling, issuing from a pale lipless mouth.

"Dancer!" she replied softly. "Thank you! We thank you! The Sol system thanks you and your comrades."

The mission families and their children, the auxiliaries, the Archive team all took her tone so readily that she knew the Dancer had worked its magic upon them. They replied softly, with love. The floor and the trees and the distant slope of the eastwall echoed with their sighing *"Thank you — thank you — "*

Then the Dancer backed away, bowing, holding out its hands and it was seen to be tired, drained of energy. The two women from the Mill hurried out, gave it support and led it gently back towards the trekker. Only the old man remained, directly opposite Taya Schwartz. Out of pure devilment she raised her surveyor's goggles and stared closely at the face of Winthrop A. North IV.

Someone had said or written, long ago, that people don't so much *change* as they grow older, they grow more like themselves. Sure, he had aged, perhaps more than she would have expected, with his healthy life, upon Wingard. But the smile he gave her was a familiar smile. He raised a hand in something between a wave and a salute; Taya returned the gesture. The Dancing Floor glowed between them like a map of the years. Then he too turned aside and rejoined his family; the trekker drove away up the dirt road to the Old Mill.

The other inhabitants of Wingard were in a euphoric state, she heard a child, Dan Jenner, crying out: *"We saw him dance! We saw him dance!"* Taya went to the sound system of the oper vehicle and did something that she hardly needed to do, with these cautious settlers, here upon Wingard.

"The presence of this being, the Dancer," she said, "and the dance we saw belongs to Wingard. It is your secret, perhaps forever. We don't want this precious survivor disturbed. I'll evaluate the trivid cassettes taken by the family at the Old Mill and prepare some for you all to see, Ranger Jenner."

She consulted briefly with the Archive team who were as happy as she had ever seen them. Knowledge, not publicity, was the mark of the good archivist. In time there might be sensational revelations of one kind or another, some things always got out, especially secrets of the Universe.

Taya drove back with the auxiliaries and sensed at once that there was something else, beside their usual cheerfulness and the excitement of the dance. She had asked them to keep a sharp look-out: their senses were keener than human senses.

"I didn't expect this," she said. "I believed that the people from the mill would tell us about the building of the floor and the crashed BTA vessel. I expected, maybe, a chance to examine the crashed vessel, hidden in the tunnel on the east wall."

"We kept a sharp look-out, Doctor," said Tom Scott. "Observed the survivor, the Dancer, you called him."

"What is it, Tom?" she demanded. "What did you find out?"

She looked around and there were smiles on all their faces.

"Surprise for all us poor wishers," said Cliff.

"Matter of the skin texture, the hair, oh everything," said Peter Miles.

"The Dancer is something we don't have a word for," said Philip Grey. "Can't say he's an *android* 'cause that comes from a word for *man*, for human. Hope this won't upset anyone. This survivor is the auxiliary of another species."

"You're sure of this?"

"We got through to that wisher, head to head, Doc," said Tom Scott. "He has a weird range of data, had to fall back on images some of the time. He gave us names to call him."

"Don't tell me," said Taya Schwartz. "Let this be *your* secret until I've evaluated the trivid material. I'm suffering from overload."

They laughed softly.

"He sure was pleased that we existed," said Cliff Watson. "The Mill folks had told him about oxper, androids, but he found it hard to believe."

the summer isles

IAN R. MacLEOD

Throughout the nineties, British writer Ian R. MacLeod has proven himself to be one of the most innovative and consistently excellent of all the decade's new writers, and his work continues to grow in power and deepen in maturity as we approach the century that looms just ahead of us. MacLeod has been underrated to date, in spite of being one of the best new writers to enter the field in many years, and it is to be hoped that in the coming decade he will finally get some of the critical recognition he deserves, as one of the richest and most distinctive voices in science fiction today. During the first nine years of the decade that's now almost past, MacLeod published a slew of strong stories in Interzone, Asimov's Science Fiction, Weird Tales, Amazing, *and* The Magazine of Fantasy & Science Fiction, *among other markets, many of which made the cut for one or another of the various Best of the Year anthologies; in 1990, in fact, he appeared in* three *different Best of the Year anthologies with three different stories, certainly a rare distinction. His first novel,* The Great Wheel, *was published in 1997, followed by a major collection of his short work,* Voyages by Starlight. *His excellent second novel remains as yet unsold, although we can hope that that situation changes soon. MacLeod's stories have appeared in our Eighth, Ninth, Tenth, Eleventh, Thirteenth, and Fifteenth Annual Collections. He lives with his wife and young daughter in the West Midlands of England.*

In the moving and eloquent story that follows, a monumental piece of work that tops even his own previous high standards, he takes us to an alternate but all-too-plausible Britain where things went a little differently in the turbulent aftermath of World War I, for a powerful, compassionate, and unforgettable look at what happens to the one man who knows things that no one is allowed to know....

ONE

O n this as on almost every Sunday evening, I find a message from my acquaintance on the wall of the third cubicle of the Gents beside Christ Church Meadow.

It's two thumbnails dug into the sleek green paint this week, which means the abandoned shed by the allotments past the rugby grounds in half an hour's time. A trail of other such marks run across the cubicle wall; what amounts nowadays to my entire sexual life. Here—Oh, happy, dangerous days!—is the special triple-mark that meant a back room in the hotel of a sympathetic but understandably wary proprietor. He's gone now, of course, has Larry Black, like so many others. Quietly taken one night for the shocks and needles of the treatment centers in the Isle of Man.

I pull the chain, clunk back the lock, and step out into the sweet Jeyes Fluid air. Placed above me on the wall as I wash my hands, with what, if you didn't know this country, you would surely imagine to be ironic intent, hangs a photograph of John Arthur. He gazes warmly across his desk, looking younger than his forty-nine years despite his grey hair. The photograph is brass-framed, well-polished. Of course, no one has dared to deface it.

Outside along St. Giles, twilight has descended, yet the warmth of this early summer day remains. A convoy of trucks lumbers around the cobbles, filled with bewildered-looking conscripts on their way to-the sprawling camps in the southeast of England. A few of the newer or expensively refurbished pubs already boom with patriotic songs. I pause to relight my pipe as I pass St. John's, then lean spluttering against a wall and cough up out a surprising quantity of stringy phlegm, watched over by a small but disapproving gargoyle. Odd, disgusting, habit—hawking and spitting. Something that, until recently, I'd only associated with old men.

There's still some life out on the playing fields. Undergrads are wandering. There are groups. Couples. Limbs entwine. Soft laughter flowers. The occasional cigarette flares. Glancing back at the towers of this city laid in shadows of hazy gold against the last flush of the sun, it's all so impossibly beautiful. It looks, in fact, exactly like an Empire Alliance poster. **Greater Britain Awake!** I smile at the thought, and wonder for a moment if there isn't some trace of reality still left in the strange dream that we in this country now seem to be living. Turning, sliding my hand into my pocket to nurse the encouraging firmness of my anticipatory erection, I cross the bridge over the Cherwell as Old Tom begins his long nightly chime.

Despite all the back-to-nature and eat-your-own greens propaganda that Home Secretary Mosley has been peddling, the shed at the far end of the allotments and the plots it once served remains abandoned, cupped as they are in a secret hollow, lost by the men who went to the War and never came back again. I lever open the door and duck inside. Tools and seeds and sweet dry manure. But no sign yet of my acquaintance as the floorboards creak beneath my feet. The darkness, even as my eyes grow accustomed to the gloom, becomes near-absolute as night settles outside. A distant bell ripples a muffled shipwreck clang. The late train to London rattles by in the distance, dead on time.

My acquaintance is late. In fact, he should have been here first. As I pushed back the door, his younger arms should already have been around me. He trembles often as not when we first lock together, does my acquaintance. After all, he has so much more to lose. For, despite the darkness and the secrecy with which we pretend to cloak our meetings, I know exactly who my acquaintance is. I have studied the lights of his house shining through the privet that he trims so neatly each fortnight, and I have watched the welcoming faces of his wife and two daughters as they greet him at his door.

Checking, occasionally, the radium glow of my watch, I let a whole hour slide by as the residues of early hope and fear sour into disappointment, and then frank anxiety. But what, after all, do I know of the demands of being a father, a husband? Of working in some grim dead-end section of the Censor's Department of the Oxford City Post Office? At ten, I lever the shed door open and step back out into the summer night, leaving my long-forgotten libido far behind me. The stars shine down implacably through the rugby H's as I make my way past lovers and drunks and dog walkers into the old alleys. I turn for a moment as I hear the whisper of footsteps. Could that be a figure, outlined against the mist of light that seeps from a doorway? But by the time I've blinked, it becomes nothing—an aging man's fancy: the paranoias of love and fear.

Then quickly along Holywell where an owl calls, and onward under the plane trees to my college and my quad, to the cool waiting sheets of my room deep in the serene heart of this ancient city.

I open my eyes next morning to the sight of my scout Christlow bearing a tray containing a steaming pot of Assam, a rack of toast, my own special jar of marmalade. Even as the disappointments of the previous evening and the cold aches that have suddenly started to assail my body wash over me, I still have to smile to find myself here.

"Lovely morning, sir." Christlow drifts through diamonds of sunlight to place the tray astride my lap. The circled cross of the EA badge on his lapel winks knowingly at me. "Oh, by the way, sir. You asked me to remind you of your appointment today."

"Appointment?"

"At ten o'clock, you were seeing your doctor. Unless, of course, you've—"

"—No. Yes." I nod in my pajamas, what's left of my hair sticking up in a grey halo, a dribble of spilt tea warming my chin—all in all, a good approximation of an absent-minded don. "Thank you, Christlow, for reminding me."

In that scarily deferential way of his, Christlow almost bows, then retreats and closes the door. With a sound like distant thunder, his trolley trundles off down the oak-floored corridor. And yes, I truly had forgotten my appointment. The dust-spangled sunlight that threads my room now seems paler and my throat begins to ache as whispers of pain and uncertainty come into my head.

Walking along High Street an hour later, I have to squeeze my way through the queue outside the Regal for the day's first showing of Olivier's *Henry V*. Many, like Christlow, wear EA badges. But all ages, all types, both sexes, every age and disability, are gathered. A mixture, most bizarrely of all, of town and gown—undergrads and workers—the two quite separate existences that Oxford so grudgingly contains.

Beyond the junction of Alfred Street I push through the little door beside the jewelers and climb the stairs to the surgery. The receptionist looks up without smiling, then returns to stabbing a finger at her typewriter. The posters in this poky waiting room are like the ones you see everywhere nowadays. **With Your Help We Can Win. Now Is The Time. Join the Empire Alliance — Be a Part of the Modernist Revolution.** There's a fetching painting of the towers and spires of this great dreaming city aglow at sunset, much as I saw them yesterday. And, of course, there's John Arthur.

"Mr. Brook. Doctor Parker will see you."

I push through the doorway, blinking. Doctor Parker is totally new to me. Fresh-faced, young, and pinkly bald, he looks, in fact, almost totally new to himself. I have no one but myself to blame for taking my chances with the National Health Service. I could have availed myself of Doctor Reichard, who comes to our college every Wednesday to see to us dons, and is available at most other times, since, on the basis of a stipend granted by George I in 1715, these attendances comprise his sole professional duty. But my complaints — shortness of breath, this cough, the odd whispering that sometimes comes upon me, the growing ache in my bones — sound all too much like the simple ravages of age. And I nurse, also, a superstitious fear that my sexual leanings will be apparent to the trained medical eye.

"Sorry about this ah . . . I've only just got . . . ," he says as he glances down at his page-a-day calendar. **Thursday 13 June 1940.** The letters seem to glow, so brightly rainbowed at their edges that I wonder if this isn't some other new symptom. "You're the ah . . . The columnist, aren't you? What was it? 'The Fingers of History'?"

" 'Figures of History.' "

"Of course. *Daily Sketch*, every Saturday. Used to find it handy at school." Then another thought strikes him. "And you knew him, didn't you? I mean, you knew John Arthur. . . ."

"That was a long time ago."

"But what's he *really* like?"

I open my mouth to give my usual noncommittal reply. But it doesn't seem worth it.

"Here we are." He shuffles the X-rays into order, then leans over the file. "Um — *Griffin Brooke*. I thought it was Geoffrey, and Brook without the e?"

"It's a sort of pen-name," I say, although in fact the *Oxford Calendar*, the door to my rooms — even the name tags Christlow sews into my gowns — also read Geoffrey Brook. Griffin Brooke, the names I was born with, now reside only in odd corners such as this, where, despite the potential for confusion, I find myself reluctant to give them up.

As my thoughts drift toward all the odd accidents in life that have brought me here — and how, indeed, Fingers of History would be a good description of some historical process or other — another part of me watches Doctor Parker as he then raises the cover of my file a few inches to peer sideways into it.

Something changes behind his eyes. But when he clears his throat and smoothes back down the papers and finally makes the effort to meet my gaze, I'm still certain that I'm fully prepared for the worst. What could be more terrible, after all, than growing old, or emphysema, bronchitis, tuberculosis? . . .

"It seems," he begins, "that a tumor has been growing in your lungs. . . . Outwardly, you're still in good enough health, but I really doubt if there's point in an operation."

Not even any need for an operation! A stupid bubble of joy rises up from my stomach, then dissolves.

I lick my lips. "How long," I ask, "have I got?"

"You'll need to make plans. I'm so terribly sorry. . . ."

Thrust upon the gleaming linoleum rivers of the new NHS, I am kept so busy at first that there is little time left for anything resembling worry. There are further X-rays at the Radcliffe, thin screens behind which I must robe and disrobe for the benefit of cold-fingered but sympathetic men who wear half-moon glasses. Nurses provide me with over-sweet tea and McVitie's Digestives. Porters seek my opinion about Arsenal's chances in the FA Cup.

I feel almost heroic. And for a while I am almost grateful for the new impetus that my condition gives to a long-planned project of mine. A book not of history, but *about* history. One which examines, much as a scientist might examine the growth of a culture, the way that events unfold, and attempts to grapple with the forces that drive them. *The Fingers of History?* The odd way that inspiration sometimes arrives when you're least looking for it, I may even have stumbled upon a title; serious and relevant to the subject, yet punning at the same time on my own small moment of popular fame in the *Daily Sketch*.

After years of grappling with the sense of being an impostor that has pervaded most of my life, I suddenly find that I am making good progress in writing the pivotal chapter about Napoleon. Was he a maker of history, or was he its servant? Of course, he was both — and yet it is often the little incidents, when history is approached from this angle, which stand large. Questions such as, what would have happened if his parents Carlo and Letizia had never met? — which normal historians would discount as ridiculous — suddenly become a way of casting new light.

But one post-hospital afternoon a week or so later, as I huddle over my desk, and the warm air drifting through my open window brings the chant and the tread of Christlow and his fellow EA members parading on the ancient grass of our college quad, the whole process suddenly seems meaningless. Now, I can see the futility of all the pages I have written. I can see, too, the insignificant and easily filled space that my whole life will soon leave. A few clothes hanging in a wardrobe, an old suitcase beneath a bed, some marks on a toilet cubicle wall. Who, after all, am I, and what possible difference does it make?

Pulling on my jacket, empty with fear, I head out into Oxford as evening floods in.

I was born in Lichfield — which, then as now, is a town that calls itself a city — in the year 1880. It's middle England, neither flat nor hilly, north or south. Barring Doctor Johnson being born and a messy siege in the Civil War, nothing much has ever happened there. My father worked for Lichfield Corporation before he died of a heart attack one evening while tending his allotment. He'd had a title that changed once or twice amid great glory and talk of more ambitious holidays, but he'd always been Assistant-this and Deputy-that—one of the great busy-but-unspecified ("Well, it's quite hard to explain what I do unless you happen to be in the same line yourself. . . .") who now so dominate this country.

My mother and I were never that stretched; we had his pension and his life insurance, and she took on a job working at Hindley's cake shop, and brought home bits of icing and angelica for me when they changed the window display. By this time, I'd already decided I wanted to be "a teacher." Until I passed into Secondary School from Stowe Street Elementary, I was always one of the brightest in my class. Even a County Scholarship to Rugby seemed within reach. And from there, yes, I was already dreaming of the Magdalene Deer, sleek bodies bathing in the Cherwell at Parson's Pleasure.

My later years in school, though, were a slog. Partly from struggling to keep pace among cleverer lads, I fell ill with something that may or may not have been scarlet fever. On my long stay away from school, a boy called Martin Dawes would call in each afternoon to deliver books and sit with me. Whilst up in my room, he would sometimes slip his hands beneath the waistband of my pajamas and toss me off, as if that, too, was a message that needed to be delivered from school. Of course, I was deeply grateful. After I had recovered, locked in the upstairs toilet with its ever-open window as my mother shuffled about in the kitchen, I would dutifully try to incorporate women into my pink imaginings as, in the absence of Martin's attentions, I stimulated myself. But at some vital moment, their chests would always flatten and their groins would engorge as they stepped toward me, cropped and clean and shining.

That, in the personal history of what I term my pre-Francis days, is the sole extent of my sexual development. There was just me, my guilty semicelibacy, and helping my mother look after her house, and watching the lads I'd known at school grow up, leave home, marry, start families. I had, by my early twenties, also come to accept my position as a Second Class Teacher for the Senior Standard Threes at Burntwood Charity. In the articles with which I began my short career in the *Daily Sketch* nearly thirty years later, I gave the impression that John Arthur was one of my brightest and most ambitious pupils there, a little comet trail across the pit-dusty Burntwood skies. Thanks to numerous flowery additions by the *Sketch's* copy editor, I also stated that he was pale-skinned, quiet, good-looking, intense, and that he possessed a slight West Country accent, this being the time before it had changed to the soft Yorkshire that we all know now—all traits that would have got him a good beating up in the playground—and that, "on summer evenings after school when the pit whistle had blown and the swallows were wheeling," he and I would walk up into "the hazy Staffordshire hills" and sit down and gaze down at "the spires of Lichfield, the pit wheels of Burntwood, and the smokestacks of Rugeley from the flowing purple heather." Now, after all these years of practice, this has become my party act. So, yes, John Arthur really is there in that classroom at Burntwood Charity with the smell of chalk dust and unwashed bodies. His hand is raised from the third row of desks to ask a more than usually pertinent question before I start to ramble on about one of my many pet subjects. That is how I recall him.

Too weary to stop, trailing cigarette smoke, memories, abstractions, I wander Oxford's new suburban streets, passing illuminated porches bearing individual nameplates; **Church House. Dawric. The Willows.** It's a quiet now, although scarcely past nine and only just getting fully dark. The houses have a sleepy look. Their curtains are drawn. Faintly, like the movement of ghosts, I can see the flicker of television screens in many darkened lounges.

A footstep scuffs in the street behind me, and the sound is so furtive and unexpected that I turn and look back, although there was nothing to see. I walk on more briskly. Beyond a patch of grass where **Ball Games Are Prohibited** lies the home of my acquaintance, with its black-and-white gable, the privet, and the long strip of drive that, in these days of ever-growing prosperity, will probably soon be graced with a Morris Ladybird "people's car" instead of his Raleigh bicycle. But the windows of the house are darkened, uncurtained. And there is something odd about the look of them. . . .

My feet crunch on something sharper than gravel as I walk up the path to my acquaintance's front door. Many of the windows in the bay are shattered, there is a pervasive, summery smell of children's urine, and a fat iron padlock has been fitted across the door's splintered frame. I see, last of all, the sign that the Oxford Constabulary have pasted across the bricks in the porch. **Take Notice Hereby** . . . but this sky is incredibly dark and deep for summer, and I can't read further than the Crown-embossed heading. I slump down on the doorstep, scattering empty milk bottles, covering my face with my hands. Suddenly, it all comes to me. This. Death. Everything.

When I look up some time later, a figure is standing watching me from the suburban night with her arms folded, head tilted, a steely glint of curlers. "I'm Mrs. Stevens," she tells me, offering a softly companionable hand to help me up, then leading me past the hedge and the dustbins into the brightness of her kitchen next door. Slumped at the table, I watch her as she boils the kettle and warms the pot.

"I know," she says. "This must be a shock to you. . . ."

"They took them all away?"

"All of them. The pity of it really." She stirs her tea and passes me mine. "Them young girls."

"Nobody did anything to stop it?"

She gazes across at me, and licks the brown line of tea that's gathered on her small mustache. "I'll tell you what they were like, Mr. Brook. In every way, I'd have said, they were a decent couple. Only odd thing I remember now is they sometimes used to leave the light on without drawing the curtains so you could see right in. . . . The lassies were nice, though. Fed our cat for us when we went up to Harrogate last year. Knew them well yourself, did you?"

"He was just an acquaintance. But when they came to the house, was it the KSG or did — "

"—and you'd never have known, would you, to look at her?"

"*Her?* You mean . . . ?"

"Ah . . ." Mrs. Stevens slaps her hand flat down on the table and leans forward, her brown eyes gleaming. "So you still don't know the truth of it? Her real name was something Polish. All Zs and Ks." She hurrumphs. "It's understandable that they want to come here, isn't it? Just as long as they don't make themselves a burden, earn a decent living, talk like we do and don't bother our children and keep themselves to themselves."

"So what was the problem?"

"She was a Jew, wasn't she? All these years they've been living next door and acting all normal and hiding it from us." Mrs. Stevens raises her shoulders and shudders theatrically. "To think of it. It's the *dishonesty*. And her nothing but a dirty little Jew."

TWO

Clouds sweep in across Oxford, thick and grey as wet cement. Rain brims over the low surrounding hills and washes away the hope of what had promised to be another spectacular summer. In the whitewashed yard of the town prison on a hissing grey dawn, two men are hanged for their part in an attempted mail robbery. In Honduras, the British prefix lost to revolution in 1919 is restored in a bloody coup. A car bomb in the Trans-Jordan kills fifteen German League of Nations soldiers. In India, as ever, there are uprisings and massacres, and I despair as I work on my book of ever making any sense of history. It seems, to quote Gibbon, little more than a register of cruelties, follies, and misfortunes.

In Britain, the Jews have always been small in number, and we've generally been "tolerant." Before the rise of Modernism, my acquaintance and his family probably had little more to fear from exposure than the occasional human turd stuffed through their letter box. After all, Jewishness isn't like homosexuality, madness, criminality, communism, militant Irishness: they can't exactly *help* being born with their grabby disgusting ways, can they? Rather like the gypsies, you see, we didn't mind them *living*, but not here, not with us. . . . In this as in so many other areas, all Modernism did when John Arthur came to power was take what people said to each other over the garden fence and turn it into Government policy.

I can well remember the *Homeland for British Jewry* newsreels: they were probably one of the defining moments of early Greater British history. There they were, the British Jews. Whole eager families of them helped by smiling Tommies as they climbed from landing craft and hauled their suitcases up onto the shingle of remote Scottish islands that had been empty but for a few sheep since the Clearances of a century before. And it was hard not to think how genuinely nice it would be to start afresh somewhere like that, to paint and make homely the grey blocks of those concrete houses, to learn the skills of shepherding, harvesting, fishing.

So many other things have happened since then that it has been easy to forget about the Jews. I remember a short piece of Pathé before Disney's *Snow White* in what must have been 1939. By then they looked rustic and sunburned, their hands callused by cold winters of weaving and dry-stone walling, their eyes bright from the wind off the sea. Since then, nothing. A blank, an empty space that I find hard to fill even in my imagination.

One morning as thunder crackles and water streams and the whole college seems to shift and creak like a ship straining at its moorings, I'm still marooned in my rooms, ill and lost in the blind alley of my book when Christlow arrives at eleven to do the cleaning.

"You know the Jews, Christlow," I chirp after clearing my throat.

"Jews sir? Yes sir. Although not personally."

He pauses in his dusting. The situation already has a forced air.

"I was wondering—it's part of my book, you see—what happened to the mixed families. Where a Jew married a gentile . . ."

"I'm sure they were treated sympathetically, sir. Although for the life of me I can't imagine there was ever very many of them."

"Of course," I nod, and force my gaze back to my desk. Christlow resumes his dusting, his lips pursed in a silent whistle, amid the rain-streaming shadows as he lifts the photos along the mantelpiece of my mother, my father—and a good-looking, dark-haired young man.

"So you'll be all right, then, sir?" he asks when he's finished, picking up his box of rags and polishes. "Fine if I leave you now?"

"Thank you, Christlow. As always," I add, laying it on thick for some reason, as if there's a deeper debt that he and I owe each other, "you've done a splendid job."

When he's gone and his footsteps have faded into the college's loose stirrings, I slide in the bolt, then cross to the gloom of my bedroom and drag my old suitcase from beneath the bed. I always keep its key in my pocket, but the hinges creak as I open them, rusty from disuse. Nothing inside has changed. The tin toys. The tennis slacks. The exercise book with the name **Francis Eveleigh** inscribed into the cardboard cover in thick childish letters. A school badge. A Gillette safety razor—his first? A pistol wrapped inside an old rag. A decent-enough herringbone jacket. A single shoe. A steel hip flask. A soldier's pass for 14–26 September 1916, cross-stamped **No Longer Valid**. Various socks and old-fashioned collarless shirts and itchy-looking undies. A copy of Morris's *News from Nowhere*. And a Touring Map of the Scottish Highlands, folded so often that the sheets threaten to break apart as I touch them.

I grab a handful of his clothes and bury my face into them, smelling Oxford damp, Oxford stone, Four Square Ready-Rubbed and Mansion House lavender floor polish. Little enough is left of Francis now. Still, that faint scent of his flesh like burnt lemon. A few dark strands of his hair . . .

What a joke I have become. My sole claim to fame is having dimly known a great man when he was still a child, and my sole claim to happiness lies almost as far back; a miracle that happened for a few days nearly thirty years ago. I suppose I've convinced myself since that homosexuals cannot really love—it's easier that way. And yet at the same time, in all the years since, Francis had always been with me.

"It really doesn't matter, Griff," I hear him say as his fingers touch my neck. He smells not of lemons now, but of the rainy oak he's been standing beneath as he watches my window from the quad. But he hasn't aged. He hasn't changed.

"No, it doesn't matter at all," he whispers as he turns me round to kiss me. "Not any of this. That's the secret of everything."

I smile to find him near me, and still shudder at the cool touch of his hands. In the moment before the thunder crackles closer over Oxford and I open my eyes, all pain is gone.

Ernie Svendsen, with his suspiciously foreign name, his long nose, his thick glasses, seems an unlikely survivor of my kind. He puts it down to something that he has on Oxford's Deputy Chief Constable, although I would have thought that would have made him a prime candidate for a hit-and-run car accident.

We meet at a park bench the next afternoon, during a break in the rain.

"Do you think they'll let them stay together?" I ask as he tosses bread from a brown paper bag to the feathered carpet of ducks that have gathered around us. "Will they send him to the Isle of Man, the girls and the mother to the Western Isles?"

Giving me a pitying look, Ernie shakes his head. "It doesn't work like that, my friend. Oh, they'll get it out of him. He'll tell them anything—lies or the truth. People always blab on so when you threaten them. . . . I shouldn't worry," he adds, seeing the expression on my face. "If something was going to happen to you, it would have happened already. Being who you are, I'm sure you'll be safe."

"I'm not who I am. I'm not anybody."

"Then you're doubly lucky."

"I keep asking myself what the point is. I mean—why?"

"I think you've forgotten what it's like, my friend."

"What?"

"Being the way we are—bent, queer. The guilt. The stupid scenes. You remember those leaflets, the promises of help, that we could be cured. Don't tell me you didn't secretly get hold of one." He sighs. "If we could just press some button—pull out something inside us—don't you think we'd all do it? Wouldn't you take that chance, if you were given it? Isn't John Arthur right in that respect—and wouldn't the Jews feel the same?"

But to change would mean re-living my life—becoming something other than what I am. Losing Francis. So I shake my head. And I've heard the stories of what happens to my kind. The drugs. The electrodes. The dirty pictures. Swimming in pools of your own piss and vomit. *That* kind of treatment that was available even before Modernism made it compulsory. "It isn't John Arthur," I say. "It's all of us. It's Britain. . . ."

Ernie chuckles. "I suppose you'll be alone now, won't you?"

"Alone?"

"Without companionship. Without a cock to suck."

I glance across the bench, wondering if Ernie's propositioning me. But his eyes behind his glasses are as far away as ever; fish in some distant sea. Sex for him, I suspect, has always been essentially a spectator sport. That's why he fits in so well. That's why he's survived. He doesn't want a real body against him. All he needs is the sharp hot memories of those he's betrayed.

"Look," I say, "I just thought you might have some information about what happens to . . . to the Jews—and to people like us. Surely somebody has to?"

"All I know is what I read in the papers, my friend. And what I see in the newsreels." His gaze travels across the silvered lawns. "I understand how it is. We're only human, after all. It's always sad when you lose someone. . . ."

He stands up, shaking the last of his breadcrumbs over the ducks, and I watch as he walks off, splashing a short cut across the lawns and then around the sodden nets of the empty tennis courts. I can't help wondering if there will be a black official KSG Rover waiting for me somewhere soon. The polite request and the arm hooked around my elbow and the people passing by too busy going about their lives to notice. The drive to a dark clearing in a wood, the cold barrel to the forehead . . . I can't help feeling selfishly afraid. But as I make my way down Holywell past the old city walls, the clouds in the west begin to thin, and the wind picks and plays with rents of blue sky as the sun flickers through. Dawdling along the narrow, unpredictable streets that wind around the backs of the colleges giving glimpses of kitchen dustbins and Wren towers, the light brightens. And Oxford. Oxford! All the years that I longed to see myself like this amid these quads and buildings, the twin shining rivers, the whispering corridors of learning.

Working on my book each evening after school in the front parlor as my mother nodded over her knitting in her chair behind me, I always knew that the dream was impossibly far away. But nourishing my one great work, I never even bothered to think of setting some more realistic target and perhaps submitting an essay on local history to the *Lichfield Mercury* or *Staffordshire Life*. It was all or nothing— and perhaps in my heart of hearts I was happy enough with nothing. One evening, I remember, the work at the parlor table was going particularly well and the hours slid by until I cracked my weary fingers and turned around to my mother to comment on the faint but foul smell that I had noticed. She sat unusually still in the dimness of the room behind me. Her head was lolling, her fingers were clenched around the knitting needles and her ball of wool had rolled from her lap in her final spasm.

THREE

Now that the rain has ended and the sun has come out, all of Britain seems to drift, held aloft on wafts of dandelion and vanilla, the dazzling boom of bandstand brass. Each morning, the *Express*, the *New Cross*, and the *Mail* vie for punning headlines and pictures of Modernist maidens in fountains, ice cream–smeared babies, fainting guardsmen. With or without me, life seems intent on going on— but I find that I remain remarkably active in any case: with Christlow's help, for example, I can manage to be fully dressed, my lungs coughed-out, my tablets taken, my limbs unstiffened, my eyes fully focused, my heartbeat and my breathing made almost regular by half past eight or nine at the latest. And thus aroused, thus fortified, I have taken a surprising number of trips out this August. This, after all, is my last chance to see anything, and I can easily afford to squander my savings by going First Class. But still, as I queue at the Oxford City Post Office for the appropriate cross-county passes that will get me to Lichfield, I can't help but wonder if the woman behind the spittle-frosted glass knew my acquaintance, and who emptied his desk upstairs in the Censor's Office, who scratched his name off the tea club . . .

Next morning, climbing aboard the *Sir Galahad* after it slides into Oxford Station, its streamlined snout oozing steam and the sense of far-away, I stumble past four senior officers of the KSG, the Knights of Saint George, as I make my way down the carriage in search of my reserved seat. They all look sleek, plump — seals basking on a sunny shore, washed by the warm waves of the future. A mother and daughter are opposite my place in the no smoking section further along. The morning sun pours over their blonde hair and their innocent blue eyes rest on me as I slump down. I feel I must look strange and sinister, already a harbinger of death, yet their manner is welcoming, and we begin to talk as the train pulls out in that absent, careless manner that strangers sometimes have. The husband, the little girl's father, is a Black Watch major who's risen through the Army ranks on merit in the way that only happens in real conflicts, and is currently on active service on the ever-troublesome India-Afghanistan border. The mother tells me she sleeps with his and John Arthur's photograph beneath her pillow. I smile as their faces shine back at me and then gaze out of the window, watching the telegraph lines rise and fall and the world flash by, carrying me on toward Lichfield.

Living in what I still thought of my mother's house back in the years before the War, alone and celibate, I still entertained thoughts of writing my book. But, after many botched attempts, I began to wonder if something else was missing. History, after all, is ever-changing, and must always be viewed from the perspective of the present. I was still as neutral in politics as I imagined myself to have become sexually, yet in my efforts to take myself seriously as a historian, I decided that politics probably lay at the cutting edge of current affairs, and I joined the local Fabian Society. It was probably a good job that I dipped my toe into the waters of political debate without any high ideals. Still, I can see with hindsight that it was an interesting time for British left wing politics. The younger and generally rowdier element (of which Francis Eveleigh was undoubtedly a member) were busily undermining the cozy nineteenth-century libertarianism of William Morris — the Morris, that is, who existed before he was re-invented by Modernism. But it was all naïvely innocent. Francis, for example, worked six days a week behind the counter of the John Menzies bookstall at Lichfield station, lived in digs, lifted his little finger when he drank tea, was secretive about his background, and spoke with a suspiciously upper-class accent. Still, I was drawn to him. I liked his youth, his enthusiasm, his good looks.

He and I began meeting occasionally after he had finished work at the station bookstall, and we would take quiet walks across the flat Staffordshire countryside. When we were alone, there was a lot less of the usual posturing and political debate, but nevertheless, the prospect of a war in Europe soon began to dominate our conversation. Francis, although supposedly a pacifist, was fascinated by the whole idea of conflict. In a white shirt, his collar loose, he would walk ahead of me as we wandered at evening along misty canal towpaths and across muddy spring fields. His body was slight and bony, yet filled with energy. He grew his hair a little longer than was then fashionable, and I loved to watch, as he walked ahead of me, the soft nest of curls that tapered toward the back of his neck.

"You understand, Griff," he said to me once as we stood to catch our breath amid the cows beneath a dripping tree. "I can work these things out when we walk together."

My heart ached. I could only smile back at him.

The idea of our taking a cycling trip to Scotland seemed to evolve naturally, gradually from this process. That was probably a good thing, for if I had planned that Francis and I could be on our own, sharing thoughts, ideas, and boarding house rooms for a whole fortnight, I am sure that love and terror would have prevented it from ever happening. But somehow, I found that we were checking maps and timetables on the basis of a vague hypothesis—playing with the whole idea, really—until suddenly we were talking proper dates and actual bookings and the thing had miraculously come about. And I was to pay. That, too, slipped easily under the yawning bridge of my uncertainties. Thank God, the idea of two men traveling together on holiday raised few suspicions in the summer of 1914. Francis, bless him, probably had a far clearer idea of where he was leading me, and what was to come. But for all of that, for absolutely everything about him, I am eternally grateful.

We ate in the dining carriage as the train pulled out of Birmingham, studying our maps. Yet we went to our shared sleeping compartment quite early, I recall, filled with that soothed, tired feeling that only the start of a long railway journey brings. In that narrow compartment, I tried to busy myself with sorting the contents of my suitcase on the lower bunk as Francis undressed beside me. Trembling, alone after he had headed up the corridor to wash, looking down at the half-erection that, absurdly, was trying to nudge its way out of my pajamas, I cursed myself for my stupidity in ever falling for the idea of this holiday. I pushed past him when he returned, and pulled down a window in the corridor and watched the fields burn with sunset as the telegraph wires rose and fell, rose and fell. By the time I finally got back to the compartment, the landscape had become a grainy patchwork and Francis was up in the top bunk, reading *News from Nowhere*. Muttering about how tired I felt, I climbed in below.

I stared up at the shape his body made against the bars of the bunk. It truly was soothing, this motion of the carriage, the steel clatter of the wheels. Eventually, when Francis turned off his light and wished me goodnight, I truly felt ready for sleep and when, about half an hour later, he began to shift down from his bunk, I simply imagined that he was heading off on a final trip to the toilets. Instead, he climbed in beside me.

His pajama shirt was already undone. He smelled faintly of soap and toothpowder, and beneath that of the warmth of his own flesh, like burnt lemon.

"This is what you want, Griff, isn't it? . . . " he said. Then he put his arms around me, and he kissed me, and nothing was ever the same.

Clatter, tee, tee . . . Even here, on the way to Lichfield, that same sense of passing. Then as now, the onward rush of a train. Stations beside canal bridges. Stations in farmyards. Stations piled with empty milk churns and mailbags in the middle of pretty nowhere. And posters, posters. Posters of the seaside and posters of the country. Posters of towns. **The Lake District for Rest and Quiet Imaginings. Take the Sunday Special and Visit Lambourn Downs,** where a smiling couple are picnicking with their two pretty daughters as colored kites dance against a cloudless sky. . . .

Francis loved the place names as we journeyed across Scotland. Mellon Udrigle. Plockton. Grey Dog. Poolewe. Smearisary. The Summer Isles. When he wasn't reading the newspapers he got hold of every day to keep track of the repercussions of the assassination of an obscure Archduke, he'd run his finger along some impossibly contoured and winding route that the pedals of our basket-fronted Northampton Humbers were supposed to carry us down, chosen entirely to include as many of those wonderful names as possible.

Alone together in those yellow-lit boarding house rooms with their great empty wardrobes, riding the creaking seas of hollowed-out double beds, his chin cupped in his hand and bare feet in the air, laughing at something, humming to himself, twiddling his toes, Francis would study his maps and his newspapers. Then he'd lay a hand across me and pull me closer with a touch that was both warmly sexual and at the same time had nothing to do with sex at all. "This is real history, Griff," he said to me once when I expressed amazement that anyone should care about what was happening in the Balkans. "How can you pretend to be a historian and then let all this pass you by?"

I remember that Francis and I were in a pub on the evening of August 4th, 1914, when Asquith announced that Britain would be at war with Germany from midnight. I knew that he was going to enlist, and I could see that he was elated. It was no use arguing. And I, too, was excited by the prospect of this new future that lay ahead of us—that night, it was impossible not to be. Suddenly, after years of trying, we British could love each other and hate the Germans. Politics and diplomacy seemed trivial compared to the raw certainties of war. Soon, we were dancing in the crowd. Francis even kissed me. That August night, nobody cared. We were all one mass of hope and humanity.

On our journey south from the Highlands, without access to a sleeping carriage now that everyone wanted to travel, I did my best to talk seriously to Francis. I needed to fix as much of him in my mind as I could. But he was teasing about his past. *Yes, I went to school but it was just a place. How do you think I learned? Do I have a brother? —well, you tell me. Go on, you know what I'm like, so guess. . . .* It was a game we'd played before, but this time it was harsher, more hurtful. As we waited on swarming platforms and changed trains and searched for seats and stood in crowded corridors, I ended up telling Francis about myself instead.

"So, Griff . . . ," He smiled as we leaned against a window by our cases and the sleepers raced by. "You want to be a Professor? Have you ever even been to Oxford? Or would that spoil the dream?"

The train rocked us on, and Lichfield, despite my willing it not to, arrived soon enough. Francis and I parted outside the station without saying very much or even shaking hands, and I walked off toward what I still thought of as my mother's house almost looking forward to being alone. In Saint Martin's Square, a brass band was playing. Men, jolly as a works outing, talking and laughing freely in the way that we British so seldom do, queued up to enlist in the Staffordshire Regiment. They beckoned me to join them, but there was no bitterness when I smiled and shook my head, such was our country's optimism.

Walking once again along the strangely shrunken streets of my home town, heavier now with the burdens of age and illness, looking over the low front wall of the house where I lived most of my life, I note the pebbledash that the new owner has added to the rendering, the replacement window frames. Hindley's Cake Shop is still there with what look like the same cakes displayed in the window, although the butcher's shop above which Francis used to live has become a gent's outfitters, and the window of his room now bears the words **Formal Dress Hire**.

I take the bus in search of Burntwood Charity. But there's no sign of the school where I started my career—or even of the road that led to it with fields on the far side, or of the pit wheels. The whole place consists of nothing but houses and a vast new "comprehensive" school. Quite remarkably when you come to think about it, John Arthur remains uncommemorated. I visit the Town Library, another old haunt, but, just as in Oxford, the Lichfield census data and the voting lists and the ratings and the parish records and pretty much every kind of document covering the period between the 1900s and the start of the thirties have been destroyed. Here, in fact, the scythes have cut even deeper. Even the *records* of the records had gone, along with the spaces they were supposed to occupy. It's as if whole decades have vanished entirely.

The War in Britain was a strange affair, like a fever. People were more sociable, strangers would talk to each other, and even I went out more often; to the theater or to the music hall, or to one of the new cinematographs. At school, I taught my lads about the many historic acts of German aggression, and had them compose outraged letters to the Kaiser about the Zeppelin bombings of Great Yarmouth.

Francis wrote me the occasional letter at first after he volunteered. *Griff, you'd hardly know me now. . . .* I could almost see him trying on his new soldierly identity. The letters were filled at first with catalogues of acquaintances and military stupidities as he was posted around various training camps and temporary barracks in southern England. They grew shorter and blander once he reached France and the rapidly solidifying Western Front. I was like the millions of puzzled relatives and loved ones who were the recipients of such letters. I put his terseness down to shortage of time, and then to the military censors. But soon, by early 1915, Francis stopped writing to me altogether.

Two years passed. I only learned about Francis by chance when, queuing for a copy of the *Post* from the John Menzies bookstall on the platform at Lichfield station, I suddenly thought I heard his name being spoken. I knew what had happened straight away, just from the voices, although none of them had known him well. I'd heard its echo many times before from teachers and children at school, and people you passed in the street talking about a son, a husband, a brother. Like so many others, Francis Eveleigh had died in the Somme Offensive.

Pushed numbly into action, prodding and probing at the facts of Francis's life in a way that I had resisted when he was still alive, I was able to discover that his parents lived in a large house set in arable countryside on the outskirts of Louth in Lincolnshire. Standing outside in my muddy shoes on a cold day as quizzical light fanned from their hall, I introduced myself to the maid as "a friend from Lichfield," and was ushered into the drawing room where Mr. and Mrs. Eveleigh stood still as china figures on either side of the unlit fire, as if they had been waiting there for a long time. Mr. Eveleigh managed a bank, while his wife (Francis's eyes and pale skin, his full dark hair that she always tied back in a bun) oscillated between various bridge clubs and civic societies. They were solid, dependable, and I was flattered and charmed that they were prepared to have anything to do with me. There was no hint, of course, that Francis and I had been lovers—or even that he'd had any kind of sexual life. But there was always a sense, somewhere amid all the weekends I was invited to the Eveleighs' house, of a shared deeper fondness.

The light was always grey at the Eveleighs' house, and a chill came to whatever part of your body was turned from the fire. Sitting in the dining room as the clocks ticked and the fire spat through interminable meals of boiled cabbage, boiled potatoes, and boiled bacon, it wasn't hard to see why Francis had gone away. But I found it easy enough to fit in, and there was always the pleasure of being able to sleep in Francis's childhood bed which still bore the imprint of his body, to slide open drawers that contained the starched uniforms of the various cheap public schools he had been forced to attend and bury my face in their folds.

Mr. Eveleigh talked endlessly about politics and the War. He'd ask me about the Jews; whether I didn't think they were involved in a conspiracy to set one half of Europe against the other. I think he even mentioned "dumping the buggers on some remote Scottish island and leaving them to get on with it." He asked if I agreed that the average working man was fundamentally lazy. He doubted whether every Tom, Dick, and Harry should be given the vote, and thought Lloyd George was just a Welsh windbag—what this country really needed was a true, strong leader. . . .

The last time I saw the Eveleighs was just after the French Capitulation. I remember that my train journey up through Peterborough and Lincoln took place in an atmosphere as feverish as it had been when Francis and I journeyed back from Scotland four years before—but also very different. Strangers were talking to strangers again, but their voices were confused, their faces were hard and angry. There were rumors already of Lloyd George's resignation and of a General Election, although, as all the major parties had supported the War, no one had any clear idea of what the campaign would be about. I bought one of the few papers that were left at a newsagent's and stared at the headline. **War Over. Allies Defeated**. It was 6 August 1918; a date, it seemed to me, that would never look right in the cold pages of history.

The Eveleighs' front door was open—which seemed like final confirmation that everything had changed. People were milling. Clients from the Bank. Friends from the bridge circle. Farmers and neighbors. Time passed. Voices grew louder, then began to fade. I was tired and had a headache by the time I found myself alone with Mr. and Mrs. Eveleigh. Still, Mr. Eveleigh insisted on spreading out a map of Belgium and France, then asking me to explain exactly who was to blame for this mess. No doubt making less sense than I imagined, I told him that the economies of all the nations had been seriously weakened, that the Bolsheviks' treaty with Germany had been a capitulation, and the promised American reinforcements had been too few, and had come too late. Once the Germans made a break in the Allied lines, the certainties of trench warfare had crumbled; tactics were suddenly about communications, swiftness, surprise. With Paris succumbing and the British and Colonial Forces clustered chaotically around Cherbourg and Dieppe, there was nothing left to do but surrender to the Germans.

"We can't leave it like this," Mr. Eveleigh said, swaying as he poured himself yet another whisky. "There'll have to be another war. . . ."

Later, Mrs. Eveleigh showed me up to my room. "You might as well have these," she said, handing me a child's exercise book with Francis's name on the cover, a couple of battered tin toys. "Oh, and there's something else." I sat on the bed and waited as she carried in a cardboard box with a War Office stamp on it. She lifted it open, filling the room with some faint other smell. Mud? Death? It was certainly unpleasant. The box proved to be half empty. There was that cheap edition of *News from Nowhere*. A spare pair of thick standard issue grey-green military socks. More odd was the pistol. It seemed well-kept and, more surprising still, a screw of yellowed paper containing a dozen of what looked like live bullets. Mrs. Eveleigh just gazed down at me as I sat on the bed and handled the thing.

"Keep that too," she said, something new and harsh in her voice. "I don't want it."

She was standing closer now. Like me, and in her own quiet way, I think she had passed into that grey hinterland that lies beyond an excess of drink. I glanced around at the familiar wallpaper, the twee pictures, expecting her to turn and leave. But she just stood there in front of me, her hands knotting and unknotting across the long line of buttons that ran down her black dress.

"I only feel as though I've lost him now," she said. "Before I knew we'd thrown away the War, it was always as if some part of him might still come back to me."

I nodded, staring up at this twisted image of Francis as a middle-aged woman. Her eyes were lost in shadow; a shade deeper than black.

"And I wonder, even now, if he ever knew a woman." She took a step closer so that our knees touched. I was looking right up at her now, the folds of her chin, the rapid rise and fall of her breasts. "I never knew what he was like," she said.

"He was . . ." I tensed my hands, feeling enclosed, threatened. But something snapped. "I loved him, Mrs. Eveleigh. I just loved him. . . ."

She took a step back and nodded severely. I had truly thought for a moment that we could somehow share our Francislessness. But, instead, I heard the sigh of her dress as she left the room, the soft clunk of the door closing.

The Eveleighs never wrote to me after that.

I never saw them again.

With half an hour to kill and the return train to Oxford delayed, I buy a *Lichfield Mercury* from the same John Menzies bookstall at the station and then share the waiting room with three members of the Young Empire Alliance. They're little more than lads, really, and yet they affect maturity and ease as they smoke their Pall Malls and stretch out in long-trousered "boy-scout" uniforms. Two of them begin to hum a tune under their breath, alternately kicking each side of my bench in rhythm. A woman in a floral hat appears at the window, and I shoot her a despairing glance before she decides not to come in. I do my best to study the paper, the **Sits Vac**, where a Decent Widow is looking for a Clean Anglo Saxon Couple to take care of her and her Nice House. The Classified columns, where various Modernist and EA self-education courses and camps are on offer, along with supposedly War Office–endorsed photographs of the Mons Archers. The photo on the back page, beside a column giving advice to Young Mr. and Mrs. Modern on setting up home, is of an elderly woman hunched in the stocks on a village green. She has been put there, the caption jokily informs us, as a "show of local outrage." Similar submissions from other readers are invited.

"I was wondering . . ." The best-looking of the YEA youths smiles. "Where's an old bastard like you going?"

"Oxford," I croak.

"Not one of them fucking eggheads, are you?"

"Well, as a matter of fact . . ."

"Tell you what . . ." He stands up. His face is tanned. His brown hair is cut so short that it would feel like velvet if you stroked it. He comes close to me and leans down. "The problem is . . ." A soft rain of his spittle touches my cheek. "I'm all out of cunting matches. Light my fag for me?"

He keeps his eyes on mine as I fumble in my coat pocket. His friends watch on, grinning. His irises are an intense, cloudless, blue. He squints slightly as the match flares, and he holds my hand to guide it toward the tip of his cigarette. Moments later, my train arrives, and I leave the waiting room a sweaty wreck, still bearing an uncomfortable erection.

My journey, though, is far from over. Summer heat has buckled the main line rails, and I end up stranded on the sun-bleached platform of a remote rural station with the faint promise of an eventual Oxford connection. There, I talk to the station master, a round-faced man whose body bulges gently from the gaps between the buttons of his uniform like rising dough.

"You know," I say, clearing my throat, taking the kind of risk that the nearness of death encourages, "I've always wondered what happened to the people who were sent north. The newspapers about five years back always used to speak of the Jews. I mean—" I hesitate, searching without success for a better word, "their relocation."

His eyes narrow as he looks at me, but the station is empty, and the rails stretch down through Leicestershire and Nottinghamshire amid nodding scoops of cow parsley and wild fennel. The air seems joined to the sky. We are safe here, alone. At other times, in other, happier places, I suspect that this station master and I might be engaged in some other kind of transaction. That is why we choose to trust each other.

"It's quieter here now," he says. "But three, four years ago, a lot of freight trains went past. Long things, they were, with slatted wooden sides, like the farmers use for market—only always at night. One of them pulled up, and this soldier got me out of bed to send a message down the line. A bad smell came off the trucks and I could hear movement inside. I thought it was just animals. But there were voices. And you could see their eyes. . . . Children's fingers poking out of the slats . . ."

The station master stands up and shuffles through the tin heat toward his little station house. He returns with something in his hands.

"I found this," he says, unfolding it, holding it out to me. "On the platform afterward."

It's a travel poster, almost like the ones for Skegness and Barmouth that are smiling down at us. A family are striding down a winding road that leads to a glittering sea. The father is grinning, beckoning us to join him while his wife holds the hands of their two daughters, who are chattering and skipping excitedly, their pig-tails dancing in mid-air. Set within the ocean, more hinted at than revealed, yet clearly the focus of the picture, lie a scatter of small islands. Looked at closely, they blur to just a few clever brush strokes, but they suggest hills and meadows, wooded glades, white beaches, and pretty shingle-roofed and whitewashed houses; a warm and happy place to live. The caption reads: **Relocate to the Summer Isles**.

The promised train does eventually arrive, and the station master and I make our farewells, briefly touching hands, a soft pressure of the flesh that I will soon be losing. I gaze out of the carriage as the train rattles on, close to tears. Oxfordshire comes. Then Oxford. Along Park End and George Street, the city is warm, summer-quiet, at peace with itself now it has lost the unwanted distraction of students, and smells sweetly of dusty bookshops, old stone, dog shit, grass clippings.

"Something for you, sir." Christlow says, nearly falling over himself to intercept me as I limp across the quad. I take the letter he's waving and climb the old oak stairs to my rooms, then stare at the crested envelope as I lean against the door, wondering if I should play a game with myself for a while and let it rest, wondering just how dangerous a letter can be . . . but already my hands are tearing at the wax seal, dragging out the one thick sheet of paper that lies inside.

Beneath a lion and unicorn, it reads:

WHITEHALL
FROM THE OFFICE OF THE PRIME MINISTER
8 August, 1940

G B —
I know it's been a *long* time, but I honestly haven't forgotten.

You may have heard that there's going to be a "National Celebration" in London before and around 21st October, Trafalgar Day. It probably still seems a long way off, but I'd really like to see you there. I promise it'll be nothing formal.

I really do hope you can make it. My staff will send you the details.

All the very best as ever,
J A.

Later that evening, I build a small fire in the grate of my rooms and feed it with the pages of my book. Everything, after all, ends this way. Napoleon, Peter the Great, Bismarck . . . all the *Figures of History*. The pages curl. Glowing fragments of paper dance up the chimney. Soon, there's barely anything left to burn. It's all over so quickly, and what is left of my life, as I open up my old suitcase and cradle Francis's old pistol in my hands, feels simpler already.

FOUR

My college principal Cumbernald comes to my rooms one evening, stretching out in one of the chairs facing the fireplace and companionably beckoning me to join him. He's a tall man, is Cumbernald. He radiates smooth affluence and, like most inferior academics, has pushed his way into administration. Yet he has risen ridiculously far, ridiculously fast. It's almost nice, as the sunlight gleams on his bald head, to think that I'm probably going to bugger up his plans for the next academic year by dying.

"About Michaelmas Term," he begins, crossing his legs to reveal a surprisingly brown length of shin. "I was thinking of giving you the old decline and fall for a change. Bit of a problem with Roberts, you see. Evidently wrote a book back in the twenties about the economics of the Roman Empire. Argued that the colonies were a drain on Rome. *Then* he keeps drawing comparisons with Britain. Even crops up in his students essays — although of course we can't expect the dear things to know any better unless we teach them, can we?"

"I'd be surprised if Roberts' book was still available."

"But that's not the point, is it? Remember *Hobson?* . . . And *Brooking?* Gone, of course. History changes. . . ."

"By the way," I say, interrupting him as he pushes on, "you'll have to do without me for the first week or so of Michaelmas."

"Oh?"

"I have a personal invitation to the Trafalgar Day celebrations from John Arthur."

I reach for the gold embossed wad of papers that arrived soon after that letter. Cumbernald studies them. He swallows audibly. "I'm sure that we can manage without you for a week or so. . . ." He smiles at me. "But you're looking a bit peaky, Brook, if you don't mind me saying so. And Eileen and the children and I, well, we have a chalet at this place outside Ross on Wye. It's very clean, very friendly, very smart. All very *modern*. We're always saying there's room enough to fit in at least one *interesting* guest. So I was wondering . . ."

Eggs and Bacon, Eggs and Bacon, Apple and Custard, Apple and Custard, Cheese and Biscuits, Cheese and Biscuits, Fish and Chips, Fish and Chips . . .

Cumbernald's two daughters are making piston-movements with their elbows, going faster and faster, pretending the Daimler's a train as we bowl along the A40 toward Wales and Gloucester. Christine's the eldest at eleven; a plump pre-adolescent who's designated "clever" and "reads a lot." Barbara's seven, thinner, more self-assured, and "sporty." Cumbernald clicks on the radio, and he and his wife Eileen argue about whether they want to listen to the Light or the Third Program. Snatches of Vera Lynn, static, and Tchaikovsky roar out from the loudspeakers—it's like the avant-garde "European" music they'd be so quick to condemn—while Christine and Barbara grow alarmingly green and listless.

It seems later than it really is when we finally arrive at Penrhos Park. The lodge, clad with logs like some fairy tale woodsman's cottage, is set in a pine-shaded clearing. Cumbernald prepares the dinner out-of-doors using a crude iron device filled with charcoal while Eileen unpacks and the children disappear into the pines. Looking over the forest crown, I see the smoke of other cooking fires rising like Indian signals. As it gets darker, Eileen sets a lantern on the outdoor table, and we watch the moths flutter into oblivion on the hot glass.

"You look a better man already," Cumbernald says, wineglass in his lap, looking pleasingly ridiculous in sandals, baggy shorts. "This is *some* place though, isn't it, eh? A real breath of England."

It's suddenly night-quiet. With the faint stirring of the pines, the distant hoot of an owl, it wouldn't take much imagination to catch the growl of a bear, the rooting chuff of a wild boar, the howl of wolves—the return of all the beasts of old to the vast Wood of Albion. Then I hear a thin shriek. The sound is so strange here, yet so familiar, that it takes me a moment to realize that it's simply the passing of a train.

"It's just a goods line," Cumbernald explains. "Never quite worked out where it's from or to. But I shouldn't worry, old chap. That's the latest I've ever heard one go by. They won't disturb your sleep. I was thinking we could go down to the Sun Area this morning, by the way. That okay with you?"

"Oh? Yes. Fine . . ."

• • •

There's eggs and bacon in the morning, which the girls have already been down to buy from the site shop so that Eileen, back in her traditional role now the cooking's indoors, can prepare them. The sound of their sizzling mingles in my head with the clack and roar of the trains that fractured my night.

The Sun Area is lavishly signposted, yet still requires a long trek past high hedges and long walls, then a queue at a turnstile. The swing doors beyond lead to a hot wooden tunnel lined with benches: some kind of changing area. Eileen Cumbernald removes her halter top and hangs it on a numbered peg. She isn't wearing a bra. Cumbernald, contrarily, first removes his shorts and his baggy y-fronts before taking off his sandals. The children, by some instantaneous process, are already naked, and scamper off to be swallowed by the bright square of light at the far end.

Cumbernald really is brown. Eileen, too; although I can see that she's not as blonde as she pretends to be. I undo a few token buttons of my shirt, wondering how easy it would be to wake up if I pinched myself. *The most amazing dream. I was with the college principal and his wife. They took all their clothes off, then asked me to do the same.* . . . Having somehow divested myself of my clothes, and hobbled into the amazing sunlight, I promise to keep an eye on the children, and sit beside the lake with a copy of something called *Future Past* while Cumbernald and Eileen go off to rustle up a team for the volleyball. Out in the distance, white sails are turning. A woman breastfeeds her child on the towel next to mine, engaging me in alarming snatches of conversation. A young Adonis strides at the water's edge. There's barely any hair on his body. Amid all this display, his genitals are disappointing—a small afterthought—but then it really is true what they say; people in the nude are impossibly decent. We should all go around like this. I can see it now—*Naturism—The Answer to the World's Troubles.* The only trouble is, I have a feeling that it was a title I drew the line at when I was stocking up for my researches on John Arthur in Blackwell's.

I squint at the book I'm supposed to be reading. *Chapter Five. The Greatness of the British Heritage—Truth or Myth?* But I can feel the air passing over me—it's strangely exhilarating—and I lie back on the towel and let the dreary pages splay in the sand. I'm part of the water, the air, the shouts and the cries. . . . Noon comes and goes. The afternoon glides by. I swim. I eat ice cream and a Melton Mowbray pork pie. I drink gallons of Vimto. By evening, as we grab our few belongings and head back up the slope, my skin is itchy and my prick, I can't help noticing, looks a bit like one of Cumbernald's barbecued sausages; cooked on just the one side.

That night, I shiver and roast, glazed in minty unguents. And the trains are busy again, banging back and forth, clanking chains and couplings, hissing brakes as they trundle back and forth. Then a creak of springs comes through the lodge's thin walls as the Cumbernalds' indulge in their own bit of coupling. And there are children's cries, too; the clatter of the showers from which they emerge like drowned figures with their hair lank, thinly naked as they walk on to be swallowed by the light. . . .

At three o'clock, feeling stiff and nauseous, I pad through the dim parlor and open the patio doors. Silvery night lies over the trees in the clearing and I can hear the breath, like a great animal sighing, of a train that must be waiting almost directly behind the lodge. Barefoot, wrapped in my crumpled sheet, I wander toward it.

The huge engine sighs in impatience, then the wheels slip as they begin to take up the tension and move again, hauling the vast burden of wagons that lie behind. They are open-backed, covered in mottled camouflage, although it's easy enough to make out the huge bodies of the Lancaster bombers as they clack past. *Eggs and Bacon, Eggs and Bacon, Apple and Custard, Apple and Custard, Cheese and Biscuits, Cheese and Biscuits, Fish and Chips, Fish and Chips.*

I shuffle back to the lodge trailing my shroud, and lie down to stare up at the grey swirling ceiling of my bedroom, wondering if I could truly perform the act that my thoughts, like the grinding of some unstoppable engine, keep returning: the one deed that would make my life mean something, and repay the debt that I owe to my acquaintance, and to Larry Black, and to all the others, the pleading fingers pushed through the slats of a railway carriage, those lost smiling families heading down the road to be swallowed in the brightness of the Summer Isles. I even owe that same debt to Francis, although the reasons are much harder to explain.

Bang bang. Scurrying KSG officers. The salty drift of cordite and smoke. I'm Charlotte Corday as she plunges her knife into Marat, I'm Gavrilo Princip and the Archduke Ferdinand, I'm John Wilkes Booth and Lincoln . . . I'm *The Fingers of History.*

Bang bang. Long after the stillness of the forest has reasserted itself, I can still hear the sound of that train.

The commonly accepted truths about John Arthur's upbringing are that he was born John Arthur of William and Mary Arthur on 21 October 1890 in a suitably pretty cottage (now open to the public) in Cornwall. Mary Arthur died in childbirth, while William Arthur and his son ended up traveling up through Britain. In the popular imagination, John Arthur never lived in a house before the age of about twelve. He slept in barns, beneath hay ricks, under the stars. He sat on milestones gazing into the future. In the more far-fetched books I've encountered on my researches, you find pictures of John Arthur hand-prints in stones, John Arthur hawthorns that lean against the prevailing wind.

A small link with Burntwood is generally made along the lines of: "William Arthur set about learning his new trade as a miner in a pit (now-disused) in Southern Staffordshire, where John also briefly attended school before heading north to the South Yorkshire village of Raughton." The famous pit at Raughton has also closed — the miners' sons and daughters now work behind the counters of gift shops, museums, pubs, and guest houses. But here, for all I know, is where a boy called John Arthur really did spend his adolescence, and where his father died in a pit accident.

At the age of fifteen, John Arthur supposedly went down the pit himself. At eighteen, he was working the roads. At twenty, he went to night school in Nottingham. At twenty-three, the War intervened. He was wounded first in Flanders in 1915, and then again at the Somme. Back at the Front by mid 1917, promoted corporal, he famously won the George Cross at Ypres, yet somehow survived that and the confusion of defeat.

By the agreed figures, John Arthur would have been twenty-seven by then. As an ex-corporal, a leader of small groups of men used to the harsh decisions and horrors of war, he would have been well equipped to make his mark in the strange and violent world of 1920's fringe politics. In Italy, Il Duce was already in power, building Romanesque temples and thumping his chest from balconies, while John Arthur was still trying to make his voice heard in the corners of East End bars and complaining about the injustice of the Treaty of Versailles. But for Britain, as South Africa plunged into civil war and the Russians expanded across Afghanistan toward the Indian border, there were only other losses to face, and then one final crushing humiliation. In 1923, the Irish Republicans defeated the British forces street by street in Dublin, then savaged them as they withdrew north.

Nothing seemed to have much value then. I, too, queued outside the grocers for ten pounds, then fifty pounds, and then a hundred pounds worth of rotten cabbage as General Election followed General Election and MacDonald succeeded Baldwin and then Baldwin took over again. India was in famine. There were street-battles and demonstrations. When Churchill took power during the Third General Strike of 1924–5 and succeeded in defeating the miners and the train drivers, then issued a "Guaranteed Pound" that people somehow actually believed in, it seemed as though the worst of Britain's post-War nightmare might soon be over. But money was still short. The Communists and the Fascists didn't go away. Neither did the reparations payments, the feeling of defeat, the whole sense of national crisis that Churchill was often so good at exploiting. In this new world order, Britain was a third-rate nation; a little island off a big continent, just like Tierra del Fuego, Ceylon, Madagascar.

I saw John Arthur once at that time, although I know that's a privilege so many people claim nowadays. I was working by then as a teacher at Lichfield Grammar, although we had to subsist on credits and half pay. I was aware of the various bus stops and bushes that the lonely men of Lichfield would sometimes frequent, but I also knew about police entrapment, the shaming articles in the *Lichfield Mercury* that were so often followed by the suicide of those named, the long prison terms, and the beating and truncheon-buggerings that generally accompanied a night in the cells. Of course, I could have tried to honor Francis's memory by seeking someone I cared about, but instead, as the twenties progressed from the time of the five-hundred-pound haddock into Churchill's empty pontificating, I became a regular weekend visitor to London. From Francis, I had taken the turn that many inverts take once love has failed them, which is to remove the holy power from sex by making it a means of humiliation, parody, comedy, degradation.

Once, wandering near midnight in an area of East End dockland houses that the police had long given up policing, I crossed toward the gaslit clamor of an end-of-terrace pub. Just half an hour before, I had been on all fours on a fire-blackened wasteground, half-choking as a fist twisted the back of my collar while an unlubricated cock was forced into me. The pub was called the Cottage Spring. Dry-throated, I made my way toward the bar, then had to give up as I was pushed and shouldered. There was a sense, I suddenly realized, that something was about to happen here.

Those were restless, anxious nights in the East End. Yet, so obsessed was I with my own sexual pursuits that I hadn't realized the many other kinds of risk I was taking. No one had noticed me when I came in, but I was sure that they would notice me now if I tried to leave. I glanced at the man nearest me and saw that his lips were moving. A whispered name, barely audible at first, but becoming clearer, was filling the air. He clambered up on the bar, then, did this man they were all calling for. His face looked pale and his hands were stained with mud or blood, yet he managed to keep an easy dignity as he balanced there with the dusty rows of glasses behind him. He raised his arms and smiled as he looked down at his people. Although he had changed much in the fifteen years since I had last seen him, it was that smile that finally made me certain. I was sure that this man—this John Arthur they were calling for—was in fact Francis Eveleigh.

I didn't wave my arms and cry out. I didn't even try to meet his eyes. Instead, I backed slowly toward a large pillar at the far end of the bar as others pushed forward to get nearer him. I hid myself from his gaze.

He's refined his technique in all the years since, has John Arthur. Nevertheless, his performance on that night was essentially the same as those since outside 10 Downing Street, and on the nation's television screens. That initial pause. The sharing, self-mocking smile that tells us that he still doesn't understand why it has to be *him*. By then, you're expecting nothing more than a calming chat, but suddenly, one of his anecdotes will twist around to some moment of national humiliation. Perhaps the forced scuttling of the fleet at Scarpa Flow in 1919, the refusal of MacDonald's petition to join the League of Nations, or Ireland. There was always Ireland. John Arthur, more clearly in control now, will gaze sadly at his audience. Truly, his eyes say, if only we could only laugh and play like innocent children . . .

When his voice rises, it is imperceptible because it always lies in the wake of the passion of his audience. He seems so calm, in fact, so reluctant, that you find yourself filled with a kind of longing. Exactly what was said on that night matters as little as his recent speeches at the Olympics, or to Fordingham's gloriously ill-fated Everest Expedition. All I know is that, despite my shock and fear, I was moved in the way that good popular music sometimes moves me. And that, when John Arthur had finished speaking and had stepped down from the bar, the men were happy to drift into the darkness toward whatever passed for their homes. For many years, I have clung to that image of John Arthur as the queller rather than the creator of violence. It's part of what has kept me sane.

I found myself momentarily rooted behind my pillar when the crowd began to thin in the Cottage Spring. Francis's hand was resting on the shoulder of a plumper, slightly older man who is now our Deputy Prime Minister, George Arkwright, and he was also talking to his then second-in-command Peter Harrison, who was executed for treason in 1938. I was surprised, as he stood there, to realize how much I still longed to hold him. Then, with that unnamed sense of being watched, he cast his eyes across the fallen tables and chairs in my direction. I just stood there with my hands in the pockets of my grubby coat, looking like the aging mess I knew I was. For a moment, John Arthur's eyes bore the trace of a smile as they met mine, a shade of what could only be recognition. Then he looked away.

Eggs and Bacon, Eggs and Bacon . . .
Back from Penrhos Park to Oxford, and the days flash by. Golden Week nears. The stones and the fields glow with anticipation. The older University hands, us fellows and dons, doctors and vicars, MA's in abstruse subjects, best-selling authors, sexual molesters, surreptitious alcoholics, athletes and aesthetes, caw and flap at each other in our black gowns as the punts still move and slow, move and slow beneath Magdalene Bridge.

Resuming my occasional traipses over to the Radcliffe, new X-rays reveal that the vast cancerous network that runs through my body has stopped growing. It's still there, still almost certainly lethal, but, to all intents and purposes, the thing's biding its time. Waiting, just as I am, while the days slip by into the maw of history.

"Couldn't help noticing, sir," Christlow says, preparatory to spitting on his cloth and wiping the small mirror above my bookshelves one morning, "that you've had an Invitation." He actually says, *Han Hinvitation,* on the traditional working class assumption that anything posh has an extra "h" in it.

"That's right," I turn from the A–Z Map of Central London I've been studying.

"Matter of fact," Christlow continues, still rubbing the mirror, "I'll be off down in London myself for the period of the celebrations. In my own minor small capacity. So we may bump into each other. . . ."

"I'll certainly keep an eye out," I say. But London's a big place.

He puts down his rag, and we find ourselves gazing at each other. I'd never realized before how much Christlow looks like Mussolini: Modernism was probably always his destiny. He clears his throat. He's probably about to ask me why I'm always hanging around now when he's cleaning my rooms, and why I've put another lock on that old suitcase. But he simply gathers up his things as if in some sudden hurry and closes the door, leaving me to my thoughts, my dreams, my desk, my studies.

I open the window to take in a great, shivering breath of Oxford air. It has a cooler feel to it this morning. The limes are dripping, sycamore seeds are spinning, soft autumn bathes the towers and rooftops and domes with light. And the bells are ringing, filling my head, my eyes, my lungs, my heart. Oh, Oxford! Oxford! I cannot bear to leave you.

But history beckons.

My moment has come.

FIVE

The narrator in William Morris's *News from Nowhere* awakes in London to find that summer has at last arrived. The air smells sweeter. The Thames runs cleaner, and the buildings along its banks have been transformed into glorious works of art. The people wear bright costumes, and smile at each other as they go about their everyday tasks. There is no poverty. Children camp in the Kensington Woods. The Houses of Parliament have been turned into a vegetable market.

A full century and a half before Morris predicted, his dream of Nowhere has come true. Truly, I think as I sip gin and gaze down from an airship droning high above the stately parks and teeming streets and the sun-flecked river, this city has never looked lovelier. The Adelphi Theater. Cleopatra's Needle. The sightseeing boats that thread their wakes across the Thames . . . the engines of the *Queen of Air and Darkness* rise in pitch as she sinks down through the skies and across the flashing lakes and lidos of Hyde Park. Eventually, after much tilting and squealing of airbags, she is safely moored to a huge gantry, and I and a dozen or so other minor dignitaries are escorted along a wobbling tunnel to the lift that bears us dizzily to the ground.

It would be rude not to smile and wave for the lenses of the Pathé News camera that follow the progression of our open top bus. Who knows, a darker thought nudges me, this image of the killer's face may be the one that makes it into history. We turn along Oxford Street into the wide new architecture of Charing Cross Road. Then Trafalgar Square, from where the Victory Spire at the end of Park Lane looks like some Jules Verne rocket, or a new secret weapon. Compared with all of this, the great government offices along Whitehall are solid and somber. To our right lies Downing Street, and, even as I watch, the gates slide open on electronic hinges, and out rolls a black Rover 3 Liter with Austin police patrol cars ahead and behind. There are no bells, no flashing lights. As the cars turn up Whitehall, I glimpse John Arthur's face, absorbed in thought as he stares from the Rover's plain unsmoked glass, and my heart freezes.

A loud-hailer calls out incoherent instructions as we disembark outside the New Dorchester's entrance on the South Bank. Reeve-Ellis, the Under Secretary who's in charge of us, lays a hand on my shoulder and steers me through the doors and across the vast main atrium where bare-breasted caryatids raise their arms to support the arches of the glass-domed roof.

"Two days before the big day now, Brook," he murmurs in that dry voice of his. "About time we had a little chat . . ."

He leads me to a door marked **No Admittance**, where plump Police Constable T3308 jumps up from his chair, his holstered pistol swinging between his legs like a cock. My skin prickles, but all that lies beyond is a long corridor bustling with the click of typewriters and the slam of filing cabinets. " 'Fraid everything's a mess here," Reeve-Ellis says as he removes his jacket in his temporary office and shrugs on a baggy grey cardigan. His little mustache bristles as he attempts a smile. I know already that Reeve-Ellis is a Balliol man, 1909 intake, and was working in the Cabinet Office when Lloyd George resigned. So he's seen it all, has toiled under every shade of administration.

"I've been meaning to ask," I begin. "Exactly how—"

"—You'll be up in the VIP seats for the afternoon parade up the Mall. Have to miss the end of *that*, though, I'm afraid, if we're going to get you across to Downing Street in time."

"So there'll be—what?—about twenty or so people in the gardens at Number Ten. And I suppose some . . . staff?"

"That's about right. It's an informal occasion."

"What if it rains?"

"We're a lucky country, Brook. It won't rain." He smiles again. "As I say, keep a space in your diary for six o'clock, Monday. Don't worry about protocol or what suit to wear—JA's the least bothered person about that kind of thing you could possibly imagine."

"I do have a new suit, actually," I say. "It was delivered to me this morning from Hawkes on Saville Row." Hand-tailored, the thing cost me a fortune, and feels quite different to any clothing I've ever worn. Just as I requested, the jacket has been tailored with an especially strong and deep inner left-side pocket to accommodate the pistol that currently lies hidden in the aged lining of the old suitcase I have brought with me.

I thought I'd already been through all the possible stages of grieving for my Francis when I discovered that he was alive again. I'd been angry. Almost suicidally miserable. Eventually, I'd come to imagine that my life was no longer under his shadow. But just knowing how I looked to him as I stood in that pub made me realize that everything about my life was still Francis, Francis, Francis. What, otherwise, was I doing in London in the first place, if not trying to wipe out my love for him?

Even in 1925, this John Arthur that he'd become was no longer a totally obscure figure, and I was soon saved the trouble of having to delve through *National Rights!* and *The Spitalfields Chronicle* to follow his activities. His was one of several names to emerge into the wider acres of political debate on the back of Churchill's use of right wing groups to help break the long succession of strikes. But John Arthur was always ahead of the rest. With his accent, his manners, he seemed both educated *and* working class. In an age of lost certainties, he made good copy. And he had a knack of simply stating the obvious— that Britain was poor, that we were shamed by the loss of Ireland and Empire— that most politicians seem to lack. Unlike William Arkwright, Peter Harrison, and the soon-to-be rising star of Jim Toller, John Arthur was never openly racist or intolerant. His carefully cultured background, the wanderings, the War record, the thuggery and unemployment of the East End, presented, like the rest of the man, so many facets that you could select the one you preferred and ignore the rest.

In the winter of 1927, John Arthur stood at a by-election in Nottinghamshire as the first-ever Empire Alliance candidate. I can well remember the moment when I picked up my newspapers from the doormat on the morning after his maiden speech in Parliament. Appropriately enough, I think it was the *Sketch* that ran a smaller by-line asking **Who Is Geoffrey Brook?** which quoted an aside in his speech about how he'd been much influenced by a teacher named Geoffrey Brook in Burntwood, Lichfield. After all, I was a distant memory to him; there was no reason why he should exactly remember my name.

Over the next few days, when the press discovered my address, I had my own small moment of fame. They called me Geoffrey, and it seemed churlish to correct them when they were so nearly right. Would it have made any difference if I had announced that, while I knew little enough about this man who called himself John Arthur, he reminded me markedly of someone else with whom I had once had a homosexual affaire? Other than betraying a trust and guaranteeing my death in some freak accident, I doubt it.

The next year, 1928, while John Arthur was joined by another 10 EA MP's at the spring General Election, and Churchill continued about the dogged business of keeping himself in power, the editor of the *Daily Sketch* approached me about writing a weekly column. At last, I felt like someone who mattered. Churchill, meanwhile, lasted until October 1929 and the Wall Street Crash. Ramsey MacDonald then became Prime Minister of a Government of National Unity while Oswald Mosley struggled to reunite Labour before giving up and joining the EA six months later, thus forcing yet another General Election. This time, John Arthur traveled from constituency to constituency by Vickers aeroplane, and such was the dangerous glamour of the EA by then that even his fat deputy George Arkwright with his trademark Homburg hat became a vote winner. Uniformed EA members marched in the streets of all the big towns, noting names as people emerged from polling stations. The EA won seventy seats. Amid an atmosphere of increasing crisis—unemployment, means tests, riots and starvation, open revolt in India, popular support for Unionist terrorist attacks in Ireland—John Arthur refused new Prime Minister Neville Chamberlain's offer of a post in his Cabinet.

Chamberlain's "get tough" policy in India over the next few months only served to increase the bloodshed, and the rest of the Empire was also starting to fray. A new Egyptian Government nationalized the Suez Canal. Welsh and Scottish Nationalists began to talk of independence. The country was in a state of collapse. Chamberlain was probably right in imagining that Britain would be torn apart by another pointless General Election. He was running out of options, but there remained one figure that the great mass of the public seemed to believe in. Not really a *politician* at all, and head of an organization that had never properly disowned violence. But controllable, surely; a useful figurehead to keep the prols happy and the bully boys at bay while the real brains got on with sorting out the mess that the country was in. It was thus without fuss or bloodshed, in a deal in which he seemingly played no part, that John Arthur was finally summoned to Number 10 and offered the only Cabinet post that he had said he would ever consider accepting.

Just after six o'clock on the chilly evening of November 10, 1932, John Arthur emerged from that famous black door to the clink of flashbulbs. In those days, traffic was still allowed along Downing Street, and he had to check left and right before he crossed over and raised his arms, smiling slightly as he looked about him. He said that he would be heading off to Buckingham Palace in a few minutes, where he planned to seek King George's advice about forming Greater Britain's first Modernist Government.

• • •

The flags and the bunting are going up as I'm chauffeur-driven across London to meet the King and Queen next morning. Tomorrow is the eve of Trafalgar Day, and there's a Thanksgiving Service at Westminster Abbey. Already the advertisements on the sides of buses for Idris Table Waters have been replaced with cheery messages to our Leader. **Greater Britain Thanks You. Here's to the Future.**

My black Daimler sweeps with a stream of others around Hyde Park Corner and through the towering gates to pull up beside the steel flagpoles in front of New Buckingham Place. I wade through a dizzy sense of unreality past the guardsmen in their busbies. I'm giving Monday's suit a trial-airing, and have even placed *News from Nowhere* in the inner pocket to give a similar weight and feel to the pistol.

Dresses rustle as the queue shuffles forward. His Highness the Duke of York stammers slightly as he greets me. I bow. Then his wife the Duchess, and their two plain daughters. A moment later I'm standing before King Edward and Queen Wallis. I glance discreetly to both sides as I bow. It would be easy for me to reach inside my jacket at this point. Click back the hammer as I pull the pistol out. Two shots, minimum, thudding into the chest at close range. Within moments, this whole Place would implode in shatters of glass and steel, drawn up through the skies in a hissing gale, back toward fairyland where it belongs.

The guests wander out through pillared archways into the afternoon's gracious warmth. There's a stir when the silver trays of sweet Merrydown Wine emerge for the loyal toast. The gardens as I explore them still feel a little like Green Park of old. The stepped orchards and monumental statues don't quite fit. The roses that amazingly still bud and flower on the trellises in this bright October sunlight look too red, too raw. You can almost smell the paint and hear the bellowing voice of the Queen of Hearts. *No! No! Sentence first—verdict afterward.* Looking around for something more filling than smoked salmon sandwiches, light-headed as my belly growls and premonitions of pain begin to dance around me, I recognize a famous face.

"Personally, I can't stand fiddling around with plates and standing up at the same time," he says affably. "Strikes me as a foreign habit."

Deputy Prime Minister Arkwright looks small and ordinary in the flesh, almost exactly like his pictures, even without the pipe and the Homburg. In fact, he really hasn't changed that much from the man I glimpsed standing with John Arthur all those years ago at the Cottage Spring. He was probably born cherubically plump, going-on-fifty.

"Hmm. Oxford," he says when I tell him who I am. "You know, I still wish I'd had a university education. And you know John from way back?"

"I taught him briefly when he was a child," I reply, conscious of the rainbowed sun gleaming on Arkwright's blood-threaded cheeks, the strange intensity, even as he chomps cocktail sausages, of his gaze. William Arkwright's the EA's comic turn. He's frequently seen on the arms of busty actresses. But he's Deputy Prime Minister *and* Home Secretary. He's the second most famous face in the country, even if he trails the first by a long way. He can hardly have come this far by accident.

"John's always so quiet about his past—not that you'd believe it if you read the press." Arkwright chews another handful of sausages. "Of course, no one gives a bugger about *my* upbringing. It's called charisma, I suppose. Some of us have to make do with hard work."

"Did you ever think you'd get this far?"

Arkwright tilts his head as the water clatters over the green brass dolphins behind us. "I'm permanently amazed, Mr. Brook. Although I know I don't look it. . . ."

I nod. I'd never realized how difficult it is to talk to someone famous, that sense of knowing them even though you don't, and the way Arkwright's looking at me as if there really is something shared between us. . . . Then I realize what's happening—and immediately wish I hadn't. It's there in his eyes. It's in that smile of his and the way he studies me. After all these years, I've finally met someone else who knows the truth about John Arthur.

"What do you think of John Arthur, Mr. Brook? I know it's been a long time, but do you like him personally?"

"He has my . . . admiration."

"Admiration." Deputy Prime Minister William Arkwright smiles at me. "I suppose that's about as much as any of us can hope for. . . ." Then he pretends to see someone else he recognizes over my shoulder, and waddles away.

Much of what happened after John Arthur became Prime Minister seemed so *traditional* that at first even the skeptics were reassured: the marches, the brass bands, the jamborees, and the improvement of the roads and the railways. The arrests certainly came. The few remaining communist and socialist MP's were immediately deprived of their seats—after the years of riots, strikes, and disturbances, that only seemed like a sensible precaution. Left wing newspapers like the *Manchester Guardian* suffered firebomb attacks. The Jews and the Irish were the subject of intimidation. Homosexuals were still routinely beaten up. In many ways, in fact, little had changed.

At this time, Britain was still supposedly a democracy. But John Arthur plainly had little time for the fripperies of a discredited political system. In his first weeks in power, he passed a short Enabling Act that effectively meant he could rule by decree. In a country without any written constitution, that was all that was needed.

It was a time of whispers. In schools, there were Modernist masters who would report any colleagues to the EA-dominated Local Education Authorities. Anxious to keep our jobs, the rest of us never quite seemed to realize that we had crossed the line from the truth and had began to peddle lies. Despite the thrill of the fresh new vision that was gripping Greater Britain, as we now called our country, there was an atmosphere of almost perpetual crisis. When I was summoned to the Headmaster's study midway through the 2B's Tuesday morning lesson one day in 1932, all the usual suspicions went though my mind. Poor results, perhaps, in the new Basic Grade exams? My sucking off that foundry worker outside the Bull at Shenstone last Saturday evening? Some new twist of the national curriculum that I had failed to absorb? The *Daily Sketch* and I had already parted company. Once again, I was a nobody, nearing retirement and easily discarded. And behind that, behind it all, was the fearsome burden of what I knew about John Arthur.

"Take a pew, take a pew. . . ." The headmaster smiled at me with alarming warmth as I slumped down. "I've received a letter this morning." He rubbed the thick vellum between his fingers as if he still didn't believe it. "From the Vice Chancellor at Oxford, in fact. It seems that they're seeking to widen their, ah, *remit*. Trying to get in some fresh educational blood. Your name, Brook, has been mentioned. . . ."

Back at the New Dorchester, surrounded by bakelite angels, deep fur rugs, soft leather chairs, a huge television set, and an ornate stained-glass frieze depicting Saint George Resting in a Forest, quite unable to rest, I put on my coat and head out into the sprawling London night. The traffic roars by as I cross Westminster Bridge, and the strung lights twinkle along the Embankment. People are *running*, amazingly enough, dressed up like athletes in shorts and vests, and there are accordionists and street vendors, floating restaurants, arm-in-arm lovers, wandering tourists. The newshoardings for the final edition *Evening Standard* proclaim **France and Britain Clash over Egypt.** You can almost feel the news hotting up as the summer cools.

Fairgrounds have been set up in all the parks, and the sickly smell of candy floss spills across all of London. Children, their faces shining with sugar, grease, and excitement, nag their parents for a last ride on one of the vast machines. I find a shooting gallery and aim and shoot, aim and shoot while the couple beside me smear their mouths across each other's faces. *Bang Bang.* Gratifyingly, several of the tin ducks sink down, and my hand hardly seems to be trembling. Further out beyond the tents and the rides lies a great bonfire. Two Spitfires swoop out of the night, agitating the sparks and trailing ribbons of smoke while lads stripped to the gleaming waist climb over each other to make trembling pyramids, marshaled by absurd middle-aged men in khaki shorts and broad-brimmed hats, and I'm enjoying the comedy and pondering the question of what else goes on in those lines of tents, when I sense that I'm being stared at from across the ring. It's Christlow, his face slippery with firelight as he marshals the next shining cluster of Modernist youth. But his eyes flick away from mine when I attempt to smile at him. He looks around as if in panic, then stumbles from sight into the trembling heat.

Everything seems tired now. Lads are yelling fuck-this and fuck-that at each other and the toilet tents have turned nasty. As I limp back along the safe, tramp- and pervert-free streets in search of a taxi, all London is suddenly, dangerously quiet, and seems to be waiting. The night staff at the New Dorchester are out with mops and vacuum cleaners in some of the communal spaces, doing their night duties, and everything in my room is immaculate, unchanged. Saint George is still at prayer in his forest of glass. The sheets of my huge bed are drum-taut. I sleepwalk over to the tall ash-and-ebony cabinet and pour out a drink from the first bottle that comes to hand to help down the tablets. Now, I notice, my hand really is shaking. I reach to the line of buttons and make the lights dim. Saint George fades, the forest darkens.

I lift my old case out from the wardrobe, sliding my hand into the flabby lining and feeling for the gnarled stock of the pistol, conscious of the weight of the metal, the pull of history, gravity, fate. Then—as now seems as good a time as any—I begin to load it. Five bullets are left out of the ten I started with, and they look newer and cleaner than I imagined. I tested the others against a dead tree stump late one evening in Readon Woods when the very stars seemed to shrink back in surprise that the damn things still worked. Now, each remaining one makes a tiny but purposeful click in the cylinder.

It was a cool day when I first arrived at Oxford, with the year's first frost covering the allotments. The sky was pale English blue and beneath it lay everything that I had ever dreamed of or expected. The bells, the bicycles. Christlow. Worn stone steps. Faded luxury. Casement widows. The college principal Cumbernald taking me for lunch at the White Horse jammed between Blackwell's and Trinity as if he really had every reason to welcome me. But by the time we'd opted—yes, why not?—for a third pint of Pedigree, I didn't even feel like an impostor. I felt as if I was gliding at last into the warm currents of a stream along which my life had always been destined to carry me.

I remember that the news vendors were selling a Special Extra Early edition of the *Oxford Evening News* as we walked back along High. Cumbernald bought a copy and we stood and read it together. Other people were doing the same, forming excited clusters, nearly blocking the street. A British Expeditionary Force had landed north of Dublin, and a task-force fleet led by HMS Hood had accepted the surrender of Belfast. All in all, it was a fine day to be British.

More fine days were to follow. There was easy victory in Ireland. The commemorative Victory Tower went up and up in London. I, meanwhile, shivered pleasurably at Christmas to the soaring music of the choir at King's. And for these new and nervous students who entered my rooms clutching essays and reading lists, I became what I had always been, which was a teacher. There were gatherings, paneled rooms, mulled wine in winter, mint teas and Japanese wallpapers in the spring, cool soft air off the river on long walks alone. Greater British forces aided Franco's victory over the communists in Spain. The Cyprus Adventure came and went. We re-took Rhodesia. I bought myself an expensive new gramophone.

The rest of the world found it easier to regard John Arthur as a kind of Fascist straight-man to Mussolini. France, Germany, and the Lowlands were too busy forming themselves into a Free Trade Community while the USA under Roosevelt, when it wasn't worrying about the threat in the Far East from a resurgent Japan, remained doggedly isolationist. In the Middle East, Britain's canny re-alignment of Egypt's King Farouk in the Modernist mold, and his conquest of Palestine with the help of British military advisors, were seen as no more than par for the course in that troubled region. After all, Britain was behaving no more aggressively than she had throughout most of history. Even now that the whole of Kent has been turned into a military camp as a precaution against some imagined Franco-German threat, the world still remains determined to think the best of us.

Meanwhile, I grew to love Oxford almost as much in reality as in the dream. Eights Week. The Encaenia Procession. Midnight chimes. The rainy climate. The bulldogs in their bowler hats checking college gardens for inebriate sleepers. The Roofs and Towers Climbing Society.

History went on. The Jews were re-located. Gypsies and tramps were forcibly "housed." Homosexuals were invited to come forward for treatment. Of course, I was panicked for a while by *that*—but by then I had my acquaintance, our discreet messages on the cubicle wall at the Gents beside Christ Church Meadow, our casual buggerings when he'd do it to me first and then I'd sometimes do it to him—my soft and easy life. I had my desk, my work, my bed. I had my books, the tea rooms, the gables, the cupolas, the stares of the Magdalene deer, the chestnuts in flower, music from the windows of buildings turned ghostly in the sunlight, young voices in the crystalline dusk, and the scent of ancient earth from the quads.

I was dazed. I was dazzled. Without even trying, I had learned how to forget.

SIX

I am dragged back toward morning by sleek sheets, a clean sense of spaciousness that cannot possibly be Oxford, and an anguished howling. My head buzzes, the light ripples. London, of course. London. The New Dorchester . . . I fumble for my tablets on the bedside table as the sirens moan, and I'm blinking and rubbing my eyes when the door to my room swings open.

"Sorry about this, Brook." Reeve-Ellis leans in. He's already dressed, and has PC T3308 in tow. "Frightful cock-up to have an air raid practice on this of all days. You know what these bongo-bongo players are like—probably think it's the Great White God coming down to impregnate their daughters. There's a good man. Just pop on that dressing gown. . . ."

It's pandemonium along the corridors. People are flapping by in odd assortments of clothing with pillow-creases on their cheeks and electrified hair. Reeve-Ellis steers me down the main stairs, then on through crowds in the main atrium. "A lot easier if we go this way," he says, and he, PC T3308, and I struggle against the flow until we reach an eddy beside the hotel souvenir shop where another PC—he's K2910 according to his shoulder badge—is standing guard at the same door marked **No Admittance** that I was led into two days before. PC K2910 follows us as we go in. The howl of the siren, the sound of people moving, suddenly grows faint. This early in the offices beyond, there are no phones ringing, no typewriters clicking.

"Along here," Reeve-Ellis says, shoving his hands into his cardigan pockets. PC K2910 keeps just behind me. PC T3308 strides ahead and opens another door marked **Emergency Exit Only** that leads to a damp and dimly lit concrete tunnel. It slams shut behind us. Here, at last, the New Dorchester's carpets and luxury give out. The passage slopes down. Water drips from tiny stalactites on the roof. The air smells gassy and damp.

We reach a gated lift which clanks us down past coils of pipework to some kind of railway platform. An earthy breeze touches our faces as we wait and the rails begin to sing before an automatic train slides in, wheezing and clicking with all the vacant purpose of a toy, hauling a line of empty mail hoppers with pull-down wooden seats. PC K2910 clambers in first, then helps Reeve-Ellis. I try taking a step back, wondering about escape.

"Might as well just get in, sir," PC T3308 says, offering a large, nail-bitten hand. Hunched in our train as we slide into the tunnel, I'm conscious of my slippered feet, my pajamas beneath the dressing gown. Grey wires along the walls rise and fall, rise and fall. I study the two policemen squatting opposite me in what light there is. PC T3308 is bigger and older, with the jowled meaty face and body of an old-fashioned copper, PC K2910 is freckled, red-headed, thin; he seems too young, in fact, to be a policeman at all.

We disembark at another mail station, and travel upward in another gated lift. Then, suddenly, the walls are almost new—painted the same municipal green that covered the walls of the Gents by Christ Church Meadow. PC T3308 grips my arm. There are doors leading into offices, but the place seems empty, abandoned, and we're still deep underground.

"It's in here." Reeve-Ellis opens a door to an office where there are three chairs and a desk, one battered-looking tin filing cabinet, and fat pipes run across the ceiling.

"You may as well sit down, Brook." Reeve-Ellis points to the chair on the far side of the desk as PC K2910 locks the door behind us, and I notice as my body settles into it that it gives off a sour, unfortunate smell. The air is warm in here, almost swimmingly hot.

"Whatever all of this is," I say, "You should know that I've no close friends or relatives. And I have terminal cancer—you can look it up in my NHS records. . . ."

"I'm afraid," Reeve-Ellis says, "that it doesn't work like that."

PC T3308 leans across and lifts my right hand from the arm rest, splaying it palm-up at the edge of the desk. He sits down on it, his fat-trousered bottom pushed virtually in my face. I hear the rasp of a belt buckle, and something jingles. I imagine that they'll start asking me questions at any moment, long before they do anything that might actually case me pain.

"If this is—" I begin just as, with a small grunt of effort, PC K2910 brings the truncheon down across the fingers of my right hand.

Alone now, I can hear Reeve-Ellis's voice as he talks to someone on the telephone in a nearby room. *Yes. No. Not yet. Just as you say* . . . I can tell from the sound of his voice that he's speaking to a superior.

I'm cradling my right hand. It's the most precious thing in the entire world. My index finger is bent back at approximately 45 degrees just above the first joint, and it's swelling and discoloring as I watch. The first and middle fingers are swelling rapidly too, although they could simply be torn and bruised rather than broken.

This is terrible—as bad as I could have imagined. Yet I've had plenty of opportunity lately to get used to pain. The thing about torture isn't the pain, I decide between bouts of shivering. It's the simple sense of wrongness.

The keys jingle. Reeve-Ellis and the two PC's re-enter the room.

"I won't piss you about, Brook," Reeve-Ellis says. "I'm no expert, anyway, at this kind of thing. . . ."

PC K2910 extracts his note pad and pencil. With that freckled narrow face of his, he still looks far too young. PC T3308 and leans back against the wall and nibbles at his nails. A sick tremor runs though me.

"Perhaps you could begin," Reeve-Ellis continues, "by telling us exactly why you're here. What all of this is about . . ."

"*You* brought me here. I'm supposed to be an honored guest, and then you . . ."

But almost before I've started, Reeve-Ellis is sighing in weary irritation. He's nodding to PC K2910 to find the keys to let him out of the room again. Once he's gone, the two PC's glance at each other, and come around to me from opposite sides of the desk. Their hook their hands beneath my armpits.

"I didn't think this was the sort of thing the London Constabulary specialized in," I say. "I always imagined this was all left to the KSG nowadays."

"Oh, we don't need those fancy boys, sir. Piss-poor at anything from what I've heard. Now, if you'll just stand up . . ."

I try to grab the chair's armrest with the fingers of my good hand, but soon I'm standing upright and the PC's are moving me toward the old grey filing cabinet in the corner of the room. I feel the agonizing pull of my tendons as they hold my damaged right hand over the open drawer. Then PC T3308 raises his boot and kicks it shut.

"These things have a pattern," Reeve-Ellis says, sitting in front of me again. "You have to accept that, Brook. What you must realize is that there's only one outcome. Which is you telling me everything."

A soft click, and there on the table, although stretched and blotched to my eyes as if in some decadent non-realist painting, lies the pistol that I inherited in some other life, some other world, from Francis.

"If you could just tell me how and why you got this thing, and what it was doing in your suitcase."

"It's a relic," I say. "It belonged to a friend of mine who died in the War."

"Can you tell me his name?"

I hesitate. A billow of black agony enfolds me. "Francis Eveleigh. As I say, he's dead."

"Where did he live?"

I tell him the name of the street in Lichfield, and then—what could it matter now?—that of Francis's parents' house in Louth. "It came back with his effects when he died at the Somme."

"And the bullets?"

"They came with the effects as well."

"So it all came to you—" Reeve-Ellis strokes his chin. "This gun, these bullets, as a memento of this Eveleigh fellow? And you've kept them with you ever since?"

"Yes."

"Ever used the gun?"

"No . . . Well, once. I wanted to make sure that it still worked."

"Did it?"

"I'm no expert. It seemed to fire."

"I see. And what did you intend to do with it?"

"What do you think?"

Reeve-Ellis frowns. "I thought we'd got past that stage, old man."

"I intended to kill John Arthur."

Reeve-Ellis nods. He seems unimpressed. Behind him, PC K2910 frowns, licks his pencil, makes a note. Somewhere, a phone is ringing.

"It was Christlow," I say, "wasn't it?"

"Who?"

"Christlow, my scout. He told you about the gun."

"We seem to be forgetting here exactly who is asking the questions." Reeve-Ellis smiles. I sense that the two PC's behind him are loosening their stance. Perhaps all this will soon be ending. Then he stands up and nods to them as he leaves the room, even though I'm screaming that I've already told him everything.

But there are more questions, the nightmare of my hand in the filing cabinet again. Pain's a strange thing. There are moments when it seems there has never been anything else in the whole universe, and others when it lies almost outside you. I think of Christ on his cross, of Torquemada and Matthew Hopkins. All those lives. And even now. Even now. In Japan. In Spain. In Russia. In Britain. I'm not lost at all. Not alone. A million twisted ghosts are with me.

I flinch as the lock slides and the door opens. Alone this time, Reeve-Ellis sits down.

"I was once John Arthur's lover," I swallow back a lump of vomit. "I bet you didn't know that?"

Reeve-Ellis frowns at me. A loose scab breaks open as the flesh on my hand parts and widens. The sensation is quite disgusting.

"I was asked to show you these," he says, laying down a brown manila envelope and sliding out four grainy enlargements of faces and upper bodies, all apparently naked. Three are white-lit against a white cloth background; the fourth—a man, I realize when I've sorted out the approximate details of these gaunt, near-bald, blotched, and virtually sexless figures—is standing against a wall. They are each holding in spider-thin hands a longer version of the kind of slot-in numbers that churches use for hymns. My vision blurs. A large part of me doesn't want to recognize these people.

"How do I know," I say, "that they're still alive?"

"You don't."

I gaze back at the photographs. Eyes that fix the camera without seeing, as if they can fill up with so many sights that light is no longer absorbed. My acquaintance, he looks younger, older, beyond time, with the thin bridge of his nose, the ridges of his cheeks, the taut drum-like skin, the sores. His wife, his children, are elfin, fairy people, blasted through into nothingness by the light that pours around them. . . .

"These people—"

"—I was just asked to show you, Brook. I don't know who they are, what they mean to you."

The lock on the door slides back. Both PC's stand close to the wall without a word, watching me and Reeve-Ellis.

"Are you proud of this?" I say to them all. "Is this how you wanted the Summer Isles?"

"Just concentrate on telling us everything, old man." Reeve-Ellis looks weary, defensive, frustrated. In spite of everything, I still have this feverish sense that there's some part of this equation that I haven't yet glimpsed. "Do you really think you could get even this close to John Arthur with a pistol unless someone wanted you to? Still, it must have been fun while it lasted, playing your stupid little game."

He picks up the photos, taps them together, and slides them back into the envelope. PC's T3308 and K2910 move toward me, grip me beneath my arms and bear me up toward the filing cabinet once again.

When I've told them more than I imagined I ever knew. When I've told them about Francis Eveleigh and about my acquaintance and about poor Larry Black at the Crown and Cushion and Ernie Svendsen who deserves it anyway and all the children I used to teach who I know are grown up by now and culpable as all we British are yet at the same time totally blameless. When I've told them about that time in the twenties when I saw Eveleigh again at the Cottage Spring except he was now really John Arthur. When I've told them everything, I'm suddenly aware of the sticky creak of the chair I'm in, and of the waiting emptiness that seems to flood around me.

"Well . . . ," Reeve-Ellis says. "I suppose we had to get there eventually." He takes PC K2910's notebook. The way he stuffs it into his pocket, I know he's going to destroy it. The two PC's are careful this time. They lift me up almost gently and, amazingly, my limbs still work as we stagger out along the corridor. We come to a door marked **Maintenance Only**, where PC K2910 fiddles with the bolts and swings it open into a shock of night air. I can hear the murmur of traffic as PC T3308 leads me into the darkness, but the sound is distant, shielded on all sides by brick and glass and concrete. The patch of sky is the same shape and color as a cooling television screen—there's even one small dot-like star in the middle. I'd always imagined that my life would end in a prettier place. A remote clearing in some wood in the Home Counties, the cry of a fox and the smell of leaves and moss . . .

I glance back. Reeve-Ellis stands in the lighted doorway, hands stuffed into his cardigan as he leans against the frame. It really is quiet here. The whole of this pre-Trafalgar Day, and the celebratory service I was expecting to attend at Westminster Abbey, has gone by. PC T3308 lets go of me and I sag to my knees, still struggling to protect the precious burden of my hand. I hear the creak of leather as he reaches to release the flap of his holster as somewhere, faintly, dimly, deep within the offices, a phone starts ringing. His breathing quickens.

"Wait!" Reeve-Ellis calls across the courtyard, and his footsteps recede. The night falls apart, pulses, regathers as I breathe the rotten air that my own body is making, trying to wish away this moment, this pain. Eventually, the phone stops. Somewhere across London, a train whistle screams. I think of a rocking sleeper carriage. A man's arms around me, his lips against mine. The gorgeous, shameless openness . . .

Reeve-Ellis's footsteps return, the lines of his body re-shape against the bright doorway.

"There's been," he calls, "a change of plan. . . ."

Reeve-Ellis drives a Triumph Imperial, a big old car from the pre-Modernist early thirties with rusty wings and a vegetable smell inside given off by the cracked leather seats. It creaks and rattles as he drives, indicating fitfully, jerking from side to side along the London streets.

"Who was that phone call from?"

"After what you've been through, old man . . . ," he says, stabbing at the brake as a taxi pushes ahead of us. "You really don't want to know. Believe me. Just count yourself as bloody lucky. . . ."

The brightening sky shines greyish-pink on the Thames as we cross Westminster Bridge. At the New Dorchester, the remnants of a fancy dress party are lingering. A Black Knight is clanking around in the remains of his armor while Robin Hood is arguing mildly about some aspect of room service with Reception. We fit in here, Reeve-Ellis and I. He's come as what he is, and I'm something from the War—or perhaps the last guest at *The Masque of the Red Death*.

Reeve-Ellis punches the button for the lift.

"The message," he says as the lighted numbers rise, "is that you carry on as before."

"What?"

"Today, old man. You still get to see John Arthur. . . ."

We arrive at my floor. My bed has been made, but otherwise nothing has changed since I left here a day ago. The nymphs still cavort across the ceiling. Saint George is still at prayer in his forest.

"Get some rest," Reeve-Ellis advises after summoning the hotel's resident nurse and doctor on the phone. "Watch the parades on television. I'll make sure someone fixes you up and sees that you're ready in time. . . ."

"Those people—the photographs you showed me."

"I don't know."

"And what about you? Aren't you afraid?"

"Of what, old man?"

"This . . ." I gesture wildly about me, nearly falling. "Hell."

"If there is a hell," Reeve-Ellis says, reaching to grasp the handle of the door, "you and me, old man—we'd probably hardly notice any difference. We'd just get on with doing the only things we know how. . . ." Then he closes the door, leaving me alone in my plush room at the New Dorchester. My wristwatch on the bedside table has stopped ticking, but the electric clock on the wall tells me it's just after six in the morning. I make the effort to slide back the wardrobe doors with my left hand and check my suitcase. The scents of Oxford still waft from inside, and everything has been left so neatly that it's almost a surprise to find that the pistol really is missing. Clambering to my feet, I swallow a handful of my tablets and study the label on the bottle, although the handwriting is indecipherable. But how would my body react if I took the whole lot? Would that be enough to do it? And the antiinflammatories, I could take all of those, too. I gaze at the stained glass frieze of Saint George. There's dragon's blood, I notice now, on his praying gauntleted hands. I've been left alone—so perhaps they're expecting this of me; a bid at suicide. But then wouldn't I have been killed already? I throw the bottle across the room with my clumsy left hand. Somehow, it actually hits the frieze, but it bounces off with a dull clunk, raining tablets. Weeping, I scuttle across the floor, picking them up, and collapse on my huge bed.

Beyond my windows, a barge sounds its horn. Lozenges of light ripple and dance with the nymphs on the ceiling. I'd press the button on the headboard that makes the doors slide back, were I able to reach it. I'd like to smell the Thames on what feels like this last of all days, I'd love to hear it innocently lapping. Here in London, it has fostered trade, cholera, prosperity, and been the muse of a thousand poets. There were bonfires upon it in the reign of Queen Elizabeth, so hard did it freeze. . . .

I see myself in front of a class of students once again, speaking these words. Francis Eveleigh is there—he's a young boy, no more than ten, and for some reason his arm is in a sling. And Cumbernald, and Christlow, and Reeve-Ellis, and my acquaintance, and the many other faces that have filled my life.

I smile down at them as they sit with their scabbed elbows and knees, their grubbily cherubic faces, the looming playtime forgotten for a while as they listen. These, I know, are my only moments of greatness. So listen, just listen. All I want to do is to tell you one last tale.

SEVEN

Monday 21 October 1940. Trafalgar Day. John Arthur's fiftieth birthday, his silver jubilee. At nine, and under clearing skies even though the forecasts had remained doubtful, the church bells begin to ring out all across the country. There had been talk of rain coming in from the North Sea, driven down over Lincolnshire and across the Fens toward London. But that was just a tease. After a glorious summer of seemingly endless celebrations, no one ever doubted the perfect autumn day this would turn out to be.

By eight o'clock, as the hotel doctor sets and splints my hand and the nurse gags my mouth with a stick to stop me biting my tongue in my agony, trestle tables are being laid in village halls and on dew-damp greens from Mablethorpe to Montgomery, from Treviscoe to Nairn. Balloons are being inflated and jellies turned out onto plates. Guardsmen are polishing their buckles and blancoing their straps while grooms feed and brush their shining mounts. We British are still unsurpassed at this kind of thing.

The doctor's manner is brisk—so unsurprised that there doesn't seem to be any point in asking whether he's used to dealing with matters of this sort. And I'm too busy weeping, anyway, until he gives me one last blissfully large injection: Floating, white as angels, the nurse and a hotel steward remain on hand to help me with the tricky process of bathing and dressing. Then I'm placed before my television set, which is already glowing, giving off a smell of warm bakelite and electricity, and my head is supported and my arm is rested. I drift in and out of the rest of the morning on the monochrome visions that come out at me. Already, the ghosts of Empire are moving from Horse Guards Parade, past Admiralty Arch, and along the Mall. Fizzing out at me in shades of grey, they turn at Palace Gardens and march back along the far side of the Mall. The Fourth Infantry. The Gurkhas. The Northamptonshire (Youth) Branch of the Empire Alliance. Bowler-hatted veterans from the War. The Metropolitan Police. The Knights of Saint George.

As noon passes, the King arrives in a white uniform. Pointedly, a gap still remains between him and Deputy Prime Minister Arkwright. It's typical of John Arthur to delay his entrance on this of all days. I can well imagine, in fact, what a delicious luxury it must be to sit in the book-lined calm of his Downing Street study, working quietly through papers while the yearning sea-roar of a whole nation and Empire drifts through the sash windows. It's hard to imagine a greater moment of power. Where to after this, Francis? Oh, *Francis*—despite everything, I almost feel as if I can almost understand. . . .

Then he arrives. John Arthur, wearing a plain grey suit, settles into his seat beside the King, and every eye, every camera, and with it, the attention of the whole world, shifts to watch him. The latter part of the parade is more military. It's hard not to be impressed by grey-black tanks of such shining bulk that they leave burning trails behind them on the television, and artillery, and bombers swooping low; the sound of their engines reaching me first overhead, trembling the warm air through my balcony windows. But through everything, even in the long minutes when he's not on the screen, my thoughts remain fixed on that one distant figure. I keep asking how it's possible for one man to change anything. And would I have killed him? I don't know. I don't know. Already, that dream seems as lost and remote as the Summer Isles that Francis and I never got around to visiting.

The procession finally ends at half past four with a final massive *boom*, and gouts of cordite and tank exhaust. The air in my room is cooler now, and the sky outside my balcony doors is already darkening.

"Here's the suit, sir, is it . . . ?"

The process of dressing me is more like armoring a knight of old; it would be easier if we had pulleys and winches. But still we get there, these hotel people and I, moving along shifting avenues of pain as the light from the television plays over us. Then triumphal music cuts short and John Arthur sits at his desk in his Downing Street study. His eyes are black pools in the moment before the dancing electrons settle in the camera; his silver hair dazzles like wet sand.

"As most of you probably know by now," he begins, arms on the desk, a small sheaf of papers in front of him, "today is a special day for me personally. As well as celebrating Admiral Nelson's famous victory at Trafalgar with all the majesty our Nation can muster, I must also celebrate my own fiftieth birthday. . . ."

A nostalgic and a personal note, then, to begin with. It must be said, though, that John Arthur doesn't look fifty. He doesn't look any age at all. The chauffeur touches my good arm, my good shoulder, but I'm still looking back at the screen as he steers me out into the corridor, trying like the rest of the world to trap a little of John Arthur's light. Outside in the grey London dusk, I sink down into the soft hide of yet another Daimler as the New Dorchester slides away. Despite everything, I feel a gathering sense of excitement as, warmly beside me, John Arthur's voice murmurs on the car radio.

"There are signs—indeed, alarming signs—that in Britain itself, this very island, we must prepare for troubles to come. I heard only this morning that Presidents De Gaulle and Von Papen have signed a treaty that draws even closer links between their economies and also those of the Low Countries, uniting their military forces into what is effectively one vast European army. . . ."

The French-and-German-threat has been a favorite theme in the popular press, but now John Arthur is giving it his own approval. I stare at my chauffeur's close-cropped neck as we drone across the empty tarmac of Westminster Bridge, wondering; does he hear those guns, the same grinding engine of history that fills my bones? Much though we British relish the threat of war, there is always a strange sense of shifting values when a fresh enemy is declared. And our main ally in this can only be Stalin's Russia, with Spain, perhaps Italy. Such a conflict would drag in America and the Colonies, China, expansionist Japan, . . .

We drive along Whitehall as the speech ends in a typically wistful finale. All this talk of war seems like a dream as we pass into Downing Street. The old Whip's Office is now the National Headquarters of the Empire Alliance, and the traffic and the tourists are kept back by those iron gates, but little else has changed here with the advent of Modernism. A London constable still stands guard at the polished black door of Number 10, just as he has done since Peel introduced them. He doesn't even wear a gun. Inside, the air smells disappointingly municipal—a bit like Oxford—of beeswax and floor polish and fried bread and half-smoked cigars; slightly of damp, even. There are voices. Other people are wandering. I look around, and glimpse one or two of the other nobodies I've come to recognize during my stay at the New Dorchester. I really am back on the tracks of the itinerary that had always been intended for me—*six o'clock, PM meets and greets* . . . It's as if the pistol, this hand, never happened. I wander through to an elegant room of wood panels and mirrors, then out into the Downing Street gardens.

Seen from the back, with its tall windows, pillars, its wrought iron and its domes, Number 10 looks a small stately home tucked into a quiet side street in the heart of London. The transformation from that terraced front is so much like all the other shams of Modernist Britain that I have to remind myself that the building has been this way since the 1730s. The willows in the garden slump limp and grey, the rose bushes are crumpled fists of paper. Paraffin lamps are carried out, shining on the guests as they move amid the mossy urns and statutes, glinting over the mirror-black waters of the ornamental pool. As they mill and chatter in the hushed tones of visitors to a consecrated building, I follow the gravel path leading to the deeper darkness beside the garden's outer wall.

A small stir arises, followed by lightning blasts of flashbulb, and a grey-haired man of slightly less than average height moves easily amid his people, one to the next, shaking hands. Their voices reach me as wordless calls; cries, murmurs, exclamations. John Arthur's shirt looks incredibly white. The lanterns seem to brighten as he passes them. I imagine my last moment of history as I step toward him from these deeper shadows and he smiles with that warmth of recognition that politicians have. Then the feel and the sound of the gun. *Bang bang.* Blood flowering blackly within the white of his shirt. His eyes fixed on mine, knowing and unknowing as he falls back.

John Arthur seems to glance in my direction as I stand hidden against the dark mass of the ilex tree. Already, discreet KSG minders are shepherding some of the guests back into the house. The garden slowly empties and the voices grow fewer and quieter as damp darkness thickens. I've seen almost all I want to see as John Arthur, arms behind his back now, white cuffs showing, looking a little tired, prepares to follow them. Then he turns and glances back. He takes a step toward the darker reaches of the garden. And I, feeling some impelling force behind me in the night, take a step forward. It's almost as if I'm still being pushed into this moment by the fingers of history.

We meet at the very edge of what remains of the light.

"It *is* you, isn't it?" John Arthur shakes his head. His voice, his whole posture, belong to a far younger man. His hands flutter white, then his eyes flicker down to my sling.

"That was done yesterday," I say, my voice more unsteady than I'd intended. "Your people did it to me when they took away the gun."

"No," he shakes his head, his gaze fixing mine so firmly that a tremor runs through me. "It wasn't *my* people, Griff. You were arrested without my authority. . . ."

Griff. A blackbird signs briefly from a bush, but otherwise there is earthy darkness, an implacable sense of silence.

"I heard that you were ill and I wanted to see you. That was all. No one told me about . . ." He runs his hand back though his sleek grey hair. It's a fair impression of distress. "No one told me about the gun. As soon as I heard you'd been arrested, I ordered your immediate release."

I study him. What am I supposed to say?

"Haven't got long to talk now, Griff," John Arthur points toward the house with his thumb. "They'll soon want me back in there."

"I thought you made your own decisions."

He laughs at that. Then he shrugs and shoves his hands into the pockets of his suit. It's a typical gesture of his; we've all seen it a million times. "But, look, I've been thinking about you these last few months. . . ." We are standing barely a pace apart now, yet he looks grainy and grey with the great house now glowing behind him. Still less than real. "I'd like for us to talk this evening, have a drink. We could go somewhere, Griff. Just you and I. I could shake this off for a while. . . ."

With that, he turns and walks back toward the house. There are many stars kindled overhead now; the night will be crisp and clear. Shadows that I hadn't noticed before separate from the trees and the ancient walls and move toward me. I almost want to run.

John Arthur is silent as he drives swiftly along Horse Guards Parade and then on through clear barricaded side streets. No one turns to stare. The speeding, blank-windowed official car is, after all, commonplace in Modernist Britain.

"You enjoyed the show?"

"The *show?*" I look over at him.

"Of course," he pushes the car faster. "You were here to kill me. . . ."

Drunk and jolly Tommies squat aside the lions as we pass Trafalgar Square. Everywhere, flags are being waved, people are leaning dangerously from windows. There will be deaths tonight. There will be conceptions. On through Covent Garden and across the Strand, then past the Inns of Court. A taxi draws up beside us as we queue to get into Cheapside. Two women in evening clothes are talking animatedly in the back.

"Tell me this, though, Griff," he says, his fingers clenching and unclenching the wheel's stitched leather. "Whatever made you think the world would change if there was no John Arthur?"

"Who would replace you? Jim Toller's too young—and nobody trusts him. People like Smith and Mosley are second-rate politicians. I suppose there was Harrison, but then he was conveniently executed. And we've all been laughing at William Arkwright for years. . . ."

"You shouldn't underestimate Bill. I've kept him close to me because he's the one person I can least trust. You're wrong about it all, in fact, Griff. The military, the bloody establishment. They all want rid of me. Why do you think I made that speech this evening? Why do you think this country has to fight? They're afraid, Griff. All of them are afraid. . . ."

Soon, we are in Whitechapel. He makes a turn and the tires squeal across the wet cobbles, then rumble to the curb of a dead end beside a scrap of wasteground. Clinging to my dignity, not waiting for him to come and help me, I climb slowly out. It's cold and dark here. The ground is sticky with litter and the air has a faintly seasidey smell of coal smoke and river silt. John Arthur opens the rear door and takes a hat from the back seat—an ordinary-looking trilby—then a dark overcoat, which he pulls on, raising the collar.

"There," he says, turning with his arms outstretched, "who would recognize me?" The transformation is, of course, complete.

My walk is slow and labored as we head past the terraced houses, and John Arthur helps me by snaking his arm around my back to support some of my weight, giving me a little lift as we step over a pothole and up onto the loose beginnings of a pavement. In odd, flashing moments, he feels almost like Francis. His breathing and way he walks is almost the same, and his skin, beneath everything, still smells faintly of burnt lemon.

Soon, we're drawing close to the sidings, tracks, and cliff-face brick warehouses of the docks, where local people have gathered for a view of the fireworks above the Thames. Mothers in slippers with scarves wrapped over their curlers. Men with fags behind their ears and the stubble of a day off work peppering their chins. They *Ohh* and *Ahh* as the sky crackles and the colors shine in gutters and ignite the myriad warehouse windows. No one notices John Arthur and I as we slip between them. He's just a slight middle-aged man helping his invalid father.

A little away from the crowd, tea chests lie heaped beside a wall. I slump down even though the air is sour here, and John Arthur sits beside me. In shadow, he risks taking off his hat, gestures toward the crowd. "They all seem so happy," he says. "A few drinks, a bed, food, some flesh to hold, some bloody fireworks . . ."

"They worship you."

"*Do* they? You tell me, Griff. You're the historian." He looks at me challeng-ingly then, does this ex-lover of mine—does this John Arthur, and something chill and terrible runs down my spine. Now, powerless as I am, I'm sure that I was right to try to kill him. "It's not enough, is it? After what we went through. I thought it might be enough when I first visited Dublin after the victory. And then again when word came through from Rhodesia." He shakes his head as sulfurous plumes of red smoke drift over London. "You don't know what the War was like, Griff. No one does who wasn't there. . . ."

He's leaning forward now, eyes fixed on nowhere as the flashes of light catch and die over the planes of his face, the silver of his hair, his elbows resting on his knees as he grips the rim of his hat, turning it over and over.

"It was all so easy when I enlisted," he says. "There were men chatting with each other on the train as it took us down to this big park north of Birmingham. Suddenly we were all the same—bosses and laborers . . . I was a rifleman, Griff. Third best shot in the training battalion when the Lee Enfields finally arrived. Went to France in December as part of Kitchener's First Army. . . . And don't believe any of the bloody rubbish about King and Regiment and Country, Griff. You fight for the bloke who's standing next to you. You put up with all the mud and the lice and the officers and the regimental bullshit for their sake."

"It must have been terrible."

"It wasn't terrible. Don't give me that. It wasn't terrible at all. I've never laughed more in my life, or felt more wanted, more as if I *belonged*. The rain. The rats. The mud. It was all like some stupid practical joke. And it was quiet a lot of the time and there were empty fields where you could lie down in the evening and stare up at a perfect sky. Then down to the town, most us of half-drunk already, and the fat white mademoiselles spitting on their fingers and saying *laver vous*. Yes, Griff, I did that too. And I had friends, mates, encounters. There were places. Nobody cared. . . ." He stares down, his silvered head bowed as the rockets whoosh and wheel, scrawling out the sky.

"We were sent to the Somme in June 1916. It was supposed to be the big push that would win the War, but we knew that we were just covering a French cock-up. I lay awake that last night. We all knew we were going over the top in the morning. Not that they told you, but you could tell from the guns. I couldn't sleep. Boom, boom, and the stink of the trenches. Boom, boom, boom. Then the big guns stopped, and that silence was the worst thing of all. We were moved up to the front line. Thousands, thousands of us. And there was silence, just men breathing and the shuffle of our feet on the duckboards and the creak and jingle of our packs. And for the first time, I knew that I'd lost it. I felt terribly afraid.

"The whistle went and men started to climb out of the trenches. A lot of them just fell back, and I thought they were being clumsy until I realized they'd been shot already. And I just stood there. It was the worst moment of my life but I knew I couldn't go back, so I started to climb up out of that trench. My mates were already running around the pool of a big shell hole miles ahead, but I was just wandering in a nightmare, looking for somewhere to hide. . . .

"I don't know when I got hit, Griff—or how long it took. But there was this heat across my side as I slid down into this long hollow. I knew it wasn't that bad. . . . I could have gone on, Griff. I could have climbed out of that ditch and gone on. But I didn't. I just crouched there the whole day. Boom, boom — I could hear the shells whistling over. The bullets rattling. But I was alone with my fear, Griff. Quite alone.

"Darkness came and the flares went up. Men with stretchers found me and hauled me out, and I looked enough of a mess to be convincing as I was taken back to the field dressing station. I was given some water and a jab of morphine and quinine and carried across the fields to a big river barge just as dawn was coming. You could still smell the coal that they'd cleared out of the barge beneath all the other stench, and you could hear the water laughing around the sides as we pulled away from the jetty.

"A few men were crying and moaning. A lot were comatose or simply asleep. There was a man with his head half-blown off on the stretcher nearest to me. He couldn't possibly live, his brains were coming out, and then he started this terrible moaning. He was trying to speak, but his jaw was so wrecked I couldn't understand what he was saying. Something *K* and something *M*. His limbs were jerking and this noise he was making just went on and on. It was a sound out of hell. Then I looked at him again with the top of his skull ripped off like an egg, and I realized what he was saying. He was saying, *Kill Me*. . . .

"I managed to stand up, and he seemed to quieten for a moment then, and look back up at me from his ruined face with his one good eye. I took strength from that, and I understood that what he wanted was what you'd do for any mate of yours in the same position. He had a pistol on his belt, but I knew that it was too late to use it here. And I was still lost, still afraid. In fact, it seemed as if was *his* strength that enabled me to take the blanket from by his feet and push it down over his face and hold it there. Of course, he began to fight and buck after a while — it takes longer than you'd imagine to kill a man — but eventually he stopped struggling. And I was glad that I still had this one soldierly act left in me. I knew that he'd died a hero's death, this man. This *soldier*.

"Perhaps it was that or the drugs I'd been given which made me do what I did next. I don't know. I felt for the waxed envelope that they'd tied to his tunic at the dressing station. His name was John Arthur, and he was a private in the Staffordshires like me, although from a different battalion. And it struck me that John Arthur was a good name for a soldier, a good name for a man. I'd always hated being Francis Eveleigh, anyway. It was all done in that moment, in the foul air of that barge with the water laughing beside me, swapping names just to see how it felt to become him. And straight away, you know, as I lay down again on my pallet and the fever began to take a bigger hold, it felt better. . . ."

John Arthur is silent for a moment as the sky above London foams with light, pushing at us like a wind.

"Didn't anyone ever suspect?"

"The rest of my platoon had been wiped out. So had John Arthur's. And I caught pneumonia, you see, Griff, so I was shipped back to England. By the time I was finally ready for active duty again, I could have been anyone for all the difference it made. So I went back to the front as S4538 Rifleman Arthur, D

Company 7th Service Battalion, The Rifle Brigade, and I knew from the first time I heard the guns that this time it would be better, this time I wouldn't feel any fear. I was even made corporal, and I won the George Cross. . . . But that's common knowledge."

"What was it like when the War ended?"

"I went up to Raughton, which was John Arthur's last address before enlisting. I found out that the Yorkshire accent I'd copied from one of the cooks was all wrong, but that didn't matter. We were like ghosts. Nobody seemed to belong anywhere then. The place was just a pit village and the address was a cheap boarding house. One or two people told me they remembered him, but I never really knew if they did. He'd been slightly older than me, but seemed to have made little impression on the world. His father had been an itinerant who'd started out in the West Country and had died in a mining accident. . . .

"But I knew I had to do something more with this new life John Arthur had given me. Do you understand that, Griff? So I jumped on a cattle truck, took the train down to London. It was cold that winter and there was the flu epidemic. Each morning under the bridges and in the shop fronts, a few extra bodies didn't wake up. And the men in suits and the women in hats who'd never done anything but complain about the rationing just wrinkled their noses and stepped over them. And there were queers like you, Griff, who'd get a man to do anything for the price of a meal. And fat cats and Jews. And the bright young things. And the colonels who were back from the War, jingling with medals and a big pension.

"But I still remembered I was John Arthur. And I began to meet people who understood that there was nothing left in all the lies that had once kept this country afloat. And you saw what it was like — Griff, that night fifteen years ago. You saw how easy it is to be John Arthur. He was always waiting there. Even now, he's leading me on."

The big display is reaching its climax. Even here, what must be two miles off, there's a sweet-sour reek of gunpowder as the flares blossom overhead. John Arthur puts his trilby hat on, straightens it, checks that his coat collar is still up, and offers me his hand again. "Come on, Griff, I'll buy you that drink. . . ."

I let him help me up, and an elderly woman in a hairnet and a housecoat glances across the road. Her hand goes up to her mouth for a moment, childlike in wonder. Is it? But no, no . . . it couldn't be. Relieved, she looks back toward the crackling sky.

John Arthur breathes easily beside me, helping me along as I wonder what I should say, what horrors I could tell him that he doesn't know already, what questions should I ask. But it's like all those letters that I never wrote to him. It's like all the promises of love that, even in that brief, glorious time when Francis and I were alone, were never given. It's like my unwritten book. It's like my whole life.

The sky is on fire now. The houses look flash-lit, pushed back into skeletons of their real selves. I stumble as renewed pain shoots through me. Our two linked shadows leap, burned and frozen ahead into the pavement, and it seems that we're at the lip of a vast wave that will soon break through everything, dissolving, destroying. Then, with one last final bellow, the display ends and we move on through the East End, the ordinary East End of London in this night of the 21st of October 1940, beneath a bruised sky, in shocked, blotchy darkness.

A public house juts at the triangular meeting of the two streets facing toward the Mudchute and the Isle of Dogs. The sign is unilluminated, painted in dark colors. If I didn't know this place already, I probably wouldn't be able to make out the words **Cottage Spring**. The room inside is smaller than the place I remember stumbling into fifteen years before. But I recognize the counter that John Arthur leapt onto, and the pattern of the mirror, now cracked, that lies behind it; there, even, is the fat pillar in the corner that I once hid behind.

There's a moment of bizarre normality as John Arthur takes off his hat, lowers his coat collar, and walks up to the bar. Two cloth-capped men are playing darts, while three underage lads sit nursing their pints, and an old man stares at his evening glass of stout. They're some of the few who couldn't be bothered to see tonight's fireworks, or even watch them at home on TV, and it's amusing to observe their reactions as they realize who's just come in. There's puzzlement, doubt — like that old woman by the docks — followed by that standard British reluctance to make a fuss.

"I'll buy everyone their next round," John Arthur says, speaking with that soft Yorkshire accent: the very image of himself, and suddenly, they're all clustered around him, breathless and eager like children at a fête when Father Christmas finally arrives. John Arthur signs beer mats, he laughs and shares a joke. He really is John Arthur now, and these are his people. The old man downs the rest of his stout, spilling most of it down his shirt, and quavers that he'd like another. The lads ask for halves of ginger beer, which John Arthur laughingly changes to pints of Fuller's that they were on before.

Outside, word of who's here must have got out, for there are children's and women's voices, the shadows of raised hands and heads shifting across the frosted windows. And I'm just standing here, tired and in pain. Drained of anger. Drained of hope. Soon to be drained of life. I shuffle closer to that pillar at the end of the bar, in need once more of its reassuring anonymity. John Arthur's forgotten about me anyway. *These* are his people. *This* is where he belongs. I'm just a name from the past that he couldn't remember well enough to get right when he made his speech to the Parliament that he later dissolved. A phone begins to ring at the back of the pub, unanswered. Somewhere, a car engine is racing.

The voices of the men are easier now. Yes, they realize, he really is just as everyone says; an ordinary bloke you could share a drink with. John Arthur looks across as the roar of an approaching car fills the street. He seems to notice me now almost as he did all those years ago. It's as if nothing has ever changed. But this time, somehow, his smile is more genuine, and as he walks over with his arms a little apart, I can't help but smile back at him.

There comes a sharp sound of banging, and the thought passes, too quickly to be fully-formed, that the fireworks have resumed. Then, one by one, the frosted windows of the Cottage Spring begin to fall in. They burst into shining veils, and splinters of wood fly out as the room explodes in a reflecting spray of collapsing mirrors. The men at the bar are jerked, thrown back, lifted. The glass is like a great watery tide, rolling and rising. John Arthur pirouettes as the last window explodes and the shining air flowers silver and red around him, then the pillar I'm beside splatters and streams before everything stops and fills with sudden, terrible silence.

As I look down at this shattered place and these broken dolls lying on the crimsoned linoleum, there comes a sudden crash as the last of the big mirrors falls, and faint, at the very edge of everything, are the sounds of crying, fumbling, moaning, weeping. Then the roar, once again, of that car. Gears smash as it turns, and I wait for more bullets, but instead something large and metallic flies through a gaping window. A thick, round-cornered box with a single wire protruding, it hits an upended table and skids hissing through the sparkling wreckage to settle beside Francis's body.

Then the car pulls away with a screech of tires in the last moment before the world erupts into darkness.

EIGHT

Every morning now, I awake not knowing who or where I am, filled with a vague sense of horror and helplessness. I do not even know if I am human, or have any real identity of my own. For a moment then, I am under the rubble again and Francis is beside me. His hand is in mine, and flutters like an insect in the moment that he dies. My life seems to float out in both directions from that point. It's like unwrapping a complex present; tearing away at silvery ribbons of the future and the past, although I know that it's all just some trick—a party game—and that I will be left clutching nothing but tangled paper, empty air.

I ungum my eyes and look out at the world, accepting the strange fact of my continued existence. But it remains a slow process even though this beamed ceiling is familiar to me; fraught with a sense of aftermath. I am Brook, yes, I am Geoffrey Brook. I am a lecturer, a teacher—in fact, a true Professor of History now. And Oxford, yes, Oxford.

I feel for my glass, my tablets, which lie a long way beyond the Chinese pheasants cavorting on my eiderdown. I sense that it is early, still dark outside my window, although a strange light seems to wash up from the quad and there is a chill to the air beyond the crackling heat of my fire. Somewhere across the rooftops and towers, a bell, distant yet clear, begins to chime the hour. When silence and equilibrium return, I slide inch by inch across the sheets until my feet drop off the edge of the bed. I am old, I think. I am old. Perhaps that is the last shock I have been waiting for.

Bunioned, barefoot, trying not to exhaust myself by coughing, I stumble through the cavorting firelight toward my window, dribbling fingers of condensation as I wipe the mullions with my wrecked and arthritic right hand and gaze at the strange whiteness. It has snowed again in the night. Of course. This is Oxford and it has snowed again in the night. . . . I have to close my eyes, then, as a twinge of pain and the rawness in my throat sets off another ugly memory.

I remember everything now. I am here. I am alive. This is the last day of the year of 1940. John Arthur is dead.

I'm still leaning there, still staring from my college window in a drugged half-doze, when the breakfast trolley rumbles toward my door. The knock sounds hesitant, mistimed, yet still I'm somehow expecting Christlow as the handle turns and the chill outer air touches my skin. But it's Allenby.

"Good morning, Professor. Terrible lot of snow in the night as you've doubtless seen. Got a nice fire going for you earlier while you were still asleep...." He slips my padded silk dressing gown from the hook near the fire where it's been warming. His breath is cool on my neck as he helps me into it; like the sense of the snow. He bends down to sheathe my feet in lambskin slippers. He's young and good-looking, is Allenby. He says all the right things; he doesn't even wear an EA badge. But he still seems like a barely competent actor, forever trying and failing to find the essential meaning of his role.

"You've got that appointment, by the way."

"Appointment?"

"Twelve o'clock at the George Hotel. Miss Flood is coming up from your publishers in London."

Then he lays the morning's papers out before me. Sheet upon warm rustling sheet that smell crisply of ink and freshly felled wood; all that history in the making. I'm tempted to ask Allenby to take the damn things away, but I know that that would seem ungrateful. And there's something—I remember now—something that still pricks my interest, although as yet I can't quite recall what.

I reach out toward the table, using my right hand like a scoop to push the *Times* into the better grip of my left. **PM Announces Immediate Inquiry into Scandal of Jewish Homeland. RAF Airlifts Aid.** The photograph beneath shows a group of people huddled outside a rough hut. They are skeleton-thin, clothed in rags. I raise it closer to my eyes, so close that their faces become collections of printed dots.

My college Daimler slides through the slush along High, Catte, and Broad. We park at the corner of George Street and the Cornmarket, where my driver helps me out onto the oystered ice of the pavement and leads me into the Ivy Restaurant. The colors that the snow and the cold have bleached out of Oxford all seem to have fled into these rooms. The ceilings are pink, the walls lean with gilded mirrors, there are flowers at every table. As is often the case now, rumor of my arrival has spread before me, and I must wait and smile and raise a trembling hand in acknowledgment as the dining room erupts into applause. But the moment isn't over-played as I shuffle toward the best table by the window where Miss Flood awaits me.

Her bracelets jangle as she sips her wine. Her fingers are restless as she picks at a bread roll, missing the chains of cigarettes that, since I succumbed to a coughing fit at one of our early meetings, she refrains from smoking in my presence.

"I was speaking to Publicity only yesterday, Geoffrey," she tells me. "And you're definitely the flagship of our spring list."

"That's good to know . . . ," I wheeze. "I received your letter with the, er, galleys only the day before yesterday."

"Try not to think of them as *galleys* or *proofs*, Geoffrey. Think of them as . . ." Miss Flood waves her hand, clutching an imaginary cigarette. "Complimentary reading material." She smiles.

I nod. What she means is that she wants to keep me well away from the tricky business of correcting my own scholarly inaccuracies, my ungrammatical turns of phrase.

Miss Flood delves into her briefcase and shows me a glossy mock-up of the dustjacket. The first print run is thirty thousand, with the presses ready to roll with another thirty thousand after that. You'll never know from the look of this book that Miss Flood's other major authors write do-it-yourselfs and whodunnits. I really can't complain.

"As to the title," she says, tapping the celluloid with a scarlet fingernail, "you'll see that we've stuck with our original idea. That, er, *other* suggestion that you made. Good though it was, I'm afraid that it didn't quite *click* with our marketing people. *Fingers* of History was too close, if you see what I mean. There are a lot of people out there who still remember your work and who'd love to have a hardback copy of your best articles. . . ."

FIGURES OF HISTORY
Geoffrey Brook

"Oh, and we've finally cleared up the copyright business. Being who you are, Geoffrey, I really didn't think that the people at the *Sketch* would resist. But we'll need to hurry you . . . ," Miss Flood says more quietly, slipping in the words when she imagines that I'm not really conscious as I gaze out of the window at the snow-softened spires, domes, towers of this city. Balliol, All Souls, Queens . . . the litany of my dreams . . . "If we're going to squeeze in that new extra chapter you were talking about."

"I've decided," I squeak, "what I want to write about. It fits in with research I was doing into the history of the Jews." *Jews* . . . My voice sounds even lighter than ever as I end the sentence, and I'm sure that the restaurant conversations fade around me. "What with all the fuss there's been in the papers these last few days about the Highlands . . ." Something sticks and crunches in my throat. "I was thinking . . . thinking that the time is right to remind people . . ."

"Geoffrey, that sounds *fascinating*." Pause. "Although everyone's hungry to hear more about your links with John Arthur."

"Of course."

"Not that I want to steer you in any particular direction."

My eyes are watering. My nose is starting to run. I fumble to find a clean corner of my handkerchief as I begin to cough and the chime of bells and the clatter of lunchtime cutlery, the waitresses' whispering and the taste of the wine and the smell of the cooking and the clangor in the kitchens and the whispers in ancient corridors and the scent of old stone and fresh snow, the dreaming towers of these rabbithole rooms—the sense of all Oxford—fractures around me.

Geoffrey Brook was born in Staffordshire, Lichfield, in 1875. He has devoted most of his life to teaching history, firstly in and around the City of his birth, where he influenced the young John Arthur, and later in his life at one of the most distinguished and ancient Oxford colleges . . .

Running my pen through the word ancient, scratching a question mark over *distinguished*, I close the file of publicity material as my college Daimler hisses slowly along High. Already, it's getting dark and the lights in the shop windows are glowing. Prices have gone up a lot recently—taxes, as well—and you'd think that people would have had enough of shopping after the frenzied weeks before Christmas. But the windows offer **Biggest Ever Sale** and **Huge Post-Xmas Discounts**, even though it won't be twelfth night until Sunday.

My college tower looms and the chill air bites as I dismiss my driver and wade unaided across the snowy quad. Wheezing, I slump down into one of the leather armchairs beside the fire in my rooms and drag my telephone, a new privilege, onto my lap and stab and turn, stab and turn, dialing out a number from the back page of the *Times*, willing all the ghosts of history to give me strength, and trying to picture a bustling newsroom filled with the same clean purposeful smell as the papers Allenby brings me. . . .

But today's New Year's Eve, and there are no newspapers tomorrow. The telephone just rings and rings.

The world already knew that John Arthur was dead by the time I was hauled out from the rubble of the Cottage Spring. I could hear it in the crowd's sobbing howls as the masonry slid and crumbled, and in the firemen's angry voices.

One of the beer-drinking lads survived for two nights at Barts inside an iron lung. Another remains alive to this day, though a mindless cripple. There were also many deaths and disablements amid the onlookers who'd gathered in the street outside. Only I, Geoffrey Brook, protected by that pillar—and, perhaps, in some strange way, by the fact that I was already close to death—truly survived. I suffered a gash along my cheek that required five stitches, a dislocated shoulder, two septic lungfuls of plaster. Of course, I had my bad right hand already, although that fact often feels as lost to me as it is to the rest of the world.

Even as I was carried to the ambulance, the flashbulbs were popping, the television lights were glaring. Three days later, as I lay propped up in my hospital bed, smoothed and groomed, sweetly drugged, the new Prime Minister William Arkwright called by at my hospital room. The flashbulbs of the many newsmen he'd brought with him popped and crackled as he shook my good left hand and grinned around his pipe. He already seemed bigger than the man I'd met in the gardens of New Buckingham Palace. "And it's Professor Brook from now on," he said as he picked up his trademark Homburg hat from my bed. "Did I mention that just now? No matter—it'll be in all tomorrow's papers."

John Arthur's death is already as much a part of his myth as everything that happened during his life. This time, unlike the fire at Old Buckingham Palace—

and unless Jim Toller and the several senior officers of the KSG commit suicide in their cells—there will even be a trial. The national mood is predominantly one of sadness and disillusion. EA badges are less frequently worn, and KSG officers suffer children's jibes as they walk the streets, implicated as they all are by association in the death of our great leader. And the British economy, it seems, is far weaker than we ever imagined, damaged by ten years of over-expenditure. Conscription is being phased out, and negotiations with France and Germany about mutual disarmament will commence in February. There is even talk—oblique, as yet—of giving India and Ireland a semblance of Home Rule, and fresh elections for a new People's Assembly.

All the rest, that last glorious summer of hope and expansion, already feels like a dream. After all, the world is becoming an increasingly dangerous place—Japan has attacked China, Stalin has annexed eastern Poland—and it's obvious that the countries of Western Europe must draw together if they are not to be swept away by Communism and a commercially belligerent America. John Arthur's threats toward France and Germany, his canny alliance with Stalin, have simply given us a top seat at the table in the negotiations to come.

I found that his picture had vanished from the Gents beside Christ Church Meadow when I made my recent farewell visit there, although the nailmarks that I and my acquaintance made in the third cubicle remain. Somehow, as I touched their soft indentations, they spoke to me of nothing but hope and human decency.

The Cumbernalds' house shines out amid a spray of car headlights as I arrive that evening.

"All terribly kitsch, I know," Eric Cumbernald assures me as I hobble past the flashing fairy lights in the front porch. "Everyone's waiting for you. . . ."

Within moments, I'm surrounded, touched, smiled at, reminded of previous meetings and promises of lunch. Grateful for the armor of my tablets, I shuffle across the carpets toward the largest and most inviting-looking chair. Cumbernald brings me a sweet sherry and a Spode plate with a sausage roll and the crowd around me thins as it becomes apparent that I'm not responding to their questions. From being a living link to John Arthur, I'm demoted to being an old relic, to be touched for luck, then forgotten. Music plays. The fire flickers. The Christmas decorations turn and sway. There are many hours to go yet before midnight and the coming of 1941.

Eileen Cumbernald sits for a while on the arm of my chair, brown as ever in a low-backed dress. Her husband Eric's impending promotion to Vice Chancellor of Oxford University has left her totally unchanged.

"I so enjoyed that time we spent together at Penrhos," she tells me. "You really must come down with us again next year. . . ."

I have to smile. It's funny, how people choose to ignore my obvious physical decline. I suppose that they imagine it's only natural. In fact, it would be wrong for me to appear too hale and hearty after surviving an explosion that killed John Arthur.

"You're even more like dead Uncle Freddie now!" Barbara Cumbernald declares delightedly as she imprisons me in her hot arms while Christine hangs back a little, looking just as pale and hot as her sister, but more clearly eldest now. "Will you tell us one of your funny stories?"

"Why don't you both tell me a story instead?" I suggest. "Tell me what you know about John Arthur."

"John Arthur," Barbara intones, her arms still around me, smelling of wine and sweat and toffee, "died a hero's death as we as a Nation celebrated Trafalgar Day. Bad people who wanted to—" But at this point, Christine begins to tickle her, and they collapse on the floor in a squealing heap.

Will the Cumbernalds' stay in this house on Raglan Street, I wonder, in the wake of Eric's promotion and the knighthood that will almost certainly follow? With the billiard room and the conservatory, the hugely expensive kitchen I got a glimpse of, they've clearly got things here exactly as they want them. But they will move, of course, ever-upward toward some semi-stately home. They'll continue to swim the warm English currents until age and frailty finally catch up with them. They'll probably even accept death with good grace—just like me, they'll have no cause to complain about the way history and these Summer Isles have treated them.

Me, I really am a full Professor now. And MA, Modern History, from my own college, too. As Cumbernald has carefully explained, my Master's can be seen as either honorary or de-facto depending upon the angle from which you choose to view it. The thing often switches back and forth even in my own befuddled mind—a strange state of existence that I suspect the scientists you used to hear about a few years ago would recognize from their studies of the hints and glimmers that apparently make up our universe. We're barely there, it seems, if you look closely enough; just energies and particles that don't belong in a particular time or place. Stare at the world too hard, breathe at it from the wrong direction, and it falls apart. Explodes.

Christlow was found drowned on a muddy bank of the Thames down by the Isle of Dogs the morning after the Cottage Spring. A presumed suicide, there were whispers on the Oxford grapevine of evidence found in his rooms of preferences that should never be entertained by a man who works with children.

I don't doubt, in fact, that he was following me. Where and how it began, and whether he always knew of my sexual dalliances, I will never know. But I'm also sure that he found the pistol in the suitcase beneath my bed. No doubt he imagined he was doing no more than his patriotic duty by reporting this fact, and my movements. But here the picture grows fuzzy, unscientific, unhistoric . . .

My thoughts always come back to the man who has most plainly benefited from John Arthur's death. More than ever now, it's clear that we all underestimated William Arkwright. He's a consummate survivor, a dealer and a fixer, a betrayer, a *politician* in the sense that John Arthur—who lived, for all his faults, by the heart, by the flame and the fire—never was. It must have been plain to Arkwright long before it was to the rest of us that Modernism was in crisis, seduced by its own myth, in danger of launching itself into economic catastrophe and a disastrous European war. So perhaps Arkwright finally persuaded the relics of an establishment that is now resurgent that enough was enough. As even the arrest of Jim

Toller and his senior KSG colleagues acknowledges, John Arthur's death was executed too professionally to be the work of mere fanatics.

From this, I soon find myself taking the kind of wild flights that, even when I was spinning through the most dangerously speculative pages of my long-projected book, I would never have considered undertaking. History—the only kind of history, anyway, that anyone ever cares about—is always reducible to solid facts that can be learned by students in hour-long lessons and then regurgitated in exams, or used to add color to television dramas, or as the embroidery in escapist novels. But what could have been more convenient than to have some dying madman kill John Arthur, alone and unaided? So I wasn't arrested. I remained an idea to be toyed with—or at least not discarded until the last appropriate moment. Even as I wandered the gardens of New Buckingham Palace, it was still quite possible that I would be allowed access to John Arthur with my gun. After all, there was no particular reason why I shouldn't succeed, other than the question mark that hung over my own character. And whom should I meet there amid the terraced fountains, but none other than William Arkwright?

It was then, I think, that I was finally weighed in the balance and found lacking. Arkwright ordered that I be arrested by his own officials, perfunctorily questioned to make sure I wasn't hiding anything, then shot while more reliable contingencies were put in hand. Only some chance enquiry from John Arthur's office about my whereabouts—that midnight phone call echoing in that shaft between the buildings—saved my life.

Did John Arthur know that an assassination attempt was likely? Was it I who led him to his killers at the Cottage Spring? But no, no. All of this is too fantastic—worse than those dreadful Modernist books that I forced myself to read. The fact is that I will never know. Perhaps in years to come when the truth is no longer potent, some hack or scholar will come up with a theory that questions the role of Jim Toller's KSG in John Arthur's death. They may even stumble across the strange fact that another figure, an obscure populist academic named Brook, was arrested in possession of a gun. Odder still, this Brook character was then released and was with John Arthur at the time of his death—survived, even, the bullets and the explosion. I cannot imagine what threads they will draw out from these odd facts. Of their nature, the true conspiracies are the ones that are least likely to be unearthed in the future. The truth, at the end of the day, remains forever silent. We are only left with history.

"*There* you are, Brook!" Cumbernald looms from the ceiling decorations and lays his hand on my shoulder. "Can't just drift off like this, you know. There's a phone call for you. A Miss *Flood*."

My knees pop and crack like tiny fireworks as he helps me up. His right arm supports me as he leads down the corridor. "You can take it in here in my study," he says, pushing open the door, watching for a few moments as I settle down on a new leather chair to make sure that I know how to operate this fancy-looking phone of his.

"*Geoffrey*, there you are!" Miss Flood sounds excited. "I got your number here from that creepy chap who works for you at the college."

"Christlow?"

"Whatever. I've marvelous news, Geoffrey. . . ."

I wait as Miss Flood burbles on, studying the ample bookshelves that cover these study walls (mostly do-it-yourselves and whodunnits, a few biographies and thin histories; a small space where my own forthcoming work will fit in easy), doing my best to banish the sense of gloomy premonition that still comes over me when people announce they have news.

". . . so Arkwright's own Private Secretary asked if it wasn't too much of a presumption. I mean, as if we'd really *mind*. Of course, we'll have to redo the dust-jacket to give his name due prominence. . . ."

"You mean Arkwright is—"

"—Yes, going to write an Introduction to your book! I know, I know. I still haven't got over it either. I haven't even started to think what this'll do to the print runs! Of course, it means that you, Geoffrey, can relax. You won't have to write *a thing more*. . . ."

Part of me drops away as I gaze down at the receiver. There are two ways, I decide, to gain a person's silence and compliance. You either take away their lives and scrub out their identity. Or you give them everything.

"So that's it, then?"

"Marvelous! And Happy New Year. Oh, Geoffrey . . . not that it matters now as far as the book's concerned, but I do have a contact for that research you were talking about. Someone in the Government who's co-ordinating the Jewish relief effort."

I cradle the phone between my shoulder and chin, searching the leather-and-ash expanse of Eric Cumbernald's desktop for something resembling a pen or a pencil. I begin to write out the number and the name that Miss Flood dictates in my left-handed scrawl, then stop half way and put down the phone without wishing her goodbye.

"Everything okay in there?" Cumbernald asks. His eyes travel down to my bit of paper. "If you want to make another call. . . ."

"I don't think I'll bother."

"In that case . . ." He slides back a cabinet front to reveal a television screen surrounded by nests of equipment, "there's something I'd very much like to show you. . . ."

I crumple the note as the comforting smell of warming valves slowly fills the room. The name Miss Flood's given me of the Home Office official who's overseeing the operation to provide food, medical treatment, and shelter to the Jews is Reeve-Ellis. The television screen snows. Then there are ghostly figures that make me think of my acquaintance and his family, huddled in their crude huts or blanketed in the hurricane wilderness. Of course, the Government has come to their rescue now. The terrible situation has been proclaimed by Ministry of Information Press Release, and the newspapers have lapped it up unquestioningly. Soon, it will be dealt with, and—a little sadder, a little wiser, a little less trustful— we Britons will watch the results on the BBC News. This Jewish Scandal has come at just the right time. It shows Arkwright as a man of honesty who is prepared to deal with the aberrations that so blackened Modernism's reputation in the rest of the world. It may even get us back into the League of Nations. In a few months—or years, perhaps, depending upon political contingencies—a similarly narrow spotlight will fall upon the treatment camps in the Isle of Man. But, even if my acquaintance and his family have survived, angel of death that I am, I realize that I must never try to contact them.

Cumbernald places a large silver disk on a spinning turntable. "I had the cine-recording transcribed to video," he explains as I watch the jumpy white outlines of Eileen, Christine, Barbara, and myself sitting outside the summer lodge in Penrhos Park on the television screen. Behind it all is a crackle and a rumble. *Eggs and bacon. Apple and custard . . .*

"Been thinking, by the way," he says, leaning against a bookshelf as he admires his camerawork. "About who should replace me as principal at college. We need someone with *reputation*, don't you think? Someone with an agile mind . . . And I don't really think you'll be surprised, Brook, when I tell you that your name was the first that came to mind."

"I'm far too old," I mutter, still gazing at the screen as Christine and Barbara run up to me, their tongues stuck out like gorgeous gargoyles, their whole futures ahead of them. "Far too ill . . ."

"Such a pity," Cumberland says, re-folding his arms, adding just the right note of regret, "even if it were true . . ." But he doesn't push it. In fact, he sounds relieved.

"Anyway," he stoops down, preparing to lift the needle from the record as the matchstick figures dance and shift, grey on white. "Time we got back into the throng, old man." Christine and Barbara dissolve into a flash of light, then shrink down through a pin dot into the blackness. "It's nearly midnight."

The lights are off now in the main room as the bells of Big Ben begin their famous chime. *Bong*—and there it is. *Bong*—a New Year is beginning. Lips and hands press against my own with the rustle of tweed and rayon, the dig of jewelry, wafts of perfume. Afterward, as I'm sipping the sweet fizzy alcohol and thinking of getting back to my tablets, my rooms, the doorbell sounds along the hall. I'm already on my way toward it in the hope that it's my driver come to rescue me when I realize that eager hands are assisting my passage, eager voices are urging me on. The doorbell sounds again. It's clearly some neighbor out first-footing with a piece of shortbread, a lump of coal. And who better than I, the famous Geoffrey Brook, to greet them?

The Cumbernalds' front door swings inward, and I'm expecting a figure, perhaps even the dark handsome stranger of tradition, to be standing on the doorstep. But the doorway remains empty, and I, pushed on, seem to travel into blackness and terrible, empty, cold.

I've been reading—or rereading, I'm really not sure now—that stained copy of William Morris's *News from Nowhere*. The curled pages, brittle with dried mud and the dusty air of nearly half a century, speak of nothing that resembles the vision of Greater Britain that came to pass. Morris hated big industry, he hated all big things, he hated terror and injustice. How, then, was his name pulled so deeply into the currents of Modernism that Blackwell's are even now trying to get rid of discounted piles of copies of *The Waters of the Wondrous Isles*? All that

Morris and Modernism ever shared was a preparedness to dream, and a love of a bright, clean, glorious past that never was. But perhaps that was enough; perhaps the dream, any dream, is always the seed from which nightmares will follow.

John Arthur is fading. His memory is twisted and pulled to suit whatever meaning people choose to give it as easily as were Morris's unread pages. It's almost as if I'm the only person left in this nation who grieves for him, or who still wishes to understand. And that last fatal night when we were together follows me even now. All the questions I should have asked, the challenges I should have made. Either I loved, I suppose, the incarnation of something evil, or John Arthur was a puppet like me, jerked by the whims of some incomprehensible greater will. Between these two horrors, I keep trying to find some middle way, a decent path that anyone might wander along in their life and find themselves unexpectedly and irrevocably lost. Francis was no monster, for all that I know that he used me much more than he loved me in the brief time that we were truly together.

So I keep thinking instead of Mrs. Stevens, my acquaintance's neighbor, who offered me tea and the bright warmth of her kitchen, and of Cumbernald, and of the woman behind the counter in the Post Office, and the doctors and the policemen, and, yes, of Christlow, and even Reeve-Ellis, and the faces you see looking out from train windows, and the children you see playing in the street. And my own face in the mirror is there, too, although haggard as death now, the stranger-corpse that will soon be all that is left of me. Francis belongs there, with us. He didn't close the cell doors himself, he didn't pull the ropes, touch the wires, kick shut the drawers of filing cabinets.

We all did that for him.

For a few short days of our Scottish holiday, Francis and I lived in a ramshackle stone cottage. The place had a rough slate floor like something carried in by the tide, thick walls with tiny windows that overlooked the beach. In storms, in winter, the thin turf roof would have leaked the sea and the wind and the rain. But the weather was like honey when we were there. The sea was like wine. Alone, miles from the world, we swam naked and caught translucent shrimps from the pools beyond the dunes.

Time stopped. The whole universe turned around us. Francis's skin was browned and bleached to lacy tidemarks by the sea and the sun, and he tasted like the shrimps; briny salt and sweet. Lying one night amid the blankets of our rough cot, my skin stiff from the sun and the soles of my feet gritty, some twist of emptiness made me reach out and open my eyes. Francis had gone from beside me, was standing naked at the open cottage doorway, looking out at the pale sea, the star-shot night.

"You see over there? . . . " he said, sensing from the change in my breathing that I was awake. "Right over there, Griff, toward the horizon? . . . "

I propped myself up, following his gaze out along the white shingle path, the low wall, the pale dunes that edged into the luminous ripple of the waves. Perhaps he was right. Perhaps there was something out there, the shining grey backs of a shoal of islands that daylight made the air too brilliant to see.

"I think we should go there, Griff," he said, his shoulders and limbs rimed with starlight. "Remember? That lovely name . . . ?"

"There won't be anything to see," I laughed, lying back in the blankets.

"There'll be no ferry. . . ."

But I could see those islands more clearly now as I closed my eyes again and the darkness began to take me. Heathered hills rolling down to dark green copses of pine. Sheep-dotted lowlands. The summer-sparking rim of the sea. I could even smell a uniquely milky scent of summer grass and flowers carried to me on the soft breeze from off the Atlantic. Yes, I thought, we will go there.

But the weather had changed in the morning when we awoke. Low grey clouds lay across the dunes and met with the sea. So we never did get to visit the Summer Isles, and Francis pushed quickly down the track as we left our cottage beneath a sky that threatened nothing but rain, cycling fast as he always cycled, forever heading on. I even feared that I, teetering with my older legs as I bumped along with my heavy suitcase strapped behind me, would never catch up. It was then, I think, as he crested the top of the first hill and vanished from sight, freewheeling eagerly down toward the farm on the headland where we would hand in the keys, that I finally lost my Francis. It was then that he was swallowed by history, and that everything else that was to happen began.

Well-anchored in my wheelchair on this steamship's juddering deck, I gaze at those famous white cliffs, as grey on this late January morning as is the sea, the sky, these circling gulls. The air is bitter and cold, filled with the groan of engines and the smoke and salt they churn in their wake. There will be no last glimpse of England—I realize that now—just this gradual fading.

Like so many other things I have done in my life, my departure has proved surprisingly easy. I could detect no resistance as my driver ferried me about Oxford and I withdrew my funds and made my travel arrangements. In any event, the number of stamps and passes required to leave this country are greatly reduced. Back in Oxford, I suppose, Allenby will have found my note by now, and passed it on to Cumbernald as he tidies his desk and prepares to leave. My letter, posted to London the day before, will probably also be waiting for Miss Flood. Of course, there will be concern about my semi-mysterious disappearance, but that will soon be followed by weary, head-shaking amusement at the thought that I still had this one last act in me.

Thus I travel, ill, wealthy, and alone. My precise plans, as the maps and the possibilities widen in my mind, remain vague. Long journeys hold no fears for me now: if you are rich enough, there are always people who will give you what you think you need. All I know is that I want to end my days somewhere far from England where the climate is dry and warm, where there are lizards on the walls and the stars are different. From Calais, I shall continue east and south for as far as this body will take me. First Class, and preferably by train. Preferably by sleeper.

Daniel Abraham, "Veritas," *Absolute Magnitude*, Summer.
Poul Anderson, "The Tale of the Cat," *Analog*, February.
Eleanor Arnason, "The Gauze Banner," *More Amazing Stories*.
——"The Venetian Method," *Tales of the Unanticipated 19*.
Catherine Asaro, "Aurora in Four Voices," *Analog*, December.
Constance Ash, "Flower Kiss," *Realms of Fantasy*, August.
Mike Ashley, "The Bridge of Fire," *Camelot Fantastic*.
Eric T. Baker, "Marooned on the Railroad to Moscow," *Science Fiction Age*, May.
Kage Baker, "Lemuria *Will* Rise!" *Asimov's*, May.
——, "The Literary Agent," *Asimov's*, July.
——, "The Wreck of the Gladstone," *Asimov's*, October/November.
Neal Barrett, Jr., "The Lizard Shoppe," *Dragon Magazine*, September.
William Barton and Michael Capabianco, "Thematic Torus in Search of a Cusp," *Amazing*, Fall.
Stephen Baxter, "The Barrier," *Interzone*, July.
——, "Dante Dreams," *Asimov's*, August.
——, "The Hydrous Astronauts," *Age of Wonder*.
——, "Moon-Calf," *Analog*, July/August.
——, "Transit," *Asimov's*, March.
——, "The Twelfth Album," *Interzone*, April.
M. Shayne Bell, "Lock Down," *Starlight 2*.
——, "The Moon Girl," *Asimov's*, June.
Gregory Benford, "A Dance to Strange Musics," *Science Fiction Age*, November.
Michael Bishop, "Sequel on Skorpiós," *Interzone*, August.
Terry Bisson, "First Fire," *Science Fiction Age*, September.
——, "Get Me to the Church on Time," *Asimov's*, May.
——, "Incident at Oak Ridge," *F&SF*, July.
Russell Blackford, "Byzantium vs the Republic of Australia," *Aurealis 20/21*.
Jayme Lynn Blaschke, "The Dust," *Interzone*, March.
James P. Blaylock, "The Old Curiosity Shop," *F&SF*, February.
Ben Bova, "The Question," *Analog*, January.
——, "Remember Caesar . . . ," *F&SF*, March.
——, "Tourist Sam," *Analog*, March.
Steven R. Boyett, "Current Affairs," *F&SF*, January.
Damien Broderick, "The Womb," *Dreaming Down-Under*.
Keith Brooke, "Segue," *Interzone*, June.
Eric Brown, "Deep Future," *Science Fiction Age*, July.
——, "Onward Station," *Interzone*, September.
——, "Venus Macabre," *Aboriginal SF*, Winter.
Simon Brown, "Imagining Ajax," *Aurealis 20/21*.
——, "With Clouds at Our Feet," *Dreaming Down-Under*.
Steven Brust, "Calling Pittsburgh," *Lord of the Fantastic*.
Pat Cadigan, "Datableed," *Asimov's*, March.

——, "What I Got for Christmas," *Interzone*, January.
Orson Scott Card, "Grinning Man," *Legends*.
Lillian Stewart Carl, "The Test of Gold," *Alternate Generals*.
Raphael Carter, "Congenital Agenesis of Gender Ideation," *Starlight 2*.
Stephan Chapman, "Minutes of the Last Meeting," *Leviathan 2*.
Eric Choi, "The Coming of the Jet," *ArrowDreams*.
Richard Chwedyk, "Auteur Theory," *F&SF*, July.
Arthur C. Clarke & Stephen Baxter, "The Wire Continuum," *Playboy*, January.
Susanna Clarke, "Mrs Mabb," *Starlight 2*.
Sarah Clemens, "Red," *Asimov's*, June.
Hal Clement, "Oh, Natural," *Absolute Magnitude*, Spring.
Brian C. Coad, "Taking Care of Daddy," *Asimov's*, January.
Hal Colebatch, "Telepath's Dance," *Choosing Names: Man-Kzin Wars VIII*.
Michael Coney, "What Are Little Girls Made Of?" *TransVersions 8/9*.
Albert E. Cowdrey, "The Great Ancestor," *F&SF*, September.
Greg Cox, "G.o.H: H.P.L," *Alternate Skiffy*.
Don D'Ammassa, "Adding It Up," *Talebones*, Fall.
Tony Daniel, "Radio Praha," *Asimov's*, March.
Avram Davidson, "Blunt," *F&SF*, October/November.
——, & Michael Swanwick, "Vergil Magus: King Without Country," *Asimov's*, July.
Stephen Dedman, "Amendment," *Science Fiction Age*, September.
——, "A Walk-On Part in the War," *Dreaming Down-Under*.
——, "Depth of Field," *Altair 2*.
——, "Founding Fathers," *Science Fiction Age*, March.
——, "Target of Opportunity," *Asimov's*, June.
——, "Transit," *Asimov's*, March.
Paul Di Filippo, "Never Let Them See You Nova," *Interzone*, March.
——, "Jack Neck and the Worrybird," *Science Fiction Age*, July.
——, "Plumage from Pegasus: Next Big Thing," *F&SF*, May.
Thomas M. Disch, "The First Annual Performance Arts Festival at the Slaughter Rock Battlefield," *Interzone*, May.
Cory Doctorow, "Fall from Grace," *Asimov's*, October/November.
——, "Jamie Spanglish in the Nile," *On Spec*, Winter.
——, "Overture, Curtain Lights," *Odyssey 6*.
William Dowding, "The Man Who Fished Forever," *Eidolon 27*.
Terry Dowling, "Downloading," *Event Horizon*, September.
——, "He Tried to Catch the Light," *Dreaming Down-Under*.
——, "The Infinite Race," *Aurealis 20/21*.
Gardner Dozois & Michael Swanwick, "Ancestral Voices," *Asimov's*, August.
L. Timmel Duchamp, "Dance at the Edge," *Bending the Landscape: SF*.
——, "A Question of Grammar," *Asimov's*, April.
——, "Portrait of the Artist as a Middle-aged Woman," *Leviathan 2*.
Tom Dupree, "With a Smile," *Mob Magic*.
S. N. Dyer, "The Experiment," *More Amazing Stories*.
——, "I Borrow Dave's Time Machine," *Science Fiction Age*, March.
——, "I Married the Stalker from Space," *Amazing*, Winter.
——, "Wild Child," *Asimov's*, March.
William R. Eakin, "Encounter in Redgunk," *Amazing*, Fall.
——, "Monogamy," *F&SF*, June.
Rosemary Edghill, "The Sword of the North," *Camelot Fantastic*.
Greg Egan, "The Planck Dive," *Asimov's*, February.
Phyllis Eisenstein, "The Island in the Lake," *F&SF*, December.

Kandis Elliot, "Evolution in Guadalajara," *Asimov's*, January.
——, "The NDE of Doctor Marceau," *Terra Incognita*, Summer.
Timons Esaias, "The Mars Convention," *Interzone*, September.
Nancy Etchemendy, "Double Silver Truth," *F&SF*, June.
Gregory Feeley, "Animae Celestes," *Asimov's*, April.
——, "Scatchophily," *Alternate Skiffy*.
Sheila Finch, "The Naked Face of God," *F&SF*, June.
——, "Reading the Bones, *F&SF*, January.
Eliot Fintushel, "Auschwitz and the Rectification of History," *Asimov's*, April.
——, "Crane Fly," *Amazing*, Fall.
——, "Galactic Business," *Crank! 8*.
——, "Honey Baby and Mademan," *Amazing*, Winter.
——, "Izzy and the Hypocrite Lecteur," *Asimov's*, February.
Marina Fitch, "Imprints," *F&SF*, March.
Michael F. Flynn, "Rules of Engagement," *Analog*, March.
Leanne Frahm, "Rain Season," *Eldolon 27*.
Esther M. Friesner, "Brown Dust," *Starlight 2*.
——, "In the Realm of Dragons," *Asimov's*, February.
——, "An Old Man's Summer," *Alternate Generals*.
——, "Totally Camelot," *Asimov's*, August.
Gregory Frost, "How Meersh the Bedeviler Lost His Toes," *Asimov's*, September.
Neil Gaiman, "Only the End of the World Again," *Lord of the Fantastic*.
R. Garcia y Robertson, "A Princess of Helium," *F&SF*, September.
——, "Starfall," *Asimov's*, July.
James Alan Gardner, "Sense of Wonder," *Amazing*, Summer.
Peter T. Garratt, "Long but without Glory," *Odyssey 4*.
Mary Gentle, "Kitsune," *Odyssey 5*.
David Gerrold, "Jumping off the Planet," *Science Fiction Age*, January.
Mark S. Geston, "The Allies," *F&SF*, May.
Alexander Glass, "Storage," *Interzone*, June.
——, "Upgrade," *Interzone*, May.
James C. Glass, "Robbie," *Talebones*, Fall.
Lisa Goldstein, "The Game This Year," *Asimov's*, December.
Ron Goulart, "My Pal Clunky," *Analog*, June.
Glenn Grant, "Thermometers Melting," *ArrowDreams*.
Dominic Green, "Queen of the Hill," *Hone*, April.
——, "That Thing over There," *Interzone*, June.
Kerry Greenwood, "Jetsam," *Dreaming Down-Under*.
Peni R. Griffin, "Alice," *Realms of Fantasy*, October.
Karen Haber, "Downsize, Downtime," *Science Fiction Age*, May.
Jack C. Halderman II, "Southern Discomfort," *Lord of the Fantastic*.
Joe Haldeman, "Odd Coupling," *Asimov's*, October/November.
Peter F. Hamilton, "A Second Chance at Eden," *A Second Chance At Eden*.
Charles L. Harness, "The Downsizing of Dr. Jain," *Analog*, September.
——, "The GUAC Bug," *Analog*, June.
Nina Kiriki Hoffman, "Gone to Heaven Shouting," *F&SF*, January.
——, "Objects of Desire," *Alien Pets*.
——, "The Somehow Not Yet Dead," *Lord of the Fantastic*.
Ernest Hogan, "Skin Dragons Talk," *Science Fiction Age*, March.
Sue Isle, "Chandriki Dance," *Tales of the Unanticipated 19*.
Michael Iwoleit, "Takeover," *Interzone*, July.
Alexander Jablokov, "Market Report," *Asimov's*, September.

Warren W. James, "Slowboat Nightmare," *Choosing Names: Man-Kzin Wars VIII*.
Ben Jeapes, "Correspondents," *Aboriginal SF*, Summer.
——, "The Fire Worker," *Altair*.
Daniel H. Jeffers, "The Value of Objects," *Asimov's*, April.
Jan Lars Jensen, "Reintroducing the Species," *On Spec*, Winter.
Gwyneth Jones, "Grazing the Long Acre," *Interzone*, January.
Janet Kagan, "The Stubbornest Broad on Earth," *Asimov's*, February.
Michael Kandel, "Wading River Dogs and More," *Asimov's*, May.
Roz Kaveney, "Instructions," *Odyssey 3*.
Fiona Kelleghan, "The Secret in the Chest," *Realms of Fantasy*, October.
James Patrick Kelly, "Fruitcake Theory," *Asimov's*, December.
——, "Lovestory," *Asimov's*, June.
——, "Bierhorst, R. G., Seera, B. L., and Jannifer, R. P., 'Proof of the Existence of God and an Afterlife,' *Journal of Experimental Psychology*. Volume 95, Spring 2007, Pages 32–36," *Asimov's*, August.
John Kessel, "Every Angel Is Terrifying," *F&SF*, October/November.
——, "The President's Channel, *Science Fiction Age*, November.
Stephen King, "The Little Sisters of Eluria," *Legends*.
Ellen Klages, "Time Gypsy," *Bending the Landscape: SF*.
Nancy Kress, "State of Nature," *Bending the Landscape: SF*.
Ellen Kushner, "The Death of the Duke," *Starlight 2*.
David J. Lake, "The Truth About Weena," *Dreaming Down-Under*.
Geoffrey A. Landis, "Outsider's Chance," *Analog*, December.
——, "Snow," *Starlight 2*.
David Langford, "A Game of Consequences," *Starlight 2*.
——, "Out of Space, Out of Time," *Science Fiction Age*, September.
Mary Soon Lee, "The Day Before They Came," *Interzone*, July.
Tanith Lee, "All the Birds of Hell," *F&SF*, October/November.
——, "The Girl Who Lost Her Looks," *Interzone*, February.
——, "Yellow and Red," *Interzone*, June.
Ursula K. Le Guin, "Dragonfly," *Legends*.
Paul Levinson, "Advantage, Bellarmine," *Analog*, January.
Anthony R. Lewis, "Plus Ultra," *Alternate Skiffy*.
Megan Lindholm, "Strays," *Warrior Princesses*.
Jame M. Lindskold, "Ki'rin and the Blue and White Tiger," *Lord of the Fantastic*.
Kelly Link, "The Specialist's Hat," *Event Horizon*, November.
Susan MacGregor, "The Vivaldi Connection," *On Spec*, Spring.
Ian R. MacLeod, "Home Time," *F&SF*, February.
Paul J. McAuley, "17," *Asimov's*, June.
——, "The Gardens of Saturn," *Interzone*, November.
——, "The Secret of My Success," *Interzone*, May.
Sally McBride, "The Queen of Yesterday," *Realms of Fantasy*, February.
Jack McDevitt, "Report from the Rear," *Aboriginal SF*, Spring.
——and Stanley Schmidt, "Good Intentions," *F&SF*, June.
Ian McDowell, "The Feasting of the Hungry Man," *Camelot Fantastic*.
Mark J. McGarry, "The Marly Gate," *F&SF*, March.
Vonda N. McIntyre, "Night Harvest," *Odyssey 4*.
Sea McMullen, "Queen of Soulmates," *Dreaming Down-Under*.
Danith McPherson, "Through the Wall to Eggshell Lake," *Asimov's*, October/November.
Barry N. Malzberg, "A Science of the Mind," *Alternate Skiffy*.
Daniel Marcus, "Binding Energy," *Asimov's*, October/November.
George R. R. Martin, "The Hedge Knight," *Legends*.

R. M. Meluch, "Vati," *Alternate Generals.*
John J. Miller, "Suicide Kings," *Lord of the Fantastic.*
Judith Moffett, "The Bradshaw," *F&SF*, October/November.
Elizabeth Moon, "Tradition," *Alternate Generals.*
Lyda Morehouse, "Everything in its Place," *Tales of the Unanticipated 19.*
Derryl Murphy, "Cold Ground," *ArrowDreams.*
Pat Murphy, "Ménage and Menagerie," *F&SF*, October/November.
Pati Nagle, "Arroyo de Oro," *Lord of the Fantastic.*
Robert L. Nansel, "Xiaoying's Journey," *Asimov's*, September.
R. Neube, "Quantum Commode Theory," *Asimov's*, October/November.
——, "King Moron," *Asimov's*, January.
Larry Niven, "Choosing Names," *Choosing Names: Man-Kzin Wars VIII.*
G. David Nordley, "A Life on Mars," *Analog*, July/August.
Jerry Oltion, "Artifacts," *Analog*, October.
Rebecca Ore, "Accelerated Grimace," *F&SF*, February.
——, "Half in Love with Easeful Rock and Roll," *Bending the Landscape: SF.*
Lawrence Person, "Crucifixion Variations," *Asimov's*, May.
Frederik Pohl, "The Golden Years of *Astounding*," *Alternate Skiffy.*
Terry Pratchett, "The Sea and Little Fishes," *Legends.*
Robert Reed, "Building the Building of the World," *Asimov's*, December.
——, "Mother Death," *Asimov's*, January.
——, "Savior," *Asimov's*, August.
——, "Whiptail," *Asimov's*, October/November.
Alastair Reynolds, "On the Oodnadatta," *Interzone*, February.
——, "Stroboscopic," *Interzone*, August.
Carrie Richerson, "The City in Morning," *Bending the Landscape: SF.*
Uncle River, "What Does the Algae Eat?" *Amazing*, Fall.
Bruce Holland Rogers, "Not Exactly a Dog," *Alien Pets.*
——, "Thirteen Ways to Water," *Black Cats and Broken Mirrors.*
Mary Rosenblum, "The Eye of God," *Asimov's*, March.
——, "The Rainmaker," *F&SF*, October/November.
Jane Routley, "To Avalon," *Dreaming Down-Under.*
Kristine Kathryn Rusch, "Coolhunting," *Science Fiction Age*, July.
——, "Echea," *Asimov's*, July.
——, "Going Native," *Amazing*, Fall.
——, "The Questing Mind," *F&SF*, May.
——, "Reflections on Life and Death," *Asimov's*, January.
Geoff Ryman, "Family," *Interzone*, January.
William Sanders, "Billy Mitchell's Overt Act," *Alternate Generals.*
——, "Ninekiller and the Neterw," *Lord of the Fantastic.*
Carter Scholz, "The Amount to Carry," *Starlight 2.*
David J. Schow, "Gills," *Weird Tales* 314.
Cecily Scutt, "Descent," *Dreaming Down-Under.*
Cynthia Seelhammer, "Gentle Horses," *F&SF*, March.
Charles Sheffield, "Brooks Too Broad for Leaping," *Bending the Landscape: SF.*
Rick Shelley, "The Beacon," *Analog*, January.
William Shunn, "Practical Ramifications of Interstellar Packet Loss," *Science Fiction Age*, September.
Robert Silverberg, "The Colonel in Autumn," *Science Fiction Age*, March.
——, "The Seventh Shrine," *Legends.*
——, "Waiting for the End," *Asimov's*, October/November.
Janni Lee Simner, "Steel Penny," *Realms of Fantasy*, June.

Bradley H. Sinor, "Back in 'The Real World,' " *Lord of the Fantastic*.
Alan Smale, "Moments of Truth," *Realms of Fantasy*, June.
S. P. Somtow, "The Hero's Celluloid Journey," *Weird Tales* 314.
Martha Soukup, "The House of Expectations," *Starlight 2*.
Bud Sparhawk, "The Ice Dragon's Song," *Analog*, July/August.
Norman Spinrad, "The Year of the Mouse," *Asimov's*, April.
Nancy Springer, "The Queen's Broidery Woman," *Camelot Fantastic*.
——, "The Time of Her Life," *More Amazing Stories*.
Brian Stableford, "The Architect of Worlds," *Camelot Fantastic*.
——, "The Piebald Plumber of Haemlin," *Interzone*, April.
——, "The Tour," *Science Fiction Age*, January.
Michael A. Stackpole, "Asgard Unlimited," *Lord of the Fantastic*.
Allen Steele, "The Flying Triangle," *Bending the Landscape: SF*.
——, "Zwart Piet's Tale, *Analog*, December.
Bruce Sterling, "Maneki Neko," *F&SF*, May.
S. M. Stirling, "The Charge of Lee's Brigade," *Alternate Generals*.
Dirk Strasser, "The Doppelganger Effect," *Dreaming Down-Under*.
Charles Stross, "Extracts from the Club Diary," *Odyssey 6*.
——, "Toast: A Con Report," *Interzone*, August.
Harry C. Stubbs, "Options," *Lamps on the Brow*.
Lucy Sussex, "Matilda Told Such Dreadful Lies," *Dreaming Down-Under*.
Michael Swanwick, "Microcosmic Dog," *Science Fiction Age*, November.
——, "Radiant Doors," *Asimov's*, September.
——, "Wild Minds," *Asimov's*, May.
——, (with Sean Swanwick), "Archaic Planets: Nine Excerpts from the Encyclopedia Galactica," *Asimov's*, December.
L. A. Taylor, "Visitors," *More Amazing Stories*.
Robert C. Taylor, "A Prisoner of History," *F&SF*, June.
Melanie Tem, "The Game," *Weird Tales* 313.
Mark W. Tiedemann, "Psyché," *F&SF*, December.
——, "Surfaces," *Bending the Landscape: SF*.
——, "With Arms to Hold the Wind," *Asimov's*, September.
Lois Tilton, "The Craft of War," *Alternate Generals*.
George Turner, "And Now Doth Time Waste Me," *Dreaming Down-Under*.
Harry Turtledove, "The Phantom Tolbukhin," *Alternate Generals*.
Mary A. Turzillo, "Chrysoberyl," *F&SF*, June.
Lisa Tuttle, "World of Strangers," *Clones and Clones*.
Paul Urayama, "Living in a Stranger," *Analog*, October.
Steven Utley, "The Here and Now," *Asimov's*, March.
James Van Pelt, "For the Love of Falmouth," *Odyssey 5*.
John Varley, "The Flying Dutchman," *Lord of the Fantastic*.
Howard Waldrop, "Mr. Goodber's Show," *Omni Online*, March.
——, "Scientifiction," *Asimov's*, March.
Ian Watson, "The Shape of Murder," *Odyssey 4*.
——, "The Shortest Night," *Asimov's*, May.
——, "Starry Night," *Altair*.
John C. Waugh, "White Lies and Alibis," *Terra Incognita*, Summer.
Don Webb, "Man of Steel Saves the World," *Interzone*, May.
——, "Meeting the Messenger," *Realms of Fantasy*, June.
David Weber, "The Captain from Kirkbean," *Alternate Generals*.
Andrew Weiner, "In Future," *Science Fiction Age*, November.
K. D. Wentworth, "Tall One," *F&SF*, April.

Michelle West, "Diamonds," *Allen Pets.*
Leslie What, "The Cost of Doing Business," *Amazing*, Winter.
——, "Say Woof," *Asimov's*, July.
Wynne Whiteford, "Night of the Wandjina," *Dreaming Down-Under.*
Rick Wilber, "Straight Changes," *F&SF*, April.
Cherry Wilder, "The Bernstein Room," *Interzone*, August.
Sean Williams, "Entre les Beaux Morts en Vie," *Dreaming Down-Under.*
Walter Jon Williams, "The Picture Business," *Asimov's*, February.
Jack Williamson, "Miss Million," *Amazing*, Winter.
——, "The Pet Rocks Mystery," *Alien Pets.*
——, "The Purchase of Earth," *Science Fiction Age*, July.
——, "The Story Roger Never Told," *Lord of the Fantastic.*
——, "Terraforming Terra," *Science Fiction Age*, November.
Robert Charles Wilson, "The Inner Inner City," *Realms of Fantasy*, October.
——, "The Observer," *The UFO Files.*
——, "Protocols of Consumption," *Realms of Fantasy*, June.
Robin Wilson, "Thanks, Diaz," *F&SF*, May.
Laurel Winter, "Fighting Gravity," *F&SF*, September.
Jane Yolen, "Flight," *Olympus.*
——, "Lost Girls," *Realms of Fantasy*, February.
George Zebrowski, "Shrinkers & Movers," *Amazing*, Winter.